The

BUCKSHAW
CHRONICLES

Volume One

The

BUCKSHAW
CHRONICLES

 *Volume One*

THE SWEETNESS AT THE BOTTOM OF THE PIE

THE WEED THAT STRINGS THE HANGMAN'S BAG

A RED HERRING WITHOUT MUSTARD

ALAN
BRADLEY

ANCHOR CANADA

contents

The Sweetness at the Bottom of the Pie

For Shirley

Unless some sweetness at the bottom lie,
Who cares for all the crinkling of the pie?
—WILLIAM KING, *The Art of Cookery* (1708)

one

IT WAS AS BLACK IN THE CLOSET AS OLD BLOOD. THEY HAD shoved me in and locked the door. I breathed heavily through my nose, fighting desperately to remain calm. I tried counting to ten on every intake of breath, and to eight as I released each one slowly into the darkness. Luckily for me, they had pulled the gag so tightly into my open mouth that my nostrils were left unobstructed, and I was able to draw in one slow lungful after another of the stale, musty air.

I tried hooking my fingernails under the silk scarf that bound my hands behind me, but since I always bit them to the quick, there was nothing to catch. Jolly good luck then that I'd remembered to put my fingertips together, using them as ten firm little bases to press my palms apart as they had pulled the knots tight.

Now I rotated my wrists, squeezing them together until I felt a bit of slack, using my thumbs to work the silk down until the knots were between my palms—then between my fingers. If they had been bright enough to think of tying my thumbs together, I should never have escaped. What utter morons they were.

With my hands free at last, I made short work of the gag.

Now for the door. But first, to be sure they were not lying in wait for me, I squatted and peered out through the keyhole at the attic. Thank heavens they had taken the key away with them. There was

no one in sight; save for its perpetual tangle of shadows, junk, and sad
bric-a-brac, the long attic was empty. The coast was clear.

Reaching above my head at the back of the closet, I unscrewed one
of the wire coat hooks from its mounting board. By sticking its curved
wing into the keyhole and levering the other end, I was able to form an
L-shaped hook which I poked into the depths of the ancient lock. A bit
of judicious fishing and fiddling yielded a gratifying click. It was almost
too easy. The door swung open and I was free.

I SKIPPED DOWN THE BROAD STONE staircase into the hall, pausing
at the door of the dining room just long enough to toss my pigtails back
over my shoulders and into their regulation position.

Father still insisted on dinner being served as the clock struck the
hour and eaten at the massive oak refectory table, just as it had been
when Mother was alive.

"Ophelia and Daphne not down yet, Flavia?" he asked peevishly,
looking up from the latest issue of *The British Philatelist*, which lay open
beside his meat and potatoes.

"I haven't seen them in ages," I said.

It was true. I hadn't seen them—not since they had gagged and
blindfolded me, then lugged me hog-tied up the attic stairs and locked
me in the closet.

Father glared at me over his spectacles for the statutory four seconds
before he went back to mumbling over his sticky treasures.

I shot him a broad smile, a smile wide enough to present him with a
good view of the wire braces that caged my teeth. Although they gave
me the look of a dirigible with the skin off, Father always liked being
reminded that he was getting his money's worth. But this time he was
too preoccupied to notice.

I hoisted the lid off the Spode vegetable dish and, from the depths of
its hand-painted butterflies and raspberries, spooned out a generous
helping of peas. Using my knife as a ruler and my fork as a prod, I marshaled the peas so that they formed meticulous rows and columns across
my plate: rank upon rank of little green spheres, spaced with a precision
that would have delighted the heart of the most exacting Swiss watch-
maker. Then, beginning at the bottom left, I speared the first pea with
my fork and ate it.

It was all Ophelia's fault. She was, after all, seventeen, and therefore expected to possess at least a modicum of the maturity she should come into as an adult. That she should gang up with Daphne, who was thirteen, simply wasn't fair. Their combined ages totalled thirty years. Thirty years!—against my eleven. It was not only unsporting, it was downright rotten. And it simply screamed out for revenge.

NEXT MORNING I WAS BUSY among the flasks and flagons of my chemical laboratory on the top floor of the east wing when Ophelia barged in without so much as a la-di-dah.

"Where's my pearl necklace?"

I shrugged. "I'm not the keeper of your trinkets."

"I know you took it. The Mint Imperials that were in my lingerie drawer are gone too, and I've observed that missing mints in this household seem always to wind up in the same grubby little mouth."

I adjusted the flame on a spirit lamp that was heating a beaker of red liquid. "If you're insinuating that my personal hygiene is not up to the same high standard as yours you can go suck my galoshes."

"Flavia!"

"Well, you can. I'm sick and tired of being blamed for everything, Feely."

But my righteous indignation was cut short as Ophelia peered short-sightedly into the ruby flask, which was just coming to the boil.

"What's that sticky mass in the bottom?" Her long manicured fingernail tapped at the glass.

"It's an experiment. Careful, Feely, it's acid!"

Ophelia's face went white. "Those are my pearls! They belonged to Mummy!"

Ophelia was the only one of Harriet's daughters who referred to her as "Mummy": the only one of us old enough to have any real memories of the flesh-and-blood woman who had carried us in her body, a fact of which Ophelia never tired of reminding us. Harriet had been killed in a mountaineering accident when I was just a year old, and she was not often spoken of at Buckshaw.

Was I jealous of Ophelia's memories? Did I resent them? I don't believe I did; it ran far deeper than that. In rather an odd way, I despised Ophelia's memories of our mother.

I looked up slowly from my work so that the round lenses of my spectacles would flash blank white semaphores of light at her. I knew that whenever I did this, Ophelia had the horrid impression that she was in the presence of some mad black-and-white German scientist in a film at the Gaumont.

"Beast!"

"Hag!" I retorted. But not until Ophelia had spun round on her heel—quite neatly, I thought—and stormed out the door.

Retribution was not long in coming, but then with Ophelia, it never was. Ophelia was not, as I was, a long-range planner who believed in letting the soup of revenge simmer to perfection.

Quite suddenly after dinner, with Father safely retired to his study to gloat over his collection of paper heads, Ophelia had too quietly put down the silver butter knife in which, like a budgerigar, she had been regarding her own reflection for the last quarter of an hour. Without preamble she said, "I'm not really your sister, you know . . . nor is Daphne. That's why we're so unlike you. I don't suppose it's ever even occurred to you that you're adopted."

I dropped my spoon with a clatter. "That's not true. I'm the spitting image of Harriet. Everybody says so."

"She picked you out at the Home for Unwed Mothers because of the striking resemblance," Ophelia said, making a distasteful face.

"How could there be a resemblance when she was an adult and I was a baby?" I was nothing if not quick on the uptake.

"Because you reminded her of her own baby pictures. Good Lord, she even dragged them along and held them up beside you for comparison."

I appealed to Daphne, whose nose was firmly stuck in a leather-bound copy of *The Castle of Otranto*. "That's not true, is it, Daffy?"

"'Fraid so," Daphne said, idly turning an onionskin page. "Father always said it would come as a bit of a shock to you. He made both of us swear never to tell. Or at least until you were eleven. He made us take an oath."

"A green Gladstone bag," Ophelia said. "I saw it with my own eyes. I watched Mummy stuffing her own baby pictures into a green Gladstone bag to drag off to the home. Although I was only six at the time—almost seven—I'll never forget her white hands . . . her fingers on the brass clasp."

I leapt up from the table and fled the room in tears. I didn't actually think of the poison until next morning at breakfast.

As with all great schemes, it was a simple one.

BUCKSHAW HAD BEEN THE HOME of our family, the de Luces, since time out of mind. The present Georgian house had been built to replace an Elizabethan original burnt to the ground by villagers who suspected the de Luces of Orange sympathies. That we had been ardent Catholics for four hundred years, and remained so, meant nothing to the inflamed citizenry of Bishop's Lacey. "Old House," as it was called, had gone up in flames, and the new house which had replaced it was now well into its third century.

Two later de Luce ancestors, Antony and William de Luce, who had disagreed about the Crimean War, had spoiled the lines of the original structure. Each of them had subsequently added a wing, William the east wing and Antony the west.

Each became a recluse in his own dominion, and each had forbidden the other ever to set foot across the black line which they caused to be painted dead center from the vestibule in the front, across the foyer, and straight through to the butler's W.C. behind the back stairs. Their two yellow brick annexes, pustulantly Victorian, folded back like the pinioned wings of a boneyard angel which, to my eyes, gave the tall windows and shutters of Buckshaw's Georgian front the prim and surprised look of an old maid whose bun is too tight.

A later de Luce, Tarquin—or Tar, as he was called—in the wake of a sensational mental breakdown, made a shambles of what had promised to be a brilliant career in chemistry, and was sent down from Oxford in the summer of Queen Victoria's Silver Jubilee.

Tar's indulgent father, solicitous of the lad's uncertain health, had spared no expense in outfitting a laboratory on the top floor of Buckshaw's east wing: a laboratory replete with German glassware, German microscopes, a German spectroscope, brass chemical balances from Lucerne, and a complexly shaped mouth-blown German Geisler tube to which Tar could attach electrical coils to study the way in which various gases fluoresce.

On a desk by the windows was a Leitz microscope, whose brass still shone with the same warm luxury as it had the day it was brought by pony cart from the train at Buckshaw Halt. Its reflecting mirror could be angled to catch the first pale rays of the morning sun, while for cloudy days or for use after dark, it was equipped with a paraffin microscope lamp by Davidson & Co. of London.

There was even an articulated human skeleton on a wheeled stand, given to Tar when he was only twelve by the great naturalist Frank Buckland, whose father had eaten the mummified heart of King Louis XIV.

Three walls of this room were lined from floor to ceiling with glass-fronted cabinets, two of them filled row upon row with chemicals in glass apothecary jars, each labeled in the meticulous copperplate hand-writing of Tar de Luce, who in the end had thwarted Fate and outlived them all. He died in 1928 at the age of sixty in the midst of his chemical kingdom, where he was found one morning by his housekeeper, one of his dead eyes still peering sightlessly through his beloved Leitz. It was rumored that he had been studying the first-order decomposition of nitrogen pent-oxide. If that was true, it was the first recorded research into a reaction which was to lead eventually to the development of the A-bomb.

Uncle Tar's laboratory had been locked up and preserved in airless silence, down through the dusty years until what Father called my "strange talents" had begun to manifest themselves, and I had been able to claim it for my own.

I still shivered with joy whenever I thought of the rainy autumn day that Chemistry had fallen into my life.

I had been scaling the bookcases in the library, pretending I was a noted Alpinist, when my foot slipped and a heavy book was knocked to the floor. As I picked it up to straighten its creased pages, I saw that it was filled not just with words, but with dozens of drawings as well. In some of them, disembodied hands poured liquids into curiously made glass containers that looked as if they might have been musical instru-ments from another world.

The book's title was *An Elementary Study of Chemistry*, and within moments it had taught me that the word *iodine* comes from a word mean-ing "violet," and that the name *bromine* was derived from a Greek word meaning "a stench." These were the sorts of things I needed to know! I slipped the fat red volume under my sweater and took it upstairs, and it wasn't until later that I noticed the name *H. de Luce* written on the flyleaf. The book had belonged to Harriet.

Soon, I found myself poring over its pages in every spare moment. There were evenings when I could hardly wait for bedtime. Harriet's book had become my secret friend.

In it were detailed all the alkali metals: metals with fabulous names like lithium and rubidium; the alkaline earths such as strontium, barium, and radium. I cheered aloud when I read that a woman, Madame Curie, had discovered radium.

And then there were the poisonous gases: phosphine, arsine (a single bubble of which has been known to prove fatal), nitrogen peroxide, hydrogen sulfide . . . the lists went on and on. When I found that precise instructions were given for formulating these compounds, I was in seventh heaven.

Once I had taught myself to make sense of the chemical equations such as $K_4FeC_6N_6 + 2K = 6KCN + Fe$ (which describes what happens when the yellow prussiate of potash is heated with potassium to produce potassium cyanide), the universe was laid open before me: It was like having stumbled upon a recipe book that had once belonged to the witch in the wood.

What intrigued me more than anything was finding out the way in which everything, all of creation—all of it!—was held together by invisible chemical bonds, and I found a strange, inexplicable comfort in knowing that somewhere, even though we couldn't see it in our own world, there was real stability.

I didn't make the obvious connection at first, between the book and the abandoned laboratory I had discovered as a child. But when I did, my life came to life—if that makes any sense.

Here in Uncle Tar's lab, row on row, were the chemistry books he had so lovingly assembled, and I soon discovered that with a little effort most of them were not too far beyond my understanding.

Simple experiments came next, and I tried to remember to follow instructions to the letter. Not to say that there weren't a few stinks and explosions, but the less said about those the better.

As time went on, my notebooks grew fatter. My work was becoming ever more sophisticated as the mysteries of Organic Chemistry revealed themselves to me, and I rejoiced in my newfound knowledge of what could be extracted so easily from nature.

My particular passion was poison.

I SLASHED AWAY at the foliage with a bamboo walking stick pinched from an elephant-foot umbrella stand in the front hall. Back here in the kitchen garden, the high redbrick walls had not yet let in the warming sun; everything was still sodden from the rain that had fallen in the night.

Making my way through the debris of last year's uncut grass, I poked along the bottom of the wall until I found what I was looking for: a patch of bright leaves whose scarlet gloss made their three-leaved clusters easy to spot among the other vines. Pulling on a pair of cotton gardening gloves that had been tucked into my belt, and launching into a loudly whistled rendition of "Bibbidi-Bobbidi-Boo," I went to work.

Later, in the safety of my sanctum sanctorum, my Holy of Holies— I had come across that delightful phrase in a biography of Thomas Jefferson and adopted it as my own—I stuffed the colorful leaves into a glass retort, taking care not to remove my gloves until their shiny foliage was safely tamped down. Now came the part I loved.

Stoppering the retort, I connected it on one side to a flask in which water was already boiling, and on the other to a coiled glass condensing tube whose open end hung suspended over an empty beaker. With the water bubbling furiously, I watched as the steam found its way through the tubing and escaped into the flask among the leaves. Already they were beginning to curl and soften as the hot vapor opened the tiny pockets between their cells, releasing the oils that were the essence of the living plant.

This was the way the ancient alchemists had practiced their art: fire and steam, steam and fire. Distillation.

How I loved this work.

Distillation. I said it aloud. "Dis-till-ation!"

I looked on in awe as the steam cooled and condensed in the coil, and wrung my hands in ecstasy as the first limpid drop of liquid hung suspended, then dropped with an audible *plop!* into the waiting receptacle.

When the water had boiled away and the operation was complete, I turned off the flame and cupped my chin in my palms to watch with fascination as the fluid in the beaker settled out into two distinct layers: the clear distilled water on the bottom, a liquid of a light yellow hue floating on top. This was the essential oil of the leaves. It was called urushiol and had been used, among other things, in the manufacture of lacquer.

Digging into the pocket of my sweater, I pulled out a shiny gold tube. I removed its cap, and couldn't help smiling as a red tip was revealed. Ophelia's lipstick, purloined from the drawer of her dressing table, along with the pearls and the Mint Imperials. And Feely—Miss Snotrag—hadn't even noticed it was gone.

Remembering the mints, I popped one into my mouth, crushing the sweet noisily between my molars.

The core of lipstick came out easily enough, and I relit the spirit lamp. Only a gentle heat was required to reduce the waxy stuff to a sticky mass. If Feely only knew that lipstick was made of fish scales, I thought, she might be a little less eager to slather the stuff all over her mouth. I must remember to tell her. I grinned. Later.

With a pipette I drew off a few millimeters of the distilled oil that floated in the beaker and then, drop by drop, dripped it gently into the ooze of the melted lipstick, giving the mixture a vigorous stir with a wooden tongue depressor.

Too thin, I thought. I fetched down a jar and added a dollop of bees-wax to restore it to its former consistency.

Time for the gloves again—and for the iron bullet mold I had pinched from Buckshaw's really quite decent firearm museum.

Odd, isn't it, that a charge of lipstick is precisely the size of a .45 caliber slug. A useful bit of information, really. I'd have to remember to think of its wider ramifications tonight when I was tucked safely into my bed. Right now, I was far too busy.

Teased from its mold and cooled under running water, the reformulated red core fitted neatly back inside its golden dispenser.

I screwed it up and down several times to make sure that it was working. Then I replaced the cap. Feely was a late sleeper and would still be dawdling over breakfast.

"WHERE'S MY LIPSTICK, you little swine? What have you done with it?"

"It's in your drawer," I said. "I noticed it when I purloined your pearls."

In my short life, bracketed by two sisters, I had of necessity become master of the forked tongue.

"It's not in my drawer. I've just looked, and it isn't there."

"Did you put on your specs?" I asked with a smirk.

Although Father had had all of us fitted with spectacles, Feely refused to wear hers and mine contained little more than window glass. I wore them only in the laboratory to protect my eyes, or to solicit sympathy.

Feely slammed down the heels of her hands on the table and stormed from the room.

I went back to plumbing the depths of my second bowl of Weetabix.

Later, I wrote in my notebook:

Friday, 2nd of June 1950, 9:42 A.M. Subject's appearance normal but grumpy.
(Isn't she always?) Onset may vary from 12 to 72 hours.

I could wait.

MRS. MULLET, WHO WAS SHORT and gray and round as a millstone and who, I'm quite sure, thought of herself as a character in a poem by A. A. Milne, was in the kitchen formulating one of her pus-like custard pies. As usual, she was struggling with the large Aga cooker that dominated the small, cramped kitchen.

"Oh, Miss Flavia! Here, help me with the oven, dear."

But before I could think of a suitable response, Father was behind me.

"Flavia, a word." His voice was as heavy as the lead weights on a deep-sea diver's boots.

I glanced at Mrs. Mullet to see how she was taking it. She always fled at the slightest whiff of unpleasantness, and once when Father raised his voice, she had rolled herself up in a carpet and refused to come out until her husband was sent for.

She eased the oven door shut as if it were made of Waterford crystal.

"I must be off," she said. "Lunch is in the warming oven."

"Thank you, Mrs. Mullet," Father said. "We'll manage." We were always managing.

She opened the kitchen door—and let out a sudden shriek like a cornered badger. "Oh, good Lord! Beggin' your pardon, Colonel de Luce, but, oh, good Lord!"

Father and I had to push a bit to see round her.

It was a bird, a jack snipe—and it was dead. It lay on its back on the doorstep, its stiff wings extended like a little pterodactyl, its eyes rather

"It's all right, Dogger!" I shouted. "I've got them covered from up here."

For a moment, I thought he hadn't heard me, but then his face turned slowly, like a sunflower, towards the sound of my voice. I held my breath. You never know what someone might do in such a state.

"Steady on, Dogger," I called out. "It's all right. They've gone."

Suddenly he went limp, like a man who has been holding a live electrical wire in which the current has just been switched off.

"Miss Flavia?" His voice quavered. "Is that you, Miss Flavia?"

"I'm coming down," I said. "I'll be there in a jiff."

Down the back stairs I ran, pell-mell, and into the kitchen. Mrs. Mullet had gone home, but her custard pie sat cooling at the open window.

No, I thought: What Dogger needed was something to drink. Father kept his Scotch locked tightly in a bookcase in his study, and I could not intrude.

Luckily, I found a pitcher of cool milk in the pantry. I poured out a tall glass of it, and dashed into the garden.

"Here, drink this," I said, holding it out to him.

Dogger took the drink in both hands, stared at it for a long moment as if he didn't know what to do with it, and then raised it unsteadily to his mouth. He drank deeply until the milk was gone. He handed me the empty glass.

For a moment, he looked vaguely beatific, like an angel by Raphael, but that impression quickly passed.

"You have a white mustache," I told him. I bent down to the cucumbers and, tearing off a large, dark green leaf from the vine, used it to wipe his upper lip.

The light was coming back into his empty eyes.

"Milk and cucumbers . . . " he said. "Cucumbers and milk . . . "

"Poison!" I shouted, jumping up and down and flapping my arms like a chicken, to show him that everything was under control. "Deadly poison!" And we both laughed a little.

He blinked.

"My!" he said, looking round the garden as if he were a princess coming awake from the deepest dream, "isn't it turning out to be a lovely day!"

FATHER DID NOT APPEAR AT LUNCH. To reassure myself, I put an ear to his study door and listened for a few minutes to the flipping of philatelic pages and an occasional clearing of the paternal throat. Nerves, I decided.

At the table, Daphne sat with her nose in Walpole (Horace), her cucumber sandwich beside her, soggy and forgotten on a plate. Ophelia, sighing endlessly, crossing, uncrossing, and recrossing her legs, stared blankly off into space, and I could only assume she was trifling in her mind with Ned Cropper, the jack-of-all-trades at the Thirteen Drakes. She was too absorbed in her haughty reverie to notice when I leaned in for a closer look at her lips as she reached absently for a cube of cane sugar, popped it into her mouth, and began sucking.

"Ah," I remarked, to no one in particular, "the pimples will be blooming in the morning."

She made a lunge for me, but my legs were faster than her flippers.

Back upstairs in my laboratory, I wrote:

Friday, 2nd of June 1950, 1:07 p.m. No visible reaction as yet. "Patience is a necessary ingredient of genius."

—(Disraeli)

TEN O'CLOCK HAD COME and gone, and still I couldn't sleep. Mostly, when the light's out I'm a lump of lead, but tonight was different. I lay on my back, hands clasped behind my head, reviewing the day.

First there had been Father. Well, no, that's not quite true. First there had been the dead bird on the doorstep—and then there had been Father. What I thought I had seen on his face was fear, but still there was some little corner of my brain that didn't seem to believe it.

To me—to all of us—Father was fearless. He had seen things during the War: horrid things that must never be put into words. He had somehow survived the years of Harriet's vanishing and presumed death. And through it all he had been stalwart, staunch, dogged, and unshakeable. Unbelievably British. Unbearably stiff upper lip. But now . . .

And then there was Dogger: Arthur Wellesley Dogger, to give him his "full patronymic" (as he called it on his better days). Dogger had come to us first as Father's valet, but then, as "the full vicissitudes of that position" (his words, not mine) bore down upon his shoulders, he found it "more copacetic" to become butler, then chauffeur, then Buckshaw's general handyman, then chauffeur again for a while. In recent months, he had rocked gently down, like a falling autumn leaf, before coming to rest in his present post of gardener, and Father had donated our Hillman estate wagon to St. Tancred's as a raffle prize.

Poor Dogger! That's what I thought, even though Daphne told me I should never say that about anyone: "It's not only condescending, it fails to take into account the future," she said.

Still, who could forget the sight of Dogger in the garden? A great simple hulk of a helpless man just standing there, hair and tools in disarray, wheelbarrow overturned, and a look on his face as if . . . as if . . .

A rustle of sound caught my ear. I turned my head and listened.

Nothing.

It is a simple fact of Nature that I happen to possess acute hearing: the kind of hearing, Father once told me, that allows its owner to hear spiderwebs clanging like horseshoes against the walls. Harriet had possessed it too, and sometimes I like to imagine I am, in a way, a rather odd remnant of her: a pair of disembodied ears drifting round the haunted halls of Buckshaw, hearing things that are sometimes better left unheard.

But, listen! There it was again! A voice reflected; hard and hollow, like a whisper in an empty biscuit tin.

I slipped out of bed and went on tiptoes to the window. Taking care not to jiggle the curtains, I peeked out into the kitchen garden just as the moon obligingly came out from behind a cloud to illuminate the scene, much as it would in a first-rate production of A Midsummer Night's Dream.

But there was nothing more to see than its silvery light dancing among the cucumbers and the roses.

And then I heard a voice: an angry voice, like the buzzing of a bee in late summer trying to fly through a closed windowpane.

I threw on one of Harriet's Japanese silk housecoats (one of the two I had rescued from the Great Purge), shoved my feet into the beaded Indian moccasins that served as slippers, and crept to the head of the stairs. The voice was coming from somewhere inside the house.

Buckshaw possessed two Grand Staircases, each one winding down in a sinuous mirror image of the other, from the first floor, coming to earth just short of the black painted line that divided the checker-tiled foyer. My staircase, from the "Tar," or east wing, terminated in that great echoing painted hall beyond which, over against the west wing, was the firearm museum, and behind it, Father's study. It was from this direction that the voice was emanating. I crept towards it.

I put an ear to the door.

"Besides, Jacko," a caddish voice was saying on the other side of the paneled wood, "how could you live in the light of discovery? How could you ever go on?"

For a queasy instant I thought George Sanders had come to Buckshaw, and was lecturing Father behind closed doors.

"Get out," Father said, his voice not angry, but in that level, controlled tone that told me he was furious. In my mind I could see his furrowed brow, his clenched fists, and his jaw muscles taut as bowstrings.

"Oh, come off it, old boy," said the oily voice. "We're in this together— always have been, always will be. You know it as well as I."

"Twining was right," Father said. "You're a loathsome, despicable excuse for a human being."

"Twining? Old Cuppa? Cuppa's been dead these thirty years, Jacko— like Jacob Marley. But, like said Marley, his ghost lingers on. As perhaps you've noticed."

"And we killed him," Father said, in a flat, dead voice.

Had I heard what I'd heard? How could he—

By taking my ear from the door and bending to peer through the keyhole I missed Father's next words. He was standing beside his desk, facing the door. The stranger's back was to me. He was excessively tall, six foot four, I guessed. With his red hair and rusty gray suit, he reminded me of the Sandhill Crane that stood stuffed in a dim corner of the firearm museum.

I reapplied my ear to the paneled door.

" . . . no statute of limitations on shame," the voice was saying. "What's a couple of thousand to you, Jacko? You must have come into a fair bit when Harriet died. Why, the insurance alone—"

"Shut your filthy mouth!" Father shouted. "Get out before I—"

Suddenly I was seized from behind and a rough hand was clapped across my mouth. My heart almost leaped out of my chest.

I was being held so tightly I couldn't manage a struggle.

"Go back to bed, Miss Flavia," a voice hissed into my ear.

It was Dogger.

"This is none of your business," he whispered. "Go back to bed."

He loosened his grip on me and I struggled free. I shot him a poisonous look.

In the near-darkness, I saw his eyes soften a little.

"Buzz off," he whispered.

I buzzed off.

Back in my room I paced up and down for a while, as I often do when I'm thwarted.

I thought about what I'd overheard. Father a murderer? That was impossible. There was probably some quite simple explanation. If only I'd heard the rest of the conversation between Father and the stranger . . . if only Dogger hadn't ambushed me in the dark. Who did he think he was?

I'll show him, I thought.

"With no further ado!" I said aloud.

I slipped José Iturbi from his green paper sleeve, gave my portable gramophone a good winding-up, and slapped the second side of Chopin's Polonaise in A flat Major onto the turntable. I threw myself across the bed and sang along:

"DAH-dah-dah-dah, DAH-dah-dah-dah, DAH-dah-dah-dah, DAH-dah-dah-dah . . . "

The music sounded as if it had been composed for a film in which someone was cranking an old Bentley that kept sputtering out: hardly a selection to float you off to dreamland . . .

WHEN I OPENED MY EYES, an oyster-colored dawn was peeping in at the windows. The hands of my brass alarm clock stood at 3:44. On Summer Time, daylight came early, and in less than a quarter of an hour, the sun should be up.

I stretched, yawned, and climbed out of bed. The gramophone had run down, frozen in mid-Polonaise, its needle lying dead in the grooves. For a fleeting moment I thought of winding it up again to give the household a Polish reveille. And then I remembered what had happened just a few hours before.

I went to the window and looked down into the garden. There was the potting shed, its glass panes clouded with the dew, and over there, an angular darkness that was Dogger's overturned wheelbarrow, forgotten in the events of yesterday.

Determined to put it right, to make up to him somehow, for something of which I was not even certain, I dressed and went quietly down the back stairs and into the kitchen.

As I passed the window, I noticed that a slice had been cut from Mrs. Mullet's custard pie. How odd, I thought; it was certainly none of the de Luces who had taken it. If there was one thing upon which we all agreed—one thing that united us as a family—it was our collective loathing of Mrs. Mullet's custard pies. Whenever she strayed from our favorite rhubarb or gooseberry to the dreaded custard, we generally begged off, feigning group illness, and sent her packing off home with the pie, and solicitous instructions to serve it up, with our compliments, to her good husband, Alf.

As I stepped outside, I saw that the silver light of dawn had transformed the garden into a magic glade, its shadows darkened by the thin band of day beyond the walls. Sparkling dew lay upon everything, and I should not have been at all surprised if a unicorn had stepped from behind a rosebush and tried to put its head in my lap.

I was walking towards the wheelbarrow when I tripped suddenly and fell forward onto my hands and knees.

"Bugger!" I said, already looking round to make sure that no one had heard me. I was now plastered with wet black loam.

"Bugger," I said again, a little less loudly.

Twisting round to see what had tripped me up, I spotted it at once: something white protruding from the cucumbers. For a teetering moment there was a part of me that fought desperately to believe it was a little rake, a cunning little cultivator with white curled tines.

But reason returned, and my mind admitted that it was a hand. A hand attached to an arm: an arm that snaked off into the cucumber patch.

And there, at the end of it, tinted an awful dewy cucumber green by the dark foliage, was a face. A face that looked for all the world like the Green Man of forest legend.

Driven by a will stronger than my own, I found myself dropping further to my hands and knees beside this apparition, partly in reverence and partly for a closer look.

When I was almost nose to nose with the thing its eyes began to open.

I was too shocked to move a muscle.

The body in the cucumbers sucked in a shuddering breath . . . and then, bubbling at the nose, exhaled it in a single word, slowly and a little sadly, directly into my face.

"*Vale*," it said.

My nostrils pinched reflexively as I got a whiff of a peculiar odor—an odor whose name was, for an instant, on the very tip of my tongue.

The eyes, as blue as the birds in the Willow pattern, looked up into mine as if staring out from some dim and smoky past, as if there were some recognition in their depths.

And then they died.

I wish I could say my heart was stricken, but it wasn't. I wish I could say my instinct was to run away, but that would not be true. Instead, I watched in awe, savoring every detail: the fluttering fingers, the almost imperceptible bronze metallic cloudiness that appeared on the skin, as if, before my very eyes, it were being breathed upon by death.

And then the utter stillness.

I wish I could say I was afraid, but I wasn't. Quite the contrary. This was by far the most interesting thing that had ever happened to me in my entire life.

three

I RACED UP THE WEST STAIRCASE. MY FIRST THOUGHT WAS TO waken Father, but something—some great invisible magnet—stopped me in my tracks. Daffy and Feely were useless in emergencies; it would be no good calling them. As quickly and as quietly as possible, I ran to the back of the house, to the little room at the top of the kitchen stairs, and tapped lightly on the door.

"Dogger!" I whispered. "It's me, Flavia."

There wasn't a sound within, and I repeated my rapping.

After about two and a half eternities, I heard Dogger's slippers shuffling across the floor. The lock gave a heavy *click* as the bolt shot back and his door opened a couple of wary inches. I could see that his face was haggard in the dawn, as if he hadn't slept.

"There's a dead body in the garden," I said. "I think you'd better come."

As I shifted from foot to foot and bit my fingernails, Dogger gave me a look that can only be described as reproachful, then vanished into the darkness of his room to dress. Five minutes later we were standing together on the garden path.

It was obvious that Dogger was no stranger to dead bodies. As if he'd been doing it all his life, he knelt and felt with his first two fingers for a pulse at the back angle of the jawbone. By his deadpan, distant look I could tell that there wasn't one.

Getting slowly to his feet, he dusted off his hands, as if they had somehow been contaminated.

"I'll inform the Colonel," he said.

"Shouldn't we call the police?" I asked.

Dogger ran his long fingers over his unshaven chin, as if he were mulling a question of earth-shattering consequence. There were severe restrictions on using the telephone at Buckshaw.

"Yes," he said at last. "I suppose we should."

We walked together, too slowly, into the house.

Dogger picked up the telephone and put the receiver to his ear, but I saw that he was keeping his finger firmly on the cradle switch. His mouth opened and closed several times and then his face went pale. His arm began shaking and I thought for a moment he was going to drop the thing. He looked at me helplessly.

"Here," I said, taking the instrument from his hands. "I'll do it."

"Bishop's Lacey two two one," I said into the telephone, thinking as I waited that Sherlock might well have smiled at the coincidence.

"Police," said an official voice at the other end of the line.

"Constable Linnet?" I said. "This is Flavia de Luce speaking from Buckshaw."

I had never done this before, and had to rely on what I'd heard on the wireless and seen in the cinema.

"I'd like to report a death," I said. "Perhaps you could send out an inspector?"

"Is it an ambulance you require, Miss Flavia?" he said. "We don't usually call out an inspector unless the circumstances are suspicious. Wait till I find a pencil . . ."

There was a maddening pause while I listened to him rummaging through stationery supplies before he continued:

"Now then, give me the name of the deceased, slowly, last name first."

"I don't know his name," I said. "He's a stranger."

That was the truth: I didn't know his name. But I did know, and knew it all too well, that the body in the garden—the body with the red hair, the body in the gray suit—was that of the man I'd spied through the study keyhole. The man Father had—

But I could hardly tell them that.

"I don't know his name," I repeated. "I've never seen him before in my life."

I had stepped over the line.

MRS. MULLET AND THE POLICE ARRIVED at the same moment, she on foot from the village and they in a blue Vauxhall sedan. As it crunched to a stop on the gravel, its front door squeaked open and a man stepped out onto the driveway.

"Miss de Luce," he said, as if pronouncing my name aloud put me in his power. "May I call you Flavia?"

I nodded assent.

"I'm Inspector Hewitt. Is your father at home?"

The Inspector was a pleasant-enough-looking man, with wavy hair, gray eyes, and a bit of a bulldog stance that reminded me of Douglas Bader, the Spitfire ace, whose photos I had seen in the back issues of *The War Illustrated* that lay in white drifts in the drawing room.

"He is," I said, "but he's rather indisposed." It was a word I had borrowed from Ophelia. "I'll show you to the corpse myself."

Mrs. Mullet's mouth fell open and her eyes goggled. "Oh, good Lord! Beggin' your pardon, Miss Flavia, but, oh, good Lord!"

If she had been wearing an apron, she'd have thrown it over her head and fled, but she didn't. Instead, she reeled in through the open door.

Two men in blue suits, who, as if awaiting instructions, had remained packed into the backseat of the car, now began to unfold themselves.

"Detective Sergeant Woolmer and Detective Sergeant Graves," Inspector Hewitt said. Sergeant Woolmer was hulking and square, with the squashed nose of a prizefighter; Sergeant Graves a chipper little blond sparrow with dimples who grinned at me as he shook my hand.

"And now if you'll be so kind," Inspector Hewitt said.

The detective sergeants unloaded their kits from the boot of the Vauxhall, and I led them in solemn procession through the house and into the garden.

Having pointed out the body, I watched in fascination as Sergeant Woolmer unpacked and mounted his camera on a wooden tripod, his fingers, fat as sausages, making surprisingly gentle microscopic adjustments to the little silver controls. As he took several covering exposures of the garden, lavishing particular attention on the cucumber patch, Sergeant Graves was opening a worn leather case in which were bottles ranged neatly row on row, and in which I glimpsed a packet of glassine envelopes.

I stepped forward eagerly, almost salivating, for a closer look.

"I wonder, Flavia," Inspector Hewitt said, stepping gingerly into the cucumbers, "if you might ask someone to organize some tea?"

He must have seen the look on my face.

"We've had rather an early start this morning. Do you think you could manage to rustle something up?"

So that was it. As at a birth, so at a death. Without so much as a kiss-me-quick-and-mind-the-marmalade, the only female in sight is enlisted to trot off and see that the water is boiled. Rustle something up, indeed! What did he take me for, some kind of cowboy?

"I'll see what can be arranged, Inspector," I said. Coldly, I hoped.

"Thank you," Inspector Hewitt said. Then, as I stamped off towards the kitchen door, he called out, "Oh, and Flavia . . . "

I turned, expectantly.

"We'll come in for it. No need for you to come out here again."

The nerve! The bloody nerve!

OPHELIA AND DAPHNE WERE already at the breakfast table. Mrs. Mullet had leaked the grim news, and there had been ample time for them to arrange themselves in poses of pretended indifference.

Ophelia's lips had still not reacted to my little preparation, and I made a mental note to record the time of my observation and the results later.

"I found a dead body in the cucumber patch," I told them.

"How very like you," Ophelia said, and went on preening her eyebrows.

Daphne had finished *The Castle of Otranto* and was now well into *Nicholas Nickleby*. But I noticed that she was biting her lower lip as she read: a sure sign of distraction.

There was an operatic silence.

"Was there a great deal of blood?" Ophelia asked at last.

"None," I said. "Not a drop."

"Whose body was it?"

"I don't know," I said, relieved at an opportunity to duck behind the truth.

"The Death of a Perfect Stranger," Daphne proclaimed in her best BBC Radio announcer's voice, dragging herself out of Dickens, but leaving a finger in to mark her place.

"How do you know it's a stranger?" I asked.

"Elementary," Daffy said. "It isn't you, it isn't me, and it isn't Feely. Mrs. Mullet is in the kitchen, Dogger is in the garden with the coppers, and Father was upstairs just a few minutes ago splashing in his bath."

I was about to tell her that it was me she had heard in the tub, but I decided not to; any mention of the bath led inevitably to gibes about my general cleanliness. But after the morning's events in the garden, I had felt the sudden need for a quick soak and a wash-up.

"He was probably poisoned," I said. "The stranger, I mean."

"It's always poison, isn't it?" Feely said with a toss of her hair. "At least in those lurid yellow detective novels. In this case, he probably made the fatal mistake of eating Mrs. Mullet's cooking."

As she pushed away the gooey remains of a coddled egg, something flashed into my mind like a cinder popping out of the grate and onto the hearth, but before I could examine it, my chain of thought was broken.

"Listen to this," Daphne said, reading aloud. "Fanny Squeers is writing a letter:

"'. . . my pa is one mask of brooses both blue and green likewise two forms are steepled in his Goar. We were kimpelled to have him carried down into the kitchen where he now lays . . .

"'. . . When your nevew that you recommended for a teacher had done this to my pa and jumped upon his body with his feet and also langwedge which I will not pollewt my pen with describing, he assaulted my ma with dreadful violence, dashed her to the earth, and drove her back comb several inches into her head. A very little more and it must have entered her skull. We have a medical certifiket that if it had, the tortershell would have affected the brain.'

"Now listen to this next bit:

"'Me and my brother were then the victims of his feury since which we have suffered very much which leads us to the arrowing belief that we have received some injury in our insides, especially as no marks of violence are visible externally. I am screaming out loud all the time I write—'"

It sounded to me like a classic case of cyanide poisoning, but I didn't much feel like sharing my insight with these two boors.

"'Screaming out loud all the time I write,'" Daffy repeated. "Imagine!"

"I know the feeling," I said, pushing my plate away, and, leaving my breakfast untouched, I made my way slowly up the east staircase to my laboratory.

WHENEVER I WAS UPSET, I made for my sanctum sanctorum. Here, among the bottles and beakers, I would allow myself to be enveloped by what I thought of as the Spirit of Chemistry. Here, sometimes, I would reenact, step by step, the discoveries of the great chemists. Or I would lift down lovingly from the bookcase a volume from Tar de Luce's treasured library, such as the English translation of Antoine Lavoisier's *Elements of Chemistry*, printed in 1790 but whose leaves, even after a hundred and sixty years, were still as crisp as butcher's paper. How I gloried in the antiquated names just waiting to be plucked from its pages: Butter of Antimony . . . Flowers of Arsenic.

"Rank poisons," Lavoisier called them, but I reveled in the recitation of their names like a hog at a spa.

"King's yellow!" I said aloud, rolling the words round in my mouth— savoring them in spite of their poisonous nature.

"Crystals of Venus! Fuming Liquor of Boyle! Oil of Ants!"

But it wasn't working this time; my mind kept flying back to Father, thinking over and over about what I had seen and heard. Who was this Twining—"Old Cuppa"—the man Father claimed they had killed? And why had Father not appeared at breakfast? That had me truly worried. Father always insisted that breakfast was "the body's banquet," and to the best of my knowledge, there was nothing on earth that would compel him to miss it.

Then, too, I thought of the passage from Dickens that Daphne had read to us: the bruises blue and green. Had Father fought with the stranger and suffered wounds that could not be hidden at the table? Or had he suffered those injuries to the insides described by Fanny Squeers: injuries that left no external marks of violence. Perhaps that was what had happened to the man with the red hair. Which should explain why I had seen no blood. Could Father be a murderer? Again?

My head was spinning. I could think of nothing better to calm it down than the Oxford English Dictionary. I fetched down the volume with the Vs. What was that word the stranger had breathed in my face? "*Vale*"! That was it.

I flipped the pages: vagabondical . . . vagrant . . . vain . . . here it was: *vale*: Farewell; good-bye; adieu. It was pronounced *val-eh*, and was the second person singular imperative of the Latin verb *valere*, to be well.

What a peculiar thing for a dying man to say to someone he didn't know.

A sudden racket from the hall interrupted my thoughts. Someone was giving the dinner gong a great old bonging. This huge disk, which looked like a leftover from the opening of a film by J. Arthur Rank, had not been sounded for ages, which could explain why I was so startled by its shattering noise.

I ran out of the laboratory and down the stairs to find an oversized man standing at the gong with the striker still in his hand.

"Coroner," he said, and I took it he was referring to himself. Although he did not trouble to give his name, I recognized him at once as Dr. Darby, one of the two partners in Bishop's Lacey's only medical practice.

Dr. Darby was the spitting image of John Bull: red face, multiple chins, and a stomach that bellied out like a sail full of wind. He was wearing a brown suit with a checked yellow waistcoat, and he carried the traditional doctor's black bag. If he remembered me as the girl whose hand he had stitched up the year before after the incident with a wayward bit of laboratory glassware, he gave no outward sign but stood there expectantly, like a hound on the scent.

Father was still nowhere in sight, nor was Dogger. I knew that Feely and Daffy would never condescend to respond to a bell ("So utterly Pavlovian," Feely said), and Mrs. Mullet always kept to her kitchen.

"The police are in the garden," I told him. "I'll show you the way."

As we stepped out into the sunshine, Inspector Hewitt looked up from examining the laces of a black shoe that protruded rather unpleasantly from the cucumbers.

"Morning, Fred," he said. "Thought you'd best come have a look."

"Um," Dr. Darby said. He opened his bag and rummaged inside for a moment before pulling out a white paper bag. He reached into it with two fingers and extracted a single crystal mint, which he popped into his mouth and sucked with noisy relish.

A moment later he had waded into the greenery and was kneeling beside the corpse.

"Anyone we know?" he asked, mumbling a bit round the mint.

"Shouldn't seem so," Inspector Hewitt said. "Empty pockets . . . no identification . . . reason to believe, though, that he's recently come from Norway."

Recently come from Norway? Surely this was a deduction worthy of the great Holmes himself—and I had heard it with my own ears! I was almost ready to forgive the Inspector his earlier rudeness. Almost . . . but not quite.

"We've launched inquiries, ports of call and so forth."

"Bloody Norwegians!" said Dr. Darby, rising and closing his bag. "Flock over here like birds to a lighthouse, where they expire and leave us to mop up. It isn't fair, is it?"

"What shall I put down as the time of death?" Inspector Hewitt asked.

"Hard to say. Always is. Well, not always, but often."

"Give or take?"

"Can't tell with cyanosis: takes a while to tell if it's coming or going, you know. Eight to twelve hours, I should say. I'll be able to tell you more after we've had our friend up on the table."

"And that would make it . . . ?"

Dr. Darby pushed back his cuff and looked at his watch.

"Well, let me see . . . it's eight twenty-two now, so that makes it no sooner than about that same hour last evening and no later than, say, midnight."

Midnight! I must have audibly sucked in air, since both Inspector Hewitt and Dr. Darby turned to look at me. How could I tell them that, just a few hours ago, the stranger from Norway had breathed his last breath into my face?

The solution was an easy one. I took to my heels. I found Dogger trimming the roses in the flower bed under the library window. The air was heavy with their scent: the delicious odor of tea chests from the Orient.

"Father not down yet, Dogger?" I asked.

"Lady Hillingdons are especially fine this year, Miss Flavia," he said, as if ice wouldn't melt in his mouth; as if our furtive encounter in the night had never taken place. Very well, I thought, I'll play his game.

"Especially fine," I said. "And Father?"

"I don't think he slept well. I expect he's having a bit of a lie-in."

A lie-in? How could he be back in bed when the place was alive with the law?

"How did he take it when you told him about the—you know—in the garden?"

Dogger turned and looked me directly in the eye. "I didn't tell him, miss."

He reached out and with a sudden snip of his secateurs, pruned a less-than-perfect bloom. It fell with a plop to the ground, where it lay with its puckered yellow face gazing up at us from the shadows.

We were both of us staring at the beheaded rose, thinking of our next move, when Inspector Hewitt came round the corner of the house.

"Flavia," he said, "I'd like a word with you."

"Inside," he added.

four

"AND THE PERSON OUTSIDE TO WHOM YOU WERE SPEAKING?"
Inspector Hewitt asked.

"Dogger," I said.

"First name?"

"Flavia," I said. I couldn't help myself.

We were sitting on one of the Regency sofas in the Rose Room. The Inspector slapped down his Biro and turned at the waist to face me.

"If you are not already aware of it, Miss de Luce—and I suspect you are—this is a murder investigation. I shall brook no frivolity. A man is dead and it is my duty to discover the why, the when, the how, and the who. And when I have done that, it is my further duty to explain it to the Crown. That means King George the Sixth, and King George the Sixth is not a frivolous man. Do I make myself clear?"

"Yes, sir," I said. "His given name is Arthur: Arthur Dogger."

"And he's the gardener here at Buckshaw?"

"He is now, yes."

The Inspector had opened a black notebook and was taking notes in a microscopic hand.

"Was he not always?"

"He's a jack-of-all-trades," I said. "He was our chauffeur until his nerve gave out . . . "

Even though I looked away, I could still feel the intensity of his detective eye.

"The war," I said. "He was a prisoner of war. Father felt that . . . he tried to—"

"I understand," Inspector Hewitt said, his voice gone suddenly soft. "Dogger's happiest in the garden."

"He's happiest in the garden."

"You're a remarkable girl, you know," he said. "In most cases I should wait to talk to you until a parent was present, but with your father indisposed . . . "

Indisposed? Oh, of course! I'd nearly forgotten my little lie.

In spite of my momentary look of puzzlement, the Inspector went on: "You mentioned Dogger's stint as chauffeur. Does your father still keep a motorcar?"

He did, in fact: an old Rolls-Royce Phantom II, which now resided in the coach house. It had actually been Harriet's, and it had not been driven since the day the news of her death had come to Buckshaw. Furthermore, although Father was not a driver himself, he would permit no one else to touch it.

Consequently, the coachwork of this magnificent old thoroughbred, with its long black bonnet and tall nickel-plated Palladian radiator with intertwined *R*s, had long ago been breached by field mice that had found their way up through the wooden floorboards and nested in its mahogany glove box. Even in its decrepitude, it was sometimes still spoken of as "The Royce," as people of quality often call these vehicles.

"Only a ploughman would call it a Rolls," Feely had said once when I'd momentarily forgotten myself in her presence.

Whenever I wanted to be alone in a place where I could count on being undisturbed, I would clamber up into the dim light of Harriet's dust-covered Roller, where I would sit for hours in the incubator-like heat, surrounded by drooping plush upholstery and cracked, nibbled leather.

At the Inspector's unexpected question, my mind flew back to a dark, stormy day the previous autumn, a day of pelting rain and a mad torrent of wind. Because the risk of falling branches had made it too dangerous to hazard a walk in the woods above Buckshaw, I had slipped away from the house and fought my way through the gale to the coach house to have a good think. Inside, the Phantom stood glinting dully in the shadows as the storm howled and screamed and beat at the windows like a tribe of hungry banshees. My hand was already on the door handle of the car before I realized there was someone inside it. I nearly leaped out of my skin. But then I realized that it was Father. He was just sitting there with tears running down his face, oblivious to the storm.

For several minutes I had stood perfectly still, afraid to move, scarce daring to breathe. But when Father reached slowly for the door handle, I had to drop silently to my hands like a gymnast and roll underneath the car. From the corner of my eye I saw one of his perfectly polished half-Wellingtons step down from the running board, and as he walked slowly away, I heard something like a shuddering sob escape him. For a long while I lay there staring up at the floorboards of Harriet's Rolls-Royce.

"Yes," I said. "There's an old Phantom in the coach house."

"And your father doesn't drive."

"No."

"I see."

The Inspector laid down his Biro and notebook as carefully as if they were made of Venetian glass.

"Flavia," he said (and I couldn't help noticing that I was no longer "Miss de Luce"), "I'm going to ask you a very important question. The way in which you answer it is crucial, do you understand?"

I nodded.

"I know that you were the one who reported this . . . incident. But who was it that first discovered the body?"

My mind went into a tailspin. Would telling the truth incriminate Father? Did the police already know that I had summoned Dogger to the cucumber patch? Obviously not; the Inspector had only just learned Dogger's identity, so it seemed reasonable to assume they had not yet questioned him. But when they did, how much would he tell them? Which of us should he protect: Father or me? Was there some new test by which they would know that the victim was still alive when I discovered him?

"I did," I blurted out. "I found the body." I felt like Cock Robin.

"Just as I thought," Inspector Hewitt said.

And here was one of those awkward silences. It was broken by the arrival of Sergeant Woolmer, who used his massive body to herd Father into the room.

"We found him in the coach house, sir," he said. "Holed up in an old motorcar."

"Who are *you*, sir?" Father demanded. He was furious, and for an instant I caught a glimpse of the man he must once have been. "Who are you, and what are you doing in my house?"

"I'm Inspector Hewitt, sir," the Inspector said, getting to his feet. "Thank you, Sergeant Woolmer."

The sergeant took two steps back until he was clear of the door frame, and then he was gone.

"Well?" Father said. "Is there a problem, Inspector?"

"I'm afraid there is, sir. A body has been found in your garden."

"What do you mean, a body? A dead body?"

Inspector Hewitt nodded. "Yes, sir," he said.

"Whose is it? The body, I mean."

It was at that moment I realized Father had no bruises, no scratches, no cuts, no abrasions . . . at least none that were visible. I also noticed that he had begun to turn white round the edges, except for his ears, which had begun to go the color of pink plasticine.

And I noticed that the Inspector had spotted it too. He did not answer Father's question at once, but left it hanging in the air.

Father turned and walked in a long arc to the liquor cabinet, touching with the tips of his fingers the horizontal surface of every piece of furniture he passed. He mixed himself a Votrix-and-gin and downed it, all with a swift, fluid efficiency that suggested more practice than I had imagined possible.

"We haven't identified the person as yet, Colonel de Luce. Actually, we were hoping you could offer us assistance."

At this, Father's face went whiter, if possible, than it had been before, and his ears burned redder.

"I'm sorry, Inspector," he said, in a voice that was nearly inaudible. "Please don't ask me to . . . I'm not very good with death, you see . . . "

Not very good with death? Father was a military man, and military men lived with death; lived *for* death; lived *on* death. To a professional soldier, oddly enough, death was life. Even I knew that.

I knew instantly, too, that Father had just told a lie, and suddenly, without warning, somewhere inside me, a little thread broke. It felt as if I had just aged a little and something old had snapped.

"I understand, sir," Inspector Hewitt said, "but unless other avenues present themselves . . . "

Father pulled a handkerchief from his pocket and mopped his forehead, then his neck.

"Bit of a shock, you know," he said, "all this . . . "

He waved an unsteady hand at his surroundings, and as he did so, Inspector Hewitt took up his notebook, flipped back the cover, and began to write. Father walked slowly to the window where he pretended to be taking in the prospect, one which I could see perfectly in my mind's eye: the artificial lake; the island with its crumbling Folly; the fountains, now dry, that had been shut off since the outbreak of war; the hills beyond.

"Have you been at home all morning?" the Inspector asked with no preliminaries.

"What?" Father spun round.

"Have you been out of the house since last evening?"

It was a long time before Father spoke.

"Yes," he said at last. "I was out this morning. In the coach house."

I had to suppress a smile. Sherlock Holmes once remarked of his brother, Mycroft, that you were as unlikely to find him outside of the Diogenes Club as you were to meet a tramcar coming down a country lane. Like Mycroft, Father had his rails, and he ran on them. Except for church and the occasional short-tempered dash to the train to attend a stamp show, Father seldom, if ever, stuck his nose out-of-doors.

"What time would that have been, Colonel?"

"Four, perhaps. Perhaps a bit earlier."

"You were in the coach house for—" Inspector Hewitt glanced at his wristwatch. "—five and a half hours? From four this morning until just now?"

"Yes, until just now," Father said. He was not accustomed to being questioned, and even though the Inspector did not notice it, I could sense the rising irritation in his voice.

"I see. Do you often go out at that time of day?"

The Inspector's question sounded casual, almost chatty, but I knew that it wasn't.

"No, not really, no, I don't," Father said. "What are you driving at?"

Inspector Hewitt tapped the tip of his nose with his Biro, as if framing his next question for a parliamentary committee. "Did you see anyone else about?"

"No," Father said. "Of course I didn't. Not a living soul."

Inspector Hewitt stopped tapping long enough to make a note. "No one?"

"No."

As if he'd known it all along, the Inspector gave a sad and gentle nod. He seemed disappointed, and sighed as he tucked his notebook into an inner pocket.

"Oh, one last question, Colonel, if you don't mind," he said suddenly, as if he had just thought of it. "What were you doing in the coach house?"

Father's gaze drifted off out the window and his jaw muscles tightened. And then he turned and looked the Inspector straight in the eye.

"I'm not prepared to tell you that, Inspector," he said.

"Very well, then," Inspector Hewitt said. "I think—"

It was at this very moment that Mrs. Mullet pushed open the door with her ample bottom, and waddled into the room with a loaded tray.

"I've brought you some nice seed biscuits," she said. "Seed biscuits and tea and a nice glass of milk for Miss Flavia."

Seed biscuits and milk! I hated Mrs. Mullet's seed biscuits the way Saint Paul hated sin. Perhaps even more so. I wanted to clamber up onto the table, and with a sausage on the end of a fork as my scepter, shout in my best Laurence Olivier voice, "Will no one rid us of this turbulent pastry cook?"

But I didn't. I kept my peace.

With a little curtsy, Mrs. Mullet set down her burden in front of Inspector Hewitt, then suddenly spotted Father, who was still standing at the window.

"Oh! Colonel de Luce. I was hoping you'd turn up. I wanted to tell you I got rid of that dead bird what we found on yesterday's doorstep."

Mrs. Mullet had somewhere picked up the idea that such reversals of phrase were not only quaint, but poetic.

Before Father could deflect the course of the conversation, Inspector Hewitt had taken up the reins.

"A dead bird on the doorstep? Tell me about it, Mrs. Mullet."

"Well, sir, me and the Colonel and Miss Flavia here was in the kitchen. I'd just took a nice custard pie out of the oven and set it to cool in the window. It was that time of day when my mind usually starts thinkin' about gettin' home to Alf. Alf is my husband, sir, and he doesn't like for me to be out gallivantin' when it's time for his tea. Says it makes him go all over fizzy-like if his digestion's thrown off its time. Once his digestion goes off, it's a sight to behold. All buckets and mops, and that."

"The time, Mrs. Mullet?"

"It was about eleven, or a quarter past. I come for four hours in the morning, from eight to twelve, and three in the afternoon, from one to four, though," she said, with a surprisingly black scowl at Father, who was too pointedly looking out the window to notice it, "I'm usually kept behind my time, what with this and that."

"And the bird?"

"The bird was on the doorstep, dead as Dorothy's donkey. A snipe, it was: one of them jack snipes. God knows I've cooked enough on 'em in my day to be certain of that. Gave me a fright, it did, lyin' there on its back with its feathers twitchin' in the wind, like, as if its skin was still alive when its heart was already dead. That's what I said to Alf. 'Alf,' I said, 'that bird was lyin' there as if its skin was still alive—'"

"You have a very keen eye, Mrs. Mullet," Inspector Hewitt said, and she puffed up like a pouter pigeon in a glow of iridescent pink. "Was there anything else?"

"Well, yes, sir, there was a stamp stuck on its little bill, almost like it was carryin' it in its mouth, like a stork carries a baby in a nappy, if you know what I mean, but in another way, not like that at all."

"A stamp, Mrs. Mullet? What sort of stamp?"

"A postage stamp, sir—but not like the ones you sees nowadays. Oh no—not like them at all. This here stamp had the Queen's head on it. Not Her Present Majesty, God bless her, but the old Queen . . . the Queen what was . . . Queen Victoria. Leastways she should have been on it if that bird's bill hadn't been stickin' through where her face ought to have been."

"You're quite sure about the stamp?"

"Cross my heart and hope to die, sir. Alf had a stamp collection when he was a lad, and he still keeps what's left of it in an old Huntley and Palmers biscuit tin under the bed in the upstairs hall. He doesn't take them out as much as he did when both of us were younger—makes him sad, he says. Still and all, I knows a Penny Black when I sees one, dead bird's bill shoved through it or no."

"Thank you, Mrs. Mullet," said Inspector Hewitt, helping himself to a seed biscuit, "you've been most helpful."

Mrs. Mullet dropped him another curtsy and went to the door.

"'It's funny,' I said to Alf, I said, 'You don't generally see jack snipes in England till September.' Many's the jack snipe I've turned on the spit and served up roasted on a nice bit of toast. Miss Harriet, God bless her soul, used to fancy nothing better than a nice—"

There was a groan behind me, and I turned just in time to see Father fold in the middle like a camp chair and slither to the floor.

I MUST SAY THAT Inspector Hewitt was very good about it. In a flash he was at Father's side, clapping an ear to his chest, loosening his tie, checking with a long finger for airway obstruction. I could see that he had not slept through his St. John Ambulance classes. A moment later he flung open the window, put first and fourth fingers to his lower lip, and let out a whistle I should have given a guinea to learn.

"Dr. Darby!" he shouted. "Up here, if you please. Quickly! Bring your bag."

As for me, I was still standing with my hand to my mouth when Dr. Darby strode into the room and knelt beside Father. After a quick one-two-three examination, he pulled a small blue vial from his bag.

"Syncope," he said to Inspector Hewitt; to Mrs. Mullet and me, "That means he's fainted. Nothing to worry about."

Phew!

He unstoppered the glass, and in the few moments before he applied it to Father's nostrils, I detected a familiar scent: It was my old friend *Ammon. Carb.*, Ammonium Carbonate, or, as I called it when we were alone together in the laboratory, *Sal Volatile*, or sometimes just plain Sal. I knew that the "ammon" part of its name came from ammonia, which was named on account of its being first discovered not far from the shrine of the god Ammon in ancient Egypt, where it was found in camel's urine. And I knew that later, in London, a man after my own heart had patented a means by which smelling salts could be extracted from Patagonian guano.

Chemistry! Chemistry! How I love it!

As Dr. Darby held the vial to his nostrils, Father gave out a snort like a bull in a field, and his eyelids flew up like roller blinds. But he uttered not a word.

"Ha! Back among the living, I see," the doctor said, as Father, in confusion, tried to prop himself up on his elbow and look round the room. In spite of his jovial tone, Dr. Darby was cradling Father like a newborn baby. "Wait a bit till you get your bearings. Just stay down on the old Axminster a minute."

Inspector Hewitt stood gravely by until it was time to help Father to his feet.

Leaning heavily on Dogger's arm—Dogger had been summoned—Father made his way carefully up the staircase to his room. Daphne and Feely put in a brief appearance: no more, really, than a couple of blanched faces behind the banisters.

Mrs. Mullet, scurrying by on her way to the kitchen, stopped to put a solicitous hand on my arm.

"Was the pie good, luv?" she asked.

I'd forgotten the pie until that moment. I took a leaf from Dr. Darby's notebook.

"Um," I said.

Inspector Hewitt and Dr. Darby had returned to the garden when I climbed slowly up the stairs to my laboratory. I watched from the window with a little sadness and almost a touch of loss as two ambulance attendants came round the side of the house and began to shift the stranger's remains onto a canvas stretcher. In the distance, Dogger was working his way round the Balaclava fountain on the east lawn, busily decapitating more of the Lady Hillingdons.

Everyone was occupied; with any luck, I could do what I needed to do and be back before anyone even realized I was gone.

I slipped downstairs and out the front door, pulled Gladys, my ancient BSA, from where she was leaning against a stone urn, and minutes later was pedaling furiously into Bishop's Lacey.

What was the name Father had mentioned?

Twining. That was it. "Old Cuppa." And I knew precisely where to find him.

five

BISHOP LACEY'S FREE LIBRARY WAS LOCATED IN COW LANE, A narrow, shady, tree-lined track that sloped from the High Street down to the river. The original building was a modest Georgian house of black brick, whose photograph had once appeared in color on the cover of *Country Life*. It had been given to the people of Bishop's Lacey by Lord Margate, a local boy who had made good (as plain old Adrian Chipping) and had gone on to fame and fortune as the sole purveyor of BeefChips, a tinned bully beef of his own invention, to Her Majesty's Government during the Boer War.

The library had existed as an oasis of silence until 1939. Then, while closed for renovations, it had taken fire when a pile of painter's rags spontaneously combusted just as Mr. Chamberlain was delivering to the British people his famous "As long as war has not begun, there is always hope that it may be prevented" speech. Since the entire adult population of Bishop's Lacey had been huddled round one another's wireless sets, no one, including the six members of the volunteer fire department, had spotted the blaze until it was far too late. By the time they arrived with their hand-operated pumping engine, nothing remained of the place but a pile of hot ashes. Fortunately, all of the books had escaped, having been stored for protection in temporary quarters.

But with the outbreak of war then, and the general fatigue since the Armistice, the original building had never been replaced. Its site was now nothing more than a weed-infested patch in Cater Street, just round the corner from the Thirteen Drakes. The property, having been given in perpetuity to the villagers of Bishop's Lacey, could not be sold, and the once-temporary premises that housed its holdings had now become the Free Library's permanent home in Cow Lane.

As I turned off the High Street, I could see the library, a low box of glass-brick and tile, which had been erected in the 1920s to house a motorcar showroom. Several of the original enamel signs bearing the names of extinct motorcars, such as the Wolseley and the Sheffield-Simplex, were still attached to one of its walls below the roofline, too high up to have attracted the attention of thieves or vandals.

Now, a quarter century after the last Lagonda had rolled out of its doors, the building had fallen, like old crockery in the servant's quarters, into a kind of chipped and broken decrepitude.

Behind and beyond the library, a warren of decaying outbuildings, like tombstones clustered round a country church, subsided into the long grass between the old showroom and the abandoned towpath that followed the river. Several of these dirt-floored hovels housed the overflow of books from the library's long gone and much larger Georgian predecessor. Makeshift structures that had once been a cluster of motor repair shops now found their dim interiors home to row upon row of unwanted books, their subjects labeled above them: History, Geography, Philosophy, Science. Still reeking of antique motor oil, rust, and primitive water closets, these wooden garages were called the stacks—and I could see why! I often came here to read and, next to my chemical laboratory at Buckshaw, it was my favorite place on earth.

I was thinking this as I arrived at the front door and turned the knob. "Oh, scissors!" I said. It was locked.

As I stepped to one side to peer in the window, I noticed a handmade sign crudely drawn with black crayon and stuck to the glass: CLOSED.

Closed? Today was Saturday. The library hours were ten o'clock to two-thirty, Thursday through Saturday; they were clearly posted in the black-framed notice beside the door. Had something happened to Miss Pickery?

I gave the door a shake, and then a good pounding. I cupped my hands to the glass and peered inside, but except for a beam of sunlight falling through motes of dust before coming to rest upon shelves of novels there was nothing to be seen.

"Miss Pickery!" I called, but there was no answer.

"Oh, scissors!" I said again. I should have to put off my researches until another time. As I stood outside in Cow Lane, it occurred to me that Heaven must be a place where the library is open twenty-four hours a day, seven days a week.

No . . . eight days a week.

I knew that Miss Pickery lived in Shoe Street. If I left my bicycle here and took a shortcut through the outbuildings at the back of the library, I'd pass behind the Thirteen Drakes, and come out beside her cottage.

I picked my way through the long wet grass, watching carefully to avoid tripping on any of the rotting bits of rusty machinery that jutted out here and there like dinosaur bones in the Gobi Desert. Daphne had described to me the effects of tetanus: One scratch from an old auto wheel and I'd be foaming at the mouth, barking like a dog, and falling to the ground in convulsions at the sight of water. I had just managed to work up a gob of spit in my mouth for practice when I heard voices.

"But how could you let him, Mary?" It was a young man's voice, coming from the inn yard.

I flattened myself behind a tree, then peeked round it. The speaker was Ned Cropper, the odd-jobs boy at the Thirteen Drakes.

Ned! The very thought of him had the same effect upon Ophelia as an injection of novocaine. She had taken it into her head that he was the spitting image of Dirk Bogarde, but the only similarity I could see was that both had arms and legs and stacks of brilliantined hair.

Ned was sitting on a beer barrel outside the back door of the inn, and a girl I recognized as Mary Stoker was sitting on another. They did not look at one another. As Ned dug an elaborate maze in the ground with the heel of his boot, Mary kept her hands clasped tightly in her lap as she gazed at nothing in midair.

Although he had spoken in an urgent undertone, I could hear every word perfectly. The plaster wall of the Thirteen Drakes functioned as a perfect sound reflector.

"I told you, Ned Cropper, I couldn't help myself, could I? He come up behind me while I was changing his sheets."

"Whyn't you let out a yell? I know you can wake the dead . . . when you feel like it."

"You don't much know my pa, do you? If he knew what that bloke had done he'd have my hide for gumboots!"

She spat into the dust.

"Mary!" The voice came from somewhere inside the inn, but still it rolled out into the yard like thunder. It was Mary's father, Tully Stoker, the innkeeper, whose abnormally loud voice played a prominent part in some of the village's most scandalous old wives' tales.

"Mary!"

Mary leaped to her feet at the sound of his voice.

"Coming!" she shouted. "I'm coming!"

She hovered: torn, as if making a decision. Suddenly she darted like an asp across to Ned and planted a sharp kiss on his mouth, then, with a flick of her apron—like a conjurer flourishing his cape—she vanished into the dark recess of the open doorway.

Ned sat for a moment longer, then wiped his mouth with the back of his hand before rolling the barrel to join the other empties along the far side of the inn yard.

"Hullo, Ned!" I shouted, and he turned, half embarrassed. I knew he'd be wondering if I'd overheard him with Mary, or witnessed the kiss. I decided to be ambiguous.

"Nice day," I said with a sappy grin.

Ned inquired after my health, and then, in order of careful precedence, about the health of Father, and of Daphne.

"They're fine," I told him.

"And Miss Ophelia?" he asked, getting round to her at last.

"Miss Ophelia? Well, to tell you the truth, Ned, we're all rather worried about her."

Ned recoiled as if a wasp had gone up his nose.

"Oh? What's the trouble? Nothing serious, I hope."

"She's gone all green," I said. "I think it's chlorosis. Dr. Darby thinks so too."

In his 1811 *Dictionary of the Vulgar Tongue*, Francis Grose called chlorosis "Love's Fever," and "The Virgin's Disease." I knew that Ned did not have the same ready access to Captain Grose's book as I did. I hugged myself inwardly.

"Ned!"

It was Tully Stoker again. Ned took a step towards the door.

"Tell her I was asking after her," he said.

I gave him a Winston Churchill V with my fingers. It was the least I could do.

SHOE STREET, like Cow Lane, ran from the High Street to the river. Miss Pickery's Tudor cottage, halfway along, looked like something you'd see on the lid of a jigsaw puzzle box. With its thatched roof and white-washed walls, its diamond-pane leaded-glass windows, and its red-painted Dutch door, it was an artist's delight, its half-timbered walls floating like a quaint old ship upon a sea of old-fashioned flowers such as anemones, hollyhocks, gillyflowers, Canterbury bells, and others whose names I didn't know.

Roger, Miss Pickery's ginger tomcat, rolled on the front doorstep, exposing his belly for a scratching. I obliged.

"Good boy, Roger," I said. "Where's Miss Pickery?"

Roger strolled slowly off in search of something interesting to stare at, and I knocked at the door. There was no answer.

I went round into the back garden. No one home.

Back in the High Street, after stopping for a look at the same old flyblown apothecary jars in the chemist's window, I was just crossing Cow Lane when I happened to glance to my left and saw someone stepping into the library. Arms outstretched, I dipped my wings and banked ninety degrees. But by the time I reached the door, whoever it was had already let themselves in. I turned the doorknob, and this time, it swung open.

The woman was putting her purse in the drawer and settling down behind the desk, and I realized I had never seen her before in my life. Her face was as wrinkled as one of those forgotten apples you sometimes find in the pocket of last year's winter jacket.

"Yes?" she said, peering over her spectacles. They teach them to do that at the Royal Academy of Library Science. The spectacles, I noted, had a slightly grayish tint, as if they had been steeped overnight in vinegar.

"I was expecting to see Miss Pickery," I said.

"Miss Pickery has been called away on a private family matter."

"Oh," I said.

"Yes, very sad. Her sister, Hetty, who lives over in Nether-Wolsey, had a tragic accident with a sewing machine. It appeared for the first few days that all might be well, but then she took a sudden turn and it seems now as if there's a real possibility she might lose the finger. Such a shame—and she with the twins. Miss Pickery, of course . . . "

"Of course," I said.

"I'm Miss Mountjoy, and I'd be happy to assist you in her stead, as it were."

Miss Mountjoy! The retired Miss Mountjoy! I had heard tales about "Miss Mountjoy and the Reign of Terror." She had been Librarian-in-Chief of the Bishop's Lacey Free Library when Noah was a sailor. All sweetness on the outside, but on the inside, "The Palace of Malice." Or so I'd been told. (Mrs. Mullet again, who reads detective novels.) The villagers still held novenas to pray she wouldn't come out of retirement.

"And how may I help you, dearie?"

If there is a thing I truly despise, it is being addressed as "dearie." When I write my magnum opus, *A Treatise Upon All Poisons*, and come to "Cyanide," I am going to put under "Uses" the phrase "Particularly efficacious in the cure of those who call one 'Dearie.'"

Still, one of my Rules of Life is this: When you want something, bite your tongue.

I smiled weakly and said, "I'd like to consult your newspaper files."

"Newspaper files!" she gurgled. "My, you do know a lot, don't you, dearie?"

"Yes," I said, trying to look modest, "I do."

"The newspapers are in chronological order on the shelves in the Drummond Room: That's the west rear, to the left, at the top of the stairs," she said with a wave of her hand.

"Thank you," I said, edging towards the staircase.

"Unless, of course, you want something earlier than last year. In that case, they'll be in one of the outbuildings. What year are you looking for, in particular?"

"I don't really know," I said. But, wait a minute—I *did* know! What was it the stranger had said in Father's study?

"Twining—Old Cuppa's been dead these—" What?

I could hear the stranger's oily voice in my head: "Old Cuppa's been dead these . . . thirty years!"

"The year 1920," I said, as cool as a trout. "I'd like to peruse your newspaper archive for 1920."

"Those are likely still in the Pit Shed—that is, if the rats haven't been at them." She said this with a bit of a leer over her spectacles as if, at the mention of rats, I might throw my hands in the air and run off screaming.

"I'll find them," I said. "Is there a key?"

Miss Mountjoy rummaged in the desk drawer and dredged up a ring of iron keys that looked as if they might once have belonged to the jailers of Edmond Dantès in *The Count of Monte Cristo*. I gave them a cheery jingle and walked out the door.

The Pit Shed was the outbuilding farthest from the library's main building. Tottering precipitously on the river's bank, it was a conglomeration of weathered boards and rusty corrugated tin, all overgrown with moss and climbing vines. In the heyday of the motor showroom, it had been the garage where autos had their oil and tires changed, their axles lubricated, and other intimate underside adjustments seen to.

Since then, neglect and erosion had reduced the place to something resembling a hermit's hovel in the woods.

I gave the key a twist and the door sprang open with a rusty groan. I stepped into the gloom, being careful to edge round the sheer sides of the deep mechanic's pit which, though it was boarded over with heavy planks, still occupied much of the room.

The place had a sharp and musky smell with more than a hint of ammonia, as if there were little animals living beneath its floorboards.

Half of the wall closest to Cow Lane was taken up with a folding door, now barred, which had once rolled back to allow motorcars to enter and park astride the pit. The glass of its four windows had been painted over, for some unfathomable reason, with a ghastly red through which the sunlight leaked, giving the room a bloody and unsettling tint.

Round the remaining three walls, rising like the frames of bunk beds, were ranged wooden shelves, each one piled high with yellowed newspapers: *The Hinley Chronicle*, *The West Counties Advertiser*, *The Morning Post-Horn*, all arranged by year and identified with faded handwritten labels.

I had no trouble finding 1920. I lifted down the top pile, choking with the cloud of dust that flew up into my face like an explosion in a flour mill as tiny shards of nibbled newsprint fell to the floor like paper snow.

Tub and loofah tonight, I thought, like it or not.

A small deal table stood near a grimy window: just enough light and enough room to spread the papers open, one at a time.

The Morning Post-Horn caught my eye: a tabloid whose front page, like the *Times of London*, was chock-full of adverts, snippets of news, and agony columns:

Lost: brown paper parcel tied with butcher's twine.
Of sentimental value to distressed owner. Generous reward offered.
Apply "Smith," c/o The White Hart, Wolverston

Or this:

Dear One: He was watching. Same time Thursday next. Bring soapstone. Bruno.

AND THEN SUDDENLY I REMEMBERED! Father had attended Greyminster . . . and wasn't Greyminster near Hinley? I tossed *The Morning Post-Horn* back onto its bier, and pulled down the first of four stacks of *The Hinley Chronicle*.

This paper had been published weekly, on Fridays. The first Friday of that year was New Year's Day, so that the year's first issue was dated the following Friday: the eighth of January, 1920.

Page followed page of holiday news—Christmas visitors from the Continent, a deferred meeting of the Ladies' Altar Guild, a "good-sized pig" for sale, Boxing Day revels at The Grange, a lost tire from a brewer's dray.

The Assizes in March were a grim catalogue of thefts, poaching, and assaults.

On and on I went, my hands blackening with ink that had dried twenty years before I was born. The summer brought more visitors from the Continent, market days, laborers wanted, Boy Scout camps, two fêtes, and several proposed road works.

After an hour I was beginning to despair. The people who read these things must have possessed superhuman eyesight, the type was so wretchedly small. Much more of this and I knew I'd have a throbbing headache.

And then I found it:

Popular Schoolmaster Plummets to Death

In a tragic accident on Monday morning, Grenville Twining, M.A. (Oxon.), 72, Latin scholar and respected housemaster at Greyminster School, near Hinley, fell to his death from the clock tower of Greyminster's Anson House. Those familiar with the facts have described the accident as "simply inexplicable."

"He climbed up onto the parapet, gathered his robes about him, and gave us the palm-down Roman Salute. *'Vale!'* he shouted down to the boys in the quad," said Timothy Greene of the sixth form at Greyminster, " . . . and down he came!"

"Vale"? My heart gave a leap. It was the same word the dying man had breathed into my face! "Farewell." It could hardly be coincidence, could it? It was just too bizarre. There *had* to be some connection—but what could it be?

Damn! My mind was racing away like mad and my wits were standing still. The Pit Shed was hardly the place for speculation; I'd think about it later.

I read on:

"The way his gown fluttered, he seemed just like a falling angel," said Toby Lonsdale, a rosy-cheeked lad who was near tears as he was shepherded away by his comrades before giving way and breaking down altogether nearby.

Mr. Twining had recently been questioned by police in the matter of a missing postage stamp: a unique and extremely valuable variation of the Penny Black.

"There is no connection," said Dr. Isaac Kissing, who has been Headmaster at Greyminster since 1915. "No connection whatsoever. Mr. Twining was revered and, if I may say so, loved by all who knew him."

The Hinley Chronicle has learned that police inquiries into both incidents are continuing.

The newspaper's date was the 24th of September, 1920.

I reshelved the paper, stepped outside, and locked the door. Miss Mountjoy was still sitting idle at her desk when I returned the key.

"Did you find what you were looking for, dearie?" she asked.

"Yes," I said, making a great show of dusting off my hands.

"May I inquire further?" she asked coyly. "I might be able to direct you to related materials."

Translation: She was perishing with nosiness.

"No, thank you, Miss Mountjoy," I said.

For some reason I suddenly felt as if my heart had been ripped out and swapped with a counterfeit made of lead.

"Are you all right, dearie?" Miss Mountjoy asked. "You seem a little peaked."

Peaked? I felt as if I were about to puke.

Perhaps it was nervousness, or perhaps it was an unconscious attempt to stave off nausea, but to my horror I found myself blurting out, "Did you ever hear of a Mr. Twining, of Greyminster School?"

She gasped. Her face went red, then gray, as if it had caught fire before my eyes and collapsed in an avalanche of ashes. She pulled a lace handkerchief from her sleeve, knotted it, and jammed it into her mouth, and for a few moments, she sat there, rocking in her chair, gripping the lace between her teeth like an eighteenth-century seaman having his leg amputated below the knee.

At last, she looked up at me with brimming eyes and said in a shaky voice, "Mr. Twining was my mother's brother."

six

WE WERE HAVING TEA. MISS MOUNTJOY HAD EXCAVATED A battered tin kettle from somewhere, and after a dig in her carry-bag, come up with a scruffy packet of Peek Freans.

I sat on a library ladder and helped myself to another biscuit.

"It was tragic," she said. "My uncle had been housemaster of Anson House forever—or so it seemed. He took great pride in his house and in his boys. He spared no pains in urging them always to do their best; to prepare themselves for life.

"He liked to joke that he spoke better Latin than Julius Caesar himself, and his Latin grammar, *Twining's Lingua Latina*—published when he was just twenty-four, by the way—was a standard text in schools round the world. I still keep a copy beside my bed, and even though I can't read much of it, I sometimes like to hold it for the comfort it brings me: *qui, quae, quod,* and all that. The words have such a comforting sound about them.

"Uncle Grenville was forever organizing things: He encouraged his boys to form a debating society, a skating club, a cycling club, a cribbage circle. He was a keen amateur conjurer, although not a very good one—you could always see the ace of diamonds peeping out of his cuffs with the bit of elastic dangling down from it. He was an enthusiastic stamp collector, and taught the boys to learn the history and the geography of the issuing countries, as well as to keep neat, orderly albums. And that was his downfall."

I stopped chewing and sat expectantly. Miss Mountjoy had slipped into a kind of reverie and seemed unlikely to go on without encouragement.

Little by little, I had come under her spell. She had talked to me woman-to-woman, and I had succumbed. I felt sorry for her . . . really I did.

"His downfall?" I asked.

"He made the great mistake of putting his trust in several wretched excuses for boyhood who had wormed themselves into his favor. They pretended great interest in his little stamp collection, and feigned an even greater interest in the collection of Dr. Kissing, the headmaster. In those days, Dr. Kissing was the world's greatest authority on the Penny Black—the world's first postage stamp—in all of its many variations. The Kissing collection was the envy—and I say that advisedly—of all the world. These vile creatures convinced Uncle Grenville to intercede and arrange a private viewing of the Head's stamps.

"While examining the crown jewel of this collection, a Penny Black of a certain peculiarity—I've forgotten the details—the stamp was destroyed."

"Destroyed?" I asked.

"Burned. One of the boys set it alight. He meant it to be a joke."

Miss Mountjoy took up her tea and drifted like a wisp of smoke to the window, where she stood looking out for what seemed like a very long time. I was beginning to think she'd forgotten about me, but then she spoke again:

"Of course, my uncle was blamed for the disaster . . . "

She turned and looked me in the eye. "And the rest of the story you've learned this morning in the Pit Shed."

"He killed himself," I said.

"He did *not* kill himself!" she shrieked. The cup and saucer fell from her hand and shattered on the tile floor. "He was murdered!"

"By whom?" I asked, getting a grip on myself, even managing to get the grammar right. Miss Mountjoy was beginning to grate on my nerves again.

"By those monsters!" she spat out. "Those obscene monsters!"

"Monsters?"

"Those boys! They killed him as surely as if they had taken a dagger into their own hands and stuck him in the heart."

"Who were they, these boys . . . these monsters, I mean? Do you remember their names?"

"Why do you want to know? What right have you coming here to stir up these ghosts?"

"I'm interested in history," I said.

She passed a hand across her eyes as if commanding herself to come out of a trance, and spoke in the slow voice of a woman drugged.

"It's so long ago," she said. "So very long ago. I really don't care to remember . . . Uncle Grenville mentioned their names, before he was—"

"Murdered?" I suggested.

"Yes, that's right, before he was murdered. Strange, isn't it? For all these years one of their names has stuck most in my mind because it reminded me of a monkey . . . a monkey on a chain, you know, with an organ grinder and a little round red hat and a tin cup."

She gave a tight, nervous little laugh.

"Jacko," I said.

Miss Mountjoy sat down heavily as if she'd been poleaxed. She stared at me with goggle eyes as if I'd just materialized from another dimension.

"Who are you, little girl?" she whispered. "Why have you come here? What's your name?"

"Flavia," I said as I paused for a moment at the door. "Flavia Sabina Dolores de Luce." The "Sabina" was real enough; "Dolores" I invented on the spot.

UNTIL I RESCUED HER from rusty oblivion, my trusty old three-speed BSA Keep Fit had languished for years in a toolshed among broken flowerpots and wooden wheelbarrows. Like so many other things at Buckshaw, she had once belonged to Harriet, who had named her *l'Hirondelle*: "the swallow." I had rechristened her Gladys.

Gladys's tires had been flat, her gears bone dry and crying out for oil, but with her own onboard tire pump and black leather tool bag behind her seat, she was entirely self-sufficient. With Dogger's help, I soon had her in tiptop running order. In the tool kit, I had found a booklet called *Cycling for Women of All Ages*, by Prunella Stack, the leader of the Women's League of Health and Beauty. On its cover was written with black ink, in beautiful, flowing script: *Harriet de Luce, Buckshaw*.

There were times when Harriet was not gone; she was everywhere.

As I raced home, past the leaning moss-covered headstones in the heaped-up churchyard of St. Tancred's, through the narrow leafy lanes, across the chalky High Road, and into the open country, I let Gladys have her head, swooping down the slopes past the rushing hedges, imagining all the while I was the pilot of one of the Spitfires which, just five years ago, had skimmed these very hedgerows like swallows as they came in to land at Leathcote.

I had learned from the booklet that if I bicycled with a poker back like Miss Gulch in *The Wizard of Oz* at the cinema, chose varied terrain, and breathed deeply, I would glow with health like the Eddystone Light, and never suffer from pimples: a useful bit of information which I wasted no time in passing along to Ophelia.

Was there ever a companion booklet, *Cycling for Men of All Ages?* I wondered. And if so, had it been written by the leader of the Men's League of Health and Handsomeness?

I pretended I was the boy Father must always have wanted: a son he could take to Scotland for salmon fishing and grouse shooting on the moors; a son he could send out to Canada to take up ice hockey. Not that Father did any of these things, but if he'd had a son, I liked to think he might have done.

My middle name should have been Laurence, like his, and when we were alone together he'd have called me Larry. How keenly disappointed he must have been when all of us had come out girls.

Had I been too cruel to that horror, Miss Mountjoy? Too vindictive? Wasn't she, after all, just a harmless and lonely old spinster? Would a Larry de Luce have been more understanding?

"Hell, no!" I shouted into the wind, and I chanted as we flew along:

Oomba-chukka! Oomba-chukka
Oomba-chukka-Boom!

But I felt no more like one of Lord Baden-Powell's blasted Boy Scouts than I did Prince Knick-Knack of Ali-Kazaam.

I was me. I was Flavia. And I loved myself, even if no one else did.

"All hail Flavia! Flavia forever!" I shouted, as Gladys and I sped through the Mulford Gates, at top speed, into the avenue of chestnuts that lined the drive at Buckshaw.

These magnificent gates, with their griffins rampant and filigreed black wrought iron, had once graced the neighboring estate of Batchley, the ancestral home of "The Dirty Mulfords." The gates were acquired for Buckshaw in the 1760s by one Brandwyn de Luce, who—after one of the Mulfords absconded with his wife—dismantled them and took them home.

The exchange of a wife for a pair of gates ("The finest this side Paradise," Brandwyn had written in his diary) seemed to have settled the matter, since the Mulfords and the de Luces remained best of friends and neighbors until the last Mulford, Tobias, sold off the estate at the time of the American Civil War and went abroad to assist his Confederate cousins.

"A WORD, FLAVIA," Inspector Hewitt said, stepping out of the front door.

Had he been waiting for me?

"Of course," I said graciously.

"Where have you been just now?"

"Am I under arrest, Inspector?" It was a joke—I hoped he'd catch on.

"I was merely curious."

He pulled a pipe from his jacket pocket, filled it, and struck a match. I watched as it burned steadily down towards his square fingertips.

"I went to the library," I said.

He lit his pipe, then pointed its stem at Gladys.

"I don't see any books."

"It was closed."

"Ah," he said.

There was a maddening calmness about the man. Even in the midst of murder he was as placid as if he were strolling in the park.

"I've spoken to Dogger," he said, and I noticed that he kept his eyes on me to gauge my reaction.

"Oh, yes?" I said, but my mind was sounding the kind of "Oogah!" warning they have on a submarine preparing to dive.

Careful! I thought. Watch your step. How much did Dogger tell him? About the strange man in the study? About the quarrel with Father? The threats?

That was the trouble with someone like Dogger: He was likely to break down for no reason whatsoever. Had he blabbed to the Inspector about the stranger in the study? Damn the man! Damn him!

"He says that you awakened him at about four A.M. and told him that there was a dead body in the garden. Is that correct?"

I held back a sigh of relief, almost choking in the process. Thank you,

Dogger! May the Lord bless you and keep you and make his face to shine upon you, always! Good old faithful Dogger. I knew I could count on you.

"Yes," I said. "That's correct."

"What happened then?"

"We went downstairs and out the kitchen door into the garden. I showed him the body. He knelt down beside it and felt for a pulse."

"And how did he do that?"

"He put his hand on the neck—under the ear."

"Hmm," the Inspector said. "And was there? Any pulse, I mean?"

"No."

"How did you know that? Did he tell you?"

"No," I said.

"Hmm," he said again. "Did you kneel down beside it too?"

"I suppose I could have. I don't think so . . . I don't remember."

The Inspector made a note. Even without seeing it, I knew what it said: Query: Did D. (1) tell F. no pulse? (2) See F. kneel BB (Beside Body)?

"That's quite understandable," he said. "It must have been rather a shock."

I brought to mind the image of the stranger lying there in the first light of dawn: the slight growth of whiskers on his chin, strands of his red hair shifting gently on the faint stirrings of the morning breeze, the pallor, the extended leg, the quivering fingers, that last, sucking breath. And that word, blown into my face . . . "*Vale.*"

The thrill of it all!

"Yes," I said, "it was devastating."

I HAD EVIDENTLY PASSED the test. Inspector Hewitt had gone into the kitchen where Sergeants Woolmer and Graves were busily setting up operations under a barrage of gossip and lettuce sandwiches from Mrs. Mullet.

As Ophelia and Daphne came down to lunch, I noticed with disappointment Ophelia's unusual clarity of complexion. Had my concoction backfired? Had I, through some freak accident of chemistry, produced a miracle facial cream?

Mrs. Mullet bustled in, grumbling as she set our soup and sandwiches on the table.

"It's not right," she said. "Me already behind my time, what with all this pother, and Alf expectin' me home, and all. The nerve of them, axin' me to dig that dead snipe out of the refuse bin," she said with a shudder, " . . . so's they could prop it up and take its likeness. It's not right. I showed them the bin and told them if they wanted the carcass so bad they could jolly well dig it out themselves; I had lunch to make. Eat your sandwiches, dear. There's nothing like cold meats in June—they're as good as a picnic."

"Dead snipe?" Daphne asked, curling her lip.

"The one as Miss Flavia and the Colonel found on my yesterday's back doorstep. It still gives me the goose-pimples, the way that thing was layin' there with its eye all frosted and its bill stickin' straight up in the air with a bit of paper stuck on it."

"Ned!" Ophelia said, slapping the table. "You were right, Daffy. It's a love token!"

Daphne had been reading *The Golden Bough* at Easter, and told Ophelia that primitive courting customs from the South Seas sometimes survived in our own enlightened times. It was simply a matter of being patient, she said.

I looked from one to the other, blankly. There were whole aeons when I didn't understand my sisters at all.

"A dead bird, stiff as a board, with its bill sticking straight up in the air? What kind of token is that?" I asked.

Daphne hid behind her book and Ophelia flushed a little. I slipped away from the table and left them tittering into their soup.

"MRS. MULLET," I said, "didn't you tell Inspector Hewitt we never see jack snipe in England until September?"

"Snipes, snipes, snipes! That's all I hear about nowadays is snipes. Step to one side, if you please—you're standin' where it wants scrubbin'."

"Why is that? Why do we never see snipe before September?"

Mrs. Mullet straightened up, dropped her brush in the bucket, and dried her soapy hands on her apron.

"Because they're somewhere else," she said triumphantly.

"Where?"

"Oh, you know . . . they're like all them birds what emigrate. They're up north somewhere. For all I know, they could be takin' tea with Father Christmas."

"By up north, how far do you mean? Scotland?"

"Scotland!" she said contemptuously. "Oh dear, no. Even my Alf's second sister, Margaret, gets as far as Scotland on her holidays, and she's no snipe.

"Although her husband is," she added.

There was a roaring in my ears, and something went "click."

"What about Norway?" I asked. "Could jack snipe summer in Norway?"

"I suppose they could, dear. You'd have to look it up."

Yes! Hadn't Inspector Hewitt told Dr. Darby that they had reason to believe the man in the garden had come from Norway? How could they possibly know that? Would the Inspector tell me if I asked?

Probably not. In that case I should have to puzzle it out for myself.

"Run along now," Mrs. Mullet said. "I can't go home till I finish this floor, and it's already one o'clock. Poor Alf's digestion is most likely in a shockin' state by now."

I stepped out the back door. The police and the coroner had gone, and taken the body with them, and the garden now seemed strangely empty. Dogger was nowhere in sight, and I sat down on a low section of the wall to have a bit of a think.

Had Ned left the dead snipe on the doorstep as a token of his love for Ophelia? She certainly seemed convinced of it. If it *had* been Ned, where did he get the thing?

Two and a half seconds later, I grabbed Gladys, threw my leg over her saddle, and, for the second time that day, was flying like the wind into the village.

Speed was of the essence. No one in Bishop's Lacey would yet know of the stranger's death. The police would not have told a soul—and nor had I.

Not until Mrs. Mullet finished her scrubbing and walked to the village would the gossip begin. But once she reached home, news of the murder at Buckshaw would spread like the Black Death. I had until then to find out what I needed to know.

seven

AS I SKIDDED TO A STOP AND LEANED GLADYS AGAINST A PILE of weathered timbers, Ned was still at work in the inn yard. He had finished with the beer barrels and was now showily unloading cheeses the size of millstones from the back of a parked lorry.

"Hoy, Flavia," he said as he saw me, jumping at the opportunity to stop work. "Fancy some cheese?"

Before I could answer he had pulled a nasty-looking jackknife from his pocket and sliced off a slab of Stilton with frightening ease. He cut one for himself and tucked into it on the spot with what Daphne would call "noisy gusto." Daphne is going to be a novelist, and copies out into an old account book phrases that strike her in her day-to-day reading. I remembered "noisy gusto" from the last time I snooped through its pages.

"Been home?" Ned asked, looking at me with a shy sideways glance. I saw what was coming. I nodded.

"And how's Miss Ophelia? Has the doctor been round?"

"Yes," I said. "I believe he saw her this morning."

Ned swallowed my deception whole.

"Still green then, is she?"

"More of a yellow than before," I said. "A shade more sulphuric than cupric."

I had learned that a lie wrapped in detail, like a horse pill in an apple, went down with greater ease. But this time, as soon as I said it, I knew that I had overstepped.

"Haw, Flavia!" Ned said. "You're making sport of me."

I let him have my best slow-dawning country-bumpkin smile.

"You've caught me out, Ned," I said. "Guilty, as charged."

He gave me back a weird mirror image of my grin. For a fraction of a second I thought he was mocking me, and I felt my temper begin to rise. But then I realized he was honestly pleased to have puzzled me out. This was my opportunity.

"Ned," I said, "if I asked you a terrifically personal question, would you answer it?"

I waited as this sunk in. Communicating with Ned was like exchanging cabled messages with a slow reader in Mongolia.

"Of course I'd answer it," he said, and the roguish twinkle in his eye tipped me off to what was coming next. "Course, I might not say the truth."

When we'd both had a good laugh, I got down to business. I'd start with the heavy artillery.

"You're frightfully keen on Ophelia, aren't you?"

Ned sucked his teeth and ran a finger round the inside of his collar. "She's a right nice girl, I'll give her that."

"But wouldn't you like to settle down with her one day in a thatched cottage and raise a litter of brats?"

By now, Ned's neck was a rising column of red, like a thick alcohol thermometer. In seconds he looked like one of those birds that inflate its gullet for mating purposes. I decided to help him out.

"Just suppose she wanted to see you but her father wouldn't allow it. Suppose one of her younger sisters could help."

Already his ruddy crop was subsiding. I thought he was going to cry.

"Do you mean it, Flavia?"

"Honest Injun," I said.

Ned stuck out his calloused fingers and gave my hand a surprisingly gentle shake. It was like shaking hands with a pineapple.

"Fingers of Friendship," he said, whatever that meant.

Fingers of Friendship? Had I just been given the secret handshake of some rustic brotherhood that met in moonlit churchyards and hidden copses? Was I now inducted, and would I be expected to take part in unspeakably bloody midnight rituals in the hedgerows? It seemed like an interesting possibility.

Ned was grinning at me like the skull on a Jolly Roger. I took the upper hand.

"Listen," I told him. "Lesson Number One: Don't leave dead birds on the loved one's doorstep. It's something that only a courting cat would do."

Ned looked blank.

"I've left flowers once or twice, hopin' she'd notice," he said. This was news to me; Ophelia must have whisked the bouquets off to her boudoir for mooning purposes before anyone else in the household spotted them.

"But dead birds? Never. You know me, Flavia. I wouldn't do a thing like that."

When I stopped to think about it for a moment, I knew that he was right; I did and he wouldn't. My next question, though, turned out to be sheer luck.

"Does Mary Stoker know you're sweet on Ophelia?" It was a phrase I had picked up at the cinema from some American film—*Meet Me in St. Louis* or *Little Women*—and this was the first opportunity I'd ever had to make use of it. Like Daphne, I remembered words, but without an account book to jot them down.

"What's Mary have to do with it? She's Tully's daughter, and there's an end of it."

"Come off it, Ned," I said. "I saw that kiss this morning as I was . . . passing by."

"She needed a little comfort. 'Twas no more than that."

"Because of whoever it was that crept up behind her?"

Ned leapt to his feet. "Damn you!" he said. "She don't want that getting out."

"As she was changing the sheets?"

"You're a devil, Flavia de Luce!" Ned roared. "Get away from me! Go home!"

"Tell her, Ned," said a quiet voice, and I turned to see Mary at the door.

She stood with one hand flat on the doorpost, the other clutching her blouse at the neck like Tess of the d'Urbervilles. Close up, I could see that she had raw red hands and a decided squint.

"Tell her," she repeated. "It can't make any difference to you now, can it?"

I detected instantly that she didn't like me. It's a fact of life that a girl can tell in a flash if another girl likes her. Feely says that there is a broken telephone connection between men and women, and we can never know which of us rang off. With a boy you never know whether he's smitten or gagging, but with a girl you can tell in the first three seconds. Between girls there is a silent and unending flow of invisible signals, like the high-frequency wireless messages between the shore and the ships at sea, and this secret flow of dots and dashes was signaling that Mary detested me.

"Go on, tell her!" Mary shouted.

Ned swallowed hard and opened his mouth, but nothing came out.

"You're Flavia de Luce, aren't you?" she said. "One of that lot from up at Buckshaw." She flung it at me like a pie in the face.

I nodded dumbly, as if I were some inbred ingrate from the squire's estate who needed coddling. Better to play along, I thought.

"Come with me," Mary said, beckoning. "Be quick about it—and keep quiet."

I followed her into a dark stone larder, and then into an enclosed wooden staircase that spiraled precipitously up to the floor above. At the top, we stepped out into what must once have been a linen press: a tall square cupboard now filled with shelves of cleaning chemicals, soaps, and waxes. In the corner, mops and brooms leaned in disarray amid an overwhelming smell of carbolic disinfectant.

"Shhh!" she said, giving my arm a vicious squeeze. Heavy footsteps were approaching, coming up the same staircase we had just ascended. We pressed back into a corner, taking care not to knock over the mops.

"That'll be the bloody day, sir, when a Cotswold horse takes the bloody purse! If I was you I'd take a flutter on Seastar, and be damned to any tips you get from some bloody skite in London what don't know his ark from his halo!"

It was Tully, exchanging confidential turf tips with someone at a volume loud enough to be heard at Epsom Downs. Another voice muttered something that ended in "Haw-haw!" as the sound of their footsteps faded away in the warren of paneled passages.

"No, this way," Mary hissed, tugging at my arm. We slipped round the corner and into a narrow corridor. She pulled a set of keys from her pocket and quietly unlocked the last door on the left. We stepped inside.

We were in a room which had not likely changed since Queen Elizabeth visited Bishop's Lacey in 1592 on one of her summer progresses. My first impressions were of a timbered ceiling, plastered panels, a tiny window with leaded panes standing ajar for air, and broad floorboards that rose and fell like the ocean swell.

Against one wall was a chipped wooden table with an *ABC Railway Guide* (October 1946) shoved under one leg to keep it from teetering. On the tabletop were an unmatched Staffordshire pitcher and ewer in pink and cream, a comb, a brush, and a small black leather case. In a corner near the open window stood a single piece of luggage: a cheap-looking steamer trunk of vulcanized fiber, plastered over with colored stickers. Beside it was a straight chair with a missing spindle. Across the room stood a wooden wardrobe of jumble-sale quality. And the bed.

"This is it," Mary said. As she locked us in, I turned to look at her closely for the first time. In the gray dishwater light from the sooty windowpanes, she looked older, harder, and more brittle than the raw-handed girl I had just seen in the bright sunlight of the inn yard.

"I expect you've never been in a room this small, have you?" she said scornfully. "You lot at Buckshaw fancy the odd visit to Bedlam, don't you? See the loonies—see how we live in our cages. Throw us a biscuit."

"I don't know what you're talking about," I said.

Mary turned her face towards me so that I was receiving the full intensity of her glare. "That sister of yours—that Ophelia—sent you with a message for Ned, and don't tell me she didn't. She fancies I'm some kind of slattern, and I'm not."

And in that instant I decided that I liked Mary, even if she didn't like me. Anyone who knew the word *slattern* was worth cultivating as a friend.

"Listen," I said, "there's no message. What I said to Ned was strictly for cover. You have to help me, Mary. I know you will. There's been a murder at Buckshaw . . . "

There! I'd said it!

" . . . and nobody knows it yet but you and me—except the murderer, of course."

She looked at me for no more than three seconds and then she asked, "Who is it that's dead, then?"

"I don't know. That's why I'm here. But it makes sense to me that if someone turns up dead in the cucumbers, and even the police don't know who he is, the most likely place he'd be staying in the neighborhood—*if* he was staying in the neighborhood—is right here at the Thirteen Drakes. Can you bring me the register?"

"Don't need to bring it to you," Mary said. "There's only one guest right now, and that's Mr. Sanders."

The more I talked to Mary the more I liked her.

"And this here's his room," she added helpfully.

"Where is he from?" I asked.

Her face clouded. "I don't know, rightly."

"Has he ever stopped here before?"

"Not so far as I know."

"Then I need to have a look at the register. Please, Mary! Please! It's important! The police will soon be here, and then it will be too late."

"I'll try . . . " she said, and, unlocking the door, slipped from the room.

As soon as she was gone, I pulled open the door of the wardrobe. Except for a pair of wooden coat hangers it was empty, and I turned my attention to the steamer trunk, which was covered over with stickers like barnacles clinging to the hull of a ship. These colorful crustaceans, however, had names: Paris, Rome, Stockholm, Amsterdam, Copenhagen, Stavanger—and more.

I tried the hasp, and to my surprise, it popped open. It was unlocked! The two halves, hinged in the middle, swung easily apart, and I found myself face-to-face with Mr. Sanders's wardrobe: a blue serge suit, two shirts, a pair of brown Oxfords (with blue serge? Even I knew better than that!), and a floppy, theatrical hat that reminded me of photographs I'd seen of G. K. Chesterton in the *Radio Times*.

I pulled out the drawers of the trunk, taking care not to disturb their contents: a pair of hairbrushes (imitation tortoiseshell), a razor (Valet AutoStrop), a tube of shaving cream (Morning Pride Brushless), a toothbrush, toothpaste (thymol: "specially recommended to arrest the germs of dental decay"), nail clippers, a straight comb (xylonite), and a pair of square cuff links (Whitby jet, with a pair of initials inset in silver: *HB*).

HB? Wasn't this Mr. Sanders's room? What could *HB* stand for?

The door flew open and a voice hissed, "What are you doing?"

I nearly flew out of my skin. It was Mary.

"I couldn't get the register. Dad was— Flavia! You can't go through a guest's luggage like that! You'll get both of us in a pickle. Stop it."

"Right-ho," I said as I finished rifling the pockets of the suit. They were empty anyway. "When was the last time you saw Mr. Sanders?"

"Yesterday. Here. At noon."

"Here? In this room?"

She gulped, and nodded, looking away. "I was changing his sheets when he come up behind me and grabbed me. Put a hand over my mouth so's I shouldn't scream. Good job Dad called from the yard just then. Rattled him a bit, it did. Don't think I didn't get in a good kick or two. Him and his filthy paws! I'd have scratched his eyes out if I'd had half the chance."

She looked at me as if she'd said too much; as if a great social gulf had suddenly opened up between us.

"I'd have scratched his eyes out and sucked the holes," I said.

Her eyes widened in horror.

"John Marston," I told her. "*The Dutch Courtesan, 1604.*"

There was a pause of approximately two hundred years. Then Mary began to giggle.

"Ooh, you are a one!" she said.

The gap had been bridged.

"Act Two," I added.

Seconds later the two of us were doubled over, hands covering our mouths, hopping about the room, snorting in unison like a pair of trained seals.

"Feely once read it to us under the blankets with a torch," I said, and for some reason, this struck both of us as being even more hilarious, and off we went again until we were nearly paralyzed from laughter.

Mary threw her arms round me and gave me a crushing hug. "You're a corker, Flavia," she said. "Really you are. Come here—take a gander at this."

She went to the table, picked up the black leather case, unfastened the strap, and lifted the lid. Nestled inside were two rows of six little glass vials, twelve in all. Eleven were filled with a liquid of a yellowish tinge; the twelfth was a quarter full. Between the rows of vials was a half-round indentation, as if some tubular object were missing.

"What do you make of it?" she whispered, as Tully's voice thundered vaguely in the distance. "Poisons, you think? A regular Dr. Crippen, our Mr. Sanders?"

I uncorked the partially filled bottle and held it to my nose. It smelled as if someone had dropped vinegar on the back of a sticking plaster: an acrid protein smell, like an alcoholic's hair burning in the next room.

"Insulin," I said. "He's a diabetic."

Mary gave me a blank look, and I suddenly knew how Archimedes felt when he said "Eureka!" in his bathtub. I grabbed Mary's arm.

"Does Mr. Sanders have red hair?" I demanded.

"Red as rhubarb. How did you know?"

She stared at me as if I were Madame Zolanda at the church fête, with a turban, a shawl, and a crystal ball.

"A wizard guess," I said.

eight

"CRIKEY!" MARY SAID, FISHING UNDER THE TABLE AND PULLING out a round metal wastepaper basket. "I almost forgot this. Dad'd have my hide for a hammock if he found out I didn't empty this thing. He's always on about germs, Dad is, even though you wouldn't think it to look at him. Good job I remembered before—oh, gawd! Just look at this mess, will you."

She pulled a wry face and held out the basket at arm's length. I peeked—tentatively—inside. You never know what you're getting into when you stick your nose in other people's rubbish.

The bottom of the wastebasket was covered with chunks and flakes of pastry: no container, just bits flung in, as if whoever had been eating it had had enough. It appeared to be the remains of a pie. As I reached in and extracted a piece of it, Mary made a gacking noise and turned her head away.

"Look at this," I said. "It's a piece of the crust, see? It's golden brown here, from the oven, with little crinkles of pastry, like decorations on one side. These other bits are from the bottom crust: They're whiter and thinner. Not very flaky, is it?

"Still," I added, "I'm famished. When you haven't eaten all day, anything looks good."

I raised the pie and opened my mouth, pretending I was about to gobble it down.

"Flavia!"

I paused with the crumbling cargo halfway to my gaping mouth. "Huh?"

"Oh, you!" Mary said. "Give it over. I'll chuck it."

Something told me this was a Bad Idea. Something else told me that the gutted pie was evidence that should be left untouched for Inspector Hewitt and the two sergeants to discover. I actually considered this for a moment.

"Got any paper?" I asked.

Mary shook her head. I opened the wardrobe and, standing on tiptoe, felt along the top shelf with my hand. As I suspected, a sheet of newspaper had been put in place to serve as a makeshift shelf liner. God bless you, Tully Stoker!

Taking care not to break them, I tipped the larger remnants of the pie slowly out onto the *Daily Mail* and folded it up into a small neat package, which I shoved into my pocket. Mary stood watching me nervously, not saying a word.

"Lab test," I said, darkly. To tell the truth, I didn't have any idea yet what I was going to do with this revolting stuff. I'd think of something later, but right now I wanted to show Mary who was in charge.

As I set the wastepaper basket down on the floor, I was startled at a sudden slight movement in its depths, and I don't mind admitting that my stomach turned a primal handspring. What was in there? Worms? A rat? Impossible: I couldn't have missed something that big.

I peered cautiously into the container and sure enough, something *was* moving at the bottom of the basket. A feather! And it was moving gently, almost imperceptibly, back and forth with the room's air currents; stirring like a dead leaf on a tree—in the same way the dead stranger's red hair had stirred in the morning breeze.

Could it have been only this morning that he died? It seemed an eternity since the unpleasantness in the garden. Unpleasantness? You liar, Flavia!

Mary looked on aghast as I reached into the basket and extracted the feather and the bit of pastry impaled upon its quill end.

"See this?" I said, holding it out towards her. She shrank back in the way Dracula is supposed to do when you threaten him with a cross. "If the feather had fallen on the pastry in the wastepaper basket, it wouldn't be attached.

"Four-and-twenty blackbirds, baked in a pie," I recited. "See?"

"You think?" Mary asked, her eyes like saucers.

"Bang on, Sherlock," I said. "This pie's filling was bird, and I think I can guess the species."

I held it out to her again. "What a pretty dish to set before the King," I said, and this time she grinned at me.

I'd do the same with Inspector Hewitt, I thought, as I pocketed the thing. Yes! I'd solve this case and present it to him wrapped up in gaily colored ribbons.

"No need for you to come out here again," he'd said to me in the garden, that saucepot. What bloody cheek!

Well, I'd show him a trick or two!

Something told me that Norway was the key. Ned hadn't been in Norway, and besides, he had sworn he didn't leave the snipe on our doorstep and I believed him, so he was out of the question—at least for now.

The stranger had come from Norway, and I had heard that straight from the horse's mouth, so to speak! Ergo (that means "therefore") the stranger could have brought the snipe with him.

In a pie.

Yes! That made sense! What better way to get a dead bird past an inquisitive H. M. Customs inspector?

Just one more step and we're home free: If the Inspector can't be asked how he knew about Norway, and nor can the stranger (obviously, since he is dead), who, then, does that leave?

And I suddenly saw it all, saw it spread out before me at my feet the way one must see from the top of a mountain. The way Harriet must have—

The way an eagle sees his prey.

I hugged myself with pleasure. If the stranger had come from Norway, dropped a dead bird on our doorstep before breakfast, and then appeared in Father's study after midnight, he must have been staying somewhere not far away. Somewhere within walking distance of Buckshaw. Somewhere such as right here in this very room at the Thirteen Drakes.

Now I knew it for certain: The corpse in the cucumbers *was* Mr. Sanders. There could be no doubt about it.

"Mary!"

It was Tully again, bellowing like a bull calf, and this time, it seemed, he was right outside the door.

"Coming, Dad!" she shouted, grabbing the wastebasket.

"Get out of here," she whispered. "Wait five minutes and then go down the back stairs—same way as we came up."

She was gone, and a moment later I heard her explaining to Tully in the hallway that she just wanted to give the wastebasket an extra clean-out, since someone left a mess in it.

"We wouldn't want somebody to die of germs they picked up at the Thirteen Drakes, would we, Dad?"

She was learning.

While I waited, I took a second look at the steamer trunk. I ran my fingers over the colored labels, trying to imagine where it had been in its travels, and what Mr. Sanders had been doing in each city: Paris, Rome, Stockholm, Amsterdam, Copenhagen, Stavanger. Paris was red, white, and blue, and so was Stavanger.

Was Stavanger in France? I wondered. It didn't sound French—unless, of course, it was pronounced "stah-vonj-yay" as in Laurence Olivier. I touched the label and it wrinkled beneath my finger, piled up like water ahead of the prow of a ship.

I repeated the test on the other stickers. Each one was pasted down tightly: as smooth as the label on a bottle of cyanide.

Back to Stavanger. It felt a little lumpier than the others, as if there were something underneath it.

The blood was humming in my veins like water in a millrace.

Again I pried the trunk open and took the safety razor from the drawer. As I extracted the blade, I thought how lucky it was that women—other than the occasional person like Miss Pickery at the library—don't need to shave. It was tough enough being a woman without having to lug all that tackle everywhere you went.

Holding the blade carefully between my thumb and forefinger (after the glassware incident I had been loudly lectured about sharp objects) I made a slit along the bottom of the label, taking great care to cut along the precise edge of a blue and red decorative line that ran nearly the full width of the paper.

As I lifted the incision slightly with the dull edge of the blade, something slid out and, with a whisper of paper, fell to the floor. It was a glassine envelope, similar to the ones I had noticed in Sergeant Graves's kit. Through its semitransparency, I could see that there was something inside, something square and opaque. I opened the envelope and gave it a tap with my finger. Something fell out into the palm of my hand: two somethings, in fact.

Two postage stamps. Two bright orange postage stamps, each in its own tiny translucent jacket. Aside from their color, they were identical to the Penny Black that had been impaled upon the jack snipe's bill. Queen Victoria's face again. What a disappointment!

I didn't doubt that Father would have gone into positive raptures about the pristine perfection of the things, the enchantment of engraving, the pleasures of perforations, and the glories of glue, but to me they were no more than the sort of thing you'd slap on a letter to dreadful Aunt Felicity in Hampshire, thanking her for her thoughtful Christmas gift of a Neddy the Squirrel Annual.

Still, why bother putting them back? If Mr. Sanders and the body in our garden were, as I knew they were, one and the same, he was well past the need for postage stamps.

No, I thought, I'll keep the things. They might come in handy someday when I need to barter my way out of a scrape with Father, who is incapable of thinking stamps and discipline at the same time.

I shoved the envelope into my pocket, licked my forefinger, and moistened the inside edge of the slit in the label on the trunk. Then, with my thumb, I ironed it shut. No one, not even Inspector Fabian of the Yard, could ever guess it had been sliced open.

My time was up. I took one last look round the room, slipped out into the dim hallway and, as Mary had instructed me, moved carefully towards the back staircase.

"You're about as useless as tights on a bull, Mary! How the bloody hell can I stay on top of things when you're letting everything go to hell in a handbasket?"

Tully was coming up the back way; one more turning of the stairs and we'd be face-to-face!

I flew on tiptoe in the other direction, through the twisting, turning labyrinth of corridors: up two steps here, down three there. A moment later, panting, I found myself at the top of the L-shaped staircase that led down to the front entrance. As far as I could see, there was no one below.

I tiptoed down, one slow step at a time.

A long hallway, hung profusely with dark, water-stained sporting prints, served as a lobby, in which centuries of sacrificed kippers had left the smell of their smoky souls clinging to the wallpaper. Only the patch of sunshine visible through the open front door relieved the gloom.

To my left was a small desk with a telephone, a telephone directory, a small glass vase of red and mauve pansies, and a ledger. The register!

Obviously, the Thirteen Drakes was not a busy beehive: Its open pages bore the names of travelers who had signed in for the past week and more. I didn't even have to touch the thing.

There it was:

2nd June 10:25 A.M. F. X. Sanders London

NO OTHER GUESTS HAD REGISTERED the day before, and none since.

But London? Inspector Hewitt had said that the dead man had come from Norway and I knew that, like King George, Inspector Hewitt was not a frivolous man.

Well, he hadn't said exactly that: He'd said that the deceased had *recently* come from Norway, which was a horse of an entirely different hue.

Before I could think this through, there was a banging from above. It was Tully again; the ubiquitous Tully. I could tell by his tone that Mary was still getting the worst of it.

"Don't look at me like that, my girl, or I'll give you reason to regret it."

And now he was clomping heavily down the main staircase! In another few seconds he'd see me. Just as I was about to make a bolt for the front door, a battered black taxicab stopped directly in front of it, the roof piled high with luggage and the wooden legs of a photographer's tripod protruding from one of its windows.

Tully was distracted for a moment.

"Here's Mr. Pemberton," he said in a stage whisper. "He's early. Now then, girl, I told you this would happen, didn't I? Get a move on and dump those dirty sheets while I find Ned."

I ran for it! Straight back past the sporting prints, into the back vestibule, and out into the inn yard.

"Ned! Come and get Mr. Pemberton's luggage."

Tully was right behind me, following me towards the back of the inn. Although momentarily dazzled by the bright sunlight, I could see that Ned was nowhere about. He must have finished unloading the lorry and gone on to other duties.

Without even thinking about it, I sprang up and into the back of the lorry, lay down, and flattened myself behind a pile of cheeses.

Peering out from between the stacked rounds I saw Tully stride out into the inn yard, look round, and mop his red face with his apron. He was dressed for pumping pints. The bar must be open, I thought.

"Ned!" he bellowed.

I knew that, standing in the bright sunlight as he was, he could not see me in the lorry's dim interior. All I had to do was lie low and keep quiet.

I was thinking that when a couple more voices were added to Tully's bellowing.

"Wot cheer, Tully," one said. "Thanks for the pint."

"S'long, mate," said the other. "See you next Saturday."

"Tell George he can hang his shirt on Seastar. Just don't tell 'im which shirt!"

It was one of those stupid things men say simply to get in the last word. There was nothing remotely funny about it. Still, they all laughed, and were probably slapping their legs, at the witticism, and a moment later I felt the lorry dip on its springs as the two climbed heavily into the cab. Then the engine grated into life and we began to move—backwards.

Tully was folding and unfolding his fingers, beckoning the lorry as it reversed, indicating with his hands the clearance between its tailgate and the inn yard wall. I couldn't jump out now without leaping straight into his arms. I'd have to wait until we drove out through the archway and turned onto the open road.

My last glimpse of the yard was of Tully walking back towards the door and Gladys leaning where I had left her against a pile of scrap lumber.

As the lorry veered sharply and then accelerated, I was beaned by a wheel of toppling Wensleydale and followed it, sliding, across the rough wooden floor. By the time I'd braced myself, the high road behind us was flashing by in a blur of green hedges, and Bishop's Lacey was receding in the distance.

Now you've done it, Flave, I thought, you might never see your family again.

As attractive as this idea seemed at first, I realized quickly that I *would* miss Father—at least a little. Ophelia and Daphne I would soon learn to live without.

Inspector Hewitt would, of course, have already jumped to the conclusion that I had committed the murder, fled the scene, and was making my way by tramp steamer to British Guiana. He would have alerted all ports to keep an eye out for an eleven-year-old murderess in pigtails and sweater.

Once they put two and two together, the police would soon set the hounds to tracking a fugitive who smelt like an Olde Worlde Cheese Shoppe. I would need to find a place to take a bath, then: a meadow stream, perhaps, where I could wash my clothes and dry them on a bramble bush. They would, naturally, interview Tully, grill Ned and Mary, and find out my means of escape from the Thirteen Drakes.

The Thirteen Drakes.

Why is it, I wondered, that the men who choose the names of our inns and public houses are so desperately unimaginative? The Thirteen Drakes, Mrs. Mullet had once told me, was given its name in the eighteenth century by a landlord who simply counted up twelve other licensed Drakes in nearby villages and added another.

Why not something of practical value, like the Thirteen Carbon Atoms, for instance? Something that could be used as a memory aid? There were thirteen carbon atoms in tridecyl, whose hydride was marsh gas. What a jolly useful name for a pub!

The Thirteen Drakes, indeed. Leave it to a man to name a place for a bird!

I was still thinking about tridecyl when, at the open tailgate of the lorry, a rounded, whitewashed stone flashed by. It had a familiar look, and I realized almost at once that it was the turnoff marker for Doddingsley. In another half mile the driver would be forced to stop—even if only for a moment—before turning either right to St. Elfrieda's or left to Nether Lacey.

I slithered to the lip of the open box just as the brakes squealed and the vehicle began to slow. A moment later, like a commando being sucked out the drop-hole of a Whitley bomber, I slipped off the tailgate and hit the dirt on all fours.

Without a backwards glance, the driver turned to the left, and as the heavy lorry and its load of cheeses lumbered away in a cloud of dust, I set off for home.

It was going to be a fair old trudge across the fields to Buckshaw.

nine

I EXPECT THAT LONG AFTER MY SISTER OPHELIA IS DEAD AND gone, whenever I think of her, the first memory that will come to mind will be her gentle touch at the piano. Seated at the keyboard of our old Broadwood grand in the drawing room, Feely becomes a different person.

Years of practice—come hell or high water—have given her the left hand of a Joe Louis and the right hand of a Beau Brummell (or so Daffy says).

Because she plays so beautifully, I have always felt it my bounden duty to be particularly rotten to her. For instance, when she is playing one of those early things by Beethoven that sounds as if it's been cribbed from Mozart, I will stop at the drop of a hat, whatever I may be doing, to stroll casually through the drawing room.

"First-rate flipper work," I'll say loudly enough to be heard above the music. "Arf! Arf! Arf!"

Ophelia has milky blue eyes: the sort of eyes I like to imagine blind Homer might have had. Although she has most of her repertoire off by heart, she occasionally shifts herself on the piano bench, folds a bit forward at the waist like an automaton, and has a good squint at the sheet music.

Once, when I remarked that she looked like a disoriented bandicoot, she leapt up from the piano bench and beat me within an inch of my life with a rolled-up piano sonata by Schubert. Ophelia has no sense of humor.

As I climbed over the last stile and Buckshaw came into view across the field, it almost took my breath away. It was from this angle and at this time of day that I loved it most. As I approached from the west, the mellow old stone glowed like saffron in the late afternoon sun, well settled into the landscape like a complacent mother hen squatting on her eggs, with the Union Jack stretching itself contentedly overhead.

The house seemed unaware of my approach, as if I were an intruder creeping up on it.

Even from a quarter of a mile away I could hear the notes of the Toccata by Pietro Domenico Paradisi—the one from his Sonata in A Major—come tripping out to meet me.

The Toccata was my favorite composition; to my mind it was the greatest musical accomplishment in the entire history of the world, but I knew that if Ophelia found that out, she would never play the piece again.

Whenever I hear this music it makes me think of flying down the steep east side of Goodger Hill; running so fast that my legs can barely keep up with themselves as I swoop from side to side, mewing into the wind, like a rapturous seagull.

When I was closer to the house, I stopped in the field and listened to the perfect flow of notes, not too *presto*—just the way I liked it. I thought of the time I heard Eileen Joyce play the Toccata on the BBC Home Service. Father had it switched on, not really listening, as he fiddled with his stamp collection. The notes had found their way through the corridors and galleries of Buckshaw, floated up the spiral staircase and into my bedroom. By the time I realized what was being played, raced down the stairs, and burst into Father's study, the music had ended.

We had stood there looking at one another, Father and I, not knowing what to say, until at last, without a word, I had backed out of the room and gone slowly back upstairs.

That's the only problem with the Toccata: It's too short.

I came round the fence and onto the terrace. Father was sitting at his desk in the window of his study, intent on whatever it was he was working at.

The Rosicrucians claim in their adverts that you can make a total stranger turn round in a crowded cinema by fixing your gaze intently on the back of his neck, and I stared at him for all I was worth.

He glanced up, but he did not see me. His mind was somewhere else.

I didn't move a muscle.

And then, as if his head were made of lead, he looked down and went on with his work, and in the drawing room, Feely moved on to something by Schumann.

WHENEVER SHE WAS THINKING ABOUT NED, Feely played Schumann. I suppose that's why they call it romantic music. Once when she was playing a Schumann sonata with an excessively dreamy look on her face, I had remarked loudly to Daffy that I simply adored bandstand music, and Feely flew into a passion—a passion that wasn't helped by my stalking out of the room and returning a few minutes later with a Bakelite ear-trumpet I had found in a closet, a tin cup, and a hand-lettered sign tied round my neck with a string: "Deafened in tragic piano accident. Please take pity."

Feely had probably forgotten that incident by now, but I hadn't. As I pretended to push past her to look out the window, I had a fleeting close-up of her face. Drat! Nothing for my notebook again.

"You're probably in trouble," she said, slamming down the lid on the keyboard. "Where have you been all day?"

"None of your horse-nails," I told her. "I'm not in your employ."

"Everyone's been looking for you. Daffy and I told them you'd run away from home, but no such bloody luck by the look of it."

"It's bloody poor form to say 'bloody,' Feely; you're not supposed to. And don't puff out your cheeks like that: It makes you look like a petulant pear. Where's Father?"

As if I didn't know.

"He hasn't stuck his nose out all day," Daffy said. "Do you suppose he's upset about what happened this morning?"

"The corpse on the premises? No, I shouldn't say so—nothing to do with him, is it?"

"That's what I thought," Feely said, and lifted the piano lid.

With a toss of her hair, she was off into the first of Bach's *Goldberg Variations*.

It was slow, but lovely nonetheless, although even on his best days Bach, to my way of thinking, couldn't hold a candle to Pietro Domenico Paradisi.

And then I remembered Gladys! I had left her at the Thirteen Drakes, where she could be spotted by anyone. If the police hadn't been there already, they soon would be.

I wondered if by now Mary or Ned had been made to tell them of my visit. But if they had, I reasoned, wouldn't Inspector Hewitt be at Buckshaw this very moment reading me the riot act?

Five minutes later, for the third time that day, I was on my way to Bishop's Lacey—this time on foot.

BY KEEPING TO THE HEDGEROWS and skulking behind trees whenever I heard the sound of an approaching vehicle, I was able to make my way, by a devious route, to the far end of the High Street which, this late in the day, was deep in its usual empty sleep.

A shortcut through Miss Bewdley's ornamental garden (water lilies, stone storks, goldfish, and a red lacquered footbridge) brought me to the brick wall that skirted the inn yard of the Thirteen Drakes, where I crouched and listened. Gladys, if no one had moved her, was directly on the other side.

Except for the hum of a far-off tractor, there wasn't a sound. Just as I was about to venture a peek over the top of the wall I heard voices. Or, to be more precise, one voice, and it was Tully's. I could have heard it even if I'd stayed home at Buckshaw with earplugs.

"Never laid eyes on the bloke in my life, Inspector. His first visit to Bishop's Lacey, I daresay. Would have remembered if he'd stopped here before: Sanders was my late wife's maiden name, God bless 'er, and I'd have marked it if someone by that name ever signed the register. You can put a fiver on that. No, he wasn't never out here in the yard; he come in the front door and went up to his room. If there's any clues, that's where you'll find 'em—there or in the saloon bar. He was in the saloon bar later for a bit. Drank a pint of half-and-half, chug-a-lug, no tip."

So the police knew! I could feel the excitement fizzing inside me like ginger beer, not because they had identified the victim, but because I had beaten them to it with one hand tied behind my back.

I allowed a smug look to flit across my face.

When the voices had faded, I used a bit of creeper for a screen and peeked over the top of the bricks. The inn yard was empty.

I vaulted over the wall, grabbed Gladys, and wheeled her furtively out into the empty High Street. Darting down Cow Lane, I retraced my tracks from earlier in the day by circling back behind the library, between the Thirteen Drakes, and along the rutted towpath beside the river, into Shoe Street, past the churchyard, and into the fields.

Bumpety-bump across the fields we went, Gladys and I. It was good to be in her company.

> *"Oh the moon shone bright on Mrs. Porter*
> *And on her daughter*
> *They wash their feet in soda water."*

It was a song Daffy had taught me, but only after exacting the promise that I would never sing it at Buckshaw. It seemed like a song for the great outdoors, and this was a perfect opportunity.

Dogger met me at the door.

"I need to talk to you, Miss Flavia," he said. I could see the tension in his eyes.

"All right," I said. "Where?"

"Greenhouse," he said, with a jerk of his thumb.

I followed him round the east side of the house and through the green door that was set into the wall of the kitchen garden. Once in the greenhouse, you might as well be in Africa; no one but Dogger ever set foot in the place.

Inside, open ventilation panes in the roof caught the afternoon sun, reflecting it down to where we stood among the potting benches and the gutta-percha hoses.

"What's up, Dogger?" I asked lightly, trying to make it sound a little bit—but not too much—like Bugs Bunny.

"The police," he said. "I have to know how much you told them about . . . "

"I've been thinking the same thing," I said. "You first."

"Well, that Inspector . . . Hewitt. He asked me some questions about this morning."

"Me too," I said. "What did you tell him?"

"I'm sorry, Miss Flavia. I had to tell him that you came and woke me when you found the body, and that I went to the garden with you."

"He already knew that."

Dogger's eyebrows flew up like a pair of seagulls.

"He did?"

"Of course he did. I told him."

Dogger let out a long slow whistle.

"Then you didn't tell him about . . . that row . . . in the study?"

"Certainly not, Dogger! What do you take me for?"

"You must never breathe a word of that, Miss Flavia. Never!"

Now here was a pretty kettle of flounders. Dogger was asking me to conspire with him in withholding information from the police. Who was he protecting? Himself? Father? Or could it be me?

These were questions I could not ask him outright. I thought I'd try a different tack.

"Of course I'll keep quiet," I said. "But why?"

Dogger picked up a trowel and began shoveling black soil into a pot. He did not look at me, but his jaw was set at an angle that signaled clearly that he had made up his mind about something.

"There are things," he said at last, "which need to be known. And there are other things which need not to be known."

"Such as?" I ventured.

The lines of his face softened and he almost smiled.

"Buzz off," he said.

IN MY LABORATORY, I pulled the paper-wrapped packet from my pocket and carefully opened out the folds.

I gave a groan of disappointment: My cycling and wall climbing had reduced the evidence to little more than particles of pastry.

"Oh, crumbs," I said, not without a little pleasure in the aptness of my words. "Now what am I going to do?"

I put the feather carefully into an envelope, and slipped it into a drawer among letters belonging to Tar de Luce that had been written and replied to when Harriet was my age. No one would ever think of looking there, and besides, as Daffy once said, the best place to hide a glum countenance is onstage at the opera.

Even in its mutilated form, the broken pastry reminded me that I had not eaten all day. Supper at Buckshaw was, by some archaic statute, always prepared earlier by Mrs. Mullet and warmed over for our consumption at nine o'clock.

I was starved, hungry enough to eat a . . . well, to eat a slice of Mrs. Mullet's icky custard pie. Odd, wasn't it? She had asked me earlier, just after Father fainted, if I had enjoyed the pie . . . and I hadn't eaten any.

When I had gone through the kitchen at four in the morning—just before I stumbled upon that body in the cucumber vines—the pie had still been on the windowsill where Mrs. Mullet had left it to cool. And there had been a piece missing.

A piece missing indeed!

Who could have taken it? I remembered wondering about that at the time. It hadn't been Father or Daffy or Feely; they would rather eat creamed worms on toast than Mrs. Mullet's cussed custard.

Nor would Dogger have eaten it; he wasn't the sort of man who helped himself to dessert. And if Mrs. Mullet had given him the slice, she wouldn't have thought I ate it, would she?

I walked downstairs and into the kitchen. The pie was gone.

The window sash was still in its raised position, just as Mrs. Mullet had left it. Had she taken the remains of the pie home to her husband, Alf?

I could telephone and ask her, I thought, but then I remembered Father's telephonic restrictions.

Father was of a generation that despised "the instrument," as he called it. Always ill at ease with the thing, he could be coaxed to talk into it only in the most dire circumstances.

Ophelia once told me that even when news had come of Harriet's death, it had to be sent by telegram because Father refused to believe anything he hadn't seen in print. The telephone at Buckshaw was subscribed to for use only in the event of fire or medical emergency. Any other use of "the instrument" required Father's personal permission, a rule which had been drummed into us from the day we climbed out of our cribs.

No, I would have to wait until tomorrow to ask Mrs. Mullet about the pie.

I took a loaf of bread from the pantry and cut a thick slice. I buttered it, then slathered on a blanket of brown sugar. I folded the bread twice in half, each time pressing it down flat with the palm of my hand. I stuck it in the warming oven and left it there for as long as it took me to sing three verses of "If I Knew You Were Comin' I'd've Baked a Cake."

It was not a true Chelsea bun, but it would have to do.

ten

EVEN THOUGH WE DE LUCES HAD BEEN ROMAN CATHOLICS since chariot races were all the rage, that did not keep us from attending St. Tancred's, Bishop's Lacey's only church and a fortress of the Church of England if ever there was one.

There were several reasons for our patronage. The first was its handy location, and another the fact that Father and the Vicar had both (although at different times) been to school at Greyminster. Besides, Father had once pointed out to us, consecration was permanent, like a tattoo. St. Tancred's, he said, had been a Roman Catholic Church before the Reformation and, in his eyes, remained one.

Consequently, every Sunday morning without exception we straggled across the fields like ducks, Father slashing intermittently at the vegetation with his Malacca walking stick, Feely, Daffy, and me in that order, and Dogger, in his Sunday best, bringing up the rear.

No one at St. Tancred's paid us the slightest attention. Some years before, there had been a minor outbreak of grumbling from the Anglicans, but all had been settled without blood or bruises by a well-timed contribution to the Organ Restoration Fund.

"Tell them we may not be praying *with* them," Father told the Vicar, "but we are at least not actively praying *against* them."

Once, when Feely lost her head and bolted for the Communion rail, Father refused to speak to her until the following Sunday. Ever since that day, whenever she so much as shifted her feet in church, Father would mutter, "Steady on, old girl." He did not need to catch her eye; his profile, which was that of the standard-bearer in some particularly ascetic Roman legion, was enough to keep us in our places. At least in public.

Now, glancing over at Feely as she knelt with her eyes closed, her fingertips touching and pointed to Heaven, and her lips shaping soft words of devotion, I had to pinch myself to keep in mind that I was sitting next to the Devil's Hairball.

The congregation at St. Tancred's had soon become accustomed to our ducking and bobbing, and we basked in Christian charity—except for the time that Daffy told the organist, Mr. Denning, that Harriet had instilled in all of us her firm belief that the story of the Flood in Genesis was derived from the racial memory of the cat family, with particular reference to the drowning of kittens.

That had caused a bit of a stir, but Father had put things right by making a handsome donation to the Roof Repair Fund, a sum he deducted from Daffy's allowance.

"Since I don't have an allowance anyway," Daffy said, "no one's the loser. It's a jolly good punishment, actually."

I listened, unmoved, as the congregation joined in the General Confession:

"We have left undone those things which we ought to have done; And we have done those things which we ought not to have done."

Dogger's words flashed into my mind:

"There are things which need to be known. And there are other things which need not to be known."

I turned round and looked at him. His eyes were closed and his lips were moving. And so, I noticed, were Father's.

Because it was Trinity Sunday we were treated to a rare old romp from Revelation all about the sardine stone, the rainbow round about the throne, the sea of glass like unto crystal, and the four beasts full of eyes before and uncomfortably behind.

I had my own opinion about the true meaning of this obviously alchemical reference, but, since I was saving it for my Ph.D. thesis, I kept it to myself. And even though we de Luces were players on the opposing team, as it were, I couldn't help envying those Anglicans the glories of their Book of Common Prayer.

The glass, too, was glorious. Above the altar, morning sunlight washed in through three windows whose stained glass had been poured in the Middle Ages by half-civilized semivagrant glassmakers who lived and caroused on the verge of Ovenhouse Wood, the thin remains of which still bordered Buckshaw to the west.

On the left panel, Jonah sprang from the mouth of the great fish, looking back over his shoulder at the thing with a look of wide-eyed indignation. From the booklet that used to be given away in the church porch, I remembered that the creature's white scales had been achieved by firing the glass with tin, while Jonah's skin had been made brown with salts of ferric iron (which, interestingly enough—to me at least—is also the antidote for arsenical poisoning).

The panel on the right portrayed Jesus emerging from his tomb, as Mary Magdalene, in a red dress (also iron, or perhaps grated particles of gold), holds out to him a purple garment (manganese dioxide) and a loaf of yellow bread (silver chloride).

I knew that these salts had been mixed with sand and the ashes of a salt marsh reed called glasswort, fired in a furnace hot enough to have given even Shadrach, Meshach, and Abednego second thoughts, and then cooled until the desired color was obtained.

The central panel was dominated by our own Saint Tancred, whose body lay at this very moment somewhere beneath our feet in the crypt. In this view, he is standing at the open door of the church in which we sit (as it looked before the Victorians improved it), welcoming with outstretched arms a multitude of parishioners. Saint Tancred has a pleasant face: He's the sort of person you would like to invite over on a Sunday afternoon to browse through back issues of the *Illustrated London News*, or maybe even *Country Life*, and, since we share his faith, I like to imagine that while he snores away eternity down below, he has a particular soft spot for all of us at Buckshaw.

As my mind swam back to the present, I realized that the Vicar was praying for the man I had found dead in the garden.

"He was a stranger among us," he said. "It is not necessary that his name be known unto us . . ."

This would be news to Inspector Hewitt, I thought.

" . . . in order for us to ask God to have mercy on his soul, and to grant him peace."

So the word was out! Mrs. Mullet, I guessed, had wasted no time in scurrying across the lane yesterday to break the news to the Vicar. I could hardly believe he had heard it from the police.

There was a sudden hollow bang as a kneeling bench slammed up, and I looked round just in time to see Miss Mountjoy edging her way crab-wise out of the pews and fleeing along the side aisle to the transept door.

"I feel nauseous," I whispered to Ophelia, who let me slide past her without batting an eye. Feely had a particular aversion to having her shoes vomited on, a useful quirk of which I took advantage from time to time.

Outside, a wind had sprung up, whipping the branches of the church-yard yews, and sending ripples running through the unmowed grass. I caught a glimpse of Miss Mountjoy disappearing among the moss-covered tombstones, heading towards the crumbling, overgrown lych-gate.

What had upset her so? For a moment I considered running after her, but then I thought better of it: The river looped round St. Tancred's in such a way that the church was virtually on an island and, through the centuries, the meandering water had cut through the ancient lane beyond the lych-gate. The only possible way for Miss Mountjoy to make her way home without retracing her steps would be to take off her shoes and wade across the now-submerged stepping-stones that had once bridged the river.

It was obvious that she wanted to be alone.

I rejoined Father as he was shaking hands with Canon Richardson. What with the murder, we de Luces were all the rage as the villagers in their Sunday finery lined up to speak with us or, sometimes, simply to touch us as if we were talismans. Everyone wanted to have a word, but nobody wanted to say anything that mattered.

"Dreadful business that, up at Buckshaw," they'd say to Father, or Feely or me.

"Nasty," we'd reply, and shake hands, and then wait for the next petitioner to shuffle forward. Only when we'd serviced the entire con-gregation were we free to make our way home for lunch.

AS WE CROSSED THE PARK, the door of a familiar blue car opened and Inspector Hewitt came across the gravel to meet us. Having already decided that police investigations were likely shelved on Sundays, I was a little surprised to see him. He gave Father a brisk nod and touched the brim of his hat to Feely, to Daffy, and to me.

"Colonel de Luce, a few words . . . in private if you please."

I watched Father closely, fearing he might faint again, but aside from a slight tightening of his knuckles on the handle of his walking stick, he seemed not at all surprised. He might even, I thought, have been preparing himself for this moment.

Dogger, meanwhile, had quietly sloped off into the house, perhaps to change his stiff old-fashioned collar and cuffs for the comfort of his gardening overalls.

Father looked round at us as if we were a gaggle of intrusive geese.

"Come into my study," he said to the Inspector, then turned and walked away.

Daffy and Feely stood gazing off into the middle distance as they are inclined to do when they don't know what to say. For a moment I thought of breaking the silence, but, on second thought, decided against it and walked away in a careless manner, whistling the "Harry Lime" theme from *The Third Man*.

Since it was Sunday, I thought it would be appropriate to go into the garden and have a look at the place where the body had lain. It would be, in a way, like those Victorian paintings of veiled widows crouching to place a handful of pathetic pansies—usually in a glass tumbler—upon the grave of their dead husband or mother. But somehow the thought made me sad, and I decided to skip the theatrics.

Without the dead man, the cucumber patch was oddly uninteresting, no more than a patch of greenery with here and there a broken stalk and something that looked suspiciously like the drag mark of a heel. In the grass, I could see the perforations where the sharp legs of Sergeant Woolmer's heavy tripod had pierced the turf.

I knew from listening to Philip Odell, the private eye on the wireless, that whenever there's a sudden and unexpected death, there's bound to be a postmortem, and I couldn't help wondering if Dr. Darby had yet had the body—as I had heard him remark to Inspector Hewitt—"up on the table." But again, that was something I dared not ask, at least not just yet.

I looked up at my bedroom window. Reflected in it, so close I could almost touch them, images of plump white clouds floated by in a sea of blue sky.

So close! Of course! The cucumber patch was directly below my window!

Why, then, had I heard nothing? Everyone knows that the killing of a human being requires the exertion of a certain amount of mechanical energy. I forget the exact formula, although I know there is one. Force applied in a short span of time (for instance a bullet), makes a great deal of noise, whereas force applied more slowly may well make no noise at all.

What did this tell me? That if the stranger had been violently attacked, it had happened somewhere else, somewhere out of earshot. If he had been attacked where I found him, the killer had used a silent method: silent and slow since, when I found him, the man had been still, although barely, alive.

"*Vale*," the dying man had said. But why would he say farewell to me? It was the word Mr. Twining had shouted before jumping to his death, but what was the connection? Was the man in the cucumbers trying to link his own death with that of Mr. Twining? Had he been there when the old man jumped? Had he been part of it?

I needed to think—and to think without distractions. The coach house was out of the question since I was now aware that, in times of trouble, I might well encounter Father sitting there in Harriet's Phantom. That left the Folly.

On the south side of Buckshaw, on an artificial island in an artificial lake, was an artificial ruin, in the shadow of which was a little Greek temple of lichen-stained marble. Now sunk deep in neglect and overgrown with nettles, there had been a time when it was one of the glories of England: a little cupola on four exquisitely slender legs that might have been a bandstand on Parnassus. Countless eighteenth-century de Luces had poled their guests out to the Folly on festive flower-strewn barges, where they had picnicked upon cold game and pastry as they watched the swans glide across the glassy water, and looked through quizzing-glasses at the hired hermit as he gaped and yawned at the doorway of his ivy-clad cave.

The island, the lake, and the Folly had been designed by Capability Brown (although this attribution had been brought into question more than once in the pages of *Notes and Queries*, which Father read avidly, but only in case matters of philatelic interest should crop up), and there was still in the library at Buckshaw a large red leather portfolio containing a signed set of the landscaper's original drawings. These inspired a little witticism on Father's part: "Let those other wise men live in their own folly," he said.

There was a family tradition that it had been on a picnic at Buckshaw Folly that John Montague, the fourth Earl of Sandwich, invented the snack which was given his name when he first slapped cold grouse between two slices of bread while playing at cribbage with Cornelius de Luce.

"History be damned," Father had said.

Now, having waded out to the island through water no more than a foot deep, I sat on the steps of the little temple with my legs drawn up and my chin on my knees.

First of all, there was Mrs. Mullet's custard pie. Where had it gone?

I let my mind drift back to the early hours of Saturday morning: envisioned myself coming down the stairs, going through the hallway to the kitchen, and—yes, the pie had certainly been on the windowsill. And there had been a single piece cut out of it.

Later, Mrs. Mullet had asked if I enjoyed the pie. Why me? I wondered. Why didn't she ask Feely or Daffy?

And then it struck me like a thunderclap! The dead man had eaten it. Yes. Everything was making sense!

Here was a diabetic who had come on a long journey from Norway, bringing with him a jack snipe concealed in a pie. I had found the remains of that pie—complete with telltale feather—at the Thirteen Drakes, and the dead bird had been dumped on our doorstep. Not having eaten—even though, according to Tully Stoker, he had been served a drink in the saloon bar—the stranger had made his way to Buckshaw on Friday night, quarreled with Father, and on his way out passed through the kitchen and helped himself to a slice of Mrs. Mullet's custard pie. And he hadn't made it through the cucumbers before it brought him down!

What kind of poison could work that quickly? I ran through the most likely possibilities. Cyanide worked in minutes: after turning blue in the face, the victim was asphyxiated almost immediately. It left behind a smell of bitter almonds. But no, the case against cyanide was that, had it been used, the victim would have been dead before I found him. (Although I have to admit that I have a soft spot for cyanide—when it comes to speed, it is right up there with the best of them. If poisons were ponies, I'd put my money on cyanide.)

But was it bitter almonds I had smelt on his last breath? I couldn't think.

Then there was curare. It, too, had an almost instant effect and again, the victim died within minutes by asphyxiation. But curare could not

kill by ingestion; to be fatal, it had to be injected. Besides that, who in
the English countryside—besides me, of course—would be likely to carry
curare in his kit?

What about tobacco? I recalled that a handful of tobacco leaves left
to soak in a jar of water in the sun for several days could easily be evaporated to a thick black molasses-like resin which brought death in seconds. But *Nicoteana* was grown in America, its fresh leaves unlikely to be
found in England, or, for that matter, in Norway.

Query: would crumbled cigarette ends, cigars, or pipe tobacco
produce an equally toxic poison?

Since nobody smoked at Buckshaw, I would have to gather my own
samples.

Query: When (and where) are the ashtrays emptied at the
Thirteen Drakes?

THE REAL QUESTION WAS THIS: Who put the poison in the pie? And,
even more to the point, if the dead man had eaten the thing by accident,
whom had it originally been intended for?

I shivered as a shadow passed across the island, and I looked up just
as a darkening cloud blotted out the sun. It was going to rain—and soon.

But before I could scramble to my feet it came pouring down in buckets, one of those sudden brief but ferocious storms of early June that
smashes flowers and plays havoc with drains. I tried to find a dry, sheltered
spot in the precise center of the open cupola where I would be most sheltered from the pelting rain—not that it made much difference, what with
the cold wind that had suddenly sprung up out of nowhere. I wrapped my
arms round myself for warmth. I'd have to wait it out, I thought.

"Hullo! Are you all right?"

A man was standing at the far edge of the lake, looking across at me
on the island. Through the sheets of falling rain, I could see no more
than dabs of damp color, which gave him the appearance of someone in
an Impressionist painting. But before I could reply, he had rolled up his
trouser legs and removed his shoes, and was swiftly wading barefoot
towards me. As he steadied himself with his long walking staff, he

reminded me of Saint Christopher carrying the Christ Child piggyback across the river, although as he drew closer, I could see that the object on his shoulders was actually a canvas knapsack.

He was dressed in a baggy walking suit and wore a hat with a wide, floppy brim: a bit like Leslie Howard, the film star, I thought. He was fiftyish, I guessed, about Father's age but dapper in spite of it.

With a waterproof artist's sketchbook in one hand, he was the very image of the strolling artist-illustrator: Olde England, and all that.

"Are you all right?" he repeated, and I realized I hadn't answered him the first time.

"Perfectly well, thank you," I said, babbling a bit too much to make up for my possible rudeness. "I was caught in the rain, you see."

"I do see," he said. "You're saturated."

"Not so much saturated as drenched," I corrected him. When it came to chemistry, I was a stickler.

He opened his knapsack and pulled out a waterproof walking cape, the sort of thing worn by hikers in the Hebrides. He wrapped it round my shoulders and I was immediately warm.

"You needn't . . . but thank you," I said.

We stood there together in the falling rain, not speaking, each of us gazing off across the lake, listening to the clatter of the downpour.

After a time he said, "Since we're to be marooned on an island together, I suppose there could be no harm in us exchanging names."

I tried to place his accent: Oxford with a touch of something else. Scandinavian, perhaps?

"I'm Flavia," I said. "Flavia de Luce."

"My name's Pemberton, Frank Pemberton. Pleased to meet you, Flavia."

Pemberton? Wasn't this the man who had arrived at the Thirteen Drakes just as I was making my escape from Tully Stoker? I wanted that visit kept quiet, so I said nothing.

We exchanged a soggy handshake, and then drew apart as strangers often do after they've touched.

The rain went on. After a bit he said, "Actually, I knew who you were."

"Did you?"

"Mmm. To anyone who takes a serious interest in English country houses, de Luce is quite a well-known name. Your family is, after all, listed in *Who's Who*."

"Do *you* take a serious interest in English country houses, Mr. Pemberton?"

He laughed. "A professional interest, I'm afraid. In fact I'm writing a book on the subject. I thought I would call it *Pemberton's Stately Homes: A Stroll Through Time*. Has rather an impressive ring, don't you think?"

"I expect it depends upon whom you're trying to impress," I said, "but it does, yes . . . rather, I mean."

"My home base is in London, of course, but I've been tramping through this part of the country for quite some time, scribbling in my notebooks. I'd rather hoped to have a look round the estate and interview your father. In fact, that's why I'm here."

"I don't think that will be possible, Mr. Pemberton," I said. "You see, there's been a sudden death at Buckshaw, and Father is . . . assisting the police with their inquiries."

Without thinking, I had pulled the phrase from remembered serials on the wireless, and, until I said it, not realized its import.

"Good Lord!" he said. "A sudden death? Not one of the family, I hope."

"No," I said. "A complete stranger. But since he was found in the garden at Buckshaw, you see, Father is bound to—"

At that moment it stopped raining as suddenly as it had begun. The sun came out to play in rainbows on the grass, and somewhere on the island, a cuckoo sang, precisely as it does at the end of the storm in Beethoven's Pastoral Symphony. I swear it did.

"I understand perfectly," he said. "I wouldn't dream of intruding. Should Colonel de Luce wish to be in contact at a later date, I'm at the Thirteen Drakes, in Bishop's Lacey. I'm sure Mr. Stoker would be happy to convey a message."

I removed the cape and handed it to him.

"Thank you," I said. "I'd best be getting back."

We waded back across the lake together like a couple of bathers holidaying at the seaside.

"It was a pleasure meeting you, Flavia," he said. "In time, I trust we shall become fast friends."

I watched as he strolled across the lawn towards the avenue of chestnuts and out of sight.

eleven

I FOUND DAFFY IN THE LIBRARY, PERCHED AT THE VERY TOP OF a wheeled ladder.

"Where's Father?" I asked.

She turned a page and went on reading as if I had never been born.

"Daffy?"

I felt my inner cauldron beginning to boil: that bubbling pot of occult brew that could so quickly transform Flavia the Invisible into Flavia the Holy Terror.

I seized one of its rungs and gave the ladder a good shake, and then a shove to start it rolling. Once in motion, it was easy enough to sustain, with Daffy clinging to the top like a paralyzed limpet as I pushed the thing down the long room.

"Stop it, Flavia! Stop it!"

As the doorway approached at an alarming rate, I braked, then ran round behind the ladder and raced off again in the opposite direction, and all the while, Daffy teetering away up top like the lookout on a whaler in a North Atlantic blow.

"Where's Father?" I shouted.

"He's still in his study with the Inspector. Stop this! Stop it!"

As she looked a little green about the gills, I stopped.

Daffy came shakily down the ladder and stepped gingerly off onto the floor. I thought for a moment she would lunge at me, but she seemed to be taking an unusually long while regaining her land legs.

"Sometimes you scare me," she said.

I was about to retort that there were times I scared myself, but then I remembered that silence can sometimes do more damage than words. I bit my tongue.

The whites of her eyes were still showing, like those of a bolted cart-horse, and I decided to take advantage of the moment.

"Where does Miss Mountjoy live?"

Daffy looked blank.

"Miss Library Mountjoy," I added.

"I have no idea," Daffy said. "I haven't used the library in the village since I was a child."

Still wide-eyed, she peered at me over her glasses.

"I was thinking of asking her advice on becoming a librarian."

It was the perfect lie. Daffy's look became almost one of respect.

"I don't know where she lives," she said. "Ask Miss Cool, at the confectionery. She knows what's under every bed in Bishop's Lacey."

"Thanks, Daff," I said as she dropped down into an upholstered wingback chair. "You're a brick."

ONE OF THE CHIEF CONVENIENCES of living near a village is that, if required, you can soon be in it. I flew along on Gladys, thinking that it might be a good idea to keep a logbook, as aeroplane pilots are made to do. By now, Gladys and I must have logged some hundreds of flying hours together, most of them in going to and from Bishop's Lacey. Now and then, with a picnic hamper strapped to her black back-skirts, we would venture even farther afield.

Once, we had ridden all morning to look at an inn where Richard Mead was said to have stayed a single night in 1747. Richard (or Dick, as I sometimes referred to him) was the author of *A Mechanical Account of Poisons in Several Essays*. Published in 1702, it was the first book on the subject in the English language, a first edition of which was the pride of my chemical library. In my bedroom portrait gallery, I kept his likeness stuck to the looking-glass alongside those of Henry Cavendish, Robert Bunsen, and Carl Wilhelm Scheele, whereas Daffy and Feely had pinups of Charles Dickens and Mario Lanza respectively.

The confectioner's shop in the Bishop's Lacey High Street stood tightly wedged between the undertaker's premises on one side and a fish shop on the other. I leaned Gladys up against the plate-glass window and seized the doorknob.

I swore curses under my breath. The place was locked as tight as Old Stink.

Why did the universe conspire against me like this? First the closet, then the library, and now the confectioner's. My life was becoming a long corridor of locked doors.

I cupped my hands at the window and peered into the interior gloom.

Miss Cool must have stepped out or perhaps, like everyone else in Bishop's Lacey, was having a family emergency. I took the knob in both hands and rattled the door, knowing as I did so that it was useless.

I remembered that Miss Cool lived in a couple of rooms behind the shop. Perhaps she had forgotten to unlock the door. Older people often do things like that: they become senile and—

But what if she's died in her sleep? I thought. Or worse . . .

I looked both ways but the High Street was empty. But wait! I had forgotten about Bolt Alley, a dark, dank tunnel of cobblestones and brick that led to the yards behind the shops. Of course! I made for it at once.

Bolt Alley smelled of the past, which was said to have once included a notorious gin mill. I gave an involuntary shiver as the sound of my footsteps echoed from its mossy walls and dripping roof. I tried not to touch the reeking green-stained bricks on either side, or to inhale its sour air, until I had edged my way out into the sunlight at the far end of the passage.

Miss Cool's tiny backyard was hemmed in with a low wall of crumbling brick. Its wooden gate was latched on the inside.

I scrambled over the wall, marched straight to the door, and gave it a good banging with the flat of my hand.

I put my ear to the panel, but nothing seemed to be moving inside.

I stepped off the walk, waded into the unkempt grass, and pressed my nose to the bottom of the sooty windowpane. The back of a dresser was blocking my view.

In one corner of the yard was a decaying doghouse—all that was left of Miss Cool's collie, Geordie, who had been run over by a speeding motorcar in the High Street.

I tugged at the sagging frame until it pulled free of the mounded earth and dragged it across the yard until it was directly under the window. Then I climbed on top of it.

From the top of the doghouse it was only one more step up until I was able to get my toes on the windowsill, where I balanced precariously on the chipped paint, my arms and legs spread out like Leonardo da Vinci's Vitruvian Man, one hand hanging on tightly to a shutter and the other trying to polish a viewing port in the grimy glass.

It was dark inside the little bedroom, but there was light enough to see the form lying on the bed; to see the white face staring back at me, its mouth gaping open in a horrid "O."

"Flavia!" Miss Cool said, scrambling to her feet, her words muffled by the window glass. "What on *earth*—?"

She snatched her false teeth from a tumbler and rammed them into her mouth, then vanished for a moment, and as I leaped to the ground I heard the sound of the bolt being shot back. The door opened inwards to reveal her standing there—like a trapped badger—in a housedress, her hand clutching and opening in nervous spasms at her throat.

"What on earth . . . ?" she repeated. "What's the matter?"

"The front door's locked," I said. "I couldn't get in."

"Of course it's locked," she said. "It's always locked on Sundays. I was having a nap."

She rubbed at her little black eyes, which were still squinting at the light.

Slowly it dawned on me that she was right. It *was* Sunday. Although it seemed aeons ago, it was only this morning that I had been sitting in St. Tancred's with my family.

I must have looked crushed.

"What is it, dear?" Miss Cool said. "That horrid business up at Buckshaw?"

So she knew about it.

"I hope you've had the good sense to keep away from the actual scene of the—"

"Yes, of course, Miss Cool," I said with a regretful smile. "But I've been asked not to talk about that. I'm sure you'll understand."

This was a lie, but a first-rate one.

"What a good child you are," she said, with a glance up at the curtained windows of an adjoining row of houses that overlooked her yard. "This is no place to talk. You'd better come inside."

She led me through a narrow hallway, on one side of it her tiny bedroom, and on the other, a miniature sitting room. And suddenly we were in the shop, behind the counter that served as the village post office. Besides being Bishop's Lacey's only confectioner, Miss Cool was also its postmistress and, as such, knew everything worth knowing—except chemistry, of course.

She watched me carefully as I looked round with interest at the tiers of shelves, each one lined with glass jars of horehound sticks, bull's-eyes, and hundreds-and-thousands.

"I'm sorry. I can't do business on a Sunday. They'd have me up before the magistrates. It's the law, you know."

I shook my head sadly.

"I'm sorry," I said. "I forgot what day it was. I didn't mean to frighten you."

"Well, no real harm done," she said, suddenly recovering her usual garrulous powers as she bustled about the shop, aimlessly touching this and that.

"Tell your father there's a new set of stamps coming out soon, but nothing to go into raptures about, at least to my way of thinking, anyways. Same old picture of King George's head, God bless 'im, but tarted up in new colors."

"Thank you, Miss Cool," I said. "I'll be sure to let him know."

"I'm sure that lot at the General Post Office up in London could come up with something better than that," she went on, "but I've heard as how they're saving up their brains for next year to celebrate the Festival of Britain."

"I wonder if you could tell me where Miss Mountjoy lives," I blurted.

"Tilda Mountjoy?" Her eyes narrowed. "Whatever could you want with her?"

"She was most helpful to me at the library, and I thought it might be nice to take her some sweets."

I gave a sweet smile to match the sentiment.

This was a shameless lie. I hadn't given the matter a moment's thought until now, when I saw that I could kill two birds with one stone.

"Ah, yes," Miss Cool said. "Margaret Pickery off to tend the sister in

Nether-Wolsey: the Singer, the needle, the finger, the twins, the way-ward husband, the bottle, the bills . . . a moment of unexpected and rewarding usefulness for Tilda Mountjoy . . .

"Acid drops," she said suddenly. "Sunday or no, acid drops would be the perfect choice."

"I'll have sixpence worth," I said.

" . . . and a shilling's worth of the horehound sticks," I added. Horehound was my secret passion.

Miss Cool tiptoed to the front of the shop and pulled down the blinds.

"Just between you and me and the gatepost," she said in a conspiratorial voice.

She scooped the acid drops into a purple paper bag of such a funereal color that it simply cried out to be filled with a scoop or two of arsenic or *nux vomica*.

"That will be one-and-six," she said, wrapping the horehound sticks in paper. I handed her two shillings and while she was still digging in her pockets I said, "That's all right, Miss Cool, I don't require change."

"What a sweet child you are." She beamed, slipping an extra horehound stick into the wrappings. "If I had children of my own, I couldn't hope to see them half so thoughtful or so generous."

I gave her a partial smile and kept the rest of it for myself as she directed me to Miss Mountjoy's house.

"Willow Villa," she said. "You can't miss it. It's orange."

WILLOW VILLA WAS, as Miss Cool had said, orange; the kind of orange you see when the scarlet cap of a Death's Head mushroom has just begun to go off. The house was hidden in the shadows beneath the flowing green skirts of a monstrous weeping willow whose branches shifted uneasily in the breeze, sweeping bare the dirt beneath it like a score of witches' brooms. Their movement made me think of a piece of seventeenth-century music that Feely sometimes played and sang—very sweetly, I must admit—when she was thinking of Ned:

The willow-tree will twist, and the willow-tree will twine,
O I wish I was in the dear youth's arms that once had the heart of mine.

The song was called "The Seeds of Love," although love was not the first thing that came to mind whenever I saw a willow; on the contrary, they always reminded me of Ophelia (Shakespeare's, not mine) who drowned herself near one.

Except for a handkerchief-sized scrap of grass at one side, Miss Mountjoy's willow filled the fenced-in yard. Even on the doorstep I could feel the dampness of the place: the tree's languid branches formed a green bell jar through which little light seemed to penetrate, giving me the odd sensation of being under water. Vivid green mosses made a stone sponge of the doorstep, and water stains stretched their sad black fingers across the face of the orange plaster.

On the door was an oxidized brass knocker with the grinning face of the Lincoln Imp. I lifted it and gave a couple of gentle taps. As I waited, I gazed absently up into the air in case anyone should be peeking out from behind the curtains.

But the dusty lace didn't stir. It was as if there was no breath of air inside the place.

To the left, a walk cobbled with old, worn bricks led round the side of the house, and after waiting at the door for a minute or two, I followed it.

The back door was almost completely hidden by long tendrils of willow leaves, all of them undulating with a slightly expectant swishing, like a garish green theater curtain about to rise.

I cupped my hands to the glass at one of the tiny windows. If I stood on tiptoe—

"What are you doing here?"

I spun round.

Miss Mountjoy was standing outside the circle of willow branches, looking in. Through the foliage, I could see only vertical stripes of her face, but what I saw made me edgy.

"It's me, Miss Mountjoy . . . Flavia," I said. "I wanted to thank you for helping me at the library."

The willow branches rustled as Miss Mountjoy stepped inside the cloak of greenery. She was holding a pair of garden shears in one hand and she said nothing. Her eyes, like two mad raisins in her wrinkled face, never left mine.

I shrank back as she stepped onto the walk, blocking my escape.

"I know well enough who you are," she said. "You're Flavia Sabina Dolores de Luce—Jacko's youngest daughter."

"You know he's my father?!" I gasped.

"Of course I know, girl. A person of my age knows a great deal."

Somehow, before I could stop it, the truth popped out of me like a cork from a bottle.

"The 'Dolores' was a lie," I said. "I sometimes fabricate things."

She took a step towards me.

"Why are you here?" she asked, her voice a harsh whisper.

I quickly plunged my hand into my pocket and fished out the bag of sweets.

"I brought you some acid drops," I said, "to apologize for my rudeness. I hope you'll accept them."

A shrill wheezing sound, which I took to depict a laugh, came out of her.

"Miss Cool's recommendation, no doubt?"

Like the village idiot in a pantomime, I gave half a dozen quick, bobbing nods.

"I was sorry to hear about the way your uncle—Mr. Twining—died," I said, and I meant it. "Honestly I was. It doesn't seem fair."

"Fair? It certainly was not fair," she said. "And yet it was not unjust. It was not even wicked. Do you know what it was?"

Of course I knew. I had heard this before, but I was not here to debate her.

"No," I whispered.

"It was murder," she said. "It was murder, pure and simple."

"And who was the murderer?" I asked. Sometimes my own tongue took me by surprise.

A rather vague look floated across Miss Mountjoy's face like a cloud across the moon, as if she had spent a lifetime preparing for the part and then, center stage in the spotlight, had forgotten her lines.

"Those boys," she said at last. "Those loathsome, detestable boys. I shall never forget them; not for all their apple cheeks and schoolboy innocence."

"One of those boys is my father," I said quietly.

Her eyes were somewhere else in time. Only slowly did they return to the present to focus upon me.

"Yes," she said. "Laurence de Luce. Jacko. Your father was called Jacko. A schoolboy sobriquet, and yet even the coroner called him that. Jacko. He said it ever so softly at the inquest, almost caressingly—as if all the court were in thrall with the name."

"My father gave evidence at the inquest?"

"Of course he testified—as did the other boys. It was the sort of thing that was done in those days. He denied everything, of course, all responsibility. A valuable postage stamp had been stolen from the headmaster's collection, and it was all, 'Oh no, sir, it wasn't me, sir!' As if the stamp had magically sprouted grubby little fingers and filched itself!"

I was about to tell her "My father is not a thief, nor is he a liar," when suddenly I knew that nothing I could say would ever change this ancient mind. I decided to take the offensive.

"Why did you walk out of church this morning?" I asked.

Miss Mountjoy recoiled as if I had thrown a glass of water in her face. "You don't mince words, do you?"

"No," I said. "It had something to do with the Vicar's praying for the stranger in our midst, didn't it? The man whose body I found in the garden at Buckshaw."

She hissed through her teeth like a teakettle. "*You* found the body? You?"

"Yes," I said.

"Then tell me this—did it have red hair?" She closed her eyes, and kept them closed awaiting my reply.

"Yes," I said. "It had red hair."

"For what we have received may the Lord make us truly thankful," she breathed, before opening her eyes again. It seemed to me not only a peculiar response, but somehow an unchristian one.

"I don't understand," I said. And I didn't.

"I recognized him at once," she said. "Even after all these years, I knew who he was as soon as I saw that shock of red hair walking out of the Thirteen Drakes. If that hadn't been enough, his swagger, that overweening cockiness, those cold blue eyes—any one of those things—would have told me that Horace Bonepenny had come back to Bishop's Lacey."

I had the feeling that we were slipping into deeper waters than I knew.

"Perhaps now you can see why I could not take part in any prayer for the repose of that boy's—that man's—rancid soul."

She reached out and took the bag of acid drops from my hand, popping one into her mouth and pocketing the rest.

"On the contrary," she continued, "I pray that he is, at this very moment, being basted in hell."

And with that, she walked into her dank Willow Villa and slammed the door.

Who on earth was Horace Bonepenny? And what had brought him back to Bishop's Lacey?

I could think of only one person who might be made to tell me.

AS I RODE UP THE AVENUE of chestnuts to Buckshaw, I could see that the blue Vauxhall was no longer at the door. Inspector Hewitt and his men had gone.

I was wheeling Gladys round to the back of the house when I heard a metallic tapping coming from the greenhouse. I moved towards the door and looked inside. It was Dogger.

He was sitting on an overturned pail, striking the thing with a trowel. Clang . . . clang . . . clang . . . clang. In the way the bell of St. Tancred's tolls for the funeral of some ancient in Bishop's Lacey, it went on and on, as if measuring the strokes of a life. Clang . . . clang . . . clang . . . clang . . .

His back was to the door, and it was obvious that he did not see me.

I crept away towards the kitchen door where I made a great and noisy ado by dropping Gladys with a loud clatter on the stone doorstep. ("Sorry, Gladys," I whispered.)

"Damn and blast!" I said, loudly enough to be heard in the greenhouse. I pretended to spot him there behind the glass.

"Oh, hullo, Dogger," I said cheerily. "Just the person I was looking for."

He did not turn immediately, and I pretended to be scraping a bit of clay from the sole of my shoe until he recovered himself.

"Miss Flavia," he said slowly. "Everyone has been looking for you."

"Well, here I am," I said. Best to take over the conversation until Dogger was fully back on the rails.

"I was talking to someone in the village who told me about somebody I thought you might be able to tell me about."

Dogger managed the ghost of a smile.

"I know I'm not putting that in the best way, but—"

"I know what you mean," he said.

"Horace Bonepenny," I blurted out. "Who is Horace Bonepenny?"

At my words, Dogger began to twitch like an experimental frog whose spinal cord has been hooked up to a galvanic battery. He licked his lips and wiped madly at his mouth with a pocket handkerchief. I could see that his eyes were beginning to dim, winking out much as the stars do just before sunrise. At the same time, he was making a great effort to pull himself together, though with little success.

"Never mind, Dogger," I said. "It doesn't matter. Forget it."

He tried to get to his feet, but was unable to lift himself from the overturned pail.

"Miss Flavia," he said, "there are questions which need to be asked, and there are questions which need not to be asked."

So there it was again: so like a law, these words that fell from Dogger's lips as naturally, and with as much finality, as if Isaiah himself had spoken them.

But those few words seemed utterly to have exhausted him, and with a loud sigh he covered his face with his hands. I wanted nothing more at that moment than to throw my arms round him and hug him, but I knew that he wasn't up to it. Instead, I settled for putting my hand on his shoulder, realizing even as I did so that the gesture was of greater comfort to me than it was to him.

"I'll go and get Father," I said. "We'll help you to your room."

Dogger turned his face slowly round towards me, a chalky white mask of tragedy. The words came out of him like stone grating upon stone.

"They've taken him away, Miss Flavia. The police have taken him away."

twelve

FEELY AND DAFFY WERE SITTING ON A FLOWERED DIVAN IN the drawing room, wrapped in one another's arms and wailing like air-raid sirens. I had taken a few steps into the room to join in with them before Ophelia spotted me.

"Where have you been, you little beast?" she hissed, springing up and coming at me like a wildcat, her eyes swollen and as red as cycle reflectors. "Everyone's been searching for you. We thought you'd drowned. Oh! How I prayed you had!"

Welcome home, Flave, I thought.

"Father's been arrested," Daffy said matter-of-factly. "They've taken him away."

"Where?" I asked.

"How should we know?" Ophelia spat contemptuously. "Wherever they take people who have been arrested, I expect. Where have you been?"

"Bishop's Lacey or Hinley?"

"What do you mean? Talk sense, you little fool."

"Bishop's Lacey or Hinley," I repeated. "There's only a one-room police station at Bishop's Lacey, so I don't expect he's been taken there. The County Constabulary is at Hinley. So they've likely taken him to Hinley."

"They'll charge him with murder," Ophelia said, "and then he'll be hanged!" She burst into tears again and turned away. For a moment I almost felt sorry for her.

I CAME OUT OF THE DRAWING ROOM and into the hallway and saw Dogger halfway up the west staircase, plodding slowly, step by step, like a condemned man ascending the steps of the scaffold.

Now was my chance!

I waited until he was out of sight at the top of the stairs, then slipped into Father's study and quietly locked the door behind me. It was the first time in my life I had ever been alone in the room.

One full wall was given over to Father's stamp albums, fat leather volumes whose colors indicated the reign of each monarch: black for Queen Victoria, red for Edward the Seventh, green for George the Fifth, and blue for our present monarch, George the Sixth. I remembered that a slim scarlet volume tucked between the green book and the blue contained only a few items—one each of the nine known variations of the four stamps issued bearing the head of Edward the Eighth before he decamped with that American woman.

I knew that Father derived endless pleasure from the countless and minute variations in his bits of confetti, but I did not know the details. Only when he became excited enough over some new tidbit of trivia in the latest issue of *The London Philatelist* to rhapsodize aloud at breakfast would we learn a little more about his happy, insulated world. Apart from those rare occasions, we were all of us, my sisters and me, babes in the wood when it came to postage stamps, while Father puttered on, mounting bits of colored paper with more fearsome relish than some men mount the heads of stags and tigers.

On the wall opposite the books stood a Jacobean sideboard whose top surface and drawers overflowed with what seemed to be no end of philatelic supplies: stamp hinges, perforation gauges, enameled trays for soaking, bottles of fluid for revealing watermarks, gum erasers, stock envelopes, page reinforcements, stamp tweezers, and a hooded ultraviolet lamp.

At the end of the room, in front of the French doors that opened onto the terrace, was Father's desk: a partner's desk the size of a playing field, which might once have seen service in Scrooge and Marley's counting house. I knew at once that its drawers would be locked—and I was right.

Where, I wondered, would Father hide a stamp in a room full of stamps? There wasn't a doubt in my mind that he *had* hidden it—as I

would have done. Father and I shared a passion for privacy, and I realized
he would never be so foolish as to put it in an obvious place.

Rather than look on top of things, or inside things, I lay flat on the
floor like a mechanic inspecting a motorcar's undercarriage, and slid
round the room on my back examining the underside of things. I looked
at the bottoms of the desk, the table, the wastepaper basket, and Father's
Windsor chair. I looked under the Turkey carpet and behind the curtains.
I looked at the back of the clock and turned over the prints on the wall.

There were far too many books to search, so I tried to think of which
of them would be least likely to be looked into. Of course! The Bible!

But a quick riffle through King James produced no more than an old
church leaflet and a mourning card for some dead de Luce from the time
of the Great Exhibition.

Then suddenly I remembered that Father had plucked the Penny
Black from the bill of the dead snipe and put it in his waistcoat pocket.
Perhaps he had left it there, meaning to dispose of it later.

Yes, that was it! The stamp wasn't here at all. What an idiot I was to
think it would be. The entire study, of course, would be at the very top
of the list of too-obvious hiding places. A wave of certainty washed over
me and I knew, with what Feely and Daffy incorrectly call "female intuition," that the stamp was somewhere else.

Trying not to make a sound, I turned the key and stepped out into the
hall. The Weird Sisters were still going at it in the drawing room, their
voices rising and falling between notes of anger and grief. I could have
listened at the door, but I chose not to. I had more important things to do.

I went, silent as a shadow, up the west staircase and into the south
wing.

As I expected, Father's room was in near-darkness as I stepped inside.
I had often glanced up at his windows from the lawn and seen the heavy
drapes pulled tightly shut.

From inside, it possessed all the gloom of a museum after hours. The
strong scent of Father's colognes and shaving lotions suggested open sar-
cophagi and canopic jars that had once been packed with ancient spices.
The finely curved legs of a Queen Anne washstand seemed almost inde-
cent beside the gloomy Gothic bed in the corner, as if some sour old
chamberlain were looking on dyspeptically as his mistress unfurled silk
stockings over her long, youthful legs.

Even the room's two clocks suggested times long past. On the chimneypiece, an ormolu monstrosity, its brass pendulum, like the curved blade in "The Pit and the Pendulum," tock-tocking away the time and flashing dully at the end of each swing in the subdued lighting of the room. On the bedside table, an exquisite little Georgian clock stood in silent disagreement: Her hands were at 3:15, his at 3:12.

I walked down the long room to the far end, and stopped.

Harriet's dressing room—which could be entered only through Father's bedroom—was forbidden territory. Father had brought us up to respect the shrine that he had made of it the day he learned of her death. He had done this by making us believe, even if we were not told so outright, that any violation of his rule would result in our being marched off in single file to the end of the garden, where we would be lined up against the brick wall and summarily shot.

The door to Harriet's room was covered with green baize, rather like a billiard table stood on end. I gave it a push and it swung open with an uneasy silence.

The room was awash in light. Through the tall windowpanes on three of its sides poured torrents of sunshine, diffused by endless swags of Italian lace, into a chamber that might have been a stage-setting for a play about the Duke and Duchess of Windsor. The dresser top was laid out with brushes and combs by Fabergé, as if Harriet had just stepped into the adjoining room for a bath. Lalique scent bottles were ringed with colorful bracelets of Bakelite and amber, while a charming little hotplate and a silver kettle stood ready to make her early morning tea. A single yellow rose was wilting in a vase of slender glass.

On an oval tray stood a tiny crystal bottle containing no more than a drop or two of scent. I picked it up, removed the stopper, and waved it languidly under my nose.

The scent was one of small blue flowers, of mountain meadows, and of ice.

A peculiar feeling passed over me—or, rather, through me, as if I were an umbrella remembering what it felt like to pop open in the rain. I looked at the label and saw that it bore a single word: *Miratrix*.

A silver cigarette case with the initials H. de L. lay beside a hand mirror whose back was embossed with the image of Flora, from Botticelli's painting *Primavera*. I had never noticed this before in prints from the original, but Flora looked hugely and happily pregnant. Could this mirror have been a gift from Father to Harriet while she was pregnant with one of us? And if so, which one: Feely? Daffy? Me? I thought it unlikely that it was me: A third girl would hardly have been a gift from the gods—at least so far as Father was concerned.

No, it was probably Ophelia the Firstborn—she who seemed to have arrived on earth with a mirror in her hand . . . perhaps this very one.

A basket chair at one of the windows made a perfect spot for reading and here, within arm's reach, was Harriet's own little library. She had brought the books back from her school days in Canada and summers with an aunt in Boston: *Anne of Green Gables* and *Jane of Lantern Hill* were next-door neighbors to *Penrod* and *Merton of the Movies*, while at the far end of the shelf leaned a dog-eared copy of *The Awful Disclosures of Maria Monk*. I had not read any of them, but from what I knew of Harriet, they were probably all of them books about free spirits and renegades.

Nearby, on a small round table, was a photo album. I lifted the cover and saw that its pages were of black pulpy paper, the captions handwritten below each black-and-white snapshot in chalky ink: Harriet (Age 2) at Morris House; Harriet (Age 15) at Miss Bodycote's Female Academy (1930—Toronto, Canada); Harriet with *Blithe Spirit*, her de Havilland Gypsy Moth (1938); Harriet in Tibet (1939).

The photos showed Harriet growing from a fat cherub with a mop of golden hair, through a tall, skinny, laughing girl (with no perceptible breasts) dressed in hockey gear, to a film star with blond bangs, standing, like Amelia Earhart, with one hand resting negligently on the rim of *Blithe Spirit*'s cockpit. There were no photographs of Father. Nor were there any of us.

In every photograph, Harriet's features were those of a woman whose design has been arrived at by taking those of Feely, Daffy, and me and shaking them in a jar before reassembling them into this grinning, confident, yet endearingly shy adventuress.

As I stared at her face, trying to see through the photographic paper to Harriet's soul, there was a light tapping at the door.

A pause—and then another tapping. And the door began to open.

It was Dogger. He stuck his head slowly into the room.

"Colonel de Luce?" he said. "Are you here?"

I froze, hardly daring even to breathe. Dogger didn't move a muscle, but gazed straight ahead in the expectant way of a well-trained servant who knows his place, relying on his ears to tell him if he was intruding.

But what was he playing at? Hadn't he just told me that the police had taken Father away? Why on earth, then, would he expect to find him here in Harriet's dressing room? Was Dogger so addled as that? Or could it be that he was shadowing me?

I parted my lips slightly and breathed in slowly through my mouth so that a wayward nose-whistle wouldn't give me away, at the same time offering up a silent prayer that I wouldn't sneeze.

Dogger stood there for the longest time, like a *tableau vivant*. I had seen etchings in the library of those ancient entertainments in which the actors were plastered with whitewash and powder before arranging themselves in motionless poses, often of a titillating nature, each supposedly representing a scene from the lives of the gods.

After a time, just as I was beginning to realize how a rabbit must feel when it "freezes," Dogger slowly withdrew his head and the door closed without a sound.

Had he seen me? And if he had, was he pretending he hadn't?

I waited, listening, but there wasn't a sound from the room next door. I knew Dogger would not linger for long, and when I judged that time enough had passed, I opened the door and peeked out.

Father's room was as I had left it, the two clocks ticking away, but now, because of my fright, they seemed louder than they had before. Realizing this was an opportunity that would never come again, I began my search using the same method as I had in Father's study, but because his bedroom was as spartan as the campaign tent of Leonidas must have been, it did not take very long.

The only book in the room was a sale catalogue from Stanley Gibbons for a stamp auction to be held in three months' time. I turned it over and flipped eagerly through its pages, but nothing tumbled out.

There were shockingly few clothes in Father's closet: a couple of old tweed jackets with leather patches at their elbows (their pockets empty), two wool sweaters, and some shirts. I dug inside his shoes and an ancient pair of regimental half-Wellingtons but found nothing.

I realized with a twinge that Father's only other clothing was his Sunday suit, which he must still have been wearing when Inspector Hewitt took him away. (I would not allow myself to use the word *arrested*.)

Perhaps he had hidden the pierced Penny Black somewhere else—in the glove box of Harriet's Rolls-Royce, for instance. For all I knew, he might already have destroyed it. Now that I stopped to think about it, that would have made most sense. The stamp itself was damaged, and therefore of no value. Something about it, though, had upset Father, and it seemed logical that as soon as he had gone to his room on Friday, he would have put a match to it at once.

That, of course, would have left its traces: paper ash in the ashtray and a burnt-out match in the wastepaper basket. It was easy enough to check since both of these were right there in front of me—and both were empty.

Perhaps he had flushed away the evidence.

Now I knew that I was clutching at straws.

Give it up, I thought; leave it to the police. Go back to your cozy lab and get on with your life's work.

I thought—but only for a moment, and with a little thrill—what lethal drops could be distilled from the entries at the Spring Flower Show; what a jolly poison could be extracted from the jonquil and what deadly liquors from the daffodil. Even the common churchyard yew, so loved by poets and by courting couples, contained within its seeds and leaves enough taxine to put paid to half the population of England.

But these pleasures would have to wait. My duty was to Father, and it had fallen upon my shoulders to help him, particularly now that he couldn't help himself. I knew that I should go to him, wherever he was, and lay my sword at his feet in the way that a medieval squire vows service to his knight. Even if I couldn't help him, I could still sit beside him, and I realized with a sudden piercing pang that I missed him dreadfully.

I was seized with a sudden idea: How many miles was it to Hinley? Could I reach there before dark? And even if I did, would I be allowed to see him?

My heart began to pound as if someone had slipped me a cup of fox-glove tea.

Time to go. I had been here long enough. I glanced at the bedside clock—3:40, it now said. The chimneypiece clock ticked solemnly on, its hands at 3:37.

Father must have been too distraught to notice, I supposed, since generally, when it came to the time of day, he was a martinet. I remembered his way of giving orders to Dogger (although not to us) in military fashion:

"Take the gladioli along to the Vicar at thirteen hundred hours, Dogger," he'd say. "He'll be expecting you. Be back by thirteen forty-five and we'll decide what to do with the duckweed."

I stared at the two clocks, hoping that something would come to me. Father had told us once, in one of his rare expansive moods, that what made him fall in love with Harriet was her ability to cogitate. "Remarkable thing in a woman, really, when you come to think of it," he had said.

And suddenly I saw. One of his clocks had been stopped—stopped for precisely three minutes. The clock on the chimneypiece.

I moved slowly towards it, as one would stalk a bird. Its dark funereal case gave it the look of a Victorian horse-drawn hearse: all knobs and glass and black shellac.

I saw my hand reaching out, small and white in the shadowed room; felt my fingers touch its cold face; felt my thumb pop open the silver catch. Now the brass pendulum was right at my fingertips, swinging to and fro, to and fro with its ghastly tock-tocking. I was almost afraid to touch the thing. I took a deep breath and grabbed the pulsing pendulum. Its inertia made it squirm heavily in my hand for a moment, like a gold-fish suddenly seized; like the telltale heart before it fell still.

I felt round the back of the weighted brass. Something was fastened there; something taped behind it: a tiny packet. I pulled at it with my fingers, felt it come free and drop into my hand. Even as I withdrew my fingers from the clock's internal organs I guessed what I was about to see . . . and I was right. There in my palm lay a little glassine envelope inside which, clearly visible, was a Penny Black postage stamp. A Penny Black with a hole in its center, such as might have been produced by the bill of a dead jack snipe. What was there about it that had frightened Father so?

I fished the stamp out for a better look. In the first place, there was Queen Victoria with a hole in her head. Unpatriotic, perhaps, but hardly enough to shake a grown man to his roots. No, there must be more.

What was it that set this stamp apart from any other of its kind? After all, hadn't the things been printed by the tens of millions, and all of them alike? Or were they?

I thought of the time that Father—in the interests of broadening our outlook—had suddenly announced that Wednesday evenings would henceforth be given over to a series of compulsory lectures (delivered by him) on various aspects of British Government. "Series A," as he called it, was to be, predictably enough, on the topic "The History of the Penny Post."

Daffy, Feely, and I had all brought notebooks to the drawing room and pretended to take notes while passing scraps of paper back and forth with scribbled messages to one another such as "Stamp Out Lectures" and "Let's Lick Boredom!"

Postage stamps, Father had explained, were printed in sheets of two hundred and forty; twenty horizontal rows of twelve, which was easy enough for me to remember since 20 is the atomic number for Calcium and 12 the number for Magnesium—all I had to do was think of CaMg. Each stamp on the sheet carried a unique two-letter identifier beginning with "AA" on the upper left stamp and progressing alphabetically from left to right until "TL" was reached at the right end of the twentieth, or bottom, row.

This scheme, Father told us, had been implemented by the Post Office to prevent forgeries, although it was not perfectly clear how this was to work. There had been rampant paranoia, he said, that dens of forgers would be toiling away day and night, from Land's End to John o'Groats, producing copies to bilk Her Victorian Majesty out of a penny per time.

I looked closely at the stamp in my hand. At the bottom, below Queen Victoria's head, was written its value: ONE PENNY. To the left of these words was the letter B, to their right, the letter H.

It looked like this: **B   ONE PENNY.   H**

"BH." The stamp had come from the second row on the printed sheet, eighth column to the right. Two-eight. Was that significant? Aside from the fact that 28 was the atomic number for Nickel, I could think of nothing.

And then I saw it! It wasn't a number at all: It was a word!

Bonepenny! Not just Bonepenny, but Bonepenny, H.! Horace Bonepenny!

Impaled on the jack snipe's bill (Yes! Father's schoolboy nickname had been "Jacko"!), the stamp had served as calling card and death threat. A threat that Father had taken in and understood at first glance.

The bird's bill had pierced the Queen's head, but left the name of its sender in clear view for anyone who had the eyes to see.

Horace Bonepenny. The *late* Horace Bonepenny.

I returned the stamp to its hiding place.

———

AT THE TOP OF THE HILL, a rotted wooden post—all that remained of an eighteenth-century gibbet—pointed two fingers in opposing directions. I could reach Hinley, I knew, by either taking the road to Doddingsley, or by following a somewhat longer, less traveled road that would take me through the village of St. Elfrieda's. The former would get me there more quickly; the latter, being more sparsely traveled, would offer less risk of being spotted in case someone reported me missing.

"Har-har-har!" I said, with vast irony. Who could care enough?

Still, I took the road to the right and pointed Gladys towards St. Elfrieda's. It was downhill all the way, and I made good speed. When I backpedaled, the Sturmey-Archer three-speed hub on Gladys's rear wheel gave off a noise like a den of enraged, venom-dripping rattle-snakes. I pretended they were right there behind me, striking at my heels. It was glorious! I hadn't felt in such fine form since the day I first produced, by successive extraction and evaporation, a synthetic curare from the bog arum in the Vicar's lily pond.

I put my feet up on the handlebars and gave Gladys her head. As we shot down the dusty hill, I yodeled a song into the wind:

> "*They call her the lass*
> *With the delicate air! . . .*"

thirteen

AT THE BOTTOM OF OAKSHOTT HILL I SUDDENLY THOUGHT OF Father and sadness came creeping back. Did they honestly believe he had murdered Horace Bonepenny? And if so, how? If Father had murdered him beneath my bedroom window, the deed had been done in utter silence. I could hardly imagine Father killing someone without raising his voice.

But before I could speculate further, the road leveled out before twisting off to Cottesmore and to Doddingsley Magna. In the shade of an ancient oak was a bus stop bench, upon which sat a familiar figure: an ancient gnome in plus fours, looking like a George Bernard Shaw who had shrunk in the wash. He sat there so placidly, his feet dangling four inches above the ground, that he might have been born on the bench and lived there all his life.

It was Maximilian Brock, one of our Buckshaw neighbors, and I prayed he hadn't seen me. It was whispered in Bishop's Lacey that Max, retired from the world of music, was now earning a secret living by writing—under feminine pseudonyms (such as Lala Dupree)—scandalous stories for American magazines with titles like *Confidential Confessions* and *Red Hot Romances*.

Because of the way he pried into the affairs of everyone he met, then spun what he was told in confidence into news-seller's gold, Max was called, at least behind his back, "The Village Pump." But as Feely's onetime piano teacher, he was someone whom I could not politely ignore.

I pulled off into the shallow ditch, pretending I hadn't seen him as I fiddled with Gladys's chain. With any luck, he'd keep looking the other way and I could hide out behind the hedge until he was gone.

"Flavia! *Haroo, mon vieux.*"

Curses! I'd been spotted. To ignore a "haroo" from Maximilian— even one from a bus stop bench—was to ignore the eleventh commandment. I pretended I had just noticed him, and laid on a bogus grin as I wheeled Gladys towards him through the weeds.

Maximilian had lived for many years in the Channel Islands, where he had been pianist with the Alderney Symphony, a position—he said— which required a great deal of patience and a good supply of detective novels.

On Alderney, it was only necessary (or so he had told me once while chatting about crime, at St. Tancred's annual Flower Show), in order to bring down the full power of the law, to stand in the middle of the town square and cry *"Haroo, haroo, mon prince. On me fait tort!"* This was called the "hue and cry," and meant, in essence, "Attention, my Prince, someone is torting me!" Or, in other words, committing a crime against me.

"And how are you, my little pelican?" Max asked, canting his head like a magpie awaiting a crumb of response even before it was offered.

"I'm all right," I said warily, remembering that Daffy had once told me that Max was like one of those spiders that paralyzed you with a bite, and didn't quit until he had sucked the last drop of juice from your life— and from the life of your family.

"And your father, the good Colonel?"

"He's keeping busy, what with one thing and another," I said. I felt my heart give a flip-flop in my breast.

"That Miss Ophelia, now," he asked. "Is she still painting her face like Jezebel and admiring herself in the tea service?"

This was too close to home, even for me. It was none of his business, but I knew that Maximilian could fly into a towering rage at the drop of a hat. Feely sometimes referred to him behind his back as "Rumpelstiltskin," and Daffy as "Alexander Pope—or lower."

Still, I had found Maximilian, in spite of his repellent habits, and perhaps because of our similarity in stature, occasionally to be an interesting and informative conversationalist—just so long as you didn't mistake his diminutive size for weakness.

"She's very well, thank you," I said. "Her complexion was quite lovely this morning."

I did not add "maddeningly."

"Max," I asked, before he could wedge in another question, "do you think I could ever learn to play that little toccata by Paradisi?"

"No," he said, without an instant's hesitation. "Your hands are not the hands of a great artist. They are the hands of a poisoner."

I grinned. This was our little joke. And it was obvious that he had not yet learned of the murder at Buckshaw.

"And the other one?" he asked. "Daphne . . . the slow sister?"

"Slow" was a reference to Daffy's prowess, or lack of it, at the piano: an endless, painful quest to place unwilling fingers upon keys that seemed to shy away from her touch. Daffy's battle with the instrument was one of the hen pitted against the fox, a losing battle that always ended in tears. And yet, because Father insisted upon it, the war went on.

One day when I found her sobbing on the bench with her head on the closed piano lid, I had whispered, "Give it up, Daff," and she had flown at me like a fighting cock.

I had even tried encouragement. Whenever I heard her at the Broadwood, I would drift into the drawing room, lean against the piano, and gaze off into the distance as if her playing had enchanted me. Usually she ignored me, but once when I said, "What a lovely piece that is! What's it called?" she had almost slammed the lid on my fingers.

"The scale of G major!" she had shrieked, and fled the room.

Buckshaw was not an easy place in which to live.

"She's well," I said. "Reading Dickens like billy-ho. Can't get a word out of her."

"Ah," Maximilian said. "Dear old Dickens."

He didn't seem to be able to think of anything further on that topic, and I dived into the momentary silence.

"Max," I said. "You're a man of the world—"

At this he preened himself, and puffed up to whatever little height he could muster.

"Not just a man of the world—a boulevardier," he said.

"Exactly," I said, wondering what the word meant. "Have you ever visited Stavanger?" It would save me looking it up in the atlas.

"What? Stavanger in Norway?"

"SNAP!" I almost shouted aloud. Horace Bonepenny had been in Norway! I took a deep breath to recover myself, hoping it would be mistaken for impatience.

"Of course in Norway," I said condescendingly. "Are there other Stavangers?"

For a moment I thought he was onto me. His eyes narrowed and I felt a chill as the thunderclouds of a Maximilian tantrum blew across the sun. But then he gave a tiny giggle, like springwater gurgling into a glass.

"Stavanger is the first stepping-stone on the Road to Hell . . . which is a railway station," he said. "I traveled over it to Trondheim, and then on to Hell, which, believe it or not, is a very small village in Norway, from which tourists often dispatch picture postcards to their friends with the message, 'Wish you were here!' and where I performed Grieg's Piano Concerto in A Minor. Grieg, incidentally, was as much a Scot as a Norwegian. Grandfather from Aberdeen, left in disgust after Culloden— must have had second thoughts, though, when he realized he'd done no more than trade the firths for the fjords.

"Trondheim was a great success, I must say . . . critics kind, public polite. But those people, they never understand their own music, you know. Played Scarlatti as well, to bring a glimpse of Italian sunshine to those snowy northern climes. Still, at the intermission I happened to hear a commercial traveler from Dublin whispering to a friend, 'It's all Grieg to me, Thor.'"

I smiled dutifully, although I had heard this ancient jest about forty-five times before.

"That was in the old days, of course, before the war. Stavanger! Yes, of course I've been there. But why do you ask?"

"How did you get there? By ship?"

Horace Bonepenny had been alive in Stavanger and now he was dead in England and I wanted to know where he had been in between.

"Of course by ship. You're not thinking of running away from home, are you, Flavia?"

"We were having a discussion—actually a row—about it last night at supper."

This was one of the ways to optimize a lie: shovel on the old frankness.

"Ophelia thought one would embark from London; Father insisted it was Hull; Daphne voted for Scarborough, but only because Anne Brontë is buried there."

"Newcastle-upon-Tyne," Maximilian said. "Actually, it's Newcastle-upon-Tyme."

There was a rumble in the distance as the Cottesmore bus approached, waddling along the lane between the hedgerows like a chicken walking a tightrope. It stopped in front of the bench, wheezing heavily as it subsided from the effort of its hard life among the hills. The door swung open with an iron groan.

"Ernie, *mon vieux*," Maximilian said. "How fares the transportation industry?"

"Board," Ernie said, looking straight ahead through the windscreen. If he caught the joke he chose to ignore it.

"No ride today, Ernie. Just using your bench to rest my kidneys."

"Benches are for the sole use of travelers awaiting a coach. It's in the rule book, Max. You know that as well as I do."

"Indeed I do, Ernie. Thank you for reminding me."

Max slid off the bench and dropped to the ground.

"Cheerio, then," he said, and tipping his hat, he set off along the road like Charlie Chaplin.

The door of the bus squealed shut as Ernie engaged the juddering gears and the coach whined into reluctant forward motion. And so we all went our separate ways: Ernie and his bus to Cottesmore, Max to his cottage, Gladys and I resuming our ride to Hinley.

THE POLICE STATION IN HINLEY was housed in a building that had once been a coaching inn. Uncomfortably hemmed in between a small park and a cinema, its half-timbered front jutted beetle-brow out over the street, the blue lamp suspended from its overhang. A cinder-block addition, painted a nondescript brown, adhered to the side of the building like cow muck to a passing railway carriage. This, I suspected, was where the cells were located.

Leaving Gladys to graze in a bicycle stand that was more than half full of official-looking black Raleighs, I went up the worn steps and in the front door.

A uniformed sergeant sat at a desk shuffling bits of paper and scratching his sparse hair with the sharpened end of a pencil. I smiled and walked on past.

"'Old on, 'old on," he rumbled. "Where do you think you're goin', miss?" he asked.

It seems to be a trait of policemen to speak in questions. I smiled as if I hadn't understood and moved towards an open door, beyond which I could see a dark passageway. More quickly than I would have believed, the sergeant was on his feet and had seized me by the arm. I was nabbed. There was nothing else to do but burst into tears.

I hated to do it, but it was the only tool I had with me.

TEN MINUTES LATER, we were sipping cocoa in the station tearoom, P. C. Glossop and I. He had told me that he had a girl just like me at home (which, somehow, I doubted), name of Elizabeth.

"She's a great 'elp to her poor mother, our Lizzie is," he said, "seeing as 'ow Missus Glossop, the wife, that is, 'ad a fall from a ladder in the happle horchard and broke 'er leg two weeks ago come Saturday."

My first thought was that he had read too many issues of *The Beano* or *The Dandy*; that he was laying it on a bit thick for entertainment purposes. But the earnest look on his face and the furrowed brow quickly told me otherwise: This was the real Constable Glossop and I would have to deal with him on his own terms.

Accordingly, I began to sob again and told him I had no mother and that she had died in far-off Tibet in a mountaineering accident and that I missed her dreadfully.

"'Ere, 'ere, miss," he said. "Cryin's not allowed in these 'ere premises. Takes away from the natural dignity of the surroundin's, so to speak. You'd best dry up now 'fore I 'ave to toss you in the clink."

I managed a pale smile, which he returned with interest.

Several detectives had slipped in for tea and a bun during my performance, each one of them giving me a silent thumbs-up smile. At least they hadn't asked any questions.

"May I see my father, please?" I asked. "His name is Colonel de Luce, and I believe you're holding him here."

Constable Glossop's face went suddenly blank and I saw that I had played my hand too quickly; that I was now up against officialdom.

"Wait 'ere," he said, and stepped out into a narrow passageway at the end of which there appeared to be a wall of black steel bars.

As soon as he was gone I had a quick look at my surroundings. I was in a dismal little room with sticks of furniture so shabby that they might have been bought directly off the tailgate of a peddler's cart, their legs chipped and dented as if they had suffered a century of kicks in the shin from government regulation boots.

In a vain attempt to cheer things up, a tiny wooden cupboard had been painted apple green, but the sink was a rust-stained relic that might have been on loan from Wormwood Scrubs. Cracked cups and crazed saucers stood sadly cheek by jowl on a draining board, and I noticed for the first time that the mullions of the window were, in fact, iron bars only halfheartedly disguised. The whole place had an odd, sharp odor that I had noticed when I first came in: It smelled as if a jar of gentleman's relish, forgotten years ago at the back of a drawer, had gone off.

Snatches of a song from *The Pirates of Penzance* flashed into my mind. "A policeman's lot is not a happy one," the D'Oyly Carte Opera Company had sung on the wireless and, as usual, Gilbert and Sullivan were right.

Suddenly I found myself thinking about leaving. This whole mission was foolhardy, no more than an impulse to save Father; something thrown up from the prehistoric part of my brain. Just get up and walk to the door, I said to myself. No one will even notice you've gone.

I listened for a moment, cocking my head like Maximilian to turn up my already acute hearing. Somewhere in the distance bass voices buzzed like bees in a far-off hive.

I slid my feet slowly one in front of the other, like some sensuous señorita doing the tango, and stopped abruptly at the door. From where I stood, I could see only one corner of the sergeant's desk outside in the hallway and, mercifully, there was no official elbow resting upon it.

I ventured a peep. The corridor was empty, and I tangoed unhindered all the way to the door and stepped outside into the daylight.

Even though I was not a prisoner, my sense of escape was immense.

I strolled casually over to the bicycle stand. Ten seconds more and I'd be on my way. And then, as if someone had thrown a pail of ice water into my face, I froze in shock: Gladys was gone! I almost screamed it aloud.

There rested all the official bicycles with their officious little lamps and government-issue carriers—but Gladys was gone!

I looked this way and that, and somehow, frighteningly, the streets seemed suddenly different now that I was on foot. Which way was home? Which way to the open road?

As if I hadn't problems enough, there was a storm coming. Black clouds were boiling in the western sky, while those scudding directly overhead were already unpleasantly purple and bruised.

Fear filled me, and then anger. How could I have been so stupid as to leave Gladys unlocked in a strange place? How would I get home? What was to become of poor Flavia?

Feely had once told me never to look vulnerable in unfamiliar surroundings, but how, I found myself wondering, does one actually go about doing that?

That was what I was thinking about when a heavy hand fell onto my shoulder and a voice said, "I think you'd better come with me."

It was Inspector Hewitt.

"THAT WOULD BE HIGHLY IRREGULAR," the Inspector said. "Most improper."

We were sitting in his office: a long narrow room that had been the saloon bar of this onetime coaching inn. It was impressively neat, a room that needed only a potted aspidistra and a piano.

A file cabinet and a desk of quite-ordinary design; a chair, a telephone, and a small bookshelf, atop which was a framed photograph of a woman in a camel-hair coat perching on the rail of a quaint stone bridge. Somehow I had expected more.

"Your father is being detained here until we are in receipt of certain information. At that time he will likely be taken elsewhere, a place which I'm not at liberty to disclose. I'm sorry, Flavia, but seeing him is out of the question."

"Is he under arrest?" I asked.

"I'm afraid so," he answered.

"But why?" This was a bad question, and I knew it as soon as it was out of my mouth. He was looking at me as if I were a child.

"Look, Flavia," he said, "I know you're upset. That's understandable. You didn't have a chance to see your father before . . . well, you were away from Buckshaw when we brought him here. These things are always very difficult for a police officer, you know, but you must understand that there are sometimes things which I would very much like to do as a friend, but which, as a representative of His Majesty, I am forbidden to do."

"I know," I said. "King George the Sixth is not a frivolous man."

Inspector Hewitt looked at me sadly. He got up from his desk and went to the window where he stood looking out at the gathering clouds, his hands clasped behind his back.

"No," he said at last, "King George is not a frivolous man."

Then suddenly, I had an idea. Like the proverbial bolt of lightning, everything fell into place as smoothly as one of those backwards cinema films in which the pieces of a jigsaw puzzle jump each into its proper place, completing itself before your very eyes.

"May I be frank with you, Inspector?" I asked.

"Of course," he said. "Please do."

"The body at Buckshaw was that of a man who arrived in Bishop's Lacey on Friday after a journey from Stavanger, in Norway. You must release Father at once, Inspector, because, you see, he didn't do it."

Although he was a little taken aback, the Inspector recovered quickly and gave me an indulgent smile.

"He didn't?"

"No," I said. "I did. I killed Horace Bonepenny."

fourteen

IT WAS ABSOLUTELY PERFECT. THERE WAS NO ONE WHO COULD prove otherwise.

I had been awakened in the night, I would claim, by a peculiar sound outside the house. I had gone downstairs and then into the garden, where I had been put upon by a prowler: a burglar, perhaps, bent on stealing Father's stamps. After a brief struggle I had overpowered him.

Hold on, Flave, that last bit seemed a little far-fetched: Horace Bonepenny was more than six feet tall and could have strangled me between his thumb and forefinger. No, we had struggled and he had died—a dicky heart perhaps, the result of some long-forgotten childhood illness. Rheumatic fever, let's say. Yes, that was it. Delayed congestive heart failure, like Beth in *Little Women*. I sent up a silent prayer to Saint Tancred to work a miracle: Please, dear Saint Tancred, let Bonepenny's autopsy confirm my fib.

"I killed Horace Bonepenny," I repeated, as if saying it twice would make it seem more credible.

Inspector Hewitt drew in a deep breath and let it out through his nose. "Tell me about it," he said.

"I heard a noise in the night, I went out into the garden, someone jumped out at me from the shadows—"

"Hold on," he said, "what part of the shadows?"

"The shadows behind the potting shed. I was struggling to get free when there was a sudden gurgle in his throat, almost as if he had suffered congestive heart failure due to a bout of rheumatic fever he suffered as a child—or something like that."

"I see," Inspector Hewitt said. "And what did you do then?"

"I went back into the house and fetched Dogger. The rest, I believe, you know."

But wait—I knew that Dogger had not told him about our joint eavesdropping on Father's quarrel with Horace Bonepenny; still, it was unlikely that Dogger would tell the Inspector I had awakened him at four in the morning without mentioning the fact that I had killed the man. Or was it?

I needed time to think this through.

"Struggling with an attacker is hardly murder," the Inspector said.

"No," I said, "but I haven't told you everything."

I riffled at lightning speed through my mental index cards: poisons unknown to science (too slow); fatal hypnotism (ditto); the secret and forbidden blows of jujitsu (unlikely; too obscure to explain). Suddenly, it began to dawn on me that martyrdom required real inventive genius—a glib tongue was not enough.

"I'm ashamed to," I added.

When in doubt, I thought, fall back on feelings. I was proud of myself for having thought of this.

"Hmm," the Inspector said. "Let's leave it for now. Did you tell Dogger you had killed this prowler?"

"No, I don't believe I did. I was too upset by it all, you see."

"Did you tell him later?"

"No, I didn't think his nerves were up to it."

"Well, this is all very interesting," Inspector Hewitt said, "but the details seem a bit sparse."

I knew that I was standing at the edge of a precipice: one step more and there would be no turning back.

"There's more," I said, "but—"

"But?"

"I'm not saying another word until you let me speak to Father."

Inspector Hewitt seemed to be trying to swallow something that wouldn't go down. He opened his mouth as if some obstruction had suddenly materialized in his throat, then closed it again. He gulped, and then did something that I had to admire, something I made a mental note to add to my own bag of tricks: He grabbed for his pocket handkerchief and transformed his astonishment into a sneeze.

"Privately," I added.

The Inspector blew his nose loudly and went back to the window, where he stood gazing out at nothing in particular, his hands again behind his back. I was beginning to learn that this meant he was thinking deeply.

"All right," he said abruptly. "Come along."

I jumped up eagerly from my chair and followed him. At the door he barred the way into the corridor with one arm and turned, his other hand floating down as gently as a feather onto my shoulder.

"I'm about to do something which I may have grave cause to regret," he said. "I'm risking my career. Don't let me down, Flavia . . . please don't let me down."

"FLAVIA!" father said. I could tell he was amazed to see me there. And then he spoiled it by adding, "Take this child away, Inspector. I beg of you, remove her."

He turned away from me and faced towards the wall.

Although the door of the room had been painted over with yellowish cream enamel, it was obvious that it was clad with steel. When the Inspector had unlocked it, I had seen that the chamber itself was little more than a small office with a fold-down cot and a surprisingly clean sink. Mercifully they had not put Father into one of the barred cages I'd glimpsed earlier.

Inspector Hewitt gave me a curt nod, as if to say, "It's up to you," then stepped outside and closed the door as quietly as possible. There was no sound of a key turning in the lock, or of a bolt shooting home, although a bright flash outside and the sudden crash of thunder might well have masked the sound.

Father must have thought that I'd gone out with the Inspector, because he gave a nervous start as he turned round and saw that I was still there.

"Go home, Flavia," he said.

Although he stood stiffly and perfectly erect, his voice was old and tired. I could see that he was trying to play the stolid English gentleman, fearless in the face of danger, and I realized with a pang that I loved him and hated him for it at the same time.

"It's raining," I said, pointing to the window. The clouds had torn themselves apart as they had done earlier at the Folly, and the rain was falling heavily once again, the fat drops clearly audible as they bounced like shot from the ledge outside the window. In a tree across the road, a solitary rook shook itself out like a wet umbrella.

"I can't go home until it stops. And someone's pinched Gladys."

"Gladys?" he said, his eyes like those of an extinct sea creature swimming up from unknown depths.

"My bicycle," I told him.

He nodded absently, and I knew he hadn't heard me.

"Who brought you here?" Father asked. "Him?" He jerked his thumb towards the door to indicate Inspector Hewitt.

"I came by myself."

"By yourself? From Buckshaw?"

"Yes," I said.

This seemed to be more than he could grasp, and he turned back to the window. I couldn't help noticing that he took up the same stance as Inspector Hewitt, with his hands clasped behind his back.

"By yourself. From Buckshaw," he said at last, as if he had just worked it out.

"Yes."

"And Daphne and Ophelia?"

"They are both well," I assured him. "Missing you terribly, of course, but they're looking after things until you come home."

If I tell a lie, my mother will die.

That was what the little girls sometimes chanted as they skipped rope in the churchyard. Well, my mother was already dead, wasn't she, so what harm could it possibly do? And who knows? Because of it, I might even have a credit in Heaven.

"Come home?" Father said at last, as something like a sigh escaped him. "That might not be for some time. No . . . that might not be for quite some time."

On the wall, beside a barred window, was pasted up a calendar from a Hinley greengrocer, bearing a picture of King George and Queen Elizabeth, each hermetically sealed in his or her own private bubble, and dressed in a way that made me think the photographer had caught them by chance on their way to a costume ball at the castle of some Bavarian princeling.

Father gave the calendar a furtive glance and began pacing restlessly back and forth in the little room, studiously avoiding my gaze. He seemed to have forgotten I was there, and had now begun making irregular little humming noises punctuated with an occasional indignant sniff as if he were defending himself before an invisible tribunal.

"I confessed just now," I said.

"Yes, yes," Father said, and went on pacing and mumbling to himself.

"I told Inspector Hewitt that *I* killed Horace Bonepenny."

Father came to as dead a stop as if he had run onto a sword. He turned and fixed me with that dreaded blue stare which was so often his weapon of choice when dealing with his daughters.

"What do you know about Horace Bonepenny?" he asked in a chill tone.

"Quite a lot, actually," I said.

Then, surprisingly, the fight went out of him all at once, just like that. One moment his cheeks were puffed out like the face of the winds that blow across medieval maps, and the next they were as hollow as a horse trader's. He sat down on the edge of the bunk, spreading out the fingers of one hand to steady himself.

"I overheard your disagreement in the study," I said. "I'm sorry if I eavesdropped. I didn't mean to, but I heard voices in the night and came downstairs. I know that he tried to blackmail you . . . I heard the quarrel. That's why I told Inspector Hewitt that I killed him."

This time it filtered through to Father.

"Killed him?" he asked. "What do you mean, killed him?"

"I didn't want them to know it was you," I said.

"Me?" Father said, rocketing up off the bed. "Good Lord! Whatever makes you think I killed the man?"

"It's all right," I said. "He most likely deserved it. I'll never tell anyone. I promise."

With my right hand I crossed my heart and hoped to die, and Father stared at me as if I were some monstrous wet creature that had just flopped out of a painting by Hieronymus Bosch.

"Flavia," he said. "Please understand this: Much as I should have liked to, I did not kill Horace Bonepenny."

"You didn't?"

I could scarcely believe it. I had already come to the conclusion that Father must have committed murder, and I could see that it was going to be hard cheese admitting I was wrong.

Still, I remembered that Feely had once told me that confession was good for the soul—this while she had my arm bent behind my back trying to force me to tell her what I had done with her diary.

"I overheard what you said about killing your housemaster, Mr. Twining. I went to the library and looked it up in the newspaper archives. I talked to Miss Mountjoy—she's Mr. Twining's niece. She remembered the names Jacko and Horace Bonepenny from the inquest. I know that he stayed at the Thirteen Drakes and that he brought a dead jack snipe from Norway hidden in a pie."

Father shook his head slowly and sadly from side to side, not in admiration of my detective skills, but like an old bear that has been shot yet refuses to lie down.

"It's true," he said. "But do you really believe your father capable of cold-blooded murder?"

When I thought about it for a moment—actually thought about it—I saw how foolish I had been. Why had I not realized this before? Cold-blooded murder was just one of the many things Father was incapable of.

"Well . . . no," I ventured.

"Flavia, look at me," he said, but when I looked up and into his eyes, I saw, for an unnerving instant, my own eyes staring back at me and I had to look away.

"Horace Bonepenny was not particularly a decent man, but he did not deserve to die. No one deserves to die," Father said, his voice fading out like a distant broadcast on the shortwave, and I knew that he was no longer speaking only to me.

"There is already so much death in the world," he added.

He sat, looking at his hands, each thumb stroking the other, his fingers engaging like the cogs of an old clock.

After a time he said, "What about Dogger?"

"He was there too," I admitted. "Outside your study . . . "

Father gave a groan.

"That is what I feared," he whispered. "That is what I feared more than anything."

And then, as the rain swept in sheets across the windowpane, Father began to talk.

fifteen

AT FIRST FATHER'S UNACCUSTOMED WORDS CAME SLOWLY AND hesitantly—jerking into reluctant motion like rusty freight cars on the railway. But then, picking up speed, they soon smoothed out into a steady flow.

"My father was not an easy man to like," he said. "He sent me away to boarding school when I was eleven. I seldom saw him again. It's odd, you know: I never knew what interested him until someone at his funeral, one of the pallbearers, chanced to remark that his passion had been netsuke. I had to look it up in the dictionary."

"It's a small Japanese carving in ivory," I said. "It's in one of Austin Freeman's Dr. Thorndyke stories."

Father ignored me and went on. "Although Greyminster was no more than a few miles from Buckshaw, in those days it might just as well have been on the moon. We were fortunate indeed in our headmaster, Dr. Kissing, a gentle soul who believed no harm could ever come to the boy who was administered daily doses of Latin, rugger, cricket, and history, and on the whole, we were treated well.

"Like most, I was a solitary boy at first, keeping to my books and weeping in the hedgerows whenever I could get away on my own. Surely, I thought, I must be the saddest child in the world; that there must be something innately horrid about me to cause my father to cast me off so heartlessly. I believed that if I could discover what it was, there might be a chance of putting things right, of somehow making it up to him.

"At night in the dorm I would tunnel under the blankets with an electric torch and examine my face in a stolen shaving mirror. I couldn't see anything particularly wrong, but then I was only a child and not really equipped to judge these things.

"But time went on, as time does, and I found myself being swept up into the life of the school. I was good at history but quite hopeless when it came to the books of Euclid, which put me somewhere in the middle ranks: neither so proficient nor so stupid as to draw attention to myself.

"Mediocrity, I discovered, was the great camouflage; the great protective coloring. Those boys who did not fail, yet did not excel, were left alone, free of the demands of the master who might wish to groom them for glory and of the school bully who might make them his scapegoat. That simple fact was the first great discovery of my life.

"It was in the fourth form, I think, that I finally began to take an interest in the things around me and, like all boys of that age, I had an insatiable taste for mystification, so that when Mr. Twining, my housemaster, proposed the founding of a conjuring circle, I found myself suddenly ablaze with new enthusiasm.

"Mr. Twining was more kindly than adept; not a very polished performer, I must admit, but he carried off his tricks with such ebullience, such good-hearted enthusiasm, that it would have been churlish of us to withhold our noisy schoolboy applause.

"He taught us, in the evenings, to turn wine into water using no more than a handkerchief and a bit of colored blotting paper; how to make a marked shilling vanish from a covered drinking glass before being extracted from Simpkins's ear. We learned the importance of 'patter,' the conjurer's line of talk, as it were; and he drilled us in spectacular shuffles which left the ace of hearts always at the bottom of the pack.

"It goes without saying that Mr. Twining was popular; *loved* might be a better word, although few of us at the time had seen enough of that emotion to recognize it for what it was.

"His greatest recognition came when the headmaster, Dr. Kissing, asked him to get up a conjuring show for Parents' Day, a happy scheme into which he threw himself wholeheartedly.

"Because of my prowess with an illusion called 'The Resurrection of Tchang Fu,' Mr. Twining was keen to have me perform it as the grand finale of the show. The stunt required two operators, and for that reason he allowed me to choose any assistant I wanted; that was how I came to know Horace Bonepenny.

"Horace had come to us from St. Cuthbert's after a fuss at that school about some missing money—just a couple of pounds, I believe it was, although at the time it seemed a fortune. I felt sorry for him, I admit. I felt he had been misused, particularly when he confided to me that his father was the cruelest of men and had done unspeakable things in the name of discipline. I hope this is not too coarse for your ears, Flavia."

"No, of course not," I said, pulling my chair closer. "Please go on."

"Horace was an extraordinarily tall boy even then, with a shock of flaming red hair. His arms were so long in the school jacket that his wrists stuck out like bare twigs beyond the cuffs. 'Bony,' the boys called him, and they ragged him without mercy about his appearance.

"To make matters worse, his fingers were impossibly long and thin and white, like the tentacles of an albino octopus, and he had that pale bleached skin one sometimes sees in redheads. It was whispered that his touch was poison. He played this up a bit, of course, snatching with pretended clumsiness at the jeering boys who danced round him, always just out of reach.

"One evening after a game of hare and hounds he was resting at a stile, panting like a fox, when a small boy named Potts danced in on tiptoe and delivered him a stinging blow across the face. It was meant to be no more than a touch, like tagging the runner, but it soon turned into something else.

"When they saw that the fearful monster, Bonepenny, was stunned, and his nose bleeding, the other boys began to pile on, and Bony was soon down, being pummeled, kicked, and savagely beaten. It was just then that I happened along.

"'Hold up!' I shouted, as loudly as I could, and to my amazement, the scuffle stopped at once. The boys began extricating themselves, one by one, from the tangle of arms and legs. There must have been something in my voice that made them obey instantly. Perhaps the fact that they had seen me perform mystifying tricks lent me some invisible air of authority, I don't know, but I do know that when I ordered them to get themselves back to Greyminster, they faded like a pack of wolves into the dusk.

"'Are you all right?' I asked Bony, helping him to his feet.

"'Faintly tender, but only in one or two widely separated spots—like Carnforth's beef,' he said, and we both laughed. Carnforth was the notorious Hinley butcher whose family had been supplying Greyminster with its boot-leather Sunday roasts of beef since the Napoleonic Wars.

"I could see that Bony was more badly beaten than he was willing to let on, but he put a brave face on it. I gave him my shoulder to lean upon, and helped him hobble back to Greyminster.

"From that day on, Bony was my shadow. He adopted my enthusiasms, and in doing so seemed almost to become a different person. There were times, in fact, when I fancied he was *becoming* me; that here before me was the part of myself for which I had been searching in the midnight mirror.

"What I do know is that we were never in better form than when we were together; what one of us couldn't do, the other could accomplish with ease. Bony seemed to have been born with a fully formed mathematical ability, and he was soon unveiling for me the mysteries of geometry and trigonometry. He made a game of it, and we spent many a happy hour calculating upon whose study the clock tower of Anson House would fall when we toppled it with a gigantic steam lever of our own invention. Another time, we worked out by triangulation an ingenious series of tunnels which, at a given signal, would collapse simultaneously, causing Greyminster and all its inhabitants to plunge into a Dantean abyss, where they would be attacked by the wasps, hornets, bees, and maggots with which we planned to stock the place."

Wasps, hornets, bees, and maggots? Could this be Father speaking? I suddenly found myself listening to him with new respect.

"How this was to be achieved," he went on, "we never really thought through, but the upshot of it all was that while I was getting chummy with old Euclid and his books of propositions, Bony, with a bit of coaching, was turning out to be a natural conjurer.

"It was the fingers, of course. Those long white appendages seemed to have a life of their own, and it wasn't long before Bony had mastered completely the arts of prestidigitation. Various objects appeared and vanished at his fingertips with such fluid grace that even I, who knew perfectly well how each illusion was done, could scarcely believe my eyes.

"And as his conjuring skill grew, so did his sense of self-worth. With a bit of magic in hand, he became a new Bony, confident, smooth, and perhaps even brash. His voice changed too. Where yesterday he had sounded like a raucous schoolboy, he seemed now, suddenly—at least, when he was performing—to possess a voice box of polished mahogany: a hypnotic professional voice which never failed to convince its hearers.

"'The Resurrection of Tchang Fu' worked like this: I decked myself out in an oversized silk kimono I had found at a church jumble sale, a beautiful bloodred thing covered with Chinese dragons and mystical markings. I plastered my face with yellow chalk and stretched a thin elastic round my head to pull my eyes up at the corners. A couple of sausage casings from Carnforth's, varnished and cut into long, curving fingernails, added a disgusting detail. All that was needed to complete my getup was a bit of burnt cork, a few wisps of frayed string for a beard, and a frightful theatrical wig.

"I would call for a volunteer from the audience—a confederate, of course, who had been rehearsed beforehand. I would bring him onstage and explain, in a comic singsong Mandarin voice, that I was about to kill him, to send him off to the Land of the Happy Ancestors. This matter-of-fact announcement never failed to fetch a gasp from the audience, and before they could recover themselves, I would pull a pistol from the folds of my robe, point it at my confederate's heart, and pull the trigger.

"A starter's pistol can make a frightful din when it's fired indoors, and the thing would go off with the most dreadful bang. My assistant would clasp his chest, squeezing in his hand a concealed paper twist of ketchup, which would ooze out horribly between his fingers. Then he would look down at the mess on his chest and gape in disbelief.

"'Help me, Jacko!' he would shriek. 'The trick's gone wrong! I'm shot!' and fall dead flat on his back.

"The audience would, by now, be sitting bolt upright in shock; several would be on their feet, and a few in tears. I would hold up a hand to quiet them.

"'Sirence!' I would hiss, fixing them with an awful stare. 'Ancestahs lequire sirence.'

"There might be a few titters of nervous laughter, but generally there was a shocked hush. I would fetch a rolled-up sheet from the shadows and drape it over my apparently dead assistant, leaving only his upturned face visible.

"Now this sheet was quite a remarkable object; one which I had manufactured in great secrecy. It was divided lengthwise into thirds by a pair of slender wooden dowels sewn into two narrow pockets that ran the length of the sheet and were, of course, invisible when the thing was rolled up.

"Squatting down and using my robe as cover, I would slip my assistant's shoes from his feet (this was easily done, since he had secretly loosened his laces just before I chose him from the audience) and stick them, toes up, on the end of the dowels.

"The shoes, you see, had been specially prepared by having a hole drilled up through each heel into which a penny nail could be inserted and pushed through to pierce the end of the dowel. The result was most convincing: a gaping corpse lying dead on the floor, its head sticking out at one end of the draped sheet and its upturned shoes at the other.

"If everything went according to plan, great red stains would by now have begun to seep through the sheet above the 'corpse's' chest, and if not, I could always add a bit from a second twist of paper sewn into my sleeve.

"Now came the important part. I would call for the lights to be lowered ('Honabuh ancestahs lequire complete dahkness!') and in the gloom I would set off a couple of flashes of magnesium paper. This had the effect of blinding the audience for a moment: just enough time for my assistant to arch his back and, as I adjusted the sheet, get his feet firmly on the floor in a squatting position. His shoes, of course, protruding from the bottom of the sheet, made it seem as if he were still lying perfectly horizontal.

"Now I would go into my Oriental mumbo jumbo, waving my hands about, summoning him back from the land of the dead. As I jabbered away in made-up incantations, my assistant would very slowly begin to raise himself from a squat until he was standing upright, supporting the projecting dowels on his shoulders, his shoes sticking out at the far end of the sheet.

"What the audience saw, of course, was a sheet-draped body that rose straight up into the air and hung floating there five feet above the floor.

"Then I would beg the happy ancestors to restore him to the Land of the Living Spirits. This would be done with many mystifying passes of my hands, after which I would set off a final flash of magnesium paper and my assistant would throw off the sheet as he leaped into the air and landed on his feet.

"The sheet, with its nailed-on shoes and its sewn-in dowels, would be thrown aside in the darkness, and we would be left to take our bows amid a storm of thunderous applause. And because he wore black socks, no one ever seemed to notice that the 'dead man' had lost his shoes.

"This was 'The Resurrection of Tchang Fu,' and that was the way I planned to stage it for Parents' Day. Bony and I would sneak off to the washhouse with our gear, where I would drill him in the niceties of the illusion.

"But it soon became apparent that Bony was not the ideal confederate. In spite of his enthusiasm, he was simply too tall. His head and feet stuck out too far beyond my doctored sheet, and it was too late to fabricate a new one. And there was the inescapable fact that while Bony was a marvel with his hands, his body and limbs were still those of an awkward and ungainly schoolboy. His stork-like knees would tremble when he was supposed to be levitating, and at one rehearsal he fell flat on his behind, bringing the whole illusion—sheet, shoes, and all—down with a crash.

"I couldn't think what to do. Bony would be devastated if I chose another assistant, and yet it was too much to hope that he would master his role in the few days remaining before the performance. I was on the verge of despair.

"It was Bony who came up with the solution.

"'Why not swap roles?' he suggested after one particularly embarrassing collapse of our props. 'Let me have a go. I'll put on the old sorcerer's robe and you shall be the floater.'

"I have to admit it was brilliant. With his face a chalky yellow, and his long thin hands projecting from the sleeves of the red kimono (made even more ghastly by three inches of sausage-skin fingernails), Bony made as remarkable a figure as has ever stalked the stage.

"And because he was a natural mimic, he had no trouble in picking up the cracked, piping voice of an ancient Mandarin. His Oriental double-talk was, if anything, better than my own, and those long twiggy fingers waving in the air like stick insects were a sight not soon to be forgotten.

"The performance itself was brilliant. With the entire school and the visiting parents as onlookers, Bony put on a show that none of them will ever forget. He was, by turns, exotic and sinister. When he called me up from the audience as his assistant, even I shivered a little at this menacing figure who was beckoning from beyond the footlights.

"And when he fired the pistol and shot me in the chest, there was pandemonium! I had taken the precaution of warming up and watering down my reservoir of ketchup blood, and the resulting stain was all too horridly real.

"One of the parents—the father of Giddings Minor—had to be physically restrained by Mr. Twining, who had foreseen that some gullible onlooker might rush the stage.

"'Steady on, dear sir,' Twining whispered in Mr. Giddings's ear, 'It's simply an illusion. These boys have done it many a time before.'

"Mr. Giddings was escorted reluctantly back to his seat, his face still burning red. Yet in spite of it, he was man enough to come up after the show and give both our hands a good cranking.

"After such a bath of gore at the death, my levitation at the resurrection was almost a letdown, if I may use the phrase, although it brought round after round of ringing applause from an audience of kind hearts who were relieved to see the hapless volunteer restored to life. At the end, we were made to come back for seven curtain calls, although I knew perfectly well that at least six of them were for my partner.

"Bony soaked up the adulation like a parched sponge. An hour after the show he was still shaking hands and being patted on the back by a tidal wave of admiring mothers and fathers who seemed to want only to touch him, although when I threw my arm across his shoulders, he gave me rather an odd look: a look which suggested, for a fleeting instant, that he had never seen me before.

"In the days that followed, I saw that a transformation had come over him. Bony had become the confident conjurer, and I was now no more than his simple assistant. He began speaking to me in a new way, and adopted a rather offhand manner, as if his earlier timidity had never existed.

"I suppose I could say he dropped me—or that was how it seemed. I often saw him with an older boy, Bob Stanley, who was someone I had never much fancied. Stanley had one of those angular, square-jawed faces that photographs well but seems hard in real life. As he had done with me, Bony seemed to take on some of Stanley's traits, in much the same way a bit of blotting paper absorbs the handwriting from a letter. I know that it was at about this time that Bony began smoking and, I suspect, tippling a bit as well.

"One day, I realized with a bit of a shock that I no longer liked him. Something had changed inside Bony or, perhaps, had crawled out. There were times when I caught him staring at me in the classroom when his eyes would seem to be at first the eyes of an aged Mandarin, and then, as they regarded me, would become cold and reptilian. I began to feel as if, in some unknowable way, something had been stolen from me.

"But there was worse to come."

Father fell silent and I waited for him to go on with his story, but instead he sat gazing out sightlessly into the falling rain. It seemed best to keep quiet and leave him to his thoughts, whatever those might be.

But I knew that, as with Horace Bonepenny, something had changed between us.

Here we were, Father and I, shut up in a plain little room, and for the first time in my life having something that might pass for a conversation. We were talking to one another almost like adults; almost like one human being to another; almost like father and daughter. And even though I couldn't think of anything to say, I felt myself wanting it to go on and on until the last star blinked out.

I wished I could hug him, but I couldn't. For some time now I had been aware that there was something in the de Luce character which discouraged any outward show of affection towards one another; any spoken statement of love. It was something in our blood.

And so we sat, Father and I, primly, like two old women at a parish tea. It was not a perfect way to live one's life, but it would have to do.

sixteen

A FLASH OF LIGHTNING BLEACHED EVERY TRACE OF COLOR from the room, and with it came a deafening crack of thunder. We both of us flinched.

"The storm is directly overhead," Father said.

Nodding to reassure him that we were in it together, I looked about at my surroundings. The brightly lighted little cubicle—its naked bulb overhead, its steel door, and its cot—the rain pouring down outside, was oddly like the control room of the submarine in *We Dive at Dawn*. I imagined the rolling thunder of the storm to be the sound of depth charges exploding immediately above our heads, and suddenly I was not quite so fearful for Father. We two, at least, were allies. I would pretend that as long as we kept still and I remained silent, nothing on earth could harm us.

Father went on as if there had been no interruption.

"We became rather strangers, Bony and I," he said. "Although we continued as members of Mr. Twining's Magic Circle, each of us pursued his own particular interests. I developed a passion for the great stage tricks: sawing a lady in half, vanishing a cage of singing canaries, that sort of thing. Of course, most of these effects were beyond my schoolboy budget, but as time went on, it seemed enough simply to read about them and learn how each one was executed.

"Bony, however, progressed to tricks which required an ever-greater degree of manual dexterity: simple effects which could be done under the spectator's nose with a minimal amount of gadgetry. He could make a nickel-plated alarm clock disappear from one hand and appear in the other before your very eyes. He never would show me how it was done.

"It was about that time that Mr. Twining had the idea of organizing a Philatelic Society, another of his great enthusiasms. He felt that in learning to collect, catalogue, and mount postage stamps from round the world, we would learn a great deal about history, geography, and neatness, to say nothing of the fact that regular discussions would promote confidence among the more shy members of the club. And since he was himself a devoted collector, he saw no reason why every one of his boys should be any less enthusiastic.

"His own collection was the eighth wonder of the world, or so it seemed to me. He specialized in British stamps, with particular attention to color variations in the printing inks. He had the uncanny ability of being able to deduce the day—sometimes the very hour—a given specimen was printed. By comparing the ever-changing microscopic cracks and variations produced by wear and stress upon the engraved printing plates, he was able to deduce an astonishing amount of detail.

"The leaves of his albums were masterpieces. The colors! And the way in which they ranged across the page, each one a dab from the palette of a Turner.

"They began, of course, with the black issues of 1840. But soon the black warms to brown, the brown to red, the red to orange, the orange to bright carmine; on to indigo, and Venetian red—a bright blossoming of color, as if to paint the bursting into bloom of the Empire itself. There's glory for you!"

I had never seen Father so alive. He was suddenly a schoolboy again, his face transformed, and shining like a polished apple.

But those words about glory: Hadn't I heard them before? Weren't they the ones spoken to Alice by Humpty Dumpty?

I sat quietly, trying to work out the connections his mind must be making.

"For all that," he went on, "Mr. Twining was not in possession of the most valuable philatelic collection at Greyminster. That honor belonged to Dr. Kissing, whose collection, although not extensive, was choice—perhaps even priceless.

"Dr. Kissing was not, as one might expect of the head of one of our great public schools, a man born either to wealth or to privilege. He was orphaned at birth and brought up by his grandfather, a bell-foundry worker in London's East End which, in those days, was better known for its crushing living conditions than for its charity, and for its crime rather than its educational opportunities.

"When he was forty-eight, the grandfather lost his right arm in a ghastly accident involving molten metal. Now no longer able to work at his trade, there was nothing for it but take to the streets as a beggar; a predicament in which he remained sunk for nearly three years.

"Five years earlier, in 1840, the London firm of Messrs. Perkins, Bacon and Petch had been appointed by the Lords of the Treasury as the sole printers of British postage stamps.

"Business prospered. In the first twelve years alone of their appointment some two billion stamps were printed, most of which eventually found their way into the dustbins of the world. Even Charles Dickens referred to their prodigious output of Queens' heads.

"Happily it was in the Fleet Street printing plant of this very firm that Dr. Kissing's grandfather found employment at last—as a sweeper. He taught himself to push a broom with one hand better than most men did with two, and because he was a firm believer in deference, punctuality, and reliability, he soon found himself one of the firm's most valued employees. Indeed, Dr. Kissing himself once told me that the senior partner, old Joshua Butters Bacon himself, always called his grandfather 'Ringer' out of respect to his former trade.

"When Dr. Kissing was still a child, his grandfather often brought home stamps that had been rejected and discarded because of irregularities in printing. These 'pretty bits of paper,' as he called them, were often his only playthings. He would spend hours arranging and rearranging the colorful scraps by shade, by variation too subtle for the human eye unaided. His greatest gift, he said, was a magnifying glass, which his grandfather bargained away from a street-seller after pawning his own mother's wedding ring for a shilling.

"Each day, on his way to and from the board school, the boy called upon as many shops and offices as he was able, offering to sweep their pavements clear of rubbish in exchange for the stamped envelopes from their wastepaper baskets.

"In time, those pretty bits of paper became the nucleus of a collection which was to be the envy of Royalty, and even when he had risen to become headmaster of Greyminster, he still possessed the little magnifying glass his grandfather had given him.

"'Simple pleasures are best,' he used to tell us.

"The young Kissing built upon the tenacity with which life had favored him as a boy and went on from scholarship to scholarship, until there came the day when old 'Ringer' was on hand in tears to see his grandson graduate with a double first at Oxford.

"Now, there is a belief among those who should know better, that the rarest of postage stamps are those freaks and mutilations that are inevitably produced as by-products of the printing process, but this is simply not so. No matter what sums such monstrosities might fetch if they are leaked upon the market, to the true collector they are never more than salvage.

"No, the real scarcities are those stamps which have been put into official circulation, legitimately or otherwise, but in very limited numbers. Sometimes a few thousand stamps may be released before a problem is noticed; sometimes a few hundred, as is the case when a single sheet manages to effect its escape from the Treasury.

"But in the entire history of the British Post Office, there has been one occasion—and one occasion only—when a single sheet of stamps was so dramatically different from its millions of fellows. This is how it came about.

"In June of 1840, a crazy potboy named Edward Oxford had fired two pistols at nearly point-blank range at Queen Victoria and Prince Albert as they rode in an open carriage. Mercifully, both shots missed their target, and the Queen, who was then four months pregnant with her first child, was unharmed.

"The attempted assassination was thought by some to be a Chartist plot, while others believed it to be a conspiracy of Orangemen who wished to set the Duke of Cumberland upon the throne of England. There was more truth in the latter than the government believed, or perhaps than they were prepared to admit. Although Oxford would pay for his crime by spending the next twenty-seven years of his life confined to Bedlam—where he seemed more sane than most of the inhabitants and many of the doctors—his handlers would remain at large, invisible in the metropolis. They had other hares to run.

"In the autumn of 1840, an apprentice pressman named Jacob Tingle was employed at the firm of Perkins, Bacon and Petch. Because he was, above all else, a creature of ambition, young Jacob was soon progressing in his trade by leaps and bounds.

"What his employers did not yet know was that Jacob Tingle was the pawn in a deadly serious game, a game to which only his shadowy masters were privy."

If there was anything that surprised me about this tale, it was the way in which Father brought it to life. I could almost reach out and touch the gentlemen in their high starched collars and stovepipe hats; the ladies in their bustled skirts and bonnets. And as the characters in his tale came to life, so did Father.

"Jacob Tingle's mission was a most secret one: He was, by whatever means were at hand, to print one sheet, and one sheet only, of Penny Black stamps, using a bright orange ink which had been provided for his mission. The vial had been handed to him, along with a retaining fee, in an alehouse adjoining St. Paul's Churchyard by a man with a broad-brimmed hat who had sat in the tavern's shadows and spoken in a stony whisper.

"When he had secretly printed this bastard sheet, he was to conceal it in a ream of ordinary Penny Blacks which were awaiting dispatch to the post offices of England. With this accomplished, Jacob's work was done. Fate would see to the rest.

"Sooner or later, somewhere in England, a sheet of orange stamps would surface, and their message would be plain enough to those with eyes to see. 'We are in your midst,' they would declare. 'We move amongst you freely and unseen.'

"The unsuspecting Post Office would have no opportunity to recall the inflammatory stamps. And once they came to light, word of their existence would spread like wildfire. Not even Her Majesty's Government could keep it quiet. The result would be terror at the highest levels.

"You see," Father went on, "although his message came too late, a secret agent had infiltrated the ranks of the conspirators and sent back word that discovery of the orange stamps was to serve as a signal to conspirators everywhere to begin a new wave of personal attacks upon the Royal Family.

"It seemed the perfect scheme. Had it failed, the perpetrators would simply have bided their time and tried again another day. But there was no need to try again; the thing went off like clockwork.

"The day after he met the stranger in St. Paul's Churchyard, there was a spectacular, and suspicious, conflagration in an alley directly behind Perkins, Bacon and Petch. As the printers and clerical staff dashed outside for a better view of the fire, Jacob coolly pulled the vial of orange ink from his pocket, inked the plate with a spare roller he had hidden behind a row of chemical bottles on a shelf, applied a damped sheet of watermarked paper, and printed the sheet. It was almost too easy.

"Before the other workers returned to their posts, Jacob had already tucked the orange sheet among its black sisters, cleaned the plate, hidden the soiled rags, and was setting up for the next run of ordinary stamps when old Joshua Butters Bacon himself strolled by and congratulated the young man on his coolness in the face of danger. He would go far in his chosen trade, the old man told him.

"And then Fate, as Fate so often does, threw a wrench into the works. What the plotters could not foresee was that the man in the broad-brimmed hat would, that very night, be struck down in the rain in Fleet Street by a runaway cart-horse, and that with his dying breath, he would revert to the faith into which he had been born and confess the plot—Jacob Tingle and all—to a rain-caped bobby whom he mistook for a cassocked Catholic priest.

"But by that time, Jacob had done his dirty work, and the sheet of orange stamps was already flying, via the night mail, to some unknown corner of England. I hope you are not finding this too boring, Harriet?"

Harriet? Had Father called me "Harriet"?

It is not unknown for fathers with a brace of daughters to reel off their names in order of birth when summoning the youngest, and I had long ago become accustomed to being called "Ophelia Daphne Flavia, damn it." But Harriet? Never! Was this a slip of the tongue, or did Father actually believe he was telling his tale to Harriet?

I wanted to shake the stuffing out of him; I wanted to hug him; I wanted to die.

I realized that the sound of my voice might break the spell, and I turned my head slowly from side to side as if it were in danger of falling off.

Outside, the wind was tearing at the vines that fringed the window as the wild rain came pelting down.

"The hue and cry was raised," Father went on at last, and I stopped holding my breath.

"Telegraphs were sent to every postmaster in the realm. To whatever corner of England the orange stamps might make their way, they were to be placed at once under lock and key, and the Treasury notified, post-haste, of their whereabouts.

"Because larger shipments of the Penny Blacks had been sent to the cities, it was thought that they would most likely make their appearance in London or Manchester; perhaps Sheffield or Bristol. As it turned out, in fact, it was none of these.

"Tucked away in one of the farthest pockets of Cornwall is the village of St. Mary-in-the-Marsh. It is a place where nothing had ever happened, and nothing was ever expected to.

"The postmaster there was one Melville Brown, an elderly gentle-man who was already some years past the usual retirement age, and was trying, with little luck, to put away a bit of his small salary to 'tide him over to the churchyard,' as he told anyone who would listen.

"As it happened—since St. Mary-in-the-Marsh was off the beaten track in more ways than one—Postmaster Brown did not receive the telegraphed directive from the Treasury, and so it was with complete surprise that, some days later, after he had unwrapped a small shipment of Penny Blacks and was counting them to see that the tally was correct, he found the missing stamps literally at his fingertips.

"Of course he spotted the orange stamps at once. Someone had made a dreadful mistake! There had not been, as there normally should have been, an official 'Instructions to Postmasters' pamphlet announcing a new color for the penny stamp. No, this was something of vast import, even though he could not say what it was.

"For a moment—but only a moment, mind you—he thought that this oddly colored sheet of stamps might be worth more than its face value. Less than half a year after their introduction, some people, most likely people up in London, he believed, who had nothing better to do with their time, had already begun collecting self-adhesive postage stamps, and putting them in little books. A stamp printed off-register or with inverted check numbers might even fetch a quid or two, and as for a whole sheet of them, why . . .

"But Melville Brown was one of those human beings who seem to be as scarce as archangels: He was an honest man. Accordingly, he at once sent off a telegraph to the Treasury, and within the hour a ministerial courier was dispatched from Paddington to retrieve the stamps and convey them back to London.

"The Government intended that the rogue sheet be destroyed at once, with all the official solemnity of a Pontifical Requiem Mass. Joshua Butters Bacon suggested rather that the stamps be placed in the printing house archive, or perhaps in the British Museum, where they could be studied by future generations.

"Queen Victoria, however, who was, as the Americans say, more than a bit of a pack rat, had her own ideas: She asked to be given a single stamp as a memento of the day she was spared an assassin's bullet; the remainder were to be destroyed by the highest-ranking officer of the firm that had printed them.

"And who could deny the Queen? By now, with British troops about to invade Beirut, the Prime Minister, Viscount Melbourne (whose name had been once linked romantically with Her Majesty's), had other things on his mind. And there the matter was allowed to rest.

"So it was that the world's only sheet of orange penny stamps was burned in a cruet on the desk of the managing director of Perkins, Bacon and Petch. But before he lit the match, Joshua Butters Bacon had, with surgical precision, snipped off two specimens—this was some years before perforations were introduced, you see: the stamp marked 'AA' from one corner, for Queen Victoria and, in great secrecy, another marked 'TL,' from the opposite corner, for himself.

"These were the stamps which would one day be known to collectors as the Ulster Avengers, although for many years before they were given that name, their very existence was a state secret.

"Years later, when Bacon's desk was moved after his death, an envelope which had somehow become lodged behind it fell to the floor. As you may have guessed, the sweeper who found it was Dr. Kissing's grandfather, Ringer. With old Bacon dead, he thought, what harm could there be in his taking home as a plaything for his three-year-old grandson the single bright-orange postage stamp which lay nestled within it?"

I felt a flush rising to my cheek, and prayed desperately that Father was too distracted to notice. How, without making the situation even worse than it was, could I tell him that both of the Ulster Avengers, one marked "AA" and the other "TL," were, at that very moment, stuffed carelessly into the bottom of my pocket?

seventeen

PART OF ME WAS POSITIVELY TWITCHING TO PULL OUT THE blasted stamps and press them into his hand, but Inspector Hewitt had put me on my honor. I could not possibly put into Father's hands anything which might have been stolen; anything which might further incriminate him.

Fortunately Father was oblivious. Even another sudden flash of lightning, followed by a sharp crack and a long roll of thunder, did not pull him back to the present.

"The Ulster Avenger marked TL, of course," he went on, "became the cornerstone of Dr. Kissing's collection. It was a well-known fact that only two such stamps were in existence. The other one—the specimen marked AA—having passed upon the death of Queen Victoria to her son, Edward the Seventh, and upon his death, to his son, George the Fifth, in whose collection it remained until recently—was stolen in broad daylight from a stamp exhibition. It has not been recovered."

"Ha!" I thought. "What about the TL?" I said aloud.

"TL, as we have seen, was tucked safely away in the safe of the headmaster's study at Greyminster. Dr. Kissing brought it out from time to time, 'in part to gloat,' he once told us, 'and in part to remember my humble beginnings in case I should ever show signs of rising above myself.'

"The Ulster Avenger was seldom shown to others, though; perhaps only to a few of the most serious philatelists. It was said that the King himself had once offered to buy the stamp, an offer that was politely but firmly declined. When that failed, the King begged, through his private secretary, special permission to view 'this marmalade phenomenon' as he called it: a request which was speedily granted and which ended with a secret after-dark visit to Greyminster by his late Royal Highness. One wonders, of course, whether he brought AA with him so that the two great stamps might be once more, if only for a few hours, reunited. That, perhaps, will forever remain one of the great mysteries of philately."

I touched my pocket lightly, and my fingertips tingled at the slight rustle of paper.

"Our old housemaster, Mr. Twining, clearly recalled the occasion, and remembered, most poignantly, how the lights in the headmaster's study burned long into that winter night.

"Which brings me back, alas, to Horace Bonepenny."

I could tell by the changed tone of his voice that Father had once more retreated into his personal past. A chill of excitement ran up my spine. I was about to get at the truth.

"Bony had, by this time, become more than an accomplished conjurer. He was now a forward, pushy young man with a brazen manner, who generally got his own way by the simple expedient of shoving harder than the other fellow.

"Besides the allowance he received from his father's solicitors, he was earning a good bit extra by performing in and around Greyminster, first at children's parties and then later, as his confidence grew, at smoking concerts and political dinners. By then he had taken on Bob Stanley as his sole confederate, and one heard tales of some of their more extravagant performances.

"But outside of the classroom I seldom saw him in those days. Having risen above the abilities of the Magic Circle, he dropped out of it, and was heard to make disparaging remarks about those 'amateur noodles' who kept up their membership.

"With its dwindling attendance, Mr. Twining finally announced that he was giving up the halls of illusion, as he called the Magic Circle, to concentrate more fully upon the Stamp Society.

"I remember the night—it was in early autumn, the first meeting of the year—that Bony suddenly showed up, all teeth and laughter and false good-fellowship. I had not seen him since the end of the last term, and he now seemed to me somehow alien and too large for the room.

"'Ah, Bonepenny,' Mr. Twining said, 'what an unexpected delight. What brings you back to these humble chambers?'

"'My feet!' Bony shouted, and most of us laughed.

"And then suddenly he dropped the pose. In an instant he was all schoolboy again, deferential and filled with humility.

"'I say, sir,' he said, 'I've been thinking all during the hols about what a jolly treat it would be if you could persuade the Head to show us that freakish stamp of his.'

"Mr. Twining's brow darkened. 'That freakish stamp, as you put it, Bonepenny, is one of the crown jewels of British philately, and I should certainly never suggest that it be trotted out for viewing by such a saucy scallywag as yourself.'

"'But, sir! Think of the future! When we lads are grown . . . have families of our own . . . '

"At that we grinned at one another and traced patterns in the carpet with our toes.

"'It will be like that scene in *Henry the Fifth,* sir,' Bony went on. 'Those families back in England home abed will count themselves accursed they were not at Greyminster to have a squint at the great Ulster Avenger! Oh please, sir! Please!'

"'I shall give you an alpha-plus for boldness, young Bonepenny, and a goose egg for your travesty of Shakespeare. Still . . . '

"We could see that Mr. Twining was softening. One corner of his mustache lifted ever so slightly.

"'Oh please, sir,' we all chimed in.

"'Well . . . ' Mr. Twining said.

"And so it was arranged. Mr. Twining spoke to Dr. Kissing, and that worthy, flattered that his boys would take an interest in such an arcane object, readily assented. The viewing was set for the following Sunday evening after Chapel, and would be conducted in the headmaster's private apartments. Invitation was by membership in the Stamp Society only, and Mrs. Kissing would cap the evening with cocoa and biscuits.

"The room was filled with smoke. Bob Stanley, who had come with Bony, was openly smoking a gasper and nobody seemed to mind. Although the sixth-form boys had privileges, this was the first time I had seen one of them light up in front of the Head. I was the last to arrive, and Mr. Twining had already filled the ashtray with the stubs of the Wills's Gold Flake cigarettes which, outside of the classroom, he smoked incessantly.

"Dr. Kissing was, as are all of the truly great headmasters, no mean showman himself. He chatted away about this and that: the weather, the cricket scores, the Old Boys' Fund, the shocking condition of the tiles on Anson House; keeping us in suspense, you know.

"Only when he had us all twitching like crickets did he say, 'Dear me, I had quite forgotten—you've come to have a look at my famous snippet.'

"By now we were boiling over like a room full of teakettles. Dr. Kissing went to his wall safe and twirled his fingertips in an elaborate dance on the dial of the combination lock.

"With a couple of clicks the thing swung open. He reached in and brought out a cigarette tin—an ordinary Gold Flake cigarette tin! That fetched a bit of a laugh, I can tell you. I couldn't help wondering if he'd had the cheek to pull out the same old container in front of the King.

"There was a bit of a hubbub, and then a hush fell over the room as he opened the lid. There inside, nestled on a bed of absorbent blotting paper, was a tiny envelope: too small, too insignificant, one would say, to hold a treasure of such great magnitude.

"With a flourish Dr. Kissing produced a pair of stamp tweezers from his waistcoat pocket and, removing the stamp as carefully as a sapper extracting a fuse from an unexploded bomb, laid it on the paper.

"We crowded round, pushing and shoving for a better view.

"'Careful, boys,' said Dr. Kissing. 'Remember your manners; gentlemen always.'

"And there it was, that storied stamp, looking just as one always knew it would look, and yet so much more . . . so much more spellbinding. We could hardly believe we were in the same room as the Ulster Avenger.

"Bony was directly behind me, leaning over my shoulder. I could feel his hot breath on my cheek, and thought I caught a whiff of pork pie and claret. Had he been drinking? I wondered.

"And then something happened which I will not forget until my dying day—and perhaps not even then. Bony darted in, snatched up the stamp, and held it high in the air between his thumb and forefinger like a priest elevating the host.

"'Watch this, sir!' he shouted. 'It's a trick!'

"We were all of us too numb to move. Before anyone could bat an eye, Bony had pulled a wooden match from his pocket, flicked it alight with his thumbnail, and held it to the corner of the Ulster Avenger.

"The stamp began blackening, then curled; a little wave of flame passed across its surface, and a moment later, there was nothing left of it but a smudge of black ash in Bony's palm. Bony lifted up his hands and in an awful voice, chanted:

'Ashes to ashes, dust to dust,
If the King can't have you, the Devil must!'

"It was appalling. There was a shocked silence. Dr. Kissing stood there with his mouth open, and Mr. Twining, who had brought us there, looked as if he had been shot in the heart.

"'It's a trick, sir,' Bony shouted, with that charnel-house grin of his. 'Now help me get it back, all of you. If we all join hands and pray together—'

"He grabbed my hand with his right, and with his left, he seized Bob Stanley's.

"'Form a circle,' he ordered. 'Join hands and form a prayer circle!'

"'Stop it!' Dr. Kissing commanded. 'Stop this insolence at once. Return the stamp to its box, Bonepenny.'

"'But, sir,' Bony said—and I swear I saw his teeth glint in the light of the flames from the fireplace—'if we don't pull together, the magic can't work. That's how magic is, you see.'

"'Put . . . the . . . stamp . . . back . . . in . . . the . . . box,' Dr. Kissing said, slowly and deliberately, his face like one of those ghastly things one finds in a trench after a battle.

"'All right then, I'll have to go it alone,' Bony said. 'But it's only fair to warn you it's much more difficult this way.'

"Never had I seen him so confident; never had I seen him so full of himself.

"He rolled up his sleeve and held those long white pointed fingers upright in the air as high as he could reach.

'Come back, come back, O Orange Queen,
Come back and tell us where you've been!'

"At this, he snapped his fingers, and suddenly there was a stamp where no stamp had been a moment earlier. An orange stamp.

"Dr. Kissing's grim face relaxed a little. He almost smiled. Mr. Twining's fingers dug deeply into my shoulder blade, and I realized for the first time that he had been hanging on to me for dear life.

"Bony reeled the stamp in for a closer look until it was almost touching the tip of his nose. At the same time he whipped an indecently large magnifying glass from his hip pocket and examined the newly materialized stamp with pursed lips.

"Then suddenly his voice was the voice of Tchang Fu, the ancient Mandarin, and I swear that even though he wore no makeup, I could clearly see the yellow skin, the long fingernails, the red dragon kimono.

"'Uh-oh! Honabuh ancestahs send long stamp!' he said, holding it out to us for our inspection. It was an ordinary Internal Revenue issue from America: a common Civil War vintage stamp which most of us had aplenty in our albums.

"He let it flutter to the floor, then gave a shrug and rolled his eyes heavenward.

'Come back, come back, O Orange Queen—'

he began again, but Dr. Kissing had seized him by the shoulders and was shaking him like a tin of paint.

"'The stamp,' he demanded, holding out his hand. 'At once.'

"Bony turned out his trouser pockets, one after another.

"'I can't seem to find it, sir,' he said. 'Something seems to have gone wrong.'

"He looked up each of his sleeves, ran a long finger round the inside of his collar, and a sudden transformation came over his face. In an instant he was a frightened schoolboy who looked as if he'd like nothing better than to make a bolt for it.

"'It's worked before, sir,' he stammered. 'Lots and lots of times.'

"His face was growing red, and I thought he was about to cry.

"'Search him,' Dr. Kissing snapped, and several of the boys, under the direction of Mr. Twining, took Bony into the lavatory where they turned him upside down and searched him from his red hair to his brown shoes.

"'It's as the boy says,' Mr. Twining said when they returned at last. 'The stamp seems to have vanished.'

"'Vanished?' Dr. Kissing said. 'Vanished? How can the bloody thing have *vanished*? Are you quite sure?'

"'*Quite* sure,' Mr. Twining said.

"A search was made of the entire room: The carpet was lifted, tables were moved, ornaments turned upside down, but all to no avail. At last Dr. Kissing crossed the room to the corner where Bony was sitting with his head sunk deeply in his hands.

"'Explain yourself, Bonepenny,' he demanded.

"'I—I can't, sir. It must have burned up. It was supposed to be switched, you see, but I must have . . . I don't . . . I can't . . . '

"And he burst into tears.

"'Go to bed, boy!' Dr. Kissing shouted. 'Leave this house and go to bed!'

"It was the first time any of us had ever heard him raise his voice above the level of pleasant conversation, and it shook us to the core.

"I glanced over at Bob Stanley and noticed that he was rocking back and forth on his toes, staring at the floor as unconcernedly as if he were waiting for a tram.

"Bony stood up and walked slowly across the room towards me. His eyes were rimmed with red as he reached out and took my hand. He gave it a flaccid shake, but it was a gesture I found myself unable to return.

"'I'm sorry, Jacko,' he said, as if I, and not Bob Stanley, were his confederate.

"I could not look him in the eye. I turned my head away until I knew that he was no longer near me.

"When Bony had slunk from the room, looking back over his shoulder, his face bloodless, Mr. Twining tried to apologize to the headmaster, but that seemed only to make matters worse.

"'Perhaps I should ring up his parents, sir,' he said.

"'Parents? No, Mr. Twining. I think it is not the parents who should be brought in.'

"Mr. Twining stood in the middle of the room wringing his hands. God knows what thoughts were racing through the poor man's mind. I can't even remember my own.

"The next morning was Monday. I was crossing the quad, tacking into the stiff breeze with Simpkins, who was prattling on about the Ulster

Avenger. The word had spread like wildfire and everywhere one looked knots of boys stood with their heads together, hands waving excitedly as they swapped the latest—and almost entirely false—rumors.

"When we were about fifty yards from Anson House, someone shouted, 'Look! Up there! On the tower! It's Mr. Twining!'

"I looked up to see the poor soul on the roof of the bell tower. He was clinging to the parapet like a tattered bat, his gown snapping in the wind. A beam of sunlight broke through between the flying clouds like a theatrical spotlight, illuminating him from behind. His whole body seemed to be aglow, and the hair sticking out from beneath his cap resembled a disk of beaten copper in the rising sun like the halo of a saint in an illuminated manuscript.

"'Careful, sir,' Simpkins shouted. 'The tiles are in shocking shape!'

"Mr. Twining looked down at his feet, as if awakening from a dream, as if bemused to find himself suddenly transported eighty feet into the air. He glanced down at the tiles and for a moment was perfectly still.

"And then he drew himself up to his full stature, holding on only with his fingertips. He raised his right arm in the Roman salute, his gown fluttering about him like the toga of some ancient Caesar on the ramparts.

"'*Vale!*' he shouted. Farewell.

"For a moment, I thought he had stepped back from the parapet. Perhaps he had changed his mind; perhaps the sun behind him dazzled my eyes. But then he was in the air, tumbling. One of the boys later told a newspaper reporter that he looked like an angel falling from Heaven, but he did not. He plummeted straight down to the ground like a stone in a sock. There is no more pleasant way of describing it."

Father paused for a long while, as if words failed him. I held my breath.

"The sound his body made when it hit the cobbles," he said at last, "has haunted my dreams from that day to this. I've seen and heard things in the war, but nothing like this. Nothing like this at all.

"He was a dear man and we murdered him. Horace Bonepenny and I murdered him as surely as if we had flung him from the tower with our own hands."

"No!" I said, reaching out and touching Father's hand. "It was nothing to do with you!"

"Ah, but it was, Flavia."

"No!" I repeated, although I was a little taken aback by my own bold-ness. Was I actually talking to Father like this? "It was nothing to do with you. Horace Bonepenny destroyed the Ulster Avenger!"

Father smiled a sad smile. "No, he didn't, my dear. You see, when I got back to my study that Sunday night and removed my jacket, I found an oddly sticky spot on my shirt cuff. I knew instantly what it was: While joining hands to form his distracting prayer circle, Bony had pushed his forefinger inside the sleeve of my jacket and stuck the Ulster Avenger to my cuff. But why me? Why not Bob Stanley? For a very good reason: If they had searched us all, the stamp would have been found in my sleeve and Bony'd have cried innocence. No wonder they couldn't find it when they turned him inside out!

"Of course, he retrieved the stamp as he shook my hand before leav-ing. Bony was a master of prestidigitation, remember, and because I had once been his accomplice, it stood to reason that I should have been so again. Who would ever have believed otherwise?"

"No!" I said.

"Yes." Father smiled. "And now there's little more to tell.

"Although nothing was ever proved against him, Bony did not return to Greyminster after that term. Someone told me he had gone abroad to escape some later unpleasantness, and I can't say I was surprised. Nor was I surprised to hear, years later, that Bob Stanley, after being ejected from medical school, had ended up in America where he had set up a philatelic shop: one of those mail-order companies that place advertise-ments in the comic papers and sell packets of stamps on approval to adolescent boys. The whole business, though, seems to have been little more than a front for his more sinister dealings with wealthy collectors.

"As for Bony, I didn't see him again for thirty years. And then, just last month, I went up to London to attend an international exhibition of stamps put on by the Royal Philatelic Society. You might remember the occasion. One of the highlights of the show was the public display of a few choice items from our present Majesty the King's collection, including the rare Ulster Avenger: AA—the twin of Dr. Kissing's stamp.

"I gave it little more than a glance; the memories it brought back were not pleasant ones. There were other exhibits I wished to see, and consequently the King's Ulster Avenger occupied no more than a few seconds of my time.

"Just before the exhibit was to close for the day, I was at the far side of the exhibition hall examining a mint sheet to which I thought I might treat myself, when I happened to glance across and catch a glimpse of shocking red hair, hair that could belong to only one person.

"It was Bony, of course. He was holding forth for the benefit of a small crowd of collectors who had gathered in front of the King's stamp. Even as I looked on, the debate became more heated, and it seemed that something Bony had said was agitating one of the curators, who shook his head vehemently as their voices rose.

"I didn't think that Bony had seen me—nor did I want him to.

"It was fortuitous that an old army friend, Jumbo Higginson, happened along at that very moment and dragged me off for a late dinner and a drink. Good old Jumbo . . . it's not the first instance where he's turned up just in the nick of time."

Something came over Father's eyes, and I saw that he had vanished down one of those personal rabbit holes which so often engulfed him. I sometimes wondered if I would ever learn to live with his sudden silences. But then, like a jammed clockwork toy that jerks abruptly back to life when it's flicked with a finger, he went on with his story as if there had been no interruption.

"When I opened the newspaper on the train home that night, and read that the King's Ulster Avenger had been switched for a counterfeit—this apparently done in full view of the general public, several irreproachable philatelists, and a pair of security guards—I knew not only who had carried off the theft, but also, at least in general terms, how the thing had been accomplished.

"Then, last Friday, when the jack snipe turned up dead on our doorstep, I knew at once that Bony had been there. 'Jack Snipe' was my nickname at Greyminster, 'Jacko' for short. The letters at the corner of the Penny Black spelled out his name. It's very complicated."

"B One Penny H," I said. "Bonepenny, Horace. At Greyminster, he was called Bony and you were Jacko, for short. Yes, I figured that out quite some time ago."

Father looked at me as if I were an asp which he was torn between pressing to his breast and flinging out the window. He rubbed his upper lip with his forefinger several times, as if to form an airtight seal, but then went on.

"Even knowing that he was somewhere nearby did not prepare me for the dreadful shock of seeing that white cadaverous face which appeared suddenly from out of the darkness at the window of my study. It was after midnight. I should have refused to speak with him, of course, but he made certain threats . . .

"He demanded I buy both of the Ulster Avengers from him: the one he had stolen recently and the one he had made to vanish years ago from Dr. Kissing's collection.

"He had it in his head, you see, that I was a wealthy man. 'It's the investment opportunity of a lifetime,' he told me.

"When I replied that I had no money, he threatened to tell the authorities that I had planned the theft of the first Ulster Avenger and commissioned the second. And Bob Stanley would back up his claim. After all, it was I who was the stamp collector, not he.

"And hadn't I been present when both of the stamps were stolen? The devil even hinted that he may have already—*may* have, mind!—planted the Ulster Avengers somewhere in my collections.

"After our quarrel, I was too upset to go to bed. When Bony had gone, I paced up and down in my study for hours, agonizing, going over and over the situation in my mind. I had always felt responsible in part for Mr. Twining's death. It's a terrible thing to admit, but it's true. It was my silence that led directly to that dear old man's suicide. If only I'd had the intestinal fortitude, as a schoolboy, to voice my suspicions, Bonepenny and Stanley should never have gotten away with it and Mr. Twining would not have been driven to take his own life. You see, Flavia, silence is sometimes the most costly of commodities.

"After a very long time and a great deal of thought, I decided—against everything I believe in—to give in to his blackmail. I would sell my collections, everything I owned, to buy his silence, and I must tell you, Flavia, that I am more ashamed of that decision than anything I have ever done in my life. Anything."

I wish I had known the right thing to say, but for once my tongue failed me, and I sat there like a mop, not able, even, to look my father in the face.

"Sometime in the small hours—it must have been four o'clock, perhaps, since it was already becoming light outside—I turned out the lamp, with the full intention of walking into the village, rousing Bonepenny from his room at the inn, and agreeing to his demands.

"But something stopped me. I can't explain it, but it's true. I stepped out onto the terrace, but rather than going round to the front of the house to the drive as I had determined to do, I found myself being drawn like a magnet to the coach house."

So! I thought. It wasn't Father who had gone out through the kitchen door. He had walked from the terrace outside his study, along the outside of the garden wall to the coach house. He had not set foot in the garden. He had not walked past the dying Horace Bonepenny.

"I needed to think," Father went on, "but I couldn't seem to bring my mind into proper focus."

"And you got into Harriet's Rolls," I blurted. Sometimes I could shoot myself.

Father stared at me with the sad kind of look the worm must give the early bird the instant before its beak snaps shut.

"Yes," he said softly. "I was tired. The last thing I remember thinking was that once Bony and Bob Stanley found I was a bankrupt, they'd give up the game for someone more promising. Not that I would ever wish this predicament on another . . .

"And then I must have fallen asleep. I don't know. It doesn't really matter. I was still there when the police found me."

"A bankrupt?" I said, astonished. I couldn't help myself. "But, Father, you have Buckshaw."

Father looked at me, his eyes moist: eyes that I had never before seen looking out of his face.

"Buckshaw belonged to Harriet, you see, and when she died, she died intestate. She didn't leave a will. The death duties—well, the death duties shall most likely consume us."

"But Buckshaw is yours!" I said. "It's been in the family for centuries."

"No," Father said sadly. "It is not mine, not mine at all. You see, Harriet was a de Luce before I married her. She was my third cousin. Buckshaw was hers. I have nothing left to invest in the place, not a sou. I am, as I have said, a virtual bankrupt."

There was a metallic tapping at the door and Inspector Hewitt stepped into the room.

"I'm sorry, Colonel de Luce," he said. "The Chief Constable, as you are undoubtedly aware, is most particular that the very shadow of the law be observed. I've allowed you as much time as I can and still escape with my skin."

Father nodded sadly.

"Come along, Flavia," the Inspector said to me. "I'll take you home."

"I can't go home yet," I said. "Someone's pinched my bicycle. I'd like to file a complaint."

"Your bicycle is in the backseat of my car."

"You've found it already?" I asked. Hallelujah! Gladys was safe and sound!

"It was never missing," he said. "I saw you park it out front and had Constable Glossop put it away for safekeeping."

"So that I couldn't escape?"

Father lifted an eyebrow at this impertinence, but said nothing.

"In part, yes," Inspector Hewitt said, "but largely because it's still raining buckets outside and it's a long old pedal uphill to Buckshaw."

I gave Father a silent hug to which, although he remained rigid as an oak, he did not seem to object.

"Try to be a good girl, Flavia," he said.

Try to be a good girl? Was that all he could think of? It was evident that our submarine had surfaced, its occupants hauled up from the vasty deeps and all the magic left below.

"I'll do my best," I said, turning away. "I'll do my very best."

"YOU MUSTN'T BE TOO HARD on your father, you know," Inspector Hewitt said as he slowed to negotiate the turn at the fingerpost which pointed to Bishop's Lacey. I glanced at him, his face lit from below by the soft glow of the Vauxhall's instrument panel. The windscreen wipers, like black scythes, swashed back and forth across the glass in the strange light of the storm.

"Do you honestly believe he murdered Horace Bonepenny?" I asked.

His reply was ages in coming, and when it did, it was burdened with a heavy sadness.

"Who else *was* there, Flavia?" he said.

"Me," I said, " . . . for instance."

Inspector Hewitt flicked on the defroster to evaporate the condensation our words were forming on the windscreen.

"You don't expect me to believe that story about the struggle and the dicky heart, do you? Because I don't. That isn't what killed Horace Bonepenny."

"It was the pie, then!" I blurted out with sudden inspiration. "He was poisoned by the pie!"

"Did you poison the pie?" he asked, almost grinning.

"No," I admitted. "But I wish I had."

"It was quite an ordinary pie," the Inspector said. "I've already had the analyst's report."

Quite an ordinary pie? This was the highest praise Mrs. Mullet's confections were ever likely to receive.

"As you've deduced," he went on, "Bonepenny did indeed indulge in a slice of pie several hours before his death. But how could you know that?"

"Who but a stranger would eat the stuff?" I asked, with just enough of a scoff in my voice to mask the sudden realization that I had made a mistake: Bonepenny hadn't been poisoned by Mrs. Mullet's pie after all. It was childish to have pretended that he had.

"I'm sorry I said that," I told him. "It just popped out. You must think me a complete bloody fool."

Inspector Hewitt didn't reply for far too long. At last he said:

> "'*Unless some sweetness at the bottom lie,*
> *Who cares for all the crinkling of the pie?*'"

"My grandmother used to say that," he added.

"What does it mean?" I asked.

"It means—well, here we are at Buckshaw. They're probably worried about you."

"OH," SAID OPHELIA IN HER careless voice. "Have you been gone? We hadn't noticed, had we, Daff?"

Daffy was showing the prominent equine whites of her eyes. She was definitely spooked but trying not to let on.

"No," she muttered, and plunged back into *Bleak House*. Daffy was, if nothing else, a rapid reader.

Had they asked, I should have told them gladly about my visit with Father, but they did not. If there was to be any grieving for his predicament, I was not to be a part of it; that much was clear. Feely and Daffy and I were like three grubs in three distinct cocoons, and sometimes I wondered why. Charles Darwin had once pointed out that the fiercest competition for survival came from one's own tribe, and as the fifth of six children—and with three older sisters—he was obviously in a position to know what he was talking about.

To me it seemed a matter of elementary chemistry: I knew that a substance tends to be dissolved by solvents that are chemically similar to it. There was no rational explanation for this; it was simply the way of Nature.

It had been a long day, and my eyelids felt as if they'd been used for oyster rakes.

"I think I'll go to bed," I said. "G'night, Feely. G'night, Daffy."

My attempt at sociability was greeted with silence and a grunt. As I was making my way up the stairs, Dogger materialized suddenly above me on the landing with a candleholder that might have been snapped up at an estate sale at Manderley.

"Colonel de Luce?" he whispered.

"He is well, Dogger," I said.

Dogger nodded a troubled nod, and we each of us trudged off to our respective quarters.

eighteen

GREYMINSTER SCHOOL LAY DOZING IN THE SUN, AS IF IT WERE dreaming of past glories. The place was precisely as I had imagined it: magnificent old stone buildings, tidy green lawns running down to the lazy river, and vast, empty playing fields that seemed to give off silent echoes of cricket matches whose players were long dead.

I leaned Gladys against a tree in the side lane by which I had entered the grounds. Behind a hedgerow, a tractor stood ticking idly, its driver nowhere in sight.

The voices of choirboys came floating across the lawns from the chapel. In spite of the bright morning sunshine, they were singing:

"Softly now the light of day
Fades upon my sight away—"

I stood listening for a moment until suddenly they broke off. Then, after a pause, the organ started up again, peevishly, and the singers went back to the beginning.

As I walked slowly across the grass of what I'm sure Father would have called "the Quad," the tall blank windows of the school stared down at me coldly and I had the sudden queer feeling an insect must have when it's placed under a microscope—the feeling of an invisible lens hovering, and something strange, perhaps, about the light.

Except for a single schoolboy dashing along and two black-gowned masters walking and talking with their heads together, the broad lawns and winding walkways of Greyminster were empty beneath a sky of deepest blue. The whole place seemed slightly unreal, like a grossly enlarged Agfacolor print: something you might see in one of those books with a name such as *Picturesque Britain*.

That limestone pile on the east side of the Quad—the one with the clock tower—must be Anson House, I thought: Father's old digs.

As I approached it, I raised my hand to shield my eyes against the glare of the sky. It was from somewhere up there among the battlements and tiles that Mr. Twining had plummeted to his death on the cobbles below; those ancient cobbles which now lay no more than a hundred feet from where I was standing.

I strolled across the grass to have a look.

Disappointingly, there were no bloodstains. Of course there wouldn't be, not after all these years. Those would have been washed away as soon as was decently possible—quite likely even before Mr. Twining's broken body had been laid to whatever passed for rest.

Other than of their constant wearing down by two hundred years of privileged feet, these cobbles told no tales. Tucked tightly in along the stone walls of Anson House, the walk was scarcely six feet wide.

I threw back my head and gazed straight up at the tower. Viewed from this angle, it rose dizzily in a sheer wall of stone that ended far, far above me in a filigree of airy ornamental stonework where fat white clouds, drifting lazily past the parapets, created the peculiar sensation that the whole structure was leaning . . . falling . . . toppling towards me. The illusion made my stomach go all queasy, and I had to look away.

Worn stone steps led enticingly from the cobbled walk, through an arched entrance, to a double door. To my left was the porter's lodge, its occupant huddled over a telephone. He did not even look up as I slipped inside.

A cool, dim corridor stretched away in front of me, to infinity it seemed, and I set out along it, lifting my feet carefully to keep from making scuffing noises on the slate floor.

On either side, a long gallery of smiling faces—some of them schoolboys and some masters—receded into the darkness, each one a

Greyminsterian who had given his life for his country, and each in his own black-lacquered frame: "That Others Might Live," it said on a gilded scroll. At the end of the corridor, set apart from the others, were photographs of three boys, their names engraved in red on little brass rectangles. Under each name were the words *Missing in Action*.

"Missing in Action?" Why wasn't Father's photo hanging there? I wondered.

Father was generally as absent as these young men whose bones were somewhere in France. I felt a little guilty at the thought, but it was true.

I think it was at that moment, there in the shadowy hall at Greyminster, that I began to realize the full extent of Father's distant nature. Yesterday I had been all too ready to throw my arms around him and hug him to jelly, but now I understood that yesterday's cozy prison scene had not been a dialogue, but a troubled monologue. It had not been me, but Harriet to whom he was speaking. And, as with the dying Horace Bonepenny, I had been no more than an unwitting confessor.

Now, just being here at Greyminster where Father's troubles had begun, it seemed all the more cold and remote and inhospitable a place.

In the gloom beyond the photos, a staircase led up to the first floor, and I climbed up it to a hallway which, like the one I had left below, also ran the length of the building. Although the doors on either side were closed, each one was fitted with a small pane of glass, which allowed me a peek into the room. They were classrooms, and all alike.

At the end of the corridor, a large corner room promised something more: A sign on its door read Chemistry Lab.

I tried the door and it opened at once. The curse was broken!

I don't know what I was expecting, but I wasn't expecting this: stained wooden tables, boring flasks, cloudy retorts, chipped test tubes, inferior Bunsen burners, and a colored wall chart of the elements containing a laughable printing error in which the positions of arsenic and selenium were interchanged. I spotted this at once and—with a nub of blue chalk from the ledge beneath the blackboard—took the liberty of correcting the mistake by drawing in a two-headed arrow. "WRONG!" I wrote beneath it, and underlined the word twice.

This so-called lab was nothing compared with my own at Buckshaw, and at the thought, my chest swelled with pride. I wanted nothing more than to bolt for home at once, just to be there, to touch my own gleaming glassware; to concoct the perfect poison just for the thrill of it.

But that pleasure would have to wait. There was work to be done.

BACK OUTSIDE IN THE CORRIDOR, I retraced my steps to the center of the building. If I had guessed accurately, I should now be directly under the tower, and the entrance to it could not be far away.

A small door in the paneling, which I had taken at first to be a broom closet, swung open to reveal a steep stone staircase. My heart skipped a beat.

And then I saw the sign. A few steps up from the bottom, a length of chain was draped across the steps, with a hand-printed card: *Tower Off Limits—Strictly Enforced.*

I was up them like a shot.

It was like being inside a nautilus shell. The stairs twisted round and round, winding their narrow way upwards in echoing sameness. There was no possible way of seeing what lay ahead or, for that matter, what lay behind. Only the few steps immediately above and below me were visible.

For a while, I counted them in a whisper as I climbed, but after a time I found that I needed my breath to fuel my legs. It was a steep ascent and I was getting a stitch in my side. I stopped for a moment to rest.

What little light there was appeared to be coming from tiny slit windows, one positioned at each complete turn of the staircase. On that side of the tower, I guessed, lay the Quad. Still short of breath, I resumed my ascent.

Then suddenly and unexpectedly the staircase ended—just like that—at a little timbered door.

It was a door such as a dwarf might pop into in the side of a forest oak: a half-rounded hatch with an iron opening for a skeleton key. And, needless to say, the stupid thing was locked.

I let out a hiss of frustration and sat down on the top step, breathing heavily.

"Damnation!" I said, and the word echoed back with startling volume from the walls.

"Hallo up there!" came a hollow, stony voice, followed by the scraping of footsteps far below.

"Damnation!" I said again, this time under my breath. I had been spotted.

"Who's up there?" the voice demanded. I put my hand over my mouth to stifle the urge to reply.

As my fingers touched my teeth, I had an idea. Father had once said there would come a time when I was grateful for the braces I had been made to wear, and he had been right. This was it.

Using my thumbs and forefingers as a dual pair of pincers, I yanked down on the braces with all the strength I could muster, and with a satisfying "click" the things popped out of my mouth and into my hand.

As the footsteps came closer and closer, climbing relentlessly up to where I was trapped against the locked door, I twisted the wire into an "L" with a loop on the end and jammed the ruined braces into the keyhole.

Father would have me horsewhipped, but I had no other choice.

The lock was old and unsophisticated, and I knew I could crack it—if only I had enough time.

"Who is it?" the voice demanded. "I know you're up there. I can hear you. The tower is off limits. Come down at once, boy."

Boy? I thought. So he hadn't actually seen me.

I eased in and out on the wire and twisted it to the left. As if it had been oiled this morning, the bolt slid smoothly back. I opened the door and stepped through, pulling it silently closed behind me. There was no time to try locking it from the inside. Besides, whoever was coming up the stairs would likely have a key.

I was in a space as dark as a coal cellar. The slit windows had ended at the top of the stairs.

The footsteps stopped outside the door. I stepped soundlessly to one side and flattened myself against the stone wall.

"Who's up here?" the voice asked. "Who is it?" And then a key was inserted, the latch clicked, the door opened, and a man stuck his head in through the opening.

The beam from his torch shot here and there, illuminating a crazy maze of ladders that twisted up into the darkness. He shone the light on each ladder, allowing his beam to climb it, rung by rung, until it vanished in the blackness far above.

I didn't move a muscle: not even my eyes. In my peripheral vision I had an impression of the man silhouetted against the open door: white hair and a fearsome mustache. He was so close I could have reached out and touched him.

There was a pause that seemed an eternity.

"Bloody rats again," he said to himself at last, and the door slammed shut, leaving me in darkness. There was the jingle of a ring of keys and then the bolt shot home.

I was locked in.

I suppose I should have let out a shout, but I didn't. I was nowhere near my wits' end. In fact, I was rather beginning to enjoy myself.

I knew that I could try picking the lock again, and creep back down the stairs, but quite possibly I'd creep straight into the porter's clutches.

Since I couldn't stay where I was forever, the only other option was up. Sticking my arms out like a sleepwalker, I slid my feet slowly one in front of the other, until my fingers touched the closest of the ladders I had seen illuminated by his torch—and up I went.

There's no real trick to climbing a ladder in the dark. In many ways, it's preferable to seeing the abyss that's always there below you. But as I climbed, my eyes became more and more accustomed to the darkness— or near-darkness. Tiny chinks in the stone and timbers were letting in pinpricks of light here and there, and I soon found I was able to make out the general outline of the ladder, black on black in the tower's gray light.

The rungs ended suddenly, and I found myself on a small wooden platform, like a sailor in the rigging. To my left, another ladder led up into the gloom.

I gave it a good shaking, and although it creaked fearsomely, it seemed solid enough. I took a deep breath, stepped onto the bottom rung, and up I went.

A minute later I had reached the top, and a smaller, shakier platform. Still another ladder, this one more narrow and spindly than the others, trembled alarmingly as I set foot upon it and began my slow, creeping ascent. Halfway up I began counting the rungs:

"Ten (approximately) . . . eleven . . . twelve . . . thirteen—"

My head smashed against something and for a moment I could see nothing but spinning stars. I hung on to the rungs for dear life, my head aching like a burst melon and the matchstick ladder vibrating in my hands like a plucked bowstring. I felt as if someone had scalped me.

As I reached up with one hand and felt above my broken head, my fingers closed around a wooden handle. I pushed up on it with all my remaining strength, and the trapdoor lifted.

In a flash I had scrambled out onto the roof of the tower, blinking like an owl in the sudden sunshine. From a square platform in its center, slate tiles sloped gently outwards to each of the four points of the compass.

The view was nothing short of magnificent. Across the Quad, beyond the slates of the chapel, vistas of different greens folded away into the hazy distance.

Still squinting, I stepped a little closer to the parapet, and I almost lost my life.

There was a sudden yawning hole at my feet, and I had to windmill my arms to keep from falling into it. As I teetered on the edge, I had a sickening glimpse of the cobbles far below shining blackly in the sun.

The gap was perhaps eighteen inches wide, with a half-inch raised lip around it, bridged every ten feet or so by a narrow finger of stone that joined the jutting parapet to the roof. This opening had evidently been designed to provide emergency drainage in case of unusually heavy rainfall.

I jumped carefully across the opening and looked over the waist-high battlements. Far below, the grass of the Quad spread off in three directions.

Tucked in tightly as it was against the wall of Anson House, the cobbled walk was not visible below the jutting battlements. How odd, I thought. If Mr. Twining had leapt out from these battlements, he could only have landed in the grass.

Unless, of course, in the thirty years that had gone by since the day of his death, the Quad had undergone substantial landscaping changes. Another dizzying look down through the opening behind me made it obvious that they had not: the cobbles below and the linden trees that lined them were positively ancient. Mr. Twining had fallen through this hole. Without a doubt.

There was a sudden noise behind me and I spun round. In the center of the roof a corpse hung, dangling from a gibbet. I had to fight to keep from crying out.

Like the bound body of a highwayman I had seen in the pages of the *Newgate Calendar*, the thing was twisting and turning in the sudden breeze. Then, without warning, its belly seemed to explode, and its guts flew up into the air in a twisted and sickening rope of scarlet, white, and blue.

With a loud *crack!* the entrails unfurled themselves, and suddenly, high above my head, at the top of the pole, the Union Jack was flapping in the wind.

As I recovered from my fright, I saw that the flag was rigged so that it could be raised and lowered from below, perhaps from the porter's lodge, by an ingenious series of cables and pulleys that terminated in the weatherproof canvas casing. It was this I had mistaken for corpse and gibbet.

I grinned stupidly at my foolishness and edged cautiously closer to the mechanism for a better look. But aside from the mechanical ingenuity of the device, there was little else of interest about it.

I had just turned and was moving back towards the open gap when I tripped and fell flat on my face, my head sticking out over the edge of the abyss.

I might have broken every bone in my body but I was afraid to move. A million miles below, or so it seemed, a pair of ant-like figures emerged from Anson House and set out across the Quad.

My first thought was that I was still alive. But then as my terror subsided, anger rushed in to take its place: anger at my own stupidity and clumsiness, anger at whatever invisible witch was blighting my life with an endless chain of locked doors, barked shins, and skinned elbows.

I got slowly to my feet and dusted myself off. Not only was my dress filthy, but I had also managed somehow to rip the sole half off my left shoe. The cause of the damage was not hard to spot: I had tripped on the sharp edge of a jutting tile which, torn from its place, now lay loose on the roof looking like one of the tablets upon which Moses had been given the Ten Commandments.

I'd better replace the slate, I thought. Otherwise the inhabitants of Anson House will find rainwater showering down on their heads and it will be no one's fault but mine.

The tile was heavier than it looked, and I had to drop to my knees as I tried to shove it back into place. Perhaps the thing had rotated, or maybe the adjoining tiles had sagged. Whatever the reason, it simply would not slide back into the dark socket from which my foot had yanked it.

I could easily slip my hand into the opening to see if there was any obstruction—but then I remembered the spiders and scorpions that are known to inhabit such grottoes.

I closed my eyes and shoved my fingers in. At the back of the cavity they encountered something—something soft.

I jerked back my hand and bent over to peer inside. There was nothing in the hole but darkness.

Carefully, I stuck my fingers in again and, with my thumb and fore-finger, plucked at whatever was in there at the back of the hole.

In the end, it came out almost effortlessly, unfolding as it emerged, like the flag that fluttered above my head. It was a length of rusty black cloth—Russell cord, I think the stuff is called—sour with mold: a school-master's gown. And rolled up tightly inside it, crushed beyond repair, was a black, square-topped mortarboard cap.

And in that instant I knew, as sure as a shilling, that these things had played a part in Mr. Twining's death. I didn't know what it was, but I would jolly well find out.

I ought to have left the things there, I know. I ought to have gone to the nearest telephone and rung up Inspector Hewitt. Instead, the first thought that popped into my mind was this: How was I going to get away from Greyminster without being noticed?

And, as it so often does when you're in a jam, the answer came at once.

I shoved my arms into the sleeves of the moldy gown, straightened the bent crown of the mortarboard and jammed it on my head, and like a large black bat, flapped my way slowly and precariously back down the cascades of trembling ladders to the locked door.

The pick I had fashioned from my braces had worked before, and now I needed it to work again. As I fidgeted the wire in the keyhole, I offered up a silent prayer to the god who governs such things.

After a great deal of scraping, a bent wire, and a couple of minor curses, my prayer was finally heard, and the bolt slid back with a sullen croak.

Before you could say "Scat!" I was down the stairs, listening at the bottom door, peering out through a crack at the long hall. The place was in empty silence.

I eased the door open, stepped quietly out into the corridor, and made my way swiftly down the gallery of lost boys, past the empty por-ter's lodge, and out into the sunshine.

There were schoolboys everywhere—or so it seemed—talking, lounging, strolling, laughing. Glorying in the outdoors with the end of term at hand.

My instinct was to hunch over in my cap and cape and skulk crab-wise away across the Quad. Would I be noticed? Of course I would; to these wolfish boys I would stand out like the wounded reindeer at the back of the herd.

No! I would throw my shoulders back and, like a boy late for the hurdles, lope off, head held high, in the direction of the lane. I could only hope that no one would notice that underneath the gown I was wearing a dress.

And nobody did; no one gave me so much as a second glance.

The farther I got from the Quad, the safer I felt, but I knew that, alone in the open, I would be far more conspicuous.

Just a few feet ahead, an ancient oak squatted comfortably on the lawn as if it had been resting there since the days of Robin Hood. As I reached out to touch it (home free!), an arm shot out from behind the trunk and grabbed my wrist.

"Ow! Let go! You're hurting me!" I yelped automatically, and my arm was released at once, even as I was still spinning round to face my assailant.

It was Detective Sergeant Graves, and he seemed every bit as surprised as I was.

"Well, well," he said with a slow grin. "Well, well, well, well, well."

I was going to make a cutting remark, but thought better of it. I knew the sergeant liked me, and I might need all the help I could get.

"The Inspector'd like the pleasure of your company," he said, pointing to a group of people who stood talking in the lane where I had left Gladys.

Sergeant Graves said no more, but as we approached, he pushed me gently in front of him towards Inspector Hewitt like a friendly terrier presenting its master with a dead rat. The torn sole of my shoe was flapping like Charlie Chaplin's Little Tramp, but although the Inspector glanced at it, he was considerate enough to keep his thoughts to himself.

Sergeant Woolmer stood towering above the blue Vauxhall, his face as large and craggy as the Matterhorn. In his shadow were a sinewy, darkly tanned man in overalls and a wizened little gentleman with a white mustache who, when he saw me, jabbed at the air excitedly with his finger.

"That's him!" he said. "That's the one!"

"Is it, indeed?" Inspector Hewitt asked, as he lifted the cap from my head and took the gown from my shoulders with the gentle deference of a valet.

The little man's pale blue eyes bulged visibly in their sockets.

"Why, it's only a girl!" he said.

I could have slapped his face.

"Ay, that's her," said the suntanned one.

"Mr. Ruggles here has reason to believe that you were up in the tower," the Inspector said, with a nod at the white mustache.

"What if I was?" I said. "I was just having a look round."

"That tower's off limits," Mr. Ruggles said loudly. "Off limits! And so it says on the sign. Can't you read?"

I gave him a graceful shrug.

"I'd have come up the ladders after you if I knew you were just a girl." And he added, in an aside to Inspector Hewitt, "Not what they used to be, my old knees.

"I knew you were up there," he went on. "I made out like I didn't so's I could ring up the police. And don't pretend you didn't pick the lock. That lock's my business, and I know it was locked as sure as I'm standing here in Fludd's Lane.

"Imagine! A girl! Tsk, tsk," he remarked, with a disbelieving shake of his head.

"Picked the lock, did you?" the Inspector asked. Even though he acted like he wasn't, I could see that he was taken aback. "Wherever did you learn a trick like that?"

I couldn't tell him, of course. Dogger was to be protected at all costs.

"Long ago and far away," I said.

The Inspector fixed me with a steely gaze. "There might be those who are satisfied with that kind of answer, Flavia, but I am not among them."

Here comes that old "King George is not a frivolous man" speech again, I thought, but Inspector Hewitt had decided to wait for my answer, no matter how long it was in coming.

"There isn't much to do at Buckshaw," I said. "Sometimes I do things just to keep from getting bored."

He held out the black gown and cap. "And that's why you're wearing this costume? To keep from getting bored?"

"It's not a costume," I said. "If you must know, I found them under a loose tile on the tower roof. They have something to do with Mr. Twining's death. I'm sure of it."

If Mr. Ruggles's eyes had bulged before, they now almost popped out of his head.

"Mr. Twining?" he said. "Mr. Twining as jumped off the tower?"

"Mr. Twining didn't jump," I said. I couldn't resist the temptation to get even with this nasty little man. "He was—"

"Thank you, Flavia," Inspector Hewitt said. "That will do. And we'll take up no more of your time, Mr. Ruggles. I know you're a busy man."

Ruggles puffed himself up like a courting pigeon, and with a nod to the Inspector and an impertinent smile at me, he set off across the lawn towards his quarters.

"Thank you for your report, Mr. Plover," the Inspector said, turning to the man in overalls, who had been standing silently by.

Mr. Plover tugged at his forelock and returned to his tractor without a word.

"Our great public schools are cities in miniature," the Inspector said, with a wave of his hand. "Mr. Plover spotted you as an intruder the instant you turned into the lane. He wasted no time in getting to the porter's lodge."

Damn the man! And damn old Ruggles too! I'd have to remember when I got home to send them a jug of pink lemonade, just to show that there were no hard feelings. It was too late in the season for anemones, so *anemonin* was out of the question. Deadly nightshade, on the other hand, although uncommon, could be found if you knew exactly where to look.

Inspector Hewitt handed the cap and gown to Sergeant Graves, who had already produced several sheets of tissue paper from his kit.

"Smashing," the sergeant said. "She might just have saved us a crawl across the slates."

The Inspector shot him a look that could have stopped a runaway horse.

"Sorry, sir," the sergeant said, his face suddenly aflame as he turned to his wrapping.

"Tell me, in detail, how you found these things," Inspector Hewitt said, as if nothing had happened. "Don't leave anything out—and don't add anything."

As I spoke he wrote it all down in his quick, minuscule hand. Because of sitting across from Feely as she wrote in her diary at breakfast, I had become rather good at reading upside down, but Inspector Hewitt's notes were no more than tiny ants marching across the page.

I told him everything: from the creak of the ladders to my near-fatal slip; from the loose tile and what lay behind it to my clever escape.

When I had finished, I saw him scribble a couple of characters beside my account, although what they were, I could not tell. He snapped the notebook shut.

"Thank you, Flavia," he said. "You've been a great help."

Well, at least he had the decency to admit it. I stood there expectantly, waiting for more.

"I'm afraid King George's coffers are not deep enough to ferry you home twice in twenty-four hours," he said, "so we'll see you on your way."

"And shall I come back with tea?" I asked.

He stood there with his feet planted in the grass, and a look on his face that might have meant anything. A minute later, Gladys's Dunlop tires were humming happily along the tarmac, leaving Inspector Hewitt—"and his ilk" as Daffy would have said—farther and farther behind.

Before I had gone a quarter of a mile, the Vauxhall overtook, and then passed me. I waved like mad as it went by, but the faces that stared out at me from its windows were grim.

A hundred feet farther on, the brake lights flashed and the car pulled over onto the verge. As I came alongside, the Inspector rolled the window down.

"We're taking you home. Sergeant Graves will load your bicycle into the boot."

"Has King George changed his mind, Inspector?" I asked haughtily.

A look crossed his face that I had never seen there before. I could almost swear it was worry.

"No," he said, "King George has not changed his mind. But *I* have."

nineteen

NOT TO BE TOO DRAMATIC ABOUT IT, THAT NIGHT I SLEPT THE sleep of the damned. I dreamt of turrets and craggy ledges where the windswept rain blew in from the ocean with the odor of violets. A pale woman in Elizabethan dress stood beside my bed and whispered in my ear that the bells would ring. An old salt in an oilcloth jacket sat atop a piling, mending nets with an awl, while far out at sea a tiny aeroplane winged its way towards the setting sun.

When at last I awoke, the sun was at the window and I had a perfectly wretched cold. Even before I went down to breakfast I had used up all the handkerchiefs from my drawer and put paid to a perfectly good bath towel. Needless to say, I was not in a good humor.

"Don't come near me," Feely said as I groped my way to the far end of the table, snuffling like a grampus.

"Die, witch," I managed, making a cross of my forefingers.

"Flavia!"

I poked at my cereal, giving it a stir with a corner of my toast. In spite of the burnt bits of crust to liven it up, the soggy muck in the bowl still tasted like cardboard.

There was a jerk, a jump in my consciousness like a badly spliced cinema film. I had fallen asleep at the table.

"What's wrong?" I heard Feely ask. "Are you all right?"

"She is stuck in her 'enervating slumbers, from the hesternal dissipation or debauch,'" Daffy said.

Daffy had recently been reading Bulwer-Lytton's *Pelham*, a few pages each night for her bedtime book, and until she finished it, we were likely to be lashed daily at breakfast with obscure phrases in a style of prose as stiff and inflexible as a parlor poker.

Hesternal, I remembered, meant, "pertaining to yesterday." I was nodding over the rest of the phrase when suddenly Feely leapt up from the table.

"Good God!" she exclaimed, quickly wrapping her dressing gown round her like a winding-sheet. "Who on earth is that?"

Someone stood silhouetted at the French doors, peering in at us through hands cupped against the glass.

"It's that writer," I said. "The country house man. Pemberton."

Feely gave a squeak and fled upstairs where I knew she would throw on her tight blue sweater set, dab powder on her morning blemishes, and float down the staircase pretending she was someone else: Olivia de Havilland, for instance. She always did that when there was a strange man on the property.

Daffy glanced up disinterestedly, and then went on reading. As usual, it was up to me.

I stepped out onto the terrace, pulling the door closed behind me.

"Good morning, Flavia," Pemberton said with a grin. "Did you sleep well?"

Did I sleep well? What kind of question was that? Here I was on the terrace, sleep in my eyes, my hair a den of nesting rats, and my nose running like a trout stream. Besides, wasn't a question about the quality of one's sleep reserved for those who had spent a night under the same roof? I wasn't sure; I'd have to look it up in *Beeton's Complete Etiquette for Ladies*. Feely had given me a copy for my last birthday, but it was still propping up the short leg of my bed.

"Not awfully," I said. "I've caught cold."

"I'm sorry to hear that. I was hoping to be able to interview your father about Buckshaw. I don't like to be a pest, but my time here is limited. Since the war, the cost of accommodation away from home, even in the most humble hostelry, such as the Thirteen Drakes, is simply shocking. One doesn't like to plead poverty, but we poor scholars still dine mostly upon bread and cheese, you know."

"Have you had breakfast, Mr. Pemberton?" I asked. "I'm sure Mrs. Mullet could manage something."

"That's very kind of you, Flavia," he said, "but Landlord Stoker laid on a veritable feast of two bangers and an egg and I live in fear for my waistcoat buttons."

I wasn't quite sure how to take this, and my cold was making me too grumpy to ask.

"Perhaps I can answer your questions," I said. "Father has been detained—"

Yes, that was it! You sly little fox, Flavia!

"Father has been detained in town."

"Oh, I don't think they're matters that would much interest you: a few knotty questions about drains and the Enclosure Acts—that sort of thing. I was hoping to put in an appendix about the architectural changes made by Antony and William de Luce in the nineteenth century. 'A House Divided' and all that."

"I've heard of an appendix being taken out," I blurted, "but this is the first time I've heard of one being put in."

Even with my nose running I could still thrust and parry with the best of them. A wet, explosive sneeze ruined the effect.

"P'raps I could just step in and have a quick look round. Make a few notes. I shan't disturb anyone."

I was trying to think of synonyms for "no" when I heard the growl of an engine, and Dogger, at the wheel of our old tractor, appeared between the trees at the end of the avenue, hauling a load of compost to the garden. Mr. Pemberton, who noticed at once that I was staring over his shoulder, turned to see what I was looking at. When he spotted Dogger coming our way, he gave a friendly wave.

"That's old Dogger, isn't it? The faithful family retainer?"

Dogger had braked, looking round to see who Pemberton might be waving at. When he saw no one, he raised his hat as if in greeting, then gave his head a scratch. He climbed down from the wheel and shambled across the lawn towards us.

"I say, Flavia," Pemberton said, glancing at his wristwatch, "I'd quite lost track of the time. I promised to meet my publisher at Nether Eaton to have a look over a shroud tomb, quite a rare one: both hands exposed and all that. Extraordinary railings. He's got a thing about tombs, has old Quarrington, so

I'd better not stand him up. If I do, why, *Pemberton's Tombs and Traceries* might never be anything more than a twinkle in its author's eye."

He hitched up his artist's knapsack and strolled down the steps, pausing at the corner of the house to close his eyes and draw in a deep, bracing lungful of the morning air.

"My regards to Colonel de Luce," he said, and then he was gone.

Dogger shuffled up the steps as if he hadn't slept. "Visitors, Miss Flavia?" he asked, removing his hat and wiping his forehead on his sleeve.

"A Mr. Pemberton," I said. "He's writing a book about country houses or tombs or something. He wanted to interview Father about Buckshaw."

"I don't believe I've heard his name," Dogger said. "But then I'm not much of a reader. Still and all, Miss Flavia . . . "

I knew that he was going to give me a homily, complete with parables and bloodcurdling instances, about talking to strangers, but he didn't. Instead he settled for touching the brim of his hat with his forefinger, and we both of us stood there gazing out across the lawn like a couple of cows. Message sent; message received. Dear old Dogger. Such was his way of teaching.

It had been Dogger, for instance, who had patiently taught me to pick locks when I had come upon him one day fiddling with the greenhouse door. He had lost the key during one of his "episodes," and was busily at work with the bent tines of a retired kitchen fork he'd found in a flowerpot.

His hands were shaking badly. Whenever Dogger was like that, you always had the feeling that if you stuck out a finger and touched him, you'd be instantly electrocuted. But in spite of that, I had offered to help, and a few minutes later he was showing me how the thing was done.

"It's easy enough, Miss Flavia," he'd said after my third try. "Just keep in mind the three *T*s: torque, tension, and tenacity. Imagine you live inside the lock. Listen to your fingertips."

"Where did you learn to do this?" I asked, marveling as the thing clicked open. It was laughably easy once you'd got the hang of it.

"Long ago and far away," Dogger had said as he stepped into the greenhouse and made himself too busy for further questioning.

ALTHOUGH SUNLIGHT WAS FLOODING in through the windows of my laboratory, I could not seem to think properly. My mind was swarming with the things Father had told me and what I had ferreted out on my own: the deaths of Mr. Twining and Horace Bonepenny.

What was the meaning of the cap and gown I had found hidden in the tiles of Anson House? Whom did they belong to, and why had they been left there?

Both Father's account, and that in the pages of *The Hinley Chronicle*, had stated that Mr. Twining was wearing his gown when he tumbled to his death. That both of them could be mistaken seemed most unlikely.

Then, too, there were the thefts of His Majesty's Ulster Avenger and its twin, which had belonged to Dr. Kissing.

Where was Dr. Kissing now? I wondered. Would Miss Mountjoy know? She seemed to know everything else. Could he possibly still be alive? Somehow it seemed doubtful. It had been thirty years since he thought he saw his precious stamp going up in smoke.

But my mind was swirling, my brain addled, and I couldn't think clearly. My sinuses were plugged, my eyes were watering, and I felt a splitting headache coming on. I needed to clear my head.

It was my own fault: I never should have let my feet get cold. Mrs. Mullet was fond of saying, "Keep warm feet and a cool head, and you'll ne'er find yourself sneezing in bed." If one did come down with a cold, there was only one thing for it, so down to the kitchen I shuffled where I found Mrs. Mullet making pastry.

"You're sniffling, dear," she said, without looking up from her rolling pin. "Let me fix you a nice mug of chicken broth." The woman could be maddeningly perceptive.

At the words *chicken broth*, she dropped her voice to a near-whisper and shot a conspiratorial look over her shoulder.

"Hot chicken broth," she said. "It's a secret Mrs. Jacobson told me at a Women's Institute tea. Been in her family since the Exodus. Mind you, I've said nothing."

Mrs. Mullet's other favorite bit of village wisdom had to do with eucalyptus. She forced Dogger to grow it for her in the greenhouse, and assiduously concealed sprigs of the stuff here and there about Buckshaw as talismans against the cold or grippe.

"Eucalyptus in the hall, no grippe or colds shall you befall," she used to crow triumphantly. And it was true. Since she had been secreting the dark waxy green leaves in unsuspected places around the house, none of us had suffered so much as a sniffle.

Until now. Something had obviously failed.

"No, thank you, Mrs. Mullet," I said. "I've just brushed my teeth."

It was a lie, but it was the best I could come up with at short notice. Besides having a whiff of martyrdom about it, my reply had the added advantage of bucking up my image in the personal cleanliness department. On my way out, I filched from the pantry a bottle of yellow granules labeled Partington's Essence of Chicken, and from a wall sconce in the hall I helped myself to a handful of eucalyptus leaves.

Upstairs in the laboratory, I took down a bottle of sodium bicarbonate which Uncle Tar, in his spidery copperplate script, had marked *sal aeratus*, as well as, in his usual meticulous manner, Sod. Bicarb. to distinguish it from potassium bicarbonate, which also was sometimes called *sal aeratus*. Pot. Bicarb. was more at home in fire extinguishers than in the tummy.

I knew the stuff as $NaHCO_3$, which the cottagers called baking soda. Somewhere I remembered hearing that the same rustics believed in the power of a good old dosing of alkali salts to flush out even the fiercest case of the common cold.

It made good chemical sense, I reasoned: If salts were a cure, and chicken broth were a cure, think of the magnificent restorative power of a glass of effervescent chicken broth! It boggled the mind. I'd patent the thing; it would be the world's first antidote against the common cold: *De Luce's Deliquescence, Flavia's Foup Formula!*

I even managed a moderately happy hum as I measured eight ounces of drinking water into a beaker, and set it over the flame to heat. Meanwhile, in a stoppered flask I boiled the torn shreds of eucalyptus leaves and watched as straw-colored drops of oil began to form at the end of the distillation coil.

When the water was at a rolling boil, I removed it from the heat and let it cool for several minutes, then dropped in two heaped teaspoons of Partington's Chicken Essence and a tablespoon of good old $NaHCO_3$.

I gave it a jolly good stir and let it foam like Vesuvius over the lip of the beaker. I pinched my nostrils shut and tossed back half of the concoction chug-a-lug.

Chicken fizz! O Lord, protect all of us who toil in the vineyards of experimental chemistry!

I unstoppered the flask and dumped the eucalyptus water, leaves and all, into the remains of the yellow soup. Then, peeling off my sweater and draping it over my head as a fume hood, I inhaled the camphoraceous steam of poultry eucalyptus, and somewhere up inside the sticky caverns of my head I thought I felt my sinuses throw their hands up into the air and surrender. I was feeling better already.

There was a sharp knock on the door and I nearly jumped out of my skin. So seldom did anyone come into this part of the house that a tap at the door was as unexpected as one of those sudden heart-clutching organ chords in a horror film when a door swings open upon a gallery of corpses. I shot back the bolt and there stood Dogger, wringing his hat like the Irish washerwoman. I could see that he had been having one of his episodes.

I reached out and touched his hands and they stilled at once. I had observed—although I did not often make use of the fact—that there were times when a touch could say things that words could not.

"What's the password?" I asked, linking my fingers together and placing both hands atop my head.

For about five and a half seconds Dogger looked blank, and then his tense jaw muscles relaxed slowly and he almost smiled. Like an automaton he meshed his fingers and copied my gesture.

"It's on the tip of my tongue," he said haltingly. Then, "I remember now: It's 'arsenic.'"

"Careful you don't swallow it," I replied. "It's poison."

With a remarkable display of sheer willpower, Dogger made himself smile. The ritual had been properly observed.

"Enter, friend," I said, and swung the door wide.

Dogger stepped inside and looked round in wonder, as if he had suddenly found himself transported to an alchemist's lab in ancient Sumer. It had been so long since he had been in this part of the house that he had forgotten the room.

"So much glass," he said shakily.

I pulled out Tar's old Windsor chair from the desk, steadying it until Dogger had folded himself between its wooden arms.

"Have a sit. I'll fix you something."

I filled a clean flask with water and set it atop a wire mesh. Dogger started at the little "pop" of the Bunsen burner as I applied the match.

"Coming up," I said. "Ready in a jiff."

The fortunate thing about lab glassware is that it boils water at the speed of light. I threw a spoonful of black leaves into a beaker. When it had gone a deep red I handed it to Dogger, who stared at it skeptically.

"It's all right," I said. "It's Tetley's."

He sipped at the tea gingerly, blowing on the surface of the drink to cool it. As he drank, I remembered that there's a reason we English are ruled more by tea than by Buckingham Palace or His Majesty's Government: Apart from the soul, the brewing of tea is the only thing that sets us apart from the great apes—or so the Vicar had remarked to Father, who had told Feely, who had told Daffy, who had told me.

"Thank you," Dogger said. "I feel quite myself now. But there's something I must tell you, Miss Flavia."

I perched on the edge of the desk, trying to look chummy.

"Fire away," I said.

"Well," Dogger began, "you know that there are occasions when I have sometimes—that is, now and then, I have times when I—"

"Of course I do, Dogger," I said. "Don't we all?"

"I don't know. I don't remember. You see, the thing of it is that, when I was—" His eyes rolled like those of a cow in the killing-pen. "I think I might have done something to someone. And now they've gone and arrested the Colonel for it."

"Are you referring to Horace Bonepenny?"

There was a crash of glassware as Dogger dropped the beaker of tea on the floor. I scrambled for a cloth and for some stupid reason dabbed at his hands, which were quite dry.

"What do you know about Horace Bonepenny?" he demanded, clamping my wrist in a steely grip. If it hadn't been Dogger I should have been terrified.

"I know all about him," I said, gently prying his fingers loose. "I looked him up at the library. I talked to Miss Mountjoy, and Father told me the whole story Sunday evening."

"You saw Colonel de Luce Sunday evening? In Hinley?"

"Yes," I said. "I bicycled over. I told you he was well. Don't you remember?"

"No," Dogger said, shaking his head. "Sometimes I don't remember."

Could this be possible? Could Dogger have encountered Horace Bonepenny somewhere inside the house, or in the garden, then grappled with him and brought about his death? Had it been an accident? Or was there more to it than that?

"Tell me what happened," I said. "Tell me as much as you can remember."

"I was sleeping," Dogger said. "I heard voices—loud voices. I got up and went along to the Colonel's study. There was someone standing in the hall."

"That was me," I said. "I was in the hall."

"That was you," Dogger said. "You were in the hall."

"Yes. You told me to buzz off."

"I did?" Dogger seemed shocked.

"Yes, you told me to go back to bed."

"A man came out of the study," Dogger said suddenly. "I ducked in beside the clock and he walked right past me. I could have reached out and touched him."

It was clear he had jumped to a point in time after I had gone back to bed.

"But you didn't—touch him, I mean."

"Not then, no. I followed him into the garden. He didn't see me. I kept to the wall behind the greenhouse. He was standing in the cucumbers . . . eating something . . . agitated . . . talking to himself . . . foulest language . . . didn't seem to notice he was off the path. And then there were the fireworks."

"Fireworks?" I asked.

"You know, Catherine wheels, skyrockets, and all that. I thought there must be a fête in the village. It's June, you know. They often have a fête in June."

There had been no fête; of that I was sure. I'd rather slog the entire length of the Amazon in perforated tennis shoes than miss a chance to pitch coconuts at the Aunt Sally and gorge myself on rock cakes and strawberries-and-cream. No, I was well up on the dates of the fêtes.

"And then what happened?" I asked. We would sort out the details later.

"I must have fallen asleep," Dogger said. "When I woke up I was lying in the grass. It was wet. I got up and went in to bed. I didn't feel well. I must have had one of my bad turns. I don't remember."

"And you think that, during your bad turn, you might have killed Horace Bonepenny?"

Dogger nodded glumly. He touched the back of his head.

"Who else *was* there?" he asked.

Who else was there? Where had I heard that before? Of course! Hadn't Inspector Hewitt used those very words about Father?

"Bow your head, Dogger," I said.

"I'm sorry, Miss Flavia. If I killed someone I didn't mean to."

"Bend down your head."

Dogger slumped down in the chair and leaned forward. As I lifted his collar he winced.

On his neck, below and behind his ear, was a filthy great purple bruise the size and shape of a shoe heel. He winced when I touched it.

I let out a low whistle.

"Fireworks, my eye!" I said. "Those were no fireworks, Dogger. You've been well and truly nobbled. And you've been walking around with this mouse on your neck for two days? It must hurt like anything."

"It does, Miss Flavia, but I've had worse."

I must have looked at him in disbelief.

"I had a look at my eyes in the mirror," he added. "Pupils the same size. Bit of concussion—but not too bad. I'll soon be over it."

I was about to ask him where he had picked up this bit of lore when he added quickly: "But that's just something I read somewhere."

I suddenly thought of a more important question.

"Dogger, how could you have killed someone if you were knocked unconscious?"

He stood there, looking like a small boy hauled in for a caning. His mouth was opening and closing but nothing was coming out.

"You were attacked!" I said. "Someone clubbed you with a shoe!"

"No, I think not, miss," he said sadly. "You see, aside from Horace Bonepenny, I was alone in the garden."

twenty

I HAD SPENT THE PAST THREE QUARTERS OF AN HOUR TRYING to talk Dogger into letting me put an ice pack on the back of his neck, but he would not allow it. Rest, he assured me, was the only thing for it, and he had wandered off to his room.

From my window, I could see Feely stretched out on a blanket on the south lawn trying to reflect sunshine onto both sides of her face with a couple of issues of the *Picture Post*. I fetched a pair of Father's old army binoculars and took a close look at her complexion. When I'd had a good squint I opened my notebook and wrote:

> Tuesday, 6th of June 1950, 9:15 A.M. Subject's appearance remains normal. 96 hours since administration. Solution too weak? Subject immune? Common knowledge that Eskimos of Baffin Island immune to poison ivy. Could this mean what I think it might?

But my heart wasn't in it. It was difficult to study Feely when Father and Dogger were so much on my mind. I needed to collect my thoughts. I turned to a fresh page and wrote:

> Possible Suspects
> FATHER: Best motive of all. Has known dead man for most of life; has been threatened with exposure; was heard quarreling with

victim shortly before murder. No one knows whereabouts at the time crime was committed. Insp. Hewitt has already arrested him and charged him with murder, so we know where the Inspector's suspicions lie!

DOGGER: Bit of a dark horse. Don't know much about his past, but do know he is fiercely loyal to Father. Overheard Father's quarrel with Bonepenny (but so did I) and may have decided to eliminate threat of exposure. Dogger subject to "episodes" during and after which memory is affected. Might he have killed Bonepenny during one of these? Could it have been an accident? But if so, who bashed Dogger on the head?

MRS. MULLET: No motive, unless to wreak vengeance upon person who left dead snipe on her kitchen doorstep. Too old.

DAPHNE de LUCE and OPHELIA GERTRUDE de LUCE: (Your secret is out, Gertie!) Don't make me laugh! These two so absorbed in book and looking-glass that they wouldn't kill cockroach on own dinner plate. Did not know deceased, had no motive, and were snoring with mouths open when Bonepenny met his end. Case closed, as far these two dimwits concerned.

MARY STOKER: Motive: Bonepenny made improper advances to her at Thirteen Drakes. Could she have followed him to Buckshaw and dispatched him in cucumbers? Seems unlikely.

TULLY STOKER: Bonepenny was guest at Thirteen Drakes. Did Tully hear what happened with Mary? Decide to seek revenge? Or is a paying guest more important than daughter's honor?

NED CROPPER: Ned sweet on Mary (plus others). Knew what happened between Mary and Bonepenny. May have decided to do him in. Good motive, but no evidence he was at Buckshaw that night. Could have killed Bonepenny somewhere else and brought him here in wheelbarrow? But so could Tully. Or Mary!

MISS MOUNTJOY: Perfect motive: Believes Bonepenny (and Father) killed her uncle, Mr. Twining. Problem is age: Can't see Mountjoy grappling with someone Bonepenny's height and strength. Unless she used some kind of poison. Query: What was the official cause of death? Would Insp. Hewitt tell me?

INSPECTOR HEWITT: Police officer. Must include only in order to be fair, complete, and objective. Was not at Buckshaw at time

of the crime, and has no known motive. (But did he attend
Greyminster?)
DETECTIVE SERGEANTS WOOLMER & GRAVES: Ditto.
FRANK PEMBERTON: Didn't arrive in Bishop's Lacey until after
the murder.
MAXIMILIAN BROCK: Gaga; too old; no motive.

I read through this list three times, hoping nothing had escaped me.
And then I saw it: something that set my mind to racing. Hadn't Horace
Bonepenny been a diabetic? I had found his vials of insulin in the kit
at the Thirteen Drakes with the syringe missing. Had he lost it? Had it
been stolen?

He had traveled, most likely by ferry, from Stavanger in Norway to
Newcastle-upon-Tyne, and from there by rail to York, where he'd have
changed trains for Doddingsley. From Doddingsley he'd have taken a bus
or taxi to Bishop's Lacey.

And, as far as I knew, in all that time, he had not eaten! The pie shell
in his room (as evidenced by the embedded feather) had been the one in
which he secreted the dead jack snipe to smuggle it into England. Hadn't
Tully Stoker told the Inspector that his guest had a drink in the saloon
bar? Yes—but there had been no mention of food!

What if, after coming to Buckshaw and threatening Father, he had
walked out of the house through the kitchen—which he almost certainly had—and had spied the custard pie on the windowsill? What if he
had helped himself to a slice, wolfed it down, stepped outside, and gone
into shock? Mrs. M's custard pies had that effect on all of us at Buckshaw,
and none of us were even diabetics!

What if it had been Mrs. Mullet's pie after all? No more than a stupid
accident? What if everyone on my list was innocent? What if Bonepenny
had not been murdered?

But if that was true, Flavia, a sad and quiet little voice inside me
said, why would Inspector Hewitt have arrested Father and laid charges
against him?

Although my nose was still running and my eyes still watering, I thought
perhaps my chicken draught was beginning to have an effect. I read again
through my list of suspects and thought until my head throbbed.

I was getting nowhere. I decided at last to go outside, sit in the grass, inhale some fresh air, and turn my mind to something entirely different: I would think about nitrous oxide, for example, N_2O, or laughing gas: something that Buckshaw and its inhabitants were sorely in need of.

Laughing gas and murder seemed strange bedfellows indeed, but were they really?

I thought of my heroine, Marie-Anne Paulze Lavoisier, one of the giants of chemistry, whose portrait, with those other immortals, was stuck up on the mirror in my bedroom, her hair like a hot-air balloon, her husband looking on adoringly, not seeming to mind her silly coiffure. Marie was a woman who knew that sadness and silliness often go hand in hand. I remembered that it was during the French Revolution, in her husband Antoine's laboratory—just as they had sealed all of their assistant's bodily orifices with pitch and beeswax, rolled him up in a tube of varnished silk, and made him breathe through a straw into Lavoisier's measuring instruments—at that very moment, with Marie-Anne standing by making sketches of the proceedings, the authorities kicked down the door, burst into the room, and hauled her husband off to the guillotine.

I had once told this grimly amusing story to Feely.

"The need for heroines is generally to be found in the sort of persons who live in cottages," she had said with a haughty sniff.

But this was getting nowhere. My thoughts were all higgledy-piggledy, like straws in a haystack. I needed to find a catalyst of some description as, for example, Kirchoff had. He had discovered that starch boiled in water remained starch but when just a few drops of sulphuric acid were added, the starch was transformed into glucose. I had once repeated the experiment to reassure myself that this was so, and it was. Ashes to ashes; starch to sugar. A little window into the Creation.

I went back into the house, which now seemed strangely silent. I stopped at the drawing room door and listened, but there was no sound of Feely at the piano or of Daffy flipping pages. I opened the door.

The room was empty. And then I remembered that my sisters had talked at breakfast about walking into Bishop's Lacey to post Father the letters that each of them had written. Aside from Mrs. Mullet, who was off in the depths of the kitchen, and Dogger, who was upstairs resting, I was, perhaps for the first time in my life, alone in the halls of Buckshaw.

I switched on the wireless for company, and as the valves warmed up, the room was filled with the sound of an operetta. It was Gilbert and

Sullivan's *Mikado*, one of my favorites. Wouldn't it be lovely, I had once thought, if Feely, Daffy, and I could be as happy and carefree as Yum-Yum and her two sisters?

> *"Three little maids from school are we,*
> *Pert as a schoolgirl well can be,*
> *Filled to the brim with girlish glee,*
> *Three little maids from school!"*

I smiled as the three of them sang:

> *"Everything is a source of fun.*
> *Nobody's safe, for we care for none!*
> *Life is a joke that's just begun!*
> *Three little maids from school!"*

Wrapped up in the music, I threw myself into an overstuffed chair and let my legs dangle over the arm, the position in which Nature intended music to be listened to, and for the first time in days I felt the muscles in my neck relaxing.

I must have fallen into a brief sleep, or perhaps only a reverie—I don't know—but when I snapped out of it, Ko-Ko, the Lord High Executioner, was singing:

> *"He's made to dwell*
> *In a dungeon cell—"*

The words made me think at once of Father, and tears sprang up in my eyes. This was no operetta, I thought. Life was not a joke that's just begun, and Feely and Daffy and I were not three little maids from school. We were three girls whose father was charged with murder. I leaped up from the chair to switch off the wireless, but as I reached for the switch, the voice of the Lord High Executioner floated grimly from the loudspeaker:

> *"My object all sublime*
> *I shall achieve in time*

To let the punishment fit the crime—
The punishment fit the crime . . . "

Let the punishment fit the crime. Of course! Flavia, Flavia, Flavia! How could you not have seen?

Like a steel ball bearing dropping into a cut-glass vase, something in my mind went *click,* and I knew as surely as I knew my own name how Horace Bonepenny had been murdered.

Only one thing more (well, two things, actually; three at most) were needed to wrap this whole thing up like a box of birthday sweets and present it, red ribbons and all, to Inspector Hewitt. Once he heard my story, he would have Father out of the clink before you could say Jack Robinson.

MRS. MULLET WAS STILL IN THE KITCHEN with her hand up a chicken.

"Mrs. M," I said, "may I speak frankly with you?"

She looked up at me and wiped her hands on her apron.

"Of course, dear," she said. "Don't you always?"

"It's about Dogger."

The smile on her face congealed as she turned away and began fussing with a ball of butcher's twine with which she was trussing the bird.

"They don't make things the way they used to," she said as it snapped. "Not even string. Why, just last week I said to Alf, I said, 'That string as you brang home from the stationer's—'"

"Please, Mrs. Mullet," I begged. "There's something I need to know. It's a matter of life and death! Please!"

She looked at me over her spectacles like a churchwarden, and for the first time ever in her presence, I felt like a little girl.

"You said once that Dogger had been in prison, that he had been made to eat rats, that he was tortured."

"That's so, dear," she said. "My Alf says I ought not to have let it slip. But we mustn't ever speak of it. Poor Dogger's nerves are all in tatters."

"How do you know that? About the prison, I mean?"

"My Alf was in the army too, you know. He served for a time with the Colonel, and with Dogger. He doesn't talk about it. Most of 'em don't. My Alf got home safely with no more harm than troubled dreams, but a lot of them didn't. It's like a brotherhood, you know, the army; like one man spread out thin as a layer of jam across the whole face of the globe. They always know where all their old mates are and what's happened to 'em. It's eerie—psychic, like."

"Did Dogger kill someone?" I asked, point-blank.

"I'm sure he did, dear. They all did. It was their job, wasn't it?"

"Besides the enemy."

"Dogger saved your father's life," she said. "In more ways than one. He was a medical orderly, or some such thing, was Dogger, and a good one. They say he fished a bullet out of your father's chest, right next to the heart. Just as he was sewin' him up, some RAF bloke went off his head from shell shock. Tried to machete everyone in the tent. Dogger stopped him."

Mrs. Mullet pulled tight the final knot and used a pair of scissors to snip off the end of the string.

"Stopped him?"

"Yes, dear. Stopped him."

"You mean he killed him."

"Afterwards, Dogger couldn't remember. He'd been having one of his moments, you see, and—"

"And Father thinks it's happened again; that Dogger has saved his life again by killing Horace Bonepenny! That's why he's taking the blame!"

"I don't know, dear, I'm sure. But if he did, it would be very like the Colonel."

That had to be it; there was no other explanation. What was it Father had said when I told him Dogger, too, had overheard his quarrel with Bonepenny? "That is what I fear more than anything." His exact words.

It was odd, really—almost ludicrous—like something out of Gilbert and Sullivan. I had tried to take the blame to protect Father. Father was taking the blame to protect Dogger. The question was this: Whom was Dogger protecting?

"Thank you, Mrs. M," I said. "I'll keep our conversation confidential. Strictly on the q.t."

"Girl to girl, like," she said, with a horrible smirking leer.

The "girl to girl" was too much. Too chummy, too belittling. Something in me that was less than noble rose up out of the depths, and I was transformed in the blink of an eye into Flavia the Pigtailed Avenger, whose assignment was to throw a wrench into this fearsome and unstoppable pie machine.

"Yes," I said. "Girl to girl. And while we're speaking girl to girl, it's probably as good a time as any to tell you that we none of us at Buckshaw really care for custard pie. In fact, we hate it."

"Oh piff, I know that well enough," she said.

"You do?" I was too taken aback to think of more than two words.

"'Course I do. Cooks know all, they say, and I'm no different than the next one. I've known that de Luces and custard don't mix since Miss Harriet was alive."

"But—"

"Why do I make them? Because Alf fancies a nice custard pie now and again. Miss Harriet used to tell me, 'The de Luces are all lofty rhubarbs and prickly gooseberries, Mrs. M, whereas your Alf's a smooth, sweet custard man. I should like you to bake an occasional custard pie to remind us of our haughty ways, and when we turn up our noses at it, why, you must take it home to your Alf as a sweet apology.' And I don't mind sayin' I've taken home a goodly number of apologies these more than twenty years past."

"Then you'll not need another," I said.

And then I fled. You couldn't see my bottom for dust.

twenty-one

I PAUSED IN THE HALLWAY, STOOD PERFECTLY STILL, AND listened. Because of its parquet floors and hardwood paneling, Buckshaw transmitted sound as perfectly as if it were the Royal Albert Hall. Even in complete silence, Buckshaw had its own unique silence; a silence I would recognize anywhere.

As quietly as I could, I picked up the telephone and gave the cradle a couple of clicks with my finger. "I'd like to place a trunk call to Doddingsley. I'm sorry, I don't have the number, but it's the inn there: the Red Fox or the Ring and Funnel. I've forgotten its name, but I think it has an R and an F in it."

"One moment, please," said the bored but efficient voice at the other end of the crackling line.

This shouldn't be too difficult, I thought. Being located across the street from the railway platform, the "RF," or whatever it was called, was the closest inn to the station and Doddingsley, after all, was no metropolis.

"The only listings I have are for the Grapes and the Jolly Coachman."

"That's it," I said. "The Jolly Coachman!"

The "RF" must have bubbled up from the sludge at the bottom of my mind.

"The number is Doddingsley two three," the voice said. "For future reference."

"Thank you," I mumbled, as the ringing at the other end began its little jig.

"Doddingsley two three. Jolly Coachman. Are you there? Cleaver, here." Cleaver, I assumed, was the proprietor.

"Yes, I'd like to speak with Mr. Pemberton, please. It's rather important."

Any barrier, I had learned—even a potential one—was best breached by pretending urgency.

"He's not here," said Cleaver.

"Oh dear," I said, laying it on a bit thick. "I'm sorry I missed him. Could you tell me when he left? Perhaps then I'll know what time to expect him."

Flave, I thought, you ought to be in Parliament.

"He left Saturday morning. Three days ago."

"Oh, thank you!" I breathed throatily, in a voice I hoped would fool the Pope. "You're awfully kind."

I rang off and returned the receiver to its cradle as gently as if it were a newly hatched chick.

"What do you think you're doing?" demanded a muffled voice.

I spun round and there was Feely, a winter scarf wrapped round the bottom part of her face.

"What are you doing?" she repeated. "You know perfectly well you're not to use the instrument."

"What are *you* doing?" I parried. "Going tobogganing?"

Feely made a grab for me and the scarf fell away to reveal a pair of red swollen lips which were the spitting image of a Cameroon mandrill's south pole.

I was too in awe to laugh. The poison ivy I had injected into her lipstick had left her mouth a blistered crater that might have done credit to Mount Popocatepetl. My experiment had succeeded after all. Loud fanfare of trumpets!

Unfortunately, I had no time to write it up; my notebook would have to wait.

MAXIMILIAN, IN MUSTARD CHECKS, was perched on the edge of the stone horse trough which lay in the shadow of the market cross, his tiny feet dangling in the air like Humpty Dumpty. He was so small I almost hadn't seen him.

"*Haroo, mon vieux*, Flavia!" he shouted, and I brought Gladys to a sliding stop at the very toes of his patent leather shoes. Trapped again! I'd better make the best of it.

"Hullo, Max," I said. "I have a question for you."

"Ho-ho!" he said. "Just like that! A question! No preliminaries? No talk of the sisters? No gossip from the great concert halls of the world?"

"Well," I said, a little embarrassed, "I did listen to *The Mikado* on the wireless."

"And how was it? Dynamically speaking? They always have an alarming tendency to shout Gilbert and Sullivan, you know."

"Enlightening," I said.

"Aha! You must tell me in what fashion. Dear Arthur composed some of the most sublime music ever written in this sceptered isle: 'The Lost Chord,' for instance. G and S fascinate me to no end. Did you know that their immortal partnership was shattered by a disagreement about the cost of a carpet?"

I looked closely at him to see if he was pulling my leg, but he seemed in earnest.

"Of course I'm simply dying to pump you about the recent unpleasantness at Buckshaw, Flavia dear, but I know your lips are thrice sealed by modesty, loyalty, and legality—and not necessarily in that order, am I correct?"

I nodded my head.

"Your question of the oracle, then?"

"Were you at Greyminster?"

Max tittered like a little yellow bird. "Oh dear, no. Nowhere quite so grand, I'm afraid. My schooling was on the Continent, Paris to be precise, and not necessarily indoors. My cousin Lombard, though, is an old Greyminsterian. He always speaks highly enough of the place—whenever he's not at the races or playing Oh Hell at Montfort's."

"Has he ever mentioned the head, Dr. Kissing?"

"The stamp wallah? Why, dear girl, he seldom speaks of anything else. He idolized the old gentleman. Claims old Kissing made him what he is today—which isn't much, but still . . . "

"I shouldn't think he's still alive? Dr. Kissing, I mean. He'd be very old, though, wouldn't he? I'm willing to bet everything I have that he's been dead for ages."

"Then you shall lose all your money!" said Max with a whoop. "Every blessed penny of it!"

ROOK'S END WAS TUCKED into the folds of a cozy bed formed by Squires Hill and the Jack O'Lantern, the latter a curious outcropping of the landscape which, from a distance, appeared to be an Iron Age tumulus but, upon approach, proved to be substantially larger and shaped like a skull.

I steered Gladys into Pooker's Lane, which ran along its jaw, or eastern edge. At the end of the lane, dense hedges bracketed the entrance to Rook's End.

Once past these ragged remnants of an earlier day, the lawns spread off to the east, west, and south, neglected and spiky. In spite of the sun, fingers of mist still floated in the shadows above the unkempt grass. Here and there the broad expanse of lawn was broken by one of those huge, sad beech trees whose massive boles and drooping branches always reminded me of a family of despondent elephants wandering lonely on the African veld.

Beneath the beeches, two antique ladies drifted in animated dialogue, as if competing for the role of Lady Macbeth. One was dressed in a diaphanous muslin nightgown, and a mobcap which seemed somehow to have escaped the eighteenth century, while her companion, enveloped in a cyanide blue tent dress, was wearing brass earrings the size of soup plates.

The house itself was what is often called romantically "a pile." Once the ancestral home of the de Lacey family, from whom Bishop's Lacey took its name (and who were said to be very distantly related to the de Luces), the place had come down in the world in stages: from being the country house of an inventive and successful Huguenot linen merchant to what it was today, a private hospital to which Daffy would instantly have assigned the name *Bleak House*. I almost wished she were here.

Two dusty motorcars huddling together in the forecourt testified to the shortage of both staff and visitors. Dumping Gladys beside an ancient monkey puzzle tree, I picked my way up the mossy, pitted steps to the front door.

A hand-inked sign said *Ring Plse.*, and I gave the enameled handle a pull. Somewhere inside the place a hollow clanking, like a cowbell Angelus, announced my arrival to persons unknown.

When nothing happened I rang again. Across the lawn, the two old ladies had begun to feign a tea party, with elaborate mincing curtsies, crooked fingers, and invisible cups and saucers.

I pressed an ear to the massive door, but other than an undertone, which must have been the sound of the building's breathing, I could hear nothing. I pushed the door open and stepped inside.

The first thing that struck me was the smell of the place: a mixture of cabbage, rubber cushions, dishwater, and death. Underlying that, like a groundsheet, was the sharp tang of the disinfectant used to swab the floors— dimethyl benzyl ammonium chloride, by the smell of it—a faint whiff of bitter almonds which was uncommonly like that of hydrogen cyanide, the gas that was used to exterminate killers in American gas chambers.

The entrance hall was painted a madhouse apple green: green walls, green woodwork, and green ceilings. The floors were covered with cheap brown linoleum so pitted with gladiatorial gouges that it might have been salvaged from the Roman Colosseum. Whenever I stepped on one of its pustulent brown blisters, the stuff let off a nasty hiss and I made a mental note to find out if color can cause nausea.

Against the far wall, in a chromium wheelchair, an ancient man sat gazing straight up into the air, mouth agape, as if expecting an imminent miracle to take place somewhere near the ceiling.

Off to one side a desk, bare except for a silver bell and a smudged card marked *Ring Plse.*, hinted at some official, yet unseen, presence.

I gave the striker four brisk strokes. At each *ting* of the bell, the old man blinked violently, but did not take his eyes from the air above his head.

Suddenly, as if she had slipped through a secret panel in the woodwork, a wisp of a woman materialized. She wore a white uniform and a blue cap, under which she was busily poking limp strands of damp straw-colored hair with one of her forefingers.

She looked as if she had been up to no good, and knew perfectly well that I knew.

"Yes?" she said, in a thin but busy, standard-issue hospital voice.

"I've come to see Dr. Kissing," I said. "I'm his great-granddaughter."

"Dr. *Isaac* Kissing?" she asked.

"Yes," I said, "Dr. Isaac Kissing. Do you keep more than one?"

Without a word the White Phantom turned on her heel and I followed, through an archway into a narrow solarium which ran the entire length of the building. Halfway along the gallery she stopped, pointed a thin finger like the third ghost in *Scrooge*, and was gone.

At the far end of the tall-windowed room, in the single ray of sunshine that penetrated the overhanging gloom of the place, an old man sat in a wicker bath chair, a halo of blue smoke rising slowly above his head. In disarray on a small table beside him, a heap of newspapers threatened to slide off onto the floor.

He was wrapped in a mouse-colored dressing gown—like Sherlock Holmes's, except that it was spotted like a leopard with burn holes. Beneath this was visible a rusty black suit and a tall winged celluloid collar of ancient vintage. His long, curling yellow-gray hair was topped with a pillbox smoking cap of plum-colored velvet, and a lighted cigarette dangled from his lips, its gray ashes drooping like a mummified garden slug.

"Hello, Flavia," he said. "I've been expecting you."

AN HOUR HAD PASSED: an hour during which I had come to realize truly, for the first time, what we had lost in the war.

We had not got off to a particularly good start, Dr. Kissing and I.

"I must warn you at the outset that I'm not at my best conversing with little girls," he announced.

I bit my lip and kept my mouth shut.

"A boy is content to be made into a civil man by caning, or any one of a number of other stratagems, but a girl, being disqualified by Nature, as it were, from such physical brutality, must remain forever something of a *terra incognita*. Don't you think?"

I recognized it as one of those questions which doesn't require an answer. I raised the corners of my lips into what I hoped was a Mona Lisa smile—or at least one that signaled the required civility.

"So you're Jacko's daughter," he said. "You're not a bit like him, you know."

"I'm told I take after my mother, Harriet," I said.

"Ah, yes. Harriet. What a great tragedy that was. How terrible for all of you."

He reached out and touched a magnifying glass that perched precipitously atop the glacier of newspapers at his side. With the same movement he pried open a tin of Players that lay on the table and selected a fresh cigarette.

"I do my best to keep up with the world as seen through the eyes of these inky scribblers. My own eyes, I must confess, having been fixed on the passing parade for ninety-five years, are much wearied by what they have seen.

"Still, I somehow manage to keep informed about such births, deaths, marriages, and convictions as transpire in our shire. And I still subscribe to *Punch* and *Lilliput*, of course.

"You have two sisters, I believe, Ophelia and Daphne?"

I confessed that such was the case.

"Jacko always had a flair for the exotic, as I recall. I was hardly surprised to read that he had named his first two offspring after a Shakespearean hysteric and a Greek pincushion."

"Sorry?"

"Daphne, shot by Eros with a love-deadening arrow before being transformed by her father into a tree."

"I meant the madwoman," I said. "Ophelia."

"Bonkers," he said, pressing out his cigarette butt in an overflowing ashtray and lighting another. "Wouldn't you agree?"

The eyes that looked out at me from his heavily lined face were as bright and beady as those of any teacher who had ever stood watch at a blackboard, pointer in hand, and I knew that I had succeeded in my plan. I was no longer a "little girl." Whereas the mythical Daphne had been transformed into a mere laurel tree, I had become a boy in the lower Fourth.

"Not really, sir," I said. "I think Shakespeare meant Ophelia to be a symbol of something—like the herbs and flowers she gathers."

"Eh?" he said. "What's that?"

"Symbolic, sir. Ophelia is the innocent victim of a murderous family whose members are all totally self-absorbed. At least that's what I think."

"I see," he said. "Most interesting.

"Still," he added suddenly, "it was most gratifying to learn that your father retained enough of his Latin to name you Flavia. She of the golden hair."

"Mine is more of a mousy brown."

"Ah."

We seemed to have reached one of those impasses that litter so many conversations with the elderly. I was beginning to think he had fallen asleep with his eyes open.

"Well," he said at last, "you'd better let me have a look at her."

"Sir?" I said.

"My Ulster Avenger. You'd better let me have a look at her. You *have* brought her along, haven't you?"

"I—yes, sir, but how—?"

"Let us deduce," he said, as quietly as if he had said *let us pray*.

"Horace Bonepenny, onetime boy conjurer and longtime fraud artist, turns up dead in the garden of his old school chum, Jacko de Luce. Why? Blackmail is most likely. Therefore, let us suppose blackmail. Within hours, Jacko's daughter is ransacking newspaper archives at Bishop's Lacey, ferreting out reports of the demise of my dear old colleague, Mr. Twining, God rest his soul. How do I know this? I should think it obvious."

"Miss Mountjoy," I said.

"Very good, my dear. Tilda Mountjoy indeed—my eyes and ears upon the village and its environs for the past quarter century."

I should have known it! Miss Mountjoy was a spook!

"But let us continue. On the last day of his life, the thief Bonepenny has chosen to take up lodgings at the Thirteen Drakes. The young fool—well, no longer young, but still a fool, for all that—then manages to get himself done in. I remarked once to Mr. Twining that that boy would come to no good end. I hesitate to point out that I was correct in my prognostication. There always was a whiff of sulphur about the lad.

"But I digress. Shortly after his launch into eternity, Bonepenny's room at the inn is rifled by a maiden fair whose name I dare not utter aloud but who now sits demurely before me, fidgeting with something in her pocket which can hardly be anything other than a certain bit of paper the shade of Dundee marmalade, upon which is printed the likeness of Her Late Majesty Queen Victoria, and bearing the check letters, TL. *Quod erat demonstrandum*. Q.E.D."

"Q.E.D." I said, and without a word I pulled the glassine envelope from my pocket and held it out to him. With trembling hands—though whether they trembled from age or excitement I could not be certain— and using the tissue-thin paper as makeshift tweezers, he peeled back the flaps of the envelope with his nicotine-stained fingers. As the orange corners of the Ulster Avengers came into view, I could not help noticing that his nicotine-stained fingertips and the stamps were of a nearly identical hue.

"Great Scott!" he said, visibly shaken. "You've found AA. This stamp belongs to His Majesty, you know. It was stolen from an exhibition in London just weeks ago. It was in all the papers."

He shot me an accusing look over his spectacles, but his gaze was drawn away almost at once to the bright treasures that lay in his hands. He seemed to have forgotten I was in the room.

"Greetings, my old friends," he whispered, as if I weren't there. "It's been far too long a time." He took up the magnifying glass and examined them closely, one at a time. "And you, my cherished little TL: What a tale *you* could tell."

"Horace Bonepenny had both of them," I volunteered. "I found them in his luggage at the inn."

"You rifled his luggage?" Dr. Kissing asked, without looking away from the magnifying glass. "Phew! The Constabulary will hardly caper in delight upon the village green when they hear of that . . . nor will you, I'll wager."

"I didn't exactly rifle his luggage," I said. "He had hidden the stamps under a travel sticker on the outside of a trunk."

"With which, of course, you just happened to be idly fiddling when out they tumbled into your hands."

"Yes," I said. "That's precisely how it happened."

"Tell me," he said suddenly, swinging round to look me in the eye, "does your father know you're here?"

"No," I said. "Father's been charged with the murder. He's under arrest in Hinley."

"Good Lord! Did he do it?"

"No, but everyone seems to think he did. For a while, even I thought so myself."

"Ah," he said. "And what do you think now?"

"I don't know," I said. "Sometimes I think one thing and sometimes another. Everything's such a muddle."

"Everything is always a muddle just before it settles in. Tell me this, Flavia: What is it that interests you above all else in the universe? What is your one great passion?"

"Chemistry," I said in less than half a heartbeat.

"Well done!" said Dr. Kissing. "I've put that same question to an army of Hottentots in my time, and they always prattle on about this and that. Babble and gush, that's all it is. You, by contrast, have put it in a word."

The wicker creaked horribly as he half twisted round in his chair to face me. For an awful moment I thought his spine had crumbled.

"Sodium nitrite," he said. "Doubtless you are acquainted with sodium nitrite."

Acquainted with it? Sodium nitrite was the antidote for cyanide poisoning, and I knew it in all its various reactions as well as I know my own name. But how had he known to choose it as an example? Was he psychic?

"Close your eyes," Dr. Kissing said. "Imagine you are holding in your hand a test tube half-filled with a thirty percent solution of hydrochloric acid. To it, you add a small amount of sodium nitrite. What do you observe?"

"I don't need to close my eyes," I said. "It becomes orange . . . orange and turbid."

"Excellent! The color of these wayward postage stamps, is it not? And then?"

"Given time, twenty or thirty minutes perhaps, it clears."

"It clears. I rest my case."

As if a great weight had been lifted from my shoulders, I grinned a stupid grin.

"You must have been a wizard teacher, sir," I said.

"Yes, so I was . . . in my day.

"And now you've brought my little treasure home to me," he said, glancing at the stamps again.

This was something I hadn't counted upon; something I hadn't really thought through. I had meant only to discover if the owner of the Ulster Avenger was still alive. After that, I would hand it over to Father, who would surrender it to the police, who would, in due course, see that it was restored to its rightful owner. Dr. Kissing spotted my hesitation at once.

"Let me pose another question," he said. "What if you had come here today and found that I'd hopped the twig, as it were; flown off to my eternal reward?"

"You mean died, sir?"

"That's the word I was fishing for: died. Yes."

"I suppose I should have given your stamp to Father."

"To keep?"

"He'd know what to do with it."

"I should think that the best person to decide that is the stamp's owner, wouldn't you agree?"

I knew that the answer was "yes" but I couldn't say it. I knew that, more than anything, I wanted to present the stamp to Father, even though it wasn't mine to give. At the same time, I wanted to give both stamps to Inspector Hewitt. But why?

Dr. Kissing lighted another cigarette and gazed out the window. At length, he plucked one of the stamps from the folder and handed me the other.

"This is AA," he said. "*It is not mine; it don't belong to me*, as the old song says. Your father may do with it as he wishes. It is not my place to decide."

I took the Ulster Avenger from him and wrapped it carefully in my handkerchief.

"On the other hand, the exquisite little TL *is* mine. Mine own, without the shadow of a doubt."

"I expect you'll be happy to be sticking it back into your album, sir," I said with resignation, slipping its mate into my pocket.

"My album?" He gave a croaking laugh that ended in a cough. "My albums are, as dear, dead Dowson put it, gone with the wind."

His old eyes turned towards the window, gazing without seeing at the lawn outside where the two old ladies still fluttered and pirouetted like exotic butterflies beneath the sun-dappled beeches.

"'I have forgot much, Cynara! Gone with the wind,
Flung roses, roses riotously with the throng,
Dancing, to put thy pale, lost lilies out of mind;
But I was desolate and sick of an old passion,
Yea, all the time, because the dance was long:
I have been faithful to thee, Cynara! In my fashion.'

"It's from his *Non Sum Qualis Eram Bonae Sub Regno Cynarae*. Perhaps you know it?"

I shook my head. "It's very beautiful," I said.

"To remain sequestered in such a place as this," Dr. Kissing said with a broad sweep of his arm, "for all its dowdy decrepitude is, as you will appreciate, a most ruinous financial undertaking."

He looked at me as if he had made a joke. When I offered no response, he pointed to the table.

"Fetch out one of those albums. The uppermost, I think, will do."

I now noticed for the first time that there was a shelf wedged in below the tabletop, upon which were two thick bound albums. I blew off the dust and handed him the top one.

"No, no . . . open it yourself."

I opened the book to the first page, which contained two stamps: one black, the other red. By the slight marks of gummy residue and the ruled lines, I could see that the page had once been filled. I turned to the next page . . . and the next. All that remained of the album was a gutted hulk: a sparse, ravaged thing that even a schoolboy might have hidden away in shame.

"The cost, you see, of housing a beating heart. One disposes of one's life one little square at a time. Not much of it left, is there?"

"But the Ulster Avenger!" I said. "It must be worth a fortune!"

"Indeed," said Dr. Kissing, glancing once more through the magnifier at his treasure.

"One reads in novels," he said, "of the reprieve that comes when the trap's already sprung; of the horse whose heart stops an inch past the finish line." He chuckled dryly, and pulled out a handkerchief to wipe his eyes. "'Too late! Too late! the maiden cried'—and all that. 'Curfew shall not ring tonight!'

"How Fate loves a jest," he went on in a half whisper. "Who said that? Cyrano de Bergerac, was it not?"

For just a fraction of a second, I thought how much Daffy would enjoy talking to this old gentleman. But only for a fraction of a second. And then I shrugged.

With a slightly amused smile, Dr. Kissing removed his cigarette from his mouth, and touched its lighted tip to the corner of the Ulster Avenger.

I felt as if a ball of fire had been thrown into my face; as if my chest had been bound with barbed wire. I blinked, and then, frozen with horror, watched as the stamp began to smolder, then burst into a tiny flame which licked slowly, inexorably, across Queen Victoria's youthful face.

As the flame reached his fingertips, Dr. Kissing opened his hand and let the dark ashes float to the floor. From beneath the hem of his dressing gown, a polished black shoe ventured out and stepped daintily on the remains then, with a few quick twists, ground them beneath the toe.

In three thunderous heartbeats, the Ulster Avenger was no more than a black smudge on the linoleum of Rook's End.

"The stamp in your pocket has just doubled in value," said Dr. Kissing. "Guard it well, Flavia. It is now the only one of its kind in the world."

twenty-two

WHENEVER I'M OUT-OF-DOORS AND FIND MYSELF WANTING TO have a first-rate think, I fling myself down on my back, throw my arms and legs out so that I look like an asterisk, and gaze at the sky. For the first little while, I'm usually entertained by my "floaters," those wormy little strings of protein that swim to and fro across one's field of vision like dark little galaxies. When I'm not in a hurry, I stand on my head to stir them up, and then lie back to watch the show, as if it were an animated cinema film.

Today, though, I'd had too much on my mind to bother, so when I had bicycled no more than a mile from Rook's End, I threw myself down on the grassy bank and stared up into the summer sky.

I could not get out of my mind something that Father had told me, namely that the two of them, he and Horace Bonepenny, had killed Mr. Twining; that they were personally responsible for his death.

Had this been no more than one of Father's fantastic ideas I should have written it off at once, but there was more to it than that. Miss Mountjoy, too, believed they had killed her uncle, and had told me so.

It was easy enough to see that Father felt a real sense of guilt. After all, he had been part of the push to view Dr. Kissing's stamp collection, and his onetime friendship with Bonepenny, even though it had cooled, made him an accomplice in a roundabout sort of way. But still . . .

No, there had to be more to it than that, but what it might be, I could not think.

I lay on the grass, staring up at the blue vault of Heaven as earnestly as those old pillar-squatting fakirs in India used to stare directly into the sun before we civilized them, but I could think of nothing properly. Directly above me, the sun was a great white zero, blazing down upon my empty head.

I visualized myself pulling on my mental thinking cap, jamming it down around my ears as I had taught myself to do. It was a tall, conical wizard's model, covered with chemical equations and formulae: a cornucopia of ideas.

Still nothing.

But wait! Yes! That was it! Father had done nothing. Nothing! He had known—or at least suspected—from the instant it happened that Bonepenny had pinched the Head's prize stamp . . . and yet he had told no one.

It was a sin of omission: one of those offenses from the ecclesiastical catalogue of crime Feely was always going on about that seemed to apply to everyone but her.

But Father's guilt was a moral thing and, as such, hardly my cup of tea.

Still, there was no denying it: Father had kept silent, and by his silence had perhaps made it seem necessary for the saintly old Mr. Twining to shoulder the blame and pay for the breach of honor with his life.

Surely there must have been some talk at the time. The natives in this part of England have never been known for their reticence; far from it. In the last century, the Hinley pond-poet Herbert Miles had referred to us as "that gaggle o' geese who gossip gaily 'pon the gladdening green," and there was a certain amount of truth in his words. People love to talk—especially when the talking involves answering the questions of others—because it makes them feel wanted. In spite of the gravy-stained copy of *Inquire Within Upon Everything* which Mrs. Mullet kept on a shelf in the pantry, I had long ago discovered that the best way to obtain answers about anything was to walk up to the closest person and ask. Inquire without.

I could not very well question Father about his silence in those schoolboy days. Even if I dared, which I did not, he was shut up in a police cell and likely to stay there. I could not ask Miss Mountjoy, who had slammed a door in my face because she viewed me as the warm flesh and blood of a cold-blooded killer. In short, I was on my own.

All day, something had been playing away in the back of my mind like a gramophone in a distant room. If only I could tune in to the melody.

The odd feeling had begun when I was browsing through the stacks of newspapers in the Pit Shed behind the library. It was something someone said . . . but what?

Sometimes, trying to catch a fleeting thought can be like trying to catch a bird in the house. You stalk it, tiptoe towards it, make a grab . . . and the bird is gone, always just beyond your fingertips, its wings . . .

Yes! Its wings!

"He looked just like a falling angel," one of the Greyminster boys had said. Toby Lonsdale—I remembered his name now. What a peculiar thing for a boy to say about a plummeting schoolmaster! And Father had compared Mr. Twining, just before he jumped, to a haloed saint in an illuminated manuscript.

The problem was that I hadn't searched far enough in the archives. *The Hinley Chronicle* had stated quite clearly that police investigations into Mr. Twining's death, and the theft of Dr. Kissing's stamp, were continuing. And what about his obituary? That would have come later, of course, but what did it say?

In two shakes of a dead lamb's tail I was aboard Gladys, pedaling furiously for Bishop's Lacey and Cow Lane.

I DIDN'T SEE THE "CLOSED" SIGN until I was ten feet from the front door of the library. Of course! Flavia, sometimes you have tapioca for brains; Feely was right about that. Today was Tuesday. The library would not open again until ten o'clock on Thursday morning.

As I walked Gladys slowly towards the river and the Pit Shed, I thought about those sappy stories they tell on *The Children's Hour*: those moral little tales of instruction such as the one about the Pony Engine ("I think I can . . . I think I can . . . ") which was able to pull an entire freight train over the mountain just because it thought it could, it thought it could. And because it never gave up. Never giving up was the key.

The key? I had returned the Pit Shed's key to Miss Mountjoy: I remembered it perfectly. But was there by chance a duplicate? A spare key hidden under a windowsill to be used in the event some forgetful character wandered off on holiday to Blackpool with the original in her pocket?

Since Bishop's Lacey was not (at least not until a few days ago) a notable hotbed of crime, a concealed key seemed a distinct possibility.

I ran my fingers along the lintel above the door, looked under the potted geraniums that lined the walkway, even lifted a couple of suspicious-looking stones.

Nothing.

I poked in the crevices of the stone wall that ran from the lane up to the door.

Still nothing. Not a sausage.

I cupped my hands to a window, and peered in at the stacks of crumbling newspapers sleeping in their cradles. So near and yet so far.

I was so exasperated I could spit, and I did.

What would Marie-Anne Paulze Lavoisier have done? I wondered. Would she have stood here fuming and foaming like one of those miniature volcanoes which results when a heap of ammonium dichromate is ignited? Somehow I doubted it. Marie-Anne would forget the chemistry and tackle the door.

I gave the doorknob a vicious twist and fell forward into the room. Some fool had been here and left the stupid thing unlocked! I hoped no one had been watching. Good thing I thought of that, though, since I realized at once that it would be wise to wheel Gladys inside where she wouldn't be spotted by passing busybodies.

Skirting the mouth of the boarded-over pit in the middle of the room, I eased my way gingerly round to the racks of yellowed newspapers.

I had no trouble finding the relevant issues of *The Hinley Chronicle*. Yes, here it was. As I thought it might, Mr. Twining's obituary had appeared on the Friday after the account of his death:

Twining, Grenville, M.A. (Oxon.) Passed away suddenly on Monday last at Greyminster School, near Hinley, at the age of seventy-two. He was predeceased by his parents, Marius and Dorothea Twining, of Winchester, Hants. He is survived by a niece, Matilda Mountjoy, of Bishop's Lacey. Mr. Twining was buried from the chapel at Greyminster, where Rev. Canon Blake-Soames, Rector of St. Tancred's, Bishop's Lacey, and Chaplain of Greyminster, led the prayers. Floral tributes were numerous.

BUT WHERE HAD THEY BURIED HIM? Had his body been returned to Winchester and laid to rest beside his parents? Had he been buried at Greyminster? Somehow I doubted it. It seemed much more likely that I would find his grave in the churchyard of St. Tancred's, no more than a two-minute walk from where I was standing.

I would leave Gladys behind in the Pit Shed; no point in attracting unnecessary attention. If I crouched down and kept behind the hedgerow that bordered the towpath, I could easily pass from here to the churchyard without being seen.

As I opened the door, a dog barked. Mrs. Fairweather, the Chairman of the Ladies' Altar Guild, was at the end of the lane with her corgi. I eased the door shut before she or the dog could spot me. I peeked out the corner of the window and watched the dog snuffling at the trunk of an oak as Mrs. Fairweather stared off into the distance, pretending she didn't know what was going on at the other end of the lead.

Blast! I'd have to wait until the dog had done its business. I looked round the room.

On either side of the door were makeshift bookcases whose rough-cut, sagging boards looked as if they'd been hammered together by a well-meaning but inept amateur carpenter.

On the right, generations of outdated reference books—year upon year of *Crockford's Clerical Directory*, *Hazell's Annual*, *Whitaker's Almanack*, *Kelly's Directories*, *Brassey's Naval Annual*—all jammed uncomfortably cheek-by-jowl on shelves of unpainted boards, their once regal bindings of red and blue and black now bleached brown by time and seeping daylight, and all of them smelling of mice.

The shelves on the left were filled with rows of identical gray volumes, each with the same gold-leaf title embossed on its spine in elaborate Gothic letters: *The Greyminsterian*; I remembered that these were the yearbooks from Father's old school. We even had a few of them at Buckshaw. I pulled one from the shelf before noticing that it was marked 1942.

I returned it to its place and ran my index finger to the left along the spines of the remaining volumes: 1930 . . . 1925 . . .

Here it was—1920! My hands shook as I took down the book and flipped quickly through it from back to front. Its pages overflowed with articles on cricket, rowing, athletics, scholarships, rugger, photography, and nature study. As far as I could see, there was not a word about the

Magic Circle or the Stamp Society. Scattered throughout were photographs in which row upon row of boys grinned, and sometimes grimaced, at the eye of the camera.

Opposite the title page was a photographic portrait edged in black. In it, a distinguished-looking gentleman in cap and gown perched casually upon the end of a desk, Latin grammar in hand as he gazed at the photographer with a look of ever-so-slight amusement. Beneath the photo was a caption: "Grenville Twining 1848–1920."

That was all. No mention of the events surrounding his death, no eulogy, and no fond recollections of the man. Had there been a conspiracy of silence?

There was more to this than met the eye.

I began slowly turning pages, scanning the articles and reading the photo captions wherever one was provided.

Two thirds of the way through the book my eye caught the name "de Luce." The photograph showed three boys in shirtsleeves and school caps sitting on a lawn beside a wicker hamper which rested on a blanket littered with what appeared to be food for a picnic: a loaf of bread, a pot of jam, tarts, apples, and jars of ginger beer.

The caption read "Omar Khayyam Revisited—Greyminster's Tuck Shop Does Us Proud. Left to right: Haviland de Luce, Horace Bonepenny, and Robert Stanley pose for a tableau from the pages of the Persian Poet."

There was no doubt that the boy on the left, cross-legged on the blanket, was Father, looking more happy and jolly and carefree than I had ever known him to be. In the center, the long, gangling lad pretending he was about to bite into a sandwich was Horace Bonepenny. I'd have recognized him even without the caption. In the photograph, his flaming red curls had registered on the film as a ghostly pale aura round his head.

I couldn't suppress a shiver as I thought of how he had looked as a corpse.

Slightly apart from his comrades, the third boy, judging by the unnatural angle at which he held his head, seemed to be taking pains to show off his best profile. He was darkly handsome and older than the other two, with a hint of the smoldering good looks of a silent movie star.

It was odd, but I had the feeling that I had seen that face before.

Suddenly I felt as if someone had dropped a lizard down my neck. Of course I had seen this face—and recently too! The third boy in the photograph was the person who only two days ago had introduced himself to me as Frank Pemberton; Frank Pemberton, who had stood with me in Buckshaw Folly in the rain; Frank Pemberton, who this very morning had told me that he was off to view a shroud tomb in Nether Eaton.

One by one the facts assembled themselves, and like Saul I saw as clearly as if the scales had been ripped from my eyes.

Frank Pemberton was Bob Stanley and Bob Stanley was "The Third Man," so to speak. It was *he* who had murdered Horace Bonepenny in the cucumber patch at Buckshaw. I'd be willing to stake my life on it.

As everything fell into place my heart pounded as if it were about to burst.

There had been something fishy about Pemberton from the outset, and again this was something I had not thought about since Sunday at the Folly. It was something he had said . . . but what?

We had talked about the weather; we had exchanged names. He had admitted that he already knew who I was, that he had looked us up in *Who's Who*. Why would he need to do that when he had known Father for most of his life? Could that have been the lie that set my invisible antennae to twitching?

There had been his accent, I remembered. Slight, but still . . .

He had told me about his book: *Pemberton's Stately Homes: A Stroll Through Time*. Plausible, I suppose.

What else had he said? Nothing of any great importance, some load of twaddle about us being fellow castaways on a desert island. That we should be friends.

The bit of tinder that had been smoldering away in the back of my mind burst suddenly into flames!

"I trust we shall become fast friends."

His exact words! But where had I heard them before?

Like a ball on a rubber string my thoughts flew back to a winter's day. Although it had been still early, the trees outside the drawing-room window had gone from yellow to orange to gray; the sky from cobalt blue to black.

Mrs. Mullet had brought in a plate of crumpets and drawn the curtains. Feely was sitting on the couch looking at herself in the back of a teaspoon, and Daffy was stretched out across Father's old stuffed chair by the fire. She was reading aloud to us from *Penrod*, a book she had commandeered from the little shelf of childhood favorites which had been preserved in Harriet's dressing room.

Penrod Schofield was twelve, a year and some months older than I, but close enough to be of passing interest. To me, Penrod seemed to be Huckleberry Finn dragged forward in time to World War I and set down in some vaguely midwestern American city. Although the book was full of stables and alleys and high board fences and delivery vans which were, in those days, still drawn by horses, the whole thing seemed to me as alien as if it had taken place upon the planet Pluto. Feely and I had sat entranced through Daffy's readings of *Scaramouche*, *Treasure Island*, and *A Tale of Two Cities*, but there was something about Penrod which made his world seem as far removed from us in time as the last Ice Age. Feely, who thought of books in terms of musical signatures, said that it was written in the key of C major.

Still, as Daffy plodded through its pages, we had laughed once or twice, here and there, at Penrod's defiance of his parents and authority, but I had wondered at the time what there was about a troublesome boy that had captured the imagination, and possibly the love, of the young Harriet de Luce. Perhaps now I could begin to guess.

The most amusing scene, I remembered, had been the one in which Penrod was being introduced to the sanctimonious Reverend Mr. Kinosling, who had patted him on the head and said, "A trost we shall bick-home fawst frainds." This was a kind of condescension with which I lived my life, and I probably laughed too loud.

The point, though, was that *Penrod* was an American book, written by an American author. It was not likely as well known here in England as it would have been abroad.

Could Pemberton—or Bob Stanley, as I now knew him to be—have come across the book, or the phrase, in England? It was possible, of course, but it seemed unlikely. And hadn't Father told me that Bob Stanley— the same Bob Stanley who was Horace Bonepenny's confederate—had gone to America and set up a shady dealing in postage stamps?

Pemberton's slight accent was American! An old Greyminsterian with just a touch of the New World.

What an imbecile I had been!

Another peek out the window showed me that Mrs. Fairweather was gone and Cow Lane was now empty. I left the book lying open on the table, slipped out the door, and made my way round the back of the Pit Shed to the river.

A hundred years ago the river Efon had been part of a canal system, although there was now little left of it but the towpath. At the foot of Cow Lane were a few rotting remnants of the pilings which had once lined the embankment, but as it flowed towards the church, the river's waters had swollen from their decaying confines to widen in places into broad pools, one of which was at the center of the low marshy area behind the church of St. Tancred.

I scrambled over the rotted lych-gate into the churchyard, where the old tombstones leaned crazily like floating buoys in an ocean of grass so long I had to wade through it as if I were a bather waist-deep at the seaside.

The earliest graves, and those of the wealthiest former parishioners, were closest to the church, while back here along the fieldstone wall were those of more recent interments.

There was also a vertical stratum. Five hundred years of constant use had given the churchyard the appearance of a risen loaf: a fat loaf of freshly baked green bread, puffed up considerably above the level of the surrounding ground. I gave a delicious shiver at the thought of the yeasty remains that lay beneath my feet.

For a while I browsed aimlessly among the tombstones, reading off the family names that one often heard mentioned in Bishop's Lacey: Coombs, Nesbit, Barker, Hoare, and Carmichael. Here, with a lamb carved on his stone, was little William, the infant son of Tully Stoker, who, had he lived, would by now have been a man of thirty, and older brother to Mary. Little William had died aged five months and four days "of a croup," it said, in the spring of 1919, the year before Mr. Twining had leaped from the clock tower at Greyminster. There was a good chance, then, that the Doctor, too, was buried somewhere nearby.

For a moment I thought I had found him: a black stone with a pointed pyramidal top had the name *Twining* crudely cut upon it. But this Twining, on closer inspection, turned out to be an Adolphus who had been lost at sea in 1809. His stone was so remarkably preserved that I couldn't resist the urge to run my fingers over its cool polished surface.

"Sleep well, Adolphus," I said. "Wherever you are."

Mr. Twining's tombstone, I knew—assuming he had one, and I found it difficult to believe otherwise—would not be one of the weathered sandstone specimens which leaned like jagged brown teeth, nor would it be one of those vast pillared monuments with drooping chains and funereal wrought-iron fences that marked the plots of Bishop Lacey's wealthiest and most aristocratic families (including any number of departed de Luces).

I put my hands on my hips and stood waist-deep in the weeds at the churchyard's perimeter. On the other side of the stone wall was the tow-path, and beyond that, the river. It was somewhere back here that Miss Mountjoy had vanished after she had fled the church, immediately after the Vicar had asked us to pray for the repose of Horace Bonepenny's soul. But where had she been going?

Over the lych-gate I climbed once more, and onto the towpath.

Now I could clearly see the stepping-stones that lay spotted among streamers of waterweed, just beneath the surface of the slow-flowing river. These wound across the widening pool to a low muddy bank on the far side, above and beyond which ran a bramble hedge bordering a field which belonged to Malplaquet Farm.

I took off my shoes and socks and stepped off onto the first stone. The water was colder than I had expected. My nose was still running slightly and my eyes watering, and the thought crossed my mind that I'd proba-bly die of pneumonia in a day or two and, before you could say "knife," become a permanent resident of St. Tancred's churchyard.

Waving my arms like semaphore signals, I made my way carefully across the water and flat-footed it through the mud of the bank. By grasping a handful of long weeds I was able to pull myself up onto the embankment, a dike of packed earth that rose up between the river and the adjoining field.

I sat down to catch my breath and wipe the muck from my feet with a hank of the wild grass which grew in knots along the hedge. Somewhere close by a yellowhammer was singing "a little bit of bread and no cheese." It suddenly went silent. I listened, but all I could hear was the distant hum of the countryside: a bagpipe drone of far-off farm machinery.

With my shoes and socks back on, I dusted myself off and began walking along the hedgerow, which seemed at first to be an impenetrable tangle of thorns and brambles. Then, just as I was about to turn and retrace my steps, I found it—a narrow cutting in the thicket, no more than a thinning, really. I pushed myself through and came out on the other side of the hedge.

A few yards back, in the direction of the church, something stuck up out of the grass. I approached it cautiously, the hair at the nape of my neck prickling in Neanderthal alarm.

It was a tombstone, and crudely carved upon it was the name Grenville Twining.

On the tilted base of the stone was a single word: *Vale!*

Vale!—the word Mr. Twining had shouted from the top of the tower! The word Horace Bonepenny had breathed into my face as he expired.

Realization swept over me like a wave: Bonepenny's dying mind had wanted only to confess to Mr. Twining's murder, and fate had granted him only one word with which to do so. In hearing his confession, I had become the only living person who could link the two deaths. Except, perhaps, for Bob Stanley. My Mr. Pemberton.

At the thought, a cold shiver ran down my spine.

There were no dates given on Mr. Twining's tombstone, almost as if whoever had buried him here had wanted to obliterate his history. Daffy had read us tales in which suicides were buried outside the churchyard or at a crossroads, but I had scarcely believed these to be any more than ecclesiastical old wives' tales. Still, I couldn't help wondering if, like Dracula, Mr. Twining was lying beneath my feet wrapped tightly in his Master's cape?

But the gown I had found hidden on the tower roof at Anson House— which was now reposing with the police—had not belonged to Mr. Twining. Father had made it clear that Mr. Twining was wearing his gown when he fell. So, too, had Toby Lonsdale, as he told *The Hinley Chronicle.*

Could they both be wrong? Father had admitted, after all, that the sun might have dazzled his eyes. What else had he told me?

I remembered his exact words as he described Mr. Twining standing on the parapet:

"His whole head seemed to be aglow," Father had said. "His hair like a disk of beaten copper in the rising sun; like a saint in an illuminated manuscript."

And then the rest of the truth rushed in upon me like a wave of nausea: It had been Horace Bonepenny up there on the ramparts. Horace Bonepenny of the flaming red hair; Horace Bonepenny the mimic; Horace Bonepenny the magician.

The whole thing had been a skillfully planned illusion!

Miss Mountjoy had been right. He *had* killed her uncle.

He and his confederate, Bob Stanley, must have lured Mr. Twining to the roof of the tower, most likely under the pretense of returning the stolen postage stamp which they had hidden there.

Father had told me of Bonepenny's extravagant mathematical calculations; his architectural prowlings would have made him as familiar with the tiles of the tower as he was with his own study.

When Mr. Twining had threatened to expose them, they had killed him, probably by bashing his head in with a brick. The fatal blow would have been impossible to detect after such a terrible fall. And then they had staged the suicide—every instant of the thing planned in cold blood. Perhaps they had even rehearsed.

It had been Mr. Twining who fell to the cobbles, but Bonepenny who trod the ramparts in the morning sun and Bonepenny, in a borrowed cap and gown, who had shouted "*Vale!*" to the boys in the Quad. "*Vale!*"—a word that could suggest only suicide.

Having done that, he had ducked down behind the parapet just as Stanley dropped the body through the drainage opening in the roof. To a sun-blinded observer on the ground, it would have appeared that the old man had fallen straight through. It was really nothing more than the Resurrection of Tchang Fu performed on a larger stage, dazzled eyes and all.

How utterly convincing it had been!

And for all these years Father had believed that it was his silence that had caused Mr. Twining to commit suicide, that it was he who was responsible for the old man's death! What a dreadful burden to bear, and how horrible!

Not for thirty years, not until I found the evidence among the tiles of Anson House, had anyone suspected it was murder. And they had almost got away with it.

I reached out and touched Mr. Twining's tombstone to steady myself.

"I see you've found him," said someone behind me, and at the sound of his voice my blood ran cold.

I spun round and found myself face-to-face with Frank Pemberton.

twenty-three

WHENEVER ONE COMES FACE-TO-FACE WITH A KILLER IN A
novel or in the cinema, his opening words are always dripping with
menace, and often from Shakespeare.

"Well, well," he will generally hiss, "'Journeys end in lovers meeting,'" or "'So wise so young, they say, do never live long.'"

But Frank Pemberton said nothing of the sort; in fact, quite the
contrary:

"Hullo, Flavia," he said with a lopsided grin. "Fancy meeting you here."

My arteries were throbbing like stink, and I could already feel the
redness rising in my face, which, in spite of the chills, had instantly
become as hot as a griddle.

A single thought went racing through my mind: I mustn't let on . . .
I mustn't let on. Mustn't show that I know he's Bob Stanley.

"Hello," I said, hoping my voice wasn't shaking. "How was the shroud
tomb?"

I knew instantly that I was fooling no one but myself. He was watching my face the way a cat watches the family canary when they're alone
in the house.

"The shroud tomb? Ah! A confection in white marble," he said.
"Remarkably like an almond marzipan, but larger, of course."

I decided to play along until I could formulate a plan.

"I expect your publisher was pleased."

"My publisher? Oh, yes. Old . . . "

"Quarrington," I said.

"Yes. Quite. Quarrington. He was ecstatic."

Pemberton—I still thought of him as Pemberton—put down his knapsack and began to unfasten the leather straps of his portfolio.

"Phew!" he said. "Rather warm, isn't it?"

He removed his jacket, threw it carelessly across his shoulder, and jerked a thumb at Mr. Twining's tombstone.

"What's the great interest?"

"He was my father's old schoolmaster," I said.

"Ah!" He sat down and lounged against the base of the stone as casually as if he were Lewis Carroll and I were Alice, picnicking upon the river Isis.

How much did he know? I wondered. I waited for him to make his opening move. I could use the time to think.

Already I was planning my escape. Could I outrun him if I took to my heels? It seemed unlikely. If I went for the river, he'd overtake me before I was halfway across. If I headed for the field towards Malplaquet Farm, I'd be less likely to find help than if I ran for the High Street.

"I understand your father is something of a philatelist," he said suddenly, looking unconcernedly off towards the farm.

"He collects stamps, yes. How did you know?"

"My publisher—old Quarrington—happened to mention it this morning over at Nether Eaton. He was thinking of asking your father to write a history of some obscure postage stamp, but couldn't think quite how best to approach him. Couldn't begin to understand it all . . . far beyond me . . . too technical . . . suggested that perhaps he should have a word with you."

It was a lie and I detected it at once. As an accomplished fibber myself, I spotted the telltale signs of an untruth before they were halfway out of his mouth: the excessive detail, the offhand delivery, and the wrapping-up of it all in casual chitchat.

"Could be worth a bundle, you know," he added. "Old Quarrington's pretty flush since he married into the Norwood millions, but don't let on I told you. I expect your father wouldn't say no to a bit of pocket change to buy a New Guinea ha'penny thingummy, would he? It must take a pretty penny to keep up a place like Buckshaw."

This was piling insult onto injury. The man must take me for a fool.

"Father's rather busy these days," I said. "But I'll mention it to him."

"Ah, yes, this—sudden death you spoke of . . . police and all that. Must be a damnable bore."

Was he going to make a move or were we going to sit here gossiping until dark? Perhaps it would be best if I took the initiative. That way, at least, I'd have the advantage of surprise. But how?

I remembered a piece of sisterly advice, which Feely once gave Daffy and me:

"If ever you're accosted by a man," she'd said, "kick him in the Casanovas and run like blue blazes!"

Although it had sounded at the time like a useful bit of intelligence, the only problem was that I didn't know where the Casanovas were located.

I'd have to think of something else.

I scraped the toe of my shoe in the sand; I would grab a handful and toss it in his eyes before he knew what had hit him. I saw him watching me.

He stood up and dusted the seat of his trousers.

"People sometimes do a thing in haste and later come to regret it," he said conversationally. Was he referring to Horace Bonepenny or to himself? Or was he warning me not to make a foolish move? "I saw you at the Thirteen Drakes, you know. You were inside the front door looking at the register when my taxi pulled up."

Curses! I had been spotted after all.

"I have friends who work there," I said. "Mary and Ned. I sometimes drop in to say hello."

"And do you always rifle the guests' rooms?"

I could feel my face going all scarlet even as he said it.

"As I suspected," he went on. "Look, Flavia, I'll be frank with you. A business associate had something in his possession that didn't belong to him. It was mine. Now, I know for a fact that, other than my associate, you and the landlord's daughter were the only two people who were in that room. I also know that Mary Stoker would have no reason to take this particular object. What am I to think?"

"Are you referring to that old stamp?" I asked.

This was going to be a tightrope act, and I was already putting on my tights. Pemberton relaxed at once.

"You admit it?" he said. "You're an even smarter girl than I gave you credit for."

"It was on the floor under the trunk," I said. "It must have fallen out. I was helping Mary clean up the room. She'd forgotten to do a few things, and her father, you see, can be—"

"I do see. So you stole my stamp and took it home."

I bit my lip, wrinkled my face a bit, and rubbed my eyes. "I didn't actually steal it. I thought someone had dropped it. No, that's not entirely true: I knew that Horace Bonepenny had dropped it, and since he was dead, he wouldn't have any further need for it. I thought I'd make a present of it to Father and he'd get over being angry with me about the Tiffany vase I smashed. There. Now you know."

Pemberton whistled. "A Tiffany vase?"

"It was an accident," I said. "I shouldn't have been playing tennis in the house."

"Well," he said, "that solves the problem, doesn't it? You hand over my stamp and it's case closed. Agreed?"

I nodded happily. "I'll run home and get it."

Pemberton burst into uncomplimentary laughter and slapped his leg. When he had recovered himself, he said, "You're very good, you know— for your age. You remind me of myself. Run home and get it indeed!"

"All right, then," I said. "I'll tell you where I hid it and you can go and get it yourself. I'll stay here. On my honor as a Girl Guide!"

I made the Girl Guide three-eared bunny salute with my fingers. I did not tell him that I was technically no longer a member of that organization, and hadn't been since I was chucked out for manufacturing ferric hydroxide to earn my Domestic Service badge. No one had seemed to care that it was the antidote for arsenic poisoning.

Pemberton glanced at his wristwatch. "It's getting late," he said. "No more time for pleasantries."

Something about his face had changed, as if a curtain had been drawn across it. There was a sudden chill in the air.

He made a lunge for me and grabbed my wrist. I let out a yelp of pain. In a few more seconds, I knew, he'd be twisting my arm behind my back. I gave in at once.

"I hid it in Father's dressing room at Buckshaw," I blurted. "There are two clocks in the room: a large one on the chimneypiece and a smaller one on the table beside his bed. The stamp is stuck to the back of the pendulum of the chimneypiece clock."

And then something dreadful happened—dreadful and, as it would turn out, quite wonderful, rolled together into one: I sneezed.

My head cold had been lingering, nearly forgotten, for most of the day. I had noticed that, in the same way they recede when you're sleeping, head colds often let up when you're too preoccupied to pay them attention. Mine was suddenly back with a vengeance.

Forgetting for a moment that the Ulster Avenger was nestled inside it, I went for my handkerchief. Pemberton, startled, must have thought my sudden move was the prelude to my bolting—or perhaps an attack upon his person.

Whatever the case, as I brought the handkerchief up towards my nose, before it was even opened he deflected my hand with a lightning-quick grab, crumpled the cotton into a ball, and rammed it, stamp and all, into my mouth.

"Right, then," he said. "We'll see what we shall see."

He pulled his jacket from his shoulder, spread it out like a matador's cape, and the last thing I saw as he threw the thing over my head was Mr. Twining's tombstone, the word "*Vale!*" carved on its base. *I bid you farewell.*

Something tightened round my temples and I guessed that Pemberton was using the straps of his portfolio to lash the jacket firmly in place.

He hoisted me up onto his shoulder and carried me back across the river as easily as a butcher does a side of beef. Before my head could stop spinning he had dumped me heavily back onto my feet.

Gripping the nape of my neck with one hand, he used the other to seize my upper arm in a vise-like grip, shoving me roughly ahead of him along the towpath.

"Just keep putting one foot in front of the other until I tell you to stop."

I tried to call out for help, but my mouth was jammed chock-full of wet handkerchief. I couldn't produce anything more than a swinish grunt. I couldn't even tell him how much he was hurting me.

I suddenly realized that I was more afraid than I had ever been in my life.

As I stumbled along, I prayed that someone would spot us; if they did, they would surely call out, and even with my head bound up in Pemberton's jacket, I would almost certainly hear them. If I did, I would wrench sharply away from him and make a dash towards the sound of their voice. But to do so prematurely, I knew, risked tumbling headlong into the river and being left there by Pemberton to drown.

"Stop here," he said suddenly, after I had been frog-marched what I judged to be a hundred yards. "Stand still."

I obeyed.

I heard him tinkering with something metallic and a moment later, what sounded like a door grating open. The Pit Shed!

"One step up," he said. "That's right . . . now three ahead. And stop."

Behind us, the door closed like a coffin lid, with a wooden groan.

"Empty your pockets," Pemberton said.

I had only one: the pocket in my sweater. There was nothing in it but the key to the kitchen door at Buckshaw. Father had always insisted that each of us carry a key at all times in case of some hypothetical emergency, and because he conducted the occasional spot check, I was never without it. As I turned my pocket inside out, I heard the key fall to the wooden floor, then bounce and skitter. A second later there was a faint clink as it landed on concrete.

"Damn," he said.

Good! The key had fallen into the service pit, I was sure of it. Now Pemberton would have to drag back the boards that covered it, and clamber down into the pit. My hands were still free: I would rip his jacket off my head, run out the door, pull the handkerchief out of my mouth, and scream like old gooseberries as I ran towards the High Street. It was less than a minute away.

I was right. Almost immediately, I heard the unmistakable sound of heavy planks being dragged across the floor. Pemberton grunted as he pulled them away from the mouth of the pit. I'd have to be careful which way I ran: one wrong step and I'd fall into the open hole and break my neck.

I hadn't moved since we came in the door, which, if I was correct, must now be behind me with the pit in front. I'd have to estimate a hundred-and-eighty-degree turn blindfolded.

Either Pemberton had a finely tuned psychic ability or he detected some minute motion of my head. Before I could do anything, he was at my side, spinning me round half a dozen times as if we were beginning a game of blindman's buff, and I was It. When he finally stopped, I was so dizzy I could barely stand up.

"Now then," he said, "we're going down. Watch your step."

I shook my head rapidly from side to side, thinking, even as I did so, how ridiculous it must look, swathed in his tweed jacket.

"Listen, Flavia, be a good girl. I'm not going to hurt you as long as you behave. As soon as I have the stamp from Buckshaw in my hands, I'll send someone to set you free. Otherwise . . . "

Otherwise?

" . . . I shall be forced to do something most unpleasant."

An image of Horace Bonepenny breathing his final breath into my face floated before my covered eyes, and I knew that Pemberton was more than capable of following through on his threat.

He dragged me by the elbow to a spot I assumed was the edge of the pit.

"Eight steps down," he said. "I'll count them. Don't worry, I'm holding on to you."

I stepped off into space.

"One," he said as my foot came down on something solid. I stood there teetering.

"Easy does it . . . two . . . three, you're almost halfway there."

I put out my right hand and felt the edge of the pit nearly level with my shoulder. As my bare knees detected the cold air in the pit, my arm began to tremble like a dead branch in the winter wind. I felt a tightness gripping at my throat.

"Good . . . four . . . five . . . just two more to go."

He was shuffling down the steps behind me, one at a time. I wondered if I could seize his arm and pull him sharply into the pit. With any luck he'd crack his head on the concrete and I'd scramble over his body to freedom.

Suddenly he froze, his fingers digging into the muscle of my upper arm. I let out a muted bellow and he relaxed his grip a little.

"Quiet!" he said in a snarl that wasn't to be trifled with.

Outside, in Cow Lane, a lorry was backing up, its gears whining in a rising and falling wail. Someone was coming!

Pemberton stood perfectly still, his quick breath rasping in the cold silence of the pit.

With my head muffled in his jacket, I could only faintly hear the voices outside, followed by the clanging of a steel tailgate.

Oddly enough, the thought that came to mind was of Feely. Why, she would demand, didn't I scream? Why didn't I rip the jacket from my head and sink my teeth into Pemberton's arm? She would want to know all the details, and no matter what I said, she would rebut every argument as if she were the Lord Chief Justice himself.

The truth was that I was having difficulty just managing to breathe. My handkerchief—a sturdy no-nonsense piece of cotton—was stuffed so tightly into my mouth that my jaws were in agony. I had to breathe through my stuffed-up nose, and even by taking the deepest breaths I was only just able to draw in enough oxygen to keep afloat.

I knew that if I began coughing I was a goner; the slightest exertion made my head spin. Besides that, I realized, a couple of men standing out there beside an idling lorry would hear nothing but the noise of its motor. Unless I could contrive something earsplitting, I'd never make myself heard. Meanwhile, it was best to keep still and to keep quiet. I would save my energy.

Someone closed the lorry's tailgate with a clang of steel; two doors slammed shut, and the thing lumbered off in first gear. We were alone again.

"Now then," Pemberton said, " . . . down you go. Two steps more."

He gave my arm a sharp pinch and I slid my foot forward.

"Seven," he said.

I paused, reluctant to take the last step that would put me in the bottom of the pit.

"One more. Careful."

As if he were helping an old lady across a busy street.

I took another step and was instantly ankle-deep in rubbish. I could hear Pemberton stirring around in the stuff with his foot. He still had a fierce grip on my arm, which he relaxed only for an instant as he bent to pick something up. Obviously the key. If he could see it, I thought, there must be a certain amount of daylight at the bottom of the pit.

The daylight at the bottom of the pit. For some unfathomable reason, the thought brought back to me Inspector Hewitt's words as he drove me home from the County Constabulary in Hinley: *Unless some sweetness at the bottom lie, Who cares for all the crinkling of the pie?*

What did it all mean? My mind was awhirl.

"I'm sorry, Flavia," Pemberton said suddenly, breaking into my thoughts, "but I'm going to have to tie you up."

Before his words had time to register, he had whipped my right hand round behind me and tied my wrists together. What had he used, I wondered. His necktie?

As he tightened it, I remembered to press my fingertips together to form an arch, just as I had done when Feely and Daffy had locked me in the closet. When had that been? Last Wednesday? It seemed a thousand years ago.

But Pemberton was no fool. He saw at once what I was up to, and without a word, he pinched the backs of my hands between his thumb and forefinger and my little arch of safety collapsed in pain. He pulled the bonds tight until my wrists were squeezed together, then double- and triple-knotted the thing, giving it a hard, tight tug at each step.

I ran a thumb over the knot and felt the slick smoothness of it. Woven silk. Yes, he had used his necktie. Precious little chance of picking my way out of *these* bonds!

My wrists were already perspiring, and I knew that the moisture would soon cause the silk to shrink. Well, not precisely: Silk, like hair, is a protein, and does not itself shrink, but the way in which it is woven can cause it to tighten mercilessly when it is wetted. After a while, the circulation in my hands would be cut off, and then . . .

"Sit," Pemberton commanded, pushing down on my shoulders—and I sat.

I heard the click of his belt buckle as he removed it, whipped it round my ankles, and pulled it tight.

He didn't say another word. His shoes grated on concrete as he climbed the steps of the pit, and then I heard the sound of the heavy boards being dragged back across its mouth.

A few moments later, all was silence. He was gone.

I was alone in the pit, and no one but Pemberton knew where I was.

I would die down here, and when eventually they found my body, they would lift me into a gleaming black hearse and transport me to some dank old morgue where they would lay me out on a stainless-steel table.

The first thing they would do would be to open my mouth and extract the soggy ball of my handkerchief, and as they spread it out flat on the table beside my white remains, an orange stamp—a stamp belonging to the King—would flutter to the floor: It was like something right out of an Agatha Christie. Someone—perhaps even Miss Christie herself—would write a detective novel about it.

I would be dead, but I'd be splashed across the front page of the *News of the World*. If I hadn't been so frightened, so exhausted, so short of breath, and in such pain, it might even have seemed amusing.

twenty-four

BEING KIDNAPPED IS NEVER QUITE THE WAY YOU IMAGINE IT WILL be. In the first place, I had not bitten and scratched my abductor. Nor had I screamed: I had gone quietly along like a lamb to the September slaughter.

The only excuse I can think of is that all my powers were being diverted to feed my racing mind, and that nothing was left over to drive my muscles. When something like this actually happens to you, the kind of rubbish that comes leaping immediately into your head can be astonishing.

I remembered, for instance, Maximilian's claim that in the Channel Islands you could raise the hue and cry merely by shouting, "*Haroo! Haroo, mon Prince! On me fait tort!*"

Easy to say but hard to do when your mouth's stopped up with cotton and your head's wrapped in a stranger's tweed jacket that fairly reeks of sweat and pomade.

Besides, I thought, there is a notable shortage of princes in England nowadays. The only ones I could think of at the moment were Princess Elizabeth's husband, Prince Philip, and their infant son, Prince Charles.

This meant that, for all practical purposes, I was on my own.

What would Marie-Anne Paulze Lavoisier have done? I wondered. Or for that matter, her husband, Antoine?

My present predicament was far too vivid a reminder of Marie-Anne's brother, cocooned in oiled silk and left to breathe through a straw. And it was unlikely, I knew, that anyone would come bursting into the Pit

Shed to haul me off to justice. There was no guillotine in Bishop's Lacey, but neither were there any miracles.

No, reflecting upon Marie-Anne and her doomed family was simply too depressing. I'd have to look to the other great chemists for inspiration.

What, then, would Robert Bunsen, for instance, or Henry Cavendish have done if they had found themselves bound and gagged at the bottom of a grease pit?

I was surprised by how quickly the answer came to mind: They would take stock.

Very well, I would take stock.

I was at the bottom of a six-foot pit, which was uncomfortably close to the dimensions of a grave. My hands and feet were tied and it would not be easy to feel my way around. With my head wrapped up in Pemberton's jacket—and doubtless tied tightly in position with its arms—I could see nothing. My hearing was muffled by the heavy cloth; my sense of taste disabled by the handkerchief stuffed in my mouth.

I was having difficulty breathing and, with my nose partially covered, the slightest exertion used up what little oxygen was reaching my lungs. I would need to remain quiet.

The sense that seemed to be working overtime was my sense of smell, and in spite of my wrapped-up head, the stench of the pit came seeping at full strength into my nostrils. At bottom, it was the sour reek of soil that has lain for many years directly beneath a human dwelling: a bitter scent of things best not thought about. Superimposed upon that background was the sweet odor of old motor oil, the sharp undulating tang of ancient petrol, carbon monoxide, tire rubber, and perhaps a faint whiff of ozone from long-burnt-out spark plugs.

And there was that trace of ammonia I had noticed before. Miss Mountjoy had mentioned rats, and I wouldn't be surprised to discover that they flourished in these neglected buildings along the riverbank.

Most unsettling was the smell of sewer gas: an unsavory soup of methane, hydrogen sulphide, sulphur dioxide, and the nitrogen oxides—the smell of decomposition and decay; the smell of the open pipe from the riverbank to the pit in which I was trussed.

I shuddered to think of the things that might even now be making their way up such a conduit. Best to give my imagination a rest, I thought, and get on with my survey of the pit.

I had almost forgotten that I was seated. Pemberton's order to sit, and his pushing me down, had been so surprising I had not noticed what it was that I sat upon. I could feel it beneath me now: flat, solid, and stable. By wiggling my behind, I was able to detect the slightest give in the thing, along with a wooden creaking sound. A large tea chest, I thought, or something very like one. Had Pemberton put it here in anticipation, before he accosted me in the churchyard?

It was then that I realized I was famished. I had eaten nothing since my skimpy breakfast, which, come to think of it, had been interrupted by the sudden appearance of Pemberton at our window. As my stomach began to send out little pangs of complaint, I began to wish I'd been more attentive to my toast and cereal.

Moreover, I was tired. More than tired: I was totally exhausted. I had not slept well, and the lingering effects of my head cold were further choking off my oxygen intake.

Relax, Flave. Keep a cool head. Pemberton will soon be arriving at Buckshaw.

I had counted on the fact that when he entered the house to retrieve the Ulster Avenger, he would be accosted by Dogger, who would put paid to him in no uncertain terms.

Good old Dogger! How I missed him. Here was this Great Unknown living under the same roof and I had never thought to ask him, face-to-face, about his past. If ever I managed to find my way out of this infernal fix, I vowed that, at the earliest opportunity, I would take him on a private picnic. I would punt with him to the Folly, where I would ply him with Marmite on bread and pump him like billy-ho for all the gory details. He would be so relieved at my escape that he would hardly dare refuse to tell me all.

The dear man had pretended that it was he who had killed Horace Bonepenny, albeit by accident during one of his spells, and he had done so to protect Father. I was sure of it. Hadn't Dogger been there with me in the corridor outside Father's study? Hadn't he overheard, as I had, the row that preceded Bonepenny's death?

Yes, whatever happened, Dogger would look after it. Dogger was fiercely loyal to Father—and to me. Loyal even unto death.

Very well, then. Dogger would tackle Pemberton and that would be that.

Or would it?

What if Pemberton actually made his way into Buckshaw undetected and gained entry to Father's dressing room? What if he stopped the chimneypiece clock, reached behind the pendulum, and found nothing there but the mutilated Penny Black? What would he do then?

The answer was a simple one: He would come back to the Pit Shed and put me to the torture.

One thing was clear: I had to escape before he could return. There was no time to waste.

My knees popped like dry twigs as I struggled to my feet.

The first and most important thing was to make a survey of the pit: to map its features and discover anything that might aid in my escape. With my hands tied behind me at the wrists, I could only map out the concrete wall by going slowly round its perimeter, my back steadied against it, using my fingertips to feel every inch of the surface. With any luck, I might find a sharp projection to use as a tool in freeing my hands.

My feet were tied so tightly I could feel my anklebones grating together, and I had to invent a kind of hopping frog gait. My every move was accompanied by the rustling of old papers underfoot.

At what I judged to be the far end of the pit, I could feel a current of cold air blowing on my ankles, as if there were an opening down near the floor. I turned and faced the wall, trying to hook a toe into something, but my bonds were too tight. Every move threatened to pitch me forward onto my face.

I could feel that my hands were quickly becoming covered with a rancid filth from the walls; the smell of the stuff alone was making me queasy.

What if, I thought, I could climb up onto the tea chest? That way, my head should be above the level of the pit, and there might be some kind of hook higher up the wall: something, perhaps, that had once been used to suspend a bag of tools, or a work light.

But first I had to find my way back to the chest.

Bound and tied as I was, this took far longer than I expected. But sooner or later, I knew, my legs would crash into the thing and, having completed my circumnavigation of the pit, I'd be back where I started.

Ten minutes later I was panting like an Ethiopian hound and still hadn't come up against the tea chest. Had I missed it? Should I carry on or go back the way I came?

Perhaps the thing was in the middle of the pit and I had been tiring myself by hopping in rectangles all round it. By what I could recall of the pit from my first visit—although it had been covered with boards and I had not actually looked down into it—I thought that it could be no more than eight feet long and six wide.

With my ankles trussed, I could hop no more than about six inches at a time in any direction: say, twelve hops by sixteen. It was easy enough to conclude that with my back to the wall, the center of the pit would be either six or eight hops away.

By now fatigue was overtaking me. I was jumping about like a grass-hopper in a jam jar and getting nowhere. Then, just when I was about to give up, I barked my shin on the tea chest. I sat down on it at once to catch my breath.

After a time, I began moving my shoulders, back a bit and to the right. When I shifted to the left, my shoulder touched concrete. This was encouraging! The box was up against the wall—or close enough to it. If I could somehow manage to climb on top of the thing, there might be a chance I could throw myself up and over the rim of the pit like a sea lion at the aquarium. Once out of the pit, there would be far more likelihood I might find some hook or projection to help me rip Pemberton's jacket from my head. Then I would be able to see what I was doing. I would free my hands, and then my feet. It all seemed so simple in theory.

As carefully as possible I turned ninety degrees so that my back was to the wall. I shifted my behind to the rear edge of the tea chest and brought my knees up until they touched the part of the jacket that was under my chin.

There was a very slightly raised edge round the top of the chest, and I was able to hook my heels onto it. Then slowly . . . carefully . . . I began to extend my legs, sliding my back, inch by inch, up the wall.

We were a right-angled triangle. The wall and the top of the chest formed the adjacent and opposite sides and I was the shaky hypotenuse.

A sudden spasm shot through my calf muscles and I wanted to scream. If I let the pain overtake me, I would tumble off the box and likely break an arm or a leg. I steeled myself and waited for the pain to pass, biting the inside of my cheek with such ferocity that I tasted, almost instantly, my own warm, salty blood.

Steady on, Flave, I told myself: There are worse things. But for the life of me, I couldn't think of one.

I don't know how long I stood there trembling but it seemed like an eternity. I was soaked through with sweat, yet cool air was blowing in from somewhere; I could still feel its draughty breath on my bare legs.

After a long struggle, I found myself at last standing upright on the tea chest. I ran my fingers over as much of the wall as I could, but it was maddeningly smooth.

Awkwardly, like an elephant ballerina, I rotated one hundred and eighty degrees until I thought I was facing the wall. I leaned forward and felt—or thought I felt—the rim of the pit beneath my chin. But with my head swaddled in Pemberton's jacket, I could not be sure.

There was no way out; not, at least, in this direction. I was like a hamster that had climbed to the top of the ladder in its cage and found there was nowhere to go but down. But surely hamsters knew in their hamster hearts that escape was futile; it was only we humans who were incapable of accepting our own helplessness.

I dropped slowly to my knees on the tea chest. Climbing down, at least, was easier than climbing up, although the rough splintered wood, and what felt painfully like a tin rim running round the top of the box, made a hash of my bare knees. From there, I was able to twist sideways into a sitting position and swing my legs over the edge until I felt them touch the floor.

Unless I could find the opening through which the cold air was entering the pit, the only way out was up. If there *was* in fact a pipe or conduit leading to the river, would it be of sufficient diameter for me to crawl through? And even if it was, would it be free of blockage, or would I suddenly crawl face-first—like a mammoth blindworm—into some ghastly thing in total darkness and become jammed in the pipe, unable to go either forward or back?

Would my bones be found in some future England by a baffled archaeologist? Would I be put on display in a glass case at the British Museum, to be stared at by the masses? My mind raced through the pros and cons.

But wait! I'd forgotten about the stairs at the end of the pit! I would sit on the bottom step and go up backwards, one step at a time. When I reached the top, I would push up with my shoulders and lift the boards that covered the pit. Why hadn't I thought of this in the first place, before I'd worn myself down to this state of quivering exhaustion?

It was then that something came over me, smothering my consciousness like a pillow. Before I could recognize my total exhaustion for what it was, before I could muster a fight, I was vanquished. I felt myself sinking to the floor amid the rustling papers: papers which, in spite of the cold air from the conduit, now seemed surprisingly warm.

I shifted a little as if to burrow into their depths, and pulling my knees up towards my chin, I was instantly asleep.

I DREAMED THAT DAFFY WAS PUTTING on a Christmas pantomime. The great hallway at Buckshaw had been transformed into an exquisite jewel box of a Viennese theater, with a red velvet curtain and a vast crystal chandelier in which the flames of a hundred candles bobbed and flickered.

Dogger and Feely and Mrs. Mullet and I sat side by side on a single row of chairs, while nearby at a wood-carver's bench, Father puttered away at his stamps.

The play was *Romeo and Juliet*, and Daffy, in a remarkable display of quick-change artistry, was playing all the parts. One moment she was Juliet on the balcony (the landing at the top of the west staircase) and the next, having vanished for no more than a blink of a magpie's eye, she reappeared on the mezzanine as Romeo.

Up and down she flew, up and down, wringing our hearts with words of tender love.

From time to time, Dogger would put a forefinger to his lips and slip quietly out of the room, returning moments later with a painted wheelbarrow spilling over with postage stamps which he would dump at Father's feet. Father, who was busily snipping stamps in half with a pair of Harriet's nail scissors, would grunt without so much as looking up, and go on about his work.

Mrs. Mullet laughed and laughed at Juliet's old nurse, blushing and shooting glances at us one and all as if there were some message encoded in the words which only she could understand. She mopped her red face with a polka-dot handkerchief, twisting it round and round in her hands before rolling it into a ball and shoving it in her mouth to stop up her hysterical laughter.

Now Daffy (as Mercutio) was describing how Mab, the Fairy Queen, gallops:

O'er ladies' lips, who straight on kisses dream,
Which oft the angry Mab with blisters plagues
Because their breaths with sweetmeats tainted are.

I took a surreptitious peek at Feely who, in spite of the fact that her lips looked like something you might see on a fishmonger's barrow, had attracted the attentions of Ned who was sitting behind her, leaning forward over her shoulder, his own lips pursed, begging a kiss. But each time Daffy flitted down from the balcony to the mezzanine below in the role of Romeo (looking, with his pencil-thin mustache, more like David Niven in *A Matter of Life and Death* than a noble Montague), Ned would leap to his feet with a volley of applause punctuated by fierce two-fingered whistles as Feely, unmoved, popped Mint Imperial after Mint Imperial into her open mouth, gasping suddenly as Romeo burst into Juliet's marbled tomb:

For here lies Juliet, and her beauty makes
This vault a feasting presence full of light.
Death, lie thou there—

I woke up. Damnation! Something was running over my feet: something wet and furry.

"Dogger!" I tried to scream, but my mouth was full of a wet mess. My jaws were aching and my head felt as if I had just been dragged from the chopping block.

I kicked out with both feet and something scuttered through the loose papers with an angry chittering noise.

A water rat. The pit was likely swarming with the things. Had they been nibbling at me while I slept? The very thought of it made me cringe.

I pulled myself upright and leaned back against the wall, my knees beneath my chin. It was too much to expect that the rats would nibble at my bonds as they did in fairy tales. They'd more than likely gnaw my knuckles to the bone and I'd be powerless to stop them.

Stow it, Flave, I thought. Don't let your imagination run away with you.

There had been several times in the past, at work in my chemical laboratory or lying in bed at night, when I unexpectedly caught myself thinking, "You are all alone with Flavia de Luce," which sometimes was a frightening thought and sometimes not. This was one of the scarier occasions.

The scurrying noises were real enough; something was rummaging about in the papers in the corner of the pit. If I moved my legs or my head, the sounds would cease for a moment, and then begin again.

How long had I been asleep? Had it been hours or minutes? Was it still daylight outside, or was it now dark?

I remembered that the library would be closed until Thursday morning, and today was only Tuesday. I could be here for a good long while.

Someone would report me missing, of course, and it would probably be Dogger. Was it too much to hope that he would catch Pemberton in the act of burgling Buckshaw? But even if he was caught, would Pemberton tell them where he had hidden me away?

Now my hands and feet were growing numb and I thought of old Ernie Forbes, whose grandchildren were made to pull him along the High Street on a little wheeled float. Ernie had lost a hand and both feet to gangrene in the war, and Feely once told me that he had to be—

Stop it, Flave! Stop being such a monstrous crybaby!

Think of something else. Think of anything.

Think, for instance, of revenge.

twenty-five

THERE ARE TIMES—ESPECIALLY WHEN I'M CONFINED—THAT my thoughts have a tendency, like the man in Stephen Leacock's story, to ride madly off in all directions.

I'm almost ashamed to admit to the things that crossed my mind at first. Most of them involved poisons, a few involved common household utensils, and all of them involved Frank Pemberton.

My mind flew back to our first encounter at the Thirteen Drakes. Although I had seen his taxi pull up at the front door, and had heard Tully Stover shout at Mary that Mr. Pemberton had arrived early, I had not actually laid eyes on the man himself. That did not take place until Sunday, at the Folly.

Although there had been several odd things about Pemberton's sudden appearance at Buckshaw, I really hadn't had time to think about them.

In the first place, he hadn't arrived in Bishop's Lacey until hours after Horace Bonepenny had expired in my face. Or had he?

When I looked up and saw Pemberton standing at the edge of the lake, I had been taken by surprise. But why? Buckshaw was my home: I had been born and lived there every minute of my life. What was so surprising about a man standing at the edge of an artificial lake?

I could feel an answer to that question nibbling at the hook I'd lowered into my subconscious. Don't look straight at it, I thought, think of something else—or at least pretend to.

It had been raining that day, or had just begun to rain. I had looked up from where I was sitting on the steps of the little ruined temple and there he was, across the water on the south side of the lake: the southeast side, to be precise. Why on earth had he made his appearance from that direction?

That was a question to which I had known the answer for quite some time.

Bishop's Lacey lay to the northeast of Buckshaw. From the Mulford Gates, at the entrance to our avenue of chestnut trees, the road ran in easy twists and turns, more or less directly into the village. And yet Pemberton had appeared from the southeast, from the direction of Doddingsley, which lay about four miles across the fields. Why then, in the name of Old Stink, I had wondered, would he choose to come that way? The choices had seemed limited, and I had quickly jotted them down in my mental notebook:

1. If (as I suspected) Pemberton was the murderer of Horace Bonepenny, could he have been, as all murderers are said to be, drawn back to the scene of the crime? Had he perhaps left something behind? Something like the murder weapon? Had he returned to Buckshaw to retrieve it?
2. Because he had already been to Buckshaw the night before, he knew the way across the fields and wanted to avoid being seen. (See 1 above)

What if on Friday, the night of the murder, Pemberton, believing that Bonepenny was carrying the Ulster Avengers, had followed him from Bishop's Lacey to Buckshaw and murdered him there?

But hold on, Flave, I thought. Hold your horses. Don't go galloping off like that.

Why wouldn't Pemberton simply waylay his victim in one of those quiet hedgerows that border nearly every lane in this part of England?

The answer had come to me as if it were sculpted in red neon tubing in Piccadilly Circus: because he wanted Father to be blamed for the crime!

Bonepenny had to be killed at Buckshaw!

Of course! With Father a virtual recluse, it was unlikely to expect that he would ever happen to be away from home. Murders—at least those in which the murderer expected to escape justice—had to be planned in advance, and often in very great detail. It was obvious that a philatelic crime needed to be pinned on a philatelist. If Father was unlikely to come to the scene of the crime, the scene of the crime would have to come to Father.

And so it had.

Although I had first formulated this chain of events—or, at least, certain of its links—hours ago, it was only now, when I was at last forced to be alone with Flavia de Luce, that I was able to fit together all the pieces.

Flavia, I'm proud of you! Marie-Anne Paulze Lavoisier would be proud of you too.

Now then: Pemberton, of course, had followed Bonepenny as far as Doddingsley; perhaps even all the way from Stavanger. Father had seen them both at the London exhibition just weeks ago—proof positive that neither one was living abroad permanently.

They had probably planned this together, this blackmailing of Father. Just as they had planned the murder of Mr. Twining. But Pemberton had a plan of his own.

Once satisfied that Bonepenny was on his way to Bishop's Lacey (where else, indeed, would he be going?), Pemberton had got off the train at Doddingsley and registered himself at the Jolly Coachman. I knew that for a fact. Then, on the night of the murder, all he had to do was walk across the fields to Bishop's Lacey.

Here, he had waited until he saw Bonepenny leave the inn and set out on foot for Buckshaw. With Bonepenny out of the way and not suspecting that he was being followed, Pemberton had searched the room at the Thirteen Drakes, and its contents—including Bonepenny's luggage—and had found nothing. He had, of course, never thought, as I had, to slit open the shipping labels.

By now, he must have been furious.

Slipping away from the inn unseen (most likely by way of that steep back staircase), he had tracked his quarry on foot to Buckshaw, where they must have quarreled in our garden. How was it, I wondered, that I hadn't heard them?

Within half an hour, he had left Bonepenny for dead, his pockets and wallet rifled. But the Ulster Avengers had not been there: Bonepenny had not had the stamps upon his person after all.

Pemberton had committed his crime and then simply walked off into the night, across the fields to the Jolly Coachman at Doddingsley.

The next morning, he had rolled up with much ado in a taxicab at the front door of the Thirteen Drakes, pretending he had just come down by rail from London. He would have to search the room again. Risky, but necessary. Surely the stamps must still be hidden there.

Parts of this sequence of events I had suspected for some time, and even though I hadn't yet put together the remaining facts, I had already verified Pemberton's presence in Doddingsley by my telephone call to Mr. Cleaver, the innkeeper of the Jolly Coachman.

In retrospect, it all seemed fairly simple.

I stopped thinking for a moment to listen to my breathing. It was slow and regular as I sat there with my head resting on my knees, which were still pulled up in an inverted V.

At this moment I thought of something Father had once told us: that Napoleon had once called the English "a nation of shopkeepers." Wrong, Napoleon!

Having just come through a war in which tons of trinitrotoluene were dumped on our heads in the dark, we were a nation of survivors, and I, Flavia Sabina de Luce, could see it even in myself.

And then I muttered part of the Twenty-third Psalm for insurance purposes. One can never be too sure.

Now: the murder.

Again the dying face of Horace Bonepenny swam before me in the dark, its mouth opening and closing like a landed fish gasping in the grass. His last word and his dying breath had come as one: "*Vale*," he had said, and it had floated from his mouth directly to my nostrils. And it had come to me on a wave of carbon tetrachloride.

There was no doubt whatsoever that it was carbon tetrachloride, one of the most fascinating of chemical compounds.

To a chemist, its sweet smell, although very transient, is unmistakable. It is not far removed in the scheme of things from the chloroform used by anesthetists in surgery.

In carbon tetrachloride (one of its many aliases) four atoms of chlorine play ring-around-a-rosy with a single atom of carbon. It is a powerful insecticide, still used now and then in stubborn cases of hookworm, those tiny, silent parasites that gorge themselves on blood sucked in darkness from the intestines of man and beast alike.

But more importantly, philatelists use carbon tetrachloride to bring out a stamp's nearly invisible watermarks. And Father kept bottles of the stuff in his study.

I thought back to Bonepenny's room at the Thirteen Drakes. What a fool I had been to think of poisoned pie! This wasn't a Grimm's fairy tale; it was the story of Flavia de Luce.

The pie shell was nothing more than that: just a shell. Before leaving Norway, Bonepenny had removed the filling, and stuffed in the jack snipe with which he planned to terrorize Father. That was how he'd smuggled the dead bird into England.

It wasn't so much what I had found in his room as what I hadn't found. And that, of course, was the single item that was missing from the little leather kit in which Bonepenny carried his diabetic supplies: a syringe.

Pemberton had come across the syringe and pocketed it when he rifled Bonepenny's room just before the murder. I was sure of it.

They were partners in crime, and no one would have known better than Pemberton the medical supplies that were essential to Bonepenny's survival.

Even if Pemberton had planned a different way of dispatching his victim—a stone to the back of the head or strangulation with a green willow withy—the syringe in Bonepenny's luggage must have seemed like a godsend. The very thought of how it was done made me shudder.

I could imagine the two of them struggling there in the moonlight. Bonepenny was tall, but not muscular. Pemberton would have brought him down as a cougar does a deer.

Out comes the hypodermic and into the base of Bonepenny's brain it goes. Just like that. It wouldn't take more than a second, and its effect would be almost instantaneous. This, I was certain, was the way in which Horace Bonepenny had met his death.

Had he ingested the stuff—and it would have been a near impossibility to force him to swallow it—a much larger quantity of the poison would have been required: a quantity which he would have promptly vomited.

Whereas five cc's injected into the base of the brain would be sufficient to bring down an ox.

The unmistakable fumes of the carbon tetrachloride would have been quickly transmitted to his mouth and nasal cavities as I had detected. But by the time Inspector Hewitt and his detective sergeants arrived, it had evaporated without a trace.

It was almost the perfect crime. In fact it would have been perfect if I had not gone down into the garden when I did.

I hadn't thought about this before. Was my continued existence all that stood between Frank Pemberton and freedom?

There was a grating noise.

I could not tell which direction it was coming from. I swiveled my head and the noise stopped instantly.

For a minute or more there was silence. I strained my ears but could hear only the sound of my own breathing, which I noticed had become more rapid—and more jagged.

There it was again! As if a piece of lumber were being dragged, with agonizing slowness, across a gritty surface.

I tried to call out "Who's there?" but the hard ball of the handkerchief in my mouth reduced my words to a muffled bleat. At the effort, my jaws felt as if someone had driven a railway spike into each side of my head.

Better to listen, I thought. Rats don't move lumber, and unless I was sadly mistaken, I was no longer alone in the Pit Shed.

Like a snake, I moved my head slowly from side to side, trying to take advantage of my superior hearing, but the heavy tweed binding my head muffled all but the loudest of sounds.

But the grating noises were not half as unnerving as the silences between them. Whatever it was in the pit was trying to keep its presence unknown. Or was it keeping quiet to unnerve me?

There was a squeak, then a faint *tick*, as if a pebble had fallen onto a large stone.

As slowly as a flower opening, I stretched my legs out in front of me, but when they met with no resistance, I pulled them back up beneath my chin. Better to be coiled up, I thought; better to present a smaller target.

For a moment, I focused my attention on my hands, which were still lashed behind me. Perhaps there had been a miracle; perhaps the silk had stretched and loosened, but no such luck. Even my numbed fingers could sense that my bonds were as tight as ever. I hadn't a hope of getting free. I really was going to die down here.

And who would miss me?

Nobody.

After a suitable period of mourning, Father would turn again to his stamps, Daphne would drag down another box of books from the

Buckshaw library, and Ophelia would discover a new shade of lipstick. And soon—too painfully soon—it would be as if I had never existed.

Nobody loved me, and that was a fact. Harriet might have when I was a baby, but she was dead.

And then, to my horror, I found myself in tears.

I was appalled. Brimming eyes were something I had fought against as long as I could remember, yet in spite of my bound-up eyes I seemed to see floating before me a kindly face, one I had forgotten in my misery. It was, of course, Dogger's face.

Dogger would be desolate if I died!

Get a grip, Flave . . . it's just a pit. What was that story Daffy read us about a pit? That tale of Edgar Allan Poe's? The one about the pendulum?

No! I wouldn't think about it. I wouldn't!

Then there was the Black Hole of Calcutta in which the Nawab of Bengal had imprisoned a hundred and forty-six British soldiers in a cell made to hold no more than three.

How many had survived a single night in that stifling oven? Twenty-three, I remembered, and by morning, stark raving mad—every last one of them.

No! Not Flavia!

My mind was like a vortex, spinning . . . spinning. I took a deep breath to calm myself, and my nostrils were filled with the smell of methane. Of course!

The pipe to the riverbank was full of the stuff. All it needed was a source of ignition to set it off and the resulting explosion would be talked about for years.

I would find the end of the pipe and kick it. If luck were on my side, the nails in the soles of my shoe would create a spark, the methane would explode, and that would be that.

The only drawback to this plan was that I would be standing at the end of the pipe when the thing went off. It would be like being strapped across the mouth of a cannon.

Well, cannon be damned! I wasn't going to die down here in this stinking pit without a struggle.

Gathering every last ounce of my remaining strength, I dug in my heels and pushed myself against the wall until I was in a standing position.

It took rather longer than I expected but at last, although teetering, I was upright.

No more time for thinking. I would find the source of the methane gas or die in the attempt.

As I made a tentative hop towards where I thought the conduit might be, a chill voice whispered into my ear:

"And now for Flavia."

twenty-six

IT WAS PEMBERTON, AND AT THE SOUND OF HIS VOICE, MY heart turned inside out. What had he meant? "And now for Flavia"? Had he already done some terrible thing to Daffy, or to Feely . . . or to Dogger?

Before I could even begin to imagine, he had seized my upper arm in a paralyzing grip, jabbing his thumb into the muscle as he had done before. I tried to scream, but nothing came out. I thought I was going to vomit.

I shook my head violently from side to side, but only after what seemed like an eternity did he release me.

"But first, Frank and Flavia are going to have a little talk," he said, in as pleasant a conversational tone as if we were strolling in the park, and I realized at that instant I was alone with a madman in my own personal Calcutta.

"I'm going to take the covering off your head, do you understand?"

I stood perfectly still, petrified.

"Listen to me, Flavia, and listen carefully. If you don't do exactly as I say, I'll kill you. It's that simple. Do you understand?"

I nodded my head a little.

"Good. Now keep still."

I could feel him tugging roughly at the knots he had tied in his jacket, and almost at once its slick silk lining began to slide across my face, then dropped away entirely.

The beam of his torch hit me like a hammer blow, blinding me with light.

I recoiled in shock. Flashing stars and patches of black flew alter-nately across my field of vision. I had been so long in darkness that even the light of a single match would have been excruciating, but Pemberton was shining a powerful torch directly—and deliberately—into my eyes.

Unable to throw up my hands to shield myself, I could only wrench my head away to one side, squeeze my eyes shut, and wait for the nausea to subside.

"Painful, isn't it?" he said. "But not half so painful as what I'm going to do if you lie to me again."

I opened my stinging eyes and tried to focus them on a dark corner of the pit.

"Look at me!" he demanded.

I turned my head and squinted at him with what must have been a truly horrible grimace. I could see nothing of the man behind the round lens of his torch, whose fierce beam was still burning into my brain like a gigantic white desert sun.

Slowly, taking his time about it, he swung the glaring beam away and pointed it at the floor. Somewhere behind the light he was no more than a voice in the darkness.

"You lied to me."

I gave something like a shrug.

"You lied to me," Pemberton repeated more loudly, and this time I could hear the strain in his voice. "There was nothing hidden in that clock but the Penny Black."

So he *had* been to Buckshaw! My heart was fluttering like a caged bird.

"Mngg," I said.

Pemberton thought this over for a moment but could make nothing of it.

"I'm going to take the handkerchief out of your mouth, but first let me show you something."

He picked up his tweed jacket from the floor of the pit and reached into the pocket. When his hand came out, it was holding a shiny object of glass and metal. It was Bonepenny's syringe! He held it out for my inspection.

"You were looking for this, weren't you? At the inn *and* in your garden? And here it was all the while!"

He laughed through his nose like a pig and sat down on the steps.

Holding the torch between his knees, he held the syringe upright as he rummaged once more in the jacket and pulled out a small brown bottle. I barely had time to read the label before he removed the stopper and swiftly filled the syringe.

"I expect you know what this stuff is, don't you, Miss Smart-Pants?"

I met his eye but gave no other sign I'd heard him.

"And don't think I don't know precisely how and where to inject it. I didn't spend all those hours in the dissecting room at the London Hospital for nothing. Once I'd knocked out old Bony, the actual injection was almost ridiculously simple: angle in a bit to the side, through the *splenius capitus* and *semispinalis capitis*, puncture the atlantoaxial ligament, and slide the needle over the arch of the axis. And whap! It's lights out. The carbon tet evaporates in no time, with hardly a trace. The perfect crime, if I may say so myself."

Just as I had deduced! But now I knew *precisely* how he'd done it! The man was stark, staring mad.

"Now listen," he said. "I'm going to take that handkerchief out of your mouth and you are going to tell me what you've done with the Ulster Avengers. One wrong word . . . one wrong move and . . . "

Holding the syringe upright, almost touching my nose, he squeezed the plunger slightly. A few drops of the carbon tetrachloride appeared for an instant, like dew, at the point of the needle, then dripped onto the floor. My nose caught the familiar reek of the stuff.

Pemberton put the torch on the steps and adjusted its position to illuminate my face. He placed the syringe beside it.

"Open," he said.

This is what rushed through my mind: He would stick a thumb and forefinger into my mouth to remove the handkerchief. I would bite down with all my might—bite them clean off!

But then what? I was still bound hand and foot, and even badly bitten, Pemberton could easily kill me.

I opened my aching jaws a little.

"Wider," he said, holding back. Then quick as a wink he darted in and fished the sodden handkerchief from my mouth. For a single instant the light of the torch was blocked by the shadow of his hand, so that he did not see, as I saw, the slightest flash of orange as the wet ball dropped in darkness to the floor.

"Thank you," I whispered hoarsely, making my first move in the second part of the game.

Pemberton seemed taken aback.

"Someone must have found them," I croaked. "The stamps, I mean. I put them in the clock—I swear it."

I knew instantly that I had gone too far. If I were telling the truth, Pemberton no longer had any reason to keep me alive. I was the only one who knew that he was a killer.

"Unless . . . " I added hastily.

"Unless? Unless what?"

He fell on my words like a jackal on a downed antelope.

"My feet," I whimpered. "The pain. I can't think. I can't . . . Please, at least loosen them—just a bit."

"All right," he said, with surprisingly little thought. "But I'm leaving your hands tied. That way you won't be going anywhere."

I nodded eagerly.

Pemberton knelt down and loosened the buckle of his belt. As the leather dropped from my ankles I gathered my strength and kicked him in the teeth.

As he reeled back, his head cracked against the concrete, and I heard the sound of a glass object hitting the floor and skipping away into the corner. Pemberton slid heavily down the wall to a sitting position as I limped towards the steps.

Up I went . . . one . . . two . . . my clumsy feet kicked the torch, which went tumbling end over end down onto the floor of the pit where it came to rest with its beam illuminating the sole of one of Pemberton's shoes.

Three . . . four . . . my feet felt like stumps hacked off at the ankles. Five . . .

Surely by now my head must be above the level of the pit, but if it was, the room was in darkness. There was no more than a faint blood-red glow from the windows in the folding door. It must be dark outside; I must have slept for hours.

As I tried to remember where the door was, there was a scrabbling in the pit. The beam of the torch arced madly across the ceiling and suddenly Pemberton was up the steps and upon me.

He threw his arms around me and squeezed until I couldn't breathe. I could hear the bones crackling in my shoulders and elbows.

I tried to kick him in the shins, but he was quickly overpowering me.

To and fro we went, across the room, like spinning tops.

"No!" he shouted, overbalancing, and fell backward into the pit, dragging me with him.

He hit the bottom with an awful thud and at the same instant I landed on top of him. I heard him gasp in the darkness. Had he broken his back? Or would he soon be on his feet again, shaking me like a rag doll?

With a sudden eruption of strength, Pemberton threw me off, and I went flying, facedown, into a corner of the pit. Like an inchworm, I wiggled my way up onto my knees, but it was too late: Pemberton had a fierce grip on my arm, and was dragging me towards the steps.

It was almost too easy: He squatted and grabbed the torch from where it had fallen, then reached out towards the stairs. I thought the syringe had been knocked to the floor, but it must have been the bottle I heard, for a moment later I caught a quick glimpse of the needle in his hand—then felt it pricking the back of my neck.

My only thought was to stall for time.

"You killed Professor Twining, didn't you?" I gasped. "You and Bonepenny."

This seemed to catch him unawares. I felt his grip relax ever so slightly.

"What makes you think that?" he breathed into my ear.

"It was Bonepenny on the roof," I said. "Bonepenny who shouted '*Vale!*' He mimicked Mr. Twining's voice. It was you who dumped his body down the hole."

Pemberton sucked air in through his nose. "Did Bonepenny tell you that?"

"I found the cap and gown," I said, "under the tiles. I figured it out myself."

"You're a very clever girl," he said, almost regretfully.

"And now you've killed Bonepenny the stamps are yours. At least, they would be if you knew where they were."

This seemed to infuriate him. He tightened his grip on my arm, again drilling the ball of his thumb into the muscle. I screamed in agony.

"Five words, Flavia," he hissed. "Where are the bloody stamps?"

In the long silence that followed, in the numbing pain, my mind took refuge in flight.

Was this the end of Flavia? I wondered.

If so, was Harriet watching over me? Was she sitting at this very moment on a cloud with her legs dangling over, saying, "Oh no, Flavia! Don't do this; don't say that! Danger, Flavia! Danger!"

If she was, I couldn't hear her; perhaps I was farther removed from Harriet than Feely and Daffy. Perhaps she had loved me less.

It was a sad fact that of Harriet's three children I was the only one who retained no real memories of her. Feely, like a miser, had experienced and hoarded seven years of her mother's love. And Daffy insisted that, even though she was hardly three when Harriet disappeared, she had a perfectly clear recollection of a slim and laughing young woman who dressed her up in a starched dress and bonnet, set her down on a blanket on a sunlit lawn, and took her photograph with a folding camera before presenting her with a gherkin pickle.

Another jab brought me back to reality—the needle was at my brain stem.

"The Ulster Avengers. Where are they?"

I pointed a finger to the corner of the pit where the handkerchief lay balled up in the shadows. As the beam of Pemberton's torch danced towards it, I looked away, then looked up, as the old-time saints were said to do when seeking for salvation.

I heard it before I saw it. There was a muffled whirring noise, as if a giant mechanical pterodactyl were flapping about outside the Pit Shed. A moment later, there was the most frightful crash and a rain of falling glass.

The room above us, beyond the mouth of the pit, erupted into brilliant yellow light, and through it clouds of steam drifted like little puffing souls of the departed.

Still rooted to the spot, I stood staring straight up into the air at the oddly familiar apparition that sat shuddering above the pit.

I've snapped, I thought. I've gone insane.

Directly above my head, trembling like a living thing, was the undercarriage of Harriet's Rolls-Royce.

Before I could blink, I heard the sound of its doors opening and feet hitting the floor above me.

Pemberton made a leap for the stairs, scrabbling up them like a trapped rat. At the top he paused, trying wildly to claw his way between the lip of the pit and the front bumper of the Phantom.

A disembodied hand appeared and seized him by the collar, dragging him up out of the pit like a fish from a pond. His shoes vanished into the light above me, and I heard a voice—Dogger's voice!—saying, "Pardon my elbow."

There was a sickening crunch and something hit the floor above me like a sack of turnips.

I was still in a daze when the apparition appeared. All in white it was, slipping easily through the narrow gap between chrome and concrete before making its rapid, flapping descent down into the pit.

As it threw its arms around me and sobbed on my shoulder, I could feel the thin body shaking like a leaf.

"Silly little fool! Silly little fool!" it cried over and over, its raw red lips pressing into my neck.

"Feely!" I said, struck stupid with surprise, "you're getting oil all over your best dress!"

OUTSIDE THE PIT SHED, in Cow Lane, it was a fantasy: Feely was on her knees sobbing, her arms wrapped fiercely round my waist. As I stood there motionless, it was as if everything dissolved between us, and for a moment Feely and I were one creature bathing in the moonlight of the shadowed lane.

And then everyone in Bishop's Lacey seemed to materialize, coming slowly forward out of the darkness, clucking like aldermen at the torchlit scene, and at the gaping hole where the door of the Pit Shed had been; telling one another what they had been doing when the sound of the crash had echoed through the village. It was like a scene from that play *Brigadoon*, where the village comes slowly back to life for a single day every hundred years.

Harriet's Phantom, its beautiful radiator punctured by having been used as a battering ram, now stood steaming quietly in front of the Pit Shed and leaking water softly into the dust. Several of the more muscular villagers—one of them Tully Stoker, I noticed—had pushed the heavy vehicle backwards to allow Feely to lead me up out of the pit and into the fierce intensity and the glare of its great round headlamps.

Feely had got to her feet but was still clinging to me like a limpet to a battleship, babbling on excitedly.

"We followed him, you see. Dogger knew that you hadn't come home, and when he spotted someone prowling round the house . . . "

These were more consecutive words than she had ever spoken to me in my entire lifetime, and I stood there savoring them a bit.

"He called the police, of course; then he said that if we followed the man . . . if we kept the headlamps off and kept well back . . . Oh, God! You should have seen us flying through the lanes!"

Good old silent Roller, I thought. Father was going to be furious, though, when he saw the damage.

Miss Mountjoy stood off to one side, pulling a woolen shawl tightly about her shoulders and glaring balefully at the splintered cavern where the door of the Pit Shed had been, as if such wholesale desecration of library property were beyond the last straw. I tried to catch her eye, but she looked nervously away in the direction of her cottage as if she'd had too much excitement for one evening and ought to be getting home.

Mrs. Mullet was there, too, with a short, roly-poly dumpling of a man visibly restraining her. This must be her husband, Alf, I thought: not at all the Jack Spratt I had imagined. Had she been by herself, Mrs. M would have dashed in and thrown her arms round me and cried, but Alf seemed to be more aware that public displays of familiarity were not quite right. When I gave her a vague smile, she dabbed at one of her eyes with a fingertip.

At that moment, Dr. Darby arrived upon the scene as casually as if he had been out for an evening stroll. In spite of his relaxed manner, I couldn't help noticing that he had brought his black medical bag. His surgery-cum-residence was just round the corner in the High Street, and he must have heard the crash of breaking wood and glass. He looked me over keenly from head to toe.

"Keeping well, Flavia?" he asked as he leaned in for a close look at my eyes.

"Perfectly well, thank you, Dr. Darby," I said pleasantly. "And you?"

He reached for his crystal mints. Before the paper sack was halfway out of his pocket, I was salivating like a dog; hours of captivity and the gag had made the inside of my mouth taste like a Victorian ball-float.

Dr. Darby rummaged for a moment among the mints, carefully selected the one that seemed most desirable, and popped it into his mouth. A moment later he was on his way home.

The little crowd made way as a motorcar turned off into Cow Lane from the High Street. As it bumped to a stop beside the stone wall, its headlamps illuminated two figures standing together beneath an oak: Mary and Ned. They did not come forward, but stood grinning at me shyly from the shadows.

Had Feely seen them there together? I don't believe she had because she was still prattling on tearfully to me about the rescue. If she had spotted them, I might quickly have found myself referee at a rustic bare-knuckles contest: up to my knees in torn-out hair. Daffy once told me that when it comes to a good dustup, it's generally the squire's daughter who gets in the first punch, and no one knows better than I that Feely has it in her. Still, I'm proud to say that I had the presence of mind—and the guts—to give Ned a furtive congratulatory thumbs-up.

The rear door of the Vauxhall opened and Inspector Hewitt climbed out. At the same time, Detective Sergeants Graves and Woolmer unfolded themselves from the front seats and stepped with surprising delicacy out into Cow Lane.

Sergeant Woolmer strode quickly to where Dogger was holding Pemberton in some kind of contorted and painful-looking grip, which caused him to be bent over like a statue of Atlas with the world on his shoulders.

"I'll take him now, sir," Sergeant Woolmer said, and a moment later I thought I heard the *snick* of nickel-plated handcuffs.

Dogger watched as Pemberton slouched off towards the police car, then turned and came slowly towards me. As he approached, Feely whispered excitedly into my ear, "It was Dogger who thought of using the tractor battery to get the Royce started up. Be sure to compliment him."

And she dropped my hand and stepped away.

Dogger stood in front of me, his hands hanging down at his sides. If he'd had a hat, he would have been twisting it. We stood there looking at one another.

I wasn't about to begin my thanks by chatting about batteries. I wanted rather to say just the right thing: brave words that would be talked about in Bishop's Lacey for years to come.

A dark shape moving in front of the Vauxhall's headlamps caught my attention as, for a moment, it cast Dogger and me into the shadows.

A familiar figure, silhouetted in black and white, stood out like a paper cutout against the glare: Father.

He began shambling slowly, almost shyly, towards me. But when he noticed Dogger at my side, he stopped and, as if he had just thought of something vitally important, turned aside to have a few quiet words with Inspector Hewitt.

Miss Cool, the postmistress, gave me a pleasant nod but kept herself well back, as if I were somehow a different Flavia than the one who— had it been only two days ago?—had bought one-and-six worth of sweets from her shop.

"Feely," I said, turning to her, "do me a favor: Pop back into the pit and fetch me my handkerchief—and be sure to bring me what's wrapped up inside it. Your dress is already filthy, so it won't make much difference. There's a good girl."

Feely's jaw dropped about a yard, and I thought for a moment she was going to punch me in the teeth. Her whole face grew as red as her lips. And then suddenly she spun on her heel and vanished into the shadows of the Pit Shed.

I turned to Dogger to deliver my soon-to-be-classic remark, but he beat me to it.

"My, Miss Flavia," he said quietly. "It's turning out to be a lovely evening, isn't it?"

twenty-seven

INSPECTOR HEWITT WAS STANDING IN THE CENTER OF MY laboratory, turning slowly round, his gaze sweeping across the scientific equipment and the chemical cabinets like the beam from a lighthouse. When he had made a complete circle, he stopped, then made another in the opposite direction.

"Extraordinary!" he said, drawing the word out. "Simply extraordinary!"

A ray of deliciously warm sunlight shone in through the tall casement windows, illuminating from within a beaker of red liquid that was just coming to a boil. I decanted half of the stuff into a china cup and handed it to the Inspector. He stared at it dubiously.

"It's tea," I said. "Assam from Fortnum and Mason. I hope you don't mind it being warmed-over."

"Warmed-over is all we drink at the station," he said. "I settle for no other."

As he sipped, he wandered slowly round the room, examining the chemical apparatus with professional interest. He took down a jar or two from the shelves and held each one up to the light, then bent down to peer through the eyepiece of my Leitz. I could see that he was having some difficulty in getting to the point.

"Beautiful bit of bone china," he said at last, raising the cup above his head to read the maker's name on the bottom.

"Quite early Spode," I said. "Albert Einstein and George Bernard

Shaw drank tea from that very cup when they visited Great-Uncle Tarquin—not both at the same time, of course."

"One wonders what they might have made of one another?" Inspector Hewitt said, glancing at me.

"One wonders," I said, glancing back.

The Inspector took another sip of his tea. Somehow, he seemed restless, as if there was something he would like to say, but couldn't find a way to begin.

"It's been a difficult case," he said. "Bizarre, really. The man whose body you found in the garden was a total stranger—or seemed to be. All we knew was that he came from Norway."

"The snipe," I said.

"I beg your pardon?"

"The dead jack snipe on our kitchen doorstep. Jack snipe are never found in England until autumn. It had to have been brought from Norway—in a pie. That's how you knew, isn't it?"

The Inspector looked puzzled.

"No," he said. "Bonepenny was wearing a new pair of shoes stamped with the name of a shoemaker in Stavanger."

"Oh," I said.

"From that, we were able to follow his trail quite easily." As he spoke, Inspector Hewitt's hands drew a map in the air. "Our inquiries here and abroad told us that he'd taken the boat from Stavanger to Newcastle-upon-Tyne, and traveled from there by rail to York, then on to Doddingsley. From Doddingsley he took a taxi to Bishop's Lacey."

Aha! Precisely as I had surmised.

"Exactly," I said. "And Pemberton—or should I say, Bob Stanley?—followed him, but stopped short at Doddingsley. He stayed at the Jolly Coachman."

One of Inspector Hewitt's eyebrows rose up like a cobra. "Oh?" he said, too casually. "How do you know that?"

"I rang up the Jolly Coachman and spoke with Mr. Cleaver."

"Is that all?"

"They were in it together, just as they were in the murder of Mr. Twining."

"Stanley denies that," he said. "Claims he had nothing to do with it. Pure as the driven snow, and all that."

"But he told me in the Pit Shed that he had killed Bonepenny! Besides that, he more or less admitted that my theory was correct: The suicide of Mr. Twining was a staged illusion."

"Well, that remains to be seen. We're looking into it, but it's going to take some time, although I must say your father has been most helpful. He's now told us the whole story of what led up to poor Twining's death. I only wish he had decided earlier to be so accommodating. We might have saved . . .

"I'm sorry," he said. "I was speculating."

"My abduction," I said.

I had to admire how quickly the Inspector changed the subject.

"Getting back to the present," he said. "Let me see if I've got this right: You think Bonepenny and Stanley were confederates?"

"They were always confederates," I said. "Bonepenny stole stamps and Stanley sold them abroad to unscrupulous collectors. But somehow they had never managed to dispose of the two Ulster Avengers; those were simply too well known. And with one of them having been stolen from the King, it would have been far too risky for any collector to be caught with them in his collection."

"Interesting," the Inspector said. "And?"

"They were planning to blackmail Father, but somewhere along the line, they must have had a falling-out. Bonepenny was coming over from Stavanger to do the deed, and at some point Stanley realized that he could follow him, kill him at Buckshaw, take the stamps, and leave the country. As simple as that. And it would all be blamed on Father. And so it was," I added, with a reproachful look.

There was an awkward silence.

"Look, Flavia," he said at last. "I didn't really have much choice, you know. There were no other viable suspects."

"What about me," I said. "I was at the scene of the crime." I waved my hand at the bottles of chemicals that lined the walls. "After all, I know a lot about poisons. I might be considered a very dangerous person."

"Hmm," the Inspector said. "An interesting point. And you *were* on the spot at the time of death. If things hadn't gone exactly as they did, it might well be your neck in the noose."

I hadn't thought of that. A goose walked over my grave and I shivered.

The Inspector went on. "Arguing against it, however, are your physical size, your lack of any real motive, and the fact that you haven't exactly made yourself scarce. Your average murderer generally gives the police as wide a berth as possible, whereas you . . . well, *ubiquitous* is the word that springs to mind. Now then, you were saying?"

"Stanley ambushed Bonepenny in our garden. Bonepenny was a diabetic, and—"

"Ah," the Inspector said, almost to himself. "Insulin! We didn't think to test for that."

"No," I said. "Not insulin: carbon tetrachloride. Bonepenny died from having carbon tetrachloride injected into his brain stem. Stanley bought a bottle of the stuff from Johns, the chemists, in Doddingsley. I saw their label on the bottle when he filled the syringe in the Pit Shed. You've probably already found it under all the rubbish."

I could tell by his face that they hadn't.

"Then it must have rolled down the pipe," I said. "There's an old drain that runs down to the river. Someone will have to fish it out."

Poor Sergeant Graves! I thought.

"Stanley stole the syringe from the kit in Bonepenny's room at the Thirteen Drakes," I added, without thinking. Damn!

The Inspector pounced. "How do you know what was in Bonepenny's room?" he asked sharply.

"Uh . . . I'm coming to that," I said. "In a few minutes.

"Stanley believed you'd never detect any possible traces of carbon tetrachloride in Bonepenny's brain. Jolly good thing you didn't. You might have assumed it came from one of Father's bottles. There are gallons of the stuff in the study."

Inspector Hewitt pulled out his notebook and scrawled a couple of words, which I assumed were *carbon tetrachloride*.

"I know it was carbon tet because Bonepenny blew the last whiff of the stuff into my face with his dying breath," I said, wrinkling my nose and making an appropriate face.

If an Inspector's complexion can be said to go white, Inspector Hewitt's complexion went white.

"You're certain about that?"

"I'm quite competent with the chlorinated hydrocarbons, thank you."

"Are you telling me that Bonepenny was still alive when you found him?"

"Only just," I said. "He . . . uh . . . passed away almost immediately."

There was another one of those long, crypt-like silences.

"Here," I said, "I'll show you how it was done."

I picked up a yellow lead pencil, gave it a couple of turns in the sharpener, and went to the corner where the articulated skeleton dangled at the end of its wire.

"This was given to my great-uncle, Tarquin, by the naturalist Frank Buckland," I said, giving the skull an affectionate rub. "I call him Yorick."

I did not tell the Inspector that Buckland, in his old age, had given his gift in recognition of young Tar's great promise. "To the Bright Future of Science," Buckland had written on his card.

I brought the sharpened point of the pencil round to the top of the spinal column, shoving it slowly in under the skull as I repeated Pemberton's words in the Pit Shed:

"'Angle in a bit to the side . . . in through the *splenius capitus* and *semispinalis capitis*, puncture the atlantoaxial ligament, and slide the needle over the—'"

"Thank you, Flavia," the Inspector said abruptly. "That's quite enough. You're quite sure that's what he said?"

"His precise words," I said. "I had to look them up in *Gray's Anatomy*. *The Children's Encyclopaedia* has several plates, but not nearly enough detail."

Inspector Hewitt rubbed his chin.

"I'm sure Dr. Darby could find the needle mark on the back of Bonepenny's neck," I added helpfully, "if he knew where to look. He might inspect the sinuses, as well. Carbon tetrachloride is stable in air, and might still be trapped there, since the man was no longer breathing.

"And," I added, "you might remind him that Bonepenny had a drink at the Thirteen Drakes just before he set out to walk to Buckshaw."

The Inspector still looked puzzled.

"The effects of carbon tetrachloride are intensified by alcohol," I explained.

"And," he asked with a casual smile, "do you have any particular theory about why the stuff might still be in his sinuses? I'm no chemist, but I believe carbon tetrachloride evaporates very rapidly."

I did have a reason, but it was not one I was willing to share with just anyone, particularly not the police. Bonepenny had been suffering from an extremely nasty head cold: a head cold which, when he breathed the word "*Vale*" into my face, he had transmitted to me. Thanks buckets, Horace! I thought.

I also suspected that Bonepenny's plugged nasal passages might well have preserved the injected carbon tetrachloride, which is insoluble in water—or in snot, for that matter—which would also have helped inhibit the intake of outside air.

"No," I said. "But you might suggest that the lab in London carry out the test suggested by the British Pharmacopoeia."

"Can't say I recall it, offhand," Inspector Hewitt said.

"It's a very pretty procedure," I said. "One that checks the limit of free chlorine when iodine is liberated from cadmium iodide. I'm sure they're familiar with it. I'd offer to do it myself, but I don't expect Scotland Yard would be comfortable handing over bits of Bonepenny's brain to an eleven-year-old."

Inspector Hewitt stared at me for what seemed several aeons.

"All right," he said at last, "let's have a dekko."

"At what?" I said, putting on my mask of injured innocence.

"Whatever you've done. Let's have a look at it."

"But I haven't done anything," I said. "I—"

"Don't play me for a fool, Flavia. No one who has had the pleasure of your acquaintance would ever believe for an instant that you haven't done your homework."

I grinned sheepishly. "It's over here," I said, moving towards a corner table upon which stood a glass tank shrouded with a damp tea towel.

I whisked the cloth away.

"Good Lord!" the Inspector said. "What in the name of—?"

He fairly gaped at the pinkish gray object that floated serenely in the tank.

"It's a nice bit of brain," I said. "I pinched it from the larder. Mrs. Mullet bought it at Carnforth's yesterday for supper tonight. She's going to be furious."

"And you've . . . ?" he said, flapping his hand.

"Yes, that's right. I've injected it with two and a half cubic centimeters of carbon tetrachloride. That's how much Bonepenny's syringe held.

"The average human brain weighs three pounds," I went on, "and that of the male perhaps a little more. I've cut an extra five ounces to allow for it."

"How did you find *that* out?" the Inspector asked.

"It's in one of the volumes of Arthur Mee's books. *The Children's Encyclopaedia* again, I think."

"And you've tested this . . . brain, for the presence of carbon tetrachloride?"

"Yes," I said, "but not until fifteen hours after I injected it. I judged that's how much time elapsed between the stuff being shot into Bonepenny's brain and the autopsy."

"And?"

"Still easily detectable," I said. "Child's play. Of course I used p-Aminodimethylaniline. That's rather a new test, but an elegant one. It was written up in *The Analyst* about five years ago. Pull up a stool and I'll show you."

"This isn't going to work, you know." Inspector Hewitt chuckled.

"Not work?" I said. "Of course it will work. I've already done it once."

"I mean you're not going to dazzle me with lab work and skate conveniently round the stamp. After all, that's what this whole thing is about, isn't it?"

He had me cornered. I had planned on saying nothing about the Ulster Avenger and then quietly handing it over to Father. Who would ever be the wiser?

"Look, I know you have it," he said. "We paid a visit to Dr. Kissing at Rook's End."

I tried to look unconvinced.

"And Bob Stanley, your Mr. Pemberton, has told us that you stole it from him."

Stole it from him? The idea! What cheek!

"It belongs to the King," I protested. "Bonepenny nicked it from an exhibition in London."

"Well, whomever it belongs to, it's stolen property, and my duty is to see that it's returned. All I need to know is how it came into your possession."

Drat the man! I could dodge it no longer. I was going to have to confess my trespasses at the Thirteen Drakes.

"Let's make a deal," I said.

Inspector Hewitt burst out laughing. "There are times, Miss de Luce," he said, "when you deserve a brass medal. And there are other times you deserve to be sent to your room with bread and water."

"And which one of those times is this?" I asked.

Hooo! Better watch your step, Flave.

He waggled his fingers at me. "I'm listening," he said.

"Well, I've been thinking," I told him. "Father's life hasn't been exactly pleasant lately. In the first place, you arrive at Buckshaw and before we know it you've charged him with murder."

"Hang on . . . hang on," the Inspector said. "We've already been through this. He was charged with murder because he confessed to it."

He did? This was something new.

"And no sooner had he done so, than along came Flavia. I had more confessions walking in the door than Our Lady of Lourdes on a Saturday night."

"I was just trying to protect him," I said. "At that point, I thought he might have done it."

"And whom was *he* trying to protect?" Inspector Hewitt asked, watching me carefully.

The answer, of course, was Dogger. That was what Father meant when he said "I feared as much" after I told him that Dogger, too, had overheard the scene in his study with Horace Bonepenny.

Father thought Dogger had killed the man; that much was clear. But why? Would Dogger have done it out of loyalty—or during one of his peculiar turns?

No—best to leave Dogger out of this. It was the least I could do.

"Probably me," I lied. "Father thought I had killed Bonepenny. After all, wasn't I the one who was found, so to speak, at the scene of the crime? He was trying to protect *me*."

"Do you really believe that?" the Inspector asked.

"It would be lovely to think so," I said.

"I'm sure he was," the Inspector said. "I'm quite sure he was. Now then, back to the stamp. I haven't forgotten about it, you know."

"Well, as I was saying, I'd like to do something for Father; something that will make him happy, even for a few hours. I'd like to give him the Ulster Avenger, even if it's only for a day or two. Let me do that, and I'll tell you everything I know. I promise."

The Inspector strolled over to the bookcase, fetched down a bound volume of the *Proceedings of the Chemical Society* for 1907, and blew a cloud of dust from the top of the spine. He leafed idly through its pages, as if looking for what to say next.

"You know," he said, "there is nothing my wife, Antigone, detests more than shopping. She told me once that she'd rather have a tooth filled than spend half an hour shopping for a leg of mutton. But shop she must, like it or not. It's her fate, she says. To dull the experience, she sometimes buys a little yellow booklet called *You and Your Stars*.

"I have to admit that up until now I've scoffed at some of the things she's read out to me at breakfast, but this morning my horoscope said, and I quote, 'Your patience will be tried to the utmost.' Do you suppose I could have been misjudging these things, Flavia?"

"Please!" I said, giving the word a gimlet twist.

"Twenty-four hours," he said, "and not a minute more."

And suddenly it all came gushing out, and I found myself babbling on about the dead jack snipe, Mrs. Mullet's really quite innocent (although inedible) custard pie, my rifling of Bonepenny's room at the inn, my finding of the stamps, my visits to Miss Mountjoy and Dr. Kissing, my encounters with Pemberton at the Folly and in the churchyard, and my captivity in the Pit Shed.

The only part I left out was the bit about my poisoning Feely's lipstick with an extract of poison ivy. Why confuse the Inspector with unnecessary details?

As I spoke, he made an occasional scribble in a little black notebook, whose pages, I noticed, were filled with arrows and cryptic signs that might have been inspired by an alchemical formulary of the Middle Ages.

"Am I in that?" I asked, pointing.

"You are," he said.

"May I have a look? Just a peek?"

Inspector Hewitt flipped the notebook shut. "No," he said. "It's a confidential police document."

"Do you actually spell out my name, or am I represented by one of those symbols?"

"You have your very own symbol," he said, shoving the book into his pocket. "Well, it's time I was getting along."

He stuck out a hand and gave me a firm handshake. "Good-bye, Flavia," he said. "It's been . . . something of an experience."

He went to the door and opened it.

"Inspector . . ."

He stopped and turned.

"What is it? My symbol, I mean."

"It's a *P*," he said. "Capital *P*."

"A *P*?" I asked, surprised. "What does *P* stand for?"

"Ah," he said, "that's best left to the imagination."

DAFFY WAS IN THE DRAWING ROOM, sprawled full-length on the carpet, reading *The Prisoner of Zenda*.

"Are you aware that you move your lips when you read?" I asked.

She ignored me. I decided to risk my life.

"Speaking of lips," I said, "where's Feely?"

"At the doctor's," she said. "She had some kind of allergic outbreak. Something she came in contact with."

Aha! My experiment had succeeded brilliantly! No one would ever know. As soon as I had a moment to myself, I'd record it in my notebook:

Tuesday, 6th of June 1950, 1:20 P.M. Success! Outcome as postulated. Justice is served.

I let out a quiet snort. Daffy must have heard it, for she rolled over and crossed her legs.

"Don't think for a moment you've got away with it," she said quietly.

"Huh?" I said. Innocent puzzlement was my specialty.

"What witch's brew did you put in her lipstick?"

"I haven't the faintest what you're talking about," I said.

"Have a peek at yourself in the looking-glass," Daffy said. "Watch you don't break it."

I turned and went slowly to the chimneypiece where a cloudy leftover from the Regency period hung sullenly reflecting the room.

I bent closer, peering at my image. At first I saw nothing other than my usual brilliant self, my violet eyes, my pale complexion: but as I stared, I began to notice more details in the ravaged mercury reflection.

There was a splotch on my neck. An angry red splotch! Where Feely had kissed me!

I let out a shriek of anguish.

"Feely said that before she'd been in the pit five seconds she'd paid you back in full."

Even before Daffy rolled over and went back to her stupid sword story, I had come up with a plan.

ONCE, WHEN I WAS ABOUT NINE, I had kept a diary about what it was like to be a de Luce, or at least what it was like to be this particular de Luce. I thought a great deal about how I felt and finally came to the conclusion that being Flavia de Luce was like being a sublimate: like the black crystal residue that is left on the cold glass of a test tube by the violet fumes of iodine. At the time, I thought it the perfect description, and nothing has happened over the past two years to change my mind.

As I have said, there is something lacking in the de Luces: some chemical bond, or lack of it, that ties their tongues whenever they are threatened by affection. It is as unlikely that one de Luce would ever tell another that she loved her as it is that one peak in the Himalayas would bend over and whisper sweet nothings to an adjacent crag.

This point was proven when Feely stole my diary, pried open the brass lock with a can opener from the kitchen, and read aloud from it while standing at the top of the great staircase dressed in clothing she had stolen from a neighbor's scarecrow.

These thoughts were in my mind as I approached the door of Father's study. I paused, unsure of myself. Did I really want to do this?

I knocked uncertainly on the door. There was a long silence before Father's voice said, "Come."

I twisted the knob and stepped into the room. At a table by the window, Father looked up for a moment from his magnifying lens, and then went on with his examination of a magenta stamp.

"May I speak?" I asked, aware, even as I said it, that it was an odd thing to be saying, and yet it seemed precisely the right choice of words.

Father put down the glass, removed his spectacles, and rubbed his eyes. He looked tired.

I reached into my pocket and pulled out the piece of blue writing paper into which I had folded the Ulster Avenger. I stepped forward like a supplicant, put the paper on his desk, and stepped back again.

Father opened it.

"Good Lord!" he said. "It's AA."

He put his spectacles back on and picked up his jeweler's loupe to peer at the stamp.

Now, I thought, comes my reward. I found myself focused on his lips, waiting for them to move.

"Where did you get this?" he said at last, in that soft voice of his that fixes its hearer like a butterfly on a pin.

"I found it," I said.

Father's gaze was military—unrelenting.

"Bonepenny must have dropped it," I said. "It's for you."

Father studied my face the way an astronomer studies a supernova.

"This is very decent of you, Flavia," he said at last, with some great effort.

And he handed me the Ulster Avenger.

"You must return it at once to its rightful owner."

"King George?"

Father nodded, somewhat sadly, I thought. "I don't know how you came to have this in your possession and I don't want to know. You've come this far on your own and now you must see it through."

"Inspector Hewitt wants me to hand it over to him."

Father shook his head. "Most kind of him," he said, "but also most official. No, Flavia, old AA here has been through many hands in its day, a few of them high and many low. You must see to it that your hands are the most worthy of them all."

"But how does one go about writing to the King?"

"I'm sure you'll find a way," Father said. "Please close the door on your way out."

AS IF TO COVER UP THE PAST, Dogger was shoveling muck from a wheelbarrow into the cucumber bed.

"Miss Flavia," he said, removing his hat and wiping his brow on his shirtsleeve.

"How should one address a letter to the King?" I asked.

Dogger leaned his shovel carefully against the greenhouse.

"Theoretically, or in actual practice?"

"In actual practice."

"Hmm," he said. "I think I should look it up somewhere."

"Hold on," I said. "Mrs. Mullet's *Inquire Within Upon Everything.*
She keeps it in the pantry."

"She's shopping in the village," Dogger said. "If we're quick about it,
we may well escape with our lives."

A minute later we were huddled in the pantry.

"Here it is," I said excitedly, as the book fell open in my hands. "But
wait—this was published sixty years ago. Would it still be correct?"

"Sure to be," Dogger said. "Things don't change as quickly in royal
circles as they do in yours and mine, nor should they."

The drawing room was empty. Daffy and Feely were off somewhere,
most likely planning their next attack.

I found a decent sheet of writing paper in a drawer, and then, dipping
the pen in the inkwell, I copied out the salutation from Mrs. Mullet's
greasy book, trying to make my handwriting as neat as possible:

Most Gracious Sovereign:

May it please Your Majesty,

Please find enclosed an item of considerable value belonging
to Your Majesty which was stolen earlier this year. How it fell
into my hands (a nice touch, I thought) is unimportant, but I can
assure Your Majesty that the criminal has been caught.

"Apprehended," Dogger said, reading over my shoulder.

I changed it.

"What else?"

"Nothing," Dogger said. "Just sign it. Kings prefer brevity."

Being careful not to blot the page, I copied the closing from the
book:

I remain, with the profoundest veneration, Your Majesty's most
faithful subject and dutiful servant.

Flavia de Luce (Miss)

"Perfect!" Dogger said.

I folded the letter neatly, making an extra-sharp crease with my thumb. I slipped it into one of Father's best envelopes and wrote the address:

> His Royal Highness King George the Sixth
> Buckingham Palace, London, SWI
> England

"Shall I mark it Personal?"

"Good idea," Dogger said.

A WEEK LATER, I was cooling my bare feet in the waters of the artificial lake, revising my notes on coniine, the chief alkaloid in poison hemlock, when Dogger appeared suddenly, waving something in his hand.

"Miss Flavia!" he called, and then he waded across to the island, boots and all.

His trouser legs were soaking wet, and although he stood there dripping like Poseidon, his grin was as bright as the summer afternoon.

He handed me an envelope that was as soft and white as goose down.

"Shall I open it?" I asked.

"I believe it's addressed to you."

Dogger winced as I tore open the flap and pulled out the single sheet of creamy paper which lay folded inside:

> My Dear Miss de Luce,
>
> I am most grateful to you for your recent communication and for the restoration of the splendid item contained therein, which has, as you must know, played a remarkable part, not only in the history of my own family, but in the history of England.
> Please accept my heartfelt thanks.

And it was signed simply "George."

acknowledgments

Whenever I pick up a new book, I always turn to the acknowledgments first because they provide me with a sort of aerial photograph of the work: a large-scale map that shows something of the wider environment in which the book was written, where it has been, and how it came to be.

No work-in-progress was ever more kindly nurtured than *The Sweetness at the Bottom of the Pie*, and it gives me tremendous pleasure to express my gratitude to the Crime Writers' Association and the panel of judges who chose the book for the Debut Dagger Award: Philip Gooden, chair of the CWA; Margaret Murphy; Emma Hargrave; Bill Massey; Sara Menguc; Keshini Naidoo; and Sarah Turner.

Additional and special thanks are due to Margaret Murphy, who not only chaired the Debut Dagger Awards Committee, but also stole time from her own hectic schedule on awards day to personally welcome a wandering alien to London.

To Meg Gardiner, Chris High, and Ann Cleeves for making me feel as if I'd known them all my life.

To Louise Penny, a Dagger winner herself, whose warm generosity and encouragement is exemplified in the beacon her website has become for aspiring writers. Louise truly knows how to "give back" for the things she has received. Besides that, her Chief Inspector Armand Gamache novels are simply terrific!

To my agent, Denise Bukowski, for flying the Atlantic to be there and, in spite of my jet lag, for getting me to the church on time.

Again, to Bill Massey, of Orion Books, who had faith enough to buy the novel—and the series—on the strength of that first handful of pages, and for treating me to a memorable lunch at the onetime Bucket of Blood, in Covent Garden, the very spot where the poet and critic John Dryden was set upon by ruffians in a passageway. No one has ever been blessed with a better editor than Bill. He is truly a kindred spirit!

To Kate Miciak and Molly Boyle, of Bantam Dell in New York, and Kristin Cochrane of Doubleday Canada, for their early faith and encouragement.

Special thanks to Janet Cooke, vice president, director of sales, the Bantam Dell Publishing Group, whose enthusiasm has contributed so much to the world of Flavia de Luce.

To Robyn Karney and Connie Munro, copy editors at Orion Books and at Bantam Dell, respectively, for their excellent and perceptive suggestions. And to Emma Wallace and Genevieve Pegg, also at Orion Books, for their enthusiastic and friendly welcome.

To the helpful and friendly staff of the British Postal Museum and Archive, at Freeling House, Phoenix Place, London, for so cheerfully answering my questions and allowing me access to materials in their care relating to the history of the Penny Black.

To my longtime Saskatoon friends and connoisseurs of crime, Mary Gilliland and Allan and Janice Cushon for putting into my hands the Edwardian equivalent of the Internet: a complete set of the eleventh edition (1911) of the *Encyclopaedia Britannica*, which must surely be every detective novelist's dream.

To David Whiteside, of the Bukowski Agency, for his yeoman work in bringing order to the necessary mountains of paperwork and red tape.

To my dear friends Dr. John and Janet Harland, who were there at every step along the way with many useful and often brilliant suggestions. Without their enthusiasm, *The Sweetness at the Bottom of the Pie* would have been a lesser book and much less fun to write.

All of these kind people have given me their best advice; if any mistakes have crept in, they are mine alone.

And finally, with love and eternal thanks to my wife, Shirley, who urged me—no, insisted that I allow Flavia and the de Luce family to emerge from the bundle of notes in which they had been languishing for far too long.

The Weed
That Strings the
Hangman's Bag

Again, for Shirley

SIR WALTER RALEIGH TO HIS SON

Three things there be that prosper up apace,
And flourish while they grow asunder far;
But on a day, they meet all in a place,
And when they meet, they one another mar.

And they be these; the Wood, the Weed, the Wag:
The Wood is that that makes the gallows tree;
The Weed is that that strings the hangman's bag;
The Wag, my pretty knave, betokens thee.

Now mark, dear boy—while these assemble not,
Green springs the tree, hemp grows, the wag is wild;
But when they meet, it makes the timber rot,
It frets the halter, and it chokes the child.

one

I WAS LYING DEAD IN THE CHURCHYARD. AN HOUR HAD CREPT by since the mourners had said their last sad farewells.

At twelve o'clock, just at the time we should otherwise have been sitting down to lunch, there had been the departure from Buckshaw: my polished rosewood coffin being brought out of the drawing room, carried slowly down the broad stone steps to the driveway, and slid with heart-breaking ease into the open door of the waiting hearse, crushing beneath it a little bouquet of wildflowers that had been laid gently inside by one of the grieving villagers.

Then there had been the long drive down the avenue of chestnuts to the Mulford Gates, whose rampant griffins looked away as we passed, though whether in sadness or in apathy I would never know.

Dogger, Father's devoted jack-of-all-trades, had paced in measured step alongside the slow hearse, his head bowed, his hand resting lightly on its roof, as if to shield my remains from something that only he could see. At the gates, one of the undertaker's mutes had finally coaxed him, by using hand signals, into a hired motorcar.

And so they had brought me to the village of Bishop's Lacey, passing somberly through the same green lanes and dusty hedgerows I had bicycled every day when I was alive.

At the heaped-up churchyard of St. Tancred's, they had taken me gently from the hearse and borne me at a snail's pace up the path beneath the limes. Here, they had put me down for a moment in the new-mown grass.

Then had come the service at the gaping grave, and there had been a note of genuine grief in the voice of the vicar as he pronounced the traditional words.

It was the first time I'd heard the Order for the Burial of the Dead from this vantage point. We had attended last year, with Father, the funeral of old Mr. Dean, the village greengrocer. His grave, in fact, was just a few yards from where I was presently lying. It had already caved in, leaving not much more than a rectangular depression in the grass that was, more often than not, filled with stagnant rainwater.

My oldest sister, Ophelia, said it collapsed because Mr. Dean had been resurrected and was no longer bodily present, while Daphne, my other sister, said it was because he had plummeted through into an older grave whose occupant had disintegrated.

I thought of the soup of bones below: the soup of which I was about to become just another ingredient.

Flavia Sabina de Luce, 1939–1950, they would cause to be carved on my gravestone, a modest and tasteful gray marble thing with no room for false sentiments.

Pity. If I'd lived long enough, I'd have left written instructions calling for a touch of Wordsworth:

A maid whom there were none to praise
And very few to love.

And if they'd balked at that, I'd have left this as my second choice:

Truest hearts by deeds unkind
To despair are most inclined.

Only Feely, who had played and sung them at the piano, would recognize the lines from Thomas Campion's Third Book of Airs, and she would be too consumed by guilty grief to tell anyone.

My thoughts were interrupted by the vicar's voice.

". . . *earth to earth, ashes to ashes, dust to dust, in sure and certain hope of the Resurrection to eternal life, through our Lord Jesus Christ; who shall change our vile body . . .*"

And suddenly they had gone, leaving me there alone—alone to listen for the worms.

This was it: the end of the road for poor Flavia.

By now the family would already be back at Buckshaw, gathered round the long refectory table: Father seated in his usual stony silence, Daffy and Feely hugging one another with slack, tearstained faces as Mrs. Mullet, our cook, brought in a platter of baked meats.

I remembered something that Daffy had once told me when she was devouring *The Odyssey*: that baked meats, in ancient Greece, were traditional funeral fare, and I had replied that, in view of Mrs. Mullet's cooking, not much had changed in two and a half thousand years.

But now that I was dead, I thought, perhaps I ought to practice being somewhat more charitable.

Dogger, of course, would be inconsolable. Dear Dogger: butler-cum-chauffeur-cum-valet-cum-gardener-cum-estate-manager: a poor shell-shocked soul whose capabilities ebbed and flowed like the Severn tides; Dogger, who had recently saved my life and forgotten it by the next morning. I should miss him terribly.

And I should miss my chemistry laboratory. I thought of all the golden hours I'd spent there in that abandoned wing of Buckshaw, blissfully alone among the flasks, the retorts, and the cheerily bubbling tubes and beakers. And to think that I'd never see them again. It was almost too much to bear.

I listened to the rising wind as it whispered overhead in the branches of the yew trees. It was already growing cool here in the shadows of St. Tancred's tower, and it would soon be dark.

Poor Flavia! Poor, stone-cold-dead Flavia.

By now, Daffy and Feely would be wishing that they hadn't been so downright rotten to their little sister during her brief eleven years on this earth.

At the thought, a tear started down my cheek.

Would Harriet be waiting to welcome me to Heaven?

Harriet was my mother, who had died in a mountaineering accident a year after I was born. Would she recognize me after ten years? Would she still be dressed in the mountain-climbing suit she was wearing when she met her end, or would she have swapped it by now for a white robe?

Well, whatever she was wearing, I knew it would be stylish.

There was a sudden clatter of wings: a noise that echoed loudly from the stone wall of the church, amplified to an alarming volume by a half acre of stained glass and the leaning gravestones that hemmed me in. I froze.

Could it be an angel—or more likely, an archangel—coming down to return Flavia's precious soul to Paradise? If I opened my eyes the merest slit, I could see through my eyelashes, but only dimly.

No such luck: It was one of the tattered jackdaws that were always hanging round St. Tancred's. These vagabonds had been nesting in the tower since its thirteenth-century stonemasons had packed up their tools and departed.

Now the idiotic bird had landed clumsily on top of a marble finger that pointed to Heaven, and was regarding me coolly, its head cocked to one side, with its bright, ridiculous boot-button eyes.

Jackdaws never learn. No matter how many times I played this trick they always, sooner or later, came flapping down from the tower to investigate. To the primeval mind of a jackdaw, any body horizontal in a churchyard could have only one meaning: food.

As I had done a dozen times before, I leapt to my feet and flung the stone that was concealed in my curled fingers. I missed—but then I nearly always did.

With an "awk" of contempt, the thing sprang into the air and flapped off behind the church, towards the river.

Now that I was on my feet, I realized I was hungry. Of course I was! I hadn't eaten since breakfast. For a moment I wondered vaguely if I might find a few leftover jam tarts or a bit of cake in the kitchen of the parish hall. The St. Tancred's Ladies' Auxiliary had gathered the night before, and there was always the chance.

As I waded through the knee-high grass, I heard a peculiar snuffling sound, and for a moment, I thought the saucy jackdaw had come back to have the last word.

I stopped and listened.

Nothing.

And then it came again.

I find it sometimes a curse and sometimes a blessing that I have inherited Harriet's acute sense of hearing, since I am able, as I am fond of telling Feely, to hear things that would make your hair stand on end.

One of the sounds to which I am particularly attuned is the sound of someone crying.

It was coming from the northwest corner of the churchyard—from somewhere near the wooden shed in which the sexton kept his grave-digging tools. As I crept slowly forward on tiptoe, the sound grew louder: Someone was having a good old-fashioned cry, of the knock-'em-down-drag-'em-out variety.

It is a simple fact of nature that while most men can walk right past a weeping woman as if their eyes are blinkered and their ears stopped up with sand, no female can ever hear the sound of another in distress without rushing instantly to her aid.

I peeped round a black marble column, and there she was, stretched out full length, facedown on the slab of a limestone tomb, her red hair flowing out across the weathered inscription like rivulets of blood. Except for the cigarette wedged stylishly erect between her fingers, she might have been a painting by one of the Pre-Raphaelites, such as Burne-Jones. I almost hated to intrude.

"Hullo," I said. "Are you all right?"

It is another simple fact of nature that one always begins such conversations with an utterly stupid remark. I was sorry the instant I'd uttered it.

"Oh! Of course I'm all right," she cried, leaping to her feet and wiping her eyes. "What do you mean by creeping up on me like that? Who are you, anyway?"

With a toss of her head she flung back her hair and stuck out her chin. She had the high cheekbones and the dramatically triangular face of a silent cinema star, and I could see by the way she bared her teeth that she was terrified.

"Flavia," I said. "My name is Flavia de Luce. I live near here—at Buckshaw."

I jerked my thumb in the general direction.

She was still staring at me like a woman in the grip of a nightmare.

"I'm sorry," I said. "I didn't mean to startle you."

She pulled herself up to her full height—which couldn't have been much more than five feet and an inch or two—and took a step towards me, like a hot-tempered version of the Botticelli *Venus* that I'd once seen on a Huntley and Palmers biscuit tin.

I stood my ground, staring at her dress. It was a creamy cotton print with a gathered bodice and a flaring skirt, covered all over with a myriad of tiny flowers, red, yellow, blue, and a bright orange the color of poppies and, I couldn't help noticing, a hem that was stained with half-dried mud.

"What's the matter?" she asked, taking an affected drag on her angled cigarette. "Never seen anyone famous before?"

Famous? I hadn't the faintest idea who she was. I had half a mind to tell her that I had indeed seen someone famous, and that it was Winston Churchill. Father had pointed him out to me from a London taxicab. Churchill had been standing in front of the Savoy with his thumbs hooked in his waistcoat pockets, talking to a man in a yellow mackintosh.

"Good old Winnie," Father had breathed, as if to himself.

"Oh, what's the use?" the woman said. "Bloody place . . . bloody people . . . bloody motorcars!" And she began to cry again.

"Is there something I can do to help?" I asked.

"Oh, go away and leave me alone," she sobbed.

Very well, then, I thought. Actually, I thought more than that, but since I'm trying to be a better person . . .

I stood there for a moment, leaning forward a bit to see if her fallen tears were reacting with the porous surface of the tombstone. Tears, I knew, were composed largely of water, sodium chloride, manganese, and potassium, while limestone was made up chiefly of calcite, which was soluble in sodium chloride—but only at high temperatures. So unless the temperature of St. Tancred's churchyard went up suddenly by several hundred degrees, it seemed unlikely that anything chemically interesting was going to be happening here.

I turned and walked away.

"Flavia . . ."

I looked back. She was reaching out a hand to me.

"I'm sorry," she said. "It's just that it's been an awfully bloody day, all round."

I stopped—then paced slowly, warily back as she wiped her eyes with the back of her hand.

"Rupert was in a foul mood to begin with—even before we left Stoatmoor this morning. We'd had rather a row, I'm afraid, and then the whole business with the van—it was simply the last straw. He's gone off to find someone to fix it, and I'm . . . well, here I am."

"I like your red hair," I said. She touched it instantly and smiled, as I somehow knew she would.

"Carrot-top, they used to call me when I was your age. Carrot-top! Fancy!"

"Carrot tops are green," I said. "Who's Rupert?"

"Who's Rupert?" she asked. "You're having me on!"

She pointed a finger and I turned to look: Parked in the lane at the corner of the churchyard was a dilapidated van—an Austin Eight. On its side panel, in showy gold circus letters, still legible through a heavy coating of mud and dust, were the words PORSON'S PUPPETS.

"Rupert Porson," she said. "Everyone knows Rupert Porson. Rupert Porson, as in Snoddy the Squirrel—*The Magic Kingdom*. Haven't you seen him on the television?"

Snoddy the Squirrel? *The Magic Kingdom?*

"We don't have the television at Buckshaw," I said. "Father says it's a filthy invention."

"Father is an uncommonly wise man," she said. "Father is undoubtedly—"

She was interrupted by the metallic rattle of a loose chain guard as the vicar came wobbling round the corner of the church. He dismounted and leaned his battered Raleigh up against a handy headstone. As he walked towards us, I reflected that Canon Denwyn Richardson was not anyone's image of a typical village vicar. He was large and bluff and hearty, and if he'd had tattoos, he might have been mistaken for the captain of one of those rusty tramp steamers that drags itself wearily from one sun-drenched port to another in whatever God-awful outposts are still left of the British Empire.

His black clerical outfit was smudged and streaked with chalky dust, as if he'd come a cropper on his bicycle.

"Blast!" he said when he spotted me. "I've lost my trouser clip and torn my cuff to ribbons," and then, dusting himself off as he walked towards us, he added, "Cynthia's going to have me on the carpet."

The woman's eyes widened and she shot me a quick glance.

"She's recently begun scratching my initials on my belongings with a needle," he went on, "but that hasn't kept me from losing things. Last week, the hectograph sheets for the parish bulletin, the week before, a brass doorknob from the vestry. Maddening, really.

"Hello, Flavia," he said. "Always nice to see you at church."

"This is our vicar, Canon Richardson," I told the redheaded woman. "Perhaps he can help."

"Denwyn," the vicar said, holding out a hand to the stranger. "We don't stand much on ceremony since the war."

The woman stuck out two or three fingers and touched his palm, but said nothing. As she extended her hand, the short sleeve of her dress slid up, and I had a quick glimpse of the ugly green and purple bruise on her upper arm. She covered it hastily with her left hand as she tugged the cotton fabric down to hide it.

"And how may I be of service?" the vicar asked, gesturing towards the van. "It is not often that we, in our bucolic little backwater, are called upon to minister to such august theater folk."

She smiled gamely. "Our van's broken down—or as good as. Something to do with the carburetor. If it had been anything electrical, I'm sure Rupert could have mended it in a flash, but I'm afraid the fuel system is beyond him."

"Dear, dear!" the vicar said. "I'm sure Bert Archer, at the garage, can put it right for you. I'll ring him up, if you like."

"Oh, no," the woman said quickly—perhaps *too* quickly—"we wouldn't want you to go to any trouble. Rupert's gone down the high street. He's probably already found someone."

"If he had, he'd be back by now," the vicar said. "Let me ring Bert. He often slips home for a nap in the afternoon. He's not as young as he was, you know—nor are any of us, if it comes to that. Still, it is a favorite maxim of mine that, when dealing with motor mechanics—even tame ones—it never does one any harm to have the blessing of the Church."

"Oh, no. It's too much trouble. I'm sure we'll be just fine."

"Nonsense," the vicar said, already moving off among the forest of gravestones and making at full speed for the rectory. "No trouble at all. I'll be back in a jiffy."

"Vicar!" the woman called. "Please—"

He stopped in mid-stride and came reluctantly back towards us.

"It's just that . . . you see, we . . ."

"Aha! A question of money, then," the vicar said.

She nodded sadly, her head down, her red hair cascading over her face.

"I'm sure something can be arranged," the vicar said. "Ah! Here's your husband now."

A little man with an oversized head and a lopsided gait was stumping towards us across the churchyard, his right leg swinging out at each step in a wide, awkward semicircle. As he approached, I saw that his calf was caged in a heavy iron brace.

He must have been in his forties, but it was difficult to tell.

In spite of his diminutive size, his barrel chest and powerful upper arms seemed ready to burst out of the seersucker suit that confined them. By contrast, his right leg was pitiful: By the way in which his trousers clung, and flapped uselessly round what lay beneath, I could see that it was little more than a matchstick. With his huge head, he looked to me like nothing so much as a giant octopus, stalking on uneven tentacles through the churchyard.

He lurched to a halt and deferentially lifted a flat, peaked motoring cap, revealing an unruly mop of pale blond hair that matched precisely his little Vandyke goatee.

"Rupert Porson, I presume?" the vicar said, giving the newcomer a jolly, hail-fellow-well-met handshake. "I'm Denwyn Richardson—and this is my young friend Flavia de Luce."

Porson nodded at me and shot an almost invisibly quick, dark glance at the woman before turning on the full beam of a searchlight smile.

"Spot of engine trouble, I understand," the vicar went on. "Quite maddening. Still, if it has brought the creator of *The Magic Kingdom* and Snoddy the Squirrel into our midst—well, it just proves the old adage, doesn't it?"

He didn't say which old adage he was referring to, nor did anyone care enough to ask.

"I was about to remark to your good wife," the vicar said, "that St. Tancred's would be honored indeed if you might see your way clear to presenting a little entertainment in the parish hall whilst your van is being repaired? I realize, of course, how much in demand you must be, but I should be negligent if I didn't at least make the attempt on behalf of the children—and yes, the grown-ups, too!—of Bishop's Lacey. It is good, now and then, to allow children to launch an attack upon their money boxes in a worthy cultural cause, don't you agree?"

"Well, Vicar," Porson said, in a honeyed voice—too big, too resonant, too mellifluous, I thought, for such a tiny man—"we do have rather a tight timetable. Our tour has been grueling, you see, and London calls. . . ."

"I understand," said the vicar.

"But," Porson added, lifting a dramatic forefinger, "nothing would delight us more than being allowed to sing for our supper, as it were. Isn't that so, Nialla? It shall be quite like the old days."

The woman nodded, but said nothing. She was staring off at the hills beyond.

"Well, then," the vicar said, rubbing his hands together vigorously, as if he were making fire, "it's all arranged. Come along and I'll show you the hall. It's rather tatty, but it does boast a stage, and the acoustics are said to be quite remarkable."

With that, the two men disappeared round the back of the church.

For a moment there seemed nothing to say. And then the woman spoke: "You wouldn't happen to have a cigarette, would you? I'm dying for a smoke."

I gave my head a rather idiotic shake.

"Hmmm," she said. "You look like the kind of kid who might have."

For the first time in my life, I was speechless.

"I don't smoke," I managed.

"And why is that?" she asked. "Too young or too wise?"

"I was thinking of taking it up next week," I said lamely. "I just hadn't actually got round to it yet."

She threw her head back and laughed toothily, like a film star. "I like you, Flavia de Luce," she said. "But I have the advantage, don't I? You've told me your name, but I haven't told you mine."

"It's Nialla," I said. "Mr. Porson called you Nialla."

She stuck out her hand, her face grave. "That's right," she said, "he did. But you can call me Mother Goose."

two

MOTHER GOOSE!

I have never much cared for flippant remarks, especially when others make them, and in particular, I don't give a frog's fundament for them when they come from an adult. It has been my experience that facetiousness in the mouth of someone old enough to know better is often no more than camouflage for something far, far worse.

And yet, in spite of that, I found myself swallowing the sharp—and deliciously nasty!—retort that was already on the tip of my tongue, and instead, managed a diluted smile.

"Mother Goose?" I repeated, dubiously.

She burst into tears again, and I was glad that I had held my tongue. I was about to be instantly rewarded by hearing something juicy.

Besides, I had already begun to detect a slight but invisible attraction between this woman and myself. Could it be pity? Or was it fear? I couldn't say: I knew only that some deep-seated chemical substance inside one of us was crying out to its long-lost complement—or was it its antidote?—in the other.

I put a hand gently on her shoulder and held out my handkerchief. She looked at it skeptically.

"It's all right," I said. "They're only grass stains."

That set her off into a remarkable contortion. She buried her face in the handkerchief, and her shoulders quaked so violently I thought for

a moment she was going to fly to pieces. To allow her time to recover—
and because I was rather embarrassed by her outburst—I wandered off a
little distance to examine the inscription on a tall, weathered gravestone
that marked the grave of one Lydia Green, who had "dyed" in 1638 at
the age of "one hundred and thirty-five yeeres."

She once warr Grene but now she waxeth white, it said on the stone,
lamented by a fewe frends.

Had Lydia lived, I reflected, she would now be four hundred and
forty-seven years old, and probably a person well worth getting to know.

"Oh, I feel such a chump."

I turned to see the woman dabbing at her eyes and giving me a damp
grin.

"I'm Nialla," she said, sticking out a hand. "Rupert's assistant."

I fought back my revulsion and gave her fingers a lightning-quick
shake. As I had suspected, her hand was wet and sticky. As soon as I was
decently able, I slid my own hand out of sight behind my back and wiped
it on the back of my skirt.

"Assistant?" The word popped out of my mouth before I could stop it.

"Oh, I know the vicar assumed that I'm Rupert's wife. But it's not like
that. Honestly! It's not like that at all."

I glanced over involuntarily at the Porson's Puppets van. She spotted
it at once.

"Well, yes . . . we do travel together. I suppose Rupert and I have
what you might call . . . a very great affection for one another. But
husband and wife . . . ?"

What kind of fool did she take me for? It was no more than a week
since Daffy had been reading aloud to Feely and me from *Oliver Twist*,
and I knew, as surely as I knew my own name, that this woman, Nialla,
was Nancy to Rupert Porson's Bill Sikes. Didn't she realize that I'd
spotted the filthy great bruise on her upper arm?

"Actually, it's such jolly fun rattling about England with Rupert. He's
recognized everywhere we go, you know. Just the day before yesterday,
for instance, we were playing at Market Selby when we were spotted in
the post office by a fat lady in a flowerpot hat.

"'Rupert Porson!' she shrieked. 'Rupert Porson uses the Royal Mail,
just like everyone else!'"

Nialla laughed. "And then she begged him for his autograph. They always do, you know. Insisted he put 'Best wishes from Snoddy the Squirrel.' When he does it that way, he always draws a couple of little nuts. She claimed she wanted it for her nephew, but I knew better. When you're on the road a lot, you develop a certain sense for these things. You can always tell."

She was prattling. If I kept quiet, it wouldn't be more than a minute before she would be confiding her size in knickers.

"Someone at the BBC told Rupert that twenty-three percent of his viewing audience is made up of childless housewives. Seems a lot, doesn't it? But there's something about *The Magic Kingdom* that satisfies one's innate desire for escape. That's the exact way they put it to Rupert: 'one's innate desire for escape.' Everyone needs to escape, don't they? In one way or another, I mean."

"Everyone but Mother Goose," I said.

She laughed. "Look, I wasn't pulling your leg. I *am* Mother Goose. At least, I am when I put on my costume. Just wait until you see it—tall witch's hat with a floppy brim and a silver buckle, a gray wig with dangling ringlets, and a great puffy dress that looks as if it once belonged to Mother Shipton. Do you know who Mother Shipton was?"

Of course I did. I knew that she was some old crone who was supposed to have lived in the sixteenth century and seen into the future, predicting, among other things, the Great Plague, the Great Fire of London, aeroplanes, battleships, and that the world would come to an end in 1881; that like those of Nostradamus, Mother Shipton's prophecies were in doggerel verse: "Fire and water shall wonders do," and all that. I also knew that there are actually still people running around loose today who believe she foresaw the use of heavy water in the making of the atomic bomb. As for myself, I didn't believe a word of it. It was nothing but a load of old tosh.

"I've heard the name," I said.

"Well, never mind. That's who I resemble when I'm all tarted up for the show."

"Brilliant," I said, not meaning it. She could see that I was a bit put off.

"What's a nice girl like you doing hanging about in a place like this?" she asked with a grin, taking in the whole of the churchyard with a wave of her hand.

"I often come here to think," I said.

This seemed to amuse her. She pursed her lips and put on an annoying, stagy voice.

"And what does Flavia de Luce think about in her quaint old country churchyard?"

"Being alone," I snapped, without meaning to be intentionally rude. I was simply being truthful.

"Being alone," she said, nodding. I could see that she was not put off by my bristling reply. "There's a lot to be said for being alone. But you and I know, don't we, Flavia, that being alone and being lonely are not at all the same thing?"

I brightened a bit. Here was someone who seemed at least to have thought through some of the same things I had.

"No," I admitted.

There was a long silence.

"Tell me about your family," Nialla said at last, quietly.

"There isn't much to tell," I said. "I have two sisters, Ophelia and Daphne. Feely's seventeen and Daffy's thirteen. Feely plays the piano and Daffy reads. Father is a philatelist. He's devoted to his stamps."

"And your mother?"

"Dead. She was killed in an accident when I was a year old."

"Good Lord!" she said. "Someone told me about a family that lived in a great rambling old mansion not far from here: an eccentric colonel and a family of girls running wild like a lot of red Indians. You're not one of *them*, are you?"

She saw instantly by the look on my face that I was.

"Oh, you poor child!" she said. "I'm sorry, I didn't mean to . . . I mean . . ."

"It's quite all right," I told her. "It's far worse than that actually, but I don't like to talk about it."

I saw the faraway look come into her eyes: the look of an adult floundering desperately to find common ground with someone younger.

"But what do you do with yourself?" she asked. "Don't you have any interests . . . or hobbies?"

"I'm keen on chemistry," I said, "and I enjoy making scrapbooks."

"Do you really?" she enthused. "Fancy that! So did I, at your age. Cigarette cards and pressed flowers: pansies, mignonettes, foxgloves, delphiniums; old buttons, valentines, poems about Granny's spinning wheel from *The Girl's Own Annual* . . . what jolly good fun it was!"

My own scrapbooks consisted of three fat purple volumes of clippings from the tide of ancient magazines and newspapers that had overflowed, and then flooded, the library and the drawing room at Buckshaw, spilling over into disused bedrooms and lumber rooms before being carted off at last to languish in damp, moldering stacks in a crypt in the cellars. From their pages, I had carefully clipped everything I could find on poisons and poisoners, until my scrapbooks were bursting at the seams with the likes of Major Herbert Rowse Armstrong, the amateur gardener and solicitor, who dispatched his wife with lovingly prepared concoctions of arsenious weed-killer; Thomas Neill Cream, Hawley Harvey Crippen, and George Chapman (remarkable, isn't it, that so many of the great poisoners' names begin with the letter C?), who with strychnine, hyoscine, and antimony respectively, sent a veritable army of wives and other women marching to their graves; Mary Ann Cotton (see what I mean?) who, after several successful trial runs on pigs, went on to poison seventeen people with arsenic; Daisy de Melker, the South African woman with a passion for poisoning plumbers: She would first marry them, and then divorce them with a dose of strychnine.

"Keeping a scrapbook is the perfect pastime for a young lady," Nialla was saying. "Genteel . . . and yet educational."

My thoughts precisely.

"My mum tossed mine in the dustbin when I ran away from home," she said with something that had it lived might have become a chuckle.

"You ran away from home?" I asked.

This fact intrigued me almost as much as her foxgloves, from which, I recalled, the vegetable alkaloid digitalin (better known to those of us who are chemists as $C_{36}H_{56}O_{14}$) could be extracted. I thought with pleasure for a moment of the several times in my laboratory I had exhausted with alcohol the leaves of foxglove plucked from the kitchen garden, watching the slender, shining needles as they crystallized, and the lovely emerald green solution that was formed when I dissolved them in hydrochloric acid and added water. The precipitated resin could, of course, be restored to its original green hue with sulfuric acid, turned light red by bromine vapor, and back to emerald green again with the addition of water. It was magical! It was also, of course, a deadly poison, and as such, was certainly far more gripping than stupid buttons and *The Girl's Own Annual*.

"Mmmm," she said. "Got tired of washing up, drying up, sweeping up, and dusting up, and listening to the people next door throwing up; tired of lying in bed at night, listening for the clatter of the prince's horse on the cobblestones."

I grinned.

"Rupert changed all that, of course," she said. "'Come with me to the Doorway of Diarbekir,' he told me. 'Come to the Orient and I will make you a princess in liquid silks and diamonds the size of market cabbages.'"

"He did?"

"No. What he actually said was, 'My bloody assistant's run out on me. Come with me to Lyme Regis at the weekend and I'll give you a guinea, six square meals, and a bag to sleep in. I'll teach you the art of manipulation,' he said, and I was bloody fool enough to think he was talking about puppets."

Before I had time to ask for details, she had jumped to her feet and dusted off her skirt.

"Speaking of Rupert," she said, "we'd better go in and see how he and the vicar are getting on. It's ominously quiet in the parish hall. Do you suppose they might already have murdered one another?"

Her flowered dress swished gracefully off among the tombstones, and I was left to trot doggedly along in her wake.

INSIDE, WE FOUND THE VICAR standing in the middle of the hall. Rupert was up on the platform, center stage, hands on hips. Had he been taking a curtain call at the Old Vic, the lighting could not have been more dramatic. As if dispatched by Fate, an unexpected ray of sunlight shone in through a stained-glass window at the rear of the hall, fixing Rupert's upturned face dead center in its round golden beam. He struck a pose, and began spouting Shakespeare:

> "When my love swears that she is made of truth,
> I do believe her though I know she lies,
> That she might think me some untutored youth,
> Unlearnèd in the world's false subtleties.
> Thus vainly thinking that she thinks me young,
> Although she knows my days are past the best,
> Simply I credit her false-speaking tongue:
> On both sides thus is simple truth suppressed."

As the vicar had mentioned, the acoustics of the hall were quite remarkable. The Victorian builders had made its interior a conch shell of curved, polished wood paneling that served as a sounding board for the faintest noise: It was like being inside a Stradivarius violin. Rupert's warm, honey-sweet voice was everywhere, wrapping us all in its rich resonance:

"But wherefore says she not she is unjust?
And wherefore say not I that I am old?
O love's best habit is in seeming trust,
And age in love, loves not to have years told.
Therefore I lie with her, and she with me,
And in our faults by lies we flattered be."

"Can you hear me now, vicar?"

The spell was instantly broken. It was as if Laurence Olivier had tossed "Woof! Woof! Testing . . . one . . . two . . . three," into the middle of "To be, or not to be."

"Brilliant!" the vicar exclaimed.

What surprised me most about Rupert's speech was that I knew what he was saying. Because of the nearly imperceptible pause at the end of each line, and the singular way in which he illustrated the shades of meaning with his long white fingers, I understood the words. Every single one of them.

As if they had been sucked in through my pores by osmosis, I knew even as they swept over me that I was hearing the bitter words of an old man to a love far younger than himself.

I glanced at Nialla. Her hand was at her throat.

In the echoing wooden silence that followed, the vicar stood stock-still, as if he were carved from black and white marble.

I was witnessing something that not all of us understood.

"Bravo! Bravo!"

The vicar's cupped hands came suddenly clapping together in a series of echoing thunderbolts. "Bravo! Sonnet one hundred and thirty-eight, unless I'm badly mistaken. And, if I may offer up my own humble opinion, perhaps never more beautifully spoken."

Rupert positively preened.

Outside, the sun went behind a cloud. Its golden beam faded in an instant, and when it had gone, we were once again just four ordinary people in a dim and dusty room.

"Splendid," Rupert said. "The hall will do splendidly."

He stumped across the stage and began clambering awkwardly down the narrow steps, the fingers of one hand splayed out against the wall for support.

"Careful!" Nialla said, taking a quick step towards him.

"Get back!" he snapped, with a look of utter ferocity. "I can manage."

She stopped short in her tracks—as if he had slapped her in the face.

"Nialla thinks I'm her child." He laughed, trying to make a joke of it.

By her murderous look, I could see that Nialla didn't think any such thing.

three

"WELL, THEN!" THE VICAR SAID BRIGHTLY, RUBBING HIS HANDS together, as if the moment hadn't happened. "That's settled. Where shall we begin?" He looked eagerly from one of them to the other.

"By unloading the van, I suppose," Rupert said. "I assume we can leave things here until the show?"

"Oh, of course . . . of course," said the vicar. "The parish hall's as safe as houses. Perhaps even a little safer."

"Then someone will need to have a look at the van . . . and we'll want a place to put up for a few days."

"Leave that department to me," the vicar said. "I'm sure I can manage something. Now then, up sleeves, and to work we go. Come along, Flavia, dear. I'm sure we'll find something suited to your special talents."

Something suited to my special talents? Somehow I doubted it—unless the subject was criminal poisoning, which was my chief delight.

But still, because I didn't feel up to going home to Buckshaw just yet, I pasted on my best Girl Guide (retired) smile for the vicar, and followed him, along with Rupert and Nialla, outside into the churchyard.

As Rupert swung open the rear doors of the van, I had my first glimpse into the life of a traveling showman. The Austin's dim interior was beautifully fitted out with row upon row of varnished drawers, each one nestled snugly above, beside, and below its neighbors: very like the boxes of shoes in a well-run boot maker's shop, with each drawer capable of sliding in and out on its own track. Piled on the floor of the van were the larger boxes—shipping crates, really—with rope handles at the ends to facilitate their being pulled out and lugged to wherever they were going. "Rupert made it all himself," Nialla said, proudly. "The drawers, the folding stage, the lighting equipment . . . made the spotlights out of old paint tins, didn't you, Rupert?"

Rupert nodded absently as he hauled away at a bundle of iron tubing.

"And that's not all. He cut the cables, made the props, painted the scenery, carved the puppets . . . everything—except *that,* of course."

She was pointing to a bulky black case with a leather handle and perforations in the side.

"What's in there? Is it an animal?"

Nialla laughed.

"Better than that. It's Rupert's pride and joy: a magnetic recorder. Had it sent him from America. Cost him a pretty penny, I can tell you. Still, it's cheaper than hiring the BBC orchestra to play the incidental music!"

Rupert had already begun to tug boxes out of the Austin, grunting as he worked. His arms were like dockyard cranes, lifting and turning . . . lifting and turning, until at last, nearly everything was piled in the grass.

"Allow me to lend a hand," the vicar said, seizing a rope handle at the end of a black coffin-shaped trunk with the word "Galligantus" stenciled upon it in white letters, as Rupert took the other end.

Nialla and I went back and forth, back and forth, with the lighter bits and pieces, and within half an hour, everything was piled up inside the parish hall in front of the stage.

"Well done!" the vicar said, dusting off the sleeves of his jacket. "Well done, indeed. Now then, would Saturday be suitable? For the show, I mean? Let me see . . . today is Thursday . . . that would give you an extra day to make ready, as well as time to have your van repaired."

"Sounds all right to me," Rupert said. Nialla nodded, even though she hadn't been asked.

"Saturday it is, then. I'll have Cynthia run off handbills on the hectograph. She can take them round the shops tomorrow . . . slap a few up in strategic places. Cynthia's such a good sport about these things."

Of the many phrases that came to mind to describe Cynthia Richardson, "good sport" was not among them; "ogress," however, was.

It was after all Cynthia, with her rodent features, who had once caught me teetering tiptoe on the altar of St. Tancred's, using one of Father's straight razors to scrape a sample of blue zafre from a medieval stained-glass window. Zafre was an impure basic arsenate of cobalt, prepared by roasting, which the craftsmen of the Middle Ages had used for painting on glass, and I was simply dying to analyze the stuff in my laboratory to determine how successful its makers had been in the essential step of freeing it of iron.

Cynthia had seized me, upended me, and spanked me on the spot, making what I thought to be unfair use of a nearby copy of *Hymns Ancient and Modern* (Standard Edition).

"What you have done, Flavia, is not worthy of congratulation," Father said when I reported this outrage to him. "You have ruined a perfectly good Thiers-Issard hollow-ground blade."

I have to admit, though, that Cynthia was a great organizer, but then, so were the men with whips who got the pyramids built. Certainly, if anyone could manage to paper Bishop's Lacey from end to end in three days with handbills, it was Cynthia Richardson.

"Hold on!" the vicar exclaimed. "I've just had the most splendid idea! Tell me what you think. Why not present *two* shows rather than one? I don't claim to be an expert in the art of the puppet theater, by any means—knowing what is possible and what is not, and so forth—but why not put on a show Saturday afternoon for the children, and another Saturday evening, when more of the grown-ups would be free to attend?"

Rupert did not reply at once, but stood rubbing his chin. Even I could see instantly that two performances would double the take at the box office.

"Well . . ." he said at last. "I suppose. It would have to be the same show both times, though . . ."

"Splendid!" said the vicar. "What's it to be, then . . . the program, that is?"

"Open with a short musical piece," Rupert said. "It's a new one I've been working up. No one's seen it yet, so this would be a good chance to try it out. Then *Jack and the Beanstalk*. They always clamor for *Jack and the Beanstalk*, young and old alike. Classic fare. Very popular."

"Smashing!" the vicar said. He pulled a folded sheet of paper and the nub of a pencil from an inner pocket and scribbled a few notes.

"How's this?" he asked, with a final flourish, then, with a pleased look on his face, read aloud what he had written:

"Direct from London!

"I hope you'll forgive the small fib and the exclamation point," he whispered to Nialla.

"Porson's Puppets

"(Operated by the acclaimed Rupert Porson. As seen on the BBC Television)

"Program

"I. A Musical Interlude
"II. Jack and the Beanstalk

(The former being presented for the first time on any stage; the latter declared to be universally popular with old and young alike.) *Saturday, July 22nd, 1950, at St. Tancred's Parish Hall, Bishop's Lacey. Performances at 2:00 p.m. and 7:00 p.m. sharp!*

". . . Otherwise they'll just dawdle in," he added. "I'll have Cynthia dash off a sketch of a little jointed figure with strings to put at the top. She's an exceedingly talented artist, you know—not that she's had as many opportunities as she'd like to express herself—oh, dear, I fear I'm rambling. I'd best away to my telephonic duties."

And with that he was gone.

"Peculiar old duck," Rupert remarked.

"He's all right," I told him. "He leads rather a sad life."

"Ah," Rupert said, "I know what you mean. Funerals, and all that."

"Yes," I said. "Funerals and all that."

But I was thinking more of Cynthia.

"Which way to the mains?" Rupert asked suddenly.

For a moment I was dumbfounded. I must have looked particularly unintelligent.

"The mains," he repeated. "The current. The electrical controls. But then I don't suppose you'd know where they are, would you?"

As it happened, I did. Only weeks before I had been press-ganged into standing backstage with Mrs. Witty, helping to throw the massive levers of the antique lighting control panel, as her first-year ballet students tripped across the boards in their recital of *The Golden Apples of the Sun*, in which Pomona (Deirdre Skidmore, in insect netting) wooed the reluctant Hyas (a red-faced Gerald Plunkett in improvised tights cut from a pair of winter-weight long johns), by presenting him with an ever-growing assortment of papier-mâché fruit.

"Stage right," I said. "Behind the black tormentor curtains."

Rupert blinked once or twice, shot me a barbed look, and clattered back up the narrow steps to the stage. For a few moments we could hear him muttering away to himself up there, punctuated by the metallic sounds of panels being opened and slammed, and switches clicked on and off.

"Don't mind him," Nialla whispered. "He's always nervous as a cat from the minute a show's booked until the final curtain falls. After that, he's generally as right as rain."

As Rupert tinkered with the electricity, Nialla began unfastening several bundles of smooth wooden posts, which were bound tightly together with leather straps.

"The stage," she told me. "It all fits together with bolts and butterfly nuts. Rupert designed and built it all himself. Mind your fingers."

I had stepped forward to help her with some of the longer pieces.

"I can do it myself, thanks," she said. "I've done it hundreds of times— got it down to a science. Only thing that needs two to lift is the floor."

A rustling sound behind me made me turn around. There stood the vicar with rather an unhappy look on his face.

"Not good news, I'm afraid," he said. "Mrs. Archer tells me that Bert has gone up to London for a training course and won't be back until tomorrow, and there's no answer at Culverhouse Farm, where I had hoped to put you up. But then Mrs. I. doesn't often answer the telephone when she's home alone. She'll be bringing the eggs down on Saturday, but by then it will be far too late. I'd offer the vicarage, of course, but Cynthia has quite forcibly reminded me that we're in the midst of painting the guest rooms: beds taken down and stowed in the hallways, armoires blockading the landings, and so forth. Maddening, really."

"Don't fret, Vicar," Rupert said from the stage.

I nearly jumped out of my skin. I'd forgotten he was there.

"We'll camp where we are, in the churchyard. We've a good tent in the van, with wool rugs and a rubber groundsheet, a little Primus stove, and beans in a tin for breakfast. We'll be as cozy as bugs in a blanket."

"Well," the vicar said, "if it were solely up to me, I—"

"Ah," Rupert said, raising a finger. "I know what you're thinking: Can't have gypsies camping among the graves. Respect for the dear departed, and all that."

"Well," said the vicar, "there might be a modicum of truth in that, but—"

"We'll set up in an unoccupied corner, won't we? No desecration, that way. Shan't be the first time we've slept in a churchyard, will it, Nialla?"

Nialla colored slightly and became fascinated with something on the floor.

"Well, I suppose it's settled then," the vicar said. "We don't really have a great deal of choice, do we? Besides, it's only for one night. What harm can there be in that?

"Dear me!" he said, glancing at his wristwatch. "How *tempus* does *fugit*! I gave Cynthia my solemn promise to return straightaway. She's preparing an early supper, you see. We always have an early supper on Thursdays, because of choir practice. I'd invite you to join us for potluck, but—"

"Not at all," Rupert interrupted. "We've imposed enough for one day, Vicar. Besides, believe it or not, Nialla's a dab hand with bacon and eggs over a churchyard bonfire. We shall eat like Corsican bandits and sleep like the dead."

Nialla sat down far too gently on an unopened box, and I could see that she was suddenly exhausted. Dark circles seemed to have formed under her eyes as quickly as storm clouds blow across the moon.

The vicar rubbed his chin. "Flavia, dear," he said, "I've had the most splendid idea. Why don't you come back bright and early tomorrow morning and lend a hand? I'm sure Porson's Puppets would be most grateful to acquire the services of an eager assistant.

"I have home visits for the sick and shut-ins tomorrow, as well as Altar Guild," he added. "You could serve as my *locum tenens*, so to speak. Offer our guests the freedom of the parish, as it were, besides serving as general factotum and all-round dogsbody."

"I'd be happy to," I said, making an almost imperceptible curtsy.

Nialla, at least, rewarded me with a smile.

Outside, at the back of the churchyard, I retrieved Gladys, my trusty bicycle, from the long grass, and moments later we were flying homewards through the sun-dappled lanes to Buckshaw.

four

"HELLO, ALL," I SAID TO FEELY'S BACK, AFTER I HAD DRIFTED inconspicuously into the drawing room.

Without turning away from the mirror in front of which she was regarding herself, Feely glanced up at my reflection in the time-rippled glass.

"You're in for it this time," she said. "Father's been looking for you all afternoon. He's just got off the telephone with Constable Linnet, in the village. I must say he seemed rather disappointed to hear that they hadn't fished your soggy little corpse out of the duck pond."

"How do you know they didn't?" I countered shrewdly. "How do you know I'm not a ghost come back to haunt you into the grave?"

"Because your shoe's untied and your nose is running," Daffy said, looking up from her book. It was *Forever Amber* and she was reading it for the second time.

"What's it about?" I had asked her on the first go-round.

"Flies in sap," she had said with a smug grin, and I had made a mental note to put it on my reading list. I adore books about the Natural Sciences.

"Aren't you going to ask me where I've been?" I said. I was simply dying to tell them about Porson's Puppets and all about Nialla.

"No," Feely answered, fingering the point of her chin as she leaned in for a closer look at herself. "No one is the slightest bit interested in what you do. You're like an unwanted dog."

"I'm not unwanted," I said.

"Oh yes you are!" she said with a hard laugh. "Name one person in this household who wants you and I'll give you a guinea. Go ahead—name one."

"Harriet!" I said. "Harriet wanted me, or she wouldn't have had me."

Feely whirled round and spat on the floor. She actually *spat*!

"For your information, Spot, Harriet fell into a profound mental bog immediately after you were born."

"Ha!" I said. "I've got you there! You told me I was adopted."

It was true. Whenever Daffy or Feely wanted to aggravate me beyond endurance, they would renew that claim.

"And so you were," she said. "Father and Harriet made an agreement to adopt you even before you were born. But when the time came, and your natural mother delivered you, you were given out by mistake to someone else—a couple in east Kent, I believe. Unfortunately they returned you. It was said to be the first time in the two-hundred-year history of the foundling hospital that anyone had returned a baby because they didn't like it.

"Harriet didn't care for you, either, once she got you home, but the papers were already signed, and the Board of Governors refused to take you back a second time. I'll never forget the day I overheard Harriet telling Father in her dressing room that she could never love such a rat-faced mewling. But what could she do?

"Well, she did what any normal woman would do in those circumstances: She fell into a deeply troubled state—and one from which she probably never recovered. She was still in the grip of it when she fell—or was it jumped?—off that mountain in Tibet. Father has always blamed you for it—surely you must realize that?"

The room went cold as ice, and suddenly I was numb from head to toe. I opened my mouth to say something, but found that my tongue had dried up and shriveled to a curled-up flap of leather. Hot tears welled up in my eyes as I fled the room.

I'd show that bloody swine Feely a thing or two. I'd have her so tied up in knots they'd have to hire a sailor to undo her for the funeral.

There is a tree that grows in Brazil, *Carica digitata*, which the natives call *chamburu*. They believe it to be such deadly poison that simply sleeping beneath its branches will cause, first of all, ever-festering sores, followed sooner or later by a wonderfully excruciating death.

Fortunately for Feely, though, *Carica digitata* does not grow in England. Fortunately for me, fool's parsley, better known as poison hemlock, does. In fact, I knew a low and marshy corner of Seaton's Meadow, not ten minutes from Buckshaw, where it was growing at that very moment. I could be there and back before supper.

I'd recently updated my notes on coniine, the active principle of the stuff. I would extract it by distilling with whatever alkali was handy—perhaps a bit of the sodium bicarbonate I kept on hand in my laboratory against Mrs. Mullet's culinary excesses. I would then, by freezing, remove by recrystallization the iridescent scales of the less powerful conhydrine. The resulting nearly pure coniine would have a deliciously mousy odor, and it would take less than half a drop of the oily stuff to put paid to old accounts.

Agitation, vomiting, convulsions, frothing at the mouth, horrendous spasms—I ticked off the highlights on my fingers as I went.

"*Sanctified cyanide*
Super-quick arsenic
Higgledy-piggledy
Into the soup.
Put out the mourning lamps
Call for the coffin clamps
Teach them to trifle with
Flavia de Luce!"

My words came echoing back to me from the high painted ceiling of the foyer and the dark polished woodwork of the galleries above. Aside from the fact that it didn't mention poison hemlock, this little poem, which I had composed for an entirely different occasion, was otherwise a perfect expression of my present feelings.

Across the black and white tiles I ran, and up the curving staircase to the east wing of the house. The "Tar" wing, as we called it, was named for Tarquin de Luce, one of Harriet's ancient uncles who had inhabited Buckshaw before us. Uncle Tar had spent the greater part of his life locked away in a magnificent Victorian chemistry laboratory at the southeast corner of the house, investigating "the crumbs of the universe," as he had written in one of his many letters to Sir James Jeans, author of *The Dynamical Theory of Gases*.

Directly below the laboratory, in the Long Gallery, there is a portrait in oils of Uncle Tar. In it, he is looking up from his microscope, his lips pressed together and his brow furrowed, as if someone with an easel, a palette, and a box of paints had rudely barged in just as he was about to discover deLucium.

"Fizz off!" his expression clearly says. "Fizz off and leave me alone!"

And so they had fizzed off—and so, eventually, had Uncle Tar.

The laboratory, and all that was in it, was now mine, and had been for a number of years. No one ever came here—which was just as well.

As I reached into my pocket and pulled out the key, something white fluttered to the floor. It was the handkerchief I had lent Nialla in the churchyard—and it was still vaguely damp to the touch.

An image rose up in my mind of Nialla as she had been when first I saw her, lying facedown upon a weathered tombstone, hair spread out like a sea of red, her hot tears sizzling in the dust.

Everything dropped into place like the tumblers in a lock. Of course!

Vengeance would have to wait.

With a pair of cuticle scissors I had pinched from Feely's vanity table, I snipped four damp disks from the linen handkerchief, taking care to avoid the green grass stains I had inflicted upon it, and cutting out only those parts diagonally opposite the stains—the spots into which Nialla had wept.

These I stuffed—with tweezers—into a test tube, which I then injected with a three-percent solution of sulfosalicylic acid to precipitate the protein. This was the so-called Ehrlich test.

As I worked, I thought with pleasure of how profoundly the great Alexander Fleming had changed the world when he accidentally sneezed into a petri dish. This was the sort of science that was dear to my heart. Who, after all, can honestly say that they have never sneezed on a culture? It could happen to anyone. It has happened to me.

After the sneeze, the magnificently observant Fleming noticed that the bacteria in the dish were shrinking back, as if in fear, from the flecks of his spattered mucus. It wasn't long before he had isolated a particular protein in his snot that repelled bacteria in much the same way that the presence of a dog foaming at the mouth keeps off burglars. He called it lysozyme, and it was this substance for which I was now testing.

Fortunately, even in high summer, the ancestral halls of Buckshaw were as cold and dank as the proverbial tomb. Room temperature in the east wing, where my laboratory was located—in spite of the heating that had been spitefully installed by warring brothers in only the west wing of the once politically divided house—was never more than sixty degrees Fahrenheit, which, as luck would have it, was precisely the temperature at which lysozyme precipitates when sulfosalicylic acid is added.

I watched, entranced, as a veil of crystals began to form, their white flakes drifting gently down in the little winter inside the test tube.

Next, I lit a Bunsen burner, and carefully warmed a beaker of water to seventy degrees. It did not take long. When the thermometer indicated that it was ready, I dipped the bottom of the test tube into the warm bath and swirled it gently.

As the newly formed precipitate dissolved, I let out a gasp of delight.

"Flavia." Father's faint voice came drifting up to the laboratory. Having traversed the front hall, floated up the curving stair, penetrated the east wing, and wended its way down the long corridor to its southernmost point, it now seeped through my closed door, its force spent, as wispy as if it had come drifting to England all the way from Ultima Thule.

"Supper," I thought I heard him call.

"IT'S DAMNABLY IRRITATING," father said.

We were seated round the long refectory table, Father at the far end, Daffy and Feely one on each side, and me at the very bottom, at Cape Horn.

"It's damnably irritating," he said again, "for one to sit here and listen to one's daughter admit that she absconded with one's eau de cologne for a bloody chemical experiment."

No matter if I denied these things or admitted my guilt, Father found it equally irritating. I simply couldn't win. I had learned that it was best to remain silent.

"Damn it, Flavia, I just bought the bloody stuff. Can't very well go up to London in this heat smelling like a shoulder of pork that's gone off, can I?"

Father was most eloquent when he was angry. I had nicked the bottle of Roger & Gallet to fill an atomizer with which I needed to spray the house after an experiment involving hydrogen sulfide had gone spectacularly wrong.

I shook my head.

"I'm sorry," I said, assuming a hangdog look and dabbing at my eye with a napkin. "I'd buy you a new bottle—but I have no money."

As if I were a tin duck in a shooting gallery, Feely glared down the long table at me in silent contempt. Daffy's nose was stuck firmly in Virginia Woolf.

"But I could make you some," I said brightly. "It's really not much more than ethanol, citrus oils, and garden herbs. I'll ask Dogger to pick me some rosemary and lavender, and I'll get some oranges and lemons and limes from Mrs. Mullet—"

"You'll do no such thing, Miss Flavia," said Mrs. Mullet, bustling— literally—into the room as she knocked open the door with one of her ample hips and dumped a large tray onto the table.

"Oh, no!" I heard Daffy whisper to Feely. "It's 'the Whiffler' again."

"The Whiffler," as we called it, was a dessert of Mrs. Mullet's own de- vising, which, so far as we could make out, consisted of a sort of clotted green jelly in sausage casings, topped with double Devon cream, and garnished with sprigs of mint and other assorted vegetable refuse. It sat there, quivering obscenely now and then, like some great beastly garden slug. I couldn't help shivering.

"Yummy," Father said. "How very yummy."

He meant it ironically, but Mrs. Mullet's antennae were not attuned to sarcasm.

"I knew you'd like it," she said. "It was no more than this morning I was sayin' to my Alf, 'It's been a while since the Colonel and those girls 'ave 'ad one of my lovely jells. They always remarks over my jells'" (this was no more than the truth), "and I loves makin' 'em for the dears.'"

She made it sound as if her employers had antlers.

Feely made a noise like a distressed passenger at the rail of the *Queen Mary* on a November crossing of the North Atlantic.

"Eat it up, dear," said Mrs. Mullet, unfazed. "It's good for you." And with that she was gone.

Father fixed me with that gaze of his. Although he had brought the latest issue of *The London Philatelist* to the table, as he always did, he had not so much as opened it. Father was a keen, not to say rabid, collector of postage stamps, his life wholly given over to gazing through a magnifying lens at a seemingly endless supply of little colored heads and scenic views. But he was not looking at stamps now—he was looking at me. The omens did not bode well.

"Where were you all afternoon?" he asked.

"At church," I answered promptly and primly and, I hoped, a little devoutly. I was a master at this kind of deflected chitchat.

"Church?" he asked. He seemed rather surprised. "Why?"

"I was helping a woman," I said. "Her van broke down."

"Ah," he said, allowing himself a half-millimeter smile. "And there you were on the spot to offer your skills as a motor mechanic."

Daffy grinned at her book, and I knew that she was listening with pleasure to my humiliation. To give her credit, Feely remained totally absorbed in polishing her fingernails on her white silk blouse.

"She's with a traveling puppet show," I said. "The vicar asked them—Rupert Porson, I mean, and Nialla—that's her name—to put on a performance in the parish hall on Saturday, and he wants me to help."

Father deflated slightly. The vicar was one of his few friends in Bishop's Lacey, and it was unlikely he would deny my services.

"Rupert is on the television," I volunteered. "He's quite famous, actually."

"Not in my circles," Father said, looking at his wristwatch and pushing his chair back from the table.

"Eight o'clock," he said. "Thursday."

He did not have to explain himself. Without a word, Daffy and Feely and I got up and made dutifully for the drawing room, all in a scattered line like a convoy.

Thursday evenings were Wireless Night at Buckshaw. Father had recently decreed that we needed to spend more time together as a family, and so it was that Wireless Night had been laid on as a supplement to his regular compulsory lecture series on Wednesdays. This week it was to be the fabulous Fifth Symphony by Ludwig van Beethoven, or "Larry" as I called him whenever I wanted to aggravate Feely. I remembered that Feely had once told us that, on the original printed score, Beethoven's given name had appeared as "Louis."

"Louis Beethoven" sounded to me like the name of one of the supporting gangsters in an Edward G. Robinson film, someone with a sallow, pockmarked face, an alarming twitch, and a Thompson submachine gun in a violin case.

"Play dat *Moonlight Snotta* thing by Louie B.," I'd snarl in my raspy mobster's voice, wandering into the room when she was practicing at the keyboard. A moment later I'd be in full flight, with Feely in hot pursuit and sheet music floating to the carpet.

Now, Feely was busily arranging herself in an artistic full-length pose on the chesterfield, like a film star. Daffy dropped down sideways into an overstuffed armchair with her legs hanging out over the side.

Father switched on the wireless, and sat down in a plain wooden chair, his back ramrod straight. As the valves were warming up, I did a handspring across the carpet, walked back across the room on my hands, and dropped into a cross-legged Buddha position with what I hoped was an inscrutable look on my face.

Father shot me a withering look, but with the program already beginning, he decided to say nothing.

After a long and boring spoken introduction by an announcer, which seemed likely to run on into the next century, the Fifth Symphony began at last.

Duh-duh-duh-DAH.

I cupped my chin in my hands, propped my elbows on my knees, and gave myself over to the music.

Father had told us that the appreciation of music was of paramount importance in the education of a decent woman. Those were his exact words, and I had come to appreciate that there was music suitable for meditation, music for writing, and music for relaxation.

With my eyes half closed, I turned my face towards the windows. From my vantage point on the floor, I could see both ends of the terrace reflected in the glass of the French doors, which stood ajar, and unless my eyes were playing me tricks, something had moved out there: Some dark form had passed by outside the window.

I didn't dare leap up to look, though. Father insisted on intent listening. Even so much as a tapping toe would meet instantly with a wicked glare and an accusatory downward-jabbing finger.

I leaned slightly forward, and saw that a man dressed all in black had just sat down on a bench beneath the rose bushes. He was leaning back, eyes closed, listening to the music as it came floating out through the open doors. It was Dogger.

Dogger was Father's Man with a capital M: gardener, chauffeur, valet, estate manager, and odd-job man. As I have said before, he had done it all.

Dogger's experiences as a prisoner of war had left something broken inside him: something that from time to time, with a ferocity beyond belief, went ripping and tearing at his brains like some ravenous beast, leaving him a trembling wreck.

But tonight he was at peace. Tonight he had dressed for the symphony in a dark suit and what might have been a regimental tie, and his shoes had been polished until they shone like mirrors. He sat motionless on the bench beneath the roses, his eyes closed, his face upturned like one of the contented Coptic saints I had seen in the art pages of *Country Life*, his shock of white hair lit from behind by an unearthly beam from the setting sun. It was pleasant to know that he was there.

I stretched contentedly, and turned my attention back to Beethoven and his mighty Fifth.

Although he was a very great musician, and a wizard composer of symphonies, Beethoven was quite often a dismal failure when it came to ending them. The Fifth was a perfect case in point.

I remembered that the end of the thing, the *allegro*, was one of those times when Beethoven just couldn't seem to find the "off" switch.

Dum . . . dum . . . dum-dum-dum, it would go, and you would think it was over.

But no—

Dum, dah, dum, dah, dum, dah, dum, dah, dum, dah, dum—DAH dum.

You'd go to get up and stretch, sighing with satisfaction at the great work you'd just listened to, and suddenly:

DAH dum. DAH dum. DAH dum. And so forth. *DAH dum*.

It was like a bit of flypaper stuck to your finger that you couldn't shake off. The bloody thing clung to life like a limpet.

I remembered that Beethoven's symphonies had sometimes been given names: the *Eroica*, the *Pastorale*, and so forth. They should have called this one the *Vampire*, because it simply refused to lie down and die.

But aside from its sticky ending, I loved the Fifth, and what I loved most about it was the fact that it was what I thought of as "running music."

I pictured myself, arms outspread, running pell-mell in the warm sunshine down Goodger Hill, swooping in broad zigzags, my pigtails flying behind me in the wind, bellowing the Fifth at the top of my lungs.

My pleasant reverie was interrupted by Father's voice.

"This is the second movement, now, *andante con moto*," he was saying loudly. Father always called out the names of the movements in a voice that was better suited to the drill hall than to the drawing room. "Means 'at a walking pace, with motion,'" he added, settling back in his chair as if, for the time being, he'd done his duty.

It seemed redundant to me: How could you have a walking pace *without* motion? It defied the laws of physics, but then, composers are not like the rest of us.

Most of them, for instance, are dead.

As I thought of being dead and of churchyards, I thought of Nialla.

Nialla! I had almost forgotten about Nialla! Father's summons to supper had come just as I was completing my chemical test. I formed in my mind an image of the slight cloudiness, the swirling flakes in the test tube, and the thrilling message they bore.

Unless I was badly mistaken, Mother Goose was pregnant.

five

I WONDERED IF SHE KNEW IT.

Even before she had risen up weeping from her limestone slab, I had noticed that Nialla was not wearing a wedding ring. Not that that meant anything: Even Oliver Twist had an unwed mother.

But then there had been the fresh mud on her dress. Although I had registered the fact in some tangled thicket of my mind, I had given it no further thought until now.

When you stopped to think about it, though, it seemed perfectly obvious that she had piddled in the churchyard. Since it hadn't rained, the fresh mud on her hem would indicate that she had done so, and hastily, at the northwest corner, away from prying eyes, behind the mound of extra soil that the sexton, Mr. Haskins, kept handy for grave-digging operations.

She must have been desperate, I decided.

Yes! That was it! There wasn't a woman on earth who would choose such an unwelcoming spot ("wretchedly insalubrious," Daffy would have called it) unless she had no other choice. The reasons were numerous, but the one that leapt immediately to mind was one I had recently come across in the pages of the *Australian Women's Weekly* while cooling my heels in the outer chamber of a dentist's surgery in Farringdon Street. "Ten Early Signs of a Blessed Event," the article had been called, and the need for frequent urination had been near the top of the list.

"Fourth movement. Allegro. Key of C major," Father boomed, as if he were a railway conductor calling out the next station.

I gave him a brisk nod to show I was paying attention, then dived back into my thoughts. Now then, where was I? Oh, yes—Oliver Twist.

Once, on a trip to London, Daffy had pointed out to us from the window of our taxicab the precise spot in Bloomsbury where Oliver's foundling hospital had stood. Although it was now a rather pleasant and leafy square, I had no trouble imagining myself plodding up those long-gone but nevertheless snowdrifted front steps, raising the huge brass door knocker, and applying for refuge. When I told them of my semi-orphan life at Buckshaw with Feely and Daffy, there would be no questions asked. I would be welcomed with open arms.

London! Damn and blast! I'd completely forgotten. Today was the day I was supposed to have gone up to the City with Father to be fitted for braces. No wonder he was peeved. While I was relishing death in the churchyard and chewing the fat with Nialla and the vicar, Father had almost certainly been steaming and fuming round the house like an over-stoked destroyer. I had the feeling I hadn't heard the last of it.

Well, too late now. Beethoven was—at last—winding his weary way homeward, like Thomas Gray's ploughman, leaving the world to darkness and to me—and to Father.

"Flavia, a word, if you please," he said, switching off the wireless with an ominous *click*.

Feely and Daffy got up from their respective places and went out of the room in silence, pausing only long enough at the door to shoot me a pair of their patented "Now you're in for it!" grimaces.

"Damn it all, Flavia," Father said when they had gone. "You knew as well as I that we had an appointment for your teeth this afternoon."

For my teeth! He made it sound as if the National Health were issuing me a full set of plaster dentures.

But what he said was true enough: I had recently destroyed a perfectly good set of wire braces by straightening them to pick a lock. Father had grumbled, of course, but had made another appointment to have me netted and dragged back up to London, to that third-floor ironmonger's shop in Farringdon Street, where I would be strapped to a board like Boris Karloff as various bits of ironmongery were shoved into my mouth, screwed in, and bolted to my gums.

"I forgot," I said. "I'm sorry. You should have reminded me at breakfast."

Father blinked. He had not expected such a vigorous—or such a neatly deflected!—response. Although he had been a career army officer, when it came to household maneuvers, he was little more than a babe-in-arms.

"Perhaps we could go tomorrow," I added brightly.

Although it may not seem so at first glance, this was a master-stroke. Father despised the telephone with a passion beyond all belief. He viewed the thing—"the instrument," as he called it—not just as a letting-down of the side by the post office, but as an outright attack on the traditions of the Royal Mail in general, and the use of postage stamps in particular. Accordingly he refused, point-blank, to use it in any but the direst of circumstances. I knew that it would take him weeks, if not months, to pick the thing up again. Even if he wrote to the dentist, it would take time for the necessary back-and-forth to be completed. In the meantime, I was off the hook.

"And remember," Father said, almost as an afterthought, "that your aunt Felicity is arriving tomorrow."

My heart sank like Professor Picard's bathyscaphe.

Father's sister descended upon us every summer from her home in Hampstead. Although she had no children of her own (perhaps because she had never married) she had, nevertheless, quite startling views upon the proper upbringing of children: views that she never tired of stating in a loud voice.

"Children ought to be horsewhipped," she used to say, "unless they are going in for politics or the Bar, in which case they ought in addition to be drowned." Which quite nicely summed up her entire philosophy. Still, like all harsh and bullying tyrants, she had a few drops of sentimentality secreted somewhere inside that would come bubbling to the surface now and then (most often at Christmas but sometimes, belatedly, for birthdays), when she would inflict her handpicked gifts upon us.

Daffy, for instance, who would be devouring *Melmoth the Wanderer*, or *Nightmare Abbey*, would receive from Aunt Felicity a copy of *The Girl's Jumbo Book*, and Feely, who never gave a thought to anything much beyond cosmetics and her own pimply hide, would rip open her parcel to find a pair of gutta-percha motoring galoshes ("Ideal for Country Breakdowns").

And yet once, when we had poked fun at Aunt Felicity in front of Father, he had become instantly as angry as I had ever seen him. But he quickly gained control of himself, touching a finger to the corner of his eye to stop a twitching nerve.

"Has it ever occurred to you," he asked, in that horrible level voice, "that your aunt Felicity is not what she may seem?"

"Do you mean to say," Feely shot back, "that this whole batty business is a pose?"

I could only look on agog at her boldness.

Father fixed her for a moment in the fierce glare of that cold blue de Luce eye, then turned on his heel and strode from the room.

"Lawks-a-mercy!" Daffy had said, but only after he had gone.

And so Aunt Felicity's ghastly gifts had continued to be received in silence—at least in my presence.

Before I could even begin to recall her trespasses on my own good nature, Father went on: "Her train gets in to Doddingsley at five past ten, and I'd like you to be there to meet her."

"But—"

"Please don't argue, Flavia. I've made plans to settle up a few accounts in the village. Ophelia is giving some sort of recital for the Women's Institute's morning tea, and Daphne simply refuses to go."

Boil me dry! I should have known that something like this would happen.

"I'll have Mundy send round a car. I'll book him when he comes tonight for Mrs. Mullet." Clarence Mundy was the owner of Bishop Lacey's only taxicab.

Mrs. Mullet was staying late to finish off the semi-annual scouring of the pots and pans: a ritual that always filled the kitchen with greasy, superheated steam, and Buckshaw's inhabitants with nausea. On these occasions, Father always insisted on sending her home afterwards by taxicab. There were various theories in circulation at Buckshaw about his reasons for doing so.

It was obvious that I couldn't be en route to or from Doddingsley with Aunt Felicity and, at the same time, be helping Rupert and Nialla set up their puppet show. I would simply have to sort out my priorities and attend to the most important matters first.

———

ALTHOUGH THERE WAS A SLIVER of gold in the eastern sky, the sun was not yet up as I barreled along the road to Bishop's Lacey. Gladys's tires were humming that busy, waspish sound they make when she's especially content.

Low fog floated in the fields on either side of the ditches, and I pretended that I was the ghost of Cathy Earnshaw flying to Heathcliff (except for the bicycle) across the Yorkshire moors. Now and then, a skeletal hand would reach out of the bramble hedges to snatch at my red woolen sweater, but Gladys and I were too fast for them.

As I pulled up alongside St. Tancred's, I could see Rupert's small white tent set up in the long grass, at the back of the built-up churchyard. He had pitched it in the potter's field: the plots where paupers had been laid to rest and where, consequently, there were bodies but no tombstones. I supposed that Rupert and Nialla had not been told of this, and I decided that they would not hear it from me.

Before I had waded more than a few feet through the sodden grass, my shoes and socks were soaking wet.

"Hello?" I called quietly. "Anyone home?"

There was no reply. Not a sound. I started as one of the curious jackdaws slipped down from the top of the tower and landed with a perfect aerodynamic plop on the crumbling limestone wall.

"Hello?" I called again. "Knock, knock. Anyone home?"

There was a rustling in the tent and Rupert stuck his head out, his haystack hair falling over his eyes, which were as red as if they were driven by electric dynamos.

"Christ, Flavia!" he said. "Is that you?"

"Sorry," I said. "I'm a bit early."

He withdrew his head into the tent like a turtle, and I heard him trying to rouse Nialla. After a few yawns and grumbles, the canvas began poking out at sudden odd angles, as if someone inside with a besom broom were sweeping up broken glass.

A few minutes later, Nialla came half crawling out of the tent. She was wearing the same dress as yesterday, and although the material looked uncomfortably damp, she had pulled out a Woodbine and lighted it even before she had fully straightened up.

"Cheers," she said, flapping an inclusive hand towards me, and causing her smoke to drift off and mingle with the fog that hung among the gravestones.

She coughed with a sudden horrid spasm, and the jackdaw, cocking its head, took several steps sideways on the wall, as if in disgust.

"You oughtn't to be smoking those things," I said.

"Better than smoking kippers," she replied, and laughed at her own joke. "Besides, what do you know?"

I knew that my late great-uncle, Tarquin de Luce, whose chemical laboratory I had inherited, had, in his student days, been hooted down and ejected bodily from the Oxford Union when he took the affirmative in a debate, Resolved: That Tobacco Is a Pernicious Weed.

I had, not long before, come across Uncle Tar's notes tucked into a diary. His meticulous chemical researches seemed to have confirmed the link between smoking and what was then called "general paralysis." Since he had been, by nature, a rather shy and retiring sort, his "utter and abject humiliation," as he put it, at the hands of his fellow students, had contributed greatly to his subsequent reclusive life.

I wrapped my arms around myself and took a step back. "Nothing," I said.

I had said too much. It was cold and clammy in the churchyard, and I had a sudden vision of the warm bed I'd climbed out of to come here and help.

Nialla blew a couple of what were supposed to be casual smoke rings straight up into the air. She watched them ascend until they had dissipated.

"I'm sorry," she said. "I'm not at my best at the crack of dawn. I didn't mean to be rude."

"It's all right," I said. But it wasn't.

A twig cracked, surprisingly loud in the muffling silence of the fog. The jackdaw unfolded its wings and flapped off to the top of a yew tree.

"Who's there?" Nialla called, making a sudden dash to the lime-stone wall and leaning over it. "Bloody kids," she said. "Trying to scare us. I heard one of them laughing."

Although I have inherited Harriet's extremely acute hearing, I had heard no more than the cracking of the twig. I did not tell Nialla that it would be strange indeed to find any of Bishop's Lacey's children in the churchyard at such an early hour.

"I'll set Rupert on them," she said. "That'll teach them a lesson. Rupert!" she called out loudly. "What are you doing in there?

"I'll bet the lazy sod's crawled back into the sack," she added with a wink.

She reached out and gave one of the guy ropes a twang, and like a parachute spilling the wind, the whole thing collapsed in a mass of slowly subsiding canvas. The tent had been pitched in the loose topsoil of the potter's field, and it crumpled at a touch.

Rupert was out of the wreckage in a flash. He seized Nialla by the wrist and twisted it up behind her back. Her cigarette fell to the grass.

"Don't ever—!" he shouted. "Don't ever—!"

Nialla motioned with her eyes towards me, and Rupert let go of her at once.

"Damn it," he said. "I was shaving. I might have cut my bloody throat."

He stuck out his chin and gave it a sideways hitch, as if he were freeing an invisible collar.

Odd, I thought. *He still has all his morning whiskers, and moreover, there's not a trace of shaving cream on his face.*

"THE DIE IS CAST," said the vicar.

He had come humming across the churchyard like a spinning top, showing black and then white through the fog, rubbing his hands together and exclaiming as he came.

"Cynthia has agreed to run up some handbills in the vestry, and we'll have them distributed before lunch. Now then, about breakfast—"

"We've eaten, thanks," Rupert said, jerking a thumb back towards the tent, which now lay neatly folded in the grass. And it was true. A few wisps of smoke were still drifting up from their doused fire. Rupert had fetched a box of wood chips from the back of the van and in surprisingly short order had an admirable campfire crackling away in the churchyard. Next, he had produced a coffeepot, a loaf of bread, and a couple of sharpened sticks to make toast of it. Nialla had even managed to find a pot of Scotch marmalade somewhere in their baggage.

"Are you quite sure?" the vicar asked. "Cynthia said to tell you that if—"

"Quite sure," Rupert said. "We're quite used to—"

"—Making do," Nialla said.

"Yes, well, then," the vicar said, "shall we go in?"

He shepherded us across the grass towards the parish hall, and as he extracted a ring of keys, I turned to look back across the churchyard toward the lych-gate. If someone *had* been there, they had since run off. A misty graveyard offers an infinite number of places to hide. Someone could well be crouching behind a tombstone not ten feet away, and you'd never know it. With one last apprehensive look at the remnants of the drifting fog, I turned and went inside.

"WELL, FLAVIA, WHAT DO YOU THINK?"

My breath was taken away. What yesterday had been a bare stage was now an exquisite little puppet theater, and such a one as might have been transported overnight by magic from eighteenth-century Salzburg.

The proscenium opening, which I guessed to be five or six feet wide, was covered with a set of red velvet draperies, richly trimmed and tasseled with gold, and embroidered with the masks of Comedy and Tragedy.

Rupert vanished backstage, and as I watched in awe, a row of footlights, red and green and amber, faded up little by little until the lower half of the curtains was a rich rainbow of velvet.

Beside me, the vicar sucked in his breath as they slowly opened. He clasped his hands in rapture.

"The Magic Kingdom," he breathed.

There, before our eyes, nestled among green hills, was a quaint country cottage, its thatched roof and half-timbered front complete in every detail, from the wooden bench beneath the window right down to the tiny tissue paper roses in the front garden.

For a moment, I wished I lived there: that I could shrink myself and crawl into that perfect little world in which every object seemed to glow as if lit from within. Once settled in the cottage, I would set up a chemical laboratory behind the tiny mullioned windows and—

The spell was broken by the sound of something falling, and a harsh "Damn!" from somewhere up in the blue painted sky.

"Nialla!" Rupert's voice said from behind the curtains. "Where's that hook for the thingumabob?"

"Sorry, Rupert," she called out, and I noticed that she took her time replying, "it must still be in the van. You were going to have it welded, remember?

"It's the thing that holds the giant up," she explained. "But then," she added, grinning at me, "we mustn't give away too many secrets. Takes all the mystery out of things, don't you think?"

Before I could answer, the door at the back of the parish hall opened, and a woman stood silhouetted against the sunlight. It was Cynthia, the vicar's wife.

She made no move to come in, but stood waiting for the vicar to come scurrying to her, which he promptly did. As she awaited his approach, she turned her face away to the outside light and, even from where I stood, I could clearly make out her cold blue eyes.

Her mouth was as pursed as if the lips were pulled tightly shut with drawstrings, and her sparse, gray-blond hair was pulled—painfully, it appeared—into an oval bun at the nape of an exceptionally long neck. In her beige taffeta blouse, mahogany-colored skirt, and brown oxfords, she looked like nothing so much as an over-wound grandfather clock.

Aside from the sound thrashing she had given me, it was hard to put a finger on what, precisely, I disliked about Cynthia Richardson. By all reports, she was a saint, a tiger, a beacon of hope to the sick, and a comfort to the bereaved. Her good works were legendary in Bishop's Lacey.

And yet . . .

There was something about her posture that just didn't ring true: a horrid slackness, a kind of limp and tired defeat that might be seen in the faces and bodies of Blitz victims in the wartime issues of the *Picture Post*. But in a vicar's wife . . . ?

All of this ran through my mind as she carried on a whispered consultation with her husband. And then, with no more than a lightning glance inside—she was gone.

"Excellent," the vicar said, breaking into a smile as he walked slowly towards us. "The Inglebys, it seems, have returned my call."

The Inglebys, Gordon and Grace, owned Culverhouse Farm, a patchwork quilt of mixed fields and ancient woods that lay to the north and west of St. Tancred's.

"Gordon's kindly offered you a place to pitch your tent at the bottom of Jubilee Field—a lovely spot. It's on the riverbank, not far from here. Walking distance, really. You'll have plenty of fresh eggs, the shade of incomparable willows, and the company of kingfishers."

"Sounds perfect," Nialla said. "A little bit of heaven."

"Cynthia tells me that Mrs. Archer rang up, too. Not such cheerful news on that front, I'm afraid. Bert's away to Cowley, on a course at the

Morris factory, and won't be home until tomorrow night. Is your van in any sort of running order?"

I knew by the worried look on the vicar's face that he was having visions of a van marked "Porson's Puppets" parked at the door of the church come Sunday morning.

"A mile or so shouldn't be a problem," Rupert said, appearing suddenly at the side of the stage. "She'll run better now she's unloaded, and I can always baby the choke."

A shadow flitted across my mind, but I let it pass.

"Splendid," said the vicar. "Flavia, dear, I wonder if you'd mind going along for the ride? You can show them the way."

six

OF COURSE WE HAD TO GO THE LONG WAY ROUND.

Had we gone on foot, it would have been no more than a shady stroll across the stepping-stones behind the church, along the riverbank by way of the old towpath that marked the southern boundary of Malplaquet Farm, and over the stile into Jubilee Field.

But by road, because there was no bridge nearby, Culverhouse Farm could be reached only by driving west towards Hinley, then, a mile west of Bishop's Lacey, turning off and winding tortuously up the steep west side of Gibbet Hill on a road whose dust was now rising up behind us in white billows. We were halfway to the top, skirting Gibbet Wood in a lane so narrow that its hedgerows scratched and tore at the sides of the jolting van.

"Don't mind my hip bones," Nialla said, laughing.

We were squeezed as tightly together in the front seat as worms in an angler's tin. With Rupert driving, Nialla and I were almost sitting on one another's lap, each with an arm across the other's shoulders.

The Austin backfired fiercely as Rupert, according to some ancient and secret formula known only to him, fiddled alternately with the choke and the throttle.

"These Inglebys, now," he shouted above the incessant string of explosions. "Tell us something about them."

The Inglebys were rather morose individuals who kept mostly to themselves. From time to time I had seen Gordon Ingleby dropping off

Grace, his tiny, doll-like wife, at the village market where, dressed always in black, she sold eggs and butter with little enthusiasm beneath a striped canopy. I knew, as did everyone else in Bishop's Lacey, that the Inglebys' seclusion had begun with the tragic death of their only child, Robin. Before that, they had been friendly and outgoing people, but ever since had turned inward. Even though five years had passed, the village still allowed them their grief.

"They farm," I said.

"Ah!" said Rupert, as if I had just rhymed off the entire Ingleby family history from the time of William the Conqueror.

The van bucked and jerked as we climbed ever higher, and Nialla and I had to brace our palms against the dashboard to keep from knocking our heads together.

"Grim old place, this," she said, nodding to the dense woods on our left. Even the few flecks of sunlight that did manage to penetrate the dense foliage seemed to be swallowed up in the dim world of the ancient trunks.

"It's called Gibbet Wood," I said. "There used to be a village nearby called Wapp's Hill, until about the eighteenth century, I think, but there's nothing left of it now. The gallows was at the old crossroads at the center of the wood. If you climb up that path you can still see the timbers. They're quite rotten, though."

"Ugh," Nialla said. "No, thank you."

I decided it was best, at least for the time being, not to tell her that it was at the crossroads in Gibbet Wood that Robin Ingleby had been found hanging.

"Good Lord!" Rupert said. "What in hell is that?"

He pointed to something dangling from a tree branch—something moving in the morning breeze.

"Mad Meg's been here," I said. "She picks up empty tins and rubbish along the roads and strings them on bits of cord. She likes shiny things. She's rather like a magpie."

A pie plate, a rusty Bovril tin, a bit of silver from a radiator shell, and a bent soup spoon, like some grotesque Gothic fishing lure, twisted slowly this way and that in the sun.

Rupert shook his head and turned his attention back to the choke and the throttle. As we reached the peak of Gibbet Hill, the motor emitted a most frightful bang, and with a sucking gurgle, died. The van jerked to a halt as Rupert threw on the hand brake.

I could see by the deep lines on his face that he was nearly exhausted. He pounded at the steering wheel with his fists.

"Don't say it," Nialla said. "We have company."

I thought for a moment she was referring to me, but her finger was pointing through the windscreen to the side of the lane, where a dark, grimy face peered out at us from the depths of a hedgerow.

"It's Mad Meg," I said. "She lives in there somewhere—somewhere in the wood."

As Meg came scuttling alongside the van, I felt Nialla shrink back.

"Don't worry, she's really quite harmless."

Meg, in a tattered outfit of rusty black bombazine, looked like a vulture that had been sucked up by a tornado and spat back out. A red glass cherry bobbed cheerfully from a wire on her black flowerpot hat.

"Ay, harmless," Meg said, conversationally, at the open window. "'Be ye therefore wise as serpents, and harmless as doves.' Hello, Flavia."

"These are my friends, Meg—Rupert and Nialla."

In view of the fact that we were crammed together cheek-by-jowl in the Austin, I thought it would be all right to call Rupert by his Christian name.

Meg took her time staring at Nialla. She reached out a filthy finger and touched Nialla's lipstick. Nialla cringed slightly, but covered it nicely with a tiny counterfeit sneeze.

"It's Tangee," she said brightly. "Theatrical Red. Changes color when you put it on. Here, give it a try."

It was a magnificent job of acting, and I had to give her top marks for the way in which she disguised her fear with an open and cheery manner.

I had to shift a bit so that she could fish in her pocket for the lipstick. As she held it out, Meg's filthy fingers snapped the golden tube from her hand. Without taking her eyes from Nialla's face, Meg painted a broad swathe of the stuff across her chapped and dirty lips, pressing them together as if she were drinking from a straw.

"Lovely!" Nialla said. "Gorgeous!"

Again she reached into her pocket and extracted an enamel powder compact, an exquisite thing of flame orange cloisonné, shaped like a butterfly. She flipped it open to reveal the little round mirror in the lid, and after a quick glance at herself, handed it over to Meg.

"Here, have a look."

In a flash, Meg had seized the compact and was scrutinizing herself in the glass, turning her head animatedly from side to side. Satisfied with what she saw, she rewarded us with a broad grin that revealed the black gaps left by several missing teeth.

"Lovely!" she muttered. "Smashing!" And she shoved the orange butterfly into her pocket.

"Here!—" Rupert made a grab for it, and Meg drew back, startled, as if noticing him for the first time. Her smile vanished as suddenly as it had appeared.

"I know you," she said darkly, her eyes fixed on his goatee. "You're the Devil, you are. Aye, that's what's gone and happened—the Devil's come back to Gibbet Wood."

And with that, she stepped backwards into the hedgerow and was gone.

Rupert climbed awkwardly out of the van and slammed the door.

"Rupert—" Nialla called out. But rather than going into the bushes after Meg, as I thought he would, Rupert walked a short distance up the road, looked round a bit, and then came slowly back, his feet stirring up the dust.

"It's only a gentle slope, and we're no more than a stone's throw from the top," he reported. "If we can push her up as far as that old chestnut, we can coast down the far side. Might even start her up again. Like to steer, Flavia?"

Although I had spent hours sitting in Harriet's old Phantom II in our coach house, it had been always for purposes of reflection or escape. I had never actually been in control of a moving motorcar. Although the idea was not unattractive at first, I quickly realized that I had no real desire to find myself hurtling out of control down the east side of Gibbet Hill, and coming to grief among the scenery.

"No," I said. "Perhaps Nialla—"

"Nialla doesn't like to drive," he snapped.

I knew at once that I had put my foot in it, so to speak. By suggesting that Nialla steer, I was at the same time suggesting that Rupert get off his backside and push—withered leg and all.

"What I meant," I said, "was that you're probably the only one of us who can get the motor started again."

It was the oldest trick in the book: Appeal to his manly vanity, and I was proud to have thought of it.

"Right," he said, clambering back into the driving seat.

Nialla scrambled out, and I behind her. Any thoughts I might have had about the wisdom of someone in her condition pushing a van uphill on a hot day were instantly put aside. And besides, I could hardly bring up the subject.

Like a flash, Nialla had darted round behind the van, pressing her back flat against the rear doors and using her powerful legs to push.

"Take off the bloody hand brake, Rupert!" she shouted.

I took up a position beside her and, with every last ounce of strength that was in me, dug in my feet and pushed.

Wonder of wonders, the stupid thing began to move. Perhaps because the puppet paraphernalia had been unloaded at the parish hall, the greatly lightened van was soon creeping, snail-like but inexorably, up towards the peak of the hill. Once we had it in motion, we turned round and shoved with our hands.

The van came to a full stop only once, and that was when Rupert threw in the clutch and turned on the ignition. A tremendous black backfire came shooting out of the tailpipe, and even without looking down, I knew that I would have to explain to Father the destruction of yet another pair of white socks.

"Don't let the clutch in now—wait until we get to the top!" Nialla shouted.

"Men!" she muttered to me. "Men and their bleeding exhaust noises."

TEN MINUTES LATER we were at the crest of Gibbet Hill. In the distance, Jubilee Field sloped away towards the river, a gently rolling blanket of flax of such electric-blue intensity that it might have caused van Gogh to weep.

"One more good heave," Nialla said, "and we're on our way."

We groaned and we grunted, pushing and shoving against the hot metal, and then suddenly, as if it had become weightless, the van began moving on its own. We were on the downside of the hill.

"Quick! Jump in!" Nialla said, and we ran alongside as the van picked up speed, bucketing and bumping down the rutted road.

We jumped onto the running board, and Nialla threw open the door. A moment later we had collapsed, hugging one another, into the seat as Rupert manipulated the engine controls. Halfway down, as the motor started at last, the van gave off an alarming backfire before settling down to an unhealthy coughing. At the bottom of the hill, Rupert touched the brakes, and we turned neatly into the lane that leads to Culverhouse Farm.

OVERHEATED FROM ITS EXERTIONS, the Austin stood sputtering and steaming like a leaky teakettle in the farmyard, which, to all intents and purposes, seemed to be abandoned. In my experience, whenever you arrived at a farm, someone always came out of the barn to greet you, wiping his oily hands on a rag and calling to a woman with a basket of eggs to bake some scones and put the tea on. At the very least, there should have been a barking dog.

Although there were no pigs in evidence, a weathered sty at the end of a row of tumbledown sheds was full of tall nettles. Beyond that was a turreted dovecote. Assorted milk pails, all of them rusty, lay scattered about the yard, and a lone hen picked halfheartedly among the weeds, watching us with its wary yellow eye.

Rupert climbed out of the van and slammed the door loudly.

"Hello?" he called. "Anyone here?"

There was no reply. He walked past a battered chopping block to the back door of the house and gave it a thunderous knocking with his fist.

"Hello? Anyone at home?"

He cupped his hands, peering in through the grimy window of what must once have been the buttery, then motioned us out of the van.

"Odd," he whispered. "There's someone standing in the middle of the room. I can see his outline against the far window." He gave the door a couple more loud bangs.

"Mr. Ingleby," I called out, "Mrs. Ingleby, it's me, Flavia de Luce. I've brought the people from the church."

There was a long silence, and then we heard the sound of heavy boots on a wooden floor. The door creaked open upon a dark interior, and a tall blond man in overalls stood blinking in the light.

I had never seen him before in my life.

"I'm Flavia de Luce," I said, "from Buckshaw." I waved my hand vaguely in its direction to the southeast. "The vicar asked me to show these people the way to Culverhouse Farm."

The blond man stepped outside, bending substantially in order to get through the low doorway without banging his head. He was what Feely would have described as "indecently gorgeous": a towering Nordic god. As this fair-haired Siegfried turned to close the door carefully behind him, I saw that there was a large, faded red circle painted on the back of his boiler suit.

It meant he was a prisoner of war.

My mind flew instantly back to the wooden block and the missing axe. Had he chopped up the Inglebys and stacked their limbs like firewood behind the kitchen stove?

What a preposterous thought. The war had been over for five years, and I had seen the Inglebys—at least Grace—as recently as last week.

Besides, I already knew that German prisoners of war were not particularly dangerous. The first ones I had seen were on my first-ever visit to a cinema, the Palace, in Hinley. As the blue-jacketed captives were marched by their armed guards into the theater and seated, Daffy had nudged me and pointed.

"The enemy!" she had whispered.

As the lights went down and the film began, Feely had leaned over and said, "Just think, you'll be sitting with them in the dark for two hours. Alone . . . if Daffy and I go for sweets."

The film was *In Which We Serve,* and I couldn't help noticing that when HMS *Torrin* was sunk in the Mediterranean by the Luftwaffe's dive-bombers, although the prisoners did not applaud the deed openly, there were nevertheless smiles among them.

"Captured Germans are to not be treated inhumanely," Father had told us when we got home, quoting something he had heard on the wireless, "but are to be shown very clearly that we regard them, officers and men, as outcasts from the society of decent men."

Although I respected Father's word—at least in principle—it was clear that the man who had greeted us at Culverhouse Farm was no outcast; not by any stretch of the imagination.

Five years after the coming of peace, he could only be wearing his bull's-eyed boiler suit out of pride.

"May I present myself? I am Dieter Schrantz," he said, with a broad smile, shaking hands with each of us in turn, beginning with Nialla. From those four words alone, I could tell that he spoke nearly perfect English. He even pronounced his own name the way any Englishman would have done, with hard *r*s and *a*s and no unpleasant snarling of his surname.

"The vicar said that you should come."

"Bloody van broke down," Rupert said, jerking his head towards the Austin with, I thought, a certain measure of aggressiveness. As if he . . .

Dieter grinned. "Don't worry, I'll help you run it down the lane to Jubilee Field. That's where you're billeted, you know, old chap."

Old chap? Dieter had obviously been in England for quite some time.

"Is Mrs. Ingleby at home?" I asked. I thought that it was probably best if Nialla was given a tour of the amenities, as it were, before she had to ask.

The shadow of a cloud passed over Dieter's face.

"Gordon's gone off up the wood somewhere," he said, gesturing to Gibbet Hill. "He likes to work alone most of the time. He'll be down presently to help Sally in the meadow. We shall see them when we take your 'bus down to the river."

"Sally" was Sally Straw, a member of the Women's Land Army, or "Land Girl," as they were called, who had been working at Culverhouse Farm since sometime during the war.

"All right," I said. "Hullo! Here's Tick and Tock."

Mrs. Ingleby's two tortoiseshell cats came ambling out of a shed, yawning and stretching in the sun. She often took them with her, for company, to the market, as she did several of her farm creatures, including, now and then, her pet goose, Matilda.

"Tick," she had informed me once, when I inquired about their names, "because she has ticks. And Tock because she chatters like a magpie."

Tock was walking directly towards me, already well launched into a meowling conversation. Tick, meanwhile, ambled off towards the dovecote, which rose up darkly from behind the warren of shabby, overgrown sheds.

"You go on ahead," I said. "I'll come down to the field in a few minutes."

I swept Tock up into my arms. "Who's a pretty pussy, then?" I cooed, watching from the corner of my eye to see if anyone was taken in. I knew that the cat was not: She had begun to squirm immediately.

But Rupert and Nialla were already piling into the van, which still stood shuddering away to itself in the yard. Dieter gave a shove and climbed onto the running board, and a moment later, with a wave, they were bumping out of the yard and into the lane that led down the slope to Jubilee Field and the river. A gentle backfire in the middle distance confirmed their departure.

The moment they were out of sight, I put Tock down in the dusty yard. "Where's Tick?" I said. "Go find her."

Tock resumed her long feline monologue, and stalked off to the dovecote.

Needless to say, I followed.

seven

THE DOVECOTE WAS A WORK OF ART. THERE'S NO OTHER WAY of putting it, and I shouldn't have been in the least surprised to hear that the National Trust had its eye on it.

It was from this remarkable specimen of architecture that Culverhouse Farm had taken its name—"culverhouse" being the old word for a dovecote. This one was a tall round tower of ancient bricks, each one the shade of a faded rose, but no two of them alike. Built in the time of Queen Anne, it had once been used to breed and raise doves for the farm's dinner table. In those days, the legs of the little dovelets were snapped to keep them fattening in the nest (this fact gleaned from the kitchen chatter of Mrs. Mullet). But times had changed. Gordon Ingleby was an avid pigeon fancier, and the birds that had lived in the tower in this century were more likely to be coddled by hand than in boiling water. At the weekends, he had sent them off by rail to some far-flung flyspeck on the map of England, where they would be released to come flapping immediately back to Culverhouse Farm. Here, they would be welcomed by the slapping-off of elaborate mechanical time clocks, much petting and bragging, and a great gorging on grain by the birds.

At least, such had been the case until little Robin Ingleby had been found hanging by the neck from the rotted gallows in Gibbet Wood. Since that day, other than a few wild specimens, there had been no more doves at Culverhouse Farm.

Poor Robin, when he died, had been the same age as I was then, and I found it hard to believe that someone so young could actually be dead. Still, it was a fact.

When one lives in a village, the more things are hushed up, the more one hears, and I remembered the undercurrent of gossip that had swept through Bishop's Lacey at the time, lapping away like the tide at the timbers beneath a pier.

"They say young Robin Ingleby's gone and killed himself." "Robin Ingleby's been done in by his parents." "The little lad's been slaughtered by Satanists. Mark my words—"

Most of these theories had been leaked to me by Mrs. Mullet, and I thought of them now as I approached the tower, gazing up in wonder at its myriad of openings.

As that monk called the lector had done in the monasteries of the Middle Ages, Daffy often read aloud to us as we ate our meals. We had recently been treated to Henry Savage Landor's description, in *Across Coveted Lands*, of the Towers of Silence, in Persia, on top of which the Parsees placed corpses in a sitting position, with a stick under the chin to keep them upright. When the crows arrived to squabble over the body, it was considered a ticket to Heaven if the right eyeball was the first one consumed. The left was not quite so auspicious.

I could not help thinking of this now, and of the author's account of the curious circular pigeon towers of Persia, each with a deep central pit for the collection of guano, whose production was the sole reason for keeping the birds.

Could there be, I wondered, some strange connection between towers, birds, death, and corruption? As I paused there for a moment, trying to think what it might be, a peculiar sound came drifting from the tower.

At first I thought it might be the muttering and cooing away to themselves of doves, high above my head in the cote. Or was it the wind?

It seemed too sustained to be either of these, rising and falling like the sound of a ghostly air-raid siren, almost at the threshold of hearing.

The sagging wooden door stood ajar, and I found that I could slip through easily into the hollow center of the tower. Tock brushed past my ankles, then vanished into the shadows in search of mice.

The sharp reek of the place slapped me in the face: the unmistakable chemical smell of dove's guano, which the great Humphry Davy had found to yield, by distillation, carbonate of ammonia, with a residuum of carbonate of lime and common salt, a finding I had once verified by experiment in my chemical laboratory at Buckshaw.

Far above my head, countless beams of sunshine slanting in through the open ports dappled the curving walls with dots of yellow light. It was as if I had stepped into the colander in which some giant strained his soup bones.

Here, inside, the wailing sound was even louder, a whirlpool of noise amplified by the circular walls, of which I was the very center. I couldn't have called out—even if I'd dared.

At the center of the room, pivoting on an ancient wooden post, was a moveable scaffold, somewhat like a library ladder, which must at one time have been used by their keepers to gain access to the doomed little birds.

The thing groaned fearsomely as I stepped onto it.

Up I went, inch by inch, hanging on for dear life, stretching my arms and legs to make impossible giant steps from one creaking crosspiece to the next. I looked down only once, and it made my head swim.

The higher I climbed, the louder the keening sound became, its echoes now coming together in a chorus of voices that seemed to congregate in some wild, high lament.

Above me, and to my left, was a vaulted opening that gave onto a niche larger than the others. By standing on tiptoe and seizing the brick ledge with my fingertips, I was able to pull myself up until my eyes were level with the floor of this grotto.

Inside, a woman knelt, her back towards me. She was singing. Her thin voice echoed from the bricks and swirled round my head:

"The robin's gone afloat.
The wind that rocks him to and fro
With a soft cradle-song and slow
Pleases him in the ebb and flow,
Rocking him in a boat."

It was Mrs. Ingleby!

In front of her, on an overturned box, a candle burned, adding its smoky odor to the stifling heat of the little brick cave. To her right was propped up a black-and-white photograph of a child: her dead son,

Robin, who grinned happily at the camera, his shock of blond hair bleached nearly white by the sun of long-gone summer days. To her left, lying on its side, as if it were hauled up on the beach to be cleaned of barnacles, was a toy sailboat.

I held my breath. She mustn't know I was here. I would climb down slowly, and—

My legs began to shake. I hadn't much of a grip, and my leather soles were already slipping on the weathered wooden frame. As I started to slide back, Mrs. Ingleby began her wail again, this time another song and, oddly, in another voice: a harsh, swashbuckling, piratical gargle:

> "So, though bold Robin's gone,
> Yet his heart lives on,
> And we drink to him with three times three."

And she let out a horrible, snuffling laugh.

I pulled myself up on tiptoe again, just in time to see her twist the cork from a tall clear bottle, and take a quick, bobbing swig. It looked to me like gin, and it was plain to see that she had been at it for some time.

With a long, shuddering sigh, she pushed the bottle back under a pile of straw and lit a new candle from the dwindling flame of the one that was dying. With drips of flowing wax, she stuck it in place beside its exhausted fellow.

And now she began another song, this one in a darker minor key; sung more slowly, and more like a dirge, pronouncing every word with an awful, exaggerated clarity:

> "Robin-Bad-fellow, wanting such a supper,
> Shall have his breakfast with a rope and butter
> To which let all his fellows be invited
> That with such deeds of darkness are delighted."

Rope and butter? Deeds of darkness?

I suddenly realized that my hair was standing completely on end, the way it did when Feely stroked her black ebonite comb on her cashmere sweater and brought it close to the nape of my neck. But while I was still trying to calculate how quickly I could scramble back down the wooden frame and make a run for it, the woman spoke: "Come up, Flavia," she said. "Come up and join in my little requiem."

Requiem? I thought. *Do I really want to scramble up into a brick cell with a woman who is at best more than a little inebriated, and at worst a homicidal maniac?*

I hauled myself up into the gloom.

As my eyes became accustomed to the candlelight, I saw that she wore a white cotton blouse with short puffed sleeves and a low peasant-girl neckline. With her raven black hair and her brightly colored dirndl skirt, she might easily be taken for a gypsy fortune-teller.

"Robin's gone," she said.

Those two words nearly broke my heart. Like everyone else in Bishop's Lacey, I had always thought that Grace Ingleby lived in her own private, insulated world: a world where Robin still played in the dusty dooryard, chasing flustered hens from fence to fence, dashing into the kitchen now and then to beg a sweet.

But it was not true: She had stood as I had done, beside the small gravestone in the churchyard of St. Tancred's, and read its simple inscription: *Robin Tennyson Ingleby, 1939–1945, Asleep in the Lamb.*

"Robin's gone," she said again, and now it was almost a moan.

"Yes," I said, "I know."

Motes of dust floated like little worlds in the pencil beams of sunlight that penetrated the chamber's gloom. I sat down in the straw.

As I did so, a pigeon clattered up from its nest, and out through the little arched window. My heart almost stopped. I had thought the pigeons long gone, and I almost sat on the stupid thing.

"I took him to the seaside," Grace went on, caressing the sailboat, oblivious to the bird. "Robin loved the seaside, you know."

I pulled my knees up under my chin and wrapped my arms around them.

"He played in the sand. Built a sand castle."

There was a long silence, and I saw that she had drifted off somewhere.

"Did you have ice cream?" I asked, as if it were the most important question in the world. I couldn't think of anything else.

"Ice cream?" She nodded her head. "They gave it to us in paper cups . . . little pointed paper cups. We wanted vanilla—we both loved vanilla, Robin and I. Funny thing, though . . ." She sighed. "When we ate it, there was a taste of chocolate . . . as if they hadn't rinsed the scoop properly."

I nodded wisely.

"That sometimes happens," I said.

She reached out and touched the sailboat again, running her finger-tips over its smooth painted hull. And then she blew out the candle.

We sat for a while in silence among the spatterings of sunshine that seeped into the red brick cave. *This must be what the womb is like*, I thought.

Hot. Waiting for something to happen.

"Why are you here?" she said at last. I noticed that she was not slurring her words as much as before.

"The vicar sent some people to camp in Jubilee Field. He asked me to show them the way." She seized my arm.

"Does Gordon know?" she demanded.

"I think he does," I said. "He told the vicar it would be all right if they camped at the bottom of the lane."

"The bottom of the lane . . ." She let out a long, slow breath. "Yes, that would be all right, wouldn't it?"

"It's a traveling puppet show," I said. "Porson's Puppets. They're putting on a performance Saturday. The vicar's asked them. Their van's broken down, you see, and . . ."

I was gripped by a sudden inspiration.

"Why don't you come?" I asked. "Everyone in the village will be there. You could sit with me, and—"

Mrs. Ingleby was staring at me with horror.

"No!" she said. "No! I couldn't do that."

"Perhaps you and Mr. Ingleby could both come, and—"

"No!"

She scrambled to her feet, raising a thick cloud of chaff, and for a few moments, as the stuff swirled round us, we stood perfectly still, like figures in a snow-globe paperweight.

"You'd better go," she said suddenly, in a throaty voice. "Please go now."

Without a word I groped my way to the opening, my eyes streaming from the dust. With surprisingly little effort, I found myself able to drop down onto the wooden vane, and begin the long climb down.

I have to admit that Jack and the Beanstalk crossed my mind.

———

THE FARMYARD WAS DESERTED. Dieter had gone down the lane with Rupert and Nialla to the river, and by now they had probably already made camp. If I was lucky, I might be just in time for a cup of tea. I felt as if I'd been up all night.

What was the time, anyway?

God blind me with a fish fork! Aunt Felicity's train was due to arrive at five past ten and I'd completely forgotten about her! Father would have my guts for garters.

Even if Aunt Felicity wasn't already fuming on the platform and frothing at the mouth, how on earth was I ever going to get to Doddingsley? It was a good six miles from Culverhouse Farm, even as the crow flies, and as far as I knew, I wasn't about to sprout wings.

Down the lane I ran, windmilling my arms as if that could propel me to a greater speed. Fortunately, it was downhill all the way, and at the bottom, I could see Rupert's van parked beneath the willows.

Dieter had the Austin's hood open and was poking around in its innards. Nialla was hanging a shirt on the bushes to dry. Gordon Ingleby was nowhere in sight, nor was Sally Straw.

"First chance I've had to break out the old Sunlight," Nialla told me. "Dieter's having a peek at the motor. Whatever took you so long?"

"What time is it?" I pleaded.

"Search me," she replied. "Rupert's the only one who owns a watch, and he's taken himself off somewhere."

As he always does. She did not actually speak the words, but her meaning was as clear as if she'd shouted them from the top of Big Ben.

"Dieter?" I asked.

Dieter shook his head. "Sorry. It was for such a long time forbidden to possess one. . . ."

"Excuse me," I interrupted, "but I have to meet a train."

Before they could answer, I was off along the towpath at top speed. It was an easy run along the old embankment, which skirted the southern edge of Jubilee Field, and within surprisingly few minutes, I was leaping across the stepping-stones to the churchyard.

The clock on the church tower showed twenty minutes to four, which was impossible: The stupid thing had probably stopped in the reign of Henry the Eighth and nobody had cared enough to set it going again.

Gladys, my trusty BSA, was exactly where I had left her at the side of the parish hall. I pushed off for Buckshaw.

As I raced past the corner of Spindle Lane, the clock set into the wall of the Thirteen Drakes showed that the time was either noon or midnight. I'm afraid I let slip rather a rude word.

Out of the village I went like the wind, southwestwards towards Buckshaw, until I came at last to the Mulford Gates, where Clarence Mundy sat waiting, perched on one of the wings of his taxicab, dragging thirstily at a cigarette. By the snowfall of butts on the road, I could tell that it was not his first.

"Hullo, Clarence," I said. "How's the time?"

"Ten hundred hours," he said, glancing at his elaborate military wristwatch. "Better climb aboard."

He let in the clutch as I did so, and we were off like a skyrocket.

As we tore along through lanes and hedgerows, Clarence worked the gear stick like a snake charmer grappling with a wilful cobra, seizing its head every few seconds and shoving it to some new quarter of the compass. Outside the windows, the countryside streamed past in an ever-accelerating blur of green, until I wanted to scream "Yarooh!"—but I restrained myself.

During the war, Clarence had flown the jumbo-sized Sunderland flying boats, endlessly patrolling the vast Atlantic for German U-boats, and, as we fairly flew along between the pressing hedgerows, he seemed still to imagine himself at the controls of one of these behemoths. At any moment, I thought, he would pull back on the steering wheel and we would lift off into the air. Perhaps, during our ascent into the summer sky, we might even catch a glimpse of Harriet.

Before she had married Father, Harriet had piloted her own de Havilland Gipsy Moth, which she had named *Blithe Spirit*, and I sometimes imagined her floating alone up there in the sunshine, dipping in and out of the puffy valleys of cumulus, with no one to answer to except the wind.

Clarence skidded to a stop at one end of the Doddingsley railway platform as the train steamed in at the other.

"Ten-oh-five," he said, glancing at wristwatch. "On the dot."

As I knew she would be, the first passenger to step down from the carriage was Aunt Felicity. In spite of the heat, she was wearing a long, light-colored motoring coat and a great solar topee, which was tied under her chin with a broad blue ribbon. Various bits protruded from her person in all directions: hatpins, umbrella handles, rolled-up magazines, newspapers, shooting sticks, and so forth. She looked like a walking bird's nest, or, rather, more like an ambulatory haystack.

"Fetch my luggage, Clarence," she said, "and mind the alligator."

"Alligator?" Clarence said, his eyebrows shooting up.

"The bag," said Aunt Felicity. "It's new from Harrods, and I won't have it ruined by a clumsy rustic on some godforsaken railway platform.

"Flavia," she said, "you may carry my hot-water bottle."

eight

DOGGER MET US AT THE FRONT DOOR. HE FISHED A CLOTH change purse from his pocket and raised his eyebrows at Clarence.

"Two bob," Clarence said, "going and coming—including the wait."

As Dogger counted out the coins, Aunt Felicity leaned back and ran her eyes over the façade of the house.

"Shocking," she said. "The place grows shabbier before one's very eyes."

I did not feel it my place to tell her that, when it came to expenses, Father was nearly at his wit's end. The house had actually belonged to Harriet, who had died young, unexpectedly, and without troubling to make a will. Now, because of what Father called "complications," it seemed unlikely that we would be able to remain at Buckshaw for much longer.

"Take my bags to my room, Dogger," Aunt Felicity said, returning her gaze to earth, "and mind the alligator."

"Yes, Miss Felicity," Dogger said, a wicker hamper already under each arm and a suitcase in each hand. "Harrods, I believe."

"Aunt Felicity's arrived," I said, slouching into the kitchen. "I'm suddenly not very hungry. I think I'll just have a lettuce sandwich and eat it in my room."

"You'll do no such thing," Mrs. Mullet said. "I've gone and made a nice aspic salad, with beets and that."

I pulled a horrid face, but when she glanced at me unexpectedly,

I remembered Nialla's dodge and cleverly transformed my grimace into a yawn, covering my mouth with my hand.

"Sorry. I was up early this morning," I said.

"So was I. More's the pity."

"I was at Ingleby's farm," I volunteered.

"So I heard," she said.

Petrify the woman! Was there nothing that escaped her ears?

"Mrs. Richardson told me you was helpin' them puppet people, her with her Judas hair, like, and him with his gampy leg."

Cynthia Richardson. I should have guessed. Obviously, the presence of the puppeteers had loosened the purse-string mouth.

"Her name's Nialla," I said, "and his is Rupert. She's quite a nice person, actually. She makes scrapbooks—or she used to, at least."

"That's all very well, I'm sure, dear, but you'll have to—"

"I met Mrs. Ingleby, too," I persisted. "In fact, we had quite an interesting chat."

Mrs. Mullet's polishing of the salad plates slowed—and stopped. She had taken the bait.

"A chat? Her? Ha! That'll be the thirsty Friday!"

"Poor soul," she added, as a quick afterthought.

"She talked about Robin, her son," I said, with a crumb of truth.

"Get away with you!"

"She said that Robin's gone."

This was too much even for Mrs. Mullet.

"Gone? I should say he is. He's deader than a doorknob these five years or more. Dead and buried. I mind the day they found him, hangin' by 'is neck in Gibbet Wood. It was a washday Monday, and I'd just hung a load on the line when Tom Batts the postman come to the gate. 'Mrs. M,' he says to me, he says, 'you'd best get ready to hear some bad news.' 'It's my Alf!' I says, and he says, 'No, it's young Robin, Gordon Ingleby's boy,' and *phoosh*! The wind went out of me just like that. I thought I was going to—"

"Who found him?" I interrupted. "Young Robin, I mean."

"Why, Mad Meg it was. Her as lives up there in Gibbet Wood. She spotted a bit of bright under a tree—that's what she calls any old bit of 'mongery she comes across: 'a bit of bright'—and when she goes to pick it up, she sees it's one of them toy shovels, them as you'd take to the beach, like, and the tin sand pail, too, lyin' right there in the woods."

"Robin's mother took him to the seaside," I was about to say, but I stopped myself just in time. I remembered that gossip withheld draws more gossip: "like flies to a magnet," as Mrs. Mullet herself had once remarked about another matter entirely.

"And then she saw 'im, swingin' by the neck from that there old scaffold," she went on. "'Is face was awful, she said—like a blackened melon."

I was beginning to regret that I hadn't brought my notebook.

"Who killed him?" I asked bluntly.

"Ah," she said, "that's the thing. Nobody knows."

"Was he murdered?"

"Might have been, for all that. But like I said, nobody knows for sure. They had what they call an ink-quest at the library—it's the same thing as a poet's mortem, Alf says. Dr. Darby got up and told them the little lad was hanged, and that's all he could rightly say. Mad Meg claimed the Devil took 'im, but you know what she's like. They called up the Inglebys, and that German what drives their tractor—Dieter, 'is name is—as well as Sally Straw. Dumb as Dorothy's donkey, the lot of 'em. Including the police."

The police? Of course!

The police would certainly have investigated Robin Ingleby's death, and if my guess was right, my old friend Inspector Hewitt would have had a hand in it.

Well, the Inspector wasn't *exactly* an old friend, but I had recently assisted him with an investigation in which he and his colleagues were completely baffled.

Rather than rely on Mrs. Mullet's village hearsay, I'd get the facts straight from the horse's mouth, so to speak. All I needed was an opportunity to bicycle over to the police station in Hinley. I would drop in casually, just in time for tea.

AS I CYCLED PAST ST. TANCRED'S, I couldn't help wondering how Rupert and Nialla were getting on. Well, I thought, as I braked and circled back, it wouldn't take long to find out.

But the door to the parish hall was locked. I gave it a good old shaking and more than a few hard knocks, but no one came to let me in. Could they still be at Culverhouse Farm?

I pushed Gladys through the churchyard to the riverbank, and lifted her across the stepping-stones. Although it was overgrown in places with weeds, and deeply rutted, the towpath brought me quickly back to Jubilee Field.

Nialla was sitting under a tree, smoking, with Dieter at her side. He scrambled to his feet as soon as he saw me.

"Well, well," she said. "Look what the cat dragged in."

"I thought you'd be at the church."

Nialla twisted the butt of her cigarette fiercely against a tree trunk. "I suppose we should be," she said, "but Rupert hasn't found his way back yet."

This struck me as rather odd, since Rupert presumably didn't know anyone in the neighborhood of Bishop's Lacey. What—or who—could have kept him away so long?

"Perhaps he's gone off to see about the van," I said, noticing that the Austin's hood was now closed and latched.

"More likely he's just gone off to have a good sulk," Nialla said. "He does that, now and again. Sometimes he just wants to be alone for a while. But he's been gone for hours.

"Dieter thought he saw him heading off in that direction," she added, pointing a finger over her shoulder.

I turned, and found myself staring up with renewed interest at Gibbet Wood.

"Flavia," Nialla said, "leave him be."

But it wasn't Rupert I wanted to see.

BY KEEPING TO THE GRASSY HEADLANDS at the edge of the field, I was able to stay clear of the growing flax as I trudged steadily on upwards. It wasn't much of a climb for me, but for Rupert, with his leg in an iron brace, it must have been torture.

What on earth would possess the man to climb back up to the top of Gibbet Hill? Did he have some notion of flushing Meg from the dense thickets, and demanding that she hand over Nialla's butterfly compact? Or was he in a sulk, threatened by Dieter's blond good looks?

I could think of a dozen more reasons, yet not one of them made perfect sense.

Above me, Gibbet Wood clung to the top of Gibbet Hill like a green skullcap. As I approached, and then entered beneath the branches of this ancient forest, it was like stepping into a painting by Arthur Rackham. Here, in the dim green gloom, the air was sharp with the smell of decay: of funguses and leaf mold, of black humus, of slithering muck, and of bark gnawed away to dust by beetles. Bright cobwebs hung suspended like little portcullises of light between the rotted tree stumps. Beneath the ancient oaks and lichen-coated hornbeams, bluebells peeped out from the deep shadows among the ferns, and there on the far side of the glade I spotted the serrated leaves of the poisonous dog's mercury that, when steeped in water, produced a gorgeous indigo poison that I had once transformed into the bright red color of arterial blood simply by adding a two-percent solution of hydrochloric acid.

I thought with pleasure of how the ammonia and amides given off by the deep compost on the forest floor provided a perfect feast for omnivorous molds that converted it to nitrogen, which they then stored in their protoplasm, where it would be fed upon by bacteria. It seemed to me a perfect world: a world in which cooperation was a fact of life.

I drew in a deep breath, sucking the sour tang into my lungs and savoring the chemical smell of decay.

But this was no time for pleasant reflections. The day was hurrying on, and I had still to find my way to the heart of Gibbet Wood.

The farther I went in among the trees, the more silent it became. Now, even the birds had become eerily still. This wood, Daffy had told me, was once a royal forest in which, many centuries ago, kings of England had hunted the wild boar. Later, the Black Death had taken most of the inhabitants of the little village that had grown up beneath its skirts.

I shivered a bit as, high in the branches above me, the leaves stirred fitfully, though whether it was from the swift passage of the ghostly royal hunters or the restless spirits of the plague victims—surely they were buried somewhere nearby?—I could not tell.

I tripped on a hummock and threw out my arms to save myself. A rotted stump of moss-covered wood was all that stood between the muck and me, and I grabbed at it instinctively.

As I regained my balance, I saw that the wood had once been square, not round. This was no branch or tree trunk, but a cut timber that had weathered and been eaten away to something that looked like gray coral. Or petrified brain matter.

My mind recognized it before I did: Only slowly did I realize that I was hanging on for dear life to the rotted remains of the old gallows.

This was the place where Robin Ingleby had died.

The backs of my upper arms bristled, as if they were being stroked with icicles.

I released my grip on the thing and took a step backwards.

Except for its frame and a shattered set of stairs, there was little left of the structure. Time and weather had crumbled all but one or two of its floorboards, reducing the platform to a few skeletal remains that stuck up out of the brambles like the bones of a dead giant's ribcage.

It was then that I heard the voices.

I have, as I have said before, an acute sense of hearing, and as I stood there under the ruined gallows, I became aware that someone was talking, although the sound was coming from some distance away.

By rotating slowly on the spot and cupping my hands behind my ears as makeshift reflectors, I quickly determined that the voices were coming from somewhere on my left, and with careful steps, I crept towards them, slipping quietly from tree to tree.

Suddenly the wood began to thin, and I had to take great care to keep out of sight. Peering round the trunk of an ash, I found myself at the edge of a large clearing that lay at the very heart of Gibbet Wood.

Here, a garden had been cultivated, and a man with a battered hat and working clothes, was hoeing away industriously among the rows of widely spaced plants.

"Well, they're all over the bloody place," he was saying to someone I could not yet see.

". . . Behind every fence post . . . hiding under every bloody hayrick."

As he removed his hat to mop his face and the top of his head with a colored handkerchief, I saw that the speaker was Gordon Ingleby.

His lips, set in a weathered face, were the startling crimson hue of what Father called "the sanguine temperament," and as I watched, he wiped away the spittle that had come with his angry words.

"Ah! 'The heavens set spies upon us,'" said the other person in a dramatic voice: a voice I recognized at once as Rupert's.

He was lounging in the shade beneath a bush, smoking a cigarette.

My heart nearly stopped in my chest! Had he spotted me?

Best to keep still, I decided. *Don't move a muscle. If I'm caught, I'll pretend I came looking for Rupert and became lost in the woods, like Goldilocks.* Because there was something in them that had the ring of truth, people always fell for fairy-tale excuses.

"Squire Morton was round again last week talking a lot of rubbish to Dieter. Prying's more like it."

"You're smarter than the lot of them, Gordon. They've all got bricks for brains."

"Maybe so," Gordon replied, "and maybe not. But like I told you, this is the end of the line. This is where Gordon gets off."

"But what about me, Gord? What about the rest of us? Are we just to be left hanging?"

"You *bastard!*" Gordon shouted, raising his hoe in the air like a battle-ax, and taking a couple of threatening steps. He was instantly livid.

Rupert scrambled awkwardly to his feet, holding out one hand defensively in front of him. "I'm sorry, Gord. I didn't mean it. It's just an expression. I didn't think."

"No, you didn't think, did you? You never do. You don't know what it's like living in my skin day and night—living with a dead woman, and the ghost of a dangling kid."

A dead woman? Could he be talking about Mrs. Ingleby?

Well, whatever the case, one thing seemed perfectly clear: This was not a conversation between two men who had met for the first time this morning. By the sound of it, Gordon and Rupert had known one another for a very long time indeed.

They stood there for a few moments, staring at one another, not knowing what to say.

"Best be getting back," Rupert said at last. "Nialla frets." He turned and walked to the far side of the clearing, then vanished into the wood.

When he had gone, Gordon wiped his face again, and I saw that his hands were shaking as he pulled a sack of tobacco and a packet of cigarette papers from his shirt pocket. He rolled a clumsy cigarette, spilling shreds of tobacco in his haste, then dug into his trouser pocket for a brass lighter, and lit up, inhaling the smoke with a deep sucking and exhaling so slowly I was sure he must be suffocating.

In a surprisingly short time he had finished. Grinding the butt into the soil with the heel of his boot, he shouldered his hoe and was gone.

I waited for about ten minutes to be sure that he wasn't coming back, then went quickly to the spot where he had been standing. From the earth beneath his heel print, I had no difficulty in retrieving the soggy remains of his cigarette. I broke a couple of leaves from one of the plants and, using them as a makeshift pot holder, picked up the butt, double-rolled it in a fresh leaf, and shoved the thing into the bottom of my pocket. Rupert, too, had left several fag ends beneath the bush where he had been sitting. These I retrieved also, and added to the others. Only then did I retrace my steps through the wood and back across the shoulder of Gibbet Hill.

NIALLA AND RUPERT WERE PERCHED on a couple of rotted pilings, letting the flowing water cool their bare feet. Dieter was nowhere in sight.

"Oh, there you are!" I said brightly. "I was looking for you everywhere."

I undid my shoes, peeled off my socks, and joined them. The sun was well down in the afternoon sky. It was probably now too late to bicycle to Hinley. By the time I got there, it would be past five o'clock, and Inspector Hewitt would be gone for the day.

My curiosity would have to wait.

For a man who had recently been threatened with the blade of a sharp hoe, Rupert was in remarkably good spirits. I could see his shriveled foot, swimming round like a pale little fish, just below the water's surface.

He reached down, dipped two fingers in the river, and flicked a couple of drops of water playfully in my direction.

"You'd better beetle off home for a decent meal and a good night's sleep. Tomorrow's the big day."

"Righty-ho," I said, scrambling to my feet. "I wouldn't miss it for the world. I'm frightfully keen on puppet shows."

nine

SUPPER HAD SOMEHOW BEEN SURVIVED, AND THE TABLE cleared. We were sitting round it just waiting for someone to think of an excuse for us to go our separate ways: Father to his stamps, Daffy to the library, Feely to her mirror, Aunt Felicity to one of the far-flung guest bedrooms, and I to my laboratory.

"And how's London these days, Lissy?" Father asked.

Since there was hardly a fortnight that passed without his traveling up there for one stamp show or another, he knew perfectly well how London was. These journeys, though, he always treated as top secret military operations. Father would rather be roasted than let Aunt Felicity know he was in the City.

"She still has all her own teeth," he used to tell us, "—and she knows how to use 'em."

Which meant, Feely said, that she wanted things her own way. Daffy said it meant she was a blood-soaked tyrant.

"London?" Aunt Felicity said. "London is always the same: all soot and pigeons and Clement Attlee. Just one damnable deprivation after another. They ought to have men with nets to capture those children one sees in Kensington and train them to run the power plants at Battersea and Bankside. With a better class of people at the switches, the current mightn't go off so frequently."

Daffy, who because of company was not allowed to read at supper, was sitting directly across the table from me, letting her eyeballs slowly and agonizingly drift towards one another, as if her brain had just died and the optic nerves and muscles were in their last throes. I would not allow her the satisfaction of a smile.

"I don't know what the world is coming to," Aunt Felicity went on. "I shudder to think of the people one meets nowadays—that man on the train, for instance. Did you see him on the platform, Flavia?"

I shook my head.

"Neither did I," she went on, "but I believe he kept back because he thought I'd whistle for the guard. Kept sticking his head into the compartment all the way down from London—asking if we were at Doddingsley yet. A rum-looking individual he was, too. Leather patches on his elbows and a bandanna round his neck like some brute of an apache dancer from Paris. It oughtn't to be allowed. I had, at last, to put him in his place.

"'When the train comes to a full stop and the signboard outside the window says "Doddingsley,"' I told him, 'we shall be at Doddingsley—and not a moment sooner.'"

Now it seemed that Daffy's brain had not only died, but that it had begun to curdle. Her right eye rolled off into one corner, while the other looked as if it were about to explode clean out of her head.

This was an effect she had been working on for years: the ability to bulge her eyes out in two different directions at the same time.

"A touch of the old exophthalmia," she had called it once, and I had begged her to teach me the trick. I had practiced in front of a looking glass until my head was splitting, but I could never manage more than a slight lateral googly.

"God moves in mysterious ways, His wonders to perform," she had said, when I reported my failure.

He did indeed. The very thought of Daffy's words had given me an idea.

"May I be excused?" I asked, already pushing back my chair. "I forgot to say my prayers this morning. I'd better see to them now."

Daffy's eyes uncrossed and her jaw dropped—I should like to think in admiration.

AS I UNLOCKED THE DOOR and walked into my laboratory, the Leitz microscope that had once belonged to Great-Uncle Tar shot me a welcoming gleam of brass. Here, close to the window, I would be able to adjust its reflecting mirror to focus a late beam of sunlight up through the specimen stage to the eyepiece.

I snipped a lozenge-shaped sample from one of the leaves I had brought from what I now thought of as the Secret Garden in Gibbet Wood, and placed it on a glass slide beneath the lens.

As I twiddled the focus, with the instrument set at one hundred times magnification, I found almost instantly what I was looking for: the barbed cystoliths that projected like thorns from the leaf's surface. I flipped the leaf over with a pair of tweezers I had pinched from Feely's mother-of-pearl vanity set. If I was correct, there would be an even greater number of these clawlike hairs on the underside—and there they were!—shifting in and out of focus beneath the snout of the lens. I sat for a few moments, staring at those stony hairs of calcium carbonate which, I remembered, had first been described by Hugh Algernon Weddell, the great botanist and globe-trotter.

More for my own amusement than anything, I placed the leaf in a test tube, into which I decanted a few ounces of dilute hydrochloric acid, then corked it and gave it a vigorous shaking. Holding it up to the light, I could see the tiny bubbles of carbon dioxide form and rise to the surface as the acid reacted with the calcium carbonate of the tiny spurs.

This test was not conclusive, though, since cystoliths were sometimes present in certain nettles, for instance. In order to confirm my findings, I would need to go a little further.

I was eternally grateful to Uncle Tar who, before his death in 1928, had bought a lifetime subscription to *Chemical Abstracts & Transactions*, which, perhaps because the editors had never been informed of his death, still arrived faithfully each month on the hall table at Buckshaw.

Piles of these enticing journals, each issue with a cover the exact blue of a mid-March sky, were now stacked in every corner of my laboratory, and it was among these—in one of the issues from 1941, in fact—that I had found a description of the then newly discovered Duquenois-Levine test. It was my own variation of this procedure that I was about to perform.

First I would need a small quantity of chloroform. Since I had used the last available bottle for a failed fireworks display on Buckshaw's south lawn to celebrate Joseph Priestley's birthday in March, I would first have to manufacture a fresh supply.

A quick raid below-stairs produced (from Mrs. Mullet's cleaning cupboard) a tin of chlorine bleaching powder, and from her pantry, a bottle of pure vanilla extract.

Safely back upstairs in the laboratory, I locked the door and rolled up my sleeves.

The tin of Bleachitol was, in reality, no more than calcium hypochlorite. Would calcium hypochlorite, I wondered, by any other name smell as sweet? Heated with acetone to a temperature of somewhere between 400 and 500 degrees Fahrenheit—or until the haloform reaction occurs—a quite decent chloroform may afterwards be extracted from the resulting acetate salts by simple distillation. This part of it was, as they say, a piece of cake.

"Yarooh!" I shouted, as I poured the results into a brown bottle and shoved home the cork.

Next, I stirred a half teaspoon of vanilla extract into a few drops of acetaldehyde (which, because the stuff is volatile and boils at room temperature, Uncle Tar had thoughtfully stored beneath a layer of argon in a sealed bottle), then tipped the mixture into a clean beaker into which I had already measured six and a half tablespoons of ethanol—plain old C_2H_5OH. This I had pinched from Father's sideboard, where it had lain unopened for ages after being brought him as a gift from a fellow philatelist who had been posted to Russia by the Foreign Office.

And now the stage was set.

Placing a fresh sample of one of the leaves into a clean test tube, I added a few drops of my alcoholic vanillin preparation (which I thought of calling the Duquenois-Levine-de-Luce reagent), and after waiting for a minute, just a nibbins of concentrated hydrochloric acid.

Again, as in my previous test, small bubbles arose in the tube as the carbon dioxide was formed, but this time, the liquid in the test tube turned quickly to a shade of blueish purple.

Excitedly, I added to the mixture a couple of drops of my homemade chloroform, which, since chloroform is not miscible in water, sank promptly to the bottom.

When the stuff had stratified into two distinct layers (the clear chloroform on the bottom and the blueish purple of the Duquenois reagent floating on top of it), I gave it a jolly good mixing up with a glass stirring rod and, holding my breath, waited for it to settle one last time.

It didn't take long: Now the chloroform layer had taken on the color of its upper blanket, the mauve of a hidden bruise.

Because I had already suspected the outcome, I didn't bother to cry "Eureka."

It wasn't parsnips Gordon Ingleby was growing in his secret glade: It was Indian hemp!

I had read about the stuff in an offprint of O'Shaughnessy's *On the Preparations of the Indian Hemp, or Gunjah; Their Effects on the Animal System in Health, and Their Utility in the Treatment of Tetanus and Other Convulsive Diseases*, a copy of which I had found tucked away in one of Uncle Tar's desk drawers.

Had Uncle Tar been using Indian hemp? Would that further explain his sudden and spectacular departure from Oxford as a young man?

Gunjah, or bhang, had long been known as an opium substitute, and Dr. O'Shaughnessy himself had reported great success in using it to treat a case of infantile convulsions.

And what more was Rupert's infantile paralysis, I thought, than muscular convulsions that would drag on cruelly, all day every day, until the last day of his life?

Testing the ends of the cigarettes that Gordon and Rupert had smoked was almost an anticlimax. The results were as I knew they would be. When I had washed up and put away the glassware (ughh!—how I loathe washing up!), I wrote in my notebook:

Friday, 21st of July 1950, 9:50 p.m.
Duquenois-Levine test of leaves and cigarette remnants from Gibbet Wood indicates presence of Indian hemp (Cannabis sativa). Gordon Ingleby growing—and smoking—the stuff. Overheard his remark that it was "the end of the line" for him. What did he mean? Who are the "rest of us" Rupert spoke of? Who is "the dead woman"? Could it be Mrs. Ingleby? Whatever is going on at Culverhouse Farm, Rupert Porson is part of it.

"And so . . ." as that man Pepys would have written: "to bed."

———

BUT I COULD NOT SLEEP. For a long while I lay staring at the ceiling, listening to the curtains as they whispered quietly to one another in the night breeze.

At Buckshaw, time does not pass as it does in other places. At Buckshaw, time seems to be controlled not by those frantic, scurrying little cogs in the hall clock that spin like hamsters in their shuttered cages, but rather by the solemn great gears that manage to creep through just one complete turn each year.

How could I be so contented, I suddenly wondered, when someone I knew personally was hiding out in the dark tower of a dovecote?

Which made me think at once, of course, of *King Lear*. Father had taken us to see John Gielgud in the title role at Stratford-upon-Avon, and although Gielgud was marvelous, it was the words of Poor Tom, the Bedlam beggar on the stormy heath (actually Edgar, in disguise), that still rang in my ears:

Child Rowland to the dark tower came;
His word was still, Fie, foh, and fum,
I smell the blood of a British man.

"Did Shakespeare steal that from *Jack and the Beanstalk?*" I had whispered in Daffy's ear. Or had the fairy tale borrowed the words from Shakespeare? "Neither," she whispered back: Both had cribbed from Thomas Nashe's *Have With You to Saffron-Walden*, which, having been staged in 1596, predated them.

Good old Daffy. There were times when I could almost forgive her for hating me.

Well, Rupert would be presenting his own version of *Jack and the Beanstalk* in just a few hours' time. I might even learn something from it.

After a while I got up, dressed, and crept outside.

I FOUND DOGGER SITTING ON a bench that overlooked the ornamental lake and the folly.

He was dressed as he had been the previous evening: dark suit, polished shoes, and a tie that probably spoke volumes to those in the know.

The full moon was rolling up the sky like a great silver cheese, and

Dogger sat bolt upright, his face upturned, as if he were basking in its rays, holding a black umbrella open above his head.

I slid quietly onto the bench beside him. He did not look at me, nor I at him, and we sat, for a time, like a couple of grave ancient astronomers studying the moon.

After a while, I said, "It's not raining, Dogger."

Somewhere, during the war, Dogger had been exposed to torrential rains: rains without mercy; rains from which there could be no shelter and no escape. Or so Mrs. Mullet had told me.

"'E takes great comfort in 'is brolly, dear," she had said. "Even when the dogs is pantin' in the dust."

Slowly, like a clockwork figure, Dogger reached up and released the lock on the umbrella's handle, allowing the ribs and the waterproof cloth to fold down like bats' wings, until his upper hand was enveloped in black.

"Do you know anything about polio?" I asked at last.

Without removing his eyes from the moon, Dogger said: "Infantile paralysis. Heine-Medin disease. Morning paralysis. Complete bed rest.

"Or so I've been told," he added, looking at me for the first time.

"Anything else?"

"Agony," he said. "Absolute agony."

"Thank you, Dogger," I said. "The roses are beautiful this year. You've put a great deal of work into them."

"*Thank you for saying so, miss,*" he said. "*The roses are beautiful every year, Dogger or no Dogger.*"

"Good night," I said, as I got up from the bench.

"Good night, Miss Flavia."

Halfway across the lawn, I stopped and looked back. Dogger had raised the umbrella again, and was sitting beneath it, straight-backed as Mary Poppins, smiling at the summer moon.

ten

"PLEASE DON'T GO WANDERING OFF TODAY, FLAVIA," FATHER said after breakfast. I had encountered him rather unexpectedly on the stairs.

"Your aunt Felicity wants to go through some family papers, and she's particularly asked that you be with her to help lift down the boxes."

"Why can't Daffy do it?" I asked. "She's the expert on libraries and so forth."

This was not entirely true, since I had charge of a magnificent Victorian chemistry library, to say nothing of Uncle Tar's papers by the ton.

I was simply hoping I wouldn't have to mention the puppet show, which was now just hours away. But Duty trumped Entertainment.

"Daphne and Ophelia have gone to the village to post some letters. They're lunching there, and going on to Foster's to look at Sheila's pony."

The dogs! Those scheming wretches!

"But I've promised the vicar," I said. "He's counting on me. They're trying to raise money for something or other—oh, I don't know. If I'm not at the church by nine, Cynthia—Mrs. Richardson, I mean—will have to come for me in her Oxford."

As I expected it would, this rather low blow gave Father real pause.

I could see his eyebrows pucker as he weighed his options, which were few: Either concede gracefully or risk coming face-to-face with the Wreck of the Hesperus.

"You are unreliable, Flavia," he said. "Utterly unreliable."

Of course I was! It was one of the things I loved most about myself.

Eleven-year-olds are supposed to be unreliable. We're past the age of being poppets: the age where people bend over and poke us in the tum with their fingers and make idiotic noises that sound like "boof-boof"— just the thought of which is enough to make me bring up my Bovril. And yet we're still not at the age where anyone ever mistakes us for a grown-up. The fact is, we're invisible—except when we choose not to be.

At the moment, I was not. I was fixed in the beam of Father's fierce-eyed tiger stare. I batted my eyelids twice: just enough not to be disrespectful.

I knew the instant he relented. I could see it in his eyes.

"Oh, very well," he said, gracious even in his defeat. "Run along. And give my compliments to the vicar."

Paint me with polka dots! I was free! Just like that!

GLADYS'S TIRES HUMMED THEIR loud song of contentment as we sped along the tarmac.

"*Summer is icumen in,*" I warbled to the world. "*Lhude sing cuccu!*"

A Jersey cow looked up from her grazing, and I stood on the pedals and gave her a shaky curtsy in passing.

I pulled up outside the parish hall just as Nialla and Rupert were coming through the long grass at the back of the churchyard.

"Did you sleep well?" I called out to them, waving.

"Like the dead," Rupert replied.

Which described perfectly what Nialla looked like. Her hair hung in long, unwashed strings, and the black circles under her red eyes reminded me of something I'd rather not think about. Either she'd ridden with witches all night from steeple to steeple, or she and Rupert had had a filthy great row.

Her silence told me it was Rupert.

"Fresh bacon . . . fresh eggs," Rupert went on, giving his chest a hearty pounding, like Tarzan, with his fists. "Sets a man up for the day."

Without so much as a glance at me, Nialla darted past and ducked into the parish hall—to the ladies' W.C., I expected.

Naturally, I followed.

Nialla was on her knees, shouting "Rope!" into the porcelain, crying and vomiting at the same time. I bolted the door.

"You're having a baby, aren't you?" I asked.

She looked up at me, her mouth gaping open, her face white. "How did you know?" she gasped.

I wanted to say "Elementary," but I knew this was no time for cheek.

"I did a lysozome test on the handkerchief you used."

Nialla scrambled to her feet and seized me by the shoulders. "Flavia, you mustn't breathe a word of this! Not a word! Nobody knows but you."

"Not even Rupert?" I asked. I could hardly believe it.

"*Especially* Rupert," she said. "He'd kill me if he knew. Promise me. Please, Flavia . . . promise me!"

"On my honor," I said, holding up three fingers in the Girl Guide salute. Although I had been chucked from that organization for insubordination (among other things), I felt it was hardly necessary to share the gruesome details with Nialla.

"Bloody good job we're camped in the country. They must have heard us for miles around, the way the two of us went at one another's throats. It was about a woman, of course. It's always about a woman, isn't it?"

This was beyond my field of expertise, but still, I tried to look attentive.

"It never takes long for Rupert to zero in on the skirt. You saw it; we weren't in Jubilee Field for half a tick when he was off up the wood with that Land Girl, Sarah, or whatever her name is."

"Sally," I said.

Although it was an interesting idea, I knew that Rupert had, in actual fact, been smoking Indian hemp in Gibbet Wood with Gordon Ingleby. But I could hardly tell Nialla that. Sally Straw had been nowhere in sight.

"I thought you said he went to see about the van."

"Oh, Flavia, you're such a—" She bit off the word in the nick of time. "Of course I said that. I didn't want to air our dirty laundry in front of a stranger."

Did she mean me—or was she referring to Dieter?

"Rupert always smudges himself with smoke, trying to cover up the scent of his tarts. I smell it on him.

"But I went a bit too far," she added ruefully. "I opened up the van and threw the first thing at him that came to hand. I shouldn't have. It was his new Jack puppet: He's been working on it for weeks. The old one's getting tatty, you see, and it tends to come apart at the worst possible moment.

"Like me," she wailed, and threw up again.

I wished that I could make myself useful, but this was one of those situations in which a bystander can do nothing to help.

"Up all the night he was, trying to fix the thing."

By the fresh marks on her neck, I could see that Rupert had done more in the night than patch up a puppet.

"Oh, I wish I were dead," she moaned.

There was a banging at the door: a sharp, rapid volley of *rat-a-tat-tat* knocks.

"Who's in there?" a woman's voice demanded, and my heart cringed. It was Cynthia Richardson.

"There may be others wishing to use the facilities," she called. "Please try to be more considerate of other people's needs."

"Just coming, Mrs. Richardson," I called out. "It's me, Flavia."

Damn the woman! How could I quickly feign illness?

I grabbed the cotton hand towel from the ring beside the sink, and gave my face a rough scrubbing. I could feel the blood rising even as I worked. I messed up my hair, ran a bit of water from the tap and mopped it across my reddening brow, and let loose a thread of spit to dangle horribly from the corner of my mouth.

Then I flushed the toilet and unbolted the door.

As I waited for Cynthia to open it, as I knew she would, I caught a glimpse of myself in the mirror: I was the very image of a malaria victim whose doctor had just stepped out to ring the undertaker.

As the knob turned and the door swung inwards, I took a couple of unsteady steps out into the hallway, puffing out my cheeks as if I were about to vomit. Cynthia shrank back against the wall.

"I'm sorry, Mrs. Richardson," I said shakily. "I've just sicked up. It must have been something I ate. Nialla's been very kind . . . but I think, with a bit of fresh air, I'll be all right."

And I tottered past her with Nialla in my wake; Cynthia didn't give her so much as a glance.

"YOU ARE TERRIFYING," NIALLA SAID. "You really are. Do you know that?"

We were sitting on a slab tomb in the churchyard as I waited for the sun to dry my feverish face. Nialla put away her lipstick and rummaged in her bag for a comb.

"Yes," I said, matter-of-factly. It was true—and there was no use denying it.

"Aha!" said a voice. "*Here* you are, then!"

A dapper little man in slacks and jacket with a yellow silk shirt was coming rapidly towards us. His neck was swathed in a mauve ascot, and an unlit pipe protruded from between his teeth. He stepped gingerly from side to side, trying not to tread directly on some of the more sunken graves.

"Oh, God!" Nialla groaned without moving her mouth, and then to him: "Hello, Mutt. Half-holiday at the monkey house, is it?"

"Where's Rupert?" he demanded. "Inside?"

"How lovely to see you, Nialla," Nialla said. "How perfectly lovely you're looking today, Nialla. Forgotten your manners, Mutt?"

Mutt—or whoever he was—turned on his heel in the grass and trod off towards the parish hall, still minding where he stepped.

"Mutt Wilmott," Nialla told me. "Rupert's producer at the BBC. They had a flaming row last week and Rupert walked out right in the middle of it. Left Mutt holding the bag with Auntie—the Corporation, I mean. But how on earth did he find us? Rupert thought we'd be quite safe here. 'Rusticating in the outback,' he called it."

"He got off the train at Doddingsley yesterday morning," I said, making a leap of deduction, but knowing I was right.

Nialla sighed. "I'd better go in. There's bound to be fireworks."

Even before we reached the door, I could hear Rupert's voice rising furiously inside the echoing hall.

"I don't care what Tony said. Tony can go sit on a paintbrush, and so can you, Mutt, come to think of it. You've shat on Rupert Porson for the last time—the lot of you."

As we entered, Rupert was halfway up the little staircase that led to the stage. Mutt stood in the middle of the hall with his hands on his hips. Neither seemed to notice we were there.

"Oh, come off it, Rupert. Tony has every right to tell you when you've overstepped the mark. And hearken unto me, Rupert, this time you *have* overstepped the mark, and by quite a long chalk at that. It's all very well for you to stir up a hornet's nest and then dodge the flak by taking your little show on the road. That's what you always do, don't you? But this time you at least owe him the courtesy of a hearing."

"I don't owe Tony a parson's whistle."

"That's where you're wrong, old boy. How many binds has he extracted you from?"

Rupert said nothing as Mutt ticked them off on his fingers.

"Well, let's see: There was the little incident with Marco. Then there was the one with Sandra Paisley—a nasty business, that. Then the thing with Sparkman and Blondel—cost the BBC a bundle, that one did. To say nothing of—"

"Shut your gob, Mutt!"

Mutt went on counting. "To say nothing of that girl in Beckenham . . . what was her name . . . Lulu? *Lulu*, for God's sake!"

"Shut up! Shut up! Shut up!"

Rupert was into a full-fledged tantrum. He came storming stiff-legged down the steps, his brace clattering dreadfully. I glanced over at Nialla, who had suddenly become as pale and as still as a painted Madonna. Her hand was at her mouth.

"Go get in your bloody Jaguar, little man, and drive it straight to hell!" Rupert snarled. "Leave me alone!"

Mutt was not intimidated. Even though they were now nose to nose, he didn't give an inch. Rather, he plucked an imaginary bit of lint from the sleeve of his jacket and pretended to watch it float to the floor.

"Didn't drive down, old boy. Came by British Rail. You know as well as I that the BBC's cutting back on expenses, what with the Festival of Britain next year, and all that."

Rupert's eyes widened as he spotted Nialla.

"Who told you we were here?" he shouted, pointing. "Her?"

"Hold on, hold on," Mutt said, his voice rising for the first time. "Don't go blaming Nialla. As a matter of fact it was a Mrs. Something right here in Bishop's Lacey. Her boy saw your van by the church and scooted off home to tell Mummy he'd hold his breath and pop if he couldn't have Porson's Puppets for his birthday party, but by the time he dragged her back, you were gone. She made a long-distance call to the BBC, and the switchboard put her through to Tony's secretary. Tony told me to come and fetch you straightaway. And here I am. End of story. So don't go blaming Nialla."

"All snug with Nialla, are you?" Rupert fumed. "Sneaking round on—"

Mutt placed the palm of his hand on Rupert's chest. "And while we're at it, Rupert, I might as well tell you that if you lay so much as a fingerprint on her again, I'll—"

Rupert shoved Mutt's hand away roughly. "Don't threaten me, you vile little snail. Not if you value living!"

"Gentlemen! Gentlemen! What on earth? You must stop this at once."

It was the vicar. He stood in the open doorway, a dark figure against the daylight.

Nialla ducked past him and fled. I quickly followed.

"DEAR LADY," THE VICAR SAID, holding out an engraved brass collection plate. "Try a cucumber and lettuce sandwich. They're said to be remarkably soothing. I made them myself." *Made them himself?* Had domestic warfare been declared at the vicarage?

We were outside in the churchyard again, quite near the spot where I had first seen Nialla weeping facedown on the gravestone. Had it been only two days ago? It seemed an eternity.

"No, thank you, Vicar," Nialla said. "I'm quite myself again, and I have things to do."

LUNCH WAS A TRIAL. Because the windows of the hall had been covered with heavy blackout curtains for the performance, we sat in near darkness as the vicar fussed with sandwiches and a jug of lemonade he must have conjured from thin air. Nialla and I sat at one end of the front row of chairs, with Mutt at the other. Rupert had vanished backstage some time before.

"We shall soon have to open the doors," said the vicar, drawing back the edge of a curtain for a peek outside. "Our public has already begun to queue up, their pockets heavy with coins of the realm."

He consulted his watch. "Ninety minutes to curtain time," he called through cupped hands. "Ninety minutes."

"Flavia," Nialla said, "be a dear—run backstage and tell Rupert to fade the music down when I begin speaking. He botched it in Fringford, and I don't want it to happen again."

I looked at her questioningly.

"Please—as a favor. I've my costume to get ready, and I don't much want to see him right now."

Actually, I didn't much want to see Rupert either. As I plodded up the steps to the stage, I thought of Sydney Carton ascending the scaffold to meet Madame Guillotine. I found the opening in the black tormentor drapes that hung on either side of the puppet stage, and stepped through into another world.

Little pools of light were everywhere, illuminating rows of electrical switches and controls, their wires and cables snaking off in all directions. Behind the stage, everything fell away into darkness, and the glow of the little lamps, gentle as it was, made it impossible to see beyond the shadows.

"Come up," said a voice from the darkness above me. It was Rupert.

"There's a ladder on the other side. Watch your step."

I felt my way round the back of the stage and found the rungs with my hands. A few steps up and I found myself standing on a raised wooden platform that ran across and above the back of the puppet stage.

A sturdy rail of black metal piping provided support for Rupert's waist as he leaned forward to operate his puppets. Although they were turned away so that I could not see their faces, several of these jointed characters were hanging from a rod behind me: an old woman, a man, and a boy, judging from their peasant clothing.

To one side, and within easy reach, the magnetic tape recorder was mounted, its two spools loaded with a shiny brown ribbon which, judging by its color, I thought must be coated with an emulsion of iron oxide.

"Nialla said to remember to lower the music volume when she starts speaking," I whispered, as if telling him a secret.

"All right," he said. "No need to whisper. The curtains absorb the sound. No one can hear us up here."

This was not a particularly comforting thought. If he were so inclined, Rupert could put his powerful hands around my neck and strangle me in luxurious silence. No one out front would be any the wiser until there was nothing left of me but a limp corpse.

"Well, I'd better be getting back," I said. "I'm helping with the tickets."

"Right," Rupert said, "but have a look at this before you go. Not many kids get a chance to come backstage."

As he spoke, he reached out and rotated a large knob, and the lights faded up on the stage below us. I nearly lost my balance as the little world seemed to materialize from nothingness beneath my feet. I found myself suddenly gazing down, like God, into a dreamy countryside of blue sky and green painted hills. Nestled in a valley was a thatched cottage with a bench in the yard, and a ramshackle cowshed.

It took my breath away.

"You made all this?"

Rupert smiled and reached for another control. As he moved it, the daylight faded away to darkness and the lights came on in the windows of the cottage.

Even though I was looking at it upside down, as it were, from above, I felt a pang—a strange and inexplicable pang that I had never felt before.

It was homesickness.

Now, even more than I had earlier when I'd first glimpsed it, I longed to be transported into that quiet little landscape, to walk up the path, to take a key from my pocket and open the cottage door, to sit down by the fireplace, to wrap my arms around myself, and to stay there forever and ever.

Rupert had been transformed, too. I could see it in his face. Lit from below, his features completely at peace, his broad features relaxed in a gentle and benevolent smile.

Leaning against the piping of the rail, he reached forward and pulled a black cotton hood from a bulky object at the side of the stage.

"Meet Galligantus the giant," he said. "Last chance before he gets his comeuppance."

It was the face of a monster, its features twisted into a look of perpetual anger and spotted with boils, its chin covered with grizzled black whiskers like carpet tacks.

I let out a squeak and took a step backwards.

"He's only papier-mâché," Rupert said. "Don't be alarmed—he's not as horrid as he looks. Poor old Galligantus—I'm quite fond of him, actually. We spend a lot of time together up here, waiting for the end of the show."

"He's . . . marvelous," I said, swallowing. "But he has no strings."

"No, he's not actually a marionette—no more than a head and shoulders, really. He has no legs. He's hinged where his waist should be, held upright out of sight just offstage, and—promise you won't repeat this: It's a trade secret."

"I promise," I said.

"At the end of the play, as Jack is chopping down the beanstalk, I only have to lift this bar—he's spring-loaded, you see, and—"

As he touched one end of it, a little metal bar flew up like a railway signal, and Galligantus tumbled forward, crashing down in front of the cottage, nearly filling the opening of the stage.

"Never fails to get a gasp from out front," Rupert said. "Always makes me laugh to hear it. I have to take care, though, that Jack and his poor old mother don't get in his way. Can't have them being smashed by a falling giant."

Reaching down and seizing Galligantus by the hair, Rupert pulled him upright and locked him back into position.

What bubbled up inexplicably from the bottom of my memory at that moment was a sermon the vicar had preached at the beginning of the year. Part of his text, taken from Genesis, was the phrase "*There were giants in the earth in those days.*" In the original Hebrew, the vicar told us, the word for giants was *nephilim*, which, he said, meant cruel bullies or fierce tyrants: not physically large, but sinister. Not monsters, but human beings filled with malevolence.

"I'd better be getting back," I said. "Thank you for showing me Galligantus."

NIALLA WAS NOWHERE IN SIGHT, and I had no time to look for her.

"Dear, dear," the vicar had said. "I don't know what to tell you to do. Just make yourself generally useful, I expect."

And so I did. For the next hour, I looked at tickets and ushered people (mostly children) to their seats. I glared at Bobby Broxton and motioned for him to take his feet off the rungs of the chair in front of him.

"It's reserved for me," I hissed menacingly.

I clambered up onto the kitchen counter and found the second teapot, which had somehow been shoved to the very back of the top shelf, and helped Mrs. Delaney place empty cups and saucers on a tea tray. I even ran up the high street to the post office to swap a ten-pound note for loose change.

"If the vicar needs coins," said Miss Cool, the postmistress, "why doesn't he break into those paper collection boxes from the Sunday school? I know the money's for missions, but he could always stuff in banknotes to replace what he's taken. Save him from imposing on His Majesty for pennies, wouldn't it? But then, vicars are not always as practical as you might think, are they, dear?"

By two o'clock, I was completely fagged out.

As I took my seat at last—front row, center—the eager buzz of the audience rose to a climax. We had a full house.

Somewhere backstage, the vicar switched off the house lights, and for a few moments we were left sitting in utter darkness.

I settled back in my chair—and the music began.

eleven

IT WAS A LITTLE THING BY MOZART: ONE OF THOSE MELODIES that make you think you've heard it before, even if you haven't.

I could imagine the reels of Rupert's tape machine winding away backstage, the strains of music being summoned up, by magnetism, from the subatomic world of iron oxide. As it had likely been nearly two hundred years since Mozart first heard them in his head, it seemed somehow appropriate that the sounds of the symphony orchestra should be stored in nothing more than particles of rust.

As the curtains opened, I was taken by surprise: Rather than the cottage and the idyllic hills I had been expecting, the stage was now totally black. Rupert had obviously masked the country setting with a dark throw-cloth.

A spotlight faded up, and in the very center of the stage there stood a miniature harpsichord, the ivories of its two keyboards starkly white against the surrounding blackness.

The music faded down, and an expectant hush fell upon the audience. We were all of us leaning forward, anticipating. . . .

A stir at one side of the stage caught our attention, and then a figure strode confidently out towards the harpsichord—it was Mozart!

Dressed in a suit of green silk, with lace at his throat, white knee-stockings, and buckled shoes, he looked as if he had stepped straight through a window from the eighteenth century and into our own. His perfectly powdered white wig framed a pink and insolent face, and he put a hand up to shade his eyes, peering out into the darkness to see who it was that had the audacity to be giggling.

Shaking his head, he went to his instrument, pulled a match from his pocket, and lit the candles: one at each end of the harpsichord's keyboards.

It was an astonishing performance! The audience erupted in applause. Every one of us knew, I think, that we were witnessing the work of a master showman.

The little Mozart seated himself on the spindled chair that stood before the keyboard, raised his hands, as if to begin—then loudly cracked his knuckles.

A great gust of laughter went up from the audience. Rupert must have recorded the close-up sound of a wooden nutcracker cracking walnuts, I thought: It sounded as if the little puppet had crushed every bone in his hands.

And then he began to play, his hands flitting easily over the keys like the shuttles in a loom. The music was the Turkish March: a lilting, driving, lively tune that made me grin.

There's no need to describe it all: From the collapsing chair to the twin keyboards that snapped at the puppet's fingers like shark's teeth, the whole thing, from beginning to end, had all of us rocking with laughter.

When at last the little figure had managed, in spite of it all, to fight his way to the final, triumphant chord, the harpsichord reared up, took a bow, and folded itself neatly up into a suitcase, which the puppet picked up. Then he strode off the stage to a storm of applause. A few of us even leapt to our feet.

The lights went down again.

There was a pause—a silence.

When the audience had settled, a strain of music—different music—came floating to our ears.

I recognized the melody at once. It was "Morning," from Edvard Grieg's *Peer Gynt* suite, and it seemed to me the perfect choice.

"Welcome to the Land of Fairy Tales," said a woman's voice as the music faded down, and a spotlight came up to reveal the most strange and remarkable character!

Seated to the right of the stage—she must have taken her place during the moments of darkness, I thought—she wore a ruff of Elizabethan lace, a black Pilgrim dress with a laced bodice, black shoes with square silver buckles, and a tiny pair of spectacles that perched precariously on the end of her nose. Her hair was a mass of gray curls, spilling out from under a tall pointed hat.

"My name is Mother Goose."

It was Nialla!

There were *oohs* and *aahs* from the audience, and she sat, smiling patiently, until the excitement died down.

"Would you like me to tell you a story?" she asked, in a voice that was not Nialla's, yet at the same time, not anyone else's.

"Yes!" everyone shouted, including the vicar.

"Very well, then," said Mother Goose. "I shall begin at the beginning, and go on till I come to the end. And then I shall stop."

You could have heard a pin drop.

"Once upon a time," she said, "in a village not far away . . ."

And as she spoke those words, the red velvet curtains with their gold tassels opened slowly to reveal the cozy cottage I had glimpsed from behind the scenes, but now I could see it in far greater detail: the diamond-paned windows, the painted hollyhocks, the three-legged milking stool . . .

". . . there lived a poor widow with a son whose name was Jack."

At that, a boy in short leather pants and an embroidered jacket and jerkin came strolling into the scene, whistling off-key to the music.

"Mother," he shouted, "are you at home? I want my supper."

As he turned to look around, his hand shielding his eyes from the light of the painted sun, the audience let out a collective gasp.

Jack's carved wooden face was a face we all recognized: It was as if Rupert had deliberately modeled the puppet's head from a photograph of Robin, the Inglebys' dead son. The likeness was uncanny.

Like a wind in the cold November woods, a wave of uneasy whispers swept through the hall.

"Shhh!" someone said at last. I think it was the vicar.

I wondered how *he* must feel at being confronted with the face of a child he had buried in the churchyard.

"Jack was a very lazy boy," Mother Goose went on. "And because he refused to work, it was not long before his mother's small savings were completely gone. There was nothing to eat in the house, and not so much as a farthing left for food."

Now the poor widow appeared, coming round the side of the cottage with a rope in her hand, and at the other end of the rope, a cow. Both of them were little more than skin and bones, but the cow had the advantage of a gorgeous pair of huge brown eyes.

"We shall have to sell the cow to the butcher," the widow said.

At this, the cow's enormous eyes turned sadly towards the widow, then towards Jack, and finally towards the audience. "*Help me!*" they seemed to say.

"Ahhhh," everyone said at once, on a rising note of sympathy.

The widow turned her back on the poor creature and walked away, leaving Jack to do the dirty work. No sooner was she gone than a peddler appeared at the gate.

"Marnin', Squire," he said to Jack. "You looks like a sharpish lad—the kind o' lad what might be needin' some beans."

"I might," said Jack.

"Jack thought of himself as a shrewd trader," Mother Goose said, "and before you could say '*Llanfairpwllgwyngyllgogerychwyrndrobwyllllanty siliogogogoch*'—which is the name of a place in Wales—he had traded the cow for a handful of beans."

The cow went all stiff-legged and dug in its heels as the peddler dragged it off, and Jack was left standing, looking at the little pile of beans in his palm.

Then suddenly his mother was back.

"Where's the cow?" she demanded. Jack pointed to the road, and held out his hand.

"You dunderhead!" the widow shrieked. "You stupid dunderhead!"

And she kicked him in the pants.

At this, a great laugh went up from the children in the audience, and I have to admit I chuckled a little myself. I'm at that age where I watch such things with two minds, one that cackles at these capers and another that never gets much beyond a rather jaded and self-conscious smile, like the Mona Lisa.

At the kick, Jack actually flew right up into the air, scattering beans everywhere.

Now, the whole audience was rocking with laughter.

"You shall sleep in the chicken coop," the widow said. "If you're hungry, you can peck for corn."

And with that, she was gone.

"Poor old I," Jack said, and stretched himself out on the bench at the cottage door.

The sunlight faded rather quickly, and suddenly it was night. A full moon shone above the folded hills. The lights in the cottage were on, their warm orange light spilling out into the yard. Jack twitched in his sleep—shifted position—and began to snore.

"But look!" said Mother Goose. "Something is stirring in the garden!"

Now the music had become mystical—the sound of a flute in an oriental bazaar.

Something was stirring in the garden! As if by magic, a thing that looked at first like a green string, and then like a green rope, began to snake up from the soil, twisting and twining like a cobra in a fakir's basket, until the top was out of sight.

As it rose into the sky, and night changed quickly to day, the stalk grew thicker and thicker, until at last it stood like a tree of emerald green, dwarfing the cottage.

Again, the music was "Morning."

Jack stretched and yawned and rolled clumsily off the bench. With hands on hips, he bent back impossibly far at the waist, trying to loosen his stiff joints. And then he spotted the beanstalk.

He reeled back as if he had been punched, fighting to keep his balance, his feet stumbling, his arms going like windmills.

"Mother!" he shouted. "Mother! Mother! Mother! Mother!"

The old lady appeared directly, broom in hand, and Jack danced crazily round her in circles, pointing.

"The beans, you see," said Mother Goose, "were magic beans, and in the night they had grown into a beanstalk that reached higher than the clouds."

Well, everyone knows the story of Jack and the Beanstalk, so there's no need for me to repeat it here. For the next hour, the tale unrolled as it has done for hundreds of years: Jack's climb, the castle in the clouds, the giant's wife and how she hid Jack in the oven, the magic harp, the bags of silver and gold—all of it was there, brought to brilliant life by Rupert's genius.

He held us captive in the palm of his hand from beginning to end, as if he were the giant, and all of us were Jack. He made us laugh and he made us cry, and sometimes both at the same time. I had never seen anything like it.

My head was buzzing with questions. How could Rupert operate lights, sound effects, music, and stage settings at the same time he was manipulating several marionettes and providing all the voices? How had he made the beanstalk grow? How could Jack and the giant run such a merry chase without their strings becoming entangled? How did the sun come up? And the moon?

Mother Goose was right: The beans *had* been magic, and they had entranced us all.

And now the end was near. Jack was scrambling down the beanstalk, bags of gold and silver at his waist. The giant wasn't far behind.

"Stop!" roared the voice of the giant. "Stop, thief, stop!"

Even before Jack reached the ground, he was calling down to his mother:

"Mother! Mother! Fetch the axe!" he cried, and taking it from her hands as he jumped to the ground, he began chopping furiously at the beanstalk, which seemed to recoil as if in pain from the sharp blade.

The music swelled to a crescendo, and there was a strange instant during which time seemed frozen. Then the beanstalk collapsed and a moment later the giant came crashing down to earth.

He landed in the front yard of the cottage, his huge torso dwarfing the dwelling, his glassy eyes staring blankly out over our heads. The giant was stone-cold dead.

The children shrieked—even some of the parents leapt to their feet.

It was, of course, Galligantus, the hinged monster I had seen before the show. But I'd had no idea how terrifying his fall and his death would be when seen from this point of view.

My heart was pounding at my ribcage. It was glorious!

"And so died Galligantus," said Mother Goose, "the cruel giant. After a time, his wife grew lonely in the sky, and found another giant to marry. Jack and his mother, now rich beyond their wildest dreams, lived, as all good people do, happily ever after.

"And we know that all of you will, too—each and every one of you."

Jack dusted off his hands, carelessly, as if killing a giant was an everyday affair.

The red curtains swept slowly closed, and as they did, all hell broke loose in the parish hall.

"It's the Devil!" shrieked a woman's voice at the back of the hall. "The Devil's took the little boy and shrinked him up! God help us! It's the Devil!"

I turned and saw someone flapping about in the open doorway. It was Mad Meg. She was pointing, jabbing her finger at the stage, but then she threw her hands up to cover her face. At that moment, the house lights came on.

The vicar was quickly at her side.

"No! No!" she shrieked. "Don't take old Meg! Leave her be!"

He somehow managed to get an arm around her shoulder, and led her gently but firmly off into the hall's kitchen where, for a minute or so, her poor cracked voice could be heard whimpering, "The Devil! The Devil! The Devil got poor Robin!"

A hush fell on the place. Parents began shepherding their children—all of them now subdued—towards the exits.

The women from the Ladies' Auxiliary did a bit of aimless tidying, then scurried away—probably to gossip, hands over mouths, I thought.

I found myself alone.

Nialla seemed to have vanished, although I had not seen her leave. Since I could hear the soft murmur of voices backstage, Rupert was presumably still up on the bridge of his puppet stage.

It was then that I thought of putting physics to work. As I have said, the hall's Victorian designers had made a perfect sound reflector of its interior. The vast expanses of the room's dark varnished paneling picked up the slightest sounds, and focused them wonderfully. By standing at the very center of the room, I found that, with my acute hearing, I could easily make out every word. One of the voices I had heard was Rupert's.

"Bloody hell!" he was saying, in a loud whisper. "Bloody hell, Nialla!"

Nialla said nothing, although I thought I heard a sob.

"Well, we shall have to put a stop to it. That's plain."

Put a stop to what? Had she told him she was pregnant? Or was he talking about his quarrel with Mutt Wilmott? Or with Gordon Ingleby?

Before I could overhear another word, the door to the kitchen opened, and the vicar came out into the hall with Mad Meg leaning on his arm, followed by Cynthia and two members of the Ladies' Auxiliary.

"It's out of the question," Cynthia was saying, "quite out of the question. The place is simply reeking with paint fumes. Furthermore, we don't have—"

"I'm afraid I must overrule you on this occasion, my dear. This poor woman needs somewhere to rest, and we can hardly send her packing back to—"

"A hovel in the woods?" Cynthia asked, a red flush rising in her cheeks.

"Flavia, dear girl," the vicar said as he spotted me. "Would you mind running ahead to the vicarage? The door is open. If you'll be kind enough to clear the books off the couch in my study . . . it doesn't much matter where you put them. We shall be along directly."

Nialla appeared suddenly from behind the curtains. "Just a moment, Vicar," she said. "I'm coming with you."

I could see that she was holding herself together, but only just.

THE VICARAGE STUDY LOOKED AS IF Charles Kingsley had just put down his pen and stepped out of the room. The bookcases, floor to ceiling, were jammed cheek-by-jowl with volumes which, to judge by their solemn bindings, could only have been of ecclesiastical interest. A cluttered, overflowing desk covered most of the room's single window, and a black horsehair sofa—an Everest of dusty books—leaned at a crazy angle on a threadbare Turkish carpet.

No sooner had I shifted the books to the floor than Nialla and the vicar arrived, leading Meg solicitously to the sofa. She seemed dazed, managing only a few vague mutters as Nialla helped her to recline and smoothed her filthy clothing.

A moment later, Dr. Darby's portly presence filled the doorway. Someone must have run up the high street to fetch him from his surgery.

"Um," he ventured, as he put down his black medical bag, opened the clasp, and had a good dig round inside. With a noisy rustle, he brought forth a paper bag and extracted a crystal mint, which he popped into his mouth.

With that detail out of the way, he bent over Meg for a closer look.

"Um," he said again, and reached into the bag for a syringe. He filled the thing from a little bottle of clear liquid, rolled up Meg's sleeve, and slid the needle into her arm.

Meg made not a sound, but looked up at him with eyes like a sledgehammered horse.

From a tall wardrobe in the corner—as if by magic—the vicar produced a pillow and a brightly colored afghan.

"Afternoon naps." He smiled, covering her gently, and Meg was snoring even before the last one of us had stepped softly from the room.

"Vicar," Nialla said abruptly, "I know you'll think it awful of me, but I have a very great favor to ask."

"Ask away," the vicar said, with a worried glance at Cynthia, who was hovering at the far end of the hall.

"I'd be eternally grateful if you could permit me a hot bath. I haven't had one for so long, I feel like something that lives under a stone."

"Of course, my dear," the vicar said. "It's upstairs at the end of the hall. Help yourself to soap and towels.

"And don't mind the little yacht," he added with a smile. "It's mine."

As Nialla climbed the stairs, a rubber heel squeaked on waxed floorboards, and Cynthia was gone.

"Cynthia has offered to run you over to Buckshaw," the vicar said, turning to me, and I knew instantly that he was fibbing. "I expect you'll be back this evening with your family?"

"Oh, of course," I said. "They're all jolly keen on Jack and the Beanstalk."

WITH GLADYS STRAPPED PRECARIOUSLY TO the roof, we crept slowly along the lane in the tired, dusty Oxford. Cynthia, like vicar's wives in general, had a tendency to over-control, steering from side to side in a series of pie crust scallops between the hedges.

Sitting beside her in the front seat, I had a good opportunity to examine her overbite, close-up and in profile. Even with her mouth shut, she showed a remarkable amount of tooth, and I found myself seriously rethinking my rebellion against braces.

"There's always something, isn't there?" she said suddenly, her face still on fire from her recent humiliation. "One is forever being rousted out of one's own house by someone more needy—not that I mind, of course. First, it was the Gypsies. Then, during the war, the evacuees. Then, last year, the Gypsies came again. Denwyn went to them in Gibbet Wood, and invited them personally, each and every one, to attend the Holy Eucharist. Not a single man jack of them ever showed up, of course. Gypsies are savages, essentially, or perhaps Roman Catholics. Not that they don't have souls—they do, naturally—but one always feels that theirs are so much shadier than one's own."

"I wonder how Nialla's getting on with her bath?" I remarked brightly, as we drove up the avenue of chestnuts to Buckshaw.

Cynthia stared straight ahead, gripping the wheel.

"NONSENSE!" AUNT FELICITY DECLARED. "We shall go as a family."

We were in the drawing room, spread as widely apart as was humanly possible.

Father muttered something about stamp albums, and I could see that Daffy was already holding her breath in an attempt to feign a fever.

"You and your girls need to get out more, Haviland. You're all of you as pale as jellyfish. It will be my treat. I shall have Clarence bring round his car as soon as we've eaten."

"But—" Father managed.

"I shall brook no buts, Haviland."

Outside, Dogger was weeding at the edge of the terrace. Aunt Felicity rapped sharply on the windowpane to get his attention.

"Yes, miss?" he said, coming to the French doors, straw hat in hand.

"Ring up Clarence and tell him we shall require a taxi for seven at six-thirty."

"Six-thirty, miss?" Dogger asked, his brow furrowed.

"Of course," Aunt Felicity said. "He'll have to make two trips. I expect you and Mrs. Mullet would both have your noses out of joint if you were left behind. Puppet shows are not just for bluebloods, you know."

"Thank you, miss," Dogger said.

I tried to catch his eye, but he was gone.

twelve

CLARENCE PULLED UP AT THE LYCH-GATE AT TWENTY MINUTES to seven. He came round the taxicab to hold the door open for Aunt Felicity, who had insisted on sitting in the front seat with him in order to, as she put it, "keep a sharp eye out for road hogs."

She had dressed herself in a sort of comic-opera cape over a voluminous red silk suit that might have been pinched from a Persian harem. Her hat was a collapsed black bag with a peacock's feather billowing out behind like smoke from the *Flying Scotsman;* on her feet were a pair of medieval slippers in mustard yellow, with long upturned points like a pair of icing bags. When we arrived at the parish hall, Father and Feely got out on the far side of the taxicab.

"Now off you go to fetch the others, Clarence," Aunt Felicity commanded, "and don't dawdle."

Clarence raised a forefinger to the peak of his cap and, with an impertinent shifting of gears, was gone.

Inside the parish hall, we found that the entire front row of chairs had been reserved for us. Aunt Felicity had certainly not skimped on the cost of tickets. She and Father were to sit front and center, with Feely and Daffy on their left. I was on Father's right, with Dogger and Mrs. Mullet (when they arrived) on our flank.

All was in readiness. The house lights had already been lowered to a level of delicious expectation. Incidental music floated from backstage, and from time to time, the red velvet curtains on the puppet stage gave an enticing twitch.

The entire population of Bishop's Lacey seemed to be there. Mutt Wilmott, I saw, had taken a seat against the wall near the back. Miss Cool was in the row behind him, listening to Cynthia Richardson, who had her ear, and behind her sat Miss Mountjoy, the niece of the late Dr. Twining, Father's old schoolmaster. To Miss Mountjoy's right, from Culverhouse Farm, Dieter Schrantz and Sally Straw, the Land Girl, sat side by side. I gave them a little wave, and both of them grinned.

"*Haroo, mon vieux*—Flavia!"

It was Maximilian Wight, our diminutive neighbor who, after several triumphant world tours as a concert pianist, had settled down at last in our village to teach music. Feely had been one of his pupils, but had begged off her lessons when Max began asking too many intrusive questions about her "paramours."

Max waved a white glove, and I waved back.

As I scanned the rows of faces, my eyes skidded to a stop on a dark-haired woman in a sage green sweater set. She was no one I had seen before, and must be, I thought, a stranger to Bishop's Lacey. Perhaps a visiting relative.

The man beside her saw me staring, and gave me a pleasant smile: Inspector Hewitt. It was not so long since I had assisted him in bringing a murderer to justice.

In a flash I was standing before them, shifting awkwardly from foot to foot as I realized I was probably intruding.

"Fancy meeting you here," the Inspector said. It was not a particularly original comment, but it neatly covered what might have been an awkward moment.

"Antigone," he told the dark-haired woman, "I'd like you to meet Flavia de Luce."

I knew for a fact that she was going to say, "Oh, yes, my husband has mentioned you," and she would say it with that little smirk that tells so much about the amused conversation that had followed.

"I'm so pleased to meet you, Flavia," she said, putting out the most beautiful hand in the world and giving me a good solid shake, "and to find that you share my love of marionettes."

If she'd told me to "fetch" I would have done it.

"I love your name," I managed.

"Do you? My father was Greek and my mother Italian. She was a ballet teacher and he was a fishmonger, so I grew up dancing in the streets of Billingsgate."

With her dark hair and sea green eyes, she was the image of Botticelli's *Flora*, whose features adorned the back of a hand mirror at Buckshaw that Father had once given to Harriet.

I wanted to ask "In what far isle is your shrine? that I might worship there," but I settled for shuffling my feet and a mumbled, "Nice to meet you, Mrs. Hewitt. I hope you and Inspector Hewitt enjoy the show."

As I slipped into my seat, the vicar strode purposefully to the front of the hall and took up a position in front of the stage. He smiled indulgently, waiting, as Daffy, Mrs. Mullet, and Dogger slid into their seats.

"Ladies and gentlemen, boys and girls, parishioners of St. Tancred's and otherwise, thank you for coming. We are honored, this evening, to welcome to our midst, the renowned puppet-showman—if he will allow me to make use of that illustrious nomenclature—Rupert Porson."

(*Applause*)

"Although Mr. Porson, or Rupert, if I may, is best known nowadays for his performances on the BBC Television of *The Magic Kingdom* which, as I'm sure all of you know, is the realm of Snoddy the Squirrel . . ."

(*Applause*)

". . . I am told on good authority that he has traveled widely, presenting his puppet artistry in all of its many forms, and has, on at least one occasion, performed before one of the crowned heads of Europe."

(*Applause*)

"But before Jack sells his mother's cow for a handful of beans—"

"Hssst! Don't give away the plot, Vicar!"

(*Tully Stoker, the proprietor and landlord of the Thirteen Drakes, greeted with hoots of laughter, including his own.*)

". . . and while the maestro prepares his enchanted strings, the Ladies' Auxiliary of St. Tancred's is pleased to present, for your musical entertainment, the Misses Puddock, Lavinia and Aurelia."

Oh, Lord! Spare us! Please spare us!

We had been saved from having to listen to them during the matinee performance only because their St. Nicholas Tea Room kept them too busy to attend.

The Misses Puddock had a death grip on public events at St. Tancred's parish hall. No matter if it was a tea put on by the Ladies' League, a whist drive by the Altar Guild, a white elephant sale by the Ladies' Auxiliary, or a spring flower show by the Vestry Guild, the Misses Puddock would perform, winter or summer, rain or shine.

Miss Lavinia would seat herself at the upright piano, rummage in her string bag, and fish out at last a tattered piece of sheet music: "Napoleon's Last Charge."

After an interminable wait—during which she would thrust her face forward until her nose was touching the music—she would sit back, her spine stiff as a poker, raise her hands above the keyboard, drop them, take a second squint at the music, and then tear into it like a grizzly bear clawing at a salmon in the Pathé newsreels.

When she was finished, her sister, Miss Aurelia, would take up her position, her white-gloved fingertips idly brushing the dusty piano top, and warble (there's no other word for what she did) "Bendemeer's Stream."

Afterwards, the chairman would announce that the Vestry Guild had voted unanimously to present the Misses Puddock with an honorarium: "a purse of appreciation," as he always put it.

And they're off!

Miss Lavinia, her eyes riveted to the music, was into "Napoleon's Last Charge," and I noticed for the first time that, as she read the music, her lips were moving. I couldn't help wondering what she was saying. There were no lyrics to the piece—could she be naming the chords? Or praying?

Mercifully, she took it at a somewhat faster gallop than usual, and the thing was soon over—at least, relatively speaking. I noticed that Feely's jaw muscles were twitching, and that Max looked as if he were biting down on a stainless-steel humbug.

Now it was Miss Aurelia's turn. Miss Lavinia pounded out the first few bars as an introduction before her sister joined in:

"There's a bower of roses by Bendemeer's Stream
And the nightingale sings round it all the day long.
At the time of my childhood 'twas like a sweet dream."

(Miss Aurelia's childhood, to look at her, must have been during George the Third.)

"To sit in the roses and hear the bird's song."

When she finished, there was a smattering of polite applause, and Miss Aurelia stood with her head cocked for a few moments, checking the piano with her fingers for dust, waiting to be coaxed into an encore. But the audience, knowing better than to encourage her, settled quickly back into their seats, and some of us crossed our arms.

As the house lights went down, I turned round for one last look at the audience. A couple of latecomers were just taking their seats on the aisle. To my horror, I saw that they were Gordon and Grace Ingleby, she in her usual dreadful black outfit, he with a bowler hat, for God's sake! And both of them looking less than happy to be there.

At first, I felt anger rushing up and fluttering within my chest. Why had no one warned them? Why had no one cared enough to keep them away?

Why hadn't I?

Crazily, the thing that popped into my mind was something Daffy once told me: It is the duty of a constitutional monarch to warn and advise.

If His Royal Majesty, King George the Sixth, had been among us this evening, he would be bound to take them aside and say something about the puppet with their dead child's face. But he was not.

Besides, it was already too late. . . . The hall was in total darkness. No one but me seemed to have noticed the Inglebys.

And then the show began. Because of the interminable Misses Puddock, I suppose, Rupert had decided to cut out the Mozart sketch and go straight for the main feature.

The red velvet curtains opened, just as they had in the afternoon, revealing the widow's cottage. The spotlight came up to illuminate Nialla in her Mother Goose costume. Grieg's "Morning" floated in the air, painting haunting images in the mind of dark forests and icy fjords.

"Once upon a time, in a village not far away," Nialla began, "there lived a widow with a son, whose name was Jack."

And in came Jack: the Jack with Robin Ingleby's face.

Again, the audible sucking-in of breath as some of the audience recognized the dead boy's features. I scarcely dared turn and look, but by pretending my skirt had become pinched in the folding mechanism of the chair, I was able to twist round in my seat just far enough to sneak a look at the Inglebys. Grace's eyes were wide and staring, but she did not cry out; she seemed frozen to the spot. Gordon was clutching at her hand, but she took no notice.

On the stage, the puppet Jack shouted: "Mother, are you at home? I want my supper."

"Jack was a very lazy boy," said Mother Goose. "And because he refused to work, it was not long before his mother's small savings were completely gone. There was nothing to eat in the house, and not so much as a farthing left for food."

As the gasps and the murmurs died down, the show went on. Rupert was in fine form, the puppets so convincing in their movements and so perfectly voiced that the audience soon fell under his enchantment—as the vicar had suggested they would.

Lighted by the colored lamps of the stage, the faces of the people around me were the faces in a painting by Toulouse-Lautrec, red, over-heated, and fiercely intent upon the little wooden actors. As Aunt Felicity crunched excitedly on a digestive mint, I noticed that even Father had a half-amused look on his face, though whether it was caused by the puppets or his sister, I could not decide.

The business of the cow and the beans and the kick in the pants was greeted with even more raucous laughter than it had been at the afternoon performance.

Mouths (including even Daffy's) fell open as the beanstalk grew while Jack slept, and the audience began nudging one another with delight. By the time Jack climbed the beanstalk into the giant's kingdom, Rupert had all of Bishop's Lacey eating out of his hand.

How was Mutt Wilmott reacting to this success? I wondered. Here was Rupert, obviously at his best in a live (so to speak) performance, with no television apparatus—wonderful as it was—standing between him and his audience. When I turned to look, I saw that Mutt was gone, and the vicar had taken his chair.

More oddly, Gordon Ingleby, too, was no longer present. His chair stood empty, but Grace still sat motionless, her vacant eyes fixed on the stage, where the giant's wife had just hidden Jack in her great stone oven.

"Fee! Fie! Fo! Fum!" the giant roared as he came into the kitchen. "I smell the blood of an Englishman!"

"Jack leapt out of the oven . . . ," said Mother Goose.

"Master! Master!" cried the charming puppet harp, plucking at its own strings in agitation. This was the part I liked best.

". . . grabbed the golden harp, and took to his heels, with the giant close behind!"

Down the beanstalk came Jack, the green leaves billowing round him. When the vegetation thinned out at last, the scene had changed to his mother's cottage. It was a marvelous effect, and I couldn't for the life of me see how Rupert had done it. I would have to ask him.

"Mother! Mother! Fetch the axe!" Jack shrieked, and the old lady came hobbling round from the garden—oh, so slowly!—with the hatchet in her hand.

Jack threw himself at the beanstalk with all his might, the axe flying fast and furious, the beanstalk shrinking back again and again as if in agony from the wickedly glinting blade.

And then, as it had done before, the beanstalk sagged, and crumpled to the ground.

Jack seemed to be looking up as, with a sound like thunder, the giant came crashing down from the sky.

For a few moments, the monster lay twitching horribly, a trickle of ruby blood oozing from the corner of its mouth, its ghastly head and shoulders filling the stage with flying sparks, as smoke and little flames rose in acrid tendrils from its burning hair and goatee. But the blank eyes that stared out unseeing into mine were not those of the hinged giant, Galligantus—they were the glazed and dying eyes of Rupert Porson.

And then the lights went out.

thirteen

PLUNGED SUDDENLY INTO DARKNESS, THE AUDIENCE SUCKED in a collective breath and released a collective gasp.

In the kitchen, someone had the presence of mind to switch on a flashlight, and after a moment brought it out, like a darting will-o'-the-wisp, into the main part of the parish hall.

How quick-witted it was of the vicar to think of closing the curtains! At least, that was what he was trying to do when he was stopped in his tracks by a loud, commanding voice: "No! No! Stand back. Don't touch anything."

It was Dogger. He had risen to his feet and was blocking the vicar's way, his arms fully extended, and seeming to be as surprised as the rest of us at his own boldness. Nialla, who had jumped up and taken a single step towards the proscenium, froze abruptly in her tracks.

All of this took place in the moving beam of the flashlight, making the scene seem like some ghastly drama played out during an air raid, illuminated by a raking searchlight.

A second voice came out of the darkness at the back of the hall: the voice of Inspector Hewitt.

"Stand still, everyone—please stay where you are. Don't move until I tell you to move."

He walked quickly to the front of the auditorium and vanished backstage as someone near the door vainly flicked a few switches, but the incandescent bulbs in their frosted glass wall sconces remained dark.

There were a few grumbles of protest until Constable Linnet—out of uniform for the evening—came to the front row of chairs, holding a hand high in the air for attention. He had brought a second flashlight, which he shone upwards upon his own face, giving him an appalling and cadaverous look.

"Please do as the Inspector says," he told the audience. "He's in charge here now."

Dr. Darby, I noticed, was already shoving his way up the crowded side aisle towards the stage.

Nialla, when I caught a glimpse of her, seemed rooted to the spot; she had not moved a muscle. Her tall Mother Goose hat was askew and, had the situation not been what it was, I might have laughed out loud at the sight of her.

My first reaction, of course, was to go to her, but I found I was being restrained by one of Father's hands, heavy on my arm.

As Rupert's body crashed to the stage, both Daffy and Feely had leapt to their feet. Father was still motioning them to sit down, but they were too excited to pay him any attention.

The Inspector reappeared in the doorway at the left of the stage. There were two of these hallways—one on either side—each leading to an exit and a short set of steps up to the stage. It was in these pens that choirs of giggling angels were usually marshaled for St. Tancred's annual Christmas Pageant.

"Constable Linnet, may I have your flashlight, please?"

PC Linnet handed over his five-cell Ever Ready, which looked like one of the sort that you see being used to search the foggy moors in the cinema. He had probably brought it along to illuminate his way home through the lanes after the show, never thinking it would come in so handy.

"May I have your attention, please," Inspector Hewitt said. "We are making every attempt to restore the lights, but it may be some time before we're able to turn them back on permanently. It may be necessary, for safety's sake, to switch the current on and off several times. I would ask you to resume your seats, and to remain there until such time as I am able to give you further instructions. There is absolutely no cause for alarm, so please remain calm."

I heard him say quietly to Constable Linnet, "Cover the stage. That banner on the balcony will do." He pointed to a wide swath of canvas that stretched across the front of the balcony, above the main door: *St. Tancred's Women's Institute*, it said, with a red and white Cross of St. George, *One Hundred Years of Service 1850–1950*.

"And when you've done that," the Inspector added, "ring up Graves and Woolmer. Give them my compliments, and ask them to come as quickly as possible."

"It's their evening for cricket, sir," said PC Linnet.

"So it is. In that case, give them my compliments *and* my regrets. I'm sure the vicar will permit you the use of the telephone?"

"Dear me!" said the vicar, looking round the hall in puzzlement. "We do have one, of course . . . for the use of the Ladies' Auxiliary and the Women's Institute, you know . . . but I fear we've been forced to keep it in a locked cupboard in the kitchen . . . so many people making long-distance calls to their friends in Devon—or even Scotland, in one instance."

"And the key?" asked Inspector Hewitt.

"I handed it to a gentleman from London, just before the performance—from the BBC, he said he was—needed to make an urgent call . . . said he'd reimburse me from his own pocket as soon as the central operator rang back with the charges. How odd, I don't see him here now.

"Still, there's always the vicarage telephone," he added.

My first impulse was to offer to pick the lock, but before I could say a word, Inspector Hewitt shook his head.

"I'm sure we can have the hinges off with no damage."
He crooked a finger at George Carew, the village carpenter, who was out of his chair like a shot.

Aside from the occasional dull glow from the backstage flashlight, we sat in darkness for what seemed like an eternity.

And then suddenly, the lights came back on, causing us all to blink and rub our eyes, and to look round at one another rather foolishly.

And there was Rupert, his dead face, frozen in a look of surprise, still occupying center stage. They would soon be covering his body with the banner, and I realized that if I were to remember the scene for future reference, I needed to make a series of indelible mental snapshots. I wouldn't have long to work.

Click!

The eyes: The pupils were hugely dilated, so much so that if I had been able to get a bit closer, I was quite sure I should have been able to see myself reflected in their convex surfaces as clearly as Jan van Eyck was reflected in the bedroom mirror in his painting of the Arnolfinis' wedding day.

Not for long, though: Rupert's corneas had already begun to film over and the whites to lose their luster.

Click!

The body was no longer twitching. The skin had taken on a milky bluish tinge. The corner of the mouth seemed to have stopped bleeding, and what little blood was still visible now appeared very slightly darker and thicker, although the red, green, and amber bulbs of the footlights might be influencing my color perception.

Click!

On the forehead, just below the scalp, was a dark discoloration the size and shape of a sixpence. Although the hair was still smoldering, filling the hall with the acrid odor one would expect whenever the sulfur-rich amino acid keratin is burnt, it was not enough to account for the smoke that was still gathering—still hanging heavily—about the lights. I could see that the curtains and the scenery were quite intact, so it must be something else that was still combusting backstage. Judging by the smell of burning grass, I guessed that it was linen—probably seersucker.

Click!

When Rupert first came crashing down, Nialla had leapt to her feet and moved towards the stage, but she then had stopped, hovering in her tracks. Oddly, no one, including me, had gone to her, and now that minutes had passed, she was walking slowly towards the kitchen with both hands cupped over her face. *Was it a delayed reaction?* I wondered. *Or something more?*

PC Linnet came clomping to the front of the auditorium, the rolled-up banner under his arm and the large jackknife with which he had cut its cords still clutched in his hand. He and the vicar made quick work of draping the canvas between two coat trees, and in so doing, blocked our view of the deceased.

Well, I was *assuming* that Rupert was deceased. Although Inspector Hewitt must surely have checked for signs of life when he first went backstage, I hadn't heard him call for an ambulance. No one, as far as I knew, had yet attempted resuscitation. No one, in fact, had seemed anxious to touch the body. Even Dr. Darby had not exactly galloped to the rescue.

All of this happened, of course, in much less time than it takes to tell about it: In actual fact, it couldn't have taken more than five minutes.

Then, as the Inspector had said they might, the lights went out again.

At first there was that sense of being plunged into what Daffy describes as "Stygian blackness," and Mrs. Mullet calls "a blind man's holiday." Mrs. Mullet, by the way, was still sitting as she had been since the show began, like a waxwork figure with a half smile on her face. I could only assume that she was still smiling zanily into the darkness.

It was that kind of darkness that seems, at first, to paralyze all of the senses.

But then one realizes that things are not quite so black as they look, nor are they as silent as they seem. Pinpoints of light, for instance, penetrated the shabby blackout curtains that had been used to cover the windows since before the war, and although there was little daylight left outside, it was enough to create a faint impression of the hall's larger features.

From behind the curtains came the sound of deliberate footsteps, and the banner, which had been draped in front of the puppet stage, was suddenly illuminated from behind by a slash of yellow light from a powerful torch.

Now began the ghastly shadow show. The outline of Dr. Darby was seen to reach down and touch the body, no doubt searching for signs of life. I could have saved him the trouble.

The shadow shook its head and a great sigh went up from the audience. It seemed clear to me that, with Rupert pronounced dead, Inspector Hewitt would now want to leave things untouched until Detective Sergeant Woolmer arrived from Hinley with his plate camera.

Aunt Felicity, meanwhile, was rummaging in her purse for more mints, and I could hear her inhaling and exhaling through her nose. To my left, Daffy was whispering to Feely, but since Father, who sat between us, was clearing his throat at regular intervals, as he does whenever he's nervous or upset, I could not quite make out her words.

After what seemed like another eternity, the lights suddenly came back on, and again, we were all left blinking.

Mrs. Mullet was dabbing at her eyes with a handkerchief, her shoulders shaking, and I realized that she was quietly crying. Dogger noticed, too. He offered her his arm, which she took without raising her eyes, and he led her off into the kitchen.

He was back in less than a minute.

"She'll be more at ease among the pots and pans," he whispered to me as he resumed his seat.

A great flash of light bleached the hall of all color for an instant, and I, along with everyone else, turned round to see that Detective Sergeant Woolmer had arrived. He had set up his bulky camera and tripod on the balcony, and had just captured all of us on film. As the flash fired a second time, it occurred to me that this second exposure would show no more than a sea of upturned white faces. Which, perhaps, was precisely what he wanted.

"Please—may I have your attention?" Inspector Hewitt had stepped out from behind the black curtains and was now standing center stage. "I'm sorry to have to tell you that there has been an unfortunate accident, and that Mr. Porson is dead."

Even though the fact should have been evident, its confirmation caused a wave of sound to break from the audience: a mixture of gasps, cries, and excited whispers. The Inspector waited patiently for it to die down.

"I'm afraid I'm going to have to ask you to remain in your seats a little longer, until we are able to take names and addresses as well as a brief statement from each one of you. This process will take some time, and for that I must apologize. When you have been interviewed, you will be free to go, although we may wish to speak with you again at some later time. Thank you for your attention."

He beckoned to someone behind me, and I saw that it was Detective Sergeant Graves. I wondered if the sergeant would remember me. I had first met him at Buckshaw during the police investigation into the death of Father's old school chum Horace Bonepenny. I kept my eyes fixed on his face as he came to the front of the hall, and at last I was rewarded with an ever-so-slight but distinct grin.

"Schoolboys!" Aunt Felicity huffed. "The police recruiters are ransacking the cradles of England."

"He's extremely experienced," I whispered. "He's already a detective sergeant."

"Poppycock!" she said, and dug for another mint.

Since the corpse had been hidden from view, there was nothing left for me to do but study the people around me.

Dieter, I noticed, was staring fixedly at Feely. Although he was sitting with Sally Straw—whose face was a petulant thundercloud—he was gazing at my sister's profile as if her hair were an altar of beaten gold.

Daffy had noticed it, too. When she saw the look of puzzlement on my face, she leaned over in front of Father and whispered, "The phrase you're fishing for is 'reverent infatuation.'" Then she leaned back and resumed not speaking to me.

Father paid us no attention. He had already retreated into his own world: a world of colored inks and perforations-per-inch; a world of albums and gum arabic; a world where our Gracious Majesty, King George the Sixth, was firmly ensconced on both the throne and the postage stamps of Great Britain; a world in which sadness—and reality—had no place.

At last the interviews began. As Inspector Hewitt and Sergeant Woolmer took on one side of the hall, Sergeant Graves and Constable Linnet attended to the other.

It was a long and weary old process. Time, as they say, hung heavily on our hands, or, to be more exact, on our behinds. Even Aunt Felicity was shifting uneasily on her more-than-ample padding.

"You may stand up and stretch," Inspector Hewitt had said at one point, "but please do not move from your places."

It was probably no more than about an hour before they got round to us, but it seemed to take forever. Father went first, to the corner where a plain wooden table with a couple of chairs had been set up. I could not hear what the Inspector asked him, nor could I hear any of his responses, which seemed to consist mainly of shaking his head in the negative.

It was not so very long since Inspector Hewitt had charged Father with the murder of Horace Bonepenny, and although Father had never said it in so many words, he still felt a certain coolness towards the constabulary. He was quickly back, and I waited patiently as Aunt Felicity, then Feely, then Daffy went up to speak quietly with the Inspector.

As each one returned to their seat, I tried to catch their eye, to get some hint of what they had been asked or what they had replied, but it was no use. Feely and Daffy both had that smarmy, sanctimonious look they get after partaking of Holy Communion, their eyes downcast and hands clasped at their waists in humbug humility. Father and Aunt Felicity were inscrutable, too.

Dogger was another matter.

Although he had borne up well under the Inspector's grilling, I noticed that he went back to his seat like a man walking a tightrope. A twitch had appeared at the corner of one eye, and his face had that strained yet vacant look that invariably preceded his attacks. Whatever it was that had happened to Dogger during the war, it had left him with an inability to be confronted close-up by any sort of officialdom.

Damn the consequences! I got up from my chair and knelt at his feet. Although Inspector Hewitt glanced in my direction, he made no move to stop me.

"Dogger," I whispered, "have you seen what I've seen?"

As I slipped into the chair beside him vacated by Mrs. Mullet, he looked at me as if he'd never seen me before in his life and then, like a pearl diver fighting his way slowly back to the surface from some great depth, he re-entered the real world, nodding his head in slow motion.

"Yes, Miss Flavia. Murder—I fear we have seen murder."

AS MY TURN AT THE TABLE APPROACHED, I suddenly became aware of my own heartbeat. I wished that I were a Tibetan lama, so that I could control its racing valves.

But before I could think about it further, Inspector Hewitt beckoned me. He was messing about with a stack of papers and forms, waiting until I had seated myself. For an idle instant, I found myself wondering where the blank forms had come from. *Woolmer and Graves must have brought them*, I decided. The Inspector certainly hadn't been carrying a briefcase before the performance.

I twisted round for a look at his wife, Antigone. Yes, there she was, sitting quietly among the villagers in her seat, radiant in spite of the situation.

"She's very beautiful," I whispered.

"Thank you," he said, not looking up from his papers, but I could tell by the corners of his mouth that he was pleased.

"Now then—name and address?"

Name and address? What was the man playing at?

"You know that already," I said.

"Of course I do"—he smiled—"but it's not official until you say it."

"Flavia de Luce—Buckshaw," I replied rather icily, and he wrote it down.

"Thank you," he said. "Now then, Flavia, what time did you arrive this evening?"

"Six-forty," I said, "on the dot. With my family. In a taxicab. Clarence Mundy's taxicab."

"And you were in the hall the whole evening?"

"Of course I was. I came over and spoke to you—don't you remember?"

"Yes. Answer the question, please."

"Yes."

I must admit that the Inspector was making me quite cross. I had hoped to be able to collaborate with him: to provide him with a richly described, minute-by-minute account of the horror that had taken place—almost in my lap—this evening. Now I could see that I was going to be treated as if I were just another gawking spectator.

"Did you see or speak to Mr. Porson before the performance?"

What did he mean by that? I had seen and spoken to Mr. Porson on several occasions over the past three days. I had driven with Mr. Porson to Culverhouse Farm and had overheard his quarrel with Gordon Ingleby in Gibbet Wood. And that was not all that I knew about Rupert Porson. Not by a long chalk.

"No," I said.

Two could play at this game.

"I see," he said. "Well, thank you. That will be all."

I had just been checkmated.

"You're free to go," he added, glancing at his wristwatch. "It's probably past your bedtime."

The nerve of the man! Past my bedtime indeed! Who did he think he was talking to?

"May I ask a question?"

"You may," he said, "although I might not be able to answer it."

"Was Rupert—Mr. Porson, I mean—electrocuted?"

He looked at me narrowly, and I could see that he was thinking carefully about his reply.

"There is that possibility. Good night, Flavia."

The man was fobbing me off. Rupert had fried like a flounder, and the Inspector knew it as well as I did.

Flashbulbs were still going off behind the puppet stage as I rejoined Father in the front row. Feely and Daffy were nowhere in sight.

"Mundy has already taken them home," he said.

"I'll be ready in a jiff," I said, walking towards the W.C. No one, anywhere, at any time in history, has ever stopped a female en route to the Baffins.

At the last moment, I changed direction and slipped into the kitchen, where I found Mrs. Mullet in full command. She had made a huge pot of tea, and had placed steaming cups in front of Nialla and Sergeant Woolmer, who sat at a side table.

Nialla saw me before the sergeant did, and her eyes flashed—but only for an instant—like a startled animal. She gave me an almost imperceptible shake of the head, but its meaning was clear.

Women's wireless at work. I rubbed my nose casually to let her know that the message had been received.

"Thank you, Miss Gilfoyle," the sergeant said. "You've been most helpful."

Gilfoyle? Was that Nialla's name? It was the first time I'd heard it.

Sergeant Woolmer drained his cup in a single draught, with no apparent ill effects.

"Champion tea, Mrs. Mullet," he said, closing his notebook. He gathered his papers, and with a pleasant nod in my direction, walked back out into the auditorium.

The man must have a stomach like a ship's boiler, I thought.

"Now then, dear, as I was saying," Mrs. Mullet said, "there's no use you goin' back to Culverhouse Farm tonight. It's rainin' cats and dogs—has been for an hour or more. The river will be mortal high—not safe to cross. 'Sides, no one would expect you to sleep in a tent in a wet field with the situation bein' what it is, if you take my meanin'. Alf's brought a brolly that's big enough for the three of us, and we're just across the way. Our Agnes's room hasn't been slept in since she left home to take up Pitman shorthand six years ago come November thirteenth. Alf and me have kept it a kind of a shrine, like. Has its own hot plate and a goose-down mattress. And don't say no, 'cause I won't hear you."

Nialla's eyes were suddenly brimming with tears, and for the life of me, I could not tell if they were tears of grief or joy.

I'D HAVE GIVEN A GUINEA to know what words passed between Father and Dogger in the backseat of the taxicab, but the simple truth is that I dropped off. With the heater turned full up against the chill of the cold night rain, and the windscreen wipers making their quiet *swish-swash* in the darkness, the urge to sleep was irresistible. Not even an owl could have stayed awake.

When Father roused me at the door of Buckshaw, I stumbled into the house and up the stairs to bed—too tired even to bother undressing.

I must have fallen asleep with my eyes open.

fourteen

THE SUN WAS STREAMING SPLENDIDLY IN AT MY CASEMENT window; the birds in the chestnuts were singing their little throats out. The first thought that came flashing into my mind was of Rupert's face: his lips pulled slightly back, his teeth showing obscenely.

I rolled over onto my back and stared at the ceiling. I always find that a blank screen helps clarify one's thoughts marvelously; helps bring them into focus.

In death Rupert had looked, I decided, remarkably like the dead dog I had once almost stepped on in a field behind the Thirteen Drakes, its fog-filled eyes staring, its yellowed fangs bared in a frozen grimace. (Although with Rupert, there had been no flies, and his teeth were quite presentable, actually.)

Somehow, the dog reminded me of something—but what?

Of course! Mutt Wilmott! The Thirteen Drakes! Mutt Wilmott would be staying at the Thirteen Drakes!

If Mrs. Mullet were to be believed, it had begun raining shortly after the evening performance began. Mutt had been there at about six-forty—say, six forty-five—I had seen him with my own eyes. He would hardly have set out for London in such a downpour. No, had he planned to leave, he would have done so before the show. It seemed obvious that he still had business to conclude with Rupert.

Ergo: He was, at this very instant, eating bacon and eggs at the

Thirteen Drakes, Bishop Lacey's sole hostelry.

Fortunately, I was already dressed.

There was a cryptlike silence in the house as I crept down the east staircase. Last night's excitement had drained everyone of their energy and they were, I guessed, still snoring away in their respective rooms like a pack of convalescent vampires.

As I was slipping out the kitchen door, however, I came to an abrupt halt. On the wooden stand beside the door, tucked between the two full bottles the milk float had left on our doorstep at dawn, was a package.

It was a pustulent purple color, with projecting top and bottom rims. The clear cellophane in which it was wrapped had protected it from last night's rain. On the lid, in gold letters, were the words *Milady Chocolates— Finest Assorted—2 lb. Duchess Selection*. Wrapped around it lengthwise was a ribbon the color of a faded red rose. The label was still attached like the Mad Hatter's hat: 10/6.

I had seen this box before. In fact, I had seen it just a few days ago in the flyblown window of Miss Cool's confectionery shop cum post office in the high street, where it had languished since time immemorial— perhaps since the war, or even longer. And I realized at once how it had made its way to the back door at Buckshaw: Ned Cropper.

Ned earned £7 a week doing chores for Tully Stoker at the Thirteen Drakes, and he was smitten with, among others, my sister Ophelia. Even though he had accompanied Tully's daughter, Mary, to *Jack and the Beanstalk* last night, it had not kept him from leaving his midnight love token on our doorstep, as an adoring tomcat drops a mouse at its owner's feet.

The chocolates were so old, I thought, they were most likely full to bursting with countless varieties of interesting molds, but unfortunately there was no time to investigate. Reluctantly, I returned to the kitchen and stuffed the box in the top compartment of the ice cabinet. I would deal with Feely later.

"NED!"

I gave him a smile, and a wave with my fingers spread generously apart, the way royalty is taught to do. With his sleeves rolled up and brilliantined hair like a wet haystack, Ned was high atop the steep-pitched roof of the Thirteen Drakes, his heels braced against a chimney pot, using a brush to slather hot pitch onto tiles that looked as if they'd been up there since King Alfred burned the cakes.

"Come down!" I shouted.

"Can't, Flavia. Got a leak in the kitchen. Tully wants this done before the Inspector shows up. Said he'd be here bright and early.

"Tully says he's counting on the early part, anyhow," he added. ". . . Whatever that means."

"I have to talk to you," I said, dropping my voice to a loud stage whisper. "I can't very well go shouting it up to the housetops."

"You'll have to come up." He pointed to a ladder that leaned against the wall. "Mind your step."

The ladder was as old as the inn, or so it seemed to me. It tottered and twisted as I climbed, creaking and groaning horribly. The ascent seemed to take forever, and I tried not to look down.

"It's about last night, isn't it?" Ned asked, as I neared the top.

Double damnation! If I was so transparent that even someone like Ned could see through me, I might as well leave it to the police.

"No," I said, "as a matter of fact it isn't, Mister Smart-Pants. A certain person asked me to thank you for your lovely gift."

"She did?" Ned said, his features broadening into a classic village idiot grin. The Folklore Society would have had him in front of a cine-camera before you could turn round three times and spit across the wind.

"She'd have come herself, but she's being detained in her tower by her wicked father who feeds her on floor sweepings and disgusting table scraps."

"Haw!" Ned said. "She didn't look too underfed last night." His features darkened, as if he had only just remembered what had taken place.

"Pretty sad, that puppet man," he said. "I feel sorry for him."

"I'm glad you do, Ned. He hadn't many friends in the world, you know. It might be nice if you expressed your condolences to Mr. Wilmott. Someone said he's staying here."

This was a lie, but a well-intentioned one.

"Is he? Dunno. All I know right now is 'Roof! Roof! Roof!'—sounds like a dog when you say it like that, doesn't it? 'Roof! Roof! Roof!'"

I shook my head and started down the shaky ladder.

"Look at yourself!" Ned said. "You're covered with tar."

"Like a roof," I said, getting a look at my filthy hands and my dress. Ned hooted with laughter and I managed a pathetic grin.

I could cheerfully have fed him to the pigs.

"It won't come off, you know. You'll still have it plastered all over you when you're an old lady."

I wondered where Ned had picked up this rustic folklore—it was probably from Tully. I knew for a fact that Michael Faraday had synthesized tetrachloroethene in the 1820s by heating hexachloroethane and piping off the chlorine as it decomposed. The resulting solvent would remove tar from fabric like stink. Unfortunately—much as I should like to have done—I hadn't the time to repeat Faraday's discovery. Instead, I would have to fall back on mayonnaise, as recommended in *The Butler and Footman's Vade Mecum*, which I had come across one rainy day while snooping through the pantry at Buckshaw.

"Perhaps Mary would know. Is she somewhere about?"

I didn't dare barge in and ask Tully about a paying guest. To be perfectly honest, I was afraid of him, although it's difficult to say why with any certainty.

"Mary? She's taken the week's wash to the laundry, then she'll most likely be off to church."

Church! Baste me with butter! I'd forgotten all about church. Father would be going purple!

"Thanks, Ned," I shouted, grabbing Gladys from the bicycle stand. "See you!"

"Not if I see you first." Ned laughed, and like Santa Claus, turned to his work.

AS I HAD FEARED, Father was standing at the front door glaring at his watch as I slid to a stop.

"Sorry!" I said. He didn't even bother asking.

Through the open door I flew and into the front hall. Daffy was sitting halfway up the west staircase with a book open in her lap. Feely wasn't down yet.

I charged up the east staircase to my bedroom, threw on my Sunday dress like a quick-change artist, scrubbed my face with a cloth, and within two minutes by the clock—barring a bit of tar on the end of my pigtails—I was ready for morning prayer.

It was then that I remembered the chocolates. I'd better retrieve them before Mrs. Mullet began to concoct her dreadful Sunday ices. If I didn't, there would be a host of cheeky questions to answer.

I tiptoed down the back stairs to the kitchen, and peered around the corner. Something nasty was just coming to the boil on the back of the cooker, but there was no one in sight.

I retrieved the chocolates from the ice cabinet and was back upstairs before you could say "Jack and the Beanstalk."

As I opened my laboratory door, my eye was arrested by a glint of glassware, which was reflecting a wayward sunbeam from the window. It was a lovely device called a Kipp's apparatus: one of Tar de Luce's splendid pieces of Victorian laboratory glass.

"A thing of beauty is a joy forever," the poet Keats had once written—or so Daffy had told me. There couldn't be a shred of doubt that Keats had written the line while contemplating a Kipp's apparatus: a device used to extract the gas resulting from a chemical reaction.

In form, it was essentially two clear glass balls mounted one above the other, a short tube connecting them, with a stoppered glass goose-neck projecting from the top globe, and a vent tube with a glass stopcock sticking out of the bottom one.

My plan took form instantly: a sure sign of divine inspiration. But I had only minutes to work before Father would come storming in to drag me down the stairs.

First, I took from a drawer one of Father's old razors—one I had nicked for an earlier experiment. I carefully slipped the faded ribbon from the chocolate box, turned it upside down, and made a careful, dead straight incision in the cellophane along the line where the ribbon had lain. A slit in the bottom and each end was all that was needed for the wrapping to open up like an oyster shell. Replacing it would be child's play.

That done, I carefully lifted the lid on the box and peered inside.

Perfect! The creams looked to be in pristine condition. I had suspected that age might have taken its toll—that opening the box might yield a sight similar to the one I had once seen in the churchyard when Mr. Haskins, the sexton, while digging a new grave, had accidentally broken through into another that was already occupied.

But then it had occurred to me that the chocolates, having been hermetically sealed—to say nothing of the preservatives that might have been added—might still seem fresh to the naked eye. Luck was on my side.

I had chosen my method because of its ability to take place at normal temperatures. Although there were other procedures that would have resulted in the same product, the one I selected was this: Into the bottom sphere of the Kipp's apparatus, I measured a quantity of ordinary iron sulfide. Into the top bulb, I carefully tipped a dilute sulfuric acid, using a glass rod to make sure that the liquid went straight into the target vessel.

I watched as the reaction began in the bottom container: a lovely chemical hubbub that invariably takes place when anything containing sulfur—including the human body—decomposes. When I judged it complete, I opened the bottom valve and let the gas escape into a rubber-stoppered flask.

Next came the part I loved best: Taking a large brass-bound glass syringe from one of Uncle Tar's desk drawers (I had often wondered if he used it to inject himself with a seven-percent solution of cocaine, like Sherlock Holmes), I shoved its needle through the rubber stopper, depressed the plunger, and then pulled it up again.

I now had a needle charged with hydrogen sulfide gas. Just one more step to go.

Sticking the needle through the rubber stopper of a test tube, I rammed the plunger down as hard as I could with both thumbs. Only fourteen atmospheric pressures were required to precipitate the gas into a liquid and, as I knew it would, it worked the first time.

I now had a test tube containing perfectly clear hydrogen sulfide in its liquid form. All that remained was to retract the plunger again, and watch it rise up into the glass of the syringe.

Carefully, I injected each chocolate with a drop or two of the stuff, touching the injection site with the glass rod (slightly warmed in the Bunsen burner) to smooth over the little hole.

I had carried out the procedure so perfectly that only the faintest whiff of rotten egg reached my nostrils. Safe inside the gooey centers, the hydrogen sulfide would remain cocooned, invisible, unsuspected, until Feely—

"Flavia!"

It was Father, shouting from the front hall.

"Coming!" I called. "I'll be there in a jiff!"

I replaced the lid of the box and then the cellophane wrapping, giving it two quick dabs of mucilage on the bottom to tack down the almost invisible incision. Then I replaced the ribbon.

As I slowly descended the curving staircase, trying desperately to look sedate and demure, I found the family gathered, waiting, in a knot at the bottom.

"I expect these are for you," I said, holding the box out to Feely. "Someone left them at the door."

She blushed a bit.

"And I have a confession to make," I added. All eyes were on me in a flash: Father's, Aunt Felicity's, Feely's, Daffy's—even Dogger's.

"I was tempted to keep them for myself," I said, eyes downcast, "but it's Sunday, and I really *am* trying hard to be a better person."

Eager hands outstretched, Feely rose to the bait like a shark to a swimmer's foot.

fifteen

WITH FATHER AND AUNT FELICITY LEADING THE WAY, AND
Dogger in the rear wearing a black bowler hat, we straggled, as we always
did, single file across the fields like ducks to a pond. The green countryside in which we were enfolded seemed as ancient and as settled in the
morning light as a canvas by Constable, and I shouldn't have been a bit
surprised to find that we were really no more than tiny figures in the background of one of his paintings, such as *The Hay Wain*, or *Dedham Vale*.

It was a perfect day. Bright prisms of dew glittered like diamonds
in the grass, although I knew that, as the day went on, they would be
vaporized by the sun.

Vaporized by the sun! Wasn't that what the universe had in store for
all of us? There would come a day when the sun exploded like a red
balloon, and everyone on earth would be reduced in less than a camera
flash to carbon. Didn't Genesis say as much? *For dust thou art, and unto dust
shalt thou return*. This was far more than dull old theology: It was precise
scientific observation! Carbon was the Great Leveler—the Grim Reaper.

Diamonds were nothing more than carbon, but carbon in a crystal
lattice that made it the hardest known mineral in nature. That was the
way we all were headed. I was sure of it. We were destined to be diamonds!

How exciting it was to think that, long after the world had ended, whatever was left of our bodies would be transformed into a dazzling blizzard of
diamond dust, blowing out towards eternity in the red glow of a dying sun.

And for Rupert Porson, the process had already begun.

"I doubt very much, Haviland," Aunt Felicity was saying, "if they'll go ahead with the service. It seems hardly right in view of what's happened."

"The Church of England, Lissy," Father replied, "like time and tide, waits for no man. Besides, the fellow died in the parish hall—not in the church proper, as it were."

"Perhaps so," she said with a sniff. "Still, I shall be put out if all this walking is for nothing."

But Father was right. As we walked alongside the stone wall that ran like a tightened belt round the banked-up churchyard, I could see the hood of Inspector Hewitt's blue Vauxhall saloon peeking out discreetly at the end of the lane. The Inspector himself was nowhere in sight as we stepped onto the porch and entered the church.

Morning Prayer was as solemn as a Requiem High Mass. I know that for a fact because we de Luces are Roman Catholics—we are in fact, virtually charter members of the club. We have seen our share of bobbing and ducking. But we regularly attend St. Tancred's because of its proximity, and because the vicar is one of Father's great friends.

"Besides," Father says, "it is one's bounden duty to trade with local firms."

This morning, the church was packed to the rafters. Even the balcony beneath the bell tower was filled to overflowing with people from the village who wanted to be as close as possible, without being unseemly, to the Scene of the Crime.

Nialla was nowhere in sight. I noticed that at once. Nor were Mrs. Mullet, or Alf, her husband. If I knew our Mrs. M, she would, at this very moment, be bombarding Nialla with sausages and questions. "Plying and prying," Daffy called it.

Cynthia was already on her knees, front and center, praying to whatever gods she wanted to bribe before the service began. She was always the first to kneel and always the first to spring to her feet again. I sometimes thought of her as St. Tancred's spiritual coxswain.

For once, because it would be about someone I had known personally, I was quite looking forward to the sermon. The vicar, I expected, would deliver something inspired by Rupert's demise—tasteful but instructional. "In the midst of life we are in death," was my guess.

But when he climbed up into the pulpit at last, the vicar was strangely subdued, and it wasn't entirely due to the fact that Cynthia was running a white-gloved forefinger along the wooden rack that held scattered copies of the Hymnary and the *Book of Common Prayer*. In fact, the vicar made no reference to the matter at all, until he had finished the sermon.

"In view of the tragic circumstances of last evening," he said in a hushed and solemn voice, "the police have requested that the parish hall be made available to them until their work is complete. Consequently, our customary refreshments, for this morning only, will be served at the vicarage. Those of you who wish to do so are cordially invited to join us after the service. And now may God the Father, God the Son, and God the Holy Ghost . . ."

Just like that! No thoughts on "the stranger in our midst," such as he had delivered when Horace Bonepenny was murdered at Buckshaw. No ruminations on the immortality of the soul . . . Nothing.

To be perfectly honest, I felt more than a little cheated.

It is never possible, at least at St. Tancred's, to burst forth from the church into the sunshine like a cork from a bottle. One must always pause at the door to shake hands with the vicar, and to make some obligatory remark about the sermon, the weather, or the crops.

Father chose the sermon, and Daffy and Feely both chose the weather—the swine!—with Daffy commenting on the remarkable clarity of the air and Feely on its warmth. That left me with little choice, and the vicar was already clasping my hand.

"How's Meg getting on?" I asked. To tell the truth, I'd forgotten all about Mad Meg until that very moment, and the question just popped into my head.

Did the vicar's face go slightly white, or had I just fancied it?

He looked to the left and then to the right, very quickly. Cynthia was hovering outside among the gravestones, already halfway along the path to the vicarage.

"I'm afraid I can't tell you," he said. "You see, she was—"

"Vicar! I have a bone to pick with you, you know!"

It was Bunny Spirling. Bunny was one of the Spirlings of Nautilus Old Hall who, as Father once remarked, had gone to the dogs by way of the horses.

Because Bunny was shaped rather like the capital letter *D*, no one could get past him, and the vicar was now wedged firmly between Bunny's ample tummy and the Gothic door frame. Aunt Felicity and Dogger, I supposed, were still penned up somewhere inside the vestibule, queuing like crewmen on a sunken submarine for their turn at the escape hatch.

As Bunny proceeded to pick his bone (something about tithing and the shocking disrepair of the padding in the kneeling benches), I saw my opportunity to escape.

"Oh, dear," I remarked to Father, "it looks as though the vicar has been detained. I'll run ahead to the vicarage and see if I can make myself useful with the cups and saucers."

There's not a father on earth who has it in him to refuse such a charitable child, and I was off like a hare.
"Morning!" I shouted to Cynthia as I flew past.

I vaulted over the stile and ran round to the front of the vicarage. The door stood open, and I could hear voices in the kitchen at the back of the house. The Women's Institute, I decided: Several of them would have slipped out of the service early to put the kettle on.

I stood in the dim hallway, listening. Time was short, but it would never do to be caught snooping. With one last look down the stretch of polished brown linoleum, I stepped into the vicar's study and closed the door behind me.

Meg, of course, was long gone, but the afghan with which the vicar had covered her yesterday still lay crumpled on the horsehair sofa, as if Meg had only just tossed it aside, got up, and left the room, leaving in her wake—to put it nicely—a woodsy smell: the smell of damp leaves, dark earth, and something-less-than-perfect personal hygiene.

But before I could put my mind to work, the door was flung open.
"What are you doing in here?"
Needless to say, it was Cynthia. She closed the door craftily behind her.
"Oh, hello, Mrs. Richardson," I said. "I just looked in to see if Meg was still here. Not that she would be, of course, but I worry about her, you see, and . . ."

When you're stumped for words, use your hands. This was a dodge that had never failed me in the past, and I hoped that it would not now.

I snatched at the wadded afghan and began to fold it. As I did so, something dropped with a barely audible plop to the carpet.

"I just thought I'd help tidy up, then see if they can put me to work in the kitchen.

"Drat!" I said, as I let a corner of the afghan escape my fingers. "Oh, sorry, Mrs. Richardson, I'm afraid I'm quite clumsy. We're so spoiled at Buckshaw, you know."

Awkwardly, I spread out the afghan on the floor, crouched in front of it, and began folding again. Under cover of its colorful woolen squares—and using my body to block Cynthia's view—I ran my fingers across the carpet.

I felt it at once: a cold, flat, metallic object. Using my thumb as a clamp, I pressed it firmly into my palm. As long as I kept my hands moving, all would be well. That was the way the sleight-of-hand magicians worked. I could always pocket the thing later.

"Here, give me that," Cynthia said.

I panicked! She had caught me out after all.

As she stepped into the room, I began a frantic jitterbug, kicking up my legs and throwing my elbows out like pikestaffs.

"Oh!" I said. "That afghan's making me itchy all over. I have a nasty allergy to wool."

I began scratching myself furiously: my arms, the back of my hands, my calves . . . anywhere, just as long as I didn't let my hands come to rest.

When I got to my neck, I shoved my hand into the top of my dress and let go the object from my palm. I felt it fall inside—and stop at my waist.

"Give me that," she repeated, snatching the afghan from my hands.

I breathed a sigh of relief as I realized that she hadn't seen whatever it was I'd retrieved. It was the afghan she wanted, and I held it out cheerily, giving myself several more houndlike scratches for insurance purposes.

"I'll go help in the kitchen," I said, moving towards the door.

"Flavia—" Cynthia said, stepping in front of the door and seizing my wrist in one rapid motion.

I looked into her pale blue watery eyes and they did not waver.

But at that instant, there was laughter outside in the hallway as the first parishioners arrived from the church.

"One thing we de Luce girls *are* good at"—I grinned into her face as I slipped round her and out the door—"is making tea!"

I had no more intention of making tea than of signing on as a coal pit donkey.

Still, I made a beeline down the hall and into the kitchen.

"Good morning, Mrs. Roberts! Good morning, Miss Roper! Just checking to see if you have enough cups and saucers?"

"Plenty, thank you, Flavia, dear," Mrs. Roberts said. She had been doing this since the dawn of time.

"But you can put the eggs in the bottom of the fridge on your way out," Miss Roper told me. "The egg lady must have left them on the kitchen counter yesterday. Nothing keeps in this weather, not the way it used to, at any rate. And while you're at it, dear, you can fill that pitcher with lemonade. Mr. Spirling likes a nice glass of lemonade after church, and as he's always so generous when the collection plate goes round, we wouldn't want to get into his bad books, would we?"

Before they could devise another task, I flew busily out the kitchen door. Later, when they had a moment—when they were washing up, perhaps—Mrs. Roberts and Miss Roper would remark to one another what a nice girl I was—and how unlike my sisters.

Outside in the churchyard, Father still stood on the cobbled walk, listening patiently to Bunny Spirling, who was telling him, word for word, what he had just said to the vicar. Father nodded from time to time, probably to keep his neck from going to sleep.

I stepped off the path and into the grass, pretending to inspect the inscription on a weathered gravestone that jutted up like a yellowed tooth from a green gum (*Hezekiah Huff 1672–1746, At Peece In Paradice*). Turning my back on the gossiping stragglers, I extracted the metal object I had dropped down the front of my dress: It was, as I knew it would be, Nialla's orange cloisonné butterfly compact. It lay cradled in the flat of my hand, gleaming softly in the warm sunlight. Meg must have dropped it while sleeping on the couch in the vicar's study.

I'd return it to Nialla later, I thought, shoving it into my pocket. She'd be happy to have it back.

As I rejoined the family, I saw that Daffy was perched on the stone wall at the front of the churchyard with her nose stuck in Robert Burton's *Anatomy of Melancholy*, her latest grand enthusiasm. How she had managed to slip such a fat volume in and out of church I could not even begin to imagine, until I came close enough to spot the neatly made tinfoil cross she had glued to its black cover. Oh, what a fraud she was! Well done, Daff!

Feely stood laughing under an oak, letting her hair fall forward to cover her face, the way she does when she wants to look like Veronica Lake. Basking in her attention, and dressed in a rough wool suit, was a tall, blond Nordic god. It took me a moment to recognize him as Dieter Schrantz, and

I realized, not without a sinking feeling, that he was already completely in Feely's thrall, hanging on her every word like a ball on a rubber string, nodding like a demented woodpecker, and grinning like a fool.

They did not even notice my look of disgust.

Aunt Felicity was talking to an elderly person with a hearing trumpet. It seemed, from their conversation, that they were old friends.

"But one mustn't arch one's back and spit!" the old lady was saying, curling her red-nailed fingers into a claw, at which they both cackled obscenely.

Dogger, meanwhile, sat patiently on a bench beneath a yew tree, his eyes closed, a slight smile on his lips, and his face upturned towards the summer sun, looking for all the world like one of those modern brass sculptures called *Sunday*.

No one paid me the slightest attention. I was on my own.

THE DOUBLE DOORS IN THE porch of the parish hall were draped with a rope, from which hung a notice: *Police Line—Do Not Cross*.

I didn't: I walked round the back of the building and went in by one of the exits.

It was pitch dark inside. At the far end of the corridor, I knew, was the door that opened into the auditorium. To my right were the several steps that led up to the stage.

I could hear the rumble of men's voices, and although I strained my ears to the utmost, I could not make out what they were saying. The black velvet curtains that lined the stage must be absorbing their words.

Unable to make any sense of the murmur, and because I didn't want to risk being caught eavesdropping, I clattered noisily up the stairs.

"Hullo!" I shouted. "Anyone for tea?"

Inspector Hewitt was standing in a pool of light talking to sergeants Woolmer and Graves. At the sight of me, he broke off at once and came striding across the stage behind the puppet theater.

"You oughtn't to be in here. Didn't you see the signs?"

"Sorry," I said, without answering his question. "I came in the back way."

"No signs in the rear, Sergeant?" the Inspector asked Graves.

"Sorry, sir," the sergeant said with a sheepish grin. "I'll see to it right away."

"Too late now," the Inspector said. "The damage is done."

Sergeant Graves lost the grin and his brow furrowed. "Sorry, sir," he said. "Entirely my fault."

"Well," the Inspector went on, "since we're almost finished, it's not a *complete* disaster. But keep it in mind for next time."

"Yes, sir."

"Now, then," the Inspector said, turning to me, "what are you doing here? And don't give me any guff about tea."

I had learned from past experience that it was best to be frank with the Inspector—at least in replying to direct questions. One could always be helpful, I reminded myself, without spilling one's guts.

"I was making notes upon a few points."

I hadn't made notes, in fact, but now that I'd thought of it, I realized it was a good idea. I'd see to it tonight.

"Notes? Why on earth would you do that?"

Because I could think of nothing to say, I said nothing. I could hardly tell the man that Dogger thought it was murder.

"And now, I'm afraid, I'm going to have to ask you to leave, Flavia."

As he spoke, I looked round desperately for something—anything!—to seize upon.

And suddenly I saw it! I almost whooped with joy. My heart welled up inside me and I could hardly keep from laughing as I spoke.

"Edgar Allan Poe!" I said aloud. *"The Purloined Letter."*

The Inspector stared at me as if I'd gone mad.

"Are you familiar with the story, Inspector?" I asked. Daffy had read it aloud to us on Christmas Eve.

"Isn't everyone?" he said. "Now, please, if you'll be so good—"

"Then you'll remember where the letter was hidden: on the mantelpiece—in plain sight—dangling from a dirty blue ribbon."

"Of course," he said, with a brief but indulgent smile.

I pointed to the wooden rail of the puppet stage, which was no more than a foot above his head.

"Has the current been switched off?" I asked.

"We're not idiots, Flavia."

"Then," I said, reaching up and almost touching the thing, "perhaps we should tell the vicar we've found his lost bicycle clip."

sixteen

IT WAS DIFFICULT, AT FIRST, TO SEE THE THING. BLACK METAL on black painted wood was nearly invisible. If it hadn't been for the patterned spray of carbon, I shouldn't have noticed it at all.

Black on black on black. I was proud of myself.

The bicycle clip was pushed down over a wooden strut, as if the strut were an ankle. Beneath it ran a length of electric flex, which connected a row of toggle switches above the stage to the colored footlights below. Even from where I stood, I could see the glint of copper wire where a section of the flex had been stripped of its insulation.

"Good Lord!" the Inspector said. "Whatever makes you think this belongs to the vicar?"

"Several things," I told him, ticking them off on my fingers. "In the first place, I heard him say on Thursday afternoon that he had lost his bicycle clip. In the second place, I know for a fact that it wasn't here yesterday afternoon before the show. Rupert let me have a good look round just before the matinee. And finally, it has the vicar's initials on it. Look here: If you squat a bit and look edge-on, you can see them: *D.R.*—Denwyn Richardson. Cynthia scratched them on with a needle because he's forever losing things."

"And you're quite sure the clip wasn't here on Saturday afternoon?"

"Positive. I was holding on to that very spot on the railing when Rupert took me up on the bridge—to show me how Galligantus worked."

"I beg your pardon?" The look on the Inspector's face was a puzzle.

"Galligantus. That's the name of the giant in *Jack and the Beanstalk*. Here, I'll show you. Is it all right to climb up there?" I asked, pointing to the bridge.

"It's extremely irregular, but carry on."

I scrambled up the ladder to the catwalk behind the puppet stage, with the Inspector hot on my heels.

Galligantus was still firmly in position.

"In the third act, as Jack is hacking away at the beanstalk, Rupert pulls this iron lever, which releases Galligantus. He's spring-loaded, you see."

There was a very long silence. Then the Inspector took out his notebook and unscrewed the cap of his biro.

"All right, Flavia," he said with a sigh, "tell me more."

"When Jack chops down the beanstalk, the giant's supposed to come crashing down from the sky. But he didn't, of course . . . Rupert did instead."

"Therefore Rupert couldn't have operated the lever. Is that what you're saying?"

"Exactly! If he had, Galligantus would have been triggered. But he wasn't, of course, because the vicar's bicycle clip was clamped over the end of the lever. Black on black. Rupert mustn't have noticed it."

"Good Lord!" the Inspector exclaimed, realizing what I was saying. "Then it wasn't—"

"A tragic accident? No, Inspector. I should hardly say so."

He let out a low whistle.

"See this? Someone's cut away the insulation from this cable," I went on, "right down to the bare wire, then shoved the bicycle clip down on top to cover it. The other end of the bicycle clip is clamped over the end of Galligantus's lever."

"Forming an electrical jumper," he said. "A deliberate short circuit."

"Precisely," I said. "Here—you can see the deposit of carbon where it arced. See where the wood beneath it is a little charred?"

Inspector Hewitt leaned in for a closer look, but said nothing.

"It seems to me," I added, " that the bicycle clip couldn't have been put there until sometime after the first performance. Otherwise, Galligantus couldn't have fallen."

"Flavia," the Inspector said, "you must promise me you will discuss this with no one. Not a word. Do you understand?"

I stared at him for a moment, as if the very thought of doing so were highly offensive.

"He was electrocuted, wasn't he?" I asked.

The Inspector nodded. "Dr. Darby thinks it most likely. We'll have the autopsy results later today."

We'll have the autopsy results? Was the Inspector including me? Did he count me as part of his team? I needed to choose my words carefully.

"My lips are sealed," I said. "Cross my heart and—"

"Thank you, Flavia," he said firmly. "A simple promise is sufficient. Now run along and let me get on with it."

Run along? What jolly cheek! What utter gall!

I'm afraid I made a rude noise on my way out.

AS I SUSPECTED SHE WOULD BE, Feely was still flirting with Dieter beneath the oaks.

Father stood near the door of the church with the perplexed look on his face of a man trying to decide if he should rush to the aid of someone who has unwittingly wandered into the tiger's cage, but can't quite make up his mind about which of the cage's two occupants is in greater need of saving from the other.

"Feely," he called out at last, "we mustn't keep Mrs. Mullet waiting."

My stomach curdled instantly. Today was Sunday, the day of the week upon which we were force-fed, like Strasbourg geese, upon one of Mrs. Mullet's failed culinary experiments, such as stuffed sow's liver brought whole to the table and passed off as Mock Denbighshire Sweet Loaf.

"Father," Feely said, taking the bull by the horns, "I'd like you to meet Dieter Schrantz."

Father, of course, like everyone else in Bishop's Lacey, was aware that there were German prisoners of war working in the neighbourhood. But until that moment, he had never been put in the position of having to converse with someone he always referred to, at home in Buckshaw's drawing room, as the Enemy.

He offered his hand.

"It's a pleasure to meet you, sir," Dieter said, and I could see that Father was taken aback by Dieter's perfect English. But before he could respond, Feely fired off the next round: "I've invited Dieter to tea," she said. "And he's accepted."

"Providing you approve, of course, sir," Dieter added.

Father seemed flustered. He pulled his spectacles from his waistcoat pocket and began polishing them on his handkerchief. Fortunately, Aunt Felicity arrived in time to intervene.

"Of course he approves!" she said. "Haviland's never been one to hold a grudge, have you, Havvie?"

Like a man in a dream, Father looked round him and remarked, to no one in particular, "Interesting weather."

I took immediate advantage of his momentary confusion.

"Go on ahead without me," I said. "I just want to pop in and make sure Nialla's all right. I'll be home directly."

And no one lifted a finger to stop me.

MRS. MULLET'S COTTAGE WAS NESTLED at the far end of Cobbler's Lane, a narrow, dusty track that ran south from the high street and ended at a stile. It was a cozy little place with hollyhocks and a ginger cat dozing in the sun. Her husband, Alf, was sitting on a bench in the yard, carving a willow whistle.

"Well, well," he said when he saw me at his gate, "to what do we owe this most prodigious great pleasure?"

"Good morning, Mr. Mullet," I said, falling effortlessly into my best prunes-and-prisms voice, "I hope you're keeping well?"

"Fair . . . fair to troublesome digestion. Sometimes kicks like a kangaroo—elsewise, burns like Rome."

"I'm sorry to hear that," I said, meaning every word of it. We de Luces were not the only ones subjected to Mrs. Mullet's culinary concoctions.

"Here," Alf said, handing me the wooden whistle. "Give 'er a blow. See if you can fetch up an elf."

I took the slender piece of wood and raised it to my lips.

"Perhaps I'd better not," I said. "I don't want to wake Nialla."

"Ha!" he said. "No fear o' that. She's gone afore the sun."

"Gone?"

I was astonished. How could she be gone?

"Where?" I asked.

"God only knows." He shrugged. "Back to Culverhouse Farm, maybe—maybe not. That's all I know. Now give us a toot."

I blew into the whistle, producing a high, shrill, piercing wail.

"Wizard tone," I said, handing it back.

"Keep it," Alf said. "I made it for you. I thought you'd be round before long."

"Smashing!" I said, because I knew it was expected of me.

AS I WALKED BACK TO BUCKSHAW, I thought how similar my life was to the lives of those swarming clerics in Anthony Trollope who seemed to spend their days buzzing from cloister to vicarage and from village to the bishop's palace like black clockwork beetles scuttling to and fro in a green maze. I had dipped into The Warden during one of our compulsory Sunday afternoon reading periods, and followed it a few weeks later by skimming bits of Barchester Towers.

I must confess that, since there was no one of my own age group in his writings, I did not care much for Trollope. Most of his fossilized clergymen, for instance, quite frankly made me want to spew my sausages. The character with whom I most identified was Mrs. Proudie, the tyrant wife of the rabbity bishop, who knew what she wanted and, for the most part, knew how to get it. Had Mrs. Proudie been keen on poisons, she might have become my favorite character in all of literature.

Although Trollope had not specifically mentioned it, there was no doubt in my mind that Mrs. Proudie had been brought up in a home with two older sisters who treated her like dirt.

Why did Ophelia and Daphne despise me so? Was it because Harriet had hated me, as they claimed? Had she, while suffering from "the baby blues," stepped off into thin air from a mountain in Tibet?

In short, the question was this: Had I killed her?

Did Father hold me responsible for her death?

Somehow the sparkle had gone out of the day as I plodded glumly along the lanes. Even the thought of Rupert's murder and its messy aftermath did little to cheer me.

I gave a couple of toots on the willow whistle, but it sounded like a baby cuckoo, fallen from its nest, crying woefully for its mother. I shoved the thing into the bottom of my pocket and trudged on.

I needed some time alone—some time to think.

SEEN FROM THE MULFORD GATES, Buckshaw always had about it a rather sad and abandoned air, as if some vital essence were missing. But now, as I walked along beneath the chestnuts, something was different. I spotted it at once. Several people were standing on the gravel sweep in the forecourt, and one of them was Father, who was pointing at the roof. I broke into a run, dashing across the lawn like a sprinter, chest out, fists going like pistons at my side.

I needn't have bothered. As I drew closer, I saw that it was only Aunt Felicity and Daffy, both standing on one side of Father, with Feely at the other.

At her right hand stood Dieter. I couldn't believe my eyes!

Feely's eyes were sparkling, her hair was shining in the summer sun, and her smile was dazzlingly perfect. In her gray skirt and canary yellow sweater set, with a single strand of Harriet's cultured pearls draped round her neck, she was more than vibrant . . . she was *beautiful*—I could have throttled her.

"Ruskin found square drip moldings abominable," Father was saying, "but he was being facetious, of course. Even the best of our British sandstone is but a pale mockery of the fine-grained marble one finds in Greece."

"Quite true, sir," Dieter agreed. "Although, was it not your Charles Dickens who thought that the Greeks used marble only because of the way it took paint and color? Still, the style and the material mean nothing when the molding is placed under a portico. It is the architect's joke, isn't it?"

Father considered for a moment, rubbing his hands together behind his back as he stood staring at the front of the house.

"By Jove!" he said at last. "You may have hit on something."

"Ah, Flavia!" Aunt Felicity said as she spotted me. "Think of the Devil and she shall appear. I should like to paint presently and you shall be my assistant. I relish the brushwork but I simply can't bear the sticky tubes and the dirty rags."

Daffy rolled her eyes and edged slowly away from her mad old aunt, fearing, I think, that she was going to be put to work as well. I relented enough to ask her one question. There were times when curiosity trumped even pride.

"What's *he* doing here?" I whispered into her ear, giving a slight tip of my head towards Dieter.

Of course I already knew, but it was a rare opportunity to talk sister-to-sister without rancor.

"Aunt Felicity insisted. Said he should walk us home and stay to tea.

"I think she's got her eye on him," she added with a coarse snicker.

Although I'm quite accustomed to Daffy's excesses, I must admit that I was shocked.

"For Feely," she explained.

Of course! No wonder Father was exercising his rusty charm! One daughter fewer would mean a one-third reduction in the number of surplus mouths he had to feed. Not that Feely ate that much—she didn't—but coupled with a similar reduction in the dose of daily insolence he would need to put up with, palming her off on Dieter was well worth the effort.

Then, too, I thought, there would be an end to the vast outlays of cash for the constant re-silvering of Buckshaw's looking glasses. Feely was hell on mirrors.

"And your father . . ." Father was saying to Dieter.

I knew it! He was already greasing the skids!

". . . I believe you said something about books?"

"He's a publisher, sir," Dieter said. "He's the 'Schrantz' of Schrantz and Markel. You may not have heard of them but they publish in German, editions of—"

"Of course! The *Luxus Ausgaben Schrantz und Markel*. Their Pliny—the one with the Dürer plates—is quite remarkable."

"Come along, Flavia," Aunt Felicity said. "You know how tiresome it is to paint brickwork once it's in shadow."

FROM A DISTANCE, I must have looked like a sinking galleon as, with Aunt Felicity's easel over my shoulder, a stretched canvas under each arm, and a wooden box of paints and brushes in each hand, I waded barefoot through the shallow waters of the ornamental lake, towards the island upon which the folly was situated. Aunt Felicity brought up the rear, carrying a three-legged stool. In her tweed suit, floppy hat, and smock, she reminded me of photos I had seen in *Country Life* of Winston Churchill dabbling with his paints at Chartwell. The only thing missing was the cigar.

"I've wanted for ages to render the south front as it was in the days of dear Uncle Tar," she shouted, as if I were on the far side of the world.

"NOW, THEN, DEAR," she said, when I had finally set up the painting gear to her satisfaction, "it's time for a quiet talk. Out here, at least, we shall not be overheard—save by the bees and the water rats."

I looked at her in astonishment.

"I expect you think I know nothing about the kind of life you lead."

This was the sort of statement of which I had learned to be exceptionally wary: Its implications were immense and, until I saw which way the conversational wind was blowing, I knew that it was best to keep quiet.

"On the contrary," she went on, "I know a great deal about what you must feel: your loneliness, your isolation, your older sisters, your preoccupied father . . ."

I was about to say that she must be mistaken, when I suddenly saw that the coming chat could be turned to my advantage.

"Yes," I said, staring off over the water and blinking, as if to stop a tear, "it *can* be difficult at times. . . ."

"That's precisely what your mother used to say about living at Buckshaw. I remember her coming here summers, as a girl, as had I before her."

Picturing Aunt Felicity as a girl was not an easy task.

"Oh, don't look so shocked, Flavia. In my youth, I used to run wild here on the island like a Pawnee princess. 'Moo-noo-tonowa,' I called myself. Pinched nice bits of beef from the larder and pretended I was cooking dog over a campfire lighted with rubbing sticks and snuff.

"Later, even in spite of the great difference in our ages, Harriet and I were always the greatest of chums. 'The Wretched Outcasts' we used to call ourselves. We would come out here to the island to talk. Once, when we hadn't seen one another for a very long time, we sat out all night in the folly, wrapped in blankets, jabbering away until the sun came up. Uncle Tar sent Pierrepoint, the old butler, to bring us Plasmon biscuits and calf's-foot jelly. He had spotted us from the windows of his laboratory, you see, and—"

"What was she like," I interrupted. "Harriet, I mean."

Aunt Felicity made a dark slash of color on her canvas, which I guessed was supposed to represent the trunk of one of the chestnuts in the drive.

"She was exactly like you," she answered. "As you very well know."

I gulped. "She was?"

"Of course she was! How could you not be aware of it?"

I could have filled her ears with the horrid tales that Feely and Daffy had told me, but I chose not to.

"*Zipped lips save ships.*"

Dogger had said that to me once when I asked him a rather personal question about Father. "Zipped lips save ships," he had answered, turning back to his deadheading, and I hadn't the nerve to ask which of the three of us were the mutes and which the vessels.

I had mumbled something unsatisfactory then, and now I found myself doing it again.

"Good heavens, child! If you want to see your mother, you have no more than to look in the glass. If you want to know her character, look inside yourself. You're so much like her it gives me the willies."

Well, then.

"Uncle Tar used to invite us down to Buckshaw for the summer," she went on, either unaware of or choosing to ignore my burning face.

"He had some extraordinary idea that the presence of young females in the house held it together in some abstruse chemical fashion—something about bonds and the unsuspected dual gender of the carbon molecule. Mad as a March hare, Tar de Luce was, but a lovely old gentleman, for all that.

"Harriet, of course, was his favorite; perhaps because she never grew weary of sitting on a tall stool in that stinking laboratory, and taking down notes as he dictated them. 'My whiz-bang assistant,' he used to call her. It was a private joke: Harriet told me once that he was referring to a spectacular experiment gone awry that might have wiped Buckshaw off the map—to say nothing of Bishop's Lacey and beyond. But she swore me to silence. I don't know why I'm telling you this."

"He was investigating the first-order decomposition of nitrogen pentoxide," I said. "It was work that led eventually to the development of the atomic bomb. There are some letters among his papers from Professor Arrhenius of Stockholm that make it quite clear what they were onto."

"And you, as it were, are left to carry the torch."

"I beg your pardon?"

"To carry on the glorious name of de Luce," she said. "Wherever it may lead you."

This was an interesting thought; it had never occurred to me that one's name could be a compass.

"And where might that be?" I asked, somewhat slyly.

"You must listen to your inspiration. You must let your inner vision be your Pole Star."

"I try," I said. I must sound to Aunt Felicity like the village idiot.

"I know you do, dear. I've heard several reports of your doings. For instance there was that horrid business with Bunpenny, or whatever his name was."

"Bonepenny," I said. "Horace. He died just over there."

I pointed across the lake to the wall of the kitchen garden.

Aunt Felicity plowed on regardless. "You must never be deflected by unpleasantness. I want you to remember that. Although it may not be apparent to others, your duty will become as clear to you as if it were a white line painted down the middle of the road. You must follow it, Flavia."

"Even when it leads to murder?" I asked, suddenly bold.

With her brush extended to arm's length, she painted in the dark shadow of a tree. "Even when it leads to murder."

We sat for a few moments in silence, Aunt Felicity dabbing away at her canvas with no particularly exciting results, and then she spoke again: "If you remember nothing else, remember this: Inspiration from outside one's self is like the heat in an oven. It makes passable Bath buns. But inspiration from *within* is like a volcano: It changes the face of the world."

I wanted to throw my arms around this dotty old bat in her George Bernard Shaw costume and hug her until the juices ran out. But I didn't. I couldn't.

I was a de Luce.

"Thank you, Aunt Felicity," I said, scrambling to my feet. "You're a brick."

seventeen

WE WERE AT TEA IN THE LIBRARY. MRS. MULLET HAD COME IN and gone out, leaving behind a vast tray of Jenny Lind cake and currant scones. To my whispered question about Nialla, she had replied with a shrug, and wrinkled her brow to remind me that she was on duty.

Feely was at the piano. It hadn't taken more than three minutes for Dieter to ask politely which of us played, and Feely had replied with her blushes. Now, sufficiently coaxed and implored, she was just beginning the second movement of Beethoven's *Pathétique* sonata.

It was a lovely piece and, as the music faded away and then welled up again, like longings in the heart, I remembered that it was the music Laurie Laurence had played in *Little Women*, as Jo, who had refused his proposal, walked away outside his window, and I wondered if Feely had chosen it subconsciously.

Father was dreamily tapping a forefinger against the edge of his saucer, which he held beautifully balanced in his hands. There were times when, for no apparent reason, I felt a huge tidal wave of love—or at least respect—for him, and this was one of them.

In the corner, Daffy was curled up like a cat in an armchair, still in the clutches of *The Anatomy of Melancholy*, and Aunt Felicity sat contentedly near the window, doing something intricate with a pair of needles and a ball of sulfur yellow wool.

Suddenly I noticed that Dieter was biting the corner of his lip, and there was a glistening at the corner of his eye. He was almost in tears, and trying not to show it.

How cruel it was of that witch, Feely, to choose something so sad and so evocative: a melody by Beethoven that could only serve as a bitter reminder to our German guest of the homeland he had left behind.

But at that instant, Feely broke off abruptly and leapt up from the keyboard.

"Oh!" she gasped, "I'm so sorry! I didn't mean to—"

And I could see that for probably the first time in her life, she was genuinely distressed. She flew to Dieter's side and held out her handkerchief—and to his eternal credit, he took it.

"No. It is I who should be sorry," he said, wiping at his eyes. "It's just that—"

"Dieter," I found my mouth suddenly blurting, "tell us how you came to be a prisoner of war. I've been simply dying to ask you. I'm frightfully keen on history, you know."

You could have heard a pin drop in Antarctica.

"Flavia!" Father finally managed—but only when it was far too late to have the effect that he intended.

But Dieter was already smiling. It seemed to me he was relieved to have got past the dampness.

"But of course!" he said. "For five years I have been waiting for someone to ask me—but no one ever has. You English are all such perfect gentlemen—even the ladies!"

Aunt Felicity shot him a look of beaming approval.

"But," Dieter added, "I must warn you—it's a long story. Are you sure you want to hear it?"

Daffy closed her book and set it aside. "I adore long stories," she said. "In fact, the longer, the better."

Dieter took up a stance on the rug in front of the fireplace, his elbow on the mantelpiece. You could almost picture him at a hunting lodge in the Black Forest.

"Well," he said, "I think you could safely say that I was shot down in England because of the Brontë sisters."

Shot down? This was something new! I was all agog.

Daffy's eyes were instantly like china doorknobs, and even Father sat up straight.

"Good Lord!" he muttered.

"I was spoiled, as a boy," Dieter began, "and I must admit to it. I was an only child, brought up in a well-to-do household by a *Kinderpflegerin* —a nursery governess.

"My father, as I have said, was a publisher, and my mother an archaeologist. Although they loved me well enough, I suppose, they were both so wrapped up in their own worlds that everything having to do with 'the boy' was left up to Drusilla. That was the governess's name—Drusilla.

"Drusilla was a very great reader of English novels. She consumed books like a whale eats krill. You never saw her without a book in her hand—in fact, she taught me to read while I was still sucking my thumb.

"Drusilla had read all of the Brontë sisters' books, of course: *Wuthering Heights, Jane Eyre, Shirley, The Tenant of Wildfell Hall*—she had them almost by heart.

"I was half in love with her, I think, and I thought that I could make her love me by reading aloud in English from her favorites.

"And that was how I became an Anglophile. From that time on, I wanted nothing more than to read English books: Dickens, of course, and Conan Doyle; Jane Austen and Thomas Hardy. When I was a bit older, Drusilla gave me for Christmas subscriptions to *The Boy's Own Annual* and *Chums*. By the time I was twelve, I was more British than many a boy from Brixton!

"Then came the wireless. From the articles in *Chums,* and with the help of a schoolboy friend who lived next door—his name was Wolfgang Zander—I was able to put together a simple single-valve wireless receiver with which we could tune in to the broadcasts of the BBC.

"We were mad about electrical gadgets, Wolfgang and I. The first thing we made was a battery-operated doorbell; the next was a telephone between my bedroom and his, with the wire strung over the rooftops and through the trees.

"Long after our families were asleep, that cotton-covered wire high in the branches buzzed long into the night with our feverish speculations. We would talk away the night, about wireless, of course, but also about English books, for Wolfgang, you see, also had been bitten by the English—and particularly the Brontë—bug.

"The adolescent imagination is a powerful force, and I suppose we saw ourselves, Wolfgang and I, as Knights of the Round Table who would come riding out from our Teutonic stronghold to rescue these Brontë sisters: these three fair, pale maidens—whose very names identify them as daughters of the Thunder-god—who were being held hostage by a monster in their cold stone tower in the north.

"Besides," he added, "there is something about young, helpless damsels in damp climates that makes every adolescent boy want to carry them off and marry them."

He paused to let his words have their effect, looking keenly from one of us to another, and as he did, I saw with a sudden shock that in Feely and Daffy and me, Dieter fancied he had found his Brontës; and in Buckshaw, his cold stone tower. We were his Charlotte, Emily, and Anne!

And there we sat, the three of us, our mouths hanging open like dogs.

My mind was reeling as Dieter went on: "But too soon we grow up," he said with a sigh. "Too soon we take on the joys of the grown-up world, but also its troubles.

"Always, there is an age when boys discover flying, and it came early to me. My parents enrolled me in the NSFK—the National Socialist Flying Corps—and when I was fourteen, I found myself suddenly alone at the controls of a *Schulgleiter*, soaring like a hawk high above the Wasserkuppe, in the hills of the Hessian Rhön.

"From the air, these mountains, even though they are of quite a different geology, bear in some places a startling resemblance to the moors of North Yorkshire."

"How do you know that?" Daffy interrupted.

"Daphne!" Father said. His pointed look added the word *manners*.

"Is it because you've bombed Sheffield?"

There was a shocked silence at her question. How bold she was! Even I would not have asked Dieter about his aerial activities over England, although I will admit that, just minutes before, that very point had crossed my mind.

"Because," Daffy added, "if you have, you must say so."

"I was coming to that," Dieter said quietly.

He continued without batting an eye.

"When the war came, and I was transferred to the Luftwaffe, I always kept the small English 'Everyman' editions of *Jane Eyre* and *Wuthering Heights* wrapped carefully in a white silk flying scarf at the bottom of my rucksack, cheek to cheek with Lord Byron and Shelley.

"I decided that when the war was over, I would enroll at a university—perhaps even Oxford, since I already had the language—where I would read English Literature. I would take a double first, and accept a teaching post at one of the great public schools, and would end my days as an honored and respected schoolmaster, somewhat like your Mr. Chips.

"'Goodbye, Herr Schrantz,' I used to say. But Fate had not yet finished with me. An order was received that I was to proceed at once to France.

"My father, it seemed, had run into an old acquaintance in Berlin: someone who was high up in the Ministry and could arrange almost anything one might desire. Father wanted to have a son who flew a fighter: one whose name was in all the headlines, not one who mooned about with his nose in a book—and an English book at that!

"Before I could protest, I found myself posted to a reconnaissance group, Luftflotte III, based in France, near Lille.

"Our aircraft were the Messerschmitt Bf 110, a twin-engine machine nicknamed the *Zerstörer*."

"The *Destroyer*," said Daffy sourly. There were times when she could be quite snappish.

"Yes," Dieter replied. "The Destroyer. These ones, though, were specially modified for reconnaissance duties. We carried no bombs."

"Spying," Daffy said. Her cheeks were a little flushed, though whether from anger or excitement, I could not tell.

"Yes, spying, if you like," Dieter agreed. "In the war, there was reconnaissance on both sides."

"He's right, you know, Daphne," Father said.

"As I was saying," Dieter went on, with a glance at Daffy, "the *Zerstörer* was a twin-engine machine with a crew of two: a pilot and a second member, who could be a wireless operator, a navigator, or a rear gunner, depending upon the mission.

"My first day on the line, as I walked towards the briefing hut, an *Oberfeldwebel*—a flight sergeant—in flying boots, clicked his heels and called out 'Herr Hauptmann! Heathcliff!' Of course it was my old chum, Wolfgang Zander.

"I looked round quickly to see if anyone had heard him, since such familiarity between ranks would not be tolerated. But no one else was within earshot.

"We shook hands happily. 'I'm your navigator,' Wolfgang said, laughing. 'Did they tell you that? Of all the navigators in the land, my name alone was chosen to be carried aloft to the wars in your tin dragon!'

"Although it was wonderful to see him again, we had to be discreet. It was a complicated situation. We developed a whole set of stratagems— rather like lovers in a Regency romance.

"We would walk to the aircraft, pointing here and there with our fingers and ducking under the fuselage, as if we were discussing the tension of cables, but our talk, of course, was of little but English novels. If anyone came close, we would switch quickly from Hardy to Hitler.

"It was during one of these inspections that the great scheme was born. I don't remember now if it was Wolfgang or I who first came up with the idea.

"We were walking around *Kathi*'s tail—*Kathi* was the thinly disguised name painted on the nose of our aircraft—when suddenly one of us, I think it might have been Wolfgang . . . or it might have been me . . . said, 'Do you suppose the heather is in bloom today on Haworth Moor?'

"It was that simple. In just those few moments, the die, as Julius Caesar remarked, was cast.

"And then, as if she had been listening at the door, Fate again stepped in. Two days later we were given an objective in South Yorkshire: a railway yard and a bicycle factory thought to be producing Rolls-Royce engines. Photographs only. 'A piece of cake,' as the RAF blokes used to say. A perfect opportunity to deliver, in person, our little gift.

"The flight across the Channel was uneventful, and for once, we were not bounced by Spitfires. The weather was beautiful, and *Kathi*'s engines were purring away like a pair of huge, contented cats.

"We arrived over the target on time—'on the dot,' as you say—and took our photographs. *Snap! Snap! Snap!* and we were finished. Mission accomplished! The next quarter of an hour belonged to us.

"The parsonage at Haworth now lay less than ten miles to the northwest, and at our speed, which was three hundred miles an hour, it was no more than two minutes away.

"The problem was that we were too high. Although we had descended to seventeen thousand feet for the photographs, for our personal mission, we needed to lose more altitude quickly. A Messerschmitt with black crosses on its wings swooping down like a hawk upon a quiet English village would hardly go unnoticed.

"I shoved the control column forward, and down and down we circled in a giant spiral, our ears popping like champagne corks. Beneath us, the heather on the moor was a sea of purple billows.

"At a thousand feet I began to pull out and dropped nearly to hedge level.

"'Get ready!' I shouted to Wolfgang.

"We came in from the east, and suddenly there it was atop its hill: the village of Haworth! We roared along, skimming the fields, barely clearing the farmhouse chimney pots.

"As we came in over the Haworth road, I caught my first glimpse of the church at the top of the steep high street: then, a hundred yards behind it, beyond the churchyard, the familiar shape of the Brontës' parsonage. It was exactly as I had always imagined it: the dark stained stones and the empty windows.

"'Now!' I shouted, and Wolfgang shoved our gift out the open port in the canopy and into the slipstream. Although I couldn't see it, I could picture our wreath arcing down through the air, tumbling over and over, its purple ribbon streaming out behind it as it fell. Later, someone would retrieve it from among the old tombstones near the parsonage door, and read the message: gold letters the color of gorse on heather-colored silk, saying *All the World Loves You——Rest in Peace*.

"It was too risky to climb back to cruising altitude. We should have to go home by hedgehopping from point to point, keeping to the open countryside. Of course, we would burn more fuel that way, but both of us were young and foolish, and we had done what we had come to do. As soon as we were spotted, we knew, all the hounds of Hell, the Hurricanes and Spitfires, would be on our tail.

"But it was a perfect August day. With a bit of luck and a tailwind, I was telling Wolfgang, we might even manage to overfly Thomas Hardy's house on the way home at no additional cost to the Reich.

"It was at that precise moment that the canopy in front of my face shattered in a rain of exploding bullets. We were hit!

"'Spitfire!' Wolfgang shouted. But it was too late. A dark shadow shot past us, then banked and turned, its red, white, and blue roundels flashing like mad eyes in the summer sun.

"'Watch out,' I yelled. 'He's coming round for another pass!'

"It was then that I noticed that our port engine temperature gauge was pinned to the top. It was overheating. I glanced to the side and, to my horror, saw the black smoke and orange flames that were billowing out from beneath the cowling. I feathered the prop and switched off the engine.

"By now the Spitfire was behind us again. In what was left of my rearview mirror, I could see his fragmented image rocking gently from side to side, riding our slipstream. He had us in his sights.

"But he held his fire. It was most unnerving.

"*Come on*, I thought. *Get it over with.* He was playing with us like a terrier with a rat.

"I don't know how long it went on. You cannot judge time when you are about to die.

"'Why doesn't he shoot?' I called out to Wolfgang, but there was no answer. With my shoulder harness locked, I could not twist round far enough in my seat to see him.

"But even on one engine, *Kathi* was easily able to stay aloft, and for what seemed like an eternity, that British hound chased the German hare across the green countryside.

"The shattered windscreen had reduced forward visibility to zero, and I had to tack sharply from side to side in order to see what lay ahead. It was a dicey situation.

"And then the other engine died. *Phut!* Just like that! I had only seconds to make a decision. The trees on a wooded hill were rushing by beneath the wings. At the edge of the wood was a sloping field. It was there that I would put her down. No wheels, I thought. Better to make a belly landing and come to a stop more quickly.

"The sound of the crash was louder than I ever could have imagined. The aircraft slewed from side to side as the earth tore at her belly, battering and banging along, lurching, bucking—it was like being thrown alive into a millrace.

"And then the unearthly silence. It took a moment to realize that we were no longer moving. I unbuckled my harness, threw back the front canopy, and jumped out onto the wing, then ran back and peered in at Wolfgang.

"'Get out!' I shouted. 'Quickly! Get out!'

"But there was no reply.

"Inside the glass canopy, in a sea of blood, Wolfgang sat with a happy smile on his face. His dead eyes were staring out almost feverishly at the green English countryside.

"I jumped down from the wing and vomited into the long grass.

"We had come to rest at the far side of the field. Now, from higher up the hillside, two men, one tall, the other short, had emerged from the trees and were clumping slowly, warily, down towards me. One of them was carrying a shotgun, the other a pitchfork.

"I stood there, not moving. As they drew near, I put one hand in the air, slowly pulled my pistol from its holster and threw it away, making sure they saw what I was doing. Then I put up the other hand.

"'You're a German,' the tall man called out as they approached.

"'Yes,' I shouted back. 'But I speak English.'

"He seemed a little taken aback.

"'Perhaps you should call the police,' I suggested, jerking my head towards the battered Messerschmitt. 'My friend is dead in there.'

"The tall man edged cautiously over to the aircraft and peered inside. The other stood his ground, staring at me as if I had landed from another planet. He drew the pitchfork back, as if he were about to jab me in the stomach.

"'Let him be, Rupert,' the man with the shotgun said. 'He's just had a bad crash.'

"Before the other man could respond, there was a high-pitched screaming in the sky, and the Spitfire shot past, lifting at the end of the field into a victory roll.

"I watched it climb straight up into the blue air, and then I said:

"'*He rises and begins to round,*

"'*He drops the silver chain of sound.*'

"The two men looked at me as if I had suddenly fallen into shock—and perhaps I had. Not until later would it come crashing home to me that poor Wolfgang was dead.

"George Meredith," I told them. "'The Lark Ascending.'"

"LATER, AT THE POLICE STATION in the village, the Spitfire pilot paid me a visit. He was with a squadron based at Catterick, and had taken his machine up to check the controls after the mechanics had made a few adjustments. He had not the slightest intention of getting into a scrap that day, he told me, but there we were, Wolfgang and I, suddenly in his gunsights over Haworth. What else could he do?

"'Hell of a prang. Bad luck, old chap,' he said. 'Damned sorry about your friend.'

"All of that was six years ago," Dieter said with a sigh. "The tall man in the field with the shotgun, as I was to find out later, was Gordon Ingleby. The other one, the man with the pitchfork, as perhaps you have already guessed, was Rupert Porson."

eighteen

RUPERT PORSON? BUT HOW COULD THE MAN WITH THE PITCH-fork have been Rupert?

My mind was spinning like a painted tin top.

The last place on earth I had ever expected Dieter's tale to end was in Jubilee Field at the Ingleby farm. But one thing now became perfectly clear: If Rupert *had* been at Culverhouse Farm six years ago, during the war, it would explain, at least in part, how the wooden face of his puppet Jack had come to be carved in the image of Robin Ingleby.

Father let out a sigh.

"I remember it well," he said. "Your machine was brought down in Jubilee Field, just below Gibbet Wood."

Dieter nodded. "I was sent for a short time to a prisoner-of-war camp with thirty or forty other Luftwaffe officers and men, where our days were spent ditching and hedging. It was backbreaking work, but at least I was still in England. Most German pilots who were captured were sent abroad to camps in Canada, where there was little hope of escape.

"When I was offered a chance to live and work on a farm, I jumped at it; although it was not compulsory, many of us did. Those who did not called us traitors, among other things.

"But the war was moving towards its end, and a lot of us knew it. Better to begin paving my own personal road to Oxford, I thought, than to leave my future to chance.

"No one was more surprised than I was to find I had been assigned to the Inglebys' farm. It amused me to think that Gordon, who only a short time before had had me at the end of a shotgun, was now helping Grace fry my kippers in the farmhouse kitchen."

"That was six years ago, you say—in 1944?" I asked.

"It was." Dieter nodded. "In September."

I couldn't help it. Before I could stifle the words, I found myself blurting, "Then you must have been at Culverhouse Farm when Robin was found hanging in Gibbet Wood."

"Flavia!" Father said, putting his cup and saucer down with a clatter. "We will have *no* gossiping about the grief of others."

Dieter's face went suddenly grim, and a fire—could it have been anger?—came into his eyes.

"It was I," he said, "who found him."

You who found him? I thought. *Impossible!* Mrs. Mullet had made it perfectly clear that it was Mad Meg who had discovered Robin's body.

There was a remarkably long silence, and then Feely leapt to her feet to refresh Dieter's teacup.

"You must excuse my little sister," she said with a brittle laugh. "She has rather an unhealthy fascination with death."

Full points, Feely, I thought. But although she had hit the nail on the head, she didn't know the half of it.

The rest of the afternoon was pretty much a thud. Father had made what I admit was a noble attempt to switch the conversation to the weather and the flax crops, while Daffy, sensing that little else was worthy of her attention, had crawled back into her book.

One by one, we made our excuses: Father to tend to his stamps, Aunt Felicity to have a nap before supper, and Daffy to the library. After a while, I grew bored with listening to Feely prattle on to Dieter about various balls and outings in the country, and made my escape to the laboratory.

I chewed on the end of my pencil for a while, and then I wrote:

Sunday, 23rd of July, 1950
WHERE IS EVERYONE? That is the burning question.
WHERE IS NIALLA? After spending the night at Mrs. Mullet's cottage, she simply disappears. (Does Inspector Hewitt know she's gone?)

WHERE IS MAD MEG? After erupting at the afternoon performance of Jack and the Beanstalk, she is taken to rest on the vicar's couch. And then she vanishes.

WHERE IS MUTT WILMOTT? He seems to have slunk off sometime during the fatal performance.

WHAT WAS RUPERT DOING AT CULVERHOUSE FARM 6 YEARS AGO? Why, when he and Dieter met at the farm on Friday, did they not admit that they already knew one another?

AND WHY, ABOVE ALL, DOES DIETER CLAIM TO BE THE ONE WHO FOUND ROBIN INGLEBY'S BODY HANGING IN GIBBET WOOD? Mrs. Mullet says it was Mad Meg, and Mrs. M is seldom wrong when it comes to village chin-wagging. YET WHY WOULD DIETER LIE ABOUT A THING LIKE THAT?

WHERE TO BEGIN? If this were a chemical experiment, the procedure would be obvious: I would start with those materials most closely to hand.

Mrs. Mullet! With any luck, she would still be puttering in the kitchen before plundering the pantry and carting off her daily booty to Alf. I ran to the top of the stairs and peered through the balustrades. Nobody in the hall.

I slid down the banister and dashed into the kitchen.

Dogger looked up from the table where, with clinical accuracy, he was excising the skin from a couple of cucumbers.

"She's gone," he said, before I could ask. "A good half hour ago."

He's a devil, that Dogger! I don't know how he does it!

"Did she say anything before she left? Anything interesting, that is?"

With Dogger in the kitchen as an audience, Mrs. M would hardly have been able to resist blathering on about how she took Nialla in (poor waif!), tucked her into a cozy bed with a hot-water bottle and a glass of watered-down sherry, and so forth, with a full account of how she slept, what they had for breakfast, and what she left on her plate.

"No." Dogger picked up a serrated bread knife and applied its edge to a loaf of new bread. "Just that the joint is in the warming oven, apple pie and clotted cream in the pantry."

Bugger!

Well, then, there was nothing for it but to make a fresh start in the morning. I'd set my alarm for sunrise, then strike out for Culverhouse

Farm and Gibbet Wood beyond. It was unlikely that there would be any clues left after all these years, but Rupert and Nialla had camped at the bottom of Jubilee Field on Friday night. If my plan were properly executed, I could be there and back before anyone at Buckshaw even knew that I was gone.

Dogger tore off a perfect square of waxed paper, and wrapped the cucumber sandwiches with hospital bed corners.

"I thought I'd make these tonight," he said, handing me the package. "I knew you'd want to get away early in the morning."

CURTAINS OF WET MIST HUNG in the fields. The morning air was damp and chill, and I breathed in deeply, trying to come fully awake, filling my nostrils and then my lungs with the rich aroma of dark soil and sodden grass.

As I bicycled into St. Tancred's churchyard, I saw that the Inspector's Vauxhall was gone, and so, I reasoned, was Rupert's body. Not that they would have left him crumpled on the puppet stage from Saturday evening until Monday morning, but I realized that the corpse would no longer be there inside the parish hall, its eyes bugging, its string of saliva congealed by now into a stalactite of spit. . . .

If I thought it had been, I might have been tempted to barge in for another look.

Behind the church, I removed my shoes and socks and wheeled Gladys through the deeper water beside the submerged stepping-stones. Saturday night's rain had increased the flow of water, which roiled about her spokes and tires, washing clean the accumulated mud and clay from my ride into Bishop's Lacey. By the time I reached the other bank, Gladys's livery was as fresh as a lady's painted carriage.

I gave my feet a final rinse, sat down on a stile, and restored my footwear.

Here, along the river, visibility was even less than it had been on the road. Trees and hedges loomed like pale shadows as I cycled along the grassy verge in a gray, wooly fog that blotted all the sound and color from the world. Except for the muted grumble of the water, all was silence.

At the bottom of Jubilee Field, Rupert's van stood forlorn beneath the willows, its gaily painted sign, "Porson's Puppets," jarringly out of place with both the location and the circumstances. There wasn't a sign of life.

I laid Gladys carefully down in the grass and tiptoed alongside the van. Perhaps Nialla had crept back and was now asleep inside, and I wouldn't want to frighten her. But the lack of condensation on the windscreen told me what I had already begun to feel: that no one was breathing inside the cold Austin.

I peered in at the windows but saw nothing unusual. I went round to the back door and gave the handle a twist. It was locked.

I walked in ever-widening circles through the grass, looking for any trace of a fire, but there was none. The campsite was as I had left it on Saturday.

As I reached the bottom of the farm lane, I was stopped in my tracks by a rope hung across the road, from which a sign was suspended. I ducked underneath to read its message.

Police Investigation———No Admittance by Order———Hinley Constabulary

Inspector Hewitt and his detectives *had* been here. But in posting their sign, they had obviously not thought of anyone coming across the swollen river. In spite of his promise to the Inspector, Sergeant Graves had still not learned his lesson about people slipping in by way of the back door.

Very well, then. Since there was nothing to see here anyway, I would move on to my next objective. Although I could not see it in the fog, I knew that Gibbet Wood lay not far ahead at the top of Gibbet Hill. It would be wet and soggy in among the trees, but I was willing to bet that the police had not been there before me.

I dragged Gladys under the barricade and pushed her slowly up the lane, which was far too steep to pedal. Halfway to the top, I shoved her behind a hawthorn hedge, and continued my climb, hemmed in on all sides with misty glimpses of blue flax.

Then suddenly the dark trees of the wood loomed out of the mist immediately in front of me. I had come upon it without realizing how close I was.

A weathered wooden sign was nailed to a tree, bearing the red words: KEEP OUT— —TRESP— —

The rest of it had been shot away by poachers.

As I had known it would be, everything in the wood was wet. I gave a shiver at the clammy coldness, steeled myself, and waded into the vegetation. Before I had gone half a dozen steps into the ferns and bracken, I was thoroughly soaked to the knees.

Something snapped in the underbrush. I froze as a dark form swooped on silent wings across my path: an owl, perhaps, mistaking the heavy morning mist for its twilight hunting time. Although it had startled me, its very presence was comforting: It meant that no one else was with me in the wood.

I pushed on, trying to follow the faint paths, any one of which, I knew, would lead me to the clearing at the very center.

Between two ancient, gnarled trees, the way was barred with what seemed to be a mossy gate, its gray wood twisted with rot. I was halfway over the crumbling barrier before I realized that I was once again at the steps of the old gallows. How many doomed souls had climbed these very stairs before being turned off the platform overhead? With a gulp, I looked up at the remnants of the structure, which now was open to the sky.

A leathery hand seized my wrist like a band of hot iron.

"What you up to, then? What you doin' snoopin' round this place?"

It was Mad Meg.

She shoved her sooty face so close to mine I could see the sandy bristles on the end of her chin. *The witch in the wood,* I thought, for one panicky moment, before I regained my senses.

"Oh, hullo, Meg," I said, as calmly as I could, trying to tame my pounding heart. "I'm glad I found you. You gave me quite a fright."

My voice was shakier than I had hoped.

"Frights as lives in Gibbet Wood," Meg said darkly. "Frights as lives here an' not elsewhere."

"Exactly," I agreed, not having the faintest idea what she was on about. "I'm glad you're here with me. Now I shan't be afraid."

"No Devil now," Meg said, rubbing her hands together. "Devil's dead and jolly good."

I remembered how frightened she had been at Rupert's performance of *Jack and the Beanstalk.* To Meg, Rupert was the Devil, who had killed Robin Ingleby, shrunk him to a wooden doll, and put him on the stage. Better to approach this indirectly.

"Did you have a nice rest at the vicarage, Meg?" I asked.

She spat on the trunk of an oak as if she were spitting in a rival witch's eye.

"Her turned me out," she said. "Took old Meg's bracelet and turned her out, so she did. 'Dirty, dirty.'"

"Mrs. Richardson?" I asked. "The vicar's wife? She turned you out?"

Meg grinned a horrid grin and set off through the trees at a near-gallop. I followed at her heels, through underbrush and ferns, deadfall, and the snags of thorns. Five minutes later and breathless, we were back where we had begun, at the foot of the rotted gallows.

"See there," she said, pointing. "That's where 'e took 'im."

"Took who, Meg?"

Robin Ingleby, she meant. I was sure of it.

"The Devil took Robin right here?" I asked.

"Turned 'im into wood, 'e did," she confided, looking over her shoulder. "Wood to wood."

"Did you actually see him? The Devil, I mean."

This was something that hadn't occurred to me before.

Was there a chance that Meg had seen someone in the wood with Robin? She lived, after all, in a shack among the trees, and it seemed unlikely that much happened within the bounds of Gibbet Wood that escaped her scrutiny.

"Meg saw," she said knowingly.

"What did he look like?"

"Meg saw. Old Meg sees plenty."

"Can you draw?" I asked, with sudden inspiration. I pulled my notebook from my pocket and handed her a stubby pencil.

"Here," I said, flipping to a blank page, "draw me the Devil. Draw him in Gibbet Wood. Draw the Devil taking Robin."

Meg gave something that I can describe only as a wet snicker. And then she squatted down, flattened the open notebook against her knee, and began to draw.

I think I was expecting something childish—nothing more than scrawled stick figures—but in Meg's sooty fingers, the pencil sprang to life. On the page, the glade in Gibbet Wood slowly appeared: a tree here, a tree there; now the rotted wood of the gallows, instantly recognizable. She had started at the margins and was working in towards the center of the page.

From time to time she clucked over her work, turning the pencil over and erasing a line. She was quite good, I have to give her that. Her sketch was probably better than I might have done myself.

And then she drew Robin.

I scarcely dared breathe as I looked on over her shoulder. Little by little, the dead boy took shape before my eyes.

He was hanging quite peacefully in midair, his neck canted to one side, a look of slightly surprised contentment on his face, as if he had suddenly and unexpectedly walked into a room full of angels. In spite of the subdued light of the wood, his neatly parted hair gave off a healthy, and therefore rather unnerving, shine. He wore a striped sweater and dark britches, their legs tucked carelessly into a pair of rubber boots. He must have died quickly, I thought.

Only then did she draw the noose that cramped his neck: a dark braided thing that dangled from the gallows into the space beneath. She shaded the rope with angry slashes of the pencil.

I breathed in deeply. Meg looked up at me triumphantly, seeking approval.

"And now the Devil," I whispered. "Draw the Devil, Meg."

She looked me straight in the eye, relishing the attention. A canny smile appeared at the corner of her mouth.

"Please, Meg—draw the Devil."

Without taking her eyes from mine, she licked a finger and thumb and turned elaborately to a fresh page. She began again, and as she drew, Gibbet Wood appeared once more at her fingertips. This second sketch grew darker than the first as Meg scrubbed at the pencil marks, smearing them to suggest the half-light of the glade. Then came the gallows, viewed this time from a slightly different angle.

How odd, I thought, *that she didn't begin with the Devil,* as most people would be tempted to do. But only when she had set the stage to her own satisfaction with trees and bushes did she begin to rough in the figure that was to be the focus of her creation.

In an approximate oval that she had left blank upon the page until now, a sketchy figure began to emerge: arms and shoulders first, followed by knees, legs, arms, hands, and feet.

It wore a black jacket, and stood on one leg in the clearing, as if captured in the midst of a frenzied dance.

Its trousers were hung by their suspenders from a low-hanging branch.

Meg shielded the paper with her left hand as she penciled in the features. When she was finished, she thrust it at me roughly, as if the paper were contaminated.

It took me a moment to recognize the face: to recognize that the figure in the glade—the Devil—was the vicar, Denwyn Richardson.

The vicar? It was too ridiculous for words. Or was it?

Just minutes earlier Meg had told me the Devil was dead, and now she was sketching him as the vicar.

What was going on in her poor addled mind?

"Are you quite sure, Meg?" I asked, tapping the notebook. "Is that the Devil?"

"Hsssst!" she said, cocking her head and putting her fingers to my lips. "Someone's comin'!"

I looked round the glade, which, even to my heightened sense of hearing, seemed perfectly silent. When I looked back, my notebook and pencil lay at my feet, and Meg had vanished among the trees. I knew there was little point in calling her back.

I stood there motionless for a few moments, listening, waiting for something, although I'm not sure what it was.

The woodland, I remembered, is an ever-changing world. From minute to minute, the shadows shift, and from hour to hour the vegetation moves with the sun. Insects tunnel in the soil, heaving it up, at first in little hummocks, and then in larger ones. From month to month, leaves grow and fall, and from year to year, the trees. Daffy once said that you can't step into the same river twice, and it's the same with forests. Five winters had come and gone since Robin Ingleby died here, and now there was nothing left to see.

I walked slowly back past the crumbling gallows and plunged into the woods. Within minutes, I was out into the open at the top of Jubilee Field.

Not twenty yards away, almost invisible in the fog, a gray Ferguson tractor was stopped in the field, and someone in a green overall and rubber boots was bending over the engine. That must have been what Meg had heard.

"Hullo!" I shouted. It's always best to announce one's self heartily when trespassing. (Even though I had invented it on the spot, this seemed to be a good general rule.)

As the figure straightened up and turned round, I realized that it was Sally Straw, the Land Army girl.

"Hello," she said, wiping her oily hands on a rag. "You're Flavia de Luce, aren't you?"

"Yes." I stuck out my hand. "And you're Sally. I've seen you at the market. I've always admired your freckles and your ginger hair."

To be most effective, flattery is always best applied with a trowel.

She gave me a broad, honest grin and a handshake that nearly crushed my fingers.

"It's all right to call me Sal," she said. "All my best friends do."

She reminded me somewhat of Joyce Grenfell, the actress: a bit mannish in the way she moved, but otherwise decidedly female.

"My Fergie's gone bust," she said, pointing to the tractor. "Might be the ignition coil. They do that sometimes, you know: get overheated and go open circuit. Then there's nothing for it but to wait for the ruddy thing to cool."

Since motors were not my forte, I nodded wisely and kept my mouth shut.

"What are you doing away out here?"

"Just rambling," I said. "I like to get away, sometimes. Go for a walk—that sort of thing."

"Lucky you," she said. "I never get away. Well, hardly ever. Dieter's taken me for a pint of half-and-half at the Thirteen Drakes a couple of times, but then there was a most god-awful flap about it. The POWs are not allowed to do that, you know. At least they weren't during the war."

"Dieter told me your sister Ophelia had him to tea yesterday," she added, somewhat cagily. I realized at once that she was fishing.

"Yes," I said, kicking carelessly at a clod of dirt, gazing off into the distance, and pretending I wasn't remotely interested. Friend or not, if she wanted gossip from me, it would have to be tit for tat.

"I saw you at the puppet show," I said. "At the church, on Saturday night. Wasn't that a corker? About Mr. Porson, I mean?"

"It was horrid," she said.

"Did you know him?"

It probably wasn't a fair question, and I fired it at her without warning: straight out of the blue.

Sally's expression became instantly guarded, and she hesitated a bit too long before answering.

"I—I've seen him around." Her lie was obvious.

"On the telly, perhaps?" I asked, perhaps too innocently. "*The Magic Kingdom*? Snoddy the Squirrel?"

I knew as soon as I said it that I'd pushed things too far.

"All right," she said, "what are you up to? Come on—out with it."

She planted her hands on her hips and fixed me with an unwavering stare.

"I don't know what you mean," I said.

"Oh, come off it. Don't give me that. Everyone for fifty miles around
knows that Flavia de Luce doesn't go walking in the woods just to put
roses in her cheeks."

Could that be true? Fifty miles? Her answer rather surprised me: I
should have thought a hundred.

"Gordon'd have your hide if he caught you in that wood," she said,
pointing to the sign.

I put on my best sheepish look, but kept quiet.

"How much do you know about all this?" Sally demanded, sweeping
her hand round in a large half-circle to take in the farm. Her meaning
was clear.

I took a deep breath. I had to trust her.

"I know that Rupert has been coming here to get cannabis for quite
a long time. I know that Gordon grows it in a patch in Gibbet Wood—not
far from where Robin was found hanging."

"And you think that Dieter and I are somehow mixed up in all this?"

"I don't know," I replied. "I hope not."

"So do I," Sally said. "So do I."

nineteen

"RUPERT WAS—A LADIES' MAN," SALLY SAID SLOWLY, AS IF reluctant to put her thoughts into words, "but then, you've probably found that out by now."

I nodded, careful not to interrupt. I had learned by observing Inspector Hewitt that silence is the best primer for a conversational pump.

"He's been coming to Culverhouse Farm off and on, for years—since well before the war. And Rupert's not the only one, you know. Gordon has a regular little army of others just like him. He supplies them with something to help manage the pain."

"Bhang," I said. I couldn't help myself. "Gunjah . . . Indian hemp, cannabis."

She looked at me with narrowed eyes, and then went on. "Some, like Rupert, come because they once had infantile paralysis—polio, they call it now—others, well, God only knows.

"You see, Gordon considers himself a kind of herbalist: someone who helps to blot out the sufferings that the doctors can't, or won't. He's very discreet about it, but then he has to be, doesn't he? Other than you, I really don't think anyone in Bishop's Lacey has ever guessed that the occasional travelers who stop by Culverhouse Farm are anything other than lost—or perhaps selling agricultural supplies.

"I've been here for eight years," Sally went on. "And don't even bother asking me: The answer is no—I'm not one of Gordon's smokers."

"I didn't expect you were," I said, fawning a little. It worked.

"I grew up in a good home," she went on, a little more eagerly. "My parents were what they used to call, in the old double-decker novels, 'poor but honest.' My mam was sick all the time, but she never would tell us what was wrong with her. Even my father didn't know. Meanwhile, I plodded on at school, got myself a bit of an education, and then the war came.

"Of course, I wanted to help out a bit with the medical bills, so I joined the WLA. Sounds simple, doesn't it? And so it was—there was no more to it than that. I was just a girl from Kent who wanted to fight Adolf Hitler, and see her mother well again.

"I was billeted, along with about forty other girls, at a Land Army hostel between here and Hinley, and that was where I first laid eyes on Rupert. Like a bee to honey that man was, make no mistake about it. He was rambling hither and yon about the countryside every summer with his little puppet show—getting back to his roots, he called it—and whenever I saw him, he seemed to have a new assistant. And she was always a bit of a knockout, if you get my meaning."

"Not long after I came to work at Culverhouse Farm, Rupert showed up for a fresh supply of smoking material. I recognized him at once as the little lame chap who was always chatting us up at the hostel, or the pub, of a weekend.

"I swore from the outset that I wouldn't get involved with him myself; I'd leave it to the other girls to take him down a notch or two. But then—"

Her gaze drifted off into another time.

So Nialla had been right! Rupert *had* gone off in search of Sally on the day they arrived. The pieces were beginning to fall into place.

Although the fog had now thinned a little, it was still quite dense, wrapping Sally and me in a misty cocoon of oddly reassuring silence. Unless they had come across us by accident, no one would know we were up here at the top of Jubilee Field. No one could have overheard us unless they had come up the length of the field from the bottom, or crept stealthily down from the wood above.

"Oh, Rupert was a charmer, make no mistake about that," Sally went on. "He could charm the—no, I mustn't say that in polite company, must I? He could charm the chickens out of the trees—and especially the hens.

"He'd start with Shakespeare, and then move on to things he'd heard in music halls. If *Romeo and Juliet* didn't do the job, he'd try his naughty recitations.

"And he got away with it, too—at least, mostly he did. Until he tried it on with Gordon's wife."

Grace Ingleby? I let out an involuntary whistle.

"That must have been quite a long time ago," I said. I knew that it sounded callous, although I didn't mean it that way.

"Years ago," Sally said. "Before Robin died. Before she went all strange. Although you wouldn't think it to look at her now, she used to be quite a stunner."

"She seems very sad," I said.

"Sad? Sad's not the word for it, Flavia. Broken is more like it. That little boy was her whole world, and the day he died, the sun went out."

"You were here then?" I asked gently. "It must have been very difficult for you."

She went on as if she hadn't heard me. "Gordon and Grace had told Robin more than once about their idyllic honeymoon by the sea, and it was something he'd always wanted to do: the sand, the seashells, the pail, the shovel, the sandcastles, the ices, the bathing machines.

"He used to dream about it. 'I dreamed the tide was coming in, Sally!' he told me once, 'and I was bobbing on the sea like a pink balloon!' Poor little tyke."

She wiped away a tear with the rough sleeve of her overall. "God! Why am I telling you all this? I must be daft."

"It's all right," I said. "I promise I won't breathe a word. I'm very good at keeping things to myself."

As a token of goodwill, I went through the motions of cross-my-heart-and-hope-to-die, but without actually saying the words.

After a quick and oddly shy glance at me, Sally went on with her story:

"Somehow they'd managed to put a bit aside for Robin's birthday. Because the harvest was so near, Gordon couldn't get away, but they agreed that Grace would take Robin to the seaside for a few days. It was the first time the two of them, mother and son, had ever been anywhere together without Gordon, and the first time Grace had taken a holiday since she was a girl.

"The weather was hot, even for late August. Grace hired a beach chair and bought a magazine. She watched Robin with his little pail, mudlarking along the water's edge. He was quite safe, she knew. She had warned him about the danger of the tides, and Robin was a most obedient little boy.

"She drifted off to sleep and slept for ages. She hadn't realized how utterly exhausted she was until she awoke and saw how far the sun had moved. The tide had gone out, and Robin was nowhere in sight. Had he disobeyed her warnings and been swept out to sea? Surely someone would have seen him. Surely someone would have wakened her."

"Did Grace tell you this?" I asked.

"Good God, no! It all came out at the inquest. They had to pry it out of her in tiny, broken pieces. Her nerves were something shocking.

"She'd wasted too much time, she said, running up and down the beach, calling out Robin's name. She ran along the edge of the water, hoping for a glimpse of his little red bathing suit; hoping to see his face among the children who were dabbling near the shore.

"Then up and down the beach again, begging the bathers to tell her if they'd seen a little boy with blond hair. It was hopeless, of course. There might have been dozens of children on the beach who answered to that description.

"And then, through sun-dazzled eyes, she saw it: a crowd gathered in the shade beneath the promenade. She burst into tears and began walking towards them, knowing what she would find: Robin had drowned, and the knot of people had gathered round to gawk. She had already begun to hate them.

"But as she drew closer, a wave of laughter went up, and she shoved her way through to the center of the crowd, not caring what they thought.

"It was a Punch and Judy show. And there, seated on the sand, tears of laughter running down his face, was her Robin. She grabbed him up and hugged him, not trusting herself to say a word. After all, it had been her fault: She had fallen asleep, and Robin had been attracted to the Punch and Judy pitch as any child would be.

"She carried him along the beach and bought him an ice, and another. Then she ran back with him to the little booth, to watch the next performance, and she joined in when he roared with laughter, and she shouted out with him 'No! No!' when Punch grabbed the policeman's stick to beat Judy on the head.

"They laughed with the rest of the crowd when Punch tricked Jack Ketch, the hangman, into sticking his own head into the noose, and—"

I had seen the traditional Punch and Judy shows nearly every year at the church fête, and I was all too familiar with the plot.

"'*I don't know how to be hanged,*'" I said, quoting Punch's famous words. "'*You'll have to show me, then I shall do it directly.*'"

"'I don't know how to be hanged,'" Sally echoed, "'You'll have to show me.' That's what Grace told the jury later, when an inquest was called into Robin's death, and those were likely her last sane words.

"Worse than that was the fact that, at the inquest, she spoke those words in that awful, strangled, quacking voice that the puppet show men use for Punch: '*I don't know how to be hanged. You'll have to show me.*'

"It was ghastly. The coroner called for a glass of water, and someone on the jury lost their nerve and laughed. Grace broke down completely. The doctor insisted that she be excused from further questioning.

"The rest of what happened that awful day at the beach, and later at the farm, had to be pieced together; each of us knew a little. I had seen Robin dragging about a length of rope he'd found in the machine shed. Later, Gordon had seen him playing cowboy at the edge of Jubilee Field. It was Dieter who found him hanging in Gibbet Wood."

"Dieter? I thought it was Mad Meg." It slipped out before I could stop myself.

Sally looked instantly away, and I realized that it was one of those times when I needed to keep my mouth shut and wait things out.

Suddenly she seemed to come to a decision. "You must remember," she said, "that we were only just out of the war. If it was known in Bishop's Lacey that Robin's body had been found hanging in the wood by a German prisoner of war, well . . . just think."

"It might have been like that scene from *Frankenstein:* furious villagers with torches, and so forth."

"Exactly," she said. "Besides, the police believed that Meg actually *had* been there before Dieter, but that she hadn't told anyone."

"How do you know that?" I asked. "What the police believed, I mean?"

Without realizing what she was doing, Sally was suddenly fluffing up her hair.

"There was a certain young police constable," she said, "whose name

I am not at liberty to mention, who used to take me, of an evening, to watch the moon rise over Goodger Hill."

"I see," I said, and I did. "They didn't want Meg to be called up at the inquest."

"Funny, isn't it," she said, "how the law can have a soft spot like that? No, someone had seen her in the village at the time Robin went missing, so she wasn't really a suspect. It was decided that because of her . . . because she was . . . well, not to put too fine a point on it, that Meg was best left out of things entirely, and that's how it was done."

"So it *was* Dieter who found the body then."

"Yes. He told me about it that same evening. He was still in shock—hardly making sense: all about how he had come racing down from Gibbet Wood, yelling himself hoarse . . . leaping fences, sliding in the mud . . . running into the yard, looking up at the empty windows. Like dead eyes, they were, he kept saying, like the windows of the Brontës' parsonage. But as I said, poor Dieter was in shock. He didn't know what he was saying."

I felt a vague stirring in my stomach, but I put it down to Mrs. Mullet's Jenny Lind cake. "And where was Rupert all this time?"

"Strange you should ask. Nobody seems to remember. Rupert came and went, often at night. As time passed, he seemed to become more and more addicted to the stuff Gordon was providing him, and his visits became more frequent. If he wasn't here when Robin died, he wasn't far away."

"I'll bet the police were all over the place."

"Of course they were! At the outset, they didn't know if it was an accident, or if Robin had been murdered."

"Murdered?" The thought had never crossed my mind. "Who on earth would murder a little boy?"

"It's been done before," Sally answered sadly. "Children have always been murdered for no good reason."

"And Robin?"

"In the end, they decided there was no evidence to support that idea. Aside from Gordon and Dieter and me—and Mad Meg, of course—no one else had been in Gibbet Wood. Robin's footprints leading up Jubilee Field and round the old scaffold made it quite clear that he had gone there alone."

"And acted out the scaffold scene from Punch and Judy," I said. "Pretending he was first Punch—and then the hangman."

"Yes. That's what they thought."

"Still," I said, "the police must have had a jolly good look round the wood."

"Almost uprooted it," she said. "Measuring tapes, plaster casts, photographs, little bags of this and that."

"Isn't it odd," I said, "that they didn't spot the patch of cannabis? It's hard to believe Inspector Hewitt would have missed it."

"This must have been before his time," Sally said. "If my memory serves me rightly, it was an Inspector Gully who was in charge of the investigation."

Aha! So *that* was who decided to keep mum about Meg. In spite of his lack of vigilance, the man must have had at least a rudimentary heart.

"And what was the outcome?" I asked. "Of the inquest, I mean."

I knew that I could look it up later, in the newspaper archive at the library, but for now I wanted to hear it in Sally's own words. She had, after all, been on the spot.

"The coroner told the jury it must reach one of three verdicts: death by unlawful killing, death by misadventure, or an open verdict."

"And?"

"They settled on 'death by misadventure,' although they had the very dickens of a time reaching an agreement."

Suddenly, I realized that the fog was lifting, and so did Sally. Although a light mist still capped the trees in the wood above us, the river and the full sloping length of Jubilee Field, looking like a hand-tinted aerial photograph, were now laid out below us in weak sunlight.

We would be clearly visible from the farmhouse.

Without another word, Sally clambered up onto the tractor's seat and engaged the starter. The engine caught at once, roared briefly, then settled into a steady ticking hum.

"I've said too much," she told me. "I don't know what I was thinking. Mind you keep your promise, Flavia. I'm going to hold you to it."

Her eyes met mine, and I saw in them a kind of pleading.

"I could get into a lot of trouble, you know," she said.

I bobbed my head but didn't actually say yes. With any luck, I could wedge in one last question.

"What do *you* think happened to Robin and to Rupert?"

With a toss of her head, Sally clenched her jaw, let in the clutch, and lurched away across the field, clods of black mud flying up from the tractor's tires before falling back to the ground like shot birds.

twenty

I RETRIEVED GLADYS FROM BEHIND THE HEDGE WHERE I HAD left her, removed the cucumber sandwiches from her carrier, and sat on a grassy bank to eat and think about the dead.

I pulled the notebook from my pocket and flipped it open to Meg's drawing: There was Robin, hanging by the neck from the gnarled timbers of the old scaffold. The expression on his face was that of a child sleeping peacefully, a slight smile at the corner of his lips.

Something in my mind went *click!* and I knew that I could put it off no longer: I would have to pay a visit to the village library—or at least the Pit Shed, the outbuilding where the back issues of newspapers were stored.

The Pit Shed was a long-defunct motorcar repair shop, which stood, surrounded by weeds, in Cow Lane, a short and rather neglected pathway that ran from Bishop Lacey's high street down to the river. The sudden recollection of my recent captivity in that moldering mausoleum gave me goose bumps.

Part of me (my quieter voice) was saying, *Give it up. Don't meddle. Go home and be with your family.* But another part was more insistent: *The library isn't open until Thursday,* it seemed to whisper. *No one will see you.*

"But the lock," I said aloud. "The place is locked."

Since when did a locked door ever stop you? replied the voice.

———

THE PIT SHED, AS I HAVE SAID, was easily reached from the riverbank. I re-crossed the water on the stepping-stones behind the church (still no sign of police cars) and followed the old towpath, which took me quickly, and with little risk of being seen, to Cow Lane.

There was no one in sight as I tried to walk nonchalantly up the path to the entrance.

I gave the door a shake, but as I had expected, it was locked. A new lock, in fact—one of the Yale design—had recently been fitted, and a hand-lettered sign placed in the window. *Positively no admittance unless accompanied by the Librarian* it said. Both the sign and the lock, I thought, had likely been put in place because of my recent escapades.

Although Dogger had given me several tutorials on the art of lock picking, the intricacies of the Yale required special tools that I did not have with me.

The door's hinges were on the inside, so there wasn't a chance of removing the pins. Even if that had been possible, it would have been foolhardy to attempt such a thing in full view of anyone passing in the high street at the end of the lane.

Round the back I went. In the long grass, directly beneath a window, lay a monster piece of rusty scrap metal, which looked as if it might have seen better days as a motor in a Daimler. I climbed on top of the things and peered in through the dirt-fogged glass.

The newspapers lay stacked in their wooden bunks as they had done for eons, and the interior had been cleared of the wreckage caused by my last visit.

As I stood on tiptoe, my foot slipped, and I nearly pitched headfirst through the windowpane. As I clutched at the sill to steady myself, something crumbled beneath my fingertips and a river of tiny grains trickled to the ground.

Wood rot, I thought. *But wait! Hang on a minute—wood rot isn't gray. This is rotten putty!*

I jumped down and within seconds was back at the window with an open-end wrench from Gladys's tool kit in my hand. As I picked away at the edges of the glass, hard wedges of putty broke off with surprisingly little effort. It was almost too easy.

When I had chipped my way round the pane, I pressed my mouth hard against the glass, and sucked for all I was worth to create a vacuum. Then I pulled my head slowly back.

Success! As the pane came free of its frame and leaned out towards me, I grasped the glass by its rough edges and lifted it carefully to the ground. In less time than it takes to tell, I had wiggled through the frame and dropped to the floor inside.

Although the broken glass from my earlier rescue had been cleared away, the place still gave me the shivers. I wasted no time in finding the issues of *The Hinley Chronicle* for the latter part of 1945.

Although Robin's exact dates hadn't been carved on his headstone, Sally's story indicated that he had died sometime after the harvest in that year. *The Hinley Chronicle* had been—and still was—published weekly, on Fridays. Consequently, there were only a couple of dozen issues covering the time between the end of June and the end of the year. I knew, though, that I would most likely find the story in an earlier issue than a later one. And so it was: Friday, 7 September, 1945.

An inquest will be held today at Almoner's Hall in Bishop's Lacey into the death of Robin Ingleby, five years of age, whose body was found on Monday in Gibbet Wood, near that village. Inspector Josiah Gully of the Hinley constabulary has declined comment at this time, but strongly urges any member of the public who may have information about the child's death to contact police authorities immediately at Hinley 5272.

Directly below this was printed the notice:

Patrons are informed that the post office and confectionery located in the high street, Bishop's Lacey, will close today (Friday, 7th inst.) at noon. Both will be open as usual on Saturday morning. Your patronage is appreciated. Letitia Cool, Proprietress.

Miss Cool was the postmistress and purveyor of sweets to the village, and there was only one reason I could think of that she would have closed her shop on a Friday.

I turned eagerly to the following week: the issue of 14 September.

An inquest convened to inquire into the death of Robin Ingleby, aged five years, of Culverhouse Farm, near Bishop's Lacey was adjourned Friday last at 3:15 p.m. after forty minutes of deliberation. The coroner recorded a verdict of Death by Misadventure, and expressed his sympathy to the bereaved parents.

And that was all. It seemed obvious that the village wanted to spare Robin's parents the grief of seeing the horrid details in print.

A quick look through the remaining papers turned up nothing more than a brief notice of the funeral, at which the pallbearers had been Gordon Ingleby, Bartram Tennyson (Robin's grandfather, who had come down from London), Dieter Schrantz, and Clarence Mundy, the taxicab proprietor. Rupert's name was not mentioned.

I replaced the newspapers in their cradle and, with no more damage to myself than a scuffed knee, shoehorned myself back out of the window.

Curses! It was beginning to rain. A black-bottomed cloud had drifted across the sun, bringing a sudden chill to the air.

I ran across the weeded lot to the river, where fat raindrops were already pocking the water with perfectly formed little craters. I scrambled down the slope and, with my bare hands, scooped out a gob of the sticky clay that formed the bank.

Then back to the Pit Shed again, where I dumped the muck in a mound on the windowsill. Taking care not to get any of it on my clothing, I rolled handfuls of the stuff between my palms, making a family of long stringy gray snakes. Then, clambering up onto the rusty motor once again, I seized the edges of the windowpane, and hoisted it gingerly back into position. With my forefinger as a makeshift putty knife, I pressed the stuff all round the edges of the glass into what looked, at least, like a tight and sturdy seal.

How long it would last was anybody's guess. If the rain didn't wash it away, it might well last forever. Not that it would need to: At the first opportunity, I thought, I would replace it by pinching some bona fide putty and the proper knife from Buckshaw, where Dogger was forever using the stuff to shore up loose panes in the decaying greenhouse.

"*The Mad Putty-Knifer has struck again!*" the villagers would whisper.

After a quick dash to the river to scrub the caked clay from my hands, I was, aside from being soaked through, almost presentable.

I picked up Gladys from the grass and strolled in a carefree manner up Cow Lane to the high street, as if butter wouldn't melt in my mouth.

MISS COOL'S CONFECTIONERY, which incorporated the village post office, was a narrow Georgian relic, hemmed in by a tearoom and an undertaker's establishment to the east and a fish shop to the west. Its flyblown display windows were sparsely strewn with faded chocolate boxes, their lids picturing plump ladies in striped stockings and feathers who grinned brazenly as they sat half astride cumbersome three-wheeled tricycles.

This was where Ned had bought the chocolates he had left on our doorstep. I was sure of it, for there on the right was the dark rectangular mark where the box had reposed since horse-drawn charabancs had rumbled past it in the high street.

For a fleeting instant I wondered if Feely had sampled my handiwork yet, but I banished the thought at once. Such pleasures would have to wait.

The bell over the door tinkled to announce my entrance, and Miss Cool looked up from behind the post office counter.

"Flavia, dear!" she said. "What a pleasant surprise. Why, you're all wet! I was just thinking about you not ten minutes ago, and here you are. Actually, it was your father I was thinking of, but it's all the same, isn't it? I've a strip of stamps here that might interest him: four Georges with an extra perforation clean through his face. Hardly seems right, does it? Quite disrespectful. Miss Reynolds over at Glebe House bought them last Friday and returned them on Saturday.

"'Too many holes in them!' she said. 'I won't have my letters to Hannah—' (that's her niece in Shropshire, dear)—'being seized for infringement of the Postal Act.'"

She handed me a glassine envelope.

"Thank you, Miss Cool," I said. "I'm sure Father will appreciate having these in his collection, and I know he'd want me to thank you for your thoughtfulness."

"You're such a good girl, Flavia," she said, blushing. "He must be very proud of you."

"Yes," I said, "he is. Very."

Actually, it was a thought that had never crossed my mind.

"You really mustn't stand around like that in wet clothing, dear. Go into my little room in the back and take off your things. I'll hang them in the kitchen to dry. You'll find a quilt at the bottom of my bed—wrap yourself up in it and we shall have a nice cozy chat."

Five minutes later, we were back in the shop, me like a blanketed Blackfoot and Miss Cool, with her tiny spectacles looking for all the world like the Factor at a Hudson's Bay trading post.

She was already moving across the shop towards the tall jar of horehound sticks.

"How many would you like today, my dear?"

"None, thank you, Miss Cool. I left home in rather a rush this morning and came away without my purse."

"Take one anyway," she said, holding out the jar. "I think I shall have one, too. Horehound sticks are meant to be shared with friends, don't you think?"

She was dead wrong about that: Horehound sticks were meant to be gobbled down in solitary gluttony, and preferably in a locked room, but I didn't dare say so. I was too busy setting my trap.

For a few minutes we sat in companionable silence, sucking on our sweets. Gray, watery light from the window seeped into the shop, illuminating from within the rows of glass sweet jars, lending them a pallid and unhealthy glow. *We must look*, I thought, *for all the world like a couple of alchemists plotting our next attack upon the elements.*

"Did Robin Ingleby like horehound sticks, Miss Cool?"

"Why, what a strange question! Whatever made you think of that?"

"Oh, I don't know," I said carelessly, running my finger along the edge of a glass display case. "I suppose it was seeing poor Robin's face on that puppet at the church hall. It was such a shock. I haven't been able to get him out of my mind."

This was true enough.

"Oh, you poor thing!" she said. "I'm sure none of us can, but no one wanted to mention it. It was almost . . . what's the word? *Obscene.* And that poor man! What a tragedy. I couldn't sleep a wink after what happened. But then, I expect it gave all of us quite a turn, didn't it?"

"You were on the jury at Robin's inquest, weren't you?"

I was becoming rather good at this. The air went out of her sails in an instant.

"Why . . . why, yes, so I was. But how on earth could you know that?"

"I think Father might have mentioned it at some time or another. He has a great deal of respect for you, Miss Cool. But surely you know that."

"A respect that is entirely mutual, I assure you," she said. "Yes, I was a member of the jury. Why do you ask?"

"Well, to be honest, my sister Ophelia and I were having an argument about it. She said that at one time, it was thought that Robin had been murdered. I disagreed. It was an accident, wasn't it?"

"I'm not sure that I'm allowed to discuss it, dear," she said. "But it was years ago, wasn't it? I think I can tell you—just among friends, mind—that the police did consider that possibility. But there was nothing in it. Not a shred of evidence. The little boy went up to the wood alone and hanged himself alone. It was an accident. We said so in our verdict—Death by Misadventure, they called it."

"But how did you know he was alone? You must be awfully clever to figure that out!"

"Why, because of his footprints, love! Because of his footprints! There were no others anywhere near that old scaffold. He went up to the wood alone."

My gaze shifted to the shop window. The downpour had begun to slacken.

"Had it rained?" I asked with sudden inspiration. "Before they found him?"

"It had, in fact," she answered. "In great bloomin' buckets."

"Ah," I said, noncommittally. "Has a Mr. Mutt Wilmott been in to pick up his mail? It would probably be poste restante."

I knew at once that I had gone too far.

"I'm sorry, dear," Miss Cool said, with a barely detectable sniff. "We are not permitted to give out information like that."

"He's a BBC producer," I said, putting on my best slightly crushed look. "Quite a famous one, actually. He's in charge of—at least he used to be—poor Mr. Porson's television program, *The Magic Kingdom*. I was hoping to get his autograph."

"If he comes in, I'll tell him you were asking," Miss Cool said, softening. "I don't believe I've had the pleasure of meeting the gentleman yet."

"Oh, thank you, Miss Cool," I babbled. "I'm frightfully keen on adding a few BBC personalities to my little collection."

Sometimes I hated myself. But not for long.

"Well, it looks as if the rain has stopped," I said. "I must really be getting along. I expect my clothes are dry enough to get me home, and

I wouldn't want Father to be worried. He has so much on his mind nowadays."

I was well aware that everyone in Bishop's Lacey knew about Father's financial difficulties. Late-paid bills in a village were as good as a signal rocket in the night. I might as well chalk up a few points for deportment.

"Such a thoughtful child, you are, Flavia," she said. "Have another horehound."

Minutes later, I was dressed and at the door. Outside, the sun had come out, and a perfect rainbow arched across the sky.

"Thank you for a lovely chat, Miss Cool, and for the horehound. It will be my treat next time—I insist."

"Ride home safely, dear," she told me. "Mind the puddles. And keep it under your hat—about the stamps, I mean. We're not supposed to let the defectives circulate."

I gave her a ghastly conspiratorial wink and a twiddle of the fingers.

She hadn't answered my question about whether Robin was fond of horehound sticks, but then it didn't really matter, did it?

twenty-one

I GAVE GLADYS A JOLLY GOOD SHAKING, AND RAINDROPS WENT flying off her frame like water from a shaggy dog. I was about to shove off for home when something in the window of the undertaker's shop caught my eye: no more than a slight movement, really.

Although it had been in business at the same location since the time of George the Third, the shop of Sowbell & Sons stood as discreet and aloof in the high street as if it were waiting for an omnibus. It was quite unusual, actually, to see anyone enter or leave the place.

I sauntered a little closer for a look, feigning a great interest in the black-edged obituary cards that were on display in the plate-glass window. Although none of the dead (*Dennison Chatfield, Arthur Bronson-Willowes, Margaret Beatrice Peddle*) were people whose names I recognized, I pored over their names intently, giving each one a rueful shake of my head.

By moving my eyes from left to right, as if I were reading the small print on the cards, and yet shifting my focus through to the shop's dim interior, I could see someone inside waving his hands as he talked. His yellow silk shirt and mauve cravat were what had caught my eye: It was Mutt Wilmott!

Before reason could apply the brakes, I had burst into the shop.

"Oh, hello, Mr. Sowbell," I said. "I hope I'm not interrupting anything. I just wanted to stop by and let you know that our little chemical experiment worked out quite admirably in the end."

I'm afraid this was varnishing the facts a little. The truth was that I had buttonholed him in St. Tancred's churchyard one Sunday after Morning Prayer, to ask his professional opinion—as an expert in preservatives, as it were—about whether a reliable embalming fluid could be inexpensively obtained by collecting, macerating, boiling, and distilling the formic acid from large numbers of red ants (*formica rufa*).

He had fingered his long jaw, scratched his head, and stared up into the branches of the yew trees for quite some time before saying he'd never really thought about it.

"It's something I'd have to look up, Miss Flavia," he said.

But I knew he would never actually do so, and I was right. The older craftsmen can be awfully tight-lipped when it comes to discussing the tricks of the trade.

He was standing now in the shadows near a dark-paneled door that led to some undoubtedly grisly back room: a room I'd give a guinea to see.

"Flavia." He nodded—somewhat warily, I thought.

"I'm afraid you'll have to excuse us," he said. "We're in the midst of rather a—"

"Well, well," Mutt Wilmott interrupted, "I do believe it's Rupert's ubiquitous young protégée, Miss . . ."

"De Luce," I said.

"Yes, of course—de Luce." He smiled condescendingly, as if he'd known it all along; as if he were only teasing.

I have to admit that, like Rupert, the man had an absolutely marvelous professional speaking voice: a rich, mellifluous flow of words that came forth as if he had a wooden organ pipe for a larynx. The BBC must breed these people on a secret farm.

"As one of Rupert's young protégées, so to speak," Mutt went on, "you'll perhaps be comforted to learn that Auntie—as we insiders call the British Broadcasting Corporation—is laying on the sort of funeral that one of her brightest stars deserves. Not quite Westminster Abbey, you understand, but the next best thing. Once Mr. Sowbell here, gets the . . . ah . . . remains back to London, the public grieving can begin: the lying in state, the floral tributes, the ruddy-faced mother of ten from Weston-super-Mare, kneeling at the bier alongside her tear-drenched children, and all with the television cameras looking on. No less a personage than the Director General himself has suggested that it might be a poignant touch to have Snoddy the Squirrel stand vigil at the foot of the coffin, mounted upon an empty glove."

"He's here?" I asked, with a gesture towards the back room. "Rupert's still here?"

"He's in good hands." Mutt Wilmott nodded, and Mr. Sowbell, with a smirk, made a humble little bow of acknowledgment.

I have never wanted anything more in my life than I wanted at that moment to ask if I could have a look at the corpse, but for once, my normally nimble mind failed me. I could not think of a single plausible reason for having a squint at Rupert's remains—as Mutt Wilmott had called them—nor could I think of an implausible one.

"How's Nialla taking it?" I asked, making a wild stab in the dark.

Mutt frowned.

"Nialla? She's taken herself off somewhere," he said. "No one seems to know where."

"Perhaps she took a room at the Thirteen Drakes," I suggested. "She might have needed a hot bath."

I was hoping Mutt would take the bait, and he did.

"She's not at the Thirteen Drakes," he replied. "I've been bivouacked there myself since I first arrived."

So! As I had suspected, Mutt Wilmott *had* been within walking distance of St. Tancred's, before, during, and perhaps after Rupert was murdered.

"Well," I said, "sorry to have bothered you."

They had their heads together before I was out the door.

AS THEY SO OFTEN DO IN SUMMER, the skies had quickly cleared. The dark overcast had moved off to the east and the birds were singing like billy-oh. Although it was still quite early in the day, and in spite of the fresh air and the warm sunshine, I found myself yawning like a cat as I rode along the lanes towards Buckshaw. Perhaps it was because I had been up before dawn; perhaps because I had been up too late the night before.

Whatever the case, I was suddenly quite fagged out. Daffy had once remarked that Samuel Pepys, the diarist, was forever climbing into bed, and Father was always going on about the remarkable restorative power of a brief nap. For once, I understood how they felt.

But how to get into the house unseen? Mrs. Mullet guarded the kitchen like a Foo Dog at the tomb of a Chinese emperor, yet if I used the front door, I ran the risk of being set upon by Aunt Felicity and assigned unwelcome duties for whatever remained of the day.

The coach house was the only place where one could easily come and go without being seen or disturbed.

I parked Gladys behind one of the great chestnut trees that lined the drive, and made my way stealthily round the side of the house.

A door in the far side of the coach house opened into what had once been a small paddock. I scaled the fence, lifted the wrought-iron latch, and slipped noiselessly inside.

Although my eyes were somewhat dazzled from the light outside, I could still make out the dark, looming form of Harriet's vintage Rolls-Royce, a Phantom II, its nickel radiator gleaming dully in the gloom. No more than a diffused and feeble light managed to find its way in through the small, dusty windows, and I knew I would have to watch my step.

Sometimes I came here to brood. I would climb aboard this palace on wheels, and in its comforting interior, I would sit in creamy leather, pretending I was Harriet, just about to engage the gears and drive off to a better life.

I took hold of the door handle and turned it quietly. If Dogger was nearby, I knew he'd be alerted by the slightest sound, and would come running to see who was burgling the coach house. *God bless the good ship Rolls-Royce, and all who sail in her*, I thought as the heavy door swung open in utter silence, and I hauled myself up into the driver's seat.

I inhaled the plush motorcar scent, as Harriet must once have done, and prepared to curl myself up into a ball. With any luck, and the near-darkness, I'd be asleep in less than a minute. There would be time enough later to think about murder.

As I stretched luxuriously, my fingers touched something: the skin of a human leg, by the feel of it. Before I could let out a scream, someone clapped a hand tightly over my mouth.

"Keep still!" a voice hissed into my ear.

My eyes rolled like a horse's in a slaughterhouse. Even in that dim light I could see the face of the person who was stifling me.

It was Nialla.

My first inclination was to bite off one of her fingers: I have a phobia about being physically restrained, and there are times when my reflexes are faster than reason.

"Don't make a sound!" she whispered, giving me a little shake. "I need your help."

Damn! She had given the female password—spoken those magic words that stretched back through the mists of time to a bond made in some primordial swamp. I was in her power. I went instantly limp and nodded my head. She removed her hand.

"Are the police looking for me?" she asked.

"I—I don't think so. I don't know," I said. "I'm not exactly one of their confidantes."

I was still a little miffed at being seized and shaken.

"Oh, come off it, Flavia," she said. "Don't go all shirty on me. I need to know. Are they looking for me?"

"I haven't seen the police since Saturday night, right after Rupert was—after Rupert—"

Although I have no qualms about the word, I couldn't bring myself to say it to Nialla's face.

"Murdered," she said, falling back into her seat. "Nor have I. That Inspector simply wouldn't stop asking me questions. It was horrid."

"Murdered?" I spat out the word as if the thought had never crossed my mind. "What makes you think Rupert was murdered?"

"It's what everyone thinks: the police, and now you. You just said 'right after Rupert was—' That implies something, doesn't it? Murdered . . . killed, what difference does it make? You certainly weren't about to say 'right after Rupert died,' and don't pretend you were. I'm not a fool, Flavia, so please don't keep treating me as if I were."

"Perhaps it was an accident," I said, stalling to get my thoughts organized.

"Would the police have spent half the night grilling the audience, if they thought it was an accident?"

She had a point.

"What's worse," she went on, "is they think I did it."

"I can see why," I said.

"What? Whose side are you on, anyway? I told you I needed help and suddenly you're accusing me of murder!"

"I am not accusing you of murder," I said. "I'm merely stating the obvious."

"Which is?"

She was becoming angrier by the minute.

"Which is," I said, taking a deep breath, "that you've been in hiding, that Rupert had been beating you, that there was Another Woman, and that you're pregnant."

In these waters, I was well in over my head, but still, determined to swim like a dog tossed off the end of a pier. Even so, the effect of my words on Nialla was quite remarkable. I thought for an instant that she was going to slap my face.

"Is it that obvious?" she asked, her lip trembling.

"It is to me," I replied. "I can't speak for anyone else."

"Do you think I did it? Killed Rupert, I mean?"

"I don't know," I said. "I shouldn't have judged you capable of such a thing, but then I'm no Spilsbury."

Although Sir Bernard had been a dab hand at fingering murderers, including those two great poisoners Dr. Crippen and Major Armstrong, he had, oddly enough, taken his own life by gassing himself in his laboratory. Still, I thought, if Spilsbury were alive, he would be the first to point out that Nialla had the means, the motive, and the opportunity.

"Stop prattling on like that," she snapped. "Do *you* think I murdered Rupert?"

"Did you?" I shot back.

"I can't answer that," she said. "You mustn't ask me."

I was no stranger to such female sparring: Eleven years under the same roof as Feely and Daffy had made me quite immune to that sort of ducking and dodging.

"All right," I persisted, "but if you didn't, then who did?"

By now, I had become accustomed to the dusky light of the coach house, and I watched as Nialla's eyes widened like luminous twin moons.

There was a long, and rather unpleasant, silence.

"If it wasn't you," I said at last, "then why are you hiding out here?"

"I'm not hiding out! I needed to get away. I told you that. The police, the Mullets—"

"I understand about the Mullets," I told her. "I'd rather spend a morning in the dentist's chair than listen to an hour of Mrs. Mullet's rattling on."

"You mustn't say things like that," Nialla said. "They were both very sweet, especially Alf. He's a lovely old gentleman—puts me in mind of my grandfather. But I needed to get away somewhere to think, to pull myself together. You don't know what it's like to come flying apart at the seams."

"Yes, I do. More than you might think. I quite often come here myself when I need to be alone."

"I must have sensed that. I thought of Buckshaw at once. No one would ever think to look for me here. The place wasn't actually that hard to find."

"You'd better get back," I said, "before they notice you're gone. The Inspector wasn't at the church when I came past. I expect they had rather a late night. Since he's already questioned you, there's no reason you shouldn't be taking a long walk in the country, is there?"

"No . . ." she said, tentatively.

"Besides," I added, getting back to my usual cheerful self, "no one but me knows you were here."

Nialla reached into the side pocket on the door of the Rolls-Royce and pulled something out. It came free with a rustle of wax paper. As she opened it out into her lap, I couldn't help noticing the razor-sharp creases in the paper.

"No one knows," she said, handing me a cucumber sandwich, ". . . but you—and one other person. Here, eat this. You must be famished."

twenty-two

"GO ON! GO ON!" DOGGER GROWLED, HIS HANDS TREMBLING like the last two leaves of autumn. He did not see me standing there, in the doorway of the greenhouse.

With one blade of his pocketknife opened at a near right angle, he was clumsily trying to hone it on a whetstone. The blade skittered crazily here and there, making ghastly grating noises on the black surface.

Poor Dogger. These episodes came upon him without warning, and almost anything could trigger them: a spoken word, a smell, or a drifting snatch of melody. He was at the mercy of his broken memory.

I backed away slowly until I was behind the garden wall. Then I began whistling softly, only gradually increasing the volume. It would sound as if I were just coming across the lawn towards the kitchen garden. Halfway to the greenhouse, I broke into song: a campfire ditty I had learned just before I was excommunicated from the Girl Guides:

"Once a jolly swagman camped by a billabong,
Under the shade of a coolibah tree,
And he sang as he watched and waited till his billy boiled,
'Who'll come a-waltzing Matilda with me?'"

I strolled square-shouldered into the greenhouse.

"G'day, mate!" I said, with a hearty, Down-Under grin.

"McCorquedale? Is that you?" Dogger called out, his voice as thin and wispy as the wind in the strings of an old harp. "Is Bennett with you? Have you got your tongues back?"

His head was cocked to one side, listening, his wrist held up to shield his eyes, which were turned blindly up to the glare of the greenhouse glass.

I felt as if I had blundered into a sanctuary, and the flesh crawled on the back of my neck.

"It's me, Dogger—Flavia," I managed.

His brows knitted themselves into a look of puzzlement. "Flavia?"

My name issued from his throat like a whisper from an abandoned well.

I could see that he was already fighting his way back from whatever had seized him, the light in his eyes coming back only warily from the depths to the surface, like golden fish in an ornamental pool.

"Miss Flavia?"

"I'm sorry," I said, taking the knife from his shaking hands. "Have I broken it? I borrowed it yesterday to cut a bit of twine, and I might have jammed the blade. If I did, I'll buy you a new one."

This was sheer fantasy—I hadn't touched the thing—but I have learned that under certain circumstances, a fib is not only permissible, but can even be an act of perfect grace. I took the knife from his hands, opened it fully, and began rubbing it in smooth circles on the surface of the stone.

"No, it's fine," I said. "Phew! I'd have been in big trouble if I'd jiggered your best knife, wouldn't I?"

I snapped the blade shut and handed it back. Dogger took it from me, his fingers now much more sure of themselves.

I turned over an empty pail and sat on it as we shared a silence.

"It was good of you to think of feeding Nialla," I said, after a while.

"She needs a friend," he said. "She's—"

"Pregnant," I blurted.

"Yes."

"But how did you know that? Surely she didn't tell you?"

"Excessive salivation," Dogger said, ". . . and telangiectasia."

"Tel- what?"

"Telangiectasia," he said in a mechanical voice, as if he were reading from an invisible book. ". . . Spider veins in proximity to the mouth, nose, and chin. Uncommon, but not unknown in early pregnancy."

"You amaze me, Dogger," I said. "How on earth do you know these things?"

"They float in my head," he replied quietly, "like corks upon the sea. I've read books, I think. I've had a lot of time on my hands."

"Ah!" I said. It was the most I'd heard him say in ages.

But Dogger's former captivity was not a topic for open discussion, and I knew that it was time to change the subject.

"Do you think she did it?" I asked. "Killed Rupert, I mean?"

Dogger knitted his eyebrows, as if thinking came to him only with the greatest effort.

"The police will think that," he said, nodding slowly. "Yes, that's what the police will think. They'll soon be along."

As it turned out, he was right.

"IT IS A WELL-KNOWN FACT," Aunt Felicity trumpeted, "that the Black Death was brought into England by lawyers. Shakespeare said we ought to have hanged the lot of them, and in light of modern sanitary reform, we now know that he was right. This will never do, Haviland!"

She stuffed a handful of papers into a dusty hatbox and clapped the lid on. "It's a perfect disgrace," she added, "the way you've let things slide. Unless something turns up, you'll soon have no option but to sell up Buckshaw and take a cold-water flat in Battersea."

"Hello, all," I said, strolling into the library, pretending for the second time in less than half an hour that I was oblivious to what was going on.

"Ah, Flavia," Father said. "I think Mrs. Mullet requires an extra pair of hands in the kitchen."

"Of course," I said. "And shall I then be allowed to go to the ball?"

Father looked puzzled. My witty repartee was completely lost on him.

"Flavia!" Aunt Felicity said. "That's no way for a child to speak to a parent. I should have thought that you'd outgrown that saucy attitude by now. I don't know why you let these girls get away with it, Haviland."

Father moved towards the window and stared out across the ornamental lake towards the folly. He was taking refuge, as he often does, in letting his eyes, at least, escape an unpleasant situation.

Suddenly he whirled round to face her.

"Damn it all, Lissy," he said, in a voice so strong I think it surprised even him. "It isn't always easy for them. No . . . it isn't always easy for them."

I think my mouth fell open as his closed.

Dear old Father! I could have hugged him, and if either of us had been other than who we were, I think I might have.

Aunt Felicity went back to rummaging among the papers.

"Statutory legacies . . . personal chattels," she said with a sniff. "Where will it all end?"

"FLAVIA," FEELY SAID, as I passed the open door of the drawing room, "a moment?"

She sounded suspiciously civil. She was up to something.

As I stepped inside, Daffy, who had been standing near the door, closed it softly behind me.

"We've been waiting for you," Feely said. "Please sit down."

"I'd rather not," I said. They had both remained standing, putting me at a disadvantage when it came to sudden flight.

"As you wish," Feely said, sitting down behind a small table and putting on her eyeglasses. Daffy stood with her back pressed against the door.

"I'm afraid we have some rather bad news for you," Feely said, toying with her spectacles like a judge at the Old Bailey.

I said nothing.

"While you've been gadding about the countryside, we've held a meeting, and we've all of us decided that you must go."

"In short, we've voted you out of the family," Daffy said. "It was unanimous."

"Unanimous?" I said. "This is just another of your stupid—"

"Dogger, of course, pleaded for leniency, but he was overruled by Aunt Felicity, who has more weight in these matters. He wanted you to be allowed to stay until the end of the week, but I'm afraid we can't permit it. It's been decided that you're to be gone by sundown."

"But—"

"Father has given instructions to Mr. Pringle, his solicitor, to draw up a Covenant of Reversion, which means, of course, that you will be returned to the Home for Unwed Mothers, who will have no option but to take you back."

"Because of the Covenant, you see," Daffy said. "It's in their Constitution. They can't say no. They can't refuse."

I clenched my fists as I felt the tears beginning to well up in my eyes. It was no good waiting upon reason.

I shoved Daffy roughly away from the door.

"Have you eaten those chocolates yet?" I demanded of Feely.

She was somewhat taken aback by the harshness in my voice.

"Well, no . . . ," she said.

"Better not," I spat. "They might be *poisoned*."

As soon as the words were out of my mouth, I knew I'd done the wrong thing.

Blast it! I'd given myself away. All that work in my laboratory wasted!

Flavia, I thought, *sometimes you're no brighter than a lightning-struck lizard.*

Angry with myself for being angry, I stalked out of the room on general principles, and nobody tried to stop me.

I TOOK A DEEP BREATH, relaxed my shoulders, and opened the kitchen door.

"Flavia," Mrs. Mullet called, "be a dear and fetch me a glass of sherry from the pantry. I've gone all-over strange. Not too much, mind, or else I shall be tipsy."

She was stretched full length in a chair by the window, her heels on the tiles, fanning herself with a small frying pan.

I did as I was bidden, and she gulped down the drink in a flash.

"What is it, Mrs. M?" I asked. "What's happened?"

"The police, dearie. They gave me such a turn, comin' for that young woman like they did."

"What young woman? You mean Nialla?"

She nodded glumly, waggling her empty glass. I refilled it.

"Such a dear, she is. Never done nobody no harm. She rapped at the kitchen door to thank me, and Alf, of course, for puttin' her up the night. Said she was movin' on—didn't want us to think she was ungrateful, like. No more the words were out of her mouth than that there Inspector whatsis—"

"Hewitt," I said.

"Hewitt. That's 'im—that's the one . . . 'E shows up in the doorway right behind 'er. Spotted 'er comin' across from the coach house, 'e did."

"And then?"

"'E asked if 'e might have a word outside. Next thing I knows, poor girl's off in the car with 'im. I 'ad to run round the front to get a good look. Proper fagged me out, so it did."

I refilled her glass.

"I shouldn't ought to, dearie," she said, "but my poor old heart's not up to such a muddlederumpus."

"You're looking better already, Mrs. M," I told her. "Is there anything I can do to help?"

"I was just about to put them things in the oven," she said, pointing to an array of dough-filled pans on the table, and heaving herself to her feet. "Open the oven door for me—that's a good girl."

Much of my life was given over to holding the oven door of the Aga as Mrs. M fed heaps of baking into its open maw. Hell, in Milton's *Paradise Lost*, had nothing to compare with my drudgery.

"Clean out of pastries, we were," she said. "When it comes to dainties, that young man of Miss Ophelia's seems to have a bottomless stomach."

Miss Ophelia's young man? Had it come to that already? Had my rambles round the village caused me to miss some sensational scene of courtship?

"Dieter?" I asked.

"Even if 'e *is* a German," she said with a nod, "'e's ever so much more refined than that rooster as keeps leavin' 'is rubbishy gifts on the kitchen doorstep."

Poor Ned! I thought. Even Mrs. Mullet was against him.

"I just 'appened to overhear a bit of what 'e said while I was dustin' the hall—about 'Eathcliff, an' all that. I mind the time me and my friend, Mrs. Waller, took the bus over to Hinley to see 'im in the cinema. *Wuthering Heights*, it was called, and a good name for it, too! That there 'Eathcliff, why, 'e kept 'is wife 'id up in the attic as if she was an old dresser! No wonder she went barmy. I know I should 'ave! Now then, what you laughin' at, miss?"

"At the idea," I said, "of Dieter mucking across Jubilee Field through rain and lightning to carry off the Fair Ophelia."

"Well, 'e might do," she said, "but not without a right fuss from Sally Straw—and, some say, the old missus herself."

"The old missus? Grace Ingleby? Surely you don't mean Grace Ingleby?"

Mrs. Mullet had suddenly gone as red as a pot of boiling beets.

"I've said too much," she said, flustered. "It's the sherry, you see. Alf always says as 'ow sherry coshes the guard what's supposed to be keepin' watch on my tongue. Now then, not another word. Off you go, dearie. And mind you—I've said nothing."

Well! I thought. *Well, well, well, well, well!*

twenty-three

THERE'S SOMETHING ABOUT POTTERING WITH POISONS THAT clarifies the mind. When the slightest slip of the hand could prove fatal, one's attention is forced to focus like a burning-glass upon the experiment, and it is then that the answers to half-formed questions so often come swarming to mind as readily as bees coming home to the hive.

With a good dollop of sulfuric acid already decanted into a freshly washed flask and warmed slightly, I gingerly added a glob of crystalline jelly, and watched in awe as it slowly dissolved, quivering and squirming in the acid bath like a translucent squidling.

I had extracted the stuff, with water and alcohol, from the roots of a Carolina jessamine plant (*Gelsemium sempervirens*) that, to my delight, I had discovered blooming blissfully away in the corner of the greenhouse, its flowers like little trumpets sculpted from fresh butter.

The plant was native to the Americas, Dogger had told me, but had been brought home to English greenhouses by travelers; this particular specimen by my mother, Harriet.

I had asked if I could have it for my laboratory, and Dogger had readily agreed.

The root contained a lovely alkaloid called gelsemine, which had lurked undetected inside the plant since the Creation, until it was teased out in 1870 by a man from Philadelphia with the charming name of Wormley, who administered the bitter poison to a rabbit, which turned a complete backwards somersault and perished in twenty minutes.

Gelsemine was a killer whose company I much enjoyed.

And now came the magic!

Into the liquid I introduced, on the tip of a knife, a small dose of $K_2Cr_2O_7$, or potassium dichromate, whose red salts, illuminated by a fortuitous beam of sunlight from the casement window, turned it the livid cherry red hue of a carbon monoxide victim's blood.

But this was only the beginning! There was more to come.

Already the cherry brilliance was fading, and the solution was taking on the impressive violet color of an old bruise. I held my breath, and—yes!—here it was, the final phase of yellow-green.

Gelsemine was one of chemistry's chameleons, shifting color with delicious abandon, and all without a trace of its former hue.

People were like that, too.

Nialla, for instance.

On the one hand, she was captive to a traveling puppeteer; a young woman who, other than the baby she was now carrying, had no family to speak of; a young woman who allowed herself to be beaten by a semi-invalid lover; a young woman now left with no money and no visible means of support. And yet, in rather a complicated way that I did not entirely understand, she did not have my complete sympathy.

Was it because she had run away from the scene of the crime, so to speak, and hidden in the coach house at Buckshaw? I could see her wanting to be alone, but she had hardly chosen the best time to do so.

Where was she now? I wondered. Had Inspector Hewitt arrested her and dragged her to a cell in Hinley?

I wrote *Nialla* on a scrap of paper.

And then there was Mutt Wilmott: a larger-than-life character, who seemed to have stepped right out of an Orson Welles film. Not to put too fine a point on it: Mutt had arrived, Rupert had died; Mutt had vanished after quarreling with Rupert, and was next seen arranging to have the body in question shipped up to London for a state funeral.

Was Mutt an assassin, hired by the BBC? Had Rupert's set-to with the mysterious Tony pushed "Auntie"—and her Director General—too far? Was Rupert's messy end on the stage of a rustic puppet theater really no more than the conclusion of a bitter contractual dispute?

What about Grace Ingleby? To be honest, the dark little woman gave me the creeps. Her shrine to a dead child in an abandoned birdhouse was enough to spook anyone—and now Mrs. Mullet was hinting that the farmer's wife was more than just a landlady to Dieter.

And Dieter! For all his Nordic godliness and passion for English literature, it seemed that he had conspired with his captors to grow and supply cannabis to what Sally Straw had called "a regular little army of others." Who were they? I wondered.

Rupert, of course, had been chief among them, and had visited the Ingleby farm with the regularity of a tramcar for many years. He had been a ladies' man—there was no doubt about it (Sally again). Of whom had he run afoul? Who wanted him dead badly enough to actually do him in?

As for Sally, both Rupert and Dieter had been keen on her. Had Rupert been shoved off into eternity by a rival in love?

Sally seemed central: She had been at the Ingleby farm for years. It was clear that she had a crush on Dieter, although whether her passions were wholly returned was another matter entirely.

And then there was Gordon Ingleby. Gordon the linen-draped saint who did for those in pain what no doctor was willing to do; Gordon the market gardener; Gordon the father of the dead child in the woods.

To say nothing of Mad Meg, who had been in Gibbet Wood when Robin died, or at least, not long afterwards.

And Cynthia—dear Cynthia Richardson, the vicar's wife, whose only passion was her hatred of sin. The sudden appearance of a pair of promiscuous puppeteers who proposed to put on a show in her husband's parish hall must have seared her soul like the lake of fire in the Book of Revelation.

In spite of all that, Cynthia's soul was no hotbed of Christian charity. What was it Meg had said when I asked about her nap at the vicarage? That Cynthia had taken away her bracelet and then turned her out because she was dirty. No doubt she was referring to Nialla's butterfly compact, but if that were the case, why had I found it tangled in the afghan in the study? Had Cynthia taken the compact from Meg and then, caught in the act by one of the dozens of villagers milling about the vicarage, hidden it away to be retrieved for her own later use?

It seemed unlikely: If there was one sin of which Cynthia Richardson was not guilty, that sin was vanity. Just one look at her was enough to know that makeup had never soiled that pale ferret face; jewelry had never dangled from that scrawny neck or brightened up those match-stick wrists. To put it politely, the woman was as plain as a pudding.

I sharpened my pencil and added six names to my list: *Mutt Wilmott, Grace Ingleby, Dieter Schrantz, Sally Straw, Mad Meg (Daffy had once told me that Meg's surname was Grosvenor, but I didn't believe her) . . .* and *Cynthia Richardson.*

I drew a line, and below it, printed in capital letters: AFFAIRS——— LOOK UP!!!

Although I had a sketchy idea of what went on between two people having an affair, I did not actually know the precise mechanical details. Once, when Father had gone away for several days to a stamp exhibition in Glasgow, Daffy had insisted upon reading *Madame Bovary* aloud to us at every meal, morning, noon, and night, including tea, and finished on the third day just as Father was walking in the door.

At the time, I had nearly died of boredom, although it has since become one of my favorite books, containing, as it does in its final chapters, what must be the finest and most exciting description of death by arsenic in all of literature. I had particularly relished the way in which the poisoned Emma had "raised herself like a galvanized corpse." But now I realized that I had been so gripped by the excitement of poor Madame Bovary's suicide that I had failed to take in the fine points of her several affairs. All I could remember was that, alone with Rodolphe by the lily pond, surrounded by duckweeds and jumping frogs, Emma Bovary—in tears, hiding her face, and with a long shudder—"gave herself up to him."

Whatever that meant. I would ask Dogger.

"DOGGER," I SAID, when I found him at last, hacking away at the weeds in the kitchen garden with a long-handled hoe, "have you read *Madame Bovary?*"

Dogger paused in his work and extracted a handkerchief from the bib pocket of his overalls. He gave his face a thorough mopping before he replied.

"A French novel, is it not?" he asked.

"Flaubert."

"Ah," Dogger said, and shoved the handkerchief back into his pocket. "The one in which a most unhappy person poisons herself with arsenic."

"Arsenic from a blue jar!" I blurted, hopping from one foot to the other with excitement.

"Yes," Dogger said, "from a blue jar. Blue, not because of any danger of decomposition or oxidation of the contents, but rather—"

"To keep it from being confused with a bottle containing a harmless substance."

"Exactly," Dogger said.

"Emma Bovary swallows the stuff due to several unhappy affairs," I said.

Dogger studiously scraped a clod of mud from the sole of his shoe with the hoe.

"She had an affair with a man named Rodolphe," I added, "and then with another, named Léon. Not at the same time, of course."

"Of course," Dogger said, and then fell silent.

"What does an affair entail, precisely?" I asked, hoping my choice of words would imply, even slightly, that I already knew the answer.

I thought for a moment that I could outwait him, even though my heart knew that trying to outwait Dogger was a mug's game.

"What did Flaubert mean," I asked at last, "when he said that Madame Bovary gave herself up to Rodolphe?"

"He meant," Dogger said, "that they became the greatest of friends. The very greatest of friends."

"Ah!" I said. "Just as I thought."

"Dogger! Come up here at once before I do myself some grave internal injury!" Aunt Felicity's voice came trumpeting down from an upstairs window.

"Coming, Miss Felicity," he called out, and then in an aside to me he said, "Miss Felicity requires assistance with her luggage."

"Her luggage?" I asked. "She's leaving?"

Dogger nodded noncommittally.

"Cheese!" I exclaimed. It was a secret prayer, whose meaning was known only to God and to me.

AUNT FELICITY WAS ALREADY HALFWAY down the west staircase in a canvas outfit that suggested Africa, rather than the wilds of Hampstead. Clarence Mundy's taxicab was at the door, and Dogger was helping Bert hoist Aunt Felicity's cargo aboard.

"We're going to miss you, Aunt Fee," Feely said.

Aunt Fee? It seemed that in my absence Feely had been ingratiating herself with Father's sister, most likely, I thought, in the hope of inheriting the de Luce family jewels: that ghastly collection of gewgaws that my grandfather de Luce (on Father's and Aunt Felicity's side) had foisted upon my grandmother who, as she received each piece, had dropped it, with thumb and forefinger, into a pasteboard box as casually as if it were a grass snake, and never looked at it again.

Feely had wasted the entire afternoon slavering over this rubbish the last time we had gone up to Hampstead for one of Aunt Felicity's compulsory teas.

"So romantic!" she had breathed, when Aunt Felicity had, rather grudgingly, I thought, lent her a pink glass pendant that would not have been out of place on a cow's udder. "I shall wear it to Rosalind Norton's coming-out, and all eyes will be on yours truly. Poor Rosalind, she's such an awful sweat!"

"I'm sorry it's turned out this way, Haviland," Aunt Felicity bellowed from the landing, "but you've well and truly botched it. All the king's horses and all the king's men couldn't put your accounts together again. I should, of course, be more than happy to rescue you from your excesses if I weren't so heavily invested in consols. There's nothing for it now but to sell those ridiculous postage stamps."

Father had drifted so silently into the hall that I had not noticed him until now. He stood, one hand holding Daffy's arm, his eyes downcast, as if he were intently studying the black and white tiles beneath his feet.

"Thank you for coming, Felicity," he said quietly, without looking up. "It was most kind of you."

I wanted to swat the woman's face!

I had actually taken half a step forward before a firm hand fell on my shoulder, stopping me in my tracks. It was Dogger.

"Will there be anything else, Miss Felicity?" he asked.

"No, thank you, Dogger," she said, rummaging in her reticule with two fingers. From its depths, like a stork pulling a fish from a pond, she extracted what looked like a shilling and handed it to him with a sigh.

"Thank you, miss," he said, pocketing the insult with ease—and without looking at it—as if it were something he did every day.

And with that Aunt Felicity was gone. A moment later, Father had stepped into the shadows of the great hall, followed closely by Daffy and Feely, and Dogger had vanished without a word into his little corridor behind the stairs.

It was like one of those electric moments just before the final curtain in a West End play: that moment when all the supporting characters have faded into the wings, leaving the heroine alone at center stage to deliver her magnificent closing line to a silent house that awaited her words with bated breath.

"Bloody hell!" I said, and stepped outdoors for a breath of fresh air.

THE PROBLEM WITH WE DE LUCES, I decided, *is that we are infested with history in much the same way that other people are infested with lice.* There have been de Luces at Buckshaw since King Harold stopped an arrow with his eye at the Battle of Hastings, and most of them have been unhappy in one complicated way or another. We seem to be born with wisps of both glory and gloom in our veins, and we can never be certain at any given moment which of the two is driving us.

On the one hand, I knew, I would never be like Aunt Felicity, but on the other, would I ever become like Harriet? Eight years after her death, Harriet was still as much a part of me as my toenails, although that's probably not the best way of putting it.

I read the books that she had owned, rode her bicycle, sat in her Rolls-Royce; Father had once, in a distracted moment, called me by her name. Even Aunt Felicity had put aside her gorgon manner long enough to tell me how much like Harriet I was.

But had she meant it as a compliment? Or a warning?

Most of the time I felt like an imposter; a changeling; a sackcloth-and-ashes stand-in for that golden girl who had been snatched up by Fate and dashed down a mountainside in an impossibly distant land. Everyone, it seemed, would be so much happier if Harriet were brought back to life and I were done away with.

These thoughts, and others, tumbled in my mind like autumn leaves in a millstream as I walked along the dusty lane towards the village. Without even noticing them, I had passed the carved griffins of the Mulford Gates, which marked the entrance to Buckshaw, and I was now within sight of Bishop's Lacey.

As I slouched along, a bit dejectedly (all right, I admit it—I was furious at Aunt Felicity for making such a chump of Dogger!) I shoved my hand into my pocket and my fingers came in contact with a round, metallic object: something that hadn't been there before—a coin.

"Hullo!" I said. "What's this?"

I pulled it out and looked at it. As soon as I saw the thing, I knew what it was and how it had made its way into my pocket. I turned it over and had a jolly good squint at the reverse.

Yes, there could be no doubt about it—no doubt whatsoever.

twenty-four

AS I LOOKED AT IT FROM ACROSS THE HIGH STREET, THE St. Nicholas Tea Room was like a picture postcard of Ye Olde England. Its upstairs rooms, with their tiny-paned bow windows, had been the residence of the present Mr. Sowbell's grandparents, in the days when they had lived above their coffin and furniture manufactory.

The Sowbell tables, sideboards, and commodes, once known far and wide for the ferocity of their black shine and the gleam of their ornate silver knobs and drawer pulls, had now fallen out of favor, and were often to be found at estate sales, standing sullen and alone in the driveway until being knocked down at the end of the day for little more than a pound or two.

"By unscrupulous sharpers who use the wood to turn Woolworth's dressers into antiques," Daffy had once told me.

The undertaker's shop, I noticed, now had a cardboard clock stuck in its window, suspended from an inverted V of black cord. The minute hand pointed to twelve, and the hour hand was missing. Mr. Sowbell had obviously gone to the Thirteen Drakes for his afternoon pint.

I crossed the street and, opening the tearoom door, stepped inside. To my right was a steep wooden staircase, with a painted blue hand pointing upwards: *Tea Room Upstairs*. Beside the stairs, a dim, narrow passageway vanished into the gloom at the rear of the building. On the wall, another helpful painted hand—this one in red, and marked *Gentlemen's and Ladies' Water Closets*—pointed the way discreetly.

I knew that the tea shop and the undertaker's shared the W.C. Feely had insisted on dragging us here for tea one autumn afternoon, and I had been gobsmacked at the sight of three women in black dresses and black veils, chattering happily away at the door to the toilet like a congress of toothy crows, before resuming their grim demeanors and slipping back into Mr. Sowbell's premises. The door through which they had vanished opened directly into the undertaker's rooms.

I was right! A discreet *Sowbell & Sons*, lettered in gold upon the dark varnish, must have been meant to remind mourners not to go blundering off into the tea shop's corridor after they had "soaped their 'ands," as Mrs. Mullet put it.

The black paneled door swung open on silent hinges.

I found myself in a dark Victorian parlor, with flocked wallpaper of black and yellow-cream. On three sides of the room were spindly wooden chairs and a small round table with a spray of artificial baby's breath. The place smelled of dust, with an underlying chemical base.

The wall at the far end of the room was bare, save for a dark framed print of Millet's *Angelus*, in which a man and a woman, obviously Flemish peasants, stand alone in a field at sunset. The woman's huge hands, which are those of a laborer, are clasped at her breast in prayer. The man has removed his hat, which he holds clutched uncomfortably in front of him. He has set aside his fork and stuck it half into the loose earth. As crows congregate above them like vultures, the couple stands with downcast eyes. Between them, half-empty on the ground, lies a wicker basket.

Max Wight had once told me that when the original of Millet's painting was exhibited in America, the sale of prints had been sluggish at best until someone thought of changing the name from *Angelus* to *Burying the Baby*.

It was beneath this print, I guessed, that the coffins were customarily parked. Since the spot was empty, it was obvious that Rupert's body, if it were still on the premises, must be in another room.

To my right was an L-shaped partition. There had to be another door behind it.

I peered round behind the half-wall and found myself looking into a room that was nearly the twin of the first. The only difference that I could see was that the flocked wallpaper was black and pink-cream, and the print on the far wall was Holman Hunt's *Light of the World*, in which

Jesus stands at the door like Diogenes seeking an honest man, with a tin lantern in His hand.

Beneath its dark frame, on trestles, was a coffin.

I crept towards it on tiptoe, my ears tuned for the slightest sound.

I ran my fingers along the highly polished woodwork, the way one might caress a piano lid before lifting it to reveal the keys. I put my thumbs under the join and felt it lift slightly.

I was in luck! The lid was not screwed down. I lifted it and looked inside.

There, like a doll in a box, lay Rupert. In life, his personality had made him seem so much larger, I had forgotten how small he really was.

Was I frightened out of my wits? I'm afraid not. Since the day I had found a body in the kitchen garden at Buckshaw, I had developed a fascination with death, with a particular emphasis on the chemistry of putrefaction.

In fact, I had already begun making notes for a definitive work which I would call *De Luce on Decomposition*, in which I would outline, step by step, the process of human cadaveric decay.

How exciting it was to reflect upon the fact that, within minutes of death, the organs of the body, lacking oxygen, begin to digest themselves! Ammonia levels start to rise and, with the assistance of bacterial action, methane (better known as marsh gas) is produced, along with hydrogen sulfide, carbon dioxide, and mercaptan, a captivating sulfur-alcohol in whose structure sulfur takes the place of oxygen—which accounts for its putrid smell.

How curious it was, I thought, that we humans had taken millions of years to crawl up out of the swamps and yet, within minutes of death, we were already tobogganing back down the slope.

My keen sense of smell told me that Mr. Sowbell had used a formalin-based embalming fluid on Rupert (a two-percent solution of formaldehyde seemed most likely, with a slight bouquet of something else: chloroform, by the smell of it) and by the slight green tint at the end of Rupert's nose, I could tell that the undertaker had skimped on the ingredients. One could only hope that the lying-in-state at the BBC would be a closed-coffin affair.

Better hurry up, though, I thought. Mr. Sowbell might walk in at any moment.

Rupert's pale hands were folded across his abdomen, with the right hand uppermost. I took hold of his fingers (it was like lifting linked sausages from the icebox) and pulled upwards.

To my amazement, his left hand came with it, and I saw at once that they had been cunningly sewn together. By twisting the cold hands and bending down for a better look beneath them, I saw what I was looking for: a blackened channel that ran from the base of his left thumb to the tips of his first and second fingers.

In spite of Mr. Sowbell's embalming efforts, Rupert was still giving off rather a scorched smell. And there could be no doubt about it: The burn on the palm of his left hand was the precise width of the lever that operated Galligantus.

A floorboard creaked.

As I closed the coffin lid, the door opened and Mr. Sowbell walked into the room. I hadn't heard him coming.

Because I was still in a half-crouch from inspecting Rupert's burned fingers, I was able to come slowly to a standing position.

"Amen," I said, crossing myself extravagantly.

"What on earth—?" said Mr. Sowbell.

"Oh, hello, Mr. Sowbell," I said in an appropriately hushed tone. "I just dropped in to pay my respects. There was no one here, but I thought a quiet prayer would be in order.

"Mr. Porson had no friends in Bishop's Lacey, you know," I added, pulling a handkerchief from my pocket and wiping away an imaginary tear. "It seemed such a shame, and I thought it would do no harm if I—I'm sorry if—"

"There, there," he said. "Death comes to us all, you know, old and young alike. . . ."

Was he threatening me, or was my imagination overheated?

"And even though we expect it," he went on, "it always comes as a shock in the end."

It certainly had for Rupert—but was the man being facetious?

Evidently not, for his long face maintained its professional polish.

"And now if you will excuse me," he said. "I must prepare him for his final journey."

Final journey? Where did they get this claptrap? Was there a phrasebook published for the undertaking trade?

I gave him my ten-years-old-going-on-eleven smile, and faked a flustered exit.

THE BELL ABOVE THE DOOR OF the St. Nicholas Tea Room jangled merrily as I stepped inside. The establishment, a bit of a climb at the top of the stairs, was owned by none other than Miss Lavinia and Miss Aurelia, the Puddock sisters: those same two relics who had provided the musical prelude to Rupert's spectacular demise.

Miss Lavinia, in a nook at the far side of the room, seemed to be locked in mortal combat with a large silver samovar. In spite of the simplicity of its task, which was the boiling of water, this Heath Robinson contraption was a bulbous squid of tubes, valves, and gauges, which spat hot water as it gurgled and hissed away like a cornered dragon.

"No tea, I'm afraid," she said over her shoulder. She could not yet see who had entered the shop.

"Anything I can do to help, Miss Puddock?" I offered cheerily.

She let out a little shriek as her hand strayed accidentally into a jet of hot steam, and the china cup she was holding crashed to the floor, where it flew into a hundred pale pieces.

"Oh, it's the little de Luce girl," she said, spinning round. "My goodness! You gave me quite a fright. I wasn't expecting to hear your voice."

Because I could see that she'd scalded her hand, I fought back my baser urges.

"Anything I can do to help?" I repeated.

"Oh, dear," she said, flustered beyond reason. "Peter always chooses to act up when Aurelia's not here. She's so much better with him than I am."

"Peter?" I asked.

"The samovar," she said, wiping her wet red hands on a tea towel. "Peter the Great."

"Here," I said, "let me—"

Without another word I took up a bowl of lemon wedges from one of the round tables and squeezed each of them into a jug of iced water. Then I grabbed a clean white table napkin, immersed it until it was soaked, wrung it out, and wrapped it around Miss Puddock's hand. She flinched as I touched her, and then relaxed.

"May I?" I asked, removing an opal brooch from her lapel and using it to pin the ends of the makeshift bandage.

"Oh! It feels better already," she said with a pained smile. "Wherever did you learn that trick?"

"Girl Guides," I lied.

Experience has taught me that an expected answer is often better than the truth. I had, in fact, quite painfully looked up the remedy in one of Mrs. Mullet's household reference books after a superheated test tube seared most of the flesh from a couple of my fingers.

"Miss Cool has always spoken so highly of you," she said. "I shall tell her she was 'bang-on,' as those nice bomber boys from the RAF used to say."

I gave her my most modest smile. "It's nothing, Miss Puddock—just jolly good luck I got here when I did. I was next door, at Mr. Sowbell's, you see, saying a prayer or two at Mr. Porson's coffin. You don't suppose it will do any harm, do you?"

I realized that I was gilding the lily with a string mop for a paintbrush, but business was business.

"Why no, dear," she said. "I think Mr. Porson would be touched."

She didn't know the half of it!

"It was so sad." I lowered my voice to a conspiratorial whisper and touched her good arm. "But I must tell you, Miss Puddock, that in spite of the tragedy on Saturday evening, my family and I enjoyed 'Napoleon's Last Charge' and 'Bendemeer's Stream.' Father said that you don't often hear music like that nowadays."

"Why, thank you, dear," she murmured damply. "It's kind of you to say so. Of course, mercifully, we didn't actually see what happened to poor Mr. Porson, being busy in the kitchen, as it were. As proprietresses of Bishop Lacey's sole tearoom, certain expectations attach, I'm afraid. Not that we resent—"

"No, of course not," I said. "But surely you must have tons of people offering to help out."

She gave a little bark. "Help? Most people don't know the meaning of the word. No, Aurelia and I were left alone in the kitchen from start to finish. Two hundred and sixty-three cups of tea we poured, but of course that's counting the ones we served after the police took charge."

"And no one offered to help?" I asked, giving her an incredulous look.

"No one. As I said, Aurelia and I were alone in the kitchen the whole while. And I was left completely on my own when Aurelia took a cup of tea to the puppeteer."

My ears went up like a flag on a pole. "She took Rupert a cup of tea?"

"Well, she tried to, dear, but the door was locked."

"The door to the stage? Across from the kitchen?"

"No, no . . . she didn't want to use that one. She'd have had to brush right past that Mother Goose, that woman who was in the spotlight, telling the story. No, Aurelia took the tea all the way round the back of the hall and down to the other door."

"The one in the opposite passage?"

"Well, yes. It's the only other one, isn't it, dear? But as I've already told you, it was locked."

"During the puppet show?"

"Why, yes. Odd, isn't it? Mr. Porson had asked us before he began if we could bring him a nice cup of tea during the show. 'Just leave it on the little table behind the stage,' he said. 'I'll find it. Puppetry's dry work, you know,' and he gave us a little wink. So why on earth would he lock the door?"

As she went on, I could already feel the facts beginning to marshal themselves in my mind.

"Those were Aurelia's exact words when she'd come all the way back with his cup of tea still in her hand. 'Whatever would possess him to lock the door?'"

"Perhaps he didn't," I said, with sudden inspiration. "Perhaps someone else did. Who has the key, do you know?"

"There are two keys to the stage door, dear. They each open the ones on either side of the stage. The vicar keeps one on his keychain, and the duplicate on a nail in his study at the vicarage. It's all because of that time he went off to Brighton for the C and S—that's the Churchwardens' and Sidesmen's—cricket match, and took Tom Stoddart with him. Tom's the locksmith, you know, and with the two of them gone, no one could get on or off the stage without a stepladder. It played havoc with the Little Theater Group's production of *King Lear*, let me tell you!"

"And there was no one else about?"

"No one, dear. Aurelia and I were in the kitchen the whole time. We had the door half closed so the light from the kitchen wouldn't spoil the darkness in the hall."

"There was no one in the passageway?"

"No, of course not. They should have had to walk through the beam of light from the kitchen door, right under our noses so to speak. Once we had the water on to boil, Aurelia and I stood right there at the crack of the door so that we could at least hear the puppet show. 'Fee! Fi! Fo! Fum.' Oh! It gives me the goose bumps just to think about it now!"

I stood perfectly still and held my breath, not moving a muscle. I kept my mouth shut and let the silence lengthen.

"Except—" she said, her gaze wavering. "I thought—"

"Yes?"

"I thought I heard a footstep in the hall. I'd just glanced over at the wall clock, and my eyes were a little dazzled by the light above the stove. I looked out and saw—"

"Do you remember the time?"

"It was twenty-five past seven. We had the tea laid on for eight o'clock, and it takes those big electric urns a long time to come to the boil. How odd that you should ask. That nice young policeman—what's his name?—the little blond fellow with the dimples and the lovely smile?"

"Detective Sergeant Graves," I said.

"Yes, that's him: Detective Sergeant Graves. Funny, isn't it? He asked me the same question, and I gave him the same answer I am going to give you."

"Which is?"

"It was the vicar's wife—Cynthia Richardson."

twenty-five

CYNTHIA, THE RODENT-FACED AVENGER! I SHOULD HAVE known! Cynthia, who doled out good works in the parish of St. Tancred's with the hand of a Herod. I could easily see her taking it upon herself to punish Rupert, the notorious womanizer. The parish hall was part of her kingdom; the spare key to the stage doors was kept on a nail in her husband's study.

How she might have come into possession of the vicar's missing bicycle clip remained something of a mystery, but mightn't it have been in the vicarage all along?

By his own admission, the vicar's absentmindedness was becoming a problem. Hence the engraved initials. Perhaps he had left home without the clip last Thursday and shredded his trouser cuff because he wasn't wearing it.

The details were unimportant. One thing I was sure of: There was more going on in the vicarage than met the eye, and whatever it was (husband dancing naked in the woods, and so forth), it seemed likely that Cynthia was at the heart of it all.

"What are you thinking, dear?" Miss Puddock's voice interrupted my thoughts. "You've suddenly gone so quiet!"

I needed time to get to the bottom of things, and I needed it now. I was unlikely to have a second chance to plumb the depths of Miss Puddock's village knowledge.

"I—I suddenly don't feel very well," I said, snatching at the edge of a table and lowering myself into one of the wire-backed chairs. "It might have been the sight of your poor scalded hand, Miss Puddock. A delayed reaction, perhaps. A touch of shock."

I suppose there must have been times when I hated myself for practicing such deceits, but I could not think of any at the moment. It was Fate, after all, who thrust me into these things, and Fate would jolly well have to stand the blame.

"Oh, you poor thing!" Miss Puddock said. "You stay right where you are, and I shall fetch you a nice cup of tea and a scone. You do like scones, don't you?"

"I l-love scones," I said, remembering suddenly that shock victims were known to shiver and shake. By the time she came back with the scones, my teeth were chattering like marbles shaken in a jar.

She removed a vase of lily of the valley (*Convallaria majalis*), whisked the starched linen cloth from one of the tables, and wrapped it round my shoulders. As the sweet smell of the flowers wafted across my nostrils, I remembered with pleasure that the plant contained a witch's brew of cardioactive glycosides, including convallatoxin and glucoconvalloside, and that even the water in which the flowers had stood was poisonous. Our ancestors had called it Our Lady's tears, or Ladder-to-Heaven, and with good reason!

"You mustn't take a chill." Miss Puddock clucked solicitously as she poured me a cup of tea from the hulking samovar.

"Peter the Great seems to be behaving himself now," I observed with a calculated tremor and a nod towards the gleaming machine.

"He's very naughty sometimes." She smiled. "It comes of his being Russian, I expect."

"Is he really Russian?" I asked, priming the pump.

"From his distinguished heads," she said, pointing to the double-headed black eagle that functioned as a hot water tap, "to his royally rounded bottom. He was manufactured in the shops of the brothers Martiniuk, the celebrated silversmiths of Odessa, and it was said that he was once used to make tea for Tsar Nicholas and his unfortunate daughters. When the city was occupied by the Reds after the Revolution, the youngest of the Martiniuks, Vladimir, who was just sixteen at the time, bundled Peter up in a wolf skin, roped him to a handcart, and fled with him on foot—on foot, fancy!—to the Netherlands, where he set up shop in one of Amsterdam's cobbled alleys, and changed his name to van den Maarten.

"Peter," she said, giving the samovar a light but affectionate pat, "was his sole possession, other than the handcart, of course. He planned to make his fortune by producing endless copies, and selling them to Dutch aristocrats, who were said to be mad about Russian tea."

"And were they?" I asked.

"I don't know," she replied, "and nor did Vladimir. He died of influenza in the great epidemic of 1918, leaving his shop and all that was in it to his landlady, Margriet van Rijn. Margriet married a farm boy from Bishop's Lacey, Arthur Elkins, who had fought in Flanders, and he brought her back with him to England not long after the end of the Great War.

"Arthur was killed when a factory chimney collapsed on him in 1924, and Margriet died of shock when they brought her the news. After her death, my sister and I found that she had willed us Peter the Great—and there was nothing for it but to open the St. Nicholas Tea Room. Twenty-five years ago, that was, and as you can see, we're still here.

"He's a very temperamental old samovar, you know," she went on, moving as if to caress his silver surface, but thinking better of it. "Of course, he's an awful old fraud. Oh, he spits boiling water and blows out fuses on occasion, but underneath it all he has a heart of gold—or at least, of silver."

"He's quite magnificent," I said.

"And doesn't he know it! Well, well, here I am talking about him as if he were a cat. When Grace was with us, she used to call him 'the Tyrant.' Imagine that! 'The Tyrant wants his polishing,' she'd say. 'The Tyrant wants his electrical contacts cleaned.'"

"Grace?" I asked.

"Grace Tennyson. Or Ingleby, as she is now."

"Grace Ingleby used to work here?"

"Oh, yes! Until she left to marry Gordon, she was our star waitress. You wouldn't think it to look at her, but she was as strong as an ox. You don't often see that in such a tiny bit of a thing.

"And she wasn't the slightest bit intimidated by Peter and his moods. Spark and spit as he may, Grace was never afraid to roll up her sleeves and have a good rummage round his innards."

"She sounds very clever," I said.

"She was all of that." Miss Puddock laughed. "All of that and more. And no wonder! One of our customers once told us—an RAF Squadron Leader, I think he was—and in confidence, of course—that Grace had the highest IQ he'd ever seen in 'the fairer sex,' as he put it: that if the people in Special Operations hadn't whisked her off to do top secret work, she might well have spent the rest of the war installing wireless sets in Spitfires."

"Top secret work?" I gasped. The thought of Grace Ingleby doing anything other than cringing in her dovecote tower, like a captive maiden waiting to be rescued by Sir Lancelot, was almost laughable.

"Of course, she would never breathe a word about it." Miss Puddock lowered her voice, in the way that people often do when they talk about the war. "They're not allowed to, you know. But then, we seldom see her nowadays. Since that tragedy with her little boy—"

"Robin," I said.

"Yes. Since then, she keeps to herself. I'm afraid she's not at all the same laughing girl who used to put Peter the Great in his place."

"Was Gordon a member of Special Operations, too?" I asked.

"Gordon?" She laughed. "Good lord, no. Gordon's 'a farmer born and a farmer he shall die,' as Shakespeare wrote, or was it Harry Lauder, or George Formby, or someone like that? My memory's gone all wormholes, and so will yours, in time."

I couldn't think what to say, and I saw at once she thought she'd offended me.

"But not for many a year, dear. No, I'm quite sure *your* memory will still be going strong when the rest of us are in our graves and paved over for parking at the bowling palaces."

"Have you seen Mrs. Ingleby recently?" I asked.

"Not since Saturday night at the parish hall. Of course I had no opportunity to chat, what with our little musicale on my mind. The rest of the evening was a nightmare, wasn't it: the death of that poor man—the puppet that was carved with Robin's face? I don't know what Gordon was thinking, bringing Grace there when she's so fragile. But then, he had no way of knowing, did he?"

"No," I said. "I don't suppose he did."

———

BY THE TIME I SET OUT FOR BUCKSHAW, it was well past lunchtime. Fortunately, Miss Puddock had wrapped a couple of buttered scones in paper and insisted upon tucking them into my pocket. I nibbled at them absently as I pedaled along the road, lost in thought.

At the end of the high street, the road made a gentle angle to the southwest as it skirted the southern perimeter of St. Tancred's churchyard.

If I hadn't glanced to my right, I mightn't have seen it: the Austin van, with "Porson's Puppets" in gold letters on its panels, parked at the side of the parish hall. Gladys's tires skidded in the dust as I applied her hand brakes and swerved into the churchyard.

As I pulled up, Nialla was stowing odds and ends in the van's interior.

"You've got it running!" I shouted. She gave me the kind of look that you might give to a bit of dog dirt in your porridge, and went on with her packing.

"It's me, Flavia," I said. "Have you forgotten me already?"

"Piss off, you little traitor," she snapped. "Leave me alone."

For an instant, I thought I was back at Buckshaw, talking to Feely. It was the kind of dismissal I've lived through a thousand times—and survived, I thought. I decided to stand my ground.

"Why? What have I done to you?"

"Oh, come off it, Flavia. You know as well as I do. You told the police I was at Buckshaw. They thought I was hiding out, or running away, or whatever you want to call it."

"I did no such thing!" I protested. "I haven't laid eyes on a policeman since I saw you in the coach house."

"But you were the only one who knew I was there."

As it always did when I was angry, my mind burned with crystal clarity.

"I knew you were there, Dogger knew you were there, and so did Mrs. Mullet, to name but three."

"I can hardly believe Dogger would peach on me."

"And nor would Mrs. Mullet," I said.

Good Lord! Was I actually defending Mrs. M?

"She may be a bloody gossip, but she's not mean," I said. "She'd never rat on you. Inspector Hewitt came to Buckshaw—probably to ask me a few more questions about Saturday night—and happened to see you walking from the coach house to the kitchen. There's no more to it than that. I'm sure of it."

I could see that Nialla was thinking about it. I wanted nothing more than to take her by the shoulders and give her a good shaking, but I had to keep in mind the fact that her emotions were being stoked by a storm of hormones: fierce clouds of hydrogen, nitrogen, oxygen, carbon, and sulfur, combining and recombining in the eternal dances of life.

It almost made me forgive her.

"Here," I said, pulling the butterfly compact dramatically from my pocket and holding it out towards her. "I believe this belongs to you."

I hugged myself in anticipation of a tidal wave of gratitude and praise. But none came.

"Thanks," Nialla said, and pocketed the thing.

Thanks? Just *thanks*? The nerve! I'd show her: I'd pretend she hadn't hurt me; pretend I didn't care.

"I can't help noticing," I remarked casually, "that you're packing the van, which means that Bert Archer's repaired it and you're about to be on your way. Since Inspector Hewitt is nowhere in sight, I expect that means you're free to go."

"Free?" she repeated, and spat in the dirt. "Free? The vicar's given me four pounds, six shillings, and eightpence from the show. Bert Archer's bill comes to seven pounds ten. It's only because the vicar put in a word for me that he's willing to let me drive to Overton to pawn whatever I can. If you call that free, then I'm free. It's all bloody well and good for Little Miss Nabob, who lives in a country house the size of Buckingham Palace, to make her smart-pants deductions. So think what you like, but don't bloody well patronize me!"

"All right," I said. "I didn't mean to. Here, take this, please."

I dug into my pocket again and pulled out the coin, the one Aunt Felicity had foisted upon Dogger, thinking it was a shilling. Dogger, in turn, had planted it in my pocket, believing, perhaps, that it would soon be spent on horehound sticks at Miss Cool's shop.

I handed it to Nialla, who looked at it with disbelief.

"Fourpence!" she said. "Bloody fourpence!"

Her tears were flowing freely as she flung it away among the tombstones.

"Yes, it *is* only fourpence," I said. "But it's fourpence in Maundy money. The coins are produced by the Royal Mint, to be handed out by the Sovereign—"

"Blow the Sovereign!" she shouted. "And blow the Royal Mint!"

"—on Maundy Thursday. They're quite rare. If I remember correctly, Bert Archer is a coin collector, and I think you'll find the Maundy fourpence will more than pay for the van."

With all the righteous dignity I could muster, I grabbed Gladys by the handlebars and shoved off for home. When I looked back from the corner of the church, Nialla was already on her hands and knees, scrabbling in the churchyard grass, and I couldn't tell whether the tears she was wiping away were tears of anger or of happiness.

twenty-six

"ALL RIGHT, DOGGER," I SAID, "THE JIG IS UP."

I had found him in the butler's pantry, polishing Father's shoes.

Dogger's duties at Buckshaw varied in direct proportion to his present capabilities, his participation in our daily life rising and descending, rather like those colored balls in Galileo's thermometer that float at different levels in a glass tube, depending on the temperature. The fact that he was doing shoes was a good sign. It indicated clearly that he had advanced once again from gardener to butler.

He looked up from his work.

"Is it?" he asked.

"Cast your mind, if you please, back to Saturday evening at the parish hall. You're sitting beside me watching *Jack and the Beanstalk* when suddenly something goes wrong backstage. Rupert comes crashing down dead, and within minutes you are telling me that you fear we have seen murder. How did you know that? How did you know it wasn't an accident?"

This question had been gnawing away at my subconscious like a rat at a rope, but until that very moment, I had not been fully aware of it.

Dogger breathed on the upper of one of Father's regimental half-wellingtons before he answered, giving the glassy black surface a final loving rub with his shirtsleeve.

"The circumstances spoke against it," he said. "Mr. Porson was a perfectionist. He manufactured all his own equipment. A puppeteer works in the dark. There's no room for error. A frayed electrical wire was out of the question."

"It wasn't frayed," I said. "I spotted it when I was backstage with Inspector Hewitt. The insulation was scraped away."

"I should have been surprised if it wasn't," he said.

"Congratulations on a brilliant deduction," I said, "although it's one that didn't occur to me."

And it certainly hadn't, because the female mind doesn't work that way.

Seen from the air, the male mind must look rather like the canals of Europe, with ideas being towed along well-worn towpaths by heavy-footed dray horses. There is never any doubt that they will, despite wind and weather, reach their destinations by following a simple series of connected lines.

But the female mind, even in my limited experience, seems more of a vast and teeming swamp, but a swamp that knows in an instant whenever a stranger—even miles away—has so much as dipped a single toe into her waters. People who talk about this phenomenon, most of whom know nothing whatsoever about it, call it "woman's intuition."

Although I had arrived at much the same conclusion as Dogger, it had been by a very different route.

In the first place, although it was obvious that Rupert had been murdered for what he had done to a woman, I think I had known almost from the moment of his death that Nialla was not his killer.

"The instant he came crashing down onto the stage," I said, "Nialla leaped to her feet and moved towards him. Her first, and automatic, impulse was to go to his aid."

Dogger rubbed his chin and nodded.

"But she forced herself to stop," I went on, "as soon as she saw the smoke and the sparks. She quickly realized that touching any part of his body could mean instant death. For her—and her baby."

"Yes," Dogger said. "I noticed that, too."

"Therefore, Nialla is not the murderer."

"I believe you can safely remove her from your list," said Dogger.

IT WASN'T UNTIL I WAS HALFWAY along the road to Culverhouse Farm that I realized how tired I was. I'd been up before the sun and had been going flat out ever since. But time was of the essence: If I didn't get there before Inspector Hewitt, I wouldn't know the gruesome details until I read about them in the *News of the World*.

This time, rather than crossing the river behind the church, I had decided to go round by the Hinley road and approach the farm from the west. By doing so, I would have the advantage of height to survey the terrain, as well as keeping to the cover of Gibbet Wood. Now that the noose was tightening, so to speak, it would never do to be ambushed by a cold-blooded killer.

By the time I was halfway up the chalky road of Gibbet Hill, I felt as if my blood were mud, and my shoes were made of lead. Under any other circumstances, I might have crawled into a quiet thicket for a nap, but it was not to be. Time was running out and, as Father was so fond of saying, "Tired is a mucker's excuse."

As I listened to the wind sighing and whispering in the treetops of Gibbet Wood, I found myself half hoping that Mad Meg would leap out and divert me from my mission. But this, too, was not to be: Aside from a yellowhammer tapping away like a busy shoemaker at the far side of the wood, there were no signs of life.

When I reached the top of the hill, Jubilee Field sloped away from me towards the river, a blanket of electric blue. At the outbreak of war, Gordon had been made to grow flax, or so Mrs. Mullet had told me, by order of HM Government, who required the stuff to manufacture parachutes. But the Battle of Britain had been years ago, and parachutes were no longer required in anywhere near the same quantity.

Still, working under the cloak of wartime necessity, it seemed that Gordon had managed to keep his secret crop of cannabis tucked handily away among the trees of Gibbet Wood, its very existence known to no more than a handful of people.

Which one of them, I wondered—if it was one of them—besides hating him passionately enough to kill, possessed sufficient electrical knowledge to have put the jolt to Rupert Porson?

A flash of light caught my eye: a reflection from the side of the road. I saw at once that it was one of Mad Meg's roadside junk ornaments, dangling by a string from a bramble bush. It was no more than a jagged bit of chrome trim, jarred loose from the radiator of some passing motorcar by the roughness of the road. Hanging beneath it, and twisting idly in the sun (it was this that had caught my eye) was a small ridged circular disk of silver which, judging by its red stains, had once been the lid on a half-pint tin of paint.

It reminded me, oddly enough, of something I had experienced the previous year when Father had taken Ophelia, Daphne, and me up to London for midnight mass at the Brompton Oratory. At the elevation of the Host, as the priest held the round white wafer (which some of us believed to be the Body of Christ) above his head for an inordinately long time, it had for just an instant caught the light from the candles and the colored reflections of the chancel, glowing with an unearthly iridescent sheen that was neither solid nor vaporous. At the time, it had seemed to me a signal that something momentous was about to happen.

Now, at the verge of Gibbet Wood, the oiled teeth of some mental cogwheel fell into place with a series of almost audible clicks.

Church. *Click!* Vicar. *Click!* Circle suspended. *Click!* Bicycle clip. *Click!* Paint lid. *Click!* Meg. *Click!*

And I saw as if in a blinding vision: The vicar had been here at Culverhouse Farm last Thursday. It was here that he had caught his trouser leg in the bicycle chain and lost his clip. He *had* been wearing it after all! And it was here in the chalky dust that he had taken a tumble. The white smudges on his black clerical garb had come from this very road.

Mad Meg, the perennial magpie, had found the clip—as she did with all shiny metallic objects dropped in the vicinity of Gibbet Wood—and Meg had picked it up and brought it with her to the vicarage.

Her turned me out. Took old Meg's bracelet and turned her out. Dirty, dirty!

Meg's words echoed in my memory. She had been talking about the vicar's wife.

It was Cynthia Richardson who had taken the bicycle clip—Meg's "bracelet"—away from her, and shooed her out of the vicarage.

From the vicarage, it was only a hop, step, and jump to the parish hall, where the thing turned up backstage, as the murder weapon, in Rupert's puppet theater.

That's the way it must have happened. I was sure of it: as sure as my name is Flavia de Luce. And I could hardly wait to tell Inspector Hewitt!

Below me, in the distance, on the far shore of a sea of blue flax, a gray Ferguson tractor was creeping slowly alongside a stone wall, towing a flatbed trailer in its wake. A flash of blond hair in the sunlight told me that the man on foot, unloading stones for wall-mending, must be Dieter, and there was no doubt that the person in overalls at the tractor's wheel was Sally. Even if they had been paying attention—which they weren't—they were too far away to spot me slinking down towards the farmhouse.

As I moved cautiously across the courtyard, the place seemed sunken in shadow: old stone piled upon old stone, with dead-eyed windows (as Sally had said) staring out blindly upon nothing. Which of the blank panes, I wondered, had been Robin's bedroom? Which of the empty windows had framed his lonely little face before that unthinkable Monday in September of 1945, when his short life had ended so abruptly at the end of a rope?

I gave a token knock at the door, and waited a respectful thirty seconds. At the end of that time I turned the knob and stepped inside.

"Mrs. Ingleby?" I called. "Mr. Ingleby? It's me, Flavia. I've come to see if you have any extra-large eggs."

I didn't think there would be a reply, and I was right. Gordon Ingleby was far too hardworking to be mooning about his house while there was still a trace of daylight outside, and Grace—well, Grace was either in her dovecote tower or wandering the hills. The inquisitive Mrs. Mullet had once asked me if I ever came upon her in my rambles about the shire.

"She's a queer one, that Grace Ingleby," she'd said. "My friend Edith—that's Edith Crowly, dear—her as was Edith Fisher before she married Jack—was walkin' over to her choir-practor's appointment in Nether Stowell—she'd missed the bus, you see—and she spotted Grace Ingleby comin' out of a copse at the bottom of Biddy's Lane which goes over the hill to nowhere.

"'Grace!' she called out to her. 'Yoo-hoo, Grace Ingleby!' but Grace slithered through a stile—those are her very words: 'slithered through a stile,' if you can picture it, and by the time she got there herself, Grace was gone. 'Gone like a dog's breath in December.' That's what she said."

When it came to village gossip, Mrs. M was infallible, like Pope Pius IX.

I moved slowly along the corridor, fairly confident that I was alone in the house. At the end of the hall, beside a round window, a grandfather clock was "tocking" away to itself, the only sound in the otherwise silent farmhouse.

I looked quickly into each room: parlor, cloakroom, kitchen, pantry . . .

Beside the clock, two steps led up to a small square landing, and by peering round the corner, I could see that a narrow stairway continued upwards to the first floor.

Tucked in beneath the stairs was a cupboard, its oddly angled door of dovetailed boards fitted out with a splendid doorknob of green and white china that could only have been Wedgwood. I would have a jolly good dig through it later.

Each step gave out its own distinctive wooden groan as I ascended: like a series of old coffin lids being pried open, I thought with a pleasant shudder.

Steady on, Flave, old girl. No sense getting the wind up.

At the top of the stairs was a second small landing, from which, at right angles, another three steps led to the upstairs corridor.

It seemed obvious that all the rooms up here were bedrooms, and I was right: A glance into each of the first two revealed cold, spartan chambers, each with a single bed, a washstand, a wardrobe, and nothing more.

The large bedroom at the front of the house was Gordon and Grace's—no doubt about it. Aside from a double dresser and a double bed with a shabby quilt, this room was as cold and sterile as the others.

I had a quick snoop in the dresser drawers: on his side socks, underwear, a wristwatch with no strap, and a greasy, much-thumbed deck of playing cards bearing the crest of the Scots Greys; on hers, slips, knickers, a bottle of prescription sleeping ampules (my old friend chloral hydrate, I noted: $C_2H_3Cl_3O_2$—a powerful hypnotic that when slipped in alcohol to American thugs was called a "Mickey Finn." In England, it was slipped to high-strung housewives by country doctors and called "something to help you sleep.").

I couldn't keep back a quick smile as I thought of the time that, using no more than alcohol, lavatory cleaner, and a bottle of chlorine bleach, I had synthesized a batch of the stuff and given it, inside a doctored apple, to Phoebe Snow, a prize pig belonging to our neighbor Max Wight. Phoebe had taken five days and seventeen hours to sleep it off and, for a while, "The Remarkable Sleeping Pig" had been the eighth wonder of the British agricultural world. Max had graciously lent her for the fête at St. Tancred's, where Phoebe could be viewed, for sixpence a time, snoring in the back of a lorry marked "Sleeping Beauty." In the end, she had raised nearly five pounds for the choir's surplice fund.

With a sigh I returned to my work.

At the back of Grace's drawer, tucked beneath a soiled linen handkerchief, was a well-thumbed Bible. I flipped open the cover and read the words on its flyleaf: *Please return to the parish church of St. Tancred's, Bishop's Lacey.*

As I was putting it back into the drawer, a slip of paper fell out and fluttered to the floor. I picked it up with my fingernails, taking great care not to leave my dabs on the thing.

The words were written in purple ink: *Grace——Please call if I may provide any further solace.* And it was signed *Denwyn.*

Denwyn Richardson—the vicar. Whom Mad Meg had seen dancing naked in nearby Gibbet Wood.

I pocketed the evidence.

All that was left now was the small bedroom at the back of the house. Robin's bedroom. It had to be. I made my way across the silent landing and stopped in front of the closed door. It was only then that I began to feel a little apprehension. What if Gordon or Grace suddenly stormed into the house and up the stairs? How could I possibly explain my invasion of their bedrooms?

I put an ear to the door's dark paneling and listened. Not a sound.

I turned the knob and stepped inside.

As I had suspected, the room was Robin's, but it was the room of a little boy who had been dead five years: a pathetically small bed, folded blankets, an empty wardrobe, and linoleum on the floor. No shrine, no candles, no framed pictures of the deceased astride a rocking horse or hanging from his knees in an apple tree. What a bitter disappointment!

It was as bare and simple as van Gogh's *Bedroom in Arles*, but without the warmth; the room was as cold and impersonal as the winter moon.

After a quick look round, there was no more to see, and I stepped outside, closing the door respectfully—almost tenderly—behind me.

And then I heard a footstep downstairs.

What was I to do? The possibilities flashed across my brain. I could gallop down the stairs in tears, pretending I had become lost and disorientated while sleepwalking. I could claim I was suffering a nervous breakdown and didn't know where I was; that I had seen, from the farmyard, a face at an upstairs window, beckoning me with a long finger: that I had thought it was Grace Ingleby in distress.

Interesting though they were, these actions would all come with consequences, and if there was one thing I did not need, it was to introduce complications to my life. No, I thought, I would sneak down the stairs and hope like mad that I would not be caught.

But the idea died almost before it was born. The instant I put my foot on it, the top step gave out a ghastly groan.

There was a flapping near the bottom of the stairs, as if a large bird were trapped in the house. I went slowly, but steadily, down the rest of the staircase. At the bottom, I stuck my head round the corner and my blood ran cold.

A beam of bright sunlight illuminated the end of the hallway. In it, a little boy in rubber boots and a sailor suit was vanishing through the open door.

twenty-seven

I WAS SURE OF IT.

He had been in the cupboard beneath the stairs all along. I stood there, stock-still at the open door, faced with a dilemma. What should I do? I knew for certain that once I stepped outside this farmhouse, I would not be likely to enter it ever again. Best to have a quick look behind the angled door now, before setting off in pursuit of the sailor-suited apparition.

Inside the dim cupboard, a length of string dangled from a naked bulb. I gave it a tug and the space sprang to feeble light. It was empty.

Empty, that is, except for a pair of child's rubber boots, very much like the ones I had just seen on the feet of the figure in the doorway.

The chief difference was that this pair of Dunlops was clodded with clay, still wet from the morning's rain.

Or the grave.

As I dashed through the open front door, I caught a glimpse of the navy blue sailor suit, just disappearing behind the machine shed. Beyond those rusty galvanized walls, I knew, was a bewildering warren of outbuildings: a maze of sagging sheds, any one of which could easily provide a dozen hiding places.

Off I loped in pursuit, like a hound on the scent. It never occurred to me to be afraid.

But then I slid to a sudden stop. Behind the machine shed, a narrow alley led off to the right. Had the fugitive darted down it to throw me off the track? I edged along the narrow passage, taking great care not to touch the neglected walls on either side. A single scratch from any one of the razor-sharp flaps of ripped tin would almost certainly end in tetanus, and I would end up hog-tied in a hospital ward, foaming at the mouth and wracked by bone-breaking spasms.

How happy Daffy and Feely would be!

"I told you she would come to no good end," Daffy would tell Father. "She should never have been allowed to run loose."

Accordingly, I inched slowly, crab-wise, along the narrow passage. When I finally reached the end, I found my way blocked on the left by a stack of battered petrol drums; on my right by a nettle-ridden pigpen.

As I edged back along the Passage of Death, which seemed, if anything, even more narrow on the return journey, I stopped to listen, but other than the distant sound of clucking hens, I could hear nothing but my own breathing.

I tiptoed softly along between the tumbledown sheds, paying close attention to my peripheral vision, aware that, at any moment, something could pounce upon me from a darkened doorway.

It wasn't until then that I noticed the tracks on the ground: tiny footprints that could only have been made by the waffle-patterned soles of a child's Dunlop rubber boot.

With all of my senses on high alert, I followed their trail.

On past the machine shed they led me; past the rusting hulk of an ancient tractor that leaned crazily to one side, missing a back wheel, looking for all the world like something half sunk in the sands, some ancient engine cast up by the sea.

Another jog to the left and I found myself at the foot of the dovecote, which towered above me like a fairy-tale castle, its piebald bricks stained almost golden by the late light of day.

Although I had been here before, it had been by a different route, and I slowly crept round it to the decrepit wooden door, the sharp pong of pigeon droppings already beginning to fill my nostrils.

Perhaps I had been wrong, I thought for a moment: Perhaps the boy in the sailor suit had run straight on past the tower, and was, by now, well away across the fields. But the footprints in the soil proved otherwise: They led straight to the dovecote door.

Something brushed against my leg and my heart nearly stopped.

"*Yow!*" said a voice.

It was Tock, the more vocal of the Inglebys' cats.

I put a finger to my lips to shush her, before I remembered that cats don't read sign language. But perhaps they do, for without another sound, she crouched low to the ground and slunk off into the shadows of the dovecote's interior.

Hesitantly, I followed her.

Inside, the place was as I remembered it: the myriad lights beaming in through chinks in the ancient brickwork; the claustrophobic, dust-choked air. This time, though, there was no banshee keening spilling out from the room above. The place was as silent as the crypt that lies beneath Death's own castle.

I put one foot onto the scaffolding and peered up to where it disappeared into the gloom above my head. The old wood let out a baleful croak, and I paused. Whoever—or whatever—was above me in the near-darkness, knew now that I had them cornered.

"Hallo!" I called out, as much to cheer myself as anything. "Hallo! It's me—Flavia! Anyone up there?"

The only sound from above was the buzzing of bees round the upper windows of the dovecote, grotesquely amplified by the tower's hollow structure.

"Don't be frightened," I called. "I'm coming up."

Little by little, one small step at a time, I began my precarious ascent. Again, I felt like Jack, this time climbing the beanstalk; dragging myself up, inch by inch, to face some unknown horror. The old wood creaked horribly, and I knew that it could crumble at any moment, dashing me down to certain death on the flagstones below, in much the same way that the giant—and Rupert—had come crashing down upon the puppet stage.

The climb seemed to go on forever. I stopped to listen: There was still no sound but that of the bees.

Up and up I went again, shifting my feet carefully from one wooden rung to the next, clutching at the crosspieces with fingers that were already beginning to grow numb.

As my eyes at last came level with the arched opening, the interior of the upper chamber came into view. A figure was hunched over the shrine to Robin Ingleby: the same figure that had fled the farmhouse.

On its knees, its back turned to me, the small apparition was dressed in a white and navy sailor suit with a middy collar and short trousers; the waffle soles of its Dunlop rubber boots were almost in my face. I could have reached out and touched them.

My knees began to tremble violently—threatening to buckle and send me plummeting down into the stony abyss.

"Help me," I said, the words brought up suddenly, inexplicably, and surprisingly, from some ancient and reptilian part of my brain.

A hand reached out, white fingers seized mine, and with surprising strength, hauled me up to safety. A moment later I found myself crouched, safe but trembling, face-to-face with the specter.

While the white sailor suit, with its crown-and-anchored jacket, and the Dunlop boots undoubtedly belonged to the dead Robin Ingleby, the strained and haggard face that stared back at me from beneath the beribboned HMS *Hood* hat was that of his tiny mother, Grace.

"You," I said, unable to restrain myself. "It was you."

Her face was sad, and suddenly very, very old. It was hard to believe that there remained in this woman a single atom of Grace Tennyson, that happy, outgoing girl who had once so cheerfully conquered the wired innards of Peter the Great, the silver samovar at the St. Nicholas Tea Room.

"Robin's gone," she said with a cough. "The Devil took him."

The Devil took him! Almost the same words Mad Meg had used in Gibbet Wood.

"And who was the Devil, Mrs. Ingleby? I thought for a while it was Rupert, but it wasn't. It was you, wasn't it?"

"Rupert's dead now," she said, touching her fingers to her temples as if she were dazed.

"Yes," I said. "Rupert's dead. He was the Punch and Judy man at the seaside, wasn't he? You had arranged to meet him there, and Robin saw you together. You were afraid he would tell Gordon."

She gave me a half-canny smile.

"At the seaside?" she said with a chuckling cough. "No, no—not at the seaside. Here . . . in the dovecote."

I had suspected for some time that the single set of footprints—the ones that had been found five years ago, leading up Jubilee Field to Gibbet Wood—had been those of Grace Ingleby, carrying the dead

Robin in her arms. In order to leave only his footprints, she had put on
her child's rubber boots. They were, after all, the same size as her own.
As if to prove it, she was wearing them now.

Five years after his death, she was still dressing up in Robin's clothing, trying desperately to conjure her son back from the dead. Or to
atone for what she had done.

"You carried him to the wood and hung him from a tree. But Robin
died *here*, didn't he? That's why you've made this his shrine, and not his
bedroom."

How matter-of-fact it sounded, this nightmare conversation with a
madwoman! I knew that if ever I made it safely home to Buckshaw, I was
going to be in need of a long, hot, steaming bath.

"I told him to stay down," she said rather petulantly. "'Go back to the
house, Robin,' I called out. 'You mustn't come up here.' But he wouldn't
listen. Little boys are like that sometimes. Disobedient."

She coughed again, and shook her head ruefully. "'I can do a trick
with the rope!' he shouted back. He'd been playing cowboy all day with
a rope he'd found in a shed."

Just as Sally had said. Grace must be telling me the truth.

"He climbed up here before we could stop him. Rupert was furious.
He grabbed at Robin to give him a shake, but his iron brace slipped on
the bricks. Robin—"

Now, silent tears were coursing down her face.

"Fell," I said. There was no need to elaborate.

"Fell," she repeated, and the way she dragged out the word made it
echo from the bricks, hovering grotesquely in the round chamber: a
sound I would never forget.

With it came an idea.

"Was it Rupert who thought of the Punch and Judy story? That Robin
had been playing out the scene with Punch and the hangman?"

"Where did you hear that?" she demanded, suddenly lucid, canny.
I thought of Mad Meg's smile in Gibbet Wood; these two women had
so much in common.

"Your evidence to the jury at the inquest," I answered. "It's public
knowledge."

I did not think it necessary to add that I had heard it from Sally.

"He made me do it," she said, wiping her eyes on the sleeve of the sailor suit, and I realized for the first time how much she looked like Robin. Once noticed, the resemblance was eerie.

"Rupert told me no one would ever know. Robin's neck was broken in the fall, and if we . . . if I . . ."

A shudder ran through her entire body.

"If I wouldn't do as he ordered, he'd tell Gordon what had been going on between us. I'd be the one to be punished. Gordon's quick with his fists, you know."

As was Rupert. I'd seen the bruises he left on Nialla's arm. Two quick-tempered men. And rather than fighting it out between them, they both had made punching bags of their women.

"Was there no one you could talk to? The vicar, for instance?"

This seemed to set her off, and she was racked by a siege of coughing. I waited until she had finished.

"The vicar," she said, gasping for breath, "is the only one who has made these past five years bearable."

"He knew about Robin?" I could hardly believe it!

"A clergyman's lips are sealed," she said. "He's never breathed a word. He tried to come to Culverhouse Farm once a week, just to let me talk. The man's a saint. His wife thought he was—"

"In love with you."

She nodded, squeezing her eyes tight shut, as if she were in excruciating pain.

"Are you all right?" I asked.

"Wait a few minutes," she said, "and I shall be fine."

Her body was crumbling before my eyes, tipping towards the opening into the shaft.

I grabbed at her arm, and as I did so, a glass bottle that she had been clutching in her fist fell to the brick floor and bounced away, clinking, into the corner, sending a pigeon clattering up towards the opening. I dragged Grace into the center of the chamber and sprang after the bottle, which had come to rest in a mound of ancient guano.

The label told me all I needed to know: *Calcium Cyanide*, it said. *Poison*.

Rat poison! The stuff was in common farm use, particularly on those farms whose henhouses attracted vermin. There was still one of the white tablets in the bottom. I removed the stopper and smelled it. Nothing.

Grace was now flat on the floor, twitching, her limbs flailing.

I dropped to my knees and sniffed her lips. The scent of bitter almonds.

The tablets of calcium cyanide, I knew, as soon as they met the moisture of her mouth, throat, and stomach, would produce hydrogen cyanide, a toxic gas that could kill in five minutes.

There was no time to waste. Her life was in my hands. I almost panicked at the thought—but I didn't.

I took a careful look round, registering every detail. Aside from the candle, the shrine, the photograph of Robin, and his toy sailboat, there was nothing in the chamber but rubble.

Well, not quite nothing. On one wall was an ancient watering device for the birds: an inverted glass bulb and tube whose gravity feed kept a dish full for the pigeons to dip their beaks into. From the clarity of the water, it seemed as if Grace had recently filled it.

A glass cock allowed the gravity feed to be turned off. I gave it a twist and pulled the full dish carefully out of its spring clips.

Grace moaned horribly on the floor, apparently no longer aware of my presence.

Treading carefully, I moved to the spot from which the pigeon had flown. Feeling gingerly in the straw with my fingertips, I was quickly rewarded. An egg. No, two little eggs!

Putting them down gently beside the dish, I picked up the sailboat. At the bottom of its tin keel was a lead weight. Damn!

I wedged the thing into the crack between two bricks in the windowsill and pulled for all I was worth—then pulled again. The third time, the weight snapped off.

Using the sharp bottom edge of the keel as a makeshift putty knife, I leaned out the opening to the wide shelf that had served for centuries as a perch.

Below me, the farmyard was empty. No sense wasting time by yelling for help.

I ground the thin keel along the ledge until I had gathered what I needed, then scraped it off, with a reluctant finger, into the water dish.

One step left.

Although their small size made it a tricky bit of work, I cracked the eggs, one at a time, the way Mrs. Mullet had taught me: a sharp rap in the middle, then using the two halves of the shell like twin egg cups, tipping the yolk back and forth from one to the other until the last of the whites had oozed away into the waiting water dish.

Taking up the glass pill bottle, I used it as a pestle: twisting, grinding, and stirring until I had perhaps half a teacup of grayish curded mud, with the slightest tinge of yellow.

So that neither of us would knock it over—Grace was now kicking feebly and pink in the face from lack of oxygen—I sat down beside her, cross-legged on the floor, and pulled her head into my lap, face upwards. She was too weak to resist.

Then seizing her nose between my thumb and forefinger, I pulled open her mouth, hoping that, in her spasms, she wouldn't bite me.

She snapped it shut at once. This was not going to be as easy as I had thought.

I pinched her nose a little tighter. Now, if she wanted to breathe at all, it was going to have to be through her mouth. I hated myself for what I was doing to her.

She struggled, her eyes bulging—and then her mouth flew open and she sucked in a breath of air—then snapped it shut again.

As slowly and as gently as I could, I leaned over and picked up the brimming dish, awaiting the proper moment.

It came sooner than I expected. With a gasp, Grace's mouth flew open, and as she sucked in air again, I dumped the contents of the dish into her mouth and slammed it shut with the heel of my hand under her chin. The empty dish fell to the floor with a crash.

But Grace was fighting me; I could see that. Some part of her was so dead set on dying that she was keeping the stuff in her mouth, refusing to swallow.

With the little finger of my right hand, I began prodding at her gullet, like a seabird digging in the sand.

We must have looked like Greek wrestlers: she with her head locked tightly in the crook of my arm, me bending over her, trembling with the sheer physical effort of trying to keep her from spitting out the nauseating mixture.

And then, just before she went limp, I heard her swallow. She was no longer resisting. I carefully pried open her mouth. Aside from a faint and distasteful glistening of foreign matter, it was empty.

I raced to the window, leaning out as far as I could into the sunshine.

My heart sank. The farmyard was still empty.

Then suddenly there was a noise of machinery in the lane, and a moment later, the gray Fergie came clattering into view, Sally bouncing at the wheel and Dieter dangling his long legs over the gate of the trailer.

"Sally! Dieter!" I shouted.

At first they didn't know where my voice was coming from. They were looking everywhere round the yard, perplexed.

"Up here—in the dovecote!"

I dug in my pocket, fished out Alf's willow whistle, and blew into it like a demented bobby.

At last they spotted me. Sally gave a wave.

"It's Grace!" I hollered. "She's taken poison! Telephone Dr. Darby and tell him to come at once."

Dieter was already dashing for the farmhouse, running full tilt, the way he must once have done when scrambling for his Messerschmitt.

"And tell him to make sure he's got amyl nitrite and sodium thiosulfate in his bag!" I shouted, in spite of a couple of wayward tears. "He's going to need them!"

twenty-eight

"PIGEON DROPPINGS?" INSPECTOR HEWITT SAID, FOR PERHAPS the third time. "You're telling me that you concocted an antidote from *pigeon droppings?*"

We were sitting in the vicar's study, sizing one another up.

"Yes," I said. "I had no other choice. Pigeon guano, when it's left outdoors in the sunlight, is remarkably high in $NaNO_3$—sodium nitrate—which is why I had to scrape it from the outside perch, rather than using the older stuff that was in the chamber. Sodium nitrate is an antidote to cyanide poisoning. I used the whites of pigeons' eggs to produce the suspension. I hope she's all right."

"She's fine," the Inspector said, "although we're seeking an opinion about whether to charge you with practicing medicine without a license."

I studied his face to see if he was teasing, but he didn't seem to be.

"But," I protested, "Dr. Darby said he couldn't have done better himself."

"Which isn't saying much," the Inspector said, looking away from me and out the window.

I saw that I had him beaten.

Inspector Hewitt had flagged me down on my way back to Buckshaw, and asked me to account for my presence at Culverhouse Farm.

A hastily fabricated story about fetching eggs for Mrs. Mullet, who wanted to make an angel food cake, seemed to have got me off the hook. At least for now.

The Inspector had assured me that Grace Ingleby was still alive; that she had been taken to the hospital at Hinley.

He did not say that my antidote had saved her life. I supposed only time would tell.

The vicar, having given up his desk and chair to Inspector Hewitt, stood like a black stork in the corner, rubbing at his eyeglasses with a linen handkerchief.

As Detective Sergeant Woolmer stood at one of the windows, pretending to polish an anastigmat lens from his precious camera, Detective Sergeant Graves glanced up from his notes just long enough to give me a beaming smile. I'd like to think that the almost imperceptible shake of his head that came with it was a sign of admiration.

And even though they're not yet aware of one another, I also like to think that Sergeant Graves will one day marry my rotten sister Ophelia and carry her off to a vine-covered cottage just far enough from Buckshaw that I can drop in whenever I feel like it for a good old gab about murder.

But now there was Dieter to take into account. Life was becoming so complicated.

"Just begin at the beginning," Inspector Hewitt said, suddenly back from his reverie. "I want to make sure we haven't missed anything."

Was I detecting a note of sarcasm? I hoped not, since I really liked the man, although he could be somewhat slow.

"Mrs. Ingleby—Grace—was having an affair with Rupert Porson. Rupert had been coming to Culverhouse Farm for years because . . . Gordon supplied him with marijuana. It eased the pain of his polio, you see."

He must have sensed my hesitation.

"No need to worry about betraying him," he said, "Mr. Ingleby has been most frank with us. It's your version I want to hear."

"Rupert and Grace arranged to meet at the seaside, years ago," I said. "Robin saw them there together. He stumbled upon them again, later, in the dovecote. Rupert made a grab for him, or something like that, and Robin tumbled down the central shaft and broke his neck. It was an accident, but still, Robin was dead. Rupert cooked up the idea of having Grace take his body, after dark, to Gibbet Wood, and hang it from a tree. Robin had been seen by several people playing with a rope.

"It was Rupert, too, who invented the story that Robin had been playing out the scene between Punch and Jack Ketch—that he had seen it at the seaside puppet show. Punch and the hangman's tale is one that's known to every child in England. No one would question the story that Robin had accidentally hanged himself. It was just bizarre enough to be true. As a well-known puppeteer, Rupert couldn't afford to have his name linked in any way with the death of a child. He needed to erase himself from the scene of Robin's death. No one but Grace knew he had been at the farm that day.

"That's why he threatened her. He told her that if she didn't do as he wanted, he would spill the beans to Gordon—sorry, I mean that he would inform Gordon that he'd been carrying on an affair with his wife. Grace would lose both her son and her husband. She was already half mad with grief and fear, so it was probably quite easy to manipulate her.

"Because she's so small, she was able to put on Robin's rubber boots to carry his body up to Gibbet Wood. She's remarkably strong for her size. I found that out when she hauled me up into the dovecote chamber. After she'd hung Robin's body from the tree, she put the boots on his feet, and went home the long way round, barefoot."

Inspector Hewitt nodded and scribbled a note in his microscopic handwriting.

"Mad Meg came upon the body hanging there, and thought it was the Devil's work. I've already given you the page from my notebook, so you've seen the drawing she made. She's quite good, actually, don't you think?"

"Um," the Inspector said. It was a bad habit he was picking up by associating too much with Dr. Darby.

"That's why she was afraid to touch him, or even tell anyone. Robin's body hung there in Gibbet Wood until Dieter found it.

"Last Saturday at the church hall, when Meg saw Robin's face on Jack, the puppet, she thought the Devil had brought the dead boy back to life, shrunk him, and put him to work on the stage. Meg has her times very badly mixed up. You can tell that from the drawing: The Robin hanging from the tree is a sight she saw five years ago. The vicar taking his clothes off in the wood is something she saw last Thursday."

The vicar went beet red, and ran a finger round the inside of his clerical collar. "Yes, well . . . you see—"

"Oh, I knew you had come a cropper, Vicar," I said. "I knew it the instant I saw you in the graveyard—the day you met Rupert and Nialla, remember? Your trouser leg was ripped, you were covered with chalky smudges from the road at Culverhouse Farm, and you'd lost your bicycle clip."

"So I had," the vicar said. "My trousers got caught up in the ruddy chain and I was catapulted into the ditch."

"Which explains why you went in among the trees of Gibbet Wood— to take off your clothes—to try to clean them up. You were afraid of what Cynthia would say—sorry, Mrs. Richardson, I mean. You said as much in the churchyard. Something about Cynthia having you on the carpet."

The vicar remained silent, and I don't think I ever admired him more than I did in that moment.

"Because you've been going to Culverhouse Farm at least once a week since Robin died five years ago, Cynthia—Mrs. Richardson, I mean— had somehow got the idea that there was more in your meetings with Grace Ingleby than met the eye. That's why you've recently been keeping your visits secret."

"I'm not really at liberty to discuss that," the vicar said. "The wearing of the dog collar puts paid to any tendency one has to be a chatterbox. But I must put in, in her defense, that Cynthia is very loyal. Her life is not always an easy one."

"Nor is Grace Ingleby's," I pointed out.

"No, nor is Grace's."

"At any rate," I went on, "Meg lives in an old shack, somewhere in the depths of Gibbet Wood. She doesn't miss much that goes on there."

Or anywhere else, I wanted to add. It had only just occurred to me that it was almost certainly Meg that Rupert and Nialla had heard prowling round near their tent in the churchyard.

"She saw you taking your trousers off beside the old gallows at the very spot where she had seen Robin hanging. That's why she drew you into her picture."

"I see," said the vicar. "At least, I *think* I see."

"Meg picked up your trouser clip in the road, meaning to use it for one of those dangling sculpture things of hers, but she recognized it as yours, and—"

"It has my initials on it," the vicar said. "Cynthia scratched them on."

"Meg can't read," I said, "but she's very observant. Look at the detail in her drawing. She even remembered the little Church of England pin in your lapel."

"Good heavens," the vicar said, coming round to peer over Inspector Hewitt's shoulder. "So she did."

"She came here on Saturday afternoon to return the trouser clip, and while she was looking for you, she happened to wander into the parish hall during Rupert's performance. When she saw the shrunken Robin on the stage, she went into a right old squiff. You and Nialla carried her off to the vicarage and tucked her in on your couch in the study. That's when the clip—and Nialla's compact—fell out of her pocket. I found the compact on the floor behind the couch the next day. I didn't find the bicycle clip because Grace Ingleby had already picked it up the day before."

"Hold on," the Inspector said. "No one's claiming to have seen Mrs. Ingleby anywhere near the vicarage—or the parish hall—on Saturday afternoon."

"Nor did they," I said. "What they *did* say was that the egg lady had been there."

Had Inspector Hewitt been the sort of man whose mouth was prone to falling open when astonished, he'd have been gaping like a gargoyle.

"Good Lord," he said flatly. "Who told you that?"

"Mrs. Roberts and Miss Roper," I said. "They were in the vicarage kitchen after church yesterday. I assumed you had questioned them."

"I believe we did," Inspector Hewitt said, cocking an eyebrow at Sergeant Graves, who flipped back through the pages of his notebook.

"Yes, sir," said Sergeant Graves. "They both gave in statements, but there was nothing said about egg ladies."

"The egg lady was Grace Ingleby, of course," I said helpfully. "She came down from Culverhouse Farm late on Saturday afternoon with eggs for the vicarage. There was no one else around. Something made her go into the vicar's study. Perhaps she heard Meg snoring, I don't know. But she found the bicycle clip on the floor, picked it up, and pocketed it."

"How can you be so sure?" asked Inspector Hewitt.

"I can't be sure," I said. "What I *can* be sure of, because he told me so, is that the vicar lost his bicycle clip last Thursday . . ."

The vicar nodded in agreement.

". . . on the road at Gibbet Hill . . . and that you and I, Inspector, found it on Sunday morning clamped to the rail of the puppet theater. The rest is mere guesswork."

The Inspector scratched at his nose, made another note, and looked up at me as if he had been shortchanged.

"Which brings us neatly back to Rupert Porson," he said.

"Yes," I replied. "Which brings us neatly back to Rupert Porson."

"About whom you are about to enlighten us."

I ignored his twitting and went on. "Grace had known Rupert for years. Perhaps since even before she met Gordon. For all I know, she might even have traveled with him at one time as his assistant."

I knew by the sudden closed look on Inspector Hewitt's face that I had hit the nail on the head. *Bravo, Flavia!* I thought. *Go to the head of the class!*

There were times when I surprised even myself.

"And even if she hadn't," I added, "she'd certainly attended some of the shows he put on round the countryside. She'd have paid particular attention to the electrical rigging. Since Rupert manufactured all of his own lighting equipment, I can hardly believe that he wouldn't have taken the opportunity to show off the details to a fellow electrician. He was rather vain about his skills, you know.

"I expect Grace took the keys from the vicarage and walked straight-away through the churchyard, to the parish hall. The afternoon performance was over by that time; the audience had gone, and so had Rupert. There was little chance of her being seen. Even if she had been spotted, no one would have paid her the slightest attention, would they? After all, she was just the egg lady. Besides, she and her husband are parishioners of St. Tancred's, so no one would have given her a second look.

"She went into the hall, and using the corridor to the left, and locking the door behind her, went up the two short flights of steps to the stage.

"She climbed up onto the bridge of the puppet stage, and scraped away the insulation from the wiring, using the bicycle clip as a kind of spoke-shave. Then she slipped the clip over the wooden framework of the stage, touching the bared electrical wire on the one side and the metal rod that released Galligantus on the other. Bob's your uncle! That's all there was to it. If you've had a close look at the clip, you've likely already found a small abrasion mark on the inside center—and perhaps slight traces of copper."

"S'truth!" Sergeant Woolmer let slip, and Inspector Hewitt shot him a look.

"Unlike most of the other suspects—except Dieter, of course, who built wireless sets as a boy in Germany—Grace Ingleby had the necessary electrical training. Before the war, before marrying Gordon, she worked in a factory installing radio sets in Spitfires. I've been told that her IQ is nearly equal in number to the Psalms."

"Dammit!" Inspector Hewitt shouted, leaping to his feet. "Sorry, Vicar. But why haven't we found these things out, Sergeant?"

He glared from one of his men to the other, including both in his exasperation.

"With respect, sir," Sergeant Woolmer ventured, "it could be because we're not Miss de Luce."

It was a bold thing to say, and a rash one. If what I'd seen in the pictures at the cinema were true, it was the sort of remark that could result in the sergeant becoming a road-mender before sunset.

After a nerve-racking silence, the Inspector said, "You're right, of course, Sergeant. We don't have the same entrée to the homes and hearths of Bishop's Lacey, do we? It's an area in which we could do better. Make a note of it."

No wonder his subordinates adored him!

"Yes, sir," said Sergeant Graves, scribbling something in his notebook.

"Then," I went on, "having set the trap, Grace went out by the hallway door at the right of the stage, and she locked that one, too—probably to keep anyone from going backstage and discovering what she had done. Not that anyone would, of course, but I expect she was under a great deal of stress. She's been planning to take her revenge on Rupert for a long time. It wasn't until she spotted the vicar's trouser clip on the floor that she saw exactly how it could be done. As I've said, she's a very intelligent woman."

"But," Inspector Hewitt said, "if both doors were locked, how did Porson get up onto the stage for the performance? He couldn't have locked himself in because he didn't have the key."

"He used that little staircase in front of the stage," I said. "It's not as steep as the two in the side halls, and it's only a single flight. Narrow stairs were difficult for Rupert because of his leg brace, and he took the shortest route. I noticed that about him last Thursday when he was checking the hall's acoustics."

"Quite an ingenious theory," Inspector Hewitt remarked. "But it doesn't explain everything. How, for instance, would the alleged murderer know that such a gimcrack bit of tin would result in Porson's death?"

"Because Rupert always leaned on a rail of iron piping as he operated the puppets. With all the lighting equipment that was hung backstage, the railing had to be grounded through the mains. The instant Rupert touched the live Galligantus lever, his lower body pressed tight against the rail as it was, with his right leg clamped in an iron brace, the current would have shot straight up his arm and through—"

"His heart," said the Inspector. "Yes, I see."

"Rather like Saint Lawrence," I said, "who, as you know, was done to death on a grill."

"Thank you, Flavia," Inspector Hewitt said. "I think you've made your point."

"Yes," I said, rather smugly, "so do I. Will that be all, then?"

Sergeant Graves was grinning away over his notebook like Scrooge over his ledgers.

Inspector Hewitt wrinkled his brow in a look that I had seen before: a look of exasperated curiosity held in firm check by years of training and a strong sense of duty.

"I think so, yes—except for one or two small points, perhaps."

I gave him that beaming, superior smile: all teeth and thin lips. I almost hated myself for doing it.

"Yes, Inspector?"

He walked to the window, his hands clasped behind his back, as I had seen him do before on several occasions. At last he turned: "Perhaps I'm a bit of a dim bulb," he said.

If he was waiting for me to contradict him, he'd be waiting until the cows came home in purple pajamas.

"Your observations on the death of Rupert Porson have been most illuminating. But try as I may, I have failed utterly to follow your reasoning in the death of Robin Ingleby.

"The boots, yes . . . perhaps. It's a possibility, I admit, but far from a certainty. Slender evidence when it comes to court. *If* the case is reopened, that is. But we shall require far more than a pair of child's boots if we are to prevail again upon their Lordships."

His tone was almost pleading. I had already decided that there were certain observations that would remain forever locked away in my brain:

choice nuggets of deduction that I would keep for my own private delectation. After all, the Inspector had far more resources at his disposal than I did.

But then I thought of his beautiful wife, Antigone. Whatever would she think of me if she found that I had thwarted him? One thing was certain: It would scotch any idea I might have had of sipping tea in the garden of their tastefully decorated maisonette.

"Very well," I said reluctantly. "There are a few more points. The first is this: When Dieter went running back to the farmyard, having just discovered Robin's dead body hanging in Gibbet Wood, the windows of the house were empty. No one was awaiting his arrival, as might have been expected. Surely the mother of a missing child would be frantic, waiting for the slightest scrap of news? But Grace Ingleby wasn't keeping watch at the windows. And why not? The reason is a simple one: She already knew that Robin was dead."

Somewhere behind me, the vicar gasped.

"I see." Inspector Hewitt nodded. "An ingenious theory . . . most ingenious. But still hardly enough to build a case upon."

"Granted," I agreed, "but there's more."

I looked from one of them to another: the vicar, Inspector Hewitt, and Sergeant Graves, their eager faces thrust forward, hanging upon my every word. Even the hulking Sergeant Woolmer slowed his polishing of the intricate lens.

"Robin Ingleby's hair was always a haystack," I told them. "'Tousled' is perhaps the proper word. You can see it in his photos. And yet when he was found hanging from the timbers of the old gallows, his hair was as neatly combed as if he'd just climbed down from the barber's chair. Meg captured it perfectly in her drawing. See?"

There was an intake of breath as everyone huddled over the page from my notebook.

"It was something that only a mother would do," I said. "She couldn't resist. Grace Ingleby wanted her son to be presentable when he was found, hanging by the neck, dead in Gibbet Wood."

"Good Lord!" Inspector Hewitt said.

twenty-nine

"GOOD LORD," FATHER EXCLAIMED. "THERE'S BROADCASTING House. They've set up cameras in Portland Place."

He got up from his chair for the umpteenth time and hurried across the drawing room to twiddle with the knobs on the television receiving set.

"Please be quiet, Haviland," Aunt Felicity said. "If they were interested in your commentary, the BBC would have sent for you."

Aunt Felicity, who had barely got home to Hampstead, had hurried back again to Buckshaw as soon as the idea came into her head. She had hired the television for the occasion ("at ruinous expense," she hastened to point out), and because of it, was now enjoying vastly increased dictatorial powers.

Early in the morning of the previous day, the workmen had begun erecting a receiving aerial on the ramparts of Buckshaw.

"It needs to be high enough to pick up the signal from the new transmitting tower at Sutton Coldfield," Aunt Felicity had said, in a voice that suggested television was her own invention. "I *had* wanted all of us to go up to London to attend the Porson obsequies," she went on, "but when Lady Burwash let slip that the Sitwells were having in the telly . . .

"No, no, don't protest, Haviland. It's educational. I'm only doing it for the good of the girls."

Several muscular workers, dressed in overalls, had lugged the set from the back of a pantechnicon and into the drawing room. There it now crouched, its single gray eye staring, like a flickering Cyclops, at those of us gathered in its baleful glow.

Daffy and Feely were huddled together on a chesterfield, feigning boredom. Father had invited the vicar and told them to watch their language.

Mrs. Mullet was enthroned in a comfortable wing-backed chair, and Dogger, who preferred not to sit in Father's presence, stood silently behind her.

"I wonder if they have televisions in Portland Place," Feely said, idly, "or whether they might, rather, be looking out their windows?"

I recognized this at once as an attempt to twit Father, whose contempt for television was legendary.

"Television is a bauble," he would reply, whenever we pleaded with him to have a receiver installed. "If God meant for pictures to be sent through the air, He'd have never given us the cinema.

"Or the National Gallery," he'd add sourly.

But in this case, he had been overruled.

"But it's History, Haviland," Aunt Felicity had said in a loud voice. "Would you have denied your daughters the opportunity to watch Henry the Fifth address his men on Crispin's Day?"

She had taken up a stance in the middle of the drawing room.

"This story shall the good man teach his son;
And Crispin Crispian shall ne'er go by,
From this day to the ending of the world,
But we in it shall be remembered;
We few, we happy few, we band of brothers—"

"Nonsense!" Father said, but Aunt Felicity, like Henry the Fifth, pushed on, undaunted:

"For he today that sheds his blood with me
Shall be my brother; be he ne'er so vile,
This day shall gentle his condition:
And gentlemen in England now abed
Shall think themselves accursed they were not here,

And hold their manhoods cheap whiles any speaks
That fought with us upon St. Crispin's day."

"That's all very well and good, but they didn't have television in 1415," Father had said rather sullenly, missing her point entirely.

But then, yesterday, something remarkable had happened. One of the mechanics, who had been in the drawing room with his eye intently upon the receiver, had begun calling instructions out the window to a companion on the lawn, who relayed them, in a drill-sergeant voice, to the man on the roof.

"Hold it, Harry! Back . . . back . . . back. No . . . you've lost it. Back t'other way . . ."

At that very moment, Father had walked into the room, planning, I think, to heap scorn upon the entire operation, when his eye was taken by something on the snow-blown screen.

"Stop!" he shouted, and his word was passed along in ever-diminishing echoes by the mechanics, out the window and up onto the ramparts.

"By George," he said. "It's the 1856 British Guiana. Back a little!" he shouted, waving his hands to illustrate.

Again his instructions were carried aloft in a verbal bucket brigade, and the picture cleared a little.

"Just as I thought," he said. "I'd know it anywhere. It's coming to auction. Turn up the sound."

As Fate would have it, the BBC was at that moment transmitting a program on the topic of stamp collecting, and a moment later, Father had pulled up a chair, fastened his wire-framed spectacles on the end of his nose, and refused to be budged.

"Quiet, Felicity!" he barked, when she tried to intervene. "This is of the utmost importance."

And so it was that Father had allowed the One-Eyed Beast to sit in his drawing room.

At least for the time being.

And now, as the hour drew near for Rupert's inhumation (a word I had heard Daffy trot out for Mrs. Mullet's benefit), Dogger drifted off to the foyer to admit the vicar who, even though he was not conducting the funeral, nevertheless felt the professional necessity of wringing the hands of each of us as he came into the room.

"Dear, dear," he said. "And to think that the poor chap expired right here in Bishop's Lacey."

No sooner had he taken a seat on the sofa than the doorbell sounded again, and a few moments later Dogger returned with an unexpected guest.

"Mr. Dieter Schrantz," he announced at the door, slipping effortlessly back into his role as butler.

Feely sprang to her feet, and came floating across the drawing room to greet Dieter, hands outstretched, palms down, as if she were walking in her sleep.

She was radiant, the vixen!

I was praying she'd trip on the rug.

"Draw the drapes, please, Dogger," Father said, and as Dogger complied, the light vanished from the room and left all of us sitting together in the gloom.

Into view on the little tube, as I have said, floated the wet pavement of Portland Place in front of Broadcasting House, as the hushed and solemn voice of the BBC announcer took up the tale (it may have been Richard Dimbleby, or perhaps it was just someone who sounded like him):

"And now, from every corner of the realm, come the children. They are brought here today by their mothers and fathers, their nurses, their governesses, and some few, I daresay, by their grandparents.

"They have been standing here in Portland Place for hours in the rain, young and old, each patiently waiting his or her turn to bid a last, sad farewell to the man who captivated their hearts; to pay their respects to Rupert Porson, the genius who kidnapped them every afternoon at four from their everyday lives and, like the Pied Piper, led them away into his Magic Kingdom. . . ."

Genius? Well, that was stretching things a bit. Rupert was a brilliant showman; there was no doubt about it. But genius? The man was a scoundrel, a womanizer, a bully, a brute.

But did that disqualify him from being a genius? I don't suppose it did. Brains and morals have nothing to do with one another. Take myself, for instance: I am often thought of as being remarkably bright, and yet my brains, more often than not, are busily devising new and interesting ways of bringing my enemies to sudden, gagging, writhing, agonizing death.

I am quite firm in my belief that poisons were put upon the earth in the first place to be discovered—and put to good use—by those of us with the wits, but not necessarily the physical strength, to . . .

The poison! I had completely forgotten about those doctored chocolates!

Had Feely actually eaten them? It seemed unlikely; if she had, she wouldn't be sitting here with such maddening calm as Dieter, like a horse breeder admiring his filly over a paddock fence, gazed appreciatively upon her better points.

The hydrogen sulfide I had injected into the sweets was not sufficient to kill, at any rate. Once inside the body—assuming that anyone was stupid enough to swallow it—it would oxidize to hydrogen sulfate, in which form it would be eliminated eventually in the urine.

Was it such a crime, this thing that I had done? Dimethyl sulfide was dumped by the boatload into artificially flavored sweets, and no one, to the best of my knowledge, had yet been hanged for it.

As my eyes became accustomed to the dimness of the drawing room, I was able to have a quick look round at the faces illuminated by the television's glow. Mrs. Mullet? No, Feely wouldn't have wasted her chocolates on Mrs. Mullet. Father and Dogger were out of the question, too, as was the vicar.

There was a remote possibility that Aunt Felicity had scarfed them, but if she had, her outraged trumpetings would have made even Sabu's elephant bolt for the hills.

Therefore, the chocolates must still be in Feely's room. If only I could slip away, unnoticed in the semi-darkness . . .

"Flavia," Father said, with a wave towards the little screen, "I know how difficult this must be for you, in particular. You may be excused, if you wish."

Salvation! Off to the poisoned chocolates!

But wait: If I slunk away now, what would Dieter think of me? As for the others, I didn't give a rap . . . well, perhaps a little for the vicar. But to be thought of as weak in the eyes of a man who had actually been shot down in flames . . .

"Thank you, Father," I said. "I think I shall manage to struggle through."

I knew it was the kind of stiff-upper-lippish response he wanted, and I was right. Having made the required parental noises, he sank back into his chair with something like a sigh.

A froggish sound went up from the depths of the chair in the corner, and I knew instantly that it was Daffy.

The television cameras were cutting away to the interior of Broad-casting House, to a large studio piled to the rafters with flowers, and there among them lay Rupert—or at least his coffin: an ornate piece of furniture that mirrored the television lights and the nearby mourners in its highly polished surface, its silver-plated handles positively glistening in the gloom.

Now another camera was showing a little girl as she approached the bier . . . hesitantly . . . tentatively—pushed forward in a series of thrusts by a self-conscious mother. The child wiped away a tear before placing a wreath of wildflowers at the rail in front of the coffin.

The scene was cut to a close-up of a full-grown woman, weeping.

Next, a man in funereal black stepped forward. He plucked three roses from the wall of floral tributes, and presented each one delicately: one to the child, one to the mother, and the third to the weeping woman. Having done so, he pulled forth a large white handkerchief, turned away from the camera, and blew his nose with grief-stricken energy.

It was Mutt Wilmott! He was stage-managing the whole thing! Just as he'd said he would! Mutt Wilmott: to the eyes of the world, a broken man.

Even at a time of national mourning, Mutt was on the spot to provide the memorable moments—the unforgettable images required by death. I almost jumped to my feet and applauded. I knew that the people who witnessed these simple devotions, either in person or on the television screen, would go on talking about them until they sat toothless on a wooden bench, in a cottage dooryard, waiting for their hearts to stop beating.

"Mutt Wilmott," the Dimbleby voice went on, "producer of Rupert Porson's The Magic Kingdom. We are told that he was devastated when news came of the puppeteer's death; that he was rushed to hospital for treatment of cardiac palpitations, but in spite of it—and against his doctor's orders—he insisted on being here today to pay tribute to his late colleague . . . although we are told on good authority that an ambulance is standing by at the ready, should it be needed. . . ."

The view from a camera we had not seen before was now cut in. Shooting from a high angle, as if from a rotunda, the view came down and down into the studio, as it might be seen through the eyes of a descending angel, getting closer and closer to the coffin until, at its very foot, it came to rest upon a remarkable figure that could have been none other than Snoddy the Squirrel.

Mounted on a wooden post perhaps, the hand puppet, with its little leather ears, protruding teeth, and question mark of a bushy tail, had been carefully arranged to gaze sadly down upon the coffin of its master, its squirrel paws crossed reverently, its squirrel head bent in an attitude of humble prayer.

There were often times—and this was one of them—when, as if in the sudden, blinding flash of a news photographer's camera—I saw it all. Death was no more than a simple masquerade—and so, moreover, was Life!—and both of them were artfully arranged by something or other: some backstage celestial Mutt Wilmott.

We were puppets, all of us, set in action upon the stage by God—or Fate—or Chemistry, call it what you will, where we would be pulled on like gloves upon the hands, and manipulated by the Rupert Porsons and Mutt Wilmotts of the world. Or the Ophelia and Daphne de Luces.

I wanted to let out a whoop!

How I wished that Nialla were here, so that I could share my discovery with her. After all, no one deserved it more. But by now, for all I knew, she was already steering the decrepit Austin van up the slopes of some Welsh mountain to some Welsh village, where, with the assistance of some hastily rustled-up, real-life Mother Goose, she would unpack her wooden crates and, later tonight, raise the curtain for the gawking villagers in some far-flung St. David's Hall, on her own personal vision of *Jack and the Beanstalk*.

With Rupert gone, which of us now was the Galligantus? I wondered. Which of us was now the monster that would come tumbling unexpectedly out of the skies and into the lives of others?

"*Heartfelt tributes continue to pour in from Land's End to John O'Groats,*" the announcer was saying, "*and from abroad.*" He paused and gave out a little sigh, as if he had been overwhelmed by the moment.

"*Here in London, and in spite of the downpour, the queue continues to grow, stretching as far as All Souls Church, and beyond into Langham Place. From above the door of Broadcasting House, the statues of Prospero and Ariel look down upon the hordes of mourners, watching, as if they too share in the common grief.*

"*Immediately following today's ceremonies at Broadcasting House,*" he went on bravely, "*Rupert Porson's coffin will be taken to Waterloo Station, and from there to its place of interment at Brookwood Cemetery, in Surrey.*"

By now, even Feely could see that we had had enough.

"Enough of this maudlin trash!" she announced, striding across the room and flipping off the switch. The picture on the television tube retracted to a tiny point of light—and vanished.

"Throw open the curtains, Daffy," she ordered, and Daffy sprang to her command. "This is so tiresome—all of it. Let's have some light for a change."

What she really wanted, of course, was to have a better squint at Dieter. Too vain to wear her spectacles, Feely had probably seen no more of Rupert's funeral than a dishwater blur. And isn't it pointless being admired at close range by an anxious swain if one is unable to see said swain's rapture?

I couldn't help but notice that Father seemed to have overlooked the way in which our first television viewing had been so abruptly terminated, and that he was already slipping away into his own private world.

Dogger and Mrs. Mullet went discreetly about their duties, leaving only Aunt Felicity to protest weakly.

"Really, Ophelia," she huffed, "you are most ungrateful. I wanted to have a closer look at the coffin handles. My charlady's son Arnold works as a set dresser at the BBC, and his services were especially requested. They gave him a guinea to ferret out some photogenic fittings."

"Sorry, Aunt Felicity," Feely said vaguely, "but funerals give me such awful gooseflesh—even on the television. I simply can't bear to watch them."

For a moment, a coolish silence hung in the air, indicating that Aunt Felicity was not so easily mollified.

"I know," Feely added brightly. "Let me offer everyone a chocolate."

And she went for an end-table drawer.

Visions of some Victorian hell flapped instantly into my mind: the caves, the flames, the burning pits, the lost souls queued up—much like those mourners outside Broadcasting House—all of them waiting to be flung by an avenging angel into the fire and molten brimstone.

Brimstone, after all, was sulfur (chemical symbol S), with whose dioxide I had stuffed the sweets. Bitten into, they would—well, that would hardly bear thinking about.

Feely was already walking towards the vicar, ripping the cellophane from the box of ancient chocolates Ned had left on the doorstep; the box with which I had so lovingly tampered.

"Vicar? Aunt Felicity?" she said, removing the lid and holding the box out at arm's length. "Have a chocolate. The almond nougats are particularly interesting."

I couldn't let this happen, but what was I to do? It was obvious that Feely had taken my earlier, blurted warning as no more than a stupid bluff.

Now the vicar was reaching for a sweet, his fingers, like the planchette on a Ouija board, hovering above the chocolates, as if some unseen spirit might direct him to the tastiest confection.

"I have dibs on the almond nougats!" I shouted. "You promised, Feely!"

I lunged forward and snatched the chocolate from the vicar's fingers, and at the same instant, contrived to stumble on the edge of the carpet, my flailing hands dashing the box from Feely's hands.

"You beast!" Feely shouted. "You filthy little beast!"

It was just like old times!

Before she could recover her wits, I had trodden on the box, and in a clumsy, windmilling—but beautifully choreographed—attempt to regain my balance, had managed to grind the whole sticky mess into the Axminster carpet.

Dieter, I noticed, had a broad grin on his face, as if it were all jolly good fun. Feely saw it, too, and I could tell that she was torn between her duchess act and swatting my face.

Meanwhile, the hydrogen sulfide fumes, which my trampling of the chocolates had released, had begun their deadly work. The room was suddenly filled with the smell of rotten eggs—and what a stench! It smelled as if a sick brontosaurus had broken wind, and I remember wondering for an instant if the drawing room would ever be the same.

All of this happened in less time than it takes to tell, and my rapid-fire reflections were broken into by the sound of Father's voice.

"Flavia," he said, in that low, flat tone he uses to express fury, "go to your room. At once." His finger trembled as he pointed.

There was no point in arguing. With shoulders hunched, as if walking in deep snow, I trudged towards the door.

Other than Father, everyone in the room was pretending that nothing had happened. Dieter was fiddling with his collar, Feely was rearranging her skirt as she perched beside him on the sofa, and Daffy was already reaching for a dog-eared copy of *King Solomon's Mines*. Even Aunt Felicity was glaring fiercely at a loose thread on the sleeve of her tweed jacket, and the vicar, who had drifted across to the French doors, stood gazing out with pretended interest in the ornamental lake and the folly beyond.

Halfway across the room, I stopped and retraced my steps. I had almost forgotten something. Digging into my pocket, I pulled out the envelope of extra-perforated stamps Miss Cool had given me, and handed it to Father.

"These are for you. I hope you like them," I said. Without looking at it, Father took the envelope from my hand, his quivering finger still point-ing. I slunk across the room.

I paused at the door . . . and turned.

"If anyone wants me," I said, "I shall be upstairs, weeping at the bottom of my closet."

acknowledgments

What better place for a confession than at the end of a mystery novel? According to the great Eric Partridge, the words knowledge and acknowledgment come from the Middle English verb knawlechen, which means not only knowledge, but also confession or admission. So I'd better admit straightaway that I'm working with the assistance of a goodly number of partners in crime.

First and foremost among these conspirators are my editors: Bill Massey of Orion Books; Kate Miciak of the Random House Publishing Group; and Kristin Cochrane of Doubleday Canada. For their unwavering faith in Flavia from the very outset, I am forever in their debt. Bill, Kate, and Kristin have become family.

Again, my dear friends Dr. John and Janet Harland have contributed beyond measure. From brilliant ideas to animated discussions over happy meals, they have never failed to be the best of patient friends.

At Orion Books, in London, Natalie Braine, Helen Richardson, and Juliet Ewers are always marvels of friendly efficiency.

My literary agent, Denise Bukowski, has worked diligently to tell the world about Flavia. Also at the Bukowski Agency, Jericho Buendia, David Whiteside, and Susan Morris have freed me from worrying about the thousands of tiny details.

My deep indebtedness to Nicole, of Apple, whose magic wand turned what might have been a tragedy into a perfect triumph of online support. Thanks again, Nicole!

At Random House, in New York City, Kate Miciak, Nita Taublib, Loyale Coles, Randall Klein, Gina Wachtel, Theresa Zoro, Gina Centrello, and Alison Masciovecchio provided a touching welcome that I will never forget. And having Susan Corcoran as one's publicist is every author's dream. And thanks to my copy editor, Connie Munro.

Thanks also to the American Booksellers Association for inviting me to their Indie Lunch at Book Expo America. Happily, I found myself seated at a table with Stanley Hadsell, of Market Block Books in Troy, New York, who epitomizes independent bookselling. We could have talked all night.

To Ann Kingman and Michael Kindness of "Books on the Nightstand," for their early and abiding faith. When I ran into Michael unexpectedly at BEA, I found out that in spite of living in the smallest town in the smallest county in the smallest state, he's one of Flavia's biggest fans.

In Houston, David Thompson and McKenna Jordan, Brenda Jordan, Michelle McNamara, and Kathryn Priest of Murder By the Book, made me understand instantly why so many people love Texas so much. Now I do, too.

Sarah Borders and Jennifer Schwartz of the Houston Public Library did double duty in arranging a question-and-answer session.

Special thanks to Jonathan Topper of Topper Stamps and Postal History in Houston, who took the time to spice up the evening with a fascinating display of Penny Blacks.

And to John Demers of Delicious Mischief, who managed to turn a steeplechase interview into a sheer delight.

Also in Houston, Random House representatives Liz Sullivan and Gianna LaMorte made me feel at home.

To that legend among booksellers, Barbara Peters of The Poisoned Pen in Scottsdale, Arizona, my profound thanks for being the perfect hostess. Although she's younger than I am, Barbara is nevertheless my long-lost twin.

Patrick Milliken, John Goodwin, and Will Hanisko, also of The Poisoned Pen, kindly allowed me a peek behind the scenes of a busy bookstore and plied me with refreshments.

Thanks, too, to Lesa Holstine and Cathy Johnson, for a very special evening during which we talked happily about everything under the sun.

Kim Garza at the Tempe Public Library put together a delightful afternoon of animated discussion. I still carry in my mind the image of all those happy faces. Thank you, Tempe!

In Westminster, Maryland, Lori Zook, Cheryl Kelly, Judy Pohlhaus, Camille Marchi, Ginny Mortorff, Wanda Rawlings, Pam Kaufman, Stacey Carlini, Sherry Drechsler plied me with soft drinks, cakes, and JuJubes (which, when we got around to recalling candy treats of long-gone movie matinees, they also taught me to pronounce correctly: It's "JOO-joo-bays," not "JOO-joobs").

Meanwhile, at Doubleday Canada, my publicist Sharon Klein has been a perfect dynamo. I must also admit that I'm in awe of Doubleday Canada's team, including Martha Leonard, as well as Heather Sanderson and Sharmila Mohammed of the Digital Team, who have brought the Flavia Fan Club to life and provided a cosy haven for visitors. And I'd be remiss indeed if I failed to extend special thanks to Brad Martin, President and CEO of Random House of Canada, who has championed Flavia from her very beginnings.

In spite of the worst blizzard of the year, Bryce Zorn and Curtis Weston of Chapters in Kelowna, British Columbia, managed a full house for the Canadian launch of the first book in this series, *The Sweetness at the Bottom of the Pie*. Thanks also to Paul Hasselback, who saw me safely home through black ice and all the windblown drifts.

Trish Kells of Random House Canada, who arranged a memorable book event in Vancouver, also acted as chauffeur and laughed at my jokes in spite of the rain.

Deb McVitie of 32 Books in North Vancouver was the charming sponsor of my first away-from-home reading and book signing. My co-readers, Hannah Holborn and Andrea Gunraj, helped to make it an unforgettable evening. If Hannah and Andrea are indicative of our up-and-coming young writers, we have no need whatsoever to worry about the future.

And finally, to my wife, Shirley, whose love, company, and patient support have allowed me the luxury of writing. Amadeus and Cleo have helped a lot, too.

A Red Herring
Without Mustard

For John and Janet Harland

. . . a cup of ale without a wench, why, alas,
'tis like an egg without salt or a red herring
without mustard.
—THOMAS LODGE AND ROBERT GREENE,
A Looking Glasse, for London and Englande (*1592*)

one

"YOU FRIGHTEN ME," THE GYPSY SAID. "NEVER HAVE I SEEN my crystal ball so filled with darkness."

She cupped her hands around the thing, as if to shield my eyes from the horrors that were swimming in its murky depths. As her fingers gripped the glass, I thought I could feel ice water trickling down inside my gullet.

At the edge of the table, a thin candle flickered, its sickly light glancing off the dangling brass hoops of the Gypsy's earrings, then flying off to die somewhere in the darkened corners of the tent.

Black hair, black eyes, black dress, red-painted cheeks, red mouth, and a voice that could only have come from smoking half a million cigarettes.

As if to confirm my suspicions, the old woman was suddenly gripped by a fit of violent coughing that rattled her crooked frame and left her gasping horribly for air. It sounded as though a large bird had somehow become entangled in her lungs and was flapping to escape.

"Are you all right?" I asked. "I'll go for help."

I thought I had seen Dr. Darby in the churchyard not ten minutes earlier, pausing to have a word or two at each stall of the church fête. But before I could make a move, the Gypsy's dusky hand had covered mine on the black velvet of the tabletop.

"No," she said. "No . . . don't do that. It happens all the time."

And she began to cough again.

I waited it out patiently, almost afraid to move.

"How old are you?" she said at last. "Ten? Twelve?"

"Eleven," I said, and she nodded her head wearily as though she'd known it all along.

"I see—a mountain," she went on, almost strangling on the words, "and the face—of the woman you will become."

In spite of the stifling heat of the darkened tent, my blood ran cold. She was seeing Harriet, of course!

Harriet was my mother, who had died in a climbing accident when I was a baby.

The Gypsy turned my hand over and dug her thumb painfully into the very center of my palm. My fingers spread—and then curled in upon themselves like the toes of a chicken's severed foot.

She took up my left hand. "This is the hand you were born with," she said, barely glancing at the palm, then letting it fall and picking up the other. " . . . and this is the hand you've grown."

She stared at it distastefully as the candle flickered. "This broken star on your Mount of Luna shows a brilliant mind turned in upon itself—a mind that wanders the roads of darkness."

This was not what I wanted to hear.

"Tell me about the woman you saw on the mountain," I said. "The one I shall become."

She coughed again, clutching her colored shawl tightly about her shoulders, as though wrapping herself against some ancient and invisible winter wind.

"Cross my palm with silver," she demanded, sticking out a grubby hand.

"But I gave you a shilling," I said. "That's what it says on the board outside."

"Messages from the Third Circle cost extra," she wheezed. "They drain the batteries of my soul."

I almost laughed out loud. Who did this old hag think she was? But still, she seemed to have spotted Harriet beyond the veil, and I couldn't let skepticism spoil even half a chance of having a few words with my dead mother.

I dug for my last shilling, and as I pressed the coin into her hand, the Gypsy's dark eyes, suddenly as bright as a jackdaw's, met mine.

"She is trying to come home," she said. "This . . . woman . . . is trying to come home from the cold. She wants you to help her."

I leapt to my feet, bashing the bottom of the table with my bare knees. It teetered, then toppled to one side as the candle slid off and fell among a tangle of dusty black hangings.

At first there was a little wisp of black smoke as the flame turned blue, then red, then quickly orange. I looked on in horror as it spread along the drapery.

In less time than it takes to tell, the entire tent was in flames.

I wish I'd had the presence of mind to throw a wet cloth over the Gypsy's eyes and lead her to safety, but instead I bolted—straight through the circle of fire that was the entranceway—and I didn't stop until I reached the coconut pitch, where I stood panting behind a canvas drape, trying to catch my breath.

Someone had brought a wind-up gramophone to the churchyard, from which the voice of Danny Kaye was issuing, made nauseously tinny by the throat of the machine's painted horn:

"Oh I've got a lov-ely bunch of coconuts.
There they are a-standin' in a row . . . "

I looked back at the Gypsy's tent just in time to see Mr. Haskins, St. Tancred's sexton, and another man whom I didn't recognize heave a tub of water, apples and all, onto the flames.

Half the villagers of Bishop's Lacey, or so it seemed, stood gaping at the rising column of black smoke, hands over mouths or fingertips to cheeks, and not a single one of them knowing what to do.

Dr. Darby was already leading the Gypsy slowly away towards the St. John's Ambulance tent, her ancient frame wracked with coughing. How small she seemed in the sunlight, I thought, and how pale.

"Oh, there you are, you odious little prawn. We've been looking for you everywhere."

It was Ophelia, the older of my two sisters. Feely was seventeen, and ranked herself right up there with the Blessed Virgin Mary, although the chief difference between them, I'm willing to bet, is that the BVM doesn't spend twenty-three hours a day peering at herself in a looking glass while picking away at her face with a pair of tweezers.

With Feely, it was always best to employ the rapid retort: "How dare you call me a prawn, you stupid sausage? Father's told you more than once it's disrespectful."

Feely made a snatch at my ear, but I sidestepped her easily. By sheer necessity, the lightning dodge had become one of my specialties.

"Where's Daffy?" I asked, hoping to divert her venomous attention.

Daffy was my other sister, two years older than me, and at thirteen already an accomplished co-torturer.

"Drooling over the books. Where else?" She pointed with her chin to a horseshoe of trestle tables on the churchyard grass, upon which the St. Tancred's Altar Guild and the Women's Institute had joined forces to set up a jumble sale of secondhand books and assorted household rubbish.

Feely had seemed not to notice the smoking remnants of the Gypsy's tent. As always, she had left her spectacles at home out of vanity, but her inattentiveness might simply have been lack of interest. For all practical purposes, Feely's enthusiasms stopped where her skin ended.

"Look at these," she said, holding a set of black earrings up to her ears. She couldn't resist showing off. "French jet. They came from Lady Trotter's estate. Glenda says they were quite fortunate to get a tanner for them."

"Glenda's right," I said. "French jet is nothing but glass."

It was true: I had recently melted down a ghastly Victorian brooch in my chemical laboratory, and found it to be completely silicaceous. It was unlikely that Feely would ever miss the thing.

"English jet is so much more interesting," I said. "It's formed from the fossilized remains of monkey-puzzle trees, you see, and—"

But Feely was already walking away, lured by the sight of Ned Cropper, the ginger-haired potboy at the Thirteen Drakes who, with a certain muscular grace, was energetically tossing wooden batons at the Aunt Sally. His third stick broke the wooden figure's clay pipe clean in two, and Feely pulled up at his side just in time to be handed the teddy bear prize by the madly blushing Ned.

"Anything worth saving from the bonfire?" I asked Daffy, who had her nose firmly stuck in what, judging by its spotty oxidized pages, might have been a first edition of *Pride and Prejudice*.

It seemed unlikely, though. Whole libraries had been turned in for salvage during the war, and nowadays there wasn't much left for the jumble sales. Whatever books remained unsold at the end of the summer season would, on Guy Fawkes Night, be carted from the basement of the parish hall, heaped up on the village green, and put to the torch.

I tipped my head sideways and took a quick squint at the stack of books

Daffy had already set aside: *On Sledge and Horseback to Outcast Siberian Lepers*, Pliny's *Natural History*, *The Martyrdom of Man*, and the first two volumes of the *Memoirs of Jacques Casanova*—the most awful piffle. Except perhaps for Pliny, who had written some ripping stuff about poisons.

I walked slowly along the table, running a finger across the books, all of them arranged with their spines upwards: Ethel M. Dell, E. M. Delafield, Warwick Deeping . . .

I had noticed on another occasion that most of the great poisoners in history had names beginning with the letter C, and now here were all of these authors beginning with a D. Was I on to something? Some secret of the universe?

I squeezed my eyes shut and concentrated: Dickens . . . Doyle . . . Dumas . . . Dostoyevsky—I had seen all of them, at one time or another, clutched in Daffy's hands.

Daffy herself was planning to become a novelist when she was older. With a name like Daphne de Luce, she couldn't fail if she tried!

"Daff!" I said. "You'll never guess—"

"Quiet!" she snapped. "I've told you not to speak to me when I'm reading."

My sister could be a most unpleasant porpoise when she felt like it.

It had not always been this way. When I was younger, for instance, and Father had recruited Daffy to hear my bedtime prayers, she had taught me to recite them in Pig Latin, and we had rolled among the down-filled pillows, laughing until we nearly split.

"Od-gay ess-blay Ather-fay, Eely-fay, and Issis-may Ullet-may. And Ogger-day, oo-tay!"

But over the years, something had changed between my sisters and me.

A little hurt, I reached for a volume that lay on top of the others: *A Looking Glasse, for London and Englande*. It was a book, I thought, that would appeal to Feely, since she was mad about mirrors. Perhaps I would purchase it myself, and store it away against the unlikely day when I might feel like giving her a gift, or a peace offering. Stranger things had happened.

Riffling through its pages, I saw at once that it was not a novel, but a play—full of characters' names and what each of them said. Someone named Adam was talking to a clown:

" . . . *a cup of ale without a wench, why, alas, 'tis like an egg without salt or a red herring without mustard."*

What a perfect motto for a certain someone, I thought, glancing across to where Ned was now grazing away at my sister's neck as she pretended not to notice. On more than one occasion I'd seen Ned sitting at his chores in the courtyard of the Thirteen Drakes with a tankard of ale— and sometimes Mary Stoker, the landlord's daughter—at his elbow. I realized with an unexpected shock that without either ale or a female within easy reach, Ned was somehow incomplete. Why hadn't I noticed that before? Perhaps, like Dr. Watson on the wireless in *A Scandal in Bohemia*, there are times that I see, but do not observe. This was something I needed to think about.

"Your handiwork, I suppose?" Daffy said suddenly, putting down a book and picking up another. She gestured towards the small knot of villagers who stood gawking at the smoking ruins of the Gypsy's tent. "It has Flavia de Luce written all over it."

"Sucks to you," I said. "I was going to help carry your stupid books home, but now you can jolly well lug them yourself."

"Oh, do stop it!" she said, clutching at my sleeve. "Please desist. My heartstrings are playing Mozart's *Requiem*, and a fugitive tear is making its way to my right eye, even as we speak."

I wandered away with a careless whistle. I'd deal with her insolence later.

"Ow! Leave off, Brookie! You're 'urtin' me."

The whining voice was coming from somewhere behind the shove ha'penny booth and, when I recognized it as belonging to Colin Prout, I stopped to listen.

By flattening myself against the stone wall of the church and keeping well back behind the canvas that draped the raffle booth, I could eavesdrop in safety. Even better, I was pleased to find that I had an unexpectedly clear view of Colin through the gaps in the booth's raw lumber.

He was dancing at the end of Brookie Harewood's arm like a great spectacled fish, his thick eyeglasses knocked askew, his dirty blond hair a hayrick, his large, damp mouth hanging open, gasping for air.

"Leave off. I didn't do nothin'."

With his other hand, Brookie took hold of the seat of Colin's baggy trousers and swiveled him round to face the smoking remains of the Gypsy's tent.

"Who did that, then, eh?" he demanded, shaking the boy to accentuate his words. "Where there's smoke, there's fire. Where there's fire, there's matches. And where there's matches, there's Colin Prout."

"'Ere," Colin said, trying to ram a hand into his pocket. "Count 'em! You just count 'em, Brookie. Same number as I had yesterday. Three. I ain't used a one."

As Brookie released his grip, Colin fell to the ground, rolled over on his elbows, dug into his trouser pocket, and produced a box of wooden matches, which he waved at his tormentor.

Brookie raised his head and sniffed the air, as if for guidance. His greasy cap and India rubber boots, his long moleskin coat and, in spite of the hot summer weather, a woolen scarf that clung like a scarlet serpent to his bulldog neck made him look like a rat catcher out of Dickens.

Before I could even wonder what to do, Colin had scrambled to his feet, and the two of them had ambled away across the churchyard, Colin dusting himself off and shrugging elaborately, as though he didn't care.

I suppose I should have stepped out from behind the booth, admitted I was responsible for the fire, and demanded that Brookie release the boy. If he refused, I could easily have run for the vicar, or called for any one of the other able-bodied men who were within earshot. But I didn't. And the simple reason, I realized with a little chill, was this: I was afraid of Brookie Harewood.

Brookie was Bishop's Lacey's riffraff.

"Brookie Harewood?" Feely had sniffed, the day Mrs. Mullet suggested that Brookie be hired to help Dogger with weeding the garden and trimming the hedges at Buckshaw. "But he's a remittance man, isn't he? Our lives wouldn't be worth tuppence with him hanging about the place."

"What's a remittance man?" I asked when Feely had flounced from the kitchen.

"I don't know, luv, I'm sure," Mrs. M had replied. "His mother's that lady as paints over in Malden Fenwick."

"Paints?" I had asked. "Houses?"

"Houses? Bless you! No, it's pitchers she paints. The gentry on 'orseback and that. P'raps she'll even paint you someday in your turn. You and Miss Ophelia and Miss Daphne."

At which I had let out a snort and dashed from the room. If I were to be painted in oils, shellacked, and framed, I would be posed in my chemical laboratory and nowhere else.

Hemmed in by beakers, bell jars, and Erlenmeyer flasks, I would be glancing up impatiently from my microscope in much the same way as my late great-uncle Tarquin de Luce is doing in his portrait, which still hangs in the picture gallery at Buckshaw. Like Uncle Tar, I would be visibly annoyed. No horses and gentry for me, thank you very much.

A light pall of smoke still hung over the churchyard. Now that most of the onlookers had wandered off, the charred and smoldering remains of the Gypsy's tent were clearly visible beside the path. But it wasn't so much the scorched circle in the grass that interested me as what had been hidden behind it: a brightly painted Gypsy caravan.

It was butter yellow with crimson shutters, and its lath-work sides, which sloped gently outwards beneath a rounded roof, gave it the look of a loaf of bread that has puffed out beyond the rim of the baking pan. From its spindly yellow wheels to its crooked tin chimney, and from its arched cathedral windows to the intricately carved wooden brackets on each side of the door, it was something that might have come rumbling out of a dream. As if to perfect the scene, an ancient, swaybacked horse was grazing in a picturesque manner among the leaning gravestones at the far corner of the churchyard.

It was a Romany cob. I recognized it at once from photographs I had seen in *Country Life*. With its feathered feet and tail, and a long mane that overhung its face (from beneath which it peered coyly out like Veronica Lake), the cob looked like a cross between a Clydesdale and a unicorn.

"Flavia, dear," said a voice behind me. It was Denwyn Richardson, the vicar of St. Tancred's. "Dr. Darby would be most obliged if you'd run in and fetch a fresh pitcher of lemonade from the ladies in the kitchen."

My ruffled glance must have made him feel guilty. Why is it that eleven-year-old girls are always treated as servants?

"I'd go for it myself, you see, but the good doctor feels that the poor lady may well be put off by my clerical collar and so forth and, well . . . "

"Happy to, Vicar," I said cheerily, and I meant it. Being the Lemonade Bearer would give me access to the St. John's Ambulance tent.

Before you could say "snap!" I had loped into the parish hall kitchen ("Excuse me. Medical emergency!"), made off with a frosty jug of iced lemonade, and was now in the dim light of the first-aid tent, pouring the stuff into a cracked tumbler.

"I hope you're all right," I said, handing it to the Gypsy. "Sorry about the tent. I'll pay for it, of course."

"Mmmm," Dr. Darby said. "No need. She's already explained that it was an accident."

The woman's awful red-rimmed eyes watched me warily as she drank.

"Dr. Darby," the vicar said, sticking his head through the flaps of the tent like a turtle, so that his dog collar wouldn't show, "if you can spare a moment . . . it's Mrs. Peasley at the skittles pitch. She's come all over queer, she says."

"Mmmm," the doctor said, snapping shut his black bag. "What you need, my old gal," he said to the Gypsy, "is a good rest." And to me: "Stay with her. I shan't be long.

"Never rains," he remarked to no one in particular on his way out.

For the longest time I stood awkwardly staring at my feet, trying to think of something to say. I dared not look the Gypsy in the eye.

"I'll pay for the tent," I repeated. "Even though it *was* an accident."

That set her off coughing again and it was evident, even to me, that the fire had taken its toll on her already shaky lungs. I waited, helpless, for the gasping to subside.

When at last it did, there was another long, unnerving silence.

"The woman," the Gypsy said at last. "The woman on the mountain. Who was she?"

"She was my mother." I said. "Her name was Harriet de Luce."

"The mountain?"

"Somewhere in Tibet, I think. She died there ten years ago. We don't often speak of it at Buckshaw."

"Buckshaw means nothing to me."

"It's where I live. South of the village," I said with a vague wave of my hand.

"Ah!" she said, fixing me with a piercing look. "The big house. Two wings folded back."

"Yes, that's it," I said. "Not far from where the river loops round."

"Yes," the woman said. "I've stopped there. Never knew what the place was called."

Stopped there? I could hardly believe it.

"The lady let my *rom* and me camp in a grove by the river. He needed to rest—"

"I know the spot!" I said. "It's called the Palings. All elder bushes and—"

"Berries," she added.

"But wait!" I said. "The lady? There's been no lady at Buckshaw since Harriet died."

The Gypsy went on as though I'd said nothing.

"A beautiful lady she was, too. Bit like you," she added, peering at me closely, "now that I see you in the light."

But then her face darkened. Was it my imagination, or was her voice growing stronger as she spoke.

"Then we got turned out," she said angrily. "They said we wasn't wanted there no more. 'Twas the summer Johnny Faa died."

"Johnny Faa?"

"My *rom*. My husband. Died in the middle of a dusty road, clutching at his chest, like, and cursing the *Gajo*—the Englishman—that had turned us out."

"And who was that?" I asked, already fearing the answer.

"Never asked his name. Straight as a ramrod on two sticks, the devil!"

Father! I was sure of it! It was Father who, after Harriet's death, had run the Gypsies off his estate.

"And Johnny Faa, your husband . . . he died because of it, you say?"

The Gypsy nodded, and I could see by the sadness in her eyes that it was true.

"Because he needed to rest?"

"Needed to rest," she repeated in a whisper, "and so do I."

And that was when it came to me. Before I could change my mind I had blurted out the words.

"You can come back to Buckshaw. Stay as long as you like. It will be all right . . . I promise."

Even as I said it I knew that there would be a great flaming row with Father, but somehow that didn't matter. Harriet had once given these people refuge and my blood would hardly allow me to do otherwise.

"We'll park your caravan at the Palings," I said, "in the bushes. No one even needs to know you're there."

Her black eyes scanned my face, darting quickly from side to side. I held out my hand to her for encouragement.

"Mmmm. Go on, old girl. Take her up on it. Spot of rest would do you a world of good."

It was Dr. Darby, who had slipped quietly back into the tent. He shot me an eighth of a wink. The doctor was one of Father's oldest friends, and I knew that he, too, could already foresee the coming battle. He had viewed the field and weighed the risks even before he spoke. I wanted to hug him.

He placed his black bag on the table, rummaged in its depths, and extracted a corked bottle.

"Take as required for cough," he said, handing it to the Gypsy. She stared at it dubiously.

"Go on," he urged, "take it. It's wicked bad luck to refuse a licensed practitioner, you know.

"I'll help with the horse," he volunteered. "Used to have one meself."

Now he was putting on the old country doctor routine and I knew that, medically speaking, we were in the clear.

Knots of people stared as the doctor shepherded us towards the caravan. In no time at all he had the Gypsy's horse in harness and the two of us settled on the wooden ledge that served as both doorstep and driving seat.

The old woman made a clucking noise and the villagers gave way on both sides as the caravan jerked into motion and began to rumble slowly along the churchyard path. From my high vantage point I looked down into the many upturned faces, but Feely's and Daffy's were not among them.

Good, I thought. They were most likely in one of the stalls stuffing their stupid faces with scones and clotted cream.

two

WE LUMBERED THROUGH THE HIGH STREET, THE SOUND OF the horse's hooves echoing loudly on the cobbles.

"What's his name?" I asked, pointing at the ancient animal.

"Gry."

"Gray?"

"Gry. 'Horse' in the Romany tongue."

I tucked that odd bit of knowledge away for future use, looking forward to the time when I would be able to trot it out in front of my know-it-all sister, Daffy. Of course she would pretend that she knew it all along.

It must have been the loud clatter of our passage that brought Miss Cool, the village postmistress, scurrying to the front of her confectionery shop. When she spotted me seated beside the Gypsy, her eyes widened and her hand flew to her mouth. In spite of the heavy plate-glass windows of the shop and the street between us, I could almost hear her gasp. The sight of Colonel Haviland de Luce's youngest daughter being carried off in a Gypsy caravan, no matter how gaily it was painted, must have been a terrible shock.

I waved my hand like a frantic dust mop, fingers spread ludicrously wide apart as if to say "What jolly fun!" What I wanted to do, actually, was to leap to my feet, strike a pose, and burst into one of those "Yo-ho for the open road!" songs they always play in the cinema musicals, but

I stifled the urge and settled for a ghastly grin and an extra twiddle of the fingers.

News of my abduction would soon be flying everywhere, like a bird loose in a cathedral. Villages were like that, and Bishop's Lacey was no exception.

"We all lives in the same shoe," Mrs. Mullet was fond of saying, "just like Old Mother 'Ubbard."

A harsh cough brought me back to reality. The Gypsy woman was now bent over double, hugging her ribs. I took the reins from her hands.

"Did you take the medicine the doctor gave you?" I asked.

She shook her head from side to side, and her eyes were like two red coals. The sooner I could get this wagon to the Palings, and the woman tucked into her own bed, the better it would be.

Now we were passing the Thirteen Drakes and Cow Lane. A little farther east, the road turned south towards Doddingsley. We were still a long way from Buckshaw and the Palings.

Just beyond the last row of cottages, a narrow lane known to locals as the Gully angled off to the right, a sunken stony cutting that skirted the west slope of Goodger Hill and cut more or less directly cross country to the southeast corner of Buckshaw and the Palings. Almost without thinking, I hauled on the reins and turned Gry's head towards the narrow lane.

After a relatively smooth first quarter mile, the caravan was now lurching alarmingly. As we went on, bumping over sharp stones, the track became more narrow and rutted. High banks pressed in on either side, so steeply mounded with tangled outcroppings of ancient tree roots that the caravan, no matter how much it teetered, could not possibly have overturned.

Just ahead, like the neck of a great green swan, the mossy branch of an ancient beech tree bent down in a huge arc across the road. There was scarcely enough space to pass beneath it.

"Robber's Roost," I volunteered. "It's where the highwaymen used to hold up the mail coaches."

There was no response from the Gypsy: She seemed uninterested. To me, Robber's Roost was a fascinating bit of local lore.

In the eighteenth century, the Gully had been the only road between Doddingsley and Bishop's Lacey. Choked with snow in the winter, flooded by icy runoffs in spring and fall, it had gained the reputation, which it still maintained after two hundred years, of being rather an unsavory, if not downright dangerous, place to hang about.

"Haunted by history," Daffy had once told me as she was inking it onto a map she was drawing of "Buckshaw & Environs."

With that sort of recommendation, the Gully should have been one of my favorite spots in all of Bishop's Lacey, but it was not. Only once had I ventured nearly its whole length on Gladys, my trusty bicycle, before a peculiar and unsettling feeling at the nape of my neck had made me turn back. It had been a dark day of high, gusty winds, cold showers, and low scudding clouds, the kind of day . . .

The Gypsy snatched the reins from my hands, gave them a sharp tug. "Hatch!" she said gruffly, and pulled the horse up short.

High on the mossy branch a child was perched, its thumb jammed firmly into its mouth.

I could tell by its red hair it was one of the Bulls.

The Gypsy woman made the sign of the cross and muttered something that sounded like "Hilda Muir."

"Ja!" she added, flicking the reins, "Ja!" and Gry jerked the caravan back into motion. As we moved slowly under the branch, the child let down its legs and began pounding with its heels on the caravan's roof, creating a horrid hollow drumming noise behind us.

If I'd obeyed my instincts, I'd have climbed up and at the very least given the brat a jolly good tongue-lashing. But one look at the Gypsy taught me that there were times to say nothing.

Rough brambles snatched at the caravan as it jolted and lurched from side to side in the lane, but the Gypsy seemed not to notice.

She was hunched over the reins, her watery eyes fixed firmly on some far-off horizon, as if only her shell were in this century, the rest of her escaped to a place far away in some dim and misty land.

The track broadened a little and a moment later we were moving slowly past a decrepit picket fence. Behind the fence were a tumbledown house that seemed to be hammered together from cast-off doors and battered shutters, and a sandy garden littered with trash which included a derelict cooker, a deep old-fashioned pram with two of its wheels missing, a number of fossilized motorcars, and, strewn everywhere, hordes of empty tins. Clustered here and there around the property stood sagging outbuildings—little more than makeshift lean-tos thrown together with rotten, mossy boards and a handful of nails.

Over it all, arising from a number of smoking rubbish heaps, hung a pall of gray acrid smoke which made the place seem like some hellish inferno from the plates of a Victorian illustrated Bible. Sitting in a washtub in the middle of the muddy yard was a small child, which jerked its thumb from its mouth the instant it saw us and broke into a loud and prolonged wailing.

Everything seemed to be coated with rust. Even the child's red hair added to the impression that we had strayed into a strange, decaying land where oxidation was king.

Oxidation, I never tire of reminding myself, is what happens when oxygen attacks. It was nibbling away at my own skin at this very moment and at the skin of the Gypsy seated beside me, although it was easy to see that she was much further gone than I was.

From my own early chemical experiments in the laboratory at Buckshaw, I had verified that in some cases, such as when iron is combusted in an atmosphere of pure oxygen, oxidation is a wolf that tears hungrily at its food: so hungrily, in fact, that the iron bursts into flames. What we call fire is really no more than our old friend oxidation working at fever pitch.

But when oxidation nibbles more slowly—more delicately, like a tortoise—at the world around us, without a flame, we call it rust and we sometimes scarcely notice as it goes about its business consuming everything from hairpins to whole civilizations. I have sometimes thought that if we could stop oxidation we could stop time, and perhaps be able to—

My pleasant thoughts were interrupted by an ear-piercing shriek.

"Gypsy! Gypsy!"

A large, redheaded woman in a sweat-stained cotton housedress came windmilling out of the house and across the yard towards us. The sleeves of her cardigan were rolled up above her rawboned elbows as if for battle.

"Gypsy! Gypsy! Clear off!" she shouted, her face as red as her hair. "Tom, get out here! That Gypsy's at the gate!"

Everyone in Bishop's Lacey knew perfectly well that Tom Bull had cleared off ages ago and that he would not likely be back. The woman was bluffing.

"'Twas you as stole my baby, and don't tell me you didn't. I seen you hangin' round here that day and I'll stand up in any court o' law and say so!"

The disappearance of the Bulls' baby girl several years earlier had been a seven-day wonder, but the unsolved case had gradually crept to the back pages of the newspapers, then faded from memory.

I glanced at the Gypsy to see how she was bearing up under the ravings of her howling accuser. She sat motionless on the driving ledge, staring straight ahead, numb to the world. It was a response that seemed to spur the other woman to an even greater frenzy.

"Tom, get yourself out here . . . and bring the ax!" the woman screeched.

Until then, she had seemed hardly to notice me, but now my gaze had become suddenly entangled with hers, and the effect was dramatic.

"I know you!" she shouted. "You're one of them de Luce girls from over at Buckshaw, ain't you? I'd rec'nize them cold blue eyes anywhere."

Cold blue eyes? Now, here was something worth thinking about. Although I had often been frozen in my tracks by Father's icy stare, I had never for an instant thought of possessing such a deadly weapon myself.

I realized, of course, that we were in a dangerous situation, the sort of predicament that can turn nasty in a flash. It was obvious that the Gypsy woman was beyond counting upon. For all practical purposes I was on my own.

"I'm afraid you're mistaken," I said, lifting my chin and narrowing my eyes to achieve the greatest effect. "My name is Margaret Vole, and this is my great-aunt Gilda Dickinson. Perhaps you've seen her in the cinema? *The Scarlet Cottage? Queen of the Moon?* But of course, how foolish of me: You wouldn't recognize her in this Gypsy costume, would you? Or in her heavy makeup? I'm sorry, I'm afraid I didn't catch your name, Miss . . . "

"B-Bull," the woman stammered, slightly taken aback. "*Mrs.* Bull."

She stared at us in utter astonishment, as if she couldn't believe her eyes.

"Lovely to meet you, Mrs. Bull," I said. "I wonder if you might offer us assistance? We're thoroughly lost, you see. We were to have joined the cine crew hours ago at Malden Fenwick. We're both of us quite hopeless when it comes to directions, aren't we, Aunt Gilda?"

There was no response from the Gypsy.

The redheaded woman had already begun to poke damp strands of hair back into position.

"Damn fools, whoever you are," she said, pointing. "There's no turning round hereabouts. Lane's too narrow. Straight on to Doddingsley you'll have to go, then back by way of Tench."

"Thanks awfully," I said in my best village-twit voice, taking the reins from the Gypsy and giving them a flick.

"Ya!" I cried, and Gry began to move at once.

We had gone about a quarter of a mile when suddenly the Gypsy spoke.

"You lie like one of us," she said.

It was hardly the sort of remark I should have expected. She must have seen the puzzled look on my face.

"You lie when you are attacked for nothing . . . for the color of your eyes."

"Yes," I said. "I suppose I do." I had never really thought of it in this way.

"So," she said, suddenly animated, as if the encounter with Mrs. Bull had warmed her blood, "you lie like us. You lie like a Gypsy."

"Is that good?" I asked. "Or bad?"

Her answer was slow in coming.

"It means you will live a long life."

The corner of her mouth twitched, as if a smile was about to escape, but she quickly suppressed it.

"In spite of the broken star on my Mount of Luna?" I couldn't resist asking.

Her creaking laugh caught me by surprise.

"Mumbo jumbo. Fortune-teller's rubbish. You weren't taken in by it, were you?"

Her laughter set off another round of coughing, and I had to wait until she regained her breath.

"But . . . the woman on the mountain . . . the woman who wants to come home from the cold . . . "

"Look," the Gypsy woman said wearily—as if she were unaccustomed to speaking—"your sisters put me up to it. They tipped me off about you and Harriet. Slipped me a couple of bob to scare the daylights out of you. No more to it than that."

I felt my blood freeze. It was as though the faucet that feeds my brain had suddenly switched from hot to cold. I stared at her.

"Sorry if I hurt you," she went on. "I never meant to . . . "

"It makes no difference," I said with a mechanical shrug. But it did. My mind was reeling. "I'm sure I shall find a way of repaying them."

"Maybe I can help," she said. "Revenge is my specialty."

Was she pulling my leg? Hadn't the woman just admitted that she was a fraud? I looked deeply into her black eyes, searching for a sign.

"Don't stare at me like that. It makes my blood itch. I said I was sorry, didn't I? And I meant it."

"Did you?" I asked rather haughtily.

"Spare us the pout. There's enough lip in the world without you adding to it."

She was right. In spite of my turning them down, the corners of my mouth flickered, then began to rise. I laughed and the Gypsy laughed with me.

"You put me in mind of that creature that was in the tent just before you. Regular thundercloud. Told her there was something buried in her past; told her it wanted digging out—wanted setting right. She went white as the garden gate."

"Why, what did you see?" I asked.

"Money!" she said with a laughing snort. "Same as I always see. Couple of quid if I played my cards right."

"And did you?"

"Pfah! A bloomin' shilling she left me—not a penny more. Like I said, she went all goosey when I told her that. Scampered out of my pitch as if she'd sat on a thistle."

We rode along in silence for a while, and I realized that we had almost reached the Palings.

TO ME, THE PALINGS WAS LIKE some lost and forgotten corner of Paradise. At the southeast angle of the Buckshaw estate, beneath a spreading tent of green and leafy branches, the river, as though twirling in its skirts, swept round to the west in a gentle bend, creating a quiet glade that was almost an island. Here, the east bank was somewhat higher than the west; the west bank more marshy than the east. If you knew precisely where to look among the trees, you could still spot the pretty arches of the little stone bridge, which dated from the time of the original Buckshaw, an Elizabethan manor house that had been put to the torch in the 1600s by irate villagers who made the wrong assumptions about our family's religious allegiances.

I turned to the Gypsy, eager to share my love of the place, but she seemed to have fallen asleep. I watched her eyelids carefully to see if she was shamming, but there wasn't so much as a flicker. Slumped against the frame of the caravan, she gave off the occasional wheeze, so that I knew she was still breathing.

In rather an odd way I found that I resented her easy slumber. I was simply itching to reel off for her, like a tour guide, some of the more fascinating bits of Buckshaw's history. But for now, I should have to keep them to myself.

The Palings, as we called it, had been one of the haunts, in his latter days, of Nicodemus Flitch, a former tailor who, in the seventeenth century, had founded the Hobblers, a religious sect named for the peculiar shackled gait they adopted as they paced out their prayers. The Hobblers' beliefs seemed to be based largely on such novel ideas as that heaven was handily located six miles above the earth's surface, and that Nicodemus Flitch had been appointed personally by God as His mouthpiece and, as such, was licensed to curse souls to eternity, whenever he felt like it.

Daffy had told me that once, when Flitch was preaching at the Palings, he had called down God's wrath upon the head of a heckler, who fell dead on the spot—and that if I didn't fork over the tin of licorice allsorts that Aunt Felicity had sent me for my birthday, she would bring the same curse crashing down upon my head.

"And don't think I can't," she had added ominously, tapping a forefinger on the book that she'd been reading. "The instructions are right here on this page."

The heckler's death was a coincidence, I had told her, and most likely due to a stroke or a heart attack. He would likely have died anyway, even if he'd decided to stay home in bed on that particular day.

"Don't bet on it," Daffy had grumbled.

In his later years Flitch, driven from London in disgrace, and steadily losing ground to the more exciting religious sects such as the Ranters, the Shakers, the Quakers, the Diggers, the Levellers, the Sliders, the Swadlers, the Tumblers, the Dunkers, the Tunkers, and yes, even the Incorrupticolians, had made his way to Bishop's Lacey, where at this very bend in the river he had begun baptizing converts to his weird faith.

Mrs. Mullet, after glancing over each of her shoulders and dropping her voice to a furtive whisper, had once told me that Nicodemus Flitch's strange brand of religion was still said to be practiced in the village, although nowadays strictly behind closed doors and drawn curtains.

"They dips their babies by the 'eels," she said, wide-eyed. "Like Killies the 'Eel in the River Stynx, my friend Mrs. Waller says 'er Bert told 'er. Don't you 'ave nothin' to do with them 'Obblers. They'll 'ave your blood for sausages."

I had grinned then and I smiled now as I recalled her words, but I shivered, too, as I thought of the Palings, and the shadows that swallowed its sunshine.

My last visit to the glade had been in spring when the clearing was carpeted with cowslips—"paigles," Mrs. Mullet called them—and primroses.

Now the grove would be hidden by the tall elder bushes that grew along the river's bank. It was too late in the season to see, and to inhale the delicious scent of, the elder flowers. Their white blossoms, like a horde of Japanese parasols, would have turned brown and vanished with the rains of June. Perhaps more cheerful was the thought that the purplish-black elderberries which took their place would soon be hanging in perfectly arranged clusters, like a picture gallery of dark bruises.

It was at the Palings, in the days of the early numbered Georges, that the river Efon had been diverted temporarily to form the ornamental lake and feed the fountains whose remnants dotted the lawns and terraces at Buckshaw. At the time of its construction, this marvel of subterranean hydraulic engineering had caused no end of hard feelings between my family and the local landowners, so that one of my ancestors, Lucius de Luce, had subsequently become known as "Leaking de Luce" to half the countryside. In his portrait, which still hangs in our picture gallery at Buckshaw, he seems rather bored, overlooking the northwest corner of his lake, with its folly, its fountains, and the—now long gone—Grecian temple. Lucius is resting the bony knuckles of one hand on a table, upon which are laid out a compass, a pocket watch, an egg, and a piece of gadgetry meant for surveyors, called a theodolite. In a wooden cage is a canary with its beak open. It is either singing or crying for help.

My cheerful musings were interrupted by a barking cough.

"Pull up," the Gypsy said, snatching the reins from my hands. Her brief nap must have done her some good, I thought. In spite of the cough, there was now more color in her dusky cheeks and her eyes seemed to burn more brightly than ever.

With a clucking noise to Gry and a quick ease that showed her familiarity with the place, she steered the caravan off the narrow road, under a leafy overhang, and onto the little bridge. Moments later, we had come to a stop in the middle of the glade.

The Gypsy climbed heavily down from her seat and began unfastening Gry's harness. As she saw to her old horse, I took the opportunity to glory in my surroundings.

Patches of poppies and nettles grew here and there, illuminated by the downward slanting bars of the afternoon sun. Never had the grass seemed so green.

Gry had noticed it, too, and was already grazing contentedly upon the long blades.

The caravan gave a sudden lurch, and there was a sound as though someone had stumbled.

I jumped down and raced round the other side.

It was evident at once that I had misread the Gypsy's condition. She had crumbled to the ground, and was hanging on for dear life to the spokes of one of the tall wooden wheels. As I reached her side, she began to cough again, more horribly than ever.

"You're exhausted," I said. "You ought to be lying down."

She mumbled something and closed her eyes.

In a flash I had climbed up onto the wagon's shafts and opened the door.

But whatever I had been expecting, it wasn't this.

Inside, the caravan was a fairy tale on wheels. Although I had no time for more than a quick glance round, I noticed an exquisite cast-iron stove in the Queen Anne style, and above it a rack of blue-willow chinaware. Hot water and tea, I thought—essentials in all emergencies. Lace curtains hung at the windows, to provide first-aid bandages if needed, and a pair of silver paraffin lamps with red glass chimneys swung gently from their mounts for steady light, a bit of heat, and a flame for the sterilizing of needles. My training as a Girl Guide, however brief, had not been entirely in vain. At the rear, a pair of carved wooden panels stood half-open, revealing a roomy bunk bed that occupied nearly the whole width of the caravan.

Back outside, I helped the Gypsy to her feet, throwing one of her arms across my shoulder.

"I've folded the steps down," I told her. "I'll help you to your bed."

Somehow, I managed to shepherd her to the front of the caravan where, by pushing and pulling, and by placing her hands upon the required holds, I was at last able to get her settled. During most of these operations, she seemed scarcely aware of her surroundings, or of me. But once tucked safely into her bunk, she appeared to revive somewhat.

"I'm going for the doctor," I said. Since I'd left Gladys parked against the back of the parish hall at the fête, I realized I'd have to hoof it later, from Buckshaw back into the village.

"No, don't do that," she said, taking a firm grip on my hand. "Make a nice cup of tea, and leave me be. A good sleep is all I need."

She must have seen the skeptical look on my face.

"Fetch the medicine," she said. "I'll have just a taste. The spoon's with the tea things."

First things first, I thought, locating the utensil among a clutter of battered silverware, and pouring it full of the treacly looking cough syrup.

"Open up, little birdie," I said with a grin. It was the formula Mrs. Mullet used to humor me into swallowing those detestable tonics and oils with which Father insisted his daughters be dosed. With her eyes fixed firmly on mine (was it my imagination, or did they warm a little?), the Gypsy opened her mouth dutifully and allowed me to insert the brimming spoon.

"Swallow, swallow, fly away," I said, pronouncing the closing words of the ritual, and turning my attention to the charming little stove. I hated to admit my ignorance: I hadn't the faintest idea how to light the thing. You might as well ask me to stoke up the boilers on the *Queen Elizabeth*.

"Not here," the Gypsy said, spotting my hesitation. "Outside. Make a fire."

At the bottom of the steps, I paused for a quick look round the grove.

Elder bushes, as I have said, were growing everywhere. I tugged at a couple of branches, trying to tear them loose, but it was not an easy task.

Too full of life, I thought; *too springy.* After something of a tug-of-war, and only by jumping vigorously on a couple of the lower branches, was I able to tear them free at last.

Five minutes later, at the center of the glade, I had gathered enough twigs and branches to have the makings of a decent campfire.

Hopefully, while muttering the Girl Guide's Prayer ("Burn, blast you!"), I lit one of the matches I had found in the caravan's locker. As the flame touched the twigs, it sizzled and went out. Another did the same.

As I am not noted for my patience, I let slip a mild curse.

If I were at home in my chemical laboratory, I thought, *I would be doing as any civilized person does and using a Bunsen burner to boil water for tea: not messing about on my knees in a clearing with a bundle of stupid green twigs.*

It was true that, before my rather abrupt departure from the Girl Guides, I had learned to start campfires, but I'd vowed that never again would I be caught dead trying to make a fire-bow from a stick and a shoe-string, or rubbing two dry sticks together like a demented squirrel.

As noted, I had all the ingredients of a roaring fire—all, that is, except one.

Wherever there are paraffin lamps, I thought, *paraffin can not be far away.* I let down the hinged side panel of the caravan and there, to my delight, was a gallon of the stuff. I unscrewed the cap of the tin, splashed a bit of it onto the waiting firewood, and before you could say "Baden-Powell," the teakettle was at a merry boil.

I was proud of myself. I really was.

"Flavia, the resourceful," I was thinking. "Flavia, the all-round good girl."

That sort of thing.

Up the steep steps of the caravan I climbed, tea in hand, balancing on my toes like a tightrope walker.

I handed the cup to the Gypsy and watched as she sipped at the steaming liquid.

"You were quick about it," she said.

I shrugged humbly. No need to tell her about the paraffin.

"You found dry sticks in the locker?" she asked.

"No," I said, "I . . . "

Her eyes grew wide with horror, and she held out the cup at arm's length.

"Not the bushes! You didn't cut the elder bushes?"

"Why, yes," I said modestly. "It was no trouble at all, I—"

The cup flew from her hands with a clatter, and scalding tea went flying in all directions. She leapt from the bunk with startling speed and shrank herself back into the corner.

"Hilda Muir!" she cried, in an eerie and desolate wail that rose and fell like an air-raid siren. "Hilda Muir!" She was pointing to the door. I turned to look, but no one was there.

"Get away from me! Get out! Get out!" Her hand trembled like a dead leaf.

I stood there, dumbfounded. What had I done?

"Oh, God! Hilda Muir! We are *all* dead!" she groaned. "Now we are *all* dead!"

three

SEEN FROM THE REAR, AT THE EDGE OF THE ORNAMENTAL lake, Buckshaw presented an aspect seldom seen by anyone other than family. Although the tall brick wall of the kitchen garden hid some parts of the house, there were two upper rooms, one at the end of each wing, that seemed to rise up above the landscape like twin towers in a fairy tale.

At the southwest corner was Harriet's boudoir, an airless preserve that was kept precisely as it had been on that terrible day ten years ago when news of her tragic death had reached Buckshaw. In spite of the Italian lace that hung at its windows, the room inside was a curiously sanitized preserve as if, like the British Museum, it had a team of silent gray-clad scrubbers who came in the night to sweep away all signs of passing time, such as cobwebs or dust.

Although I thought it unlikely, my sisters believed that it was Father who was the keeper of Harriet's shrine. Once, hiding on the stairs, I had overheard Feely telling Daffy, "He cleans in the night to atone for his sins."

"Bloodstains and the like," Daffy had whispered dramatically.

Far too agog for sleep, I had lain in bed for hours, open-eyed and wondering what she meant.

Now, at the southeast corner of the house, the upstairs windows of my chemical laboratory reflected the slow passage of the clouds as they drifted across the dark glass like fat sheep in a blue meadow, giving no hint to the outside world of the pleasure palace that lay within.

I looked up at the panes happily, hugging myself, visualizing the array of gleaming glassware that awaited my pleasure. The indulgent father of my great-uncle Tarquin de Luce had built the laboratory for his son during the reign of Queen Victoria. Uncle Tar had been sent down from Oxford amidst some sort of scandal that had never been quite fully explained—at least in my presence—and it was here at Buckshaw that he had begun his glorious, if cloistered, chemical career.

After Uncle Tar's death, the laboratory was left to keep its secrets to itself: locked and forgotten by people who were more concerned with taxes and drainage than with cunningly shaped vessels of glass.

Until I came along, that is, and claimed it for my own.

I wrinkled my nose in pleasure at the memory.

As I approached the kitchen door, I felt proud of myself to have thought of using the least conspicuous entrance. With Daffy and Feely forever scheming and plotting against me, one could never be too careful. But the excitement of the fête and the moving of the Gypsy's caravan to the Palings had caused me to miss lunch. Right now, even a slice of Mrs. Mullet's stomach-churning cabbage cake would probably be bearable if taken with a glass of ice-cold milk to freeze the taste buds. By this late in the afternoon Mrs. M would have gone home for the day, and I would have the kitchen to myself.

I opened the door and stepped inside.

"Got you!" said a grating voice at my ear, and everything went dark as a sack was pulled over my head.

I struggled, but it did no good. My hands and arms were useless, as the mouth of the sack was tied tightly about my thighs.

Before I could scream, my assailants—of whom I was quite sure there were two, judging by the number of hands that were grabbing at my limbs—turned me head over heels. Now I was upside down, standing on my head, with someone grasping my ankles.

I was suffocating, fighting for breath, my lungs filled with the sharp earthy smell of the potatoes that had recently occupied the sack. I could feel the blood rushing to my head.

Damn! I should have thought sooner of kicking them. Too late now.

"Make all the noise you want," hissed a second voice. "There's no one here to save you."

With a sinking feeling I realized that this was true. Father had gone up to London to a philatelic auction, and Dogger had gone with him to shop for secateurs and boot polish.

The idea of burglars inside Buckshaw was unthinkable.

That left Daffy and Feely.

In an odd way I wished it had been burglars.

I recalled that in the entire house there was only one doorknob that squeaked: the door to the cellar stairs.

It squeaked now.

A moment later, like a shot deer, I was being hoisted up onto the shoulders of my captors and roughly borne, headfirst, down into the cellars.

At the bottom of the stairs they dumped me heavily onto the flagstones, banging my elbow, and I heard my own voice shrieking with pain as it came echoing back from the vaulted ceilings—followed by the sound of my own ragged breathing.

Someone's shoes shifted in the grit not far from where I lay sprawled.

"Pray silence!" croaked a hollow voice, which sounded artificial, like that of a tin robot.

I let out another shriek, and I'm afraid I might even have whimpered a little.

"Pray silence!"

Whether it was from the sudden shock or the clammy coldness of the cellars I could not be certain, but I had begun to shiver. Would they take this as a sign of weakness? It is said that in certain small animals it is instinctive when in danger to play dead, and I realized that I was one of them.

I took shallow breaths and tried not to move a muscle.

"Free her, Garbax!"

"Yes, O Three-Eyed One."

It sometimes amused my sisters to slip suddenly into the roles of bizarre alien creatures: creatures even more bizarre and alien than they were already in everyday life. Both of them knew it was a trick that for some reason I found particularly upsetting.

I had already learned that sisterhood, like Loch Ness, has things that lurk unseen beneath the surface, but I think it was only now that I realized that of all the invisible strings that tied the three of us together, the dark ones were the strongest.

"Stop it, Daffy. Stop it, Feely!" I shouted. "You're frightening me."

I gave my legs a couple of convincing froglike kicks, as if I were on the verge of a seizure.

The sack was suddenly whisked away, spinning me round so that I now lay facedown upon the stones.

A single candle, stuck to the top of a wooden cask, flickered fitfully, its pale light sending dark shapes dancing everywhere among the stone arches of the cellar.

As my eyes became accustomed to the gloom, I saw my sisters' faces looming grotesquely in the shadows. They had drawn black circles round their eyes and their mouths with burnt cork, and I understood instantly the message that this was intended to convey: "Beware! You are in the hands of savages!"

Now I could see the cause of the distorted robot voice I had heard: Feely had been speaking into the mouth of an empty cocoa tin.

"'French jet is nothing but glass,'" she spat, chucking the tin to the floor where it fell with a nerve-wracking clatter. "Your very words. What have you done with Mummy's brooch?"

"It was an accident," I whined untruthfully.

Feely's frozen silence lent me a bit of confidence.

"I dropped it and stepped on it. If it were real jet it mightn't have shattered."

"Hand it over."

"I can't, Feely. There was nothing left but little chips. I melted them down for slag."

Actually, I had hit the thing with a hammer and reduced it to black sand.

"Slag? Whatever do you want with slag?"

It would be a mistake to tell her that I was working on a new kind of ceramic flask, one that would stand up to the temperatures produced by a super-oxygenated Bunsen burner.

"Nothing," I said. "I was just mucking about."

"Oddly enough, I believe you," Feely said. "That's what you pixy changelings do best, isn't it? Muck about?"

My puzzlement must have been evident on my face.

"Changelings," Daffy said in a weird voice. "The pixies come in the night and steal a healthy baby from its crib. They leave an ugly shriveled changeling like you in its place, and the mother desolate."

"If you don't believe it," Feely said, "go stand in front of a looking glass."

"I'm not a changeling," I protested, my anger rising. "Harriet loved me more than she did either of you two morons!"

"Did she?" Feely sneered. "Then why did she used to leave you sleeping in front of an open window every night, hoping that the pixies would bring back the real Flavia?"

"She didn't!" I shouted.

"I'm afraid she did. I was there. I saw. I remember."

"No! It's not true."

"Yes, it is. I used to cling to her and cry, 'Mummy! Mummy! Please make the pixies bring back my baby sister.'"

"Flavia? Daphne? Ophelia?"

It was Father!

His voice came at parade-square volume from the direction of the kitchen staircase, amplified by the stone walls and echoing from arch to arch.

All three of our heads snapped round just in time to see his boots, his trousers, his upper body, and finally his face come into sight as he descended the stairs.

"What's the meaning of this?" he asked, peering round at the three of us in the near-darkness. "What have you done to yourselves?"

With the backs of their hands and their forearms, Feely and Daffy were already trying to scrub the black markings from their faces.

"We were only playing Prawns and Trivets," Daffy said before I could answer. She pointed accusingly at me. "She gives us jolly good what-for when it's her turn to play the Begum, but when it's ours she always . . . "

Well done, Daff, I thought. I couldn't have concocted a better spur-of-the-moment excuse myself.

"I'm surprised at you, Ophelia," Father said. "I shouldn't have thought . . ."

And then he stopped, unable to find the required words. There were times when he seemed almost—what was it . . . *afraid?* . . . of my oldest sister.

Feely rubbed at her face, smearing her cork makeup horribly. I nearly laughed out loud, but then I realized what she was doing. In a bid for sympathy, she was spreading the stuff to create dark, theatrical circles under her eyes.

The vixen! Like an actress applying her makeup onstage, it was a bold and brazen performance, which I couldn't help admiring.

Father looked on in thrall, like a man fascinated by a cobra.

"Are you all right, Flavia?" he said at last, not budging from his position on the third step from the bottom.

"Yes, Father," I said.

I was going to add "Thank you for asking" but I stopped myself just in time. I didn't want to overdo it.

Father looked slowly from one of us to another with his sad eyes, as if there were no words left in the world from which to choose.

"There will be a parley at seven o'clock," he said at last. "In the drawing room."

With a final glance at each of us, he turned and trudged slowly up the stairs.

"THE THING OF IT IS," Father was saying, "you girls just don't seem to understand . . . "

And he was right: We no more understood his world than he did ours.

His was a world of confetti: a brightly colored universe of royal profiles and scenic views on sticky bits of paper; a world of pyramids and battleships, of rickety suspension bridges in far-flung corners of the globe, of deep harbors, lonely watchtowers, and the heads of famous men. In short, Father was a stamp collector, or a "philatelist," as he preferred to call himself, and to be called by others.

His every waking moment was spent in peering through a magnifying lens at paper scraps in an eternal search for flaws. The discovery of a single microscopic crack in a printing plate, which had resulted in an unwanted hair on Queen Victoria's chin, could send him into raptures.

First would come the official photograph, and elation. He would bring out of storage, and set up on its tripod in his study, an ancient plate camera with a peculiar attachment called a macroscopic lens, which allowed him to take a close-up of the specimen. This, when developed, would produce an image large enough to fill an entire page of a book. Sometimes, as he fussed happily over these operations, we would catch snatches of *H.M.S. Pinafore* or *The Gondoliers* drifting like fugitives through the house.

Then would come the written paper which he would submit to *The London Philatelist* or suchlike, and with it would come a certain crankiness.

Every morning Father would bring to the breakfast table reams of writing paper which he would fill, page after laborious page, with his minuscule handwriting.

For weeks he would be unapproachable, and would remain so until such time as he had scribbled the last word—and more—on the topic of the queen's superfluous whisker.

Once, when we were lying on the south lawn looking up into the blue vault of a perfect summer sky, I had suggested to Feely that Father's quest for imperfections was not limited to stamps, but was sometimes expanded to include his daughters.

"Shut your filthy mouth!" she'd snapped.

"The thing of it is," Father repeated, bringing me back to the present, "you girls don't appear to understand the gravity of the situation."

Mainly he meant me.

Feely had ratted, of course, and the story of how I had vaporized one of Harriet's dreadful Victorian brooches had come tumbling out of her mouth as happily as the waters of a babbling brook.

"You had no right to remove it from your mother's dressing room," Father said, and for a moment his cold blue stare was shifted to my sister.

"I'm sorry," Feely said. "I was going to wear it to church on Sunday to impress Dieter. It was quite wrong of me. I should have asked permission."

It was quite wrong of me? Had I heard what I thought I'd heard, or were my ears playing hob with me? It was more likely that the sun and the moon should suddenly dance a jolly jig in the heavens than that one of my sisters should apologize. It was simply unheard of.

The Dieter Feely had mentioned was Dieter Schrantz, of Culverhouse Farm, a former German prisoner of war who had chosen to remain behind in England after the armistice. Feely had him in her sights.

"Yes," Father said. "You should have."

As he turned his attention to me, I could not help noticing that the folds of skin at the outer corners of his hooded eyes—those folds that I so often thought of as making him look so aristocratic—were hanging more heavily than usual, giving him a look of deeper sadness than I had ever seen.

"Flavia," he said in a flat and weary voice that wounded me more than a pointed weapon.

"Yes, sir?"

"What is to be done with you?"

"I'm sorry, Father. I didn't mean to break the brooch. I dropped it and stepped on it by accident, and it just crumbled. Gosh, it must have been very old to be so brittle!"

He gave an almost imperceptible wince, followed instantly by one of those looks that meant I had touched upon a topic that was not open for discussion. With a long sigh he shifted his gaze to the window. Something in my words had sent his mind fleeing to safety beyond the hills.

"Did you have an enjoyable trip up to London?" I ventured. "To the philatelic exhibition, I mean?"

The word "philatelic" drew him back quickly.

"I hope you found some decent stamps for your collection."

He let out another sigh: this one frighteningly like a death rattle. "I did not go to London to buy stamps, Flavia. I went there to sell them."

Even Feely gasped.

"Our days at Buckshaw may be drawing to a close," Father said. "As you are well aware, the house itself belonged to your mother, and when she died without leaving a will . . . "

He spread his hands in a gesture of helplessness that reminded me of a stricken butterfly.

He had deflated so suddenly in front of us that I could scarcely believe it.

"I had hoped to take her brooch to someone whom I know . . . "

For quite a few moments his words did not register.

I knew that in recent years the cost of maintaining Buckshaw had become positively ruinous, to say nothing of the taxes and the looming death duty. For years Father had managed to keep "the snarling taxmen," as he called them, at bay, but now the wolves must be howling once again on the doorstep.

There had been hints from time to time of our predicament, but the threat had always seemed unreal: no more than a distant cloud on a summer horizon.

I remembered that for a time, Father had pinned his hopes on Aunt Felicity, his sister who lived in Hampstead. Daffy had suggested that many of his so-called "philatelic jaunts" were, in fact, calls upon Aunt Felicity to touch her for a loan—or to beg her to fork over whatever remained of the family jewels.

In the end, his sister must have turned him down. Just recently, and with our own ears, we had heard her tell him he must think about selling his philatelic collection. "Those ridiculous postage stamps," she had called them, to be precise.

"Something will turn up," Daffy remarked brightly. "It always does."

"Only in Dickens, Daphne," Father said. "Only in Dickens."

Daffy had been reading *David Copperfield* for the umpteenth time. "Boning up on pawnshops," she had answered when I asked her why.

Only now did it occur to me that Father had intended to take Harriet's brooch—the one I had destroyed—to a pawnbroker.

"May I be excused?" I asked. "I'm suddenly not feeling well."

IT WAS TRUE. I must have fallen asleep the instant my head touched the pillow.

Now, hours later, I was suddenly awake. The hands of my alarm clock, which I had carefully dabbed with my own formulation of phosphorescent paint, told me that it was several minutes past two in the morning.

I lay in bed watching the dark shadows of the trees as they twitched restlessly on the ceiling. Ever since a territorial dispute between two of my distant ancestors had ended in a bitter stalemate—and a black line painted in the middle of the foyer—this wing of the house had remained unheated. Time and the weather had taken their toll, causing the wallpaper of nearly every room—mine was mustard yellow with scarlet worms—to peel away in great sheets which hung in forlorn flaps, while the paper from the ceilings hung down in great loose swags whose contents were probably best not thought about.

Sometimes, especially in winter, I liked to pretend that I lived beneath an iceberg in an Arctic sea; that the coldness was no more than a dream, and that when I awoke, there would be a roaring fire in the rusty fireplace and hot steam rising from the tin hip-bath that stood in the corner behind the door.

There never was, of course, but I couldn't really complain. I slept here by choice, not by necessity. Here in the east wing—the so-called "Tar" wing—of Buckshaw, I could work away to my heart's content until all hours in my chemical laboratory. Since they faced south and east, my windows could be ablaze with light and no one outside would see them—no one, that is, except perhaps the foxes and badgers that inhabited the island and the ruined folly in the middle of the ornamental lake, or perhaps the occasional poacher whose footprints and discarded shell casings I sometimes found in my rambles through the Palings.

The Palings! I had almost forgotten.

My abduction at the kitchen door by Feely and Daffy, my subsequent imprisonment in the cellars, my shaming at the hands of Father, and finally my fatigue: All of those had conspired to make me put the Gypsy clean out of my mind.

I leapt from my bed, somewhat surprised to find myself still fully clothed. I *must* have been tired!

Shoes in hand, I crept down the great curving staircase to the foyer, where I stopped to listen in the middle of that vast expanse of black-and-white tiling. To an observer in one of the galleries above, I must have looked like a pawn in some grand and Gothic game of chess.

A pawn? Pfah, Flavia! Admit it: surely something more than a pawn!

The house was in utter silence. Father and Feely, I knew, would be dreaming their respective dreams: Father of perforated bits of paper and Feely of living in a castle built entirely of mirrors in which she could see herself reflected again and again from every possible aspect.

Upstairs, at the far end of the west wing, Daffy would still be awake, though, goggling by candlelight, as she loved to do, at the Gustave Doré engravings in *Gargantua and Pantagruel*. I had found the fat calf-bound volume hidden under her mattress while rifling her room in search of a packet of chewing gum that an American serviceman had given to Feely, who had come across him sitting on a stile one morning as she was walking into the village to post a letter. His name was Carl, and he was from St. Louis, in America. He told her she was the spitting image of Elizabeth Taylor in *National Velvet*. Feely, of course, had come home preening and hidden the gum, as she always does with such tributes, in her lingerie drawer, from which Daffy had pinched it. And I in my turn from her.

For weeks afterwards it was "Carl-this" and "Carl-that" with Feely prattling endlessly on about the muddy Mississippi, its length, its twists and bends, and how to spell it properly without making a fool of oneself. We were given the distinct impression that she had personally conceived and executed the formation of that great river, with God standing helplessly on the sidelines, little more than a plumber's assistant.

I smiled at the thought.

It was at that precise instant that I heard it: a metallic *click*.

For a couple of heartbeats, I stood perfectly still, trying to decide from which direction it had come.

The drawing room, I thought, and immediately began tiptoeing in that direction. In my bare feet, I was able to move in perfect silence, keeping an ear out for the slightest sound. Although there are times when I have cursed the painfully acute sense of hearing I've inherited from Harriet, this was not one of them.

As I moved at a snail's pace along the corridor, a crack of light suddenly appeared beneath the drawing-room door. *Who could be in there at this time of night?* I wondered. Whoever it was, it certainly wasn't a de Luce.

Should I call for help, or tackle the intruder myself?

I seized the knob, turned it ever so slowly, and opened the door: a foolhardy action, I suppose, but after all, I *was* in my own home. No sense in letting Daffy or Feely take all the credit for catching a burglar.

Accustomed to the darkness, my eyes were somewhat dazzled by the light of an ancient paraffin lamp that was kept for use during electrical interruptions, and so at first I didn't see anyone there. In fact, it took a moment for me to realize that someone—a stranger in rubber boots— was crouched by the fireplace, his hand on one of the brass firedogs that had been cast into the shape of foxes.

The whites of his eyes flashed as he looked up into the mirror and saw me standing behind him in the open doorway.

His moleskin coat and his scarlet scarf flared out as he came to his feet and spun quickly round.

"Crikey, gal! You might have given me a heart attack!"

It was Brookie Harewood.

four

THE MAN HAD BEEN DRINKING. I NOTICED THAT AT ONCE. Even from where I stood I could detect the smell of alcohol—that and the powerful fishy odor that accompanies a person who wears a creel with as much pride as another might wear a kilt and sporran.

I closed the door quietly behind me.

"What are you doing here?" I asked, putting on my sternest face.

Actually, what I was thinking was that Buckshaw, in the small hours of the morning, was becoming a virtual Paddington Station. It wasn't more than a couple of months since I had found Horace Bonepenny in a heated nocturnal argument with Father. Well, Bonepenny was now in his grave, and yet here was another intruder to take his place.

Brookie raised his cap and tugged at his forelock—the ancient signal of submission to one's better. If he were a dog, it would be much the same thing as prostrating himself and rolling over to expose his belly.

"Answer me, please," I said. "What are you *doing* here?"

He fiddled a bit with the wicker creel on his hip before he replied.

"You caught me fair and square, miss," he said, shooting me a disarming smile. I noticed, much to my annoyance, that he had perfect teeth.

"But I didn't mean no harm. I'll admit I was on the estate hoping to do a bit of business rabbitwise. Nothing like a nice pot of rabbit stew for a weak chest, is there?"

He knocked his rib cage with a clenched fist and forced a cough that, since I had done it so often myself, didn't fool me for an instant. Neither did his fake gamekeeper dialect. If, as Mrs. Mullet claimed, Brookie's mother was a society artist, he had probably been schooled at Eton, or some such place. The grubbing voice was meant to gain him sympathy. That, too, was an old trick. I had used it myself, and because of that, I found myself resenting it.

"The Colonel's no shooter," he went on, "and all the world knows that for a fact. So where's the harm in ridding the place of a pest that does no more than eat your garden and dig holes in your shrubbery? Where's the harm in that, eh?"

I noticed that he was repeating himself—almost certainly a sign that he was lying. I didn't know the answer to his question, so I remained silent, my arms crossed.

"But then I saw a light inside the house," he went on. " 'Hullo!' I said to myself, 'What's this, then, Brookie? Who could be up at this ungodly hour?' I said. 'Could someone be sick?' I know the Colonel doesn't use a motor-car, you see, and then I thought, 'What if someone's needed to run into the village to fetch the doctor?' "

There was truth in what he said. Harriet's ancient Rolls-Royce—a Phantom II—was kept in the coach house as a sort of private chapel, a place that both Father and I went—though never at the same time, of course—whenever we wanted to escape what Father called "the vicissitudes of daily life."

What he meant, of course, was Daffy and Feely—and sometimes me.

Although Father missed Harriet dreadfully, he never spoke of her. His grief was so deep that Harriet's name had been put at the top of the Buckshaw Blacklist: things that were never to be spoken of if you valued your life.

I confess that Brookie's words caught me off guard. Before I could frame a reply he went on: "But then I thought, 'No, there's more to it than that. If someone was sick at Buckshaw there'd be more lights on than one. There'd be lights in the kitchen—someone heating water, someone dashing about . . .' "

"We might have used the telephone," I protested, instinctively resist-ing Brookie's attempt to spin a web.

But he had a point. Father loathed the telephone, and allowed it to be used only in the most extreme emergencies. At two-thirty in the morning, it would be quicker to cycle—or even run!—into Bishop's

Lacey than to arouse Miss Runciman at the telephone exchange and ask
her to ring up the sleeping Dr. Darby.

By the time *that* tedious game of Button, Button, Who's Got the
Button had been completed, we might all of us be dead.

As if he were the squire and I the intruder, Brookie, his rubber-booted
feet spread wide and his hands clasped behind him, had now taken up a
stance in front of the fireplace, midway between the two brass foxes that
had belonged to Harriet's grandfather. He didn't lean an elbow on the
mantel, but he might as well have.

Before I could say another word, he gave a quick, nervous glance to
the right and to the left and dropped his voice to a husky whisper: " *'But
wait, Brookie, old man,'* I thought. *'Hold on, Brookie, old chum. Mightn't
this be the famous Gray Lady of Buckshaw that you're seeing?'* After all,
miss, everyone knows that there's sometimes lights seen hereabouts that
have no easy explanation."

Gray Lady of Buckshaw? I'd never heard of such an apparition. How
laughably superstitious these villagers were! Did the man take me for a fool?

"Or is the family specter not mentioned in polite company?"

Family specter? I had the sudden feeling that someone had tossed a
bucket of ice water over my heart.

Could the Gray Lady of Buckshaw be the ghost of my mother, Harriet?

Brookie laughed. "Silly thought, wasn't it?" he went on. "No spooks
for me, thank you very much! More likely a housebreaker with his eye
on the Colonel's silver. Lot of that going on nowadays, since the war."

"I think you'd better go now," I said, my voice trembling. "Father's a
light sleeper. If he wakes up and finds you here, there's no telling what
he'll do. He sleeps with his service revolver on the night table."

"Well, I'll be on my way, then," Brookie said casually. "Glad to know
the family's come to no harm. We worry about you lot, you know, all of
us down in the village. No telling what can happen when you're way out
here, cut off, as it were . . . "

"Thank you," I said. "We're very grateful, I'm sure. And now, if you
don't mind—"

I unlocked one of the French doors and opened it wide.

"Good night, miss," he said, and with a grin he vanished into the
darkness.

I counted slowly to ten—and then I followed him.

BROOKIE WAS NOWHERE IN SIGHT. The shadows had swallowed him whole. I stood listening for a few moments on the terrace, but the night was eerily silent.

Overhead, the stars twinkled like a million little lanterns, and I recognized the constellation called the Pleiades, the Seven Sisters, named for the family of girls in Greek mythology who were so saddened by their father's fate—he was the famous Atlas who was doomed to carry the heavens on his shoulders—that they committed suicide.

I thought of the rain-swept afternoon I had spent in the greenhouse with Dogger, helping him cut the eyes from a small mountain of potatoes, and listening to a tale that had been handed down by word of mouth for thousands of years.

"What a stupid thing to do!" I said. "Why would they kill themselves?"

"The Greeks are a dramatic race," Dogger had answered. "They *invented* the drama."

"How do you know all these things?"

"They swim in my head," he said, "like dolphins." And then he had lapsed into his customary silence.

Somewhere across the lawn an owl hooted, bringing me back with a start to the present. I realized that I was still holding my shoes in my hand. What a fool I must have looked to Brookie Harewood!

Behind me, except for the paraffin lamp that still burned in the drawing room, Buckshaw was all in darkness. It was too early for breakfast and too late to go back to bed.

I stepped back into the house, put on my shoes, and turned down the wick. By now, the Gypsy woman would be rested and be over her fright. With any luck, I could manage an invitation to a Gypsy breakfast over an open campfire. And with a bit more luck, I might even find out who Hilda Muir was, and why we were all dead.

I PAUSED AT THE EDGE OF the Palings, waiting for my eyes to become accustomed to the deeper gloom among the trees.

A wooded glade in darkness is an eerie place, I thought; *a place where almost anything could happen.*

Pixies . . . Hilda Muir . . . the Gray Lady of Buckshaw . . .

I gave myself a mental shake. "*Stop it, Flavia!*" a voice inside me said, and I took its advice.

The caravan was still there: I could see several stars and a patch of the Milky Way reflected in one of its curtained windows. The sound of munching somewhere in the darkness told me that Gry was grazing not far away.

I approached the caravan slowly.

"Hel-lo," I sang, keeping the tone light, in view of the Gypsy's earlier frame of mind. "It's me, Flavia. Knock-knock. Anyone at home?"

There was no reply. I waited a moment, then made my way round to the back of the caravan. When I touched its wooden side to steady myself, my hand came away wet with the cold dew.

"Anyone here? It's me, Flavia." I gave a light rap with my knuckles.

There was a faint glow in the rear window: the sort of glow that might be given off by a lamp turned down for the night.

Suddenly something wet and horrid and slobbering touched the side of my face. I leapt back, my arms windmilling.

"Cheeses!" I yelped.

There was a rustling noise and a hot breath on the back of my neck, followed by the sweet smell of wet grass.

Then Gry was nuzzling at my ear.

"Creekers, Gry!" I said, spinning round. "Creekers!"

I touched his warm face in the darkness and found it oddly comforting: much more so than I should ever have guessed. I touched my forehead to his, and for a few moments as my heart slowed we stood there in the starlight, communicating in a way that is far older than words.

If only you could talk, I thought. *If only you could talk.*

"Hel-lo," I called again, giving Gry's muzzle one last rub and turning towards the caravan. But still, there was no reply.

The wagon teetered a bit on its springs as I stepped onto the shafts and clambered up towards the driving seat. The ornamental door handle was cold in my hand as I gave it a twist. The door swung open—it had not been locked.

"Hello?"

I stepped inside and reached for the paraffin lamp that glowed dully above the stove. As I turned up the wick, the glass shade sprang to light with a horrid sticky red brilliance.

Blood! There was blood everywhere. The stove and the curtains were splattered with the stuff. There was blood on the lampshade—blood on my hands.

Something dripped from the ceiling onto my face. I shrank back in revulsion—and perhaps a little fright.

And then I saw the Gypsy—she was lying crumpled at my feet: a black tumbled heap lying perfectly still in a pool of her own blood. I had almost stepped on her.

I knelt at her side and took her wrist between my thumb and forefinger. *Could that thin stirring possibly be a pulse?*

If it was, I needed help, and needed it quickly. Mucking about would do no good.

I was about to step out onto the driving seat when something stopped me in my tracks. I sniffed the air, which was sharp with the coppery, metallic smell of blood.

Blood, yes—but something more than blood. Something out of place. I sniffed again. What could it be?

Fish! The caravan reeked of blood and fish!

Had the Gypsy woman caught and cooked a fish in my absence? I thought not; there was no sign of a fire or utensils. Besides, I thought, she had been too weak and tired to do so. And there had certainly been no fishy smell about the caravan when I left it earlier.

I stepped outside, closed the door behind me, and leapt to the ground.

Running back to Buckshaw for help was out of the question. It would take far too long. By the time the proper people had been awakened and Dr. Darby summoned, the Gypsy might well be dead—if she wasn't already.

"Gry!" I called, and the old horse came shuffling towards me. Without further thought, I leapt onto his back, flung my arms round his neck, and gave his ribs a gentle kick with my heels. Moments later we were trotting across the bridge, then turning north into the leafy narrowness of the Gully.

In spite of the darkness, Gry kept up a steady pace, as if he were familiar with this rutted lane. As we went along, I learned quickly to balance on his bony spine, ducking down as overhanging branches snatched at my clothing, and wishing I'd been foresighted enough to bring a sweater. I'd forgotten how cold the nights could be at the end of summer.

On we trotted, the Gypsy's horse outdoing himself. Perhaps he sensed a hearty meal at the end of his journey.

Soon we would be passing the tumbledown residence of the Bulls, and I knew that we would not pass unnoticed. Even in broad daylight there were seldom travelers in the narrow lane. In the middle of the night, the unaccustomed sound of Gry's hooves on the road would surely be heard by one of the half-wild Bull family.

Yes, there it was: just ahead of us on the right. I could smell it. Even in the dark I could see the gray curtain of smoke that hung about the place. Spotted here and there about the property, the embers of the smoldering rubbish tips glowed like red eyes in the night. In spite of the lateness of the hour, the windows of the house were blazing with light.

No good begging for help here, I thought. Mrs. Bull had made no bones about her hatred of the Gypsy.

Seizing a handful of Gry's thick mane, I tugged at it gently. As if he had been trained from birth to this primitive means of control, the old horse slowed to a shamble. At the change of pace, one of his hooves struck a rock in the rutted road.

"Shhh!" I whispered into his ear. "Tiptoe!"

I knew that we had to keep moving. The Gypsy woman needed help desperately, and the Bulls' was not the place to seek it.

A door banged as someone came out into the yard—on the far side of the house, by the sound of it.

Gry stopped instantly and refused to move. I wanted to whisper into his ear to keep going, that he was a good horse—a remarkable horse— yet I hardly dared breathe. But Gry stood as motionless in the lane as if he were a purebred pointer. Could it be that a Gypsy's horse knew more about stealth than I did? Had years of traveling the unfriendly roads taught him more low cunning than even I possessed?

I made a note to think more about this when we were no longer in peril.

By the sound of it, the person in the yard was now rummaging through a lot of old pots, muttering to themselves whenever they stopped the clatter. The light from the house, I knew, would cast me into deeper darkness. Better, though, to make myself smaller and less visible than a rider on horseback.

I waited until the next round of banging began, and slipped silently to the ground. Using Gry as a shield, I kept well behind him so that my white face would not be spotted in the darkness.

When you're in a predicament time slows to a crawl. I could not begin to guess how long we stood rooted to the spot in the lane; it was probably no more than a few minutes. But almost immediately I found myself shifting my weight uneasily from foot to foot and shivering in the gloom while Gry, the old dear, had apparently fallen asleep. He didn't move a muscle.

And then the racket stopped abruptly.

Had the person in the garden sensed our presence? Were they lying in wait—ready to spring—on the far side of the house?

More time leaked past. I couldn't move. My heart was pounding crazily in my chest. It seemed impossible that whoever was in the Bulls' garden could fail to hear it.

They must be keeping still . . . listening, as I was.

Suddenly there came to my nostrils the sharp reek of a safety match; the unmistakeably acrid odor of phosphorus reacting with potassium chlorate. This was quickly followed by the smell of a burning cigarette.

I smiled. Mrs. Bull was taking a break from her brats.

But not for long. A door banged and a dark shape fluttered across behind one of the closed curtains.

Before I could talk myself out of it I began moving along the lane—slowly at first, and then more quickly. Gry walked quietly behind me. When we reached the trees at the far edge of the property, I scrambled up onto his back and urged him on.

"Dr. Darby's surgery," I said. "And make it snappy!"

As if he understood.

THE SURGERY WAS SITUATED IN the high street, just round the corner from Cow Lane. I lifted the knocker—a brass serpent on a staff—and pounded at the door. Almost instantly, or so it seemed, an upstairs window flew open with a sharp wooden groan and Dr. Darby's head appeared, his gray, wispy hair tousled from sleeping.

"The bell," he said grumpily. "Please use the bell."

I gave the button a token jab with my thumb, and somewhere in the depths of the house a muted buzzing went off.

"It's the Gypsy woman," I called up to him. "The one from the fête. I think someone's tried to kill her."

The window slammed shut.

It couldn't have been more than a minute before the front door opened and Dr. Darby stepped outside, shrugging himself into his jacket. "My car's in the back," he said. "Come along."

"But what about Gry?" I asked, pointing at the old horse, which stood quietly in the street.

"Bring him round to the stable," he said. "Aesculapius will be glad of his company."

Aesculapius was the ancient horse that had pulled Dr. Darby's buggy until about ten years ago, when the doctor had finally caved in to pressure from patients and purchased a tired old bull-nosed Morris—an open two-seater that Daffy referred to as "The Wreck of the Hesperus."

I hugged Gry's neck as he sidled into the stall with an almost audible sigh.

"Quickly," Dr. Darby said, tossing his bag into the back of the car.

A few moments later we were veering off the high street and into the Gully.

"The Palings, you said?"

I nodded, hanging on for dear life. Once, I fancied I caught Dr. Darby stealing a glance at my bloody hands in the dim light of the instrument panel, but whatever he might have been thinking, he kept it to himself.

We rocketed along the narrow lane, the Morris's headlamps illuminating the green tunnel of the trees and hedgerows with bounces of brightness. We sped past the Bulls' place so quickly that I almost missed it, although my mind did manage to register the fact that the house was now in total darkness.

AS WE SHOT ACROSS THE LITTLE stone bridge and into the grove, the Morris nearly became airborne, then bounced heavily on its springs as Dr. Darby brought it to a skidding halt just inches from the Gypsy's caravan. Even in the dark his knowledge of Bishop's Lacey's lanes and byways was remarkable, I thought.

"Stay here," he barked. "If I need you, I'll call." He threw open the driver's door, walked briskly round the caravan, and was gone.

Alone in the darkness, I gave an involuntary shiver.

To be perfectly honest, my stomach was a bit queasy. I don't mind death, but injury makes me nervous. It would all depend upon what Dr. Darby found inside the caravan.

I shifted restlessly in the Morris, trying to sift through these rather unexpected feelings. Was the Gypsy woman dead? The thought that she might be was appalling.

Although Death and I were not exactly old friends, we did have a nodding acquaintance. Twice before in my life I had encountered corpses, and each one had given me—

"Flavia!" The doctor was at the caravan's door. "Fetch a screwdriver. It's in the tool kit in the boot."

A screwdriver? What kind of—

It was perhaps just as well that my speculations were interrupted.

"Quickly. Bring it here."

At any other time I might have balked at his insolence in ordering me about like a lackey, but I bit my tongue. In fact, I even forgave him a little.

As Dr. Darby began loosening the screws of the door hinges, I couldn't help thinking what remarkably strong hands he had for an older man. If he hadn't used them to save lives, he might have made a wizard carpenter.

"Unscrew the last few," he said. "I'll take the weight of the door. That's it . . . good girl."

Even without knowing what we were doing, I was his willing slave.

As we worked, I caught glimpses of the Gypsy beyond, in the caravan's interior. Dr. Darby had lifted her from the floor to her bed where she lay motionless, her head wrapped in surgical gauze. I could not tell if she was dead or alive and it seemed awkward to ask.

At last the door came free of the frame, and for an instant, Dr. Darby held it in front of him like a shield. The image of a crusader crossed my mind.

"Easy now—put it down here."

He maneuvered the heavy panel carefully onto the caravan's floor, where it fit with not an inch to spare between the stove and the upholstered seats. Then, plucking two pillows from the bed, he placed them lengthwise on the door, before wrapping the Gypsy in a sheet and ever so gently lifting her from the bunk onto the makeshift stretcher.

Again I was struck with his compact strength. The woman must have weighed almost as much as he did.

"Quickly now," he said. "We must get her to the hospital."

So! The Gypsy *was* alive. Death had been thwarted—at least for now.

Pulling a second sheet from the bed, Dr. Darby tore it into long strips, which he worked swiftly into position under the door, then round and round the Gypsy, fastening the ends with a series of expert knots.

He had positioned her so that her feet were closest to the empty door frame, and now I watched as he eased past her and leapt to the ground outside.

I heard the Morris's starter grind—and then engage. The motor roared and moments later I saw him backing his machine towards the caravan.

Now he was clambering back aboard.

"Take this end," he said, pointing to the Gypsy's feet. "It's lighter."

He scrambled past me, seized the end of the door that lay beneath her head, and began sliding it towards the doorway.

"Into the offside seat," he said. "That's it . . . easy now."

I had suddenly seen what he was trying to do, and as Dr. Darby lifted the head of the door, I guided its foot down into the space between the passenger's seat and the instrument panel.

With surprisingly little struggle, our task was finished. With the Gypsy jutting up at a rigid angle, the little Morris looked like an oversized wood-working plane; the Gypsy herself like a mummy lashed to a board.

It isn't the neatest of arrangements, I remember thinking, *but it will do*.

"You'll have to stay here," Dr. Darby said, wedging himself in behind the steering wheel. "There's not room for the three of us in the old bus. Just stay put and don't touch anything. I'll send the police as soon as I'm able."

What he meant, of course, was that I was in far less physical danger if I remained in one spot, rather than risking the possibility of flushing out the Gypsy's attacker by walking home alone to Buckshaw.

I gave the doctor a halfhearted thumbs-up. More than that would have been out of place.

He let in the clutch and the car, with its weird cargo, began teetering slowly across the grove. As it crept over the humpbacked bridge, I had my last glimpse of the Gypsy, her face dead white in the light of a sudden moon.

five

NOW I WAS TRULY ALONE.

Or was I?

Not a leaf stirred. Something went *plop* in the water nearby, and I held my breath. An otter, perhaps? Or something worse?

Could the Gypsy's attacker still be here in the Palings? Still hiding . . . still watching . . . from somewhere in the trees?

It was a stupid thought, and I realized it instantly. I'd learned quite early in life that the mind loves nothing better than to spook itself with outlandish stories, as if the various coils of the brain were no more than a troop of roly-poly Girl Guides huddled over a campfire in the darkness of the skull.

Still, I gave a little shiver as the moon slipped behind a cloud. It had been cool enough when I'd first come here with the Gypsy, chilly when I'd ridden Gry into the village for Dr. Darby, and now, I realized, I was beastly cold.

The lights of the caravan glowed invitingly, warm patches of orange in the blue darkness. If a wisp of smoke had been floating up from the tin chimney, the scene might have been one of those frameable tear-away prints in the weekly magazines: *A Gypsy Moon*, for instance.

It was Dr. Darby who had left the lamp burning. Should I scramble aboard and turn it out?

Vague thoughts of saving paraffin crossed my mind, and even vaguer thoughts of being a good citizen.

Saints on skates! I was looking for an excuse to get inside the caravan and have a jolly good gander at the scene of the crime. Why not admit it?

"*Don't touch anything*," Dr. Darby had said. Well, I wouldn't. I'd keep my hands in my pockets.

Besides, my footprints were already everywhere on the floor. What harm would a few more do? Could the police distinguish between two sets of bloody footprints made less than an hour apart? *We shall see*, I thought.

Even as I clambered up onto the footboard I realized that I should have to work quickly. Having arrived at the hospital in Hinley, Dr. Darby would soon be calling the police—or instructing someone else to call them.

There wasn't a second to waste.

A quick look round showed that the Gypsy lived a frugal life indeed. As far as I could discover, there were no personal papers or documents, no letters, and no books—not even a Bible. I had seen the woman make the sign of the cross and it struck me as odd that a copy of the scriptures should not have its place in her traveling home.

In a bin beside the stove, a supply of vegetables looked rather the worse for wear, as if they had been snatched hastily from a farmer's field rather than purchased clean from a village market: potatoes, beets, turnips, onions, all jumbled together.

I shoved my hand into the bin and rummaged around at the bottom. Nothing but clay-covered vegetables.

I don't know what I was looking for, but I would if I found it. If I were a Gypsy, I thought, the bottom of the veggie bin would have been high on my list of hiding places.

But now my hands were thoroughly covered not only with dried blood, but also with soil. I wiped them on a grubby towel that hung on a nearby nail, but I could see at once that this would never do. I turned to the tin basin, took down a rose-and-briar ewer from the shelf, and poured water over my filthy hands, one at a time. Bits of earth and caked blood turned it quickly to a muddy red.

A goose walked over my grave and I shuddered slightly. Red blood cells, I remembered from my chemical experiments, were really not much more than a happy soup of water, sodium, potassium, chloride, and phosphorus. Mix them together in the proper proportions, though, and they formed a viscous liquid jelly: a jelly with mystic capabilities, one that could contain in its scarlet complexities not just nobility but also treachery.

Again I wiped my hands on the towel, and was about to chuck the contents of the basin outside onto the grass when it struck me: *Don't be a fool, Flavia! You're leaving a trail of evidence that's as plain to see as an advert on a hoarding!*

Inspector Hewitt would have a conniption. And I had no doubt it would be he—four in the morning or not—who responded to the doctor's call.

If questioned about it later, Dr. Darby would surely remember that I hadn't washed or wiped the blood from my hands in his presence. And, unless caught out by the evidence, I could hardly admit to disobeying his orders by reentering the caravan after he had gone.

Like a tightrope walker, I teetered my way down the shafts of the wagon, the basin held out in front of me at arm's length like an offering.

I made my way to the river's edge, put down the basin, and undid my laces. The ruin of another pair of shoes would drive Father into a frenzy.

I waded barefoot into the water, wincing at the sudden coldness. Closer to the middle, where the sluggish current was even slightly stronger, would be the safest place to empty the basin; closer in might leave telltale residue on the grassy bank, and for the first time in my life I offered up a bit of thanks for the convenience of a shortish skirt.

Knee-deep in the flowing water, I lowered the basin and let the current wash away the telltale fluids. As the clotted contents combined with the river and floated off to God-knows-where, I gave a sigh of relief. The evidence—at least this bit of it—was now safely beyond the recall of Inspector Hewitt and his men.

As I waded back towards the riverbank, I stepped heavily on a submerged stone and stubbed my toe. I nearly went face-first into the water, and only a clumsy windmilling of my arms saved me. The basin, too, acted as a kind of counterweight, and I arrived breathless, but upright, at the riverbank.

But wait! The towel! The prints of my dirty and bloody hands were all over the thing.

Back to the caravan I dashed. As I had thought it would be, the towel was stained with a pair of remarkably clear Flavia-sized handprints. Rattling good luck I had thought of it!

One more trip to the river's edge; one more wade into the chilly water, where I scrubbed and rinsed the towel several times over, grimacing as I wrung it out with a series of surprisingly fierce twists. Only when the water that dribbled back into the river was perfectly clear in the moonlight did I retrace my steps to the bank.

With the towel safely back on its nail in the caravan, I began to breathe normally. Even if they analyzed the cotton strands, the police would find nothing out of the ordinary. I gave a little snort of satisfaction.

Look at me, I thought. *Here I am behaving like a criminal.* Surely the police would never suspect me of attacking the Gypsy. Or would they?

Wasn't I, after all, the last person to be seen in her company? Our departure from the fête in the Gypsy's caravan had been about as discreet as a circus parade. And then there had been the set-to in the Gully with Mrs. Bull, who I suspected would be only too happy to fabricate evidence against a member of the de Luce family.

What was it she had said? *"You're one of them de Luce girls from over at Buckshaw."* I could still hear her raw voice: *"I'd rec'nize them cold blue eyes anywhere."*

Harsh words, those. What grievance could she possibly have against us?

My thoughts were interrupted by a distant sound: the noise of a motorcar bumping its bottom on a stony road. This was followed by a mechanical grinding as it shifted down into a lower gear.

The police!

I leapt to the ground and made for the bridge. There was enough time—but just barely—to assume the pose of a faithful lookout. I scrambled up onto the stone parapet and arranged myself as carefully as if I were sitting for a statue of Wendy, from *Peter Pan*: seated primly, leaning slightly forward in eager relief, palms pressed flat to the stone for support, brow neatly furrowed with concern. I hoped I wouldn't look too smarmy.

Not a minute too soon. The car's headlamps were already flashing between the trees to my left, and seconds later, a blue Vauxhall was chuddering to a stop at the bridge.

Fixed in the spotlight of the powerful beams, I turned my head slowly to face them, at the same time lifting my hand ever so languidly, as if to shield my eyes from their harsh and unrelenting glare.

I couldn't help wondering how it looked to the Inspector.

There was an unnerving pause, rather like the one that occurs between the time the houselights go down, but before the orchestra strikes up the first notes of the overture.

A car door slammed heavily, and Inspector Hewitt came walking slowly into the converging beams of light.

"Flavia de Luce," he said in a flat, matter-of-fact voice: too flat to be able to tell if he was thrilled or disgusted to find me waiting for him at the scene of the crime.

"Good morning, Inspector," I said. "I'm very happy to see you."

I was half hoping that he would return the compliment but he did not. In the recent past I had assisted him with several baffling investigations. By rights he should be bubbling over with gratitude—but was he?

The Inspector walked slowly to the highest point in the middle of the humpbacked bridge and stared off towards the glade where the caravan was parked.

"You've left your footprints in the dew," he said.

I followed his gaze, and sure enough: Lit by the low angle of the Vauxhall's headlamps, and although Dr. Darby's footprints and the tire tracks left by his car had already lightened somewhat, the impressions of my every step lay black and fresh in the wet, silvery grass of the glade, leading straight back to the caravan's door.

"I had to make water," I said. It was the classic female excuse, and no male in recorded history had ever questioned it.

"I see," the Inspector said, and left it at that.

Later, I would have a quick piddle behind the caravan for insurance purposes. No one would be any the wiser.

A silence had fallen, each of us waiting, I think, to see what the other would say. It was like a game: First one to speak is the Booby.

It was Inspector Hewitt.

"You've got goose-bumps," he said, looking at me attentively. "Best go sit in the car."

He had already reached the far side of the bridge before he turned back. "There's a blanket in the boot," he said, and then vanished in the shadows.

I felt my temper rising. Here was this man—a man in an ordinary business suit, without so much as a badge on his shoulder—dismissing me from the scene of a crime that I had come to think of as my very own. After all, hadn't I been the first to discover it?

Had Marie Curie been dismissed after discovering polonium? Or radium? Had someone told *her* to run along?

It simply wasn't fair.

A crime scene, of course, wasn't exactly an atom-shattering discovery, but the Inspector might at least have said "Thank you." After all, hadn't the attack upon the Gypsy taken place within the grounds of Buckshaw, my ancestral home? Hadn't her life likely been saved by my horseback expedition into the night to summon help?

Surely I was entitled to at least a nod. But no—

"Go and sit in the car," Inspector Hewitt had said, and now—as I realized with a sinking feeling that the law doesn't know the meaning of the word "gratitude"—I felt my fingers curling slowly into involuntary fists.

Even though he had been on the scene for no more than a few moments, I knew that a wall had already gone up between the Inspector and myself. If the man was expecting cooperation from Flavia de Luce, he would bloody well have to work for it.

six

THE NERVE OF THE MAN!

I resolved to tell him nothing.

In the glade, across the humpbacked bridge, I could see his shadow moving slowly across the curtained window of the caravan. I imagined him stepping carefully between the bloodstains on the floor.

To my surprise the light was extinguished, and moments later the Inspector came walking back across the bridge.

He seemed surprised to see me standing where he had left me. Without a word, he walked to the boot, took out a tartan blanket, and wrapped it round my shoulders.

I yanked the thing off and handed it back to him. To my surprise, I noticed that my hands were shaking.

"I'm not cold, thank you very much," I said icily.

"Perhaps not," he said, wrapping the blanket round me once again, "but you're in shock."

In shock? Fancy that! I've never been in shock before. This was entirely new and uncharted territory.

With a hand on my shoulder and another on my arm, Inspector Hewitt walked me to the car and held open the door. I dropped into the seat like a stone, and suddenly I was shaking like a leaf.

"We'd better get you home," he said, climbing into the driver's seat and switching on the ignition. As a blast of hot air from the car's heater engulfed me, I wondered vaguely how it could have warmed up so quickly. Perhaps it was a special model, made solely for the police . . . something intentionally designed to induce a stupor. Perhaps . . .

And I remember nothing more until we were grinding to a stop on the gravel sweep at Buckshaw's front entrance. I had no recollection whatever of having been driven back through the Gully, along the high street, past St. Tancred's, and so to Buckshaw. But here we were, so I must have been.

Dogger, surprisingly, was at the door—as if he had been waiting up all night. With his prematurely white hair illuminated from behind by the lights of the foyer, he seemed to me like a gaunt Saint Peter at the pearly gates, welcoming me home.

"I could have walked," I said to the Inspector. "It was no more than a half mile."

"Of course you could," Inspector Hewitt said. "But this trip is at His Majesty's expense."

Was he teasing me? Twice in the recent past the Inspector had driven me home, and upon one of those occasions he had made it clear that when it came to petrol consumption the coffers of the King were not bottomless.

"Are you sure?" I asked, oddly fuddled.

"Straight out of his personal change purse."

As if in a dream, I found myself plodding heavily up the steps to the front door. When I reached the top, Dogger fussed with the blanket round my shoulders.

"Off to bed with you, Miss Flavia. I'll be along with a hot drink directly."

As I trudged exhausted up the curving staircase, I could hear quiet words being exchanged between Dogger and the Inspector, but could not make out a single one of them.

Upstairs, in the east wing, I walked into my bedroom and without even removing His Majesty's tartan blanket, fell facedown onto my bed.

I WAS GAZING AT A CUP OF COCOA on my night table.

As I focused on the thick brown skin that had formed upon its surface like ice on a muddy pond, something at the root of my tongue leapt like a little goat and my stomach turned over. There are not many things that I despise, but chiefest among them is skin on milk. I loathe it with a passion.

Not even the thought of the marvelous chemical change that forms the stuff—the milk's proteins churned and ripped apart by the heat of boiling, then reassembling themselves as they cool into a jellied skin—was enough to console me. I would rather eat a cobweb.

Of course by now the cocoa would be as cold as ditch water. For various complicated reasons reaching back into my family's past, Buckshaw's east wing was, as I have said, unheated, but I could hardly complain. I occupied this part of the house by choice, rather than by necessity. Dogger must have—

Dogger!

In an instant the whole of the previous day's events came storming into my consciousness like a wayward crash of thunder, and like those fierce sharp bolts of lightning that are said to strike upwards from the earth to the sky, so did these thoughts arrive in curiously reversed order: first, Inspector Hewitt and Dr. Darby, the Gully, and then the blood—the blood!—my sisters, Daffy and Feely, the Gypsy and Gry, her horse, and finally the church fête—all of these tumbling in upon one another in tattered but nevertheless sharply etched detail.

Had I been hit by lightning? Was that why I felt so curiously electrified: like a comb rubbed with tissue paper?

No, that wasn't it—but something in my mind was evading itself.

Oh, well, I thought, *I'll turn over and go back to sleep.*

But I couldn't manage it. The morning sun streaming in at the windows was painful to look at, and my eyes were as gritty as if someone had pitched a bucket of sand into them.

Perhaps a bath would buck me up. I smiled at the thought. Daffy would be dumbstruck if she knew of my bathing without being threatened. "Filthy Flavia," she called me, at least when Father wasn't around.

Daffy herself loved nothing better than to subside into a steaming tub with a book, where she would stay until the water had gone cold.

"It's like reading in one's own coffin," she would say afterwards, "but without the stench."

I did not share her enthusiasm.

A light tapping at the door interrupted these thoughts. I wrapped myself tightly in the tartan blanket and, like a penguin, waddled across the room.

It was Dogger, a fresh cup of steaming cocoa in his hand.

"Good morning, Miss Flavia," he said. He did not ask how I was feeling, but nonetheless, I was aware of his keen scrutiny.

"Good morning," I replied. "Please put it on the table. Sorry about the one you brought last night. I was too tired to drink it."

With a nod, Dogger swapped the cups.

"The Colonel wishes to see you in the drawing room," he said. "Inspector Hewitt is with him."

Blast and double blast! I hadn't had time to think things through. How much was I going to tell the Inspector and how much was I going to keep to myself?

To say nothing of Father! What would he say when he heard that his youngest daughter had been out all night, wading around in the blood of a Gypsy he had once evicted from his estate?

Dogger must have sensed my uneasiness.

"I believe the Inspector is inquiring about your health, miss. I shall tell them you'll be down directly."

BATHED AND RIGGED UP IN a ribboned dress, I came slowly down the stairs. Feely turned from a mirror in the foyer in which she had been examining her face.

"Now you're for it," she said.

"Fizz off," I replied pleasantly.

"Half the Hinley Constabulary on your tail and still you have time to be saucy to your sister. I hope you won't expect a visit from me when you're in the clink."

I swept past her with all the dignity I could muster, trying to gather my wits as I walked across the foyer. At the door of the drawing room, I paused to form a little prayer: "May the Lord bless me and keep me and make His face to shine upon me; may He fill me with great grace and lightning-quick thinking."

I opened the door.

Inspector Hewitt came to his feet. He had been sitting in the overstuffed armchair in which Daffy was usually lounging sideways with a book. Father stood in front of the mantelpiece, the dark side of his face reflected in the mirror.

"Ah, Flavia," he said. "The Inspector was just telling me that a woman's life has been saved by your prompt action. Well done."

Well done? . . . Well done?

Was this my father speaking? Or was one of the Old Gods merely using him as a ventriloquist's dummy to deliver to me a personal commendation from Mount Olympus?

But no—Father was a most unlikely messenger. Not once in my eleven years could I recall him praising me, and now that he had done so, I hadn't the faintest idea how to respond.

The Inspector extracted me from a sticky situation.

"Well done, indeed," he said. "They tell me that in spite of the ferocity of the attack, she's come out of it with no more than a fractured skull. At her age, of course . . ."

Father interrupted. "Dr. Darby rang up to express his commendations, Flavia, but Dogger told him you were sleeping. I took the message myself."

Father on the telephone? I could hardly believe it! Father only allowed "the instrument," as he called it, to be kept in the house with the express understanding that it be used only in the direst of emergencies: the Apocalypse, for instance.

But Dr. Darby was one of Father's friends. In due course, I knew, the good doctor would be sternly lectured on his breach of household standing orders, but ultimately would live to tell the tale.

"Still," Father said, his face clouding a little, "you're going to have to explain what you were doing wandering round the Palings in the middle of the night."

"That poor Gypsy woman," I said, changing the subject. "Her tent burned down at the fête. She had nowhere to go."

As I talked, I watched Father's face for any sign of balking. Hadn't he, after all, been the one who had driven Johnny Faa and his wife from the Buckshaw estate? Had he forgotten the incident? He was almost certainly not aware that his actions had caused the Gypsy's husband to fall dead in the road, and I wasn't about to tell him.

"I thought of the vicar's sermon, the one about Christian charity—"

"Yes, yes, Flavia," Father said. "Most commendable."

"I told her she could camp in the Palings, but only for one night. I knew that you'd—"

"Thank you, Flavia, that's quite enough."

"—approve."

Poor Father: outflanked, outgunned, and outwitted. I almost felt sorry for him.

He crooked a forefinger and touched the angled joint to each side of his clipped mustache in turn: right and then left—a kind of suppressed, nervous preening that had probably been practiced by military officers since time immemorial. I'd be willing to bet that if Julius Caesar had a mustache he knuckled it in precisely the same way.

"Inspector Hewitt would like a word with you. Because it concerns confidential information about individuals with whom I am not acquainted, I shall leave you alone."

With a nod to the Inspector, Father left the room. I heard the door of his study open, and then close, as he sought refuge among his postage stamps.

"Now then," the Inspector said, flipping open his notebook and unscrewing the cap of his Biro. "From the beginning."

"I couldn't sleep, you see," I began.

"Not *that* beginning," Inspector Hewitt said without looking up. "Tell me about the church fête."

"I'd gone into the Gypsy's tent to have my fortune told."

"And did you?"

"No," I lied.

The last thing on earth I wanted to share with the Inspector was the woman on the mountain—the woman who wanted to come home from the cold. Nor did I care to tell him about the woman that I was in the process of becoming.

"I knocked her candle over, and before I knew it, I . . . I . . . "

Much to my surprise, my lower lip was trembling at the recollection.

"Yes, we've heard about that. The vicar was able to provide us with a very good account, as was Dr. Darby."

I gulped, wondering if anyone had reported how I'd hidden behind a pitch as the Gypsy's tent burned to ashes.

"Poor girl," he said tenderly. "You've had quite a series of shocks, haven't you?"

I nodded.

"If I'd had any idea of what you'd already been through, I'd have taken you to the hospital directly."

"It's all right," I said gamely. "I'll be all right."

"Will you?" the Inspector asked.

"No," I said, struggling with tears.

And suddenly it all came pouring out: From the fête to the Palings, not forgetting the seething Mrs. Bull; from my frankly fabricated tale of awakening in the night to fret about the Gypsy woman's welfare to my discovery of her lying in a pool of her own blood in the caravan, I left out not a single detail.

Except Brookie Harewood, of course.

I was saving him for myself.

It was a magnificent performance, if I do say so. As I had been forced to learn at a very young age, there's no better way to mask a lie—or at least a glaring omission—than to wrap it in an emotional outpouring of truth.

During it all, Inspector Hewitt's Biro fairly flew over the pages, getting every scrap of it down for the record. *He must have studied one of the shorthand methods*, I thought idly as he scribbled. Later, he would expand these notes into a longer, neater, more legible form.

Perhaps he would dictate them to his wife, Antigone. I had met her not long before at a puppet show in the parish hall. Would she remember me?

In my mind I could see her seated at a typewriter at the kitchen table in their tastefully decorated cottage, her back ramrod straight in a position of perfect posture, her fingers hovering eagerly over the keys. She would be wearing hooped earrings, and a silk blouse of oyster gray.

"Flavia de Luce?" she would be saying, her large, dark eyes looking up at her husband. "Why, isn't she that charming girl I met at St. Tancred's, dear?"

Inspector Hewitt's eyes would crinkle at the corners.

"One and the same, my love," he would tell her, shaking his head at the memory of me. "One and the same."

We had reached the end of my statement, the point at which the Inspector himself had arrived upon the scene in the Palings.

"That will do for now," he said, flipping closed his notebook and shoving it into the inside pocket of his jacket. "I've asked Sergeant Graves to come round later to take your fingerprints. Quite routine, of course."

I wrinkled my brow, but secretly I couldn't have been more delighted. The dimpled detective sergeant with his winks and grins had come to be one of my favorites among the Hinley Constabulary.

"I expect they'll be all over everything," I said helpfully. "Mine and Dr. Darby's."

"And those of the Gypsy woman's attacker," he might have added, but he did not. Rather, he stood up and stuck his hand out to be shaken, as formally as if he were being received at a royal garden party.

"Thank you, Flavia," he said. "You've been of great assistance . . . as always."

As always? Was the Inspector twitting me?

But no—his handshake was firm and he looked me straight in the eye.

I'm afraid I smirked.

seven

"DOGGER!" I SAID. "THEY'RE COMING TO TAKE MY FINGERPRINTS!"

Dogger looked up from the vast array of silverware he was polishing on the kitchen table. For just a moment his face was a complete blank, and then he said, "I trust they will be returned to you in good order."

I blinked. Was Dogger making a joke? I hoped desperately that he was.

Dogger had suffered the most awful privations in the Far East during the war. His mind now seemed sometimes to consist of no more than a crazy tangle of broken suspension bridges joining the past with the present. If he had ever made a joke before, I had never heard of it. This, then, could be a momentous occasion.

"Oh! Ha ha ha." I laughed too loudly. "That's very good, Dogger. Returned to me in good order . . . I must remember to tell that one to Mrs. Mullet."

I had no intention whatever of sharing this precious moment with our cook, but sometimes flattery does not know when to stop.

Dogger formed a faint smile as he returned a fish fork to the cutlery chest and selected another. The de Luce silverware was kept in a dark folding cabinet which, when opened, presented a remarkable array of fish forks, toddy ladles, mote spoons, marrow scoops, lobster picks, sugar nips, grape shears, and pudding trowels, all arranged in steps, like so many silvery salmon leaping up the stony staircase of a whisky-colored stream somewhere in Scotland.

Dogger had lugged this heavy box to the kitchen table for the ritual cleaning of the cutlery, a seemingly endless task that occupied a great deal of his time, and one that I never tired of watching.

Mrs. Mullet loved to tell about how, as a child, I had been found on top of the table playing with the dolls I had contrived by clothing a family of sterling silver forks in folded napkins. Their identical faces—long noses and round cheeks—were just barely suggested by the engraved *D L* on the top of each handle, and required a great leap of the imagination to make them out at all.

"The Mumpeters," I had called them: Mother Mumpeter, Father Mumpeter, and the three little Mumpeter girls, all of whom—even though they were burdened with three or four legs each—I had made to walk and dance and sing gaily upon the tabletop.

I could still remember Grindlestick, the three-legged waif I had fashioned from a pickle fork (which Father referred to as a trifid), who performed the most amazing acrobatics until I jammed one of her legs in a crack and broke it off.

"Better than the 'ippodrome, it were," Mrs. M would tell me as she wiped away a tear of laughter. "Poor little tyke."

I still don't know if she meant Grindlestick or me.

Now, as I watched him at his work, I wondered if Dogger had known about the Mumpeters. It was likely that he did, since Mrs. Mullet, when it came to gossip, was equaled only by the *News of the World*.

I knew that there would never be a better time to dig for information: Mrs. M was away from her usual post in the kitchen and Dogger seemed to be at a peak of alertness. I took a deep breath and plunged directly in: "I found Brookie Harewood in the drawing room last night," I said. "Actually, it was past two in the morning."

Dogger finished polishing a grapefruit knife, then put it down and aligned it perfectly with its mates on a strip of green baize.

"What was he doing?" he asked.

"Nothing. Just standing by the fireplace. No, wait! He was crouched down, touching one of the firedogs."

These fire irons had belonged to Harriet, and although they had different faces, each was that of a wily fox. Harriet had used them as the main characters in the bedtime stories she'd invented for Daffy and Feely: a fact of which they never tired of reminding me.

To be perfectly truthful, I bitterly resented the fact that my mother had spun so many tales of the make-believe world for my sisters but not for me. She had died before I was old enough to receive my due.

"Which of the two irons was he touching?" Dogger asked, already halfway to his feet.

"The Sally Fox," I said. "The one on the right."

Sally Fox and Shoppo were the names Harriet had given to the cunning pair, who had gone jauntily adventuring through an imaginary world—a world that had been lost with Harriet's death. From time to time, Feely and Daffy, trying to resuscitate the warm and happy feeling of bygone days, had made up their own tales about the two crafty foxes, but in recent years they had, for some reason, stopped trying. Perhaps they had grown too old for fairy tales.

I followed as Dogger walked from the kitchen through to the foyer and made for the drawing room in the west wing.

He paused for a moment, listening at the door, then seemed to vanish through its panels like a wisp of smoke, as so many of the older servants are able to do.

He went straight to the Sally Fox, regarding her as solemnly as if he were a priest come to administer the last rites. When he had finished, he moved a few feet to his left and repeated the same performance with Shoppo.

"Most odd," he said.

"Odd?"

"*Most* odd. This one," he said, pointing to the Sally Fox, "has been missing for several weeks."

"Missing?"

"It was not here yesterday. I did not inform the Colonel because I knew he would worry. At first I thought I might have misplaced it myself during one of my—my . . . "

"Reveries," I suggested.

Dogger nodded. "Thank you," he said.

Dogger suffered occasional terrors during which his very being was snatched away for a while by unseen forces and hurled into some horrid abyss. At such times his soul seemed to be replaying old atrocities, as he was once more thrown into the company of his dear old comrades-in-arms, their restless spirits dragged back from death by his love for them.

"A month ago it was Shoppo: here one day, gone the next. And then he reappeared. I thought I must be imagining things."

"Are you sure, Dogger?"

"Yes, Miss Flavia—quite sure."

I thought for a moment of telling him I had taken the firedogs, but I couldn't bring myself to mouth the lie. There was something in Dogger that demanded truth.

"Perhaps Daffy borrowed them for one of her drawing sessions."

Daffy's occasional pencil sketches usually began well enough but then, quite often, took a spectacularly wrong turn. The Virgin Mary would suddenly sprout buck teeth, for instance, or an impromptu cartoon of Father seated at the dinner table would turn into a man with no eyes. Whenever this happened, Daffy would set the drawing aside and go back to her reading. For weeks afterwards we would keep finding, stuffed into the crevices of the chesterfield and under the cushions of the drawing-room chairs, the pages she had ripped from her sketchbook.

"Perhaps," Dogger said. "Perhaps not."

I think it was at that moment, without realizing it, that I began to see the solution to the puzzle of the fire irons.

"Is Mrs. Mullet here today?"

I knew perfectly well that she was but I hadn't seen her in the kitchen.

"She's outside having a word with Simpkins, the milk-float man. Something about a wood chip in the butter."

I'd have to wait until Dogger put away the cutlery before I tackled Mrs. M.

I wanted to be alone with her.

"THEM TRADESMEN DON'T GIVE A FLICK," Mrs. Mullet said disgustedly, her arms white to the elbows with flour. "Really, they don't. One day it's a fly in the clotted cream, and the next it's a—well, you really don't want to know, dear. But one thing's as clear as dishwater. If you lets 'em get away with it, there's never any tellin' what they'll bring round next time. Keep quiet about a toothpick in today's butter and next thing you know you'll be findin' a doorknob in the cottage cheese. I don't like it, dear, but it's the way of the world."

How on earth, I wondered, could I bring the conversation around from tradesmen to Brookie Harewood without seeming to do so?

"Perhaps we should eat more fish," I suggested. "Some of the fishermen in the village sell it fresh from their creels. Brookie Harewood, for instance."

Mrs. Mullet looked at me sharply. "Hmph! Brookie Harewood! He's no more than a poacher. I'm surprised the Colonel hasn't run him off the Palings. Them are *your* fish he's sellin' at the cottage gates."

"I suppose he has to earn a living."

"Livin'?" She bristled, giving the great mound of bread dough an extra pummel. "He don't need to make a livin' no more than Grace's goose. Not with that mother of his over in Malden Fenwick sendin' him reg'lar checks to stay away. He's a layabout, plain and simple, that one is, and a rascal to boot."

"A remittance man?" I asked.

Daffy had once told me about the black-sheep son of our neighbors, the Blatchfords, who was paid to keep well away in Canada. "Two pounds ten shillings per mile per year," she said. "He lives in the Queen Charlotte Islands to maximize his pension."

"Mittens man or not, he's no good, and that's a fact," said Mrs. Mullet. "He's managed to get in with a bad lot."

"Colin Prout?" I suggested, thinking of the way Brookie had bullied the boy at the fête.

"Colin Prout's no more than Brookie Harewood's spare fingers, or so I've 'eard. No, I was talkin' about Reggie Pettibone an' that lot what 'as the shop in the 'igh street."

"The antiques place?"

Pettibone's Antiques & Quality Goods was just a few doors west of the Thirteen Drakes. Although I had passed it often, I had never been inside.

Mrs. Mullet sniffed.

"Antiques, my sitter!" she exclaimed. "Sorry, dear, but that's 'ow I feels about it. That Reggie Pettibone give us two pounds six and three last year for a table me and Alf bought new at the Army and Navy when first we was married. Three weeks later we spots it in 'is window with silver knobs and fifty-five guineas on it! And a sign what says 'Georgian Whist Table by Chippendale.' We knew it was ours because Alf reckernized the burn mark on the leg where 'e raked it with an 'ot poker whilst 'e was tryin' to fish out a coal what 'ad popped out of the grate and rolled under it when our Agnes was just a mite."

"And Brookie's in with Pettibone?"

"I should say he is. Thick as thieves. Tight as the jaws off a nutcracker, them two."

"What does his mother think of that, I wonder?"

"Pfaw!" Mrs. Mullet said. "A fat lot she cares about 'im. 'Er with 'er paints and brushes! She does the 'orses and 'ounds crowd, you know—that lot o' swells. Charges 'em a pretty penny, too, I'll wager. Brookie and 'is under'anded ways 'as brought 'er nothin' but shame. To my mind, she don't rightly care what 'e gets 'isself up to so long as 'e keeps clear of Malden Fenwick."

"Thank you, Mrs. M," I said. "I enjoy talking to you. You always have such interesting stories to tell."

"Mind you, I've said nothing," she said in an undertone, raising a finger. "My lips are sealed."

And in rather an odd way, there was truth in what she said. Since I first came into the room I had been waiting for her to ask me about the Gypsy, or why the police had turned up at Buckshaw, but she had done neither. Was it possible she didn't know about either of these events?

It seemed unlikely. Mrs. M's recent chin-wag at the kitchen door with the milk-float man was likely to have resulted in more swapping of intelligence than a chin-wag between Lord Haw-Haw and Mata Hari.

I was already across the kitchen with my hand on the door when she said it: "Don't go wandering too far off, dear. That nice officer—the one with the dimples—will be round soon to 'ave your fingerprints."

Curse the woman! Was she eavesdropping from behind every closed door at Buckshaw? Or was she truly clairvoyant?

"Oh, yes," I replied lamely. "Thanks for reminding me, Mrs. M. I'd almost forgotten about him."

THE DOORBELL RANG AS I came through the passage beneath the stairs. I put on a sprint but Feely beat me to it.

I skidded to a stop on the foyer's checkerboard tiles just as she swung open the front door to reveal Detective Sergeant Graves standing on the doorstep, small black box in hand and his jaw already halfway to the ground.

I have to admit that Feely had never looked more beautiful: From her salmon-colored silk blouse to her sage green mohair sweater (both of which, as I knew from my own snooping expeditions, she had pinched from Harriet's dressing room), from her perfect honey-colored hair to her sparkling blue eyes (having, of course, left her black-rimmed spectacles, as she always did, stuffed behind the pillows on the chesterfield), she was a close-up from a Technicolor cinema film.

She had planned this, the hag!

"Sergeant Graves, I presume?" she said in a low, husky voice—one I had never heard her use before. "Come in. We've been expecting you."

We? What in the old malarkey was she playing at?

"I'm Flavia's sister, Ophelia," she was saying, extending a coral-encrusted wrist and a long white hand that made the Lady of Shalott's fingers look like meathooks.

I could have killed her!

What right did Feely have to insert herself, without so much as a by-your-leave, between me and the man who had come to Buckshaw expressly to take my fingerprints? It was unforgiveable!

Still, I mustn't forget that I'd had more than one daydream in which the chipper little sergeant married my older sister and lived in a flower-choked cottage where I would be able to drop in for afternoon tea and happy professional chats about criminal poisoners.

Sergeant Graves had finally recovered enough of his wits to say "Yes," and bumble his way into the foyer.

"Would you like a cup of tea and a biscuit, Sergeant?" Feely asked, managing to suggest in her tone that the poor dear was overworked, dog-tired, and malnourished.

"I *am* quite thirsty, come to think of it," he managed with a bashful grin. "And hungry," he added.

Feely stepped back and ushered him towards the drawing room.

I followed like a neglected hound.

"You may set up your gear here," Feely told him, indicating a Regency table that stood near a window. "How dreadfully trying the life of a police officer must be. All firearms and criminals and hobnail boots."

Sergeant Graves had the good grace not to slug her. In fact, he seemed to be enjoying himself.

"It *is* a hard life, Miss Ophelia," he said, "at least most of the time."

His dimpled grin suggested that this was one of the easier moments.

"I'll ring for Mrs. Mullet," Feely said, reaching for a velvet pull that hung near the mantelpiece, and which probably hadn't been used since

George the Third was foaming at the mouth. Mrs. M would have kidney failure when the bell in the kitchen went off right above her head.

"What about the dabs?" I asked. It was a term I had picked up from Philip Odell, the private eye on the wireless. "Inspector Hewitt will be dead keen on having a squint at them."

Feely laughed a laugh like a tinkling silver bell. "You must forgive my little sister, Sergeant," she said. "I'm afraid she's been left alone too much."

Left alone? I almost laughed out loud! What would the sergeant say if I told him about the Inquisition in the Buckshaw cellars? About how Feely and Daffy had trussed me up in a smelly potato sack and flung me onto the stony floor?

"Dabs it is, then," said the sergeant, opening the clasps and flinging open his kit. "I suppose you'll be wanting to have a dekko at the chemicals and so forth," he added, giving me a wink.

If I'd had my way, he'd have been sanctified on the spot: *Saint Detective Sergeant Graves*. Come to think of it, I didn't even know his given name, but now was not the time to ask.

"This," he said, extracting the first of two small glass bottles, "is fingerprint powder."

"Mercury-based, I assume? Fine enough to give good definition to the loops and whorls, and so on?"

This, too, I had learned from Philip Odell. It had stuck in my mind because of its chemical connection.

The sergeant grinned and pulled out the second bottle, this one darker than the first.

"Go on," he said. "See if you can guess this one."

Guess? I thought. *The poor deluded man!*

"Graphite-based," I said. "More coarse than the mercury, but shows up better on certain surfaces."

"Top marks!" the sergeant said.

I turned away as if to wipe a bit of grit from my eye and stuck out my tongue at Feely.

"But surely these are for dusting?" I protested. " . . . and not needed for recording prints?"

"Right enough," the sergeant said. "I just thought you'd be interested in seeing the tools of the trade."

"Oh, I am indeed," I said quickly. "Thank you for the thought."

I did not suppose it would be polite to mention that I had upstairs in my chemical laboratory enough mercury and graphite to supply the needs of the Hinley Constabulary until well into the next century. Great-uncle Tar had been, among many other things, a hoarder.

"Mercury," I said, touching the bottle. "Fancy that!"

Sergeant Graves was now removing from its protective padding a rectangular sheet of plain glass, followed in quick succession by a bottle of ink and a roller.

Deftly he applied five or six drops of the ink to the surface of the glass, then rolled it smooth until the plate was uniformly covered with the black ooze.

"Now then," he said, taking my right wrist, and spreading my fingers until they were just hovering above the glass, "relax—let me do the work."

With no more than a slight pressure, he pushed my fingertips down and into the ink, one at a time, rolling each one from left to right on the ball of my fingertip. Then, moving my hand to a white card, which was marked with ten squares—one for each finger—he made the prints.

"Oh, Sergeant Graves!" Feely said. "You must take mine, too!"

"*Oh, Sergeant Graves! You must take mine, too!*"

I could have swatted her.

"Happy to, Miss Ophelia," he said, taking up her hand and dropping mine.

"Better ink the glass again," I said, "otherwise you might make a bad impression."

The sergeant's ears went a bit pink, but he soldiered on. In no time at all he had recoated the glass with a fresh film, and was taking up Feely's hand as if it were some venerable object.

"Did you know that, in the Holy Land, they have the fingerprints of the angel Gabriel?" I asked, trying desperately to regain his attention. "At least they used to. Dr. Robert Richardson and the Earl of Belmore saw them at Nazareth. Remember, Feely?"

For nearly a week—before our recent set-to—Daffy had been reading aloud to us at the breakfast table from an odd volume of the doctor's *Travels along the Mediterranean and Parts Adjacent*, and some of its many wonders were still fresh in my mind.

"They also showed him the Virgin Mary's Kitchen, at the Chapel of the Incarnation. They still have the cinders, the fire irons, the cutlery—"

Something in the back room of my brain was thinking about our own fire irons: the Sally Fox and Shoppo firedogs that had once belonged to Harriet.

"That will be quite enough, thank you, Flavia," Feely said. "You may fetch me a rag to wipe my fingers on."

"Fetch it yourself," I flung at her, and stalked from the room.

Compared with my life, Cinderella was a spoiled brat.

eight

ALONE AT LAST!

Whenever I'm with other people, part of me shrinks a little. Only when I am alone can I fully enjoy my own company.

In the kitchen garden, I grabbed my faithful old BSA Keep-Fit from the greenhouse. The bicycle had once belonged to Harriet, who had called her *l'Hirondelle*, "the Swallow": a word that reminded me so much of being force-fed cod-liver oil with a gag-inducing spoon that I had renamed her "Gladys." Who, for goodness' sake, wants to ride a bicycle with a name that sounds like a sickroom nurse?

And Gladys was much more down-to-earth than *l'Hirondelle*: an adventurous female with Dunlop tires, three speeds, and a forgiving dis-position. She never complained and she never tired, and neither, when I was in her company, did I.

I pedaled southeast from Buckshaw, wobbling slowly along the edge of the ornamental lake. To my left was a somewhat flat expanse called the Visto which had been cleared by Sir George de Luce in the mid-nineteenth century to serve as what he described in his diary as a "coign of vantage": a grassy green plain across which one was supposed to contemplate the blue enfolding hills.

In recent times, however, the Visto had been allowed to become little more than an overgrown cow pasture: a place where nettles ran riot and the contemplator's clothing was at risk of being ripped to tatters.

It was here that Harriet had kept *Blithe Spirit*, her de Havilland Gypsy Moth, which she had flown regularly up to London to meet her friends.

All that remained now of those happy days were the three iron rings, still rusting somewhere among the weeds, to which *Blithe Spirit* had long ago been tethered.

Once, when I had asked Father how Buckshaw looked from the air, he had gone all tight around the temples.

"Ask your aunt Felicity," he'd said gruffly. "She's flown."

I'd made a mental note to do so.

From the Visto an overgrown path ran south, crossing here and there long-abandoned lawns and hedges, which gave way eventually to copses and scrub. I followed the narrow track, and soon arrived at the Palings.

The Gypsy's caravan was as I had left it, although the ground bore signs of many "hobnail boots," as Feely had called them.

Why was I drawn back here? I wondered. Was it because the Gypsy had been under my protection? I had, after all, offered her sanctuary in the Palings and she had accepted. If amends were to be made, I would make them on my own—not because I was made to do so by a sense of shame.

Gry was grazing contentedly near the elders at the far side of the grove. Someone had brought him back to the Palings. They had even thought to bring a bale of fresh hay to the clearing, and he was making short work of it. He looked up at me without curiosity and then went back to his food.

"Who's a good boy, then?" I asked him, realizing, even as I said it, that these were words to be used in addressing a parrot.

"Good Gry," I said. "Splendid horse."

Gry paid not the slightest attention.

Something fastened to one of the tree trunks near the bridge caught my eye: a white wooden panel about six feet from the ground. I walked round the other side for a closer look.

Police Investigation—No Admittance by Order—Hinley Constabulary

The signboard was facing east—away from Buckshaw. Obviously it was meant to deter those hordes of the idly curious who flock to places where blood has been shed like crows to a winter oak.

I was, after all, on my own property. I could hardly be trespassing. Besides, I could always claim that I hadn't seen the thing.

I put a foot carefully onto one of the caravan's shafts and, waving my arms for balance like an aerialist, made my way slowly, heel to toe, up the slope to the driving board. To my surprise, the door had been replaced.

I paused to prepare myself—took a deep breath—then opened the door and stepped inside.

The blood had been cleaned up—I saw that at once. The floor was newly scrubbed and the sharp clean smell of Sunlight soap still hung in the air.

It wasn't dark inside the caravan, but neither was it light. I took a step towards the rear and froze in my tracks.

Someone was lying on the bed!

Suddenly my heart was pounding in a frenzy, and my eyes felt as if they were about to pop out of their sockets. I hardly dared breathe.

In the gloom of the drawn curtains I could see that it was a woman—no, not a woman—a girl. A few years older than me, perhaps. Her hair was raven black, her complexion tawny, and she was wrapped in a shapeless garment of black crepe.

As I stood motionless, staring at her face, her dark eyes opened slowly—and met mine.

With a quick, powerful spring she leapt from the bed, snatching something from a shelf, and I suddenly found myself wedged sharply against the wall, my arm twisted behind my back and a knife at my throat.

"Let go! You're hurting me!" I managed to squeeze the words out through the pain.

"Who are you? What are you doing here?" she hissed. "Tell me before I slit your gullet."

I could feel the knife's blade against my windpipe.

"Flavia de Luce," I gasped.

Damn it all! I was beginning to cry.

I caught a glimpse of myself in the mirror: her arm beneath my chin . . . my bulging eyes . . . the knife—the knife!

"That's a butter knife," I croaked in desperation.

It was one of those moments that might later seem amusing, but it wasn't now. I was trembling with fear and anger.

I felt my head jerk as she pulled back to look at the blade, and then I was being pushed away.

"Get out of here," she said roughly. "Get away—now—before I take the razor to you."

I didn't need a second invitation. The girl was obviously mad.

I stumbled towards the door and jumped to the ground. I grabbed Gladys and was halfway to the trees when—

"Wait!"

Her voice echoed in the glade.

"Did you say your name was Flavia? Flavia de Luce?"

I did not reply, but stopped at the edge of the grove, making sure that I kept Gry between us as a makeshift barrier.

"Please," she said. "Wait. I'm sorry. I didn't know who you were. They told me you saved Fenella's life."

"Fenella?" I managed, my voice shaking, still hollowed out by fear.

"Fenella Faa. You brought the doctor to her . . . here . . . last night."

I must have looked a perfect fool as I stood there with my mouth open like a goldfish. My brain needed time to catch up as the girl flip-flopped suddenly from holding a blade at my throat to being sorry. I was not accustomed to apologies, and this one—probably the first I had ever received in my life—caught me off guard.

"Who are you?" I asked.

"Porcelain," she said, jumping down from the caravan. "Porcelain Lee—Fenella's my gram."

She was coming towards me through the grass, her arms extended in biblical forgiveness.

"Let me hug you," she said. "I need to thank you."

I'm afraid I shrank back a little.

"Don't worry, I won't bite," she said, and suddenly she was upon me, her arms enfolding me in a tight embrace, her chin resting sharply on my shoulder.

"Thank you, Flavia de Luce," she whispered in my ear, as if we had been friends forever. "Thank you."

Since I was still half expecting a dagger to be plunged between my shoulder blades, I'm afraid I did not return her hug, which I received in stiff silence, rather like one of the sentries at Buckingham Palace pretending he doesn't notice the liberties being taken by an excessively affectionate tourist.

"You're welcome," I managed. "How is she? Fenella, I mean."

Using the Gypsy's first name did not come easily to me. In spite of the fact that Daffy and I have always referred to our own mother as Harriet (only Feely, who is older, seems to have the right to call her Mummy), it still felt excessively saucy to call a stranger's grandmother by her given name.

"She'll be all right, they think. Too early to tell. But if it hadn't been for you—"

Tears were beginning to well up in her dark eyes.

"It was nothing," I said uncomfortably. "She needed help. I was there."

Was it really that simple? Or did something deeper lie beneath?

"How did you hear—about this?" I asked, waving at the glade.

"The coppers tracked me down in London. Found my name and all that on a scrap of paper in her handbag. I begged a ride off a bloke with a lorry in Covent Garden, and he brought me as far as Doddingsley. I walked the rest of the way. Got here no more than an hour ago."

Four gold stars to Inspector Hewitt and his men, I thought. Searching the caravan for Fenella Faa's handbag had never crossed my mind.

"Where are you staying? At the Thirteen Drakes?"

"Blimey!" she said in a feigned Cockney accent. "That's a larf, that is!"

I must have looked offended.

"I couldn't rub two shillings together if my life depended on it," she said, waving her hands expansively at the grove. "So I expect right here is where I'll stay."

"Here? In the caravan?"

I looked at her aghast.

"Why not? It's Fenella's, isn't it? That means it's as good as mine. All I have to do is find out who's the nob that owns this bit of green, and—"

"It's called the Palings," I said, "and it belongs to my father."

Actually it didn't: It belonged to Harriet, but I didn't feel that I needed to explain our family's legal difficulties to a semi-ragamuffin stranger who had just threatened my life.

"Coo!" she said. "I'm sorry. I never thought."

"But you can't stay here," I went on. "It's a crime scene. Didn't you see the sign?"

"'Course I did. Didn't you?"

I chose to ignore this childish response. "Whoever attacked your gram might still be hanging about. Until the police find out who and why, it isn't safe to be here after dark."

This was a part, but not all, of the truth.

Every bit as important as Porcelain's physical safety was the sudden gnawing need I felt to make amends to the family of Fenella Faa: to correct an old wrong committed by my father. For the first time in my life I found myself seized by hereditary guilt.

"So you'll have to stay at Buckshaw," I blurted.

There! I'd done it. I'd made the leap. But even as I spoke, I knew that I would soon regret my words.

Father, for instance, would be furious.

Even when his beloved Harriet had invited the Gypsies to stay at Buckshaw, Father had driven them off. If she had failed, I didn't stand a chance.

Perhaps that was why I did it.

"My father's quite eccentric," I said. "At least, he has some odd ideas. He won't allow guests at Buckshaw, other than his own sister. I'll have to sneak you in."

Porcelain seemed quite alarmed at the thought. "I don't want to make trouble."

"Nonsense," I said, sounding like Aunt Felicity, the Human Steamroller. "It will be no trouble at all. Nobody ever comes into the east wing. They won't even know you're there.

"Bring your things," I ordered.

Until that moment I hadn't noticed how haggard Porcelain was looking. With her black crepe dress and the black circles under her eyes, she looked like someone made up for a masquerade party: "The Grim Reaper as a Young Woman."

"I've nothing," she said. "Just what you see." She tugged apologetically at her heavy hem. "This is Fenella's," she said. "I had to wash out my own things in the river this morning, and they aren't dry."

Wash out her things? Why would she need to do that? Since it didn't seem to be any of my business, I didn't ask—perhaps I could find an excuse to bring it up later.

"Off we go, then," I said, trying to sound cheerful. "Buckshaw awaits."

I picked up Gladys and wheeled her along beside me. Porcelain trudged a few steps behind, her eyes downcast.

"It isn't awfully far," I said, after a while. "I expect you'll be happy to get some sleep."

I turned and saw her nodding in response, but she did not speak. She shuffled along behind me, drained, and not even the ornamental dolphins of the Poseidon fountain made her take her eyes from the ground.

"These were made in the eighteenth century," I told her, "so they're rather elderly. They used to spout water from their mouths."

Again a nod.

We were taking a shortcut across the Trafalgar Lawn, an abandoned series of terraces that lay to the southeast of the house. Sir George de Luce, who planned it as a tribute to Admiral Nelson and his victory over the Spanish, which had taken place some forty years earlier, had laid it out at about the same time as the Visto.

By the simple expedient of tapping into Lucius "Leaking" de Luce's earlier and extensive subterranean waterworks, Sir George had planned to activate his glorious fountained landscape as a surprise for his bride.

And so he had begun on a work of landscape architecture that would rival or even surpass the spectacle of the ornamental lake, but speculation during the Railway Mania had scotched his fortunes. With most of his capital gone, what had been planned as a noble avenue of fountains, with Buckshaw as its focal point, had been abandoned to the elements.

Now, after a century of rain and snow, sun and wind, and the nocturnal visits of the villagers who came at night to steal stone for their garden walls, the Trafalgar Lawn and its statues were like a sculptor's scrapyard, with various bits of stone cherubs, mossy Tritons, and sea nymphs jutting up out of the ground here and there like stone swimmers from a shipwreck waiting to be rescued from a sea of earth.

Only Poseidon had survived, lounging with his net atop a crumbling base, brooding in marble over his broken family, his three-pronged trident like a lightning rod, sticking up towards whatever might be left of the ancient Greek heavens.

"Here's old Poseidon," I said, turning to haul Gladys up yet another set of crumbled steps. "His photograph was in *Country Life* a couple of years ago. Rather splendid, isn't he?"

Porcelain had come suddenly to a dead stop, her hand covering her mouth, her hollowed-out eyes staring upwards, as wide and as dark as the pit. Then she let out a cry like a small animal.

I followed her gaze, and saw at once the thing that had frozen her in her tracks.

Dangling from Poseidon's trident, like a scarecrow hung on a coat hook, was a dark figure.

"It's Brookie Harewood," I said, even before I saw his face.

nine

ONE OF THE TRIDENT'S TINES HAD PIERCED BROOKIE'S LONG moleskin coat at the neck, and he swung slightly in the breeze, looking rather casual in his flat cap and scarlet scarf, as if he were enjoying one of the roundabouts at an amusement pier.

For a moment, I thought he might have fallen. Perhaps in an excess of alcoholic high spirits he'd been attempting to scale the statue. Perhaps he had slipped from Poseidon's head and fallen onto the trident.

That idea was short-lived, however. I saw almost at once that his hands were tied behind his back. But that wasn't the worst of it.

As I came round full front-on, the sun glinted brightly on something that seemed to be projecting from Brookie's mouth.

"Stay here," I told Porcelain, even though I could see that there wasn't a chance of her moving.

I leaned Gladys against the lower of the three seashell bowls that comprised the fountain, then climbed up her tubular frame until finally I was standing on her seat, from which point I could get a knee up onto the rough stone rim.

The bowl of the thing was filled with a disgusting broth of black water, dead leaves, and mold, the result of a century of neglect, and it smelled to high heaven.

By standing on the rim, I was able to clamber up onto the fountain's middle bowl, and finally the highest one. I was now level with Brookie's knees, staring up into his unseeing eyes. His face was a horrid fish-belly white.

He was quite dead, of course.

After the initial shock of realizing that someone I had spoken to just hours before was no longer in the land of the living, I began to feel oddly excited.

I have no fear of the dead. Indeed, in my own limited experience I have found them to produce in me a feeling that is quite the opposite of fear. A dead body is much more fascinating than a live one, and I have learned that most corpses tell better stories. I'd had the good fortune of seeing several of them in my time; in fact, Brookie was my third.

As I teetered on the edge of the sculptured stone seashell, I could see clearly what it was that had glinted in the sun. Projecting from one of Brookie's nostrils—not his mouth—was an object that first appeared to be a round silver medallion: a flat, perforated disk with a handle attached. On the end of it was suspended a single drop of Brookie's blood.

The image punched out of the disk was that of a lobster, and engraved on the handle was the de Luce monogram.

D L.

It was a silver lobster pick—one of the set that belonged to Buckshaw.

The last time I'd seen one of these sharp-pointed utensils, Dogger had been rubbing it with silver polish at the kitchen table.

The business end of the thing, I recalled, ended in two little tines that stuck out like the horns on a snail's head. These prongs, which had been designed to pry the pink meat from the cracks and crevices of a boiled lobster, were now lodged firmly somewhere deep in Brookie Harewood's brain.

Death by family silver, I thought, before I could turn off that part of my mind.

A little moan from below reminded me that Porcelain was still there.

Her face was nearly as white as Brookie's, and I saw that she was trembling.

"For God's sake, Flavia," she said in a quavering voice, "come down—let's get out of here. I think I'm going to throw up."

"It's Brookie Harewood," I said, and I think I offered up a silent prayer for the repose of the poacher's soul.

Protect him, O Lord, and let heaven be bountifully supplied with trout streams.

The thought of trout reminded me of Colin Prout. I'd almost forgotten the boy. Would Colin breathe a sigh of relief when he heard that his tormentor was dead? Or would he grieve?

Brookie's mother would be in the same quandary. And so, I realized, would almost everyone in Bishop's Lacey.

I put one foot on Poseidon's knee and hauled myself up by his muscular elbow. I was now slightly above Brookie and looking down at something that had caught my eye. In the notch between two of the trident's prongs was a shiny spot the size of a sixpence, as if someone had given the bronze a bit of a polish with a rag.

I memorized the shape of the thing, then began to climb down slowly, taking great care not to touch Brookie's body.

"Come on," I said to Porcelain, giving her arm a shake. "Let's get out of here before they think one of us did it."

I did not tell her that the back of Brookie's skull was a bloody mess.

WE PAUSED FOR A MOMENT behind one of the rose hedges which, at this time of year, were in their second bloom. From the direction of the kitchen garden came the sound of Dogger scraping old soil from flowerpots with a trowel. Mrs. Mullet, I knew, had probably gone for the day.

"Stay here," I whispered, "while I scout things out."

Porcelain seemed barely to have heard me. White with fright and fatigue, she stood stock-still among the roses like one of Buckshaw's statues, over which someone, as a joke, had flung an old black dress.

I flitted, invisibly I hoped, across the grass and the graveled drive to the kitchen door. Flattening myself against it, I pressed my ear to the heavy wood.

As I've said, I had inherited from Harriet an almost freakish sense of hearing. Any clatter of pots and pans or the hum of conversation would be instantly audible. Mrs. Mullet talked constantly to herself as she worked, and even though I guessed she had gone for the day, one could never be too careful. If Feely and Daffy were planning another ambush, surely their giggles and their tittering would give them away.

But I could hear nothing.

I opened the door and stepped into an empty kitchen.

My first priority was to get Porcelain into the house and stick her safely away in a place where her presence would be unsuspected. That done, I would call the police.

The telephone at Buckshaw was kept out of sight in a small cupboard in the narrow passageway that connected the foyer with the kitchen. As I have said, Father loathed "the instrument," and all of us at Buckshaw were forbidden to use the thing.

As I tiptoed along the passage, I heard the unmistakeable sound of shoe leather on tiles. It was Father, most likely. Daffy and Feely's shoes were more feminine, and made a softer, more shuffling sound.

I ducked into the telephone cubicle and quietly pulled the door shut. I would sit on the little Oriental bench in the darkness and wait it out.

In the foyer, the footsteps slowed—and stopped. I held my breath.

After what seemed like two and a half eternities, they moved away, towards the west wing and Father's study, I thought.

At that instant—right at my elbow!—the telephone rang . . . then rang again.

A few moments later, the footsteps returned, advancing towards the foyer. I picked up the receiver and pressed it tightly against my chest. If the ringing stopped suddenly, Father would think that the caller had rung off.

"Hello? Hello?" I could hear a tinny voice saying to my breastbone. "Are you there?"

Outside, in the foyer, the footsteps stopped—and then retreated.

"Are you there? Hello? Hello?" the muffled voice was now shouting, rather irately.

I put the receiver to my ear and whispered into the mouthpiece. "Hello? Flavia de Luce speaking."

"Constable Linnet here, at Bishop's Lacey. Inspector Hewitt has been attempting to get in touch with you."

"Oh, Constable Linnet," I breathed in my best Olivia de Havilland voice. "I was just about to ring you. I'm so glad you called. The most awful thing has just happened at Buckshaw!"

That chore done, I beat a rapid retreat to the rosebushes.

"Come on," I said to Porcelain, who was standing precisely as I had left her. "There's no time to waste!"

In less than a minute, we were creeping stealthily up the wide staircase of Buckshaw's east wing.

———

"BLIMEY," PORCELAIN SAID when she saw my bedroom. "It's like a bloomin' parade square!"

"And every bit as cold," I replied. "Climb under the quilt. I'll go fix a hot water bottle."

A quick trip next door to my laboratory, five minutes with a Bunsen burner, and I had filled a red rubber bag with boiling water, ready to shove in under Porcelain's feet.

I hoisted a corner of my mattress and pulled out a box of chocolates I'd nicked from the kitchen doorstep, where Ned, the smitten potboy, was forever leaving tributes to Feely. Since Miss Snotrag never knew they'd arrived, she could hardly miss them, could she? I reminded myself to tell Ned, the next time I saw him, how much his gift had been appreciated. I just wouldn't tell him by whom.

"Help yourself," I said, ripping the cellophane from the box. "They may not be as fresh as the flowers in May, but at least they're not crawling with maggots."

Ned's budget could only afford chocolates that had been left in the shop window for a quarter century or more.

Porcelain stopped with a vanilla cream halfway to her mouth.

"Go ahead," I told her. "I was teasing."

Actually I wasn't, but there was no point in upsetting the girl.

Meaning to close the drapes, I went to the window, where I paused to have a quick look outside. There was no one in sight.

Beyond the lawns, I could see one corner of the Visto, and to the south—Poseidon! I'd completely forgotten that I could see the fountain from my bedroom window.

Was it possible that—? I rubbed my eyes and looked again.

Yes! There he was—Brookie Harewood, from this distance, no more than a dark doll hanging from the sea god's trident. I could easily slip back for another look before the police turned up. And if they *did* arrive while I was at the scene, I'd tell them that I'd been waiting for them; keeping an eye on Brookie, making sure that nothing was touched. And so forth.

"You look exhausted," I said, turning to Porcelain.

Her eyelids were already flickering as I drew the drapes.

"Sleep tight," I said, but I don't think she heard me.

The doorbell rang as I came down the stairs. Rats! Just when I thought I was alone. I counted to ten and opened the door—just as the bell rang again.

Inspector Hewitt was standing there, his finger still on the button, a slightly embarrassed look on his face, as if he were a small boy who'd been caught playing Knock-Knock-Run.

They certainly don't believe in letting the grass grow under their feet, I thought. It had been less than ten minutes since I'd spoken to Constable Linnet.

The Inspector seemed a little taken aback to see me at the door.

"Ah," he said. "The ubiquitous Flavia de Luce."

"Good afternoon, Inspector," I said, in a butter-wouldn't-melt-in-her-heart voice. "Won't you come in?"

"Thank you, no," he replied. "I understand there's been another . . . incident."

"An incident," I said, falling into the game. "It's Brookie Harewood, I'm afraid. The quickest way to the Trafalgar Lawn is through here," I added, pointing towards the east. "Follow me and I'll show you."

"Hold on," Inspector Hewitt said. "You'll do no such thing. I want you to keep completely out of this. Do you understand, Flavia?"

"It *is* our property, Inspector," I said, just to remind him that he was talking to a de Luce.

"Yes, and it's *my* investigation. So much as one of your fingerprints at the scene and I'll have you up on charges. Do you understand?"

What insolence! It didn't deserve an answer. I could have said "My fingerprints are already at the scene, Inspector," but I didn't. I spun on my heel and slammed the door in his face.

Inside, I quickly clapped my ear to the panel and listened for all I was worth.

Although it sounded like a dry chuckle, the sound I heard must really have been a little cry of dismay from the Inspector at having so foolishly lost the services of a first-rate mind.

Damn and blast the man! He'd regret his high-handed manner. Oh yes he would—he'd regret it!

Up the stairs I flew to my chemical laboratory. I unlocked the heavy door, stepped into the room, and almost instantly relaxed as a deep feeling of peace came over me.

There was something special about the place: The way in which the light fell so softly through the tall leaded casement windows, the warm brass glow of the Leitz microscope that had once belonged to Uncle Tar and was now so satisfyingly mine, the crisp—almost eager—shine of the laboratory's glassware, the cabinets filled with neatly labeled bottles of chemicals (including some quite remarkable poisons), and the rows upon rows of books—all of these lent to the room something I can only describe as a sense of sanctuary.

I took one of the tall laboratory stools and lifted it onto a counter near the windows. Then, from the bottom drawer of the desk—which, because it contained his diaries and documents, I still thought of as being Uncle Tar's—I removed a pair of German binoculars. Their lenses, I had learned from one of the books in his library, had been made from a special sand found only in the Thuringian Forest near the village of Martinroda, in Germany, which, because of its aluminum oxide content, produced an image of remarkable clarity. Which was precisely what I needed!

With the binoculars hung round my neck, I used a chair to climb up onto the countertop, then scaled the stool, where I teetered uneasily atop my improvised observation tower, my head almost touching the ceiling.

Using one hand to steady myself against the window frame, and the binoculars pressed to my eyes with the other, I used whatever fingers were left to turn the focusing knob.

As the hedges surrounding the Trafalgar Lawn sprang into sharp detail, I realized that the view from the laboratory, and from this angle, should be much better than the one I'd had from my bedroom window.

Yes—there was Poseidon, gazing out upon his invisible ocean, oblivious to the dark bundle dangling from his trident. But now I had a good view of the entire fountain.

With distance collapsed by the powerful lenses, I could also see Inspector Hewitt as he came into view from behind the fountain, raised a hand to shield his eyes from the sun, and stood gazing up at Brookie's body. He pursed his lips and I could almost hear in my mind the little whistle that escaped him.

I wondered if he knew he was being watched.

The image in the binoculars faded suddenly, was restored—and then faded again. I took the glasses away from my eyes and realized that a sudden cloud had blotted out the sun. Although it was too far to the west for me to actually see it, I could tell by the darkness that had fallen on the landscape that we were in for a storm.

I raised the binoculars again just in time to see that the Inspector was now looking directly at me. I gasped—then realized that it was a trick of the optics; of course he couldn't see me. He must be looking up at the storm clouds that were gathering over Buckshaw.

He turned away, then turned again, and now it appeared as if he was talking to somebody, and so he was. As I looked on, Detective Sergeant Woolmer came round the base of the fountain carrying a heavy kit, closely followed by Dr. Darby and Detective Sergeant Graves. *They must all have come in the same car,* I thought, *and driven round by way of the Gully and the Palings*.

Before you could say Jack Robinson, Sergeant Woolmer had set up his folding tripod and attached the heavy police camera. I marveled at how deftly his stubby fingers handled the delicate controls, and how quickly he managed to take his initial exposures.

There was a sudden, blinding flash of lightning, followed almost instantly by an ear-splitting clap of thunder, and I nearly toppled off the stool. I let the binoculars fall free to dangle round my neck, and slapped both hands against the windowpanes to regain my balance.

What was it Daffy had once told me during a summer downpour?

"Stay away from windows during a thunderstorm, you silly moke."

Now here I was, with lightning licking at the transom, pinned against the glass like a butterfly to a card in the Natural History Museum.

"Even if the lightning misses you," she'd added, "the breath will be sucked from your lungs by the sound of the thunder, and you'll be turned inside out like a red sock."

The lightning flashed again and the thunder roared, and now the rain was coming down in sweeping sheets, pounding on the roof like the roll of kettledrums. A sudden wind had sprung up, and the trees in the park pitched wildly in its gusts.

Actually it was quite exhilarating. *Daffy be damned,* I thought. If I practiced a bit, I could even come to love the thunder and the lightning.

I straightened up, adjusted my balance, and raised the glasses to my eyes.

What I saw was like a scene from Hell. In the watery green light, blown by the wind and illuminated by erratic flashes of lightning, the three policemen were removing Brookie's body from the trident. They had looped a rope under his armpits, and were lowering him slowly, almost tenderly to the ground. Towering above them in the rain, Poseidon, like a monstrous stone Satan with his pitchfork at the ready, still stared out across his watery world as if he were bored stiff with the antics of mere humans.

Inspector Hewitt reached out to touch the rope and ease the body's descent, his hair plastered flat against his forehead by the rain, and for a moment, I had the feeling that I was watching some horrific passion play.

And perhaps I was.

Only when Sergeant Woolmer had fetched a bit of tarpaulin from his kit and covered Brookie's body did the men seem to think of sheltering themselves. Although it provided precious little protection, Dr. Darby held his black medical bag above his head and stood there motionless, looking miserable in the rain.

Inspector Hewitt had unfolded a small transparent raincoat and slipped it on over his saturated clothing. It seemed like something that a chambermaid might wear, and I wondered if his lovely wife, Antigone, had slipped it into his pocket for emergencies such as this.

Sergeant Woolmer stood stolid in the downpour, as if his bulk were protection enough against the wind and rain, while Sergeant Graves, who was the only one of the four small enough to do so, had tucked himself comfortably under the lowest bowl of the fountain on the down-wind side, where he squatted as dry as a duck.

Then suddenly, as quickly as it had begun, the storm was over. The dark cloud was now drifting off to the east as the sun reappeared and the birds renewed their interrupted songs.

Sergeant Woolmer removed the waterproof covering with which he had draped his camera, and began photographing the fountain from every imaginable angle. As he began his close-ups, an ambulance came into view, teetering its way across the rough ground between the Palings and the Trafalgar Lawn.

After a few words with the driver, Dr. Darby helped shift Brookie's shrouded body onto a stretcher, then climbed into the passenger's seat.

As the ambulance bumped slowly away, swerving to avoid the half-buried statuary, I noticed that a rainbow had appeared. An eerie yellow light had come upon the landscape, making it seem like some garish painting by a madman.

On the far side of the Trafalgar Lawn, at the edge of the trees, something moved. I swiveled a bit and refocused quickly, just in time to see a figure vanish into the wood.

Another poacher, I thought, *watching the police; not wanting to be seen.*

I made a slow sweep of the tree trunks, but whoever had been there was gone.

I found the ambulance again with the binoculars, and watched until it vanished behind a distant hedge. When it was lost to view, I climbed down from the stool and locked up the laboratory.

If I wanted to search Brookie's digs before the police got there, I'd have to get cracking.

ten

THE ONLY PROBLEM WAS THIS: I HADN'T THE FAINTEST IDEA where Brookie lived.

I could have made another visit to the telephone closet, I suppose, but in Buckshaw's foyer I was risking an encounter with Father, or worse—with Daffy or Feely. Besides, it seemed most unlikely that a ne'-er-do-well such as Brookie would be listed in the directory.

Rather than risk being caught, I slipped stealthily into the picture gallery, which occupied nearly the entire ground floor of the east wing.

An army of de Luce ancestors gazed down upon me as I passed, in whose faces I recognized, uncomfortably, aspects of my own. *I wouldn't have liked most of them*, I thought, *and most of them wouldn't have liked me.*

I did a cartwheel just to show them that I didn't care.

Still, because the old boy deserved it, I gave Uncle Tar's portrait a brisk Girl Guide salute, even though I'd been drummed out of that organization, quite unfairly I thought, by a woman with no sense of humor whatsoever. *"Honestly, Miss Pashley,"* I'd have told her, had I been given half a chance, *"the ferric hydroxide was only meant to be a joke."*

At the far end of the gallery was a box room which, in Buckshaw's glory days, had been used for the framing and repair of the portraits and landscapes that made up my family's art collection.

A couple of deal shelves and the workbench in the room were still littered with dusty tins of paint and varnish whose contents had dried out at about the same time as Queen Victoria, and from which brush handles stuck up here and there like fossilized rats' tails.

Everyone but me seemed to have forgotten that this room had a most useful feature: a sashed window that could be raised easily from both inside and out—and all the more so since I had taken to lubricating its slides with lard pinched from the pantry.

On the outside wall, directly below the window casing and halfway to the ground, a brick had half crumbled away—its slow decay encouraged somewhat, I'll admit, by my hacking at it with one of Dogger's trowels: a perfect foothold for anyone who wished to leave or get back into the house without attracting undue attention.

As I scrambled out the window and climbed to the ground, I almost stepped on Dogger, who was on his knees in the wet grass. He got to his feet, lifted his hat, and replaced it.

"Good afternoon, Miss Flavia."

"Good afternoon, Dogger."

"Lovely rain."

"Quite lovely."

Dogger glanced up at the golden sky, then went on with his weeding.

The very best people are like that. They don't entangle you like flypaper.

GLADYS'S TIRES HUMMED HAPPILY as we shot past St. Tancred's and into the high street. She was enjoying the day as much as I was.

Ahead on my left, a few doors from the Thirteen Drakes, was Reggie Pettibone's antiques shop. I was making a mental note to pay it a visit later when the door flew open and a spectacled boy came hurtling into the street.

It was Colin Prout.

I swerved to avoid hitting him, and Gladys went into a long shuddering slide.

"Colin!" I shouted as I came to a stop. I had very nearly taken a bad tumble.

But Colin had already crossed the high street and vanished into Bolt Alley, a narrow, reeking passage that led to a lane behind the shops.

Needless to say, I followed, offering up fresh praise for the invention of the Sturmey-Archer three-speed shifter.

Into the lane I sped, but Colin was already disappearing round the corner at the far end. A few seconds more, having taken a roughly circular route, and he would be back in the high street.

I was right. By the time I caught sight of him again, he was cutting into Cow Lane, as if the hounds of Hell were at his heels.

Rather than following, I applied the brakes.

Where Cow Lane ended at the river, I knew, Colin would veer to the left and follow the old towpath that ran behind the Thirteen Drakes. He would not risk going to ground anywhere along the old canal for fear of being boxed in behind the shops.

I turned completely round and went back the way I'd come, making a broad sweeping turn into Shoe Street, where Miss Pickery, the new librarian, lived in the last cottage. I braked, dismounted, and, leaning Gladys against her fence, climbed quickly over the stile and crept into position behind one of the tall poplars that lined the towpath.

Just in time! Here was Colin hurrying towards me, and all the while looking nervously back over his shoulder.

"Hello, Colin," I said, stepping directly into his path.

Colin stopped as if he had walked into a brick wall, but the shifting of his pale eyes, magnified like oysters by his thick lenses, signaled that he was about to make a break for it.

"The police are looking for you, you know. Do you want me to tell them where you are?"

It was a bald-faced lie: one of my specialties.

"N-n-n-no."

His face had gone as white as tissue paper, and I thought for a moment he was going to blubber. But before I could tighten the screws, he blurted out: "I never done it, Flavia! Honest! Whatever they think I done, I didn't."

In spite of his tangle of words I knew what he meant. "Didn't do what, Colin? What is it you haven't done?"

"Nothin'. I 'aven't done nothin'."

"Where's Brookie?" I asked casually. "I need to see him about a pair of fire irons."

My words had the desired effect. Colin's arms swung round like the vanes on a weathercock, his fingers pointing north, south, west, east. He finally settled on the latter, indicating that Brookie was to be found somewhere beyond the Thirteen Drakes.

"Last time I seen him 'e was unloading 'is van."

His van? Could Brookie have a van? Somehow the idea seemed ludicrous—as if the scarecrow from *The Wizard of Oz* had been spotted behind the wheel of a Bedford lorry—and yet . . .

"Thanks awfully, Colin," I told him. "You're a wonder."

With a scrub at his eyes and a tug at his hair, he was over the stile and up Shoe Street like a whirling dervish. And then he was gone.

Had I just made a colossal mistake? Perhaps I had, but I could hardly carry out my inquiries with someone like Colin drooling over my shoulder.

Only then did a cold horror of an idea come slithering across my mind. What if—

But no, if there'd been blood on Colin's clothing, I'd surely have noticed it.

As I walked back to retrieve Gladys, I was taken with a rattling good idea. In all of Bishop's Lacey there were very few vans, most of which were known to me on sight: the ironmonger's, the butcher's, the electrician's, and so forth. Each one had the name of its owner in prominent letters on the side panels; each was unique and unmistakeable. A quick ride up the high street would account for most of them, and a strange van would stand out like a sore thumb.

And so it did.

A few minutes later I had pedaled a zigzag path throughout the village without any luck. But as I swept round the bend at the east end of the high street, I could hardly believe my eyes.

Parked in front of Willow Villa was a disreputable green van that, although its rusty panels were blank, had Brookie Harewood written all over it.

Willow Villa was aptly named for the fact that it was completely hidden beneath the drooping tassels of a giant tree, which was just as well since the house was painted a hideous shade of orange. It belonged to Tilda Mountjoy, whom I had met under rather unhappy circumstances a few months earlier. Miss Mountjoy was the retired Librarian-in-Chief of the Bishop's Lacey Free Library where, it was said, even the books had lived in fear of her. Now, with nothing but time on her hands, she had become a freelance holy terror.

Although I was not anxious to renew our acquaintance, there was nothing for it but to open her gate, push my way through the net of dangling fronds, squelch through the mosses underfoot, and beard the dragon in her den.

My excuse? I would tell her that, while out bicycling, I had been overcome with a sudden faintness. Seeing Brookie's van, I thought that perhaps he would be kind enough to load Gladys into the rear and drive me home. Father, I was sure, would be filled with eternal gratitude, etc., etc., etc.

Under the willow's branches, lichens flourished on the doorstep and the air was as cool and dank as a mausoleum.

I had already raised the corroded brass knocker, which was in the shape of the Lincoln Imp, when the door flew open and there stood Miss Mountjoy—covered with blood!

I don't know which of us was the most startled to see the other, but for a peculiar moment we both of us stood perfectly still, staring wide-eyed at each other.

The front of her dress and the sleeves of her gray cardigan were soaked with the stuff, and her face was an open wound. A few fresh drops of scarlet had already plopped to the floor before she lifted a bloody handkerchief and clapped it to her face.

"Nosebleed," she said. "I get them all the time."

With her mouth and nose muffled by the stained linen, it sounded as if she had said "I give them all the twine," but I knew what she meant.

"Gosh, Miss Mountjoy," I blurted. "Let me help you."

I seized her arm and before she could protest, steered her towards the kitchen through a dark hallway lined with heavy Tudor sideboards.

"Sit down," I said, pulling out a chair, and to my surprise, she did.

My experience with nosebleeds was limited but practical. I remembered one of Feely's birthday parties at which Sheila Foster's nose had erupted on the croquet lawn and Dogger had stanched it with someone's handkerchief dipped in a solution of copper sulfate from the greenhouse.

Willow Villa, however, didn't seem likely to have a supply of Blue Vitriol, as the solution was called, although I knew that, given no more than half a teacup of dilute sulfuric acid, a couple of pennies, and the battery from Gladys's bicycle lamp, I could whip up enough of the stuff to do the trick. But this was no time for chemistry.

I grabbed for an ornamental iron key that hung from a nail near the fireplace and clapped it to the back of her neck.

She let out a shriek, and came halfway out of the chair.

"Easy now," I said, as if talking to a horse (a quick vision of clinging to Gry's mane in the darkness came to mind). "Easy."

Miss Mountjoy sat rigid, her shoulders hunched. Now was the time.

"Is Brookie here?" I said conversationally. "I saw his van outside."

Miss Mountjoy's head snapped back and I felt her stiffen even more under my hand. She slowly removed the bloody handkerchief from her nose and said with perfect cold clarity, "Harewood will never set foot in this house again."

I blinked. Was Miss Mountjoy merely stating her determination, or was there something more ominous in her words? Did she know that Brookie was dead?

As she twisted round to glare at me, I saw that her nosebleed had stopped.

I let the silence lengthen, a useful trick I had picked up from Inspector Hewitt.

"The man's a thief," she said at last. "I should never have trusted him. I don't know what I was thinking."

"Can I bring you anything, Miss Mountjoy? A glass of water? A damp cloth?"

It was time to ingratiate myself.

Without a word I went to the sink and wetted a hand towel. I wrung it out and gave it to her. As she wiped the blood from her face and hands, I looked away discreetly, taking the opportunity to examine the kitchen.

It was a square room with a low ceiling. A small green Aga crouched in the corner and there was a plain, scrubbed deal table with a single chair: the one in which Miss Mountjoy was presently sitting. A plate rail ran round two sides of the room, upon which were displayed an assortment of blue and white plates and platters—mostly Staffordshire, by the look of them: village greens and country scenes, for the most part. I counted eleven, with an empty space about a foot and a half in diameter where a twelfth plate must once have hung.

Filtered through the willow branches outside, the weak green light that seeped in through the two small windows above the sink gave the plates a weird and watery tint, which reminded me of what the Trafalgar Lawn had looked like after the rain: after the taking down of Brookie's body from the Poseidon fountain.

At the entrance to the narrow passage through which we had entered the kitchen was a chipped wooden cabinet, on top of which was a cluster of identical bottles, all of them medicinal-looking.

Only as I read their labels did the smell hit me. *How odd*, I thought: the sense of smell is usually lightning fast, often speedier than that of sight or hearing.

But now there was no doubt about it. The whole room—even Miss Mountjoy herself—reeked of cod-liver oil.

Perhaps until that moment the sight of Miss Mountjoy's nosebleed and her blood-splattered clothing had overwhelmed my sense of smell. Although I had first noticed the fishy odor when I saw her dripping blood at the door, and again when I had applied the cold key to the nape of her neck, my brain must have labeled the fact as not immediately important, and tucked it away for later consideration.

My experience of cod-liver oil was vast. Much of my life had been spent fleeing the oncoming Mrs. Mullet, who, with uncorked bottle and a spoon the size of a garden spade, pursued me up and down the corridors and staircases of Buckshaw—even in my dreams.

Who in their right mind would want to swallow something that looked like discarded engine oil and was squeezed out of fish livers that had been left to rot in the sun? The stuff was used in the tanning of leather, and I couldn't help wondering what it would do to one's insides.

"Open up, dearie," I could hear Mrs. Mullet calling as she trundled after me. "It's good for you."

"No! No!" I would shriek. "No acid! Please don't make me drink acid!"

And it was true—I wasn't just making this up. I had analyzed the stuff in my laboratory and found it to contain a catalogue of acids, among them oleic, margaric, acetic, butyric, fellic, cholic, and phosphoric, to say nothing of the oxides, calcium and sodium.

In the end, I had made a bargain with Mrs. M: She would allow me to take the cod-liver oil alone in my room at bedtime, and I would stop screaming like a tortured banshee and kicking at her ankles. I swore it on my mother's grave.

Harriet, of course, had no grave. Her body was somewhere in the snows of Tibet.

Happy to be relieved of a difficult and unwanted task, Mrs. Mullet had pretended to be scandalized, but cheerfully handed over both spoon and bottle.

My mind came snapping back to the present like a rubber ball on an elastic string.

"Trouble with antiques, was it?" I heard myself say. "You're not alone in that, Miss Mountjoy."

Although I almost missed it, her rapid glance upwards, towards the spot where the missing plate had hung, told me I had hit the bull's-eye.

She saw me following her gaze.

"It was from the time of Hongwu, the first Ming emperor. He told me he knew a man—"

"Brookie?" I interrupted.

She nodded.

"He said he knew someone who could have the piece assessed discreetly, and at reasonable cost. Things have been difficult since the war, you see, and I thought of—"

"Yes, I know, Miss Mountjoy," I said. "I understand."

With Father's financial difficulties, and the blizzard of past-due accounts that arrived with every postal delivery being the subject of much idle chitchat in Bishop's Lacey, there was no need for her to explain her own poverty.

Her look formed a bond between us. "Partners in debt," it seemed to say.

"He told me the railway had broken it. He'd packed the plate in straw, he said, and put it in a barrel, but somehow—he'd taken out no insurance, of course, trying to keep expenses down—trying not to burden me with additional—and then—"

"Someone spotted it in an antiques shop," I blurted.

She nodded. "My niece, Julia. In Pimlico. She said, 'Auntie, you'll never guess what I saw today: the mate to your Ming!'

"She was standing right there where you are, and just as you did, she looked up and saw the empty space on the shelf. 'Oh, Auntie!' she said. 'Oh, Auntie.'

"We tried to get the plate back, of course, but the man said he had it on consignment from an MP who lived in the next street. Couldn't give out names because of confidentiality. Julia was all for going to the police, but I reminded her that Uncle Jamieson, who brought the piece into the family, was not always on the up-and-up. I'm sorry to have to tell you that story, Flavia, but I've always made it a point to be scrupulously honest."

I nodded and gave her a little look of disappointment. "But Brookie Harewood," I said. "How did *he* come to get his hands on the plate?"

"Because he's my tenant. He lives in my coach house, you see."

Brookie? Here? In Miss Mountjoy's coach house? This was news to me.

"Oh, yes," I said. "Of course he does. I'd forgotten. Well, then, I'd better be getting along. I think you'd best lie down for a while, Miss Mountjoy. You're still quite pale. A nosebleed takes so much out of one, doesn't it? Iron, and so forth. You must be quite worn out."

I led her to the little parlor I had seen at the front of the house and helped her recline on a horsehair settee. I covered her with an afghan, and left her clutching at it with white fingers.

"I'll see myself out," I said.

eleven

LIKE AN ACTOR IN THE PANTOMIME MUDDLING HIS WAY OUT from behind the curtains, I pushed aside the hanging willow branches and stepped out from the green gloom and into the blinding glare of the sun's spotlight.

Time was running out. Inspector Hewitt and his men were probably minutes away and my work was hardly begun.

Since Brookie's van was directly in front of me, I'd begin there. I glanced quickly up and down the street. There was no one in sight.

One of the van's windows was rolled all the way down: obviously just as Brookie had left it. Here was a bit of luck!

Father was always going on about the importance of carrying a hand-kerchief at all times, and for once he was right. Opening the door would leave my fingerprints on the nickel-plated handle. A clean bit of linen was just the ticket.

But the handle wouldn't budge, although it did give off an alarming groan that hinted of extensive rust beneath. One thing that I didn't need was to have a van door fall off and go clattering into the street.

I stepped up onto the running board (another metallic groan) and used my elbows to lever myself into position. With my stomach on the bottom of the window frame, I was able to hinge the top half of my body into the van, leaving my legs and feet sticking straight out in the air for balance.

With the handkerchief wrapped round my hand, I pressed on the glove compartment's release button, and when it popped open, reached inside and pulled out a small packet. It was, as I thought it might be, the registration papers for the van.

I almost let out a cheer! Now I would find out Brookie's real address, which I somehow doubted would be Willow Villa.

Edward Sampson, the document said. *Rye Road, East Finching.*

I knew well enough where East Finching was: It lay about five miles by road to the north of Bishop's Lacey.

But who was Edward Sampson? Other than being the owner of the van from which my bottom was probably projecting like a lobster's claw from a trap—I hadn't the faintest idea.

I shoved the papers back into the glove compartment and pushed home the panel.

Now for the coach house.

"Come along, Gladys," I said, taking her from where she had been waiting. No sense having my presence detected by leaving her parked in plain view.

Because of the peculiar shape of Miss Mountjoy's property, the coach house was located at the end of a hedge-lined L-shaped lane that ran along one side and across the back. I tucked Gladys out of sight behind a box hedge and proceeded on foot.

As I approached the building, I could see that the term "coach house" was no more than a courtesy title. In fact, it was almost a joke.

The building was square, with bricks on the bottom floor and boards on the top. The windows were coated with the kind of opaque film that tells of neglect and cobwebs; the kind of windows that watch you.

The door had once been painted, but had blistered away to reveal gray, weathered wood that matched the unpainted boards of the upper story.

I wrapped my hand in the handkerchief and tried the latch. The door was locked.

The first-floor windows were too high to gain entry, and the tangle of ivy on a broken trellis too fragile to climb. A rickety ladder leaned wearily against the wall, too dangerous to be pressed into service. I decided to try round the back.

I had to be careful. Only a sagging wooden fence and a narrow walkway separated the rear of the coach house from Miss Mountjoy's overhanging willow tree: I'd have to crouch and run, like a commando on the beach.

At the end of the fence, on the left side of the walkway, was a wire compound attached to the coach house, from which issued, as I approached, an excited clucking. Inside the compound, there was a cage no more than two feet high—rather less, in fact—and in it was the biggest rooster I had ever seen: so large that he had to strut about his cage with stooped shoulders.

As soon as he saw me the bird made for the wires that separated us, fluttering up towards my face with a frightening rustle of wings. My first instinct was to take to my heels—but then I saw the pleading look in his marmalade eye.

He was hungry!

I took a handful of feed from a box that was nailed to the framework of the cage and tossed it through the mesh. The rooster fell upon the stuff like a wolf upon Russian travelers, his comb, as red as paper poppies, bobbing busily up and down as if it were driven by steam.

As he feasted, I noticed a hatch on the far side of the cage that opened into the coach house. It was no more than rooster-sized, but it would do.

Throwing a couple more handfuls of feed to distract the bird, I turned to the wire fence. It was only about seven feet high, but too far to leap up and grasp the upper frame. I tried to swarm up the mesh, but my shoes could find no grip.

Undefeated, I sat down and removed my shoes and socks.

When I come to write my autobiography, I must remember to record the fact that a chicken-wire fence *can* be scaled by a girl in bare feet, but only by one who is willing to suffer the tortures of the damned to satisfy her curiosity.

As I climbed, my toes stuck through the hexagons of the wire mesh, each strand like the blades of a cheese cutter. By the time I reached the top, my feet felt as if they belonged to Scott of the Antarctic.

As I dropped to the ground on the inside of the enclosure the rooster made a lunge for me. Since I hadn't thought to bring a pocketful of feed to appease the famished bird, I was at his mercy.

He threw himself at my bare knees and I made a dive for the hatchway.

It was a tight fit, and I could only squirm my way painfully through the opening as the enraged bird pecked furiously at my legs—but moments later I was inside the coach house: still inside a wired partition, but inside.

And so was the rooster, who had followed me in, and was now flinging himself upon me like an avenging fury.

Seized by a sudden inspiration, I squatted, caught the bird's eye, then with a loud hissing, rose up suddenly to my full height, weaving my head and flicking my tongue in and out like a king cobra.

It worked! In his feeble rooster brain, some age-old instinct whispered a sudden, wordless tale of terror that involved a chicken and a snake, and taking to his heels, he shot out through the hatch like a feathered cannonball.

I poked my fingers through the mesh and rotated the strip of wood that served as a latch, then stepped into the corridor.

I suppose my mind had been filled with images of dusty box stalls, of shriveled harness hanging from wooden pegs, of currycombs and benches, and perhaps a long-abandoned phaeton carriage lurking in some dim corner. Perhaps I was thinking of our own coach house at Buckshaw.

But whatever the case, I was totally unprepared for what I saw.

Beneath the low, beamed ceiling of what had once been a stable, couches upholstered in green and pink silk were jammed together like buses in Piccadilly Circus. Cameo jars and vases—some of them surely Wedgwood—stood here and there on tables whose old wood managed to glow even in the dim light. Carved cabinets and elaborately inlaid tables receded into the shadows, while nearby horse stalls overflowed with Royal Albert ewers and Oriental screens.

The place was a warehouse—and, I thought, no ordinary one at that!

Against one wall, almost hidden by a massive sideboard, was an exquisitely carved Georgian chimneypiece, in front of which, half-unrolled, was a rich and elaborate carpet. Something very much like it had been pointed out to me on more than one occasion by Feely's friend and toady, Sheila Foster, who managed to drag their carpet into even the most casual conversation: "The Archbishop of Canterbury was down for the weekend, you know. As he was pinching my cheek, he dropped a crumb of his Dundee cake on our dear old Aubusson."

I had just stepped forward to have a closer look at the thing when something caught my eye: a gleam in a dark corner by the chimneypiece.

I sucked in my breath, for there in Miss Mountjoy's coach house stood Sally Fox and Shoppo—Harriet's brass fire irons!

What on earth—? I thought. *How can this be?*

I had seen the firedogs just hours before in the drawing room at Buckshaw. Brookie Harewood couldn't possibly have crept back into the house and stolen them because Brookie was dead. But who else could have brought them here?

Could it have been Colin Prout? Colin was, after all, Brookie's puppet, and I had found him hanging about the neighborhood just minutes ago.

Did Colin live here with Brookie? Miss Mountjoy had referred to Brookie as her tenant, which surely meant that he lived here. I hadn't seen any sign of a kitchen or sleeping quarters, but perhaps they lay somewhere beyond the vast expanse of furniture or upstairs on the first floor.

As I retraced my steps to the central corridor, a car door slammed in the lane outside.

Crackers! It could well be Inspector Hewitt.

I ducked down and waddled my way towards a window, where I pressed myself flat against the back of a massive ebony armoire, round which I could peek out without being seen.

But it was not Inspector Hewitt who was coming towards the door: It was a walking bulldog. The man's shirtsleeves were rolled to his elbows, revealing arms that, except for their excessive hairiness, might have been a pair of Christmas hams. His shirt, open at the neck, revealed a forest of black, springy chest hair, and his fists clenched and unclenched as he strode purposefully towards the door.

Whoever he was, it was clear that he was unhappy. The man was powerful enough to tear me open like a packet of cigarettes. I couldn't let him find me here.

It was unnerving to work my way back through the maze of furniture. Twice I startled at a movement close by, only to find that it was a reflection of myself in an uncovered mirror.

The man was already opening the door as I reached the caged cubicle. I slipped inside—thank goodness for bare feet and straw on the floor!—then lowered myself to hands and knees, then flat on my face, and began to crawl through the narrow hole to the outside.

The rooster was on me like a champion fighting cock. As I crawled, I tried to keep my hands up to protect my face, but the bird's spurs were razor sharp. Before I was even halfway through, my wrists were bleeding.

Up the wire wall I swarmed, the rooster throwing himself again and again at my feet and legs. There was no time even to think of what the wire mesh was doing to my toes. At the top, I threw myself over the wooden bar and dropped heavily to the ground.

"Who's there?" Inside the coach house, the man's voice sounded as if he was no more than a few feet away. But unless he got down on his belly and crawled, he could not follow me—could not even see me in the outside pen.

He would have to return to his car, then come round behind the coach house in the lane.

I heard his footsteps retreating on the wooden floor.

Again I made a crouching scuttle along the crumbling fence—but wait: I'd forgotten my shoes and socks!

Back again I went to retrieve them, my breath now coming in quick painful gasps. Once more along the fence and I ducked behind the hedge where I had left Gladys.

Just in time. I froze behind the box hedge—trying not to breathe—as the human bulldog went lumbering past.

"Who's there?" he demanded again, and I heard the rooster throw himself at the wire mesh with a wild crowing.

A few more coarse oaths and my pursuer was gone. I cannot bring myself to record his exact words, but will keep them in mind against the day I can put them to good use.

I waited for a minute or two to be sure, then dragged Gladys from behind the hedge and set off for home.

As I pedaled along I did my best to look like a respectable English girl out for a bracing bicycle ride in the fresh air.

But somehow I doubted that my charade would convince anyone: My hands and face were filthy, my wrists and ankles were bleeding, my knees were scraped to the bone, and my clothing would have to be tossed in the dustbin.

Father would not be amused.

And what if, in my absence, they had discovered Porcelain in my bedroom? What if she had awakened and wandered downstairs? Or into Father's study!

Although I had never before cringed on a bicycle, I cringed.

"I CAUGHT HER CRAWLING IN at one of the windows of the picture gallery," Feely said. "Like a common housebreaker. Can you imagine? I'd gone there to study the Maggs painting of Ajax, and—"

Maggs was a ruffian painter who had lived in the vicinity of Bishop's Lacey during the Regency, and Ajax a horse that had been bought on a whim by one of my ancestors, Florizel de Luce. Ajax had rewarded his new owner by going on to win enough races that Florizel was able to have himself elected to a rotten borough.

"Thank you, Ophelia," Father said.

Feely cast down humble eyes and drifted out the door, where she would sit on the chair in the hallway to eavesdrop comfortably upon my humiliation.

"Do you know what day it is, Flavia?" Father began.

"Sunday," I said without hesitation, although yesterday's fête at St. Tancred's seemed as far removed in time as the last ice age.

"Precisely," Father said. "And what have we done on Sundays since time immemorial?"

"Gone to church," I replied like a trained macaw.

Church! I'd forgotten all about it.

"I'd thought to let you lie in this morning to recover from that nasty business in the Palings. Next thing I know, there's an inspector at the door and you're wanted for fingerprinting.

"Now I'm informed that there's a dead body on the Trafalgar Lawn and that you're nosing about the village asking impertinent questions."

"Miss Mountjoy?" I ventured.

Give a little, learn a lot. That was going to be my Motto of the Month. I would have to remember to jot it down in my notebook.

But wait! How could Miss Mountjoy have known about the body on the lawn? Unless—

"Miss Mountjoy," Father confirmed. "She telephoned to ask if you'd got home safely."

The old harpy! She must have got up from her settee and been peering out through the trailing seaweed fronds of the willow tree, spying on my encounters with the rooster and the bulldog-man.

"How very kind of her," I said. "I must remember to send her a card."

I'd send her a card, all right. It would be the Ace of Spades, and I'd mail it anonymously from somewhere other than Bishop's Lacey. Philip Odell, the detective on the wireless, had once investigated such a case, and it had been a cracking good story—one of his best adventures.

"And your dress!" Father went on. "What have you done to your dress?"

My dress? Hadn't Miss Mountjoy described to him fully what she'd seen?

Hold on!—perhaps she hadn't after all. Perhaps Father was still unaware of what had taken place at the coach house.

God bless you, Miss Mountjoy! I thought. *May you live forever in the company of those saints and martyrs who refused to tell them where the church plate was buried.*

But wasn't Father going to remark upon my cuts and abrasions?

Apparently not.

And it was at that moment, I think, it began to dawn upon me—truly dawn upon me—that there were things that were never mentioned in polite company no matter what; that blue blood was heavier than red; that manners and appearances and the stiff upper lip were all of them more important, even, than life itself.

"Flavia," Father repeated, fighting to keep from wringing his hands, "I asked you a question. What have you done to your dress?"

I looked down at myself as if noticing the damage for the first time.

"My dress?" I said, smoothing it down and making sure he had a good view of my bloodied wrist and knees. "Oh, I'm sorry, Father. It's nothing. I had a bit of a prang with my bicycle. Jolly bad luck, but still—I'll rinse it out at once and mend it myself. It'll be a piece of cake."

My acute hearing detected the sound of a coarse snicker in the hallway.

But I'd like to believe that what I saw in Father's eyes was pride.

twelve

PORCELAIN WAS SLEEPING THE SLEEP OF THE DEAD. I HAD
worried in vain.

I stood looking down at her as she lay on my bed in much the same
position as when I had left her. The dark swatches under her eyes seemed
to have lightened, and her breathing was almost imperceptible.

Two seconds later there was a flurry of furious motion and I was
pinned to the bed with Porcelain's thumbs pressing into my windpipe.

"Fiend!" I thought she hissed.

I struggled to get free but I couldn't move. Bright stars were bursting in my brain as I clawed at her hands. I wasn't getting enough oxygen.
I tried to pull away.

But I was no match for her. She was bigger and stronger than me, and
already I could feel myself becoming languid and uncaring. How easy it
would be to give in . . .

But no!

I stopped trying to fight her hands and instead took hold of her nose
with my thumb and forefinger. With my last remaining strength I gave it
a most vicious twist.

"Flavia!"

She seemed suddenly surprised to see me—as if we were old friends
who had met unexpectedly in front of a lovely Vermeer in the National
Gallery.

Her hands withdrew themselves from my throat, but still I couldn't seem to breathe. I rolled off the bed and onto the floor, seized with a fit of coughing.

"What are you doing?" she demanded, looking round in puzzlement.

"What are *you* doing?" I croaked. "You've crushed my windpipe!"

"Oh, God!" she said. "How awful. I'm sorry, Flavia—really I am. I was dreaming I was in Fenella's caravan and there was some horrid . . . beast! . . . standing over me. I think it was—"

"Yes?"

She looked away from me. "I . . . I'm sorry. I can't tell you."

"I'll keep it to myself. I promise."

"No, it's no good. I mustn't."

"All right, then," I said. "Don't. In fact, I forbid you to tell me."

"Flavia—"

"No," I said, and I meant it. "I don't want to know. Let's talk about something else."

I knew that if I bided my time, whatever it was that Porcelain was withholding would come spilling out like minced pork from Mrs. Mullet's meat grinder.

Which reminded me that I hadn't eaten for ages.

"Are you hungry?" I asked.

"Starving. You must have heard my tummy rumbling."

I hadn't, but I pretended I had, and nodded wisely.

"Stay here. I'll bring something from the kitchen."

TEN MINUTES LATER I was back with a bowl of food nicked from the pantry.

"Follow me," I said. "Next door."

Porcelain looked round wide-eyed as we entered my chemical laboratory. "What is this place? Are we supposed to be in here?"

"Of course we are," I told her. "It's where I do my experiments."

"Like magic?" she asked, glancing around at the glassware.

"Yes," I said. "Like magic. Now then, you take these . . . "

She jumped at the *pop* of the Bunsen burner as I put a match to it.

"Hold them over the flame," I said, handing her a couple of bangers and a pair of nickel-plated test tube clamps. "Not too close—it's exceedingly hot."

I broke six eggs into a borosilicate evaporating dish and stirred them with a glass rod over a second burner. Almost immediately the laboratory was filled with mouthwatering aromas.

"Now for toast," I said. "You can do two slices at a time," I said. "Use the tongs again. Do both sides, then turn them inside out."

By necessity, I had become quite an accomplished laboratory chef. Once, just recently, when Father had banished me to my room, I had even made myself a spotted dick by steaming suet from the larder in a wide-neck Erlenmeyer flask. And because water boils at only 212 degrees Fahrenheit, while nylon doesn't melt until it is heated to 417 degrees, I had verified my theory that one of Feely's precious stockings would make a perfect pudding bag.

If there's anything more delicious than a sausage roasted over an open Bunsen burner, I can't imagine what it might be—unless it's the feeling of freedom that comes of eating it with the bare fingers and letting the fat fall where it may. Porcelain and I tore into our food like cannibals after a missionary famine, and before long there was nothing left but crumbs.

As two cups of water came to the boil in a glass beaker, I took down from the shelf where it was kept, alphabetically, between the arsenic and the cyanide, an apothecary jar marked *Camellia sinensis*.

"Don't worry," I said. "It's only tea."

Now there fell between us one of those silences that occur when two people are getting to know each other: not yet warm and friendly, but neither cold nor wary.

"I wonder how your gram is doing?" I said at last. "Fenella, I should say."

"Well enough, I expect. She's a hard old bird."

"Tough, you mean." Her answer had surprised me.

"I mean hard."

She deliberately let go of the glass test tube she'd been toying with and watched it shatter on the floor.

"But she'll not be broken," she said.

I begged to differ but I kept my mouth shut. Porcelain had not seen her grandmother, as I had, sprawled in a pool of her own blood.

"Life can kill you, but only if you let it. She used to tell me that."

"You must have loved her awfully," I said, realizing even as I spoke that I made it sound as if Fenella were already dead.

"Yes, sometimes very much," Porcelain said reflectively, "—and sometimes not at all."

She must have seen my startled reaction.

"Love's not some big river that flows on and on forever, and if you believe it is, you're a bloody fool. It can be dammed up until nothing's left but a trickle . . . "

"Or stopped completely," I added.

She did not reply.

I let my gaze wander out the window and across the Visto and I thought about the kinds of love I knew, which were not very many. After a while I thought about Brookie Harewood. Who had hated him enough to kill him, I wondered, and hang him from Poseidon's trident? Or had Brookie's death come about through fear rather than hate?

Well, whatever the case, Brookie would be laid out on a wheeled trolley in Hinley by now, and someone—his next of kin—would have been asked to identify the body.

As an attendant in a white coat lifted the corner of a sheet to reveal Brookie's dead face, a woman would step forward. She would gasp, clap a handkerchief to her mouth, and quickly turn her head away.

I knew how it was done: I'd seen it in the cinema.

And unless I missed my bet, the woman would be his mother: the artist who lived in Malden Fenwick.

But perhaps I was wrong: Perhaps they would spare a mother the grief. Perhaps the woman who was stepping forward was just a friend. But no—Brookie didn't seem the type to have ladies as friends. Not many women would fancy spending their nights sneaking about the countryside in rubber boots and handling dead fish.

I was so wrapped up in my thoughts that I hadn't heard Porcelain begin speaking.

"—but never in summer," she was saying. "In summer she'd chuck all that and take to the roads with Johnny Faa, and not a penny between them. Like a couple of kids, they were. Johnny was a tinker when he was younger, but he'd given it up for some reason he would never explain. Still, he made friends easily enough, and his way with a fiddle meant that he spoke every language under the sun. They lived on whatever Fenella could get by telling the fortunes of fools."

"I was one of those fools," I told her.

"Yes," Porcelain said. She was not going to spare my feelings.

"Did you travel with them?" I asked.

"Once or twice when I was younger. Lunita didn't much like me being with them."

"Lunita?"

"My mother. She was their only child. Gypsies like large families, you know, but she was all they had. Their hearts were broken in half when she ran off with a *Gajo*—an Englishman from Tunbridge Wells."

"Your father?"

Porcelain nodded sadly. "She used to tell me my father was a prince—that he rode on the back of a pure white horse that was faster than the wind. His jacket was of spun gold and his sleeves of finest silk. He could talk to the birds in their own language and make himself invisible whenever the fancy took him.

"Some of that was true—he was specially good at the invisible dodge."

As Porcelain spoke, there appeared in my mind a thought as sudden and as uninvited as a shooting star in the night sky: Would I trade my father for hers?

I brushed it away.

"Tell me about your mother," I said, perhaps a little too eagerly.

"There's little enough to tell. She was on her own. She couldn't go home, if you can call it that, because Fenella and Johnny—mostly Fenella—wouldn't have her. She'd me to care for, and she hadn't a friend in the world."

"How awful," I said. "How did she manage?"

"By doing the only thing she knew. She had the gift of the cards, so she told fortunes. Sometimes, when things got bad, she would send me to Fenella and Johnny for a while. They cared for me well enough, but when I was with them they never asked about Lunita."

"And you never told them."

"No. But when the war came, things were different. We'd been living in a frightful old bed-sitter in Moorgate, where Lunita told fortunes behind a bedsheet strung up across the room. I was only four at the time, so I don't remember much about it in those days, apart from a spider that lived in a hole in the bathroom wall.

"We'd been there for, oh, I think about four years, so I must have been eight when one day a sign went up in the window of the empty house next door, and the landlady told Lunita that the place was being turned into a servicemen's club.

"Suddenly she was making more money than she knew what to do with. I think she felt guilty about all the Canadians, the Americans, the New Zealanders, and the Australians—even the Poles—that came flocking in their uniforms to our rooms to have their cards turned. She didn't want anyone to think she was profiting by the war.

"I'll never forget the day I found her weeping in the W.C. 'Those poor boys!' I remember her sobbing. 'They all ask the same question: *Will I go home alive?*'"

"And what did she tell them?"

"'You will go home in greater glory than ever you came.' She told them all the same, every one of them: half-a-crown a time."

"That's very sad," I said.

"Sad? No, not sad. Those were the best days of our lives. We just didn't realize it at the time.

"There was one particular officer that was always hanging round the club: tall bloke with a little blond mustache. I used to see him in the street, coming and going. Never had much to say, but he always seemed to be keeping an eye out for something. One day, just for a lark, Lunita invited him in and told his fortune. Wouldn't take a penny for it because it happened to be a Sunday.

"Within a day or two she was working for MI-something. They wouldn't tell her what, but it seemed that whatever she'd seen in his cards, she'd hit the nail on the head.

"Some boffin in Whitehall was trying to work out what Hitler's next move was going to be, and he'd heard through the grapevine about the Gypsy who spread the cards in Moorgate.

"They invited Lunita straightaway to lunch at the Savoy. At first, it might have been no more than a game. Maybe they wanted word to get about that they were desperate enough to pin their hopes on a Gypsy.

"But again, the things she told them were so close to the top-secret truth that they couldn't believe their ears. They'd never heard anything like it.

"At first, they thought she was a spy, and they had a scientist from Bletchley Park come up to London to interrogate her. He was hardly through the door before she told him he was lucky to be alive: that an illness had saved his life.

"And it was true. He'd just been attached to the Americans as a liaison officer when a sudden attack of appendicitis had kept him from taking part in a rehearsal for D-day—Exercise Tiger, it was called. The thing had been badly botched—hundreds killed. It was all hushed up, of course. Nobody knew about it at the time.

"Needless to say, the bloke was flabbergasted. She passed the test with flying colors, and within days—within hours—they had us set up in our own posh flat in Bloomsbury."

"She must have remarkable powers," I said.

Porcelain's body went slack. "Had," she said flatly. "She died a month later. A V1 rocket in the street outside the Air Ministry. Six years ago. In June."

"I'm sorry," I said, and I was. At last we had something in common, Porcelain and I, even if it was no more than a mother who had died too young and left us to grow up on our own.

How I longed to tell her about Harriet—but somehow I could not. The grief in the room belonged to Porcelain, and I realized, almost at once, that it would be selfish to rob her of it in any way.

I set about cleaning up the shattered glass from the test tube she had dropped.

"Here," she said. "I should be doing that."

"It's all right," I told her. "I'm used to it."

It was one of those made-up excuses that I generally despise, but how could I tell her the truth: that I was unwilling to share with anyone the picking up of the pieces.

Was this a fleeting glimpse of being a woman? I wondered.

I hoped it was . . . and also that it was not.

WE WERE SITTING ON MY BED, Porcelain with her back against the head, and I cross-legged at the foot.

"I expect you'll be wanting to visit your gram," I said.

Porcelain shrugged, and I think I understood her.

"The police don't know you're here yet. I suppose we'd better tell them."

"I suppose."

"Let's leave it till the morning," I told her. "I'm too tired to think."

And it was true: My eyelids felt as if they had been hung with lead sinkers. I was simply too exhausted to deal with the problems at hand. The greatest of these would be to keep secret Porcelain's presence in the house. The last thing I needed was to look on helplessly as Father drove away the granddaughter of Fenella and Johnny Faa.

Fenella was in hospital in Hinley and, for all I knew, she might be dead by now. If I was to get to the bottom of the attack upon her at the Palings—and, I suspected, the murder of Brookie Harewood—I would have to attract as little attention as possible.

It was only a matter of time before Inspector Hewitt would be at the door, demanding details about how I had discovered Brookie's body. I needed time to review which facts I would tell him and which I would not. Or did I?

My mind was a whirl. *Heigh-ho!* I thought. *What jolly sport is the world of Flavia de Luce.*

Next thing I knew it was morning, and sunlight was pouring in through the windows.

thirteen

I ROLLED OVER AND BLINKED. I HAD BEEN SPRAWLED ACROSS the bottom of the bed, my head twisted painfully against the footboard. At the top of the bed, Porcelain was tucked in with my blanket pulled over her shoulders, her head on my pillow, sleeping away for all she was worth like some Oriental princess.

For a moment I felt my resentment rising, but when I remembered the tale she had told me last night, I let the resentment melt into pity.

I glanced at the clock and saw, to my horror, that I had overslept. I was late for breakfast. Father insisted that dishes at the table arrive and be taken away with military precision.

Taking great care not to awaken Porcelain, I made a quick change of clothing, took a swipe at my hair with a brush, and crept down to breakfast.

Father, as usual, was immersed in the latest number of *The London Philatelist*, and seemed hardly to notice my arrival: a sure sign that another philatelic auction was about to take place. If our financial condition was as precarious as he claimed, he'd need to be sharp about current prices. As he ate, he made little notes on a napkin with the stub of a pencil, his mind in another world.

As I slipped into my chair, Feely fixed me with the cold and stony stare she had perfected by watching Queen Mary in the newsreels.

"You have a pimple on your face," I said matter-of-factly as I poured milk on my Weetabix.

She pretended she didn't hear me, but less than a minute later I was gratified to see her hand rise automatically to her cheek and begin its exploration. It was like watching a crab crawl slowly across the seabed in one of the full-colored short subjects at the cinema: *The Living Ocean*, or something like that.

"Careful, Feely!" I said. "It's going to explode."

Daffy looked up from her book—the copy of *A Looking Glasse, for London and Englande* I had found at the fête. She'd picked it up herself, the swine!

I made a note to steal it later.

"What does it mean where it says 'a red herring without mustard'?" I asked, pointing.

Daffy loved the slightest opportunity to show off her superior knowledge.

I had already reviewed in my mind what I knew about mustard, which was precious little. I knew, for instance, that it contained, among other things, the acids oleic, erucic, behenic, and stearic. I knew that stearic acid was found in beef and mutton suet because I had once subjected one of Mrs. Mullet's greasy Sunday roasts to chemical analysis, and I had looked up the fact that erucic acid gets its name from the Greek word meaning "to vomit."

"Red herring, in the sixteenth and seventeenth centuries, was considered an inferior dish," Daffy replied, with an especially withering look at me on the word "inferior."

I glanced over at Father to see if he was looking, but he wasn't.

"Nicholas Breton called it 'a good gross dish for a coarse stomach,'" she went on, squirming and preening in her chair. "He also said that old ling—that's another fish, in case you don't know—is like 'a blew coat without caugnisaunce,' which means a servant who doesn't wear his master's badge of arms."

"Daphne, please . . . " Father said, without looking up, and she subsided.

I knew that they were referring—over my head, they thought—to Dogger. Warfare at Buckshaw was like that: invisible and sometimes silent.

"Pass the toast, please," Daffy said, as quietly and politely as if she were addressing a stranger in an A.B.C. tea shop: as if the last eleven years of my life hadn't happened.

"They're having a new badminton court at Fosters'," Feely remarked suddenly to no one in particular. "Sheila's going to use the old one to park her Daimler."

Father grunted, but I could tell he was no longer listening.

"She's such a saucy stick," Feely went on. "She had Copley bring out little dishes of dessert onto the south lawn, but instead of ices she served snails—*escargots*! We ate them raw, like oysters, as the cinema stars do. It was ever so amusing."

"You'd better be careful," I said. "The snail gatherers sometimes pick up leeches by mistake. If you swallow a leech, it will eat its way out of your stomach from the inside."

Feely's face drained slowly, like a washbasin.

"There was something in *The Hinley Chronicle*," I added helpfully, "three weeks ago, if I remember correctly, about a man from St. Elfrieda's—not that far from here, really—who swallowed a leech and they had to—"

But Feely had scraped back her chair and fled.

"Are you provoking your sister again, Flavia," Father asked, looking up from his journal, but leaving a forefinger on the page to mark his place.

"I was trying to discuss current events," I said. "But she doesn't seem much interested."

"Ah," Father said, and went back to reading about plate flaws in the 1840 tuppenny blue.

With Father present at the table, we were at least semi-civilized.

I made my escape with surprisingly little difficulty.

MRS. MULLET WAS IN THE KITCHEN torturing the corpse of a chicken with a ball of butcher's twine.

"No good roastin' 'em 'less you truss properly," she said. "That's what Mrs. Chadwick up at Norton Old Hall used to tell me, and she ought to know. She was the one that learned me—mind you that was back in the days of Lady Rex-Wells, long before you was born, dear. 'Truss 'em up three-times-three,' she used to say, 'and you'll never have to rake out your oven.' What are you laughin' at, miss?"

A nervous titter had escaped me as a sudden image—of being tied up in a similar way by my own flesh and blood—had flashed across my mind.

The very thought of it reminded me that I had not yet taken my revenge. Certainly, there had been my little leech joke, but that was a mere warm-up: no more than a prelude to vengeance. The fact was that I had simply been too busy.

As Mrs. M slid the doomed bird into the maw of the open Aga, I took the opportunity to pinch a pot of strawberry jam from the pantry.

"Three-times-three," I said with an awful grimace and a horrid wink at Mrs. Mullet, as if I were giving the password of a secret society—one in which she and I were the only members. At the same time, I gave her a Winston Churchill "V for Victory" sign with my right hand, to divert attention from the jam jar in my left.

Safely back upstairs, I opened the bedroom door as quietly as possible. There was no need to disturb Porcelain. I would leave a note telling her that I'd be back later, and that was all. No need to say where I was going.

But no note was necessary: The bed was perfectly made and Porcelain was gone.

Confound her! I thought. Hadn't she understood that she was to keep to my room and out of sight? I thought I had made that perfectly clear, but perhaps I hadn't.

Where was she now? Wandering the halls of Buckshaw—where she would surely be caught? Or had she returned to the caravan in the Palings?

I'd been intending to accompany her to the police station in Bishop's Lacey so that she could make her presence known to Constable Linnet. By being on the spot, I'd be not only doing my duty, but putting myself in the perfect position to overhear anything that passed between Porcelain and the police. PC Linnet would, in turn, inform his superiors in Hinley, who would pass the word to Inspector Hewitt. And I'd be the recipient of his grateful thanks.

It could have been so simple. Damn the girl!

Back through the kitchen I trudged with a second-degree wink to Mrs. Mullet and a muttered "Three-times-three."

Gladys was waiting by the garden wall and Dogger was in the greenhouse, intent upon his work.

But as I pedaled away, I was aware of his eyes upon my back.

MALDEN FENWICK LAY TO THE east of Bishop's Lacey, not far beyond Chipford.

Although I had never been there before, the place had a familiar look: and no wonder. "The Prettiest Village in England," as it was sometimes called, had been photographed almost to distraction. Its Elizabethan and Georgian cottages, thatched and timbered, with their hollyhocks and diamond-paned windows, its duck pond and its tithe barn had appeared not just in hundreds of books and magazines, but as the setting for several popular films, such as *Honey for Sale* and *Miss Jenks Goes to War*.

"Trellis Terraces," Daffy called it.

This was the place where Brookie Harewood's mother lived and had her studio, although I hadn't the faintest idea which of the cottages might be hers.

A green charabanc was parked in front of The Bull, its passengers spilling forth into the high street, cameras at the ready, fanning out in every direction with dangling arms, like a gaggle of gunfighters.

Several elderly villagers, caught out-of-doors in their gardens, began furtively fluffing up their hair or straightening their ties even as shutters began to click.

I parked Gladys against an ancient elm and walked round the coach.

"Good morning," I said to a lady in a sun hat, as if I were helping to organize the tea. "Welcome to Malden Fenwick. And where are *you* from?"

"Oh, Mel," she said, turning to a man behind her, "listen to her accent! Isn't she adorable? We're from Yonkers, New York, sweetheart. I'll bet you don't know where that is."

As a matter of fact, I did: Yonkers was the home of Leo Baekeland, the Belgian chemist who had accidentally discovered *polyoxybenzylmethylenglycolanhydride*, better known as Bakelite, while working to produce a synthetic replacement for shellac which, until Baekeland came along, had been made from the secretions of the lac beetle.

"Oh, yes," I said. "I think I've heard of Yonkers."

I attached myself to Mel, who was busily arming his camera as he strolled off towards a wash-painted cottage, dragging along behind him, with slack bones and downcast eyes, a sulking daughter who looked fed to the gills with transatlantic travel.

Shifting from foot to foot, I waited as he fired off a couple of shots of a white-haired woman in tweeds who was perched precariously on a ladder, deadheading a climbing rosebush.

As Mel wandered off in search of new memories, I lingered for a moment at the gate pretending to admire the garden and then, as if awakening from a partial trance, put on my best attempt at an American accent.

"Say," I called out, pointing to the village green. "Isn't this where whatsername lives? The painter lady?"

"Vanetta Harewood. Glebe Cottage," the woman said cheerily, waving her secateurs. "Last one on the right."

It was so easy I was almost ashamed of myself.

So that was her name: "Vanetta." Vanetta Harewood. It certainly had the right ring to it for someone who painted the gentry with their hounds and horses.

Barging in on a freshly bereaved mother was not, perhaps, in the best of taste, but there were things I needed to know before the police knew them. I owed as much to Fenella Faa, and to a lesser degree, to my own family. Why, for instance, had I found Vanetta Harewood's son in the drawing room at Buckshaw in the middle of the night, just before he was murdered?

I didn't expect his mother knew the answer to that, but mightn't she give me some scrap of information that would allow me to find it out for myself?

As the woman with the secateurs had said, Glebe Cottage was the last one on the right. It was twice the size of the others—as if two cottages had been shoved together end-to-end like dominos to form a larger one. Each half had its own front door, its own leaded window, and its own chimney; each half of the house was the mirror image of the other.

There was only one gate, though, and on it was a small brass plaque upon which was engraved: *Vanetta Harewood—Portraitist*.

My mind flew back to a spring evening upon which Daffy, during one of Father's compulsory literary evenings, had read aloud to us excerpts from Boswell's *The Life of Samuel Johnson, LL.D.*, and I remembered that Johnson had declared portrait painting to be an improper employment for a woman. "Public practice of any art, and staring in men's faces, is very indelicate in a female," he had said.

Well, I'd seen Dr. Johnson's face in the book's frontispiece, and I couldn't imagine anyone, male *or* female, wanting to stare into it for any length of time—the man was an absolute toad!

Behind the gate, the garden of Glebe Cottage was a mass of electric blue; the tall delphiniums in their second blooming seemed to stand on tiptoe behind the salvia, trying desperately to be first to touch the sky.

Dogger had once told me that although delphiniums could be made to bloom again by cutting them down low after their first flowering, no honest gardener would dream of doing so, since it weakened the stock.

Whatever else she might be, Vanetta Harewood was not an honest gardener.

I touched my finger to the china doorbell button and gave it a jab. As I waited for someone to answer, I stepped back and stared up in an interested way at the sky, pursing my lips as if I were whistling carelessly. You never knew: Someone might be peeking out from behind the curtains and it was important to look harmless.

I waited—then pushed the button again. There was a scurrying inside the house, followed by a grating noise directly behind the door, as if someone were moving a barricade of furniture.

As the door opened, I almost gasped aloud. Standing in front of me was a muscular woman in riding breeches and a lavender blouse. Her short gray hair lay tightly against her head like an aluminum helmet.

She screwed a tortoiseshell monocle into her eye and peered at me. "Yes?"

"Mrs. Harewood?"

"No," she said, and shut the door in my face.

Very well, then!

I remembered Father remarking once that if rudeness was not attributable to ignorance, it could be taken as a sure sign that one was speaking to a member of the aristocracy. I pushed the bell again. I would ask for directions.

But this time the door stayed closed, and the house behind it remained in silence.

But wait! The cottage had *two* front doors. I had simply chosen the wrong one.

I gave myself a knuckle on the head and walked to the other door. I raised the door knocker and gave it a gentle tap.

The door flew open instantly, and there stood Riding Breeches, glaring at me for all she was worth, though not through her monocle this time.

"May I speak to Mrs. Harewood?" I ventured. "It's about—"

"No!" she said loudly. "Go away!"

But before she could slam the door, a voice came from somewhere inside the house.

"Who is it, Ursula?"

"A girl selling something," she called over her shoulder, and to me, "Go away. We don't want any biscuits."

I saw my opportunity and I took it.

"Mrs. Harewood," I shouted. "It's about Brookie!"

It was as if I had cast a spell and frozen time. For what seemed like forever, the woman at the door stood perfectly motionless, gaping at me as if she were a life-sized painted cutout from a picture book. She didn't even breathe.

"Mrs. Harewood—please! It's Flavia de Luce, from Bishop's Lacey."

"Show her in, Ursula," the voice said.

As I brushed past her and into the narrow hallway, Ursula didn't move a muscle.

"In here," the voice said, and I moved towards it.

I suppose I was half expecting to find a decayed Miss Haversham, clinging to her moldy treasures in the curtained cave of her drawing room. What I found was altogether different.

Vanetta Harewood stood in a beam of sunlight at the bow window, and she turned to hold out her hands to me as I entered.

"Thank you for coming," she said.

She looked, I thought, to be about forty-five. But surely she must be much older than that. How on earth could such a beautiful creature be the mother of that middle-aged layabout, Brookie Harewood?

She wore a smart dark suit with an Oriental silk at her neck, and her fingers were afire with diamonds.

"I must apologize for Ursula," she said, taking my hand in hers, "but she's fiercely protective of me. Perhaps too fiercely."

I nodded dumbly.

"In my profession, privacy is paramount, you see, and now, with all this . . . "

She made a wide sweep of her hands to take in the entire world.

"I understand," I said. "I'm sorry about Brookie."

She turned and took a cigarette from a silver box, lit it with a silver lighter that might have been a scale model of Aladdin's lamp, and blew out a long jet of smoke which, oddly enough, was also silver in the sunlight.

"Brookie was a good boy," she said, "but he did not grow up to be a good man. He had the fatal gift of making people believe him."

I wasn't sure what she meant, but I nodded anyway.

"His life was not an easy one," she said reflectively. "Not as easy as it might seem."

And then, quite suddenly—"Now tell me, why have you come?"

Her question caught me by surprise. Why *had* I come?

"Oh, don't be embarrassed, child. If you're here to express your condolences, you have already done so, for which I thank you. You may leave, if you wish."

"Brookie was at Buckshaw," I blurted. "I found him in the drawing room in the middle of the night."

I could have cut out my tongue! There was no need for his mother to know this—no need at all, and even less for me to tell her.

But part of me knew that it was safe enough. Vanetta Harewood was a professional woman. She would no more want the midnight ramblings of her son brought to light than . . . than I would.

"I am going to ask you a very great favor, Flavia. Tell the police if you must, but if you feel it isn't essential . . . "

She had walked back to the window, where she stood staring out into the past. "You see, Brookie had his . . . demons, if you will. If there is no need to make them public, then—"

"I won't tell anyone, Mrs. Harewood," I said. "I promise."

She turned back to me and came across the room slowly. "You're a remarkably intelligent girl, Flavia," she said. And then, after thinking for a couple of seconds, she added, "Come with me; there's something I wish to show you."

Down a step we went, and then up another, into the part of the house whose door I had first knocked upon. Low timbered ceilings made her stoop more than once as we went from room to room.

"Ursula's studio," she said, with a wave of a hand at a room that seemed full of twigs and branches.

"Basketry," she explained. "Ursula is a devotee of traditional crafts. Her willow baskets have taken prizes both here and on the Continent.

"To tell you the truth," she went on, lowering her voice to a confidential whisper, "the smell of her chemical preparations sometimes drives me out of the house, but then, it's all she has, poor dear."

Chemical preparations? My ears went up like those of an old warhorse at the sound of the bugle.

"Mostly sulfur," she said. "Ursula uses the fumes to bleach the willow withies. They end up as white as polished bones, you know, but oh dear—the smell!"

I could foresee that I was going to have a late night poring over books in Uncle Tar's chemical library. Already my mind was racing ahead to the chemical possibilities of salicin ($C_{13}H_{18}O_7$)—which was discovered in willow bark in 1831 by Leroux—and good old sulfur (S). I already knew from personal experience that certain willow catkins, kept in a sealed box for several weeks, give off the most dreadful odor of dead fish, a fact which I had filed away for future use.

"Through here," Mrs. Harewood said, ducking to keep her head from banging on an exceptionally low beam. "Mind your head and watch your step."

Her studio was a glorious place. Clear north light flooded in through the angled transom windows overhead, making it seem like a room suddenly stumbled upon in a forest glade.

A large wooden easel stood in the light, and on it was a half-finished portrait of Flossie, the sister of Feely's friend Sheila Foster. Flossie was sitting in a large upholstered chair, one leg curled under her, petting an enormous white Persian cat that nestled in her lap. The cat, at least, looked almost human.

Actually, Flossie didn't look that bad, either. She was not my favorite living person, but I didn't hold that against her. The portrait captured perfectly, in a way that even a camera can't, her air of highly polished dopiness.

"Well, what do you think?"

I looked around at the tubes of paints, the daubed rags, and the profusion of camel-hair brushes that jutted up all around me from tins, glasses, and bottles like reeds in a December marsh.

"It's a very nice studio," I said. "Is that what you wanted to show me?"

I pointed a finger at Flossie's portrait.

"Good heavens, no!" she said.

I had not noticed it before but at the far end of the studio, away from the windows, were two shadowy corners in which perhaps a dozen unframed paintings were leaning with their faces against the wall, their paper-sealed backsides towards the room.

Vanetta (by now I was thinking of her as "Vanetta," rather than

"Mrs. Harewood") bent over them, shifting each one as if she were rif-fling through the record cards in a giant index file.

"Ah! Here it is," she said at last, pulling a large canvas from among the others.

Keeping its back towards me, she carried the painting to the easel. After shifting Flossie to a nearby wooden chair, she turned it round and lifted it into place.

She stepped back without a word, giving me an unobstructed view of the portrait.

My heart stopped.

It was Harriet.

fourteen

HARRIET. MY MOTHER.

She is sitting on the window box of the drawing room at Buckshaw. At her right hand, my sister Ophelia, aged about seven, plays with a cat's cradle of red wool, its strands entangling her fingers like slender scarlet snakes. To Harriet's left, my other sister, Daphne, although she is too young to read, uses a forefinger to mark her place in a large book: *Grimm's Fairy Tales*.

Harriet gazes tenderly down, a slight smile on her lips, like a Madonna, at the white bundle which she holds supported in the crook of her left arm: a child—a baby dressed in a white, trailing garment of elaborate and frothy lace—could it be a baptismal gown?

I want to look at the mother but my eyes are drawn repeatedly back to the child.

It is, of course, me.

"Ten years ago," Vanetta was saying, "I went to Buckshaw on a winter day."

She was now standing behind me.

"How well I remember it. There had been a killing frost overnight. Everything was covered with ice. I rang up your mother and suggested that we leave it until another day, but she wouldn't hear of it. She was going away, she said, and she wanted the portrait as a gift for your father. She meant to give it to him as a surprise when she returned."

My head was spinning.

"Of course, she never did," she added softly, "and frankly I've not since had the heart to hand it over to him, the poor man. He grieves so."

Grieves? Although I had never thought about it in precisely this way, it was true. Father did grieve, but he did so in private, and mostly in silence.

"The painting, I suppose, belongs to him, since your mother paid me for it in advance. She was a very trusting person."

Was she? I wanted to say. *I wouldn't know. I didn't know her as well as you did.*

Suddenly, I needed to get out of this place—to be outdoors again where I could breathe my own breath.

"I think you'd better keep it, Mrs. Harewood—at least for now. I wouldn't want to upset Father."

Hold on! I thought. My whole life was given over to upsetting Father—or at least to going against his wishes. Why now was I filled with a sudden desire to comfort him, and to have him hug me?

Not that I would, of course, because in real life we de Luces don't do that sort of thing.

But still, some unknowable part of the universe had changed, as if one of the four great turtles that are said to support the world on their backs had suddenly shifted its weight from one foot to another.

"I have to go now," I said, backing, for some reason, towards the door. "I'm sorry to hear about Brookie. I know he had lots of friends in Bishop's Lacey."

Actually, I knew no such thing! Why was I saying this? It was as if my mouth were possessed, and I had no way of stopping its flow of words.

All I really knew about Brookie Harewood was that he was a poacher and a layabout—and that I had surprised him in his midnight prowling. That and the fact that he had claimed to have seen the Gray Lady of Buckshaw.

"Good-bye, then," I said. As I stepped into the hallway, Ursula turned rapidly away and scuttled out of sight with a wicker basket in her hand. But not so quickly that I missed the look of pure hatred that she shot me.

AS I BICYCLED WESTWARD towards Bishop's Lacey, I thought of what I had seen. I'd gone to Malden Fenwick in search of clues to the behavior of Brookie Harewood—surely it was he who had attacked Fenella Faa in the Palings, for who else could have been abroad at Buckshaw that night? But instead, I had come away with a new image of Harriet, my mother: an image that was not as happy as it might have been.

Why, for instance, did it gnaw at my heart so much to see Feely and Daffy, like two contented slugs, secure and basking in her glow, while I lay helpless, wrapped up like a little mummy in white cloth; of no more interest than a bundle from the butcher?

Had Harriet loved me? My sisters were forever claiming that she did not: that, in fact, she despised me; that she had fallen into a deep depression after I was born—a depression that had, perhaps, resulted in her death.

And yet, in the painting, which must have been made just before she set out on her final journey, there was not a trace of unhappiness. Harriet's eyes had been upon *me* and the look on her face had shown, if anything, a trace of amusement.

Something about the portrait nagged at my mind: some half-forgotten thing that had tried to surface as I stood staring at the easel in Vanetta Harewood's studio. But what was it?

Hard as I tried, I couldn't think of it.

Relax, Flavia, I thought. *Calm down. Think about something else.*

I had long ago discovered that when a word or formula refused to come to mind, the best thing for it was to think of something else: tigers, for instance, or oatmeal. Then, when the fugitive word was least expecting it, I would suddenly turn the full blaze of my attention back onto it, catching the culprit in the beam of my mental torch before it could sneak off again into the darkness.

"Thought-stalking," I called the technique, and I was proud of myself for having invented it.

I let my mind drift away towards tigers, and the first one that came to mind was the tiger in William Blake's poem: the one that burned away with fearful symmetry in the forests of the night.

Once, when I was younger, Daffy had driven me into hysterics by wrapping herself in the tiger-skin rug from Buckshaw's firearm museum and creeping into my bedroom in the middle of the night, while reciting the poem in a deep and fearsome snarl: "*Tyger, tyger, burning bright . . .*"

She had never forgiven me for throwing my alarm clock. She still had the scar on her chin.

And now I thought of oatmeal: in the winter, great steaming ladles of the stuff, gray, like lava dished from a volcano on the moon. Mrs. Mullet, under orders from Father—

Mrs. Mullet! Of course!

It was something she'd told me when I'd asked about Brookie Harewood. "His mother's that woman as paints over in Malden Fenwick."

"P'raps she'll even paint you in your turn," Mrs. M had added. "*In your turn.*"

Which meant that Mrs. M knew about the portrait of Harriet! She must have been in on the secret sittings.

"Tiger!" I shouted. "Tye-ger!"

My words echoed back from the hedgerows on either side of the narrow lane. Something ahead of me bolted for cover.

An animal, perhaps? A deer? No, not an animal—a human.

It was Porcelain. I was sure of it. She was still wearing Fenella's black crepe dress.

I brought Gladys to a skidding stop.

"Porcelain?" I called. "Is that you?"

There was no answer.

"Porcelain? It's me, Flavia."

What a foolish thing to say. Porcelain had hidden in the hedgerow *because* it was me. But why?

Although I couldn't see her, she was probably close enough to touch. I could feel her eyes upon me.

"Porcelain? What is it? What's the matter?"

The eerie silence lengthened. It was like one of those parlor séances when you're waiting for the dial on the Ouija board to move.

"All right," I said at last, "take your time. I'm sitting down and I'm not moving until you come out."

There was another long wait, and then the bushes rustled and Porcelain stepped out into the lane. The look on her face suggested that she was on her way to the guillotine.

"What's the matter?" I asked. "What's happened?"

As I took a step towards her, she moved away, keeping a safe distance between us.

"The police took me to see Fenella," she said shakily. "In the hospital."

Oh, no! I thought. *She's died of her injuries. Let it not be true.*

"I'm sorry," I said, taking another step. Porcelain fell back, raising her hands as if to fend me off.

"Sorry?" she said in a strange voice. "What for? No!—Stay where you are!"

"Sorry for whatever's happened to Fenella. I did everything I could to help her."

"For God's sake, Flavia," Porcelain screamed, "stop it! You bloody well tried to kill her, and you know you did. And now you want to kill me!"

Her words hit me like a body blow, knocking the wind completely out of me. I couldn't breathe; my head was spinning, my mind was spinning, and there was a sound in my head like a swarm of locusts.

"I—"

But it was no good—I couldn't speak.

"Fenella told me all about it. You and your family have hated us for years. Your father drove Fenella and Johnny Faa off your estate and that's why Johnny died. You took her back to their old camping place so that you could finish the job, and you very nearly did, didn't you?"

"That's insane," I managed. "Why would I want to—"

"You were the only one that knew she was camped there."

"Look, Porcelain," I said. "I know you're upset. I understand that. But if I wanted to kill Fenella, why would I bother going for Dr. Darby? Wouldn't I simply let her die?"

"I—I don't know. You're confusing me now. Maybe you wanted an excuse—just in case you hadn't killed her."

"If I'd wanted to kill her, I'd have killed her," I said, exasperated. "I'd have kept at it until I was finished. I wouldn't have botched it. Do you understand?"

Her eyes widened, but I could see that I had made my point.

"And as for being the only one around that night, what about Brookie Harewood? He was roaming around at Buckshaw—I even caught him in our drawing room. Do you think I killed him, too? Do you think someone who weighs less than five stone murdered Brookie—who probably weighs thirteen—and hung him up like a bit of washing from Poseidon's trident?"

"Well . . ."

"Oh, come off it, Porcelain! I don't think Fenella saw her attacker. If she had, she wouldn't have blamed it on me. She's badly injured and she's confused. She's letting her mind fill in the blanks."

She stood there in the lane staring at me as if I were the cobra in a snake charmer's basket, and had suddenly begun to speak.

"Come on," I said, getting Gladys ready to go. "Hop on. We'll go back to Buckshaw and find some grub."

"No," she said. "I'm going back to the caravan."

"It isn't safe," I said. Perhaps by presenting the nasty facts without varnish I could change her mind. "Whoever bashed in Fenella's skull and stuck a lobster pick up Brookie's nostril is still wandering about. Come on."

"No," she said. "I told you, I'm going back to the caravan."

"Why? Are you afraid of me?"

Her answer came a little too quickly for my liking.

"Yes," she said. "I am."

"All right, then," I said softly. "Be a fool. See if I care."

I put a foot on a pedal and prepared to push off.

"Flavia—"

I turned and looked at her over my shoulder.

"I told Inspector Hewitt what Fenella said."

Wonderful, I thought. *Just bloody wonderful.*

SOMEONE ONCE SAID THAT music has charms to soothe a savage breast—or was it "beast"? Daffy would know for sure, but since I wasn't speaking to her, I could hardly ask.

But for me, music wasn't half as relaxing as revenge. To my way of thinking, the settling of scores has a calming effect upon the mind that beats music by a Welsh mile. The encounter with Porcelain had left me breathing noisily through my nose like a boar at bay and I needed time to simmer down.

Stepping through the door into my laboratory was like gaining sanctuary in a quiet church: The rows of bottled chemicals were my stained-glass windows, the chemical bench my altar. Chemistry has more gods than Mount Olympus, and here in my solitude I could pray in peace to the greatest of them: Joseph Louis Gay-Lussac (who, when he found a young assistant in a linen draper's shop surreptitiously reading a chemistry text which she kept hidden under the counter, promptly dumped his fiancée and married the girl); William Perkin (who had found a way of making purple dye for the robes of emperors without using the spit of mollusks); and Carl Wilhelm Scheele, who probably discovered oxygen, and—more thrilling even than that—hydrogen cyanide, my personal pick as the last word in poisons.

I began by washing my hands. I always did this in a ceremonial way, but today they needed to be dry.

I had brought with me to the laboratory an object that was normally strapped to Gladys's seat. Gladys had come fully equipped from the factory with a tire repair kit, and it was this tin box with the name of Messrs. Dunlop on the lid that I now deposited on my workbench.

But first I closed my eyes and focused on the object of my attentions: my beloved sister, Ophelia Gertrude de Luce, whose mission in life is to revive the Spanish Inquisition with me as the sole victim. With Daffy's connivance, her recent torture of me in the cellars had been the last straw. And now the dreadful clock of revenge was about to strike!

Feely's great weakness was the mirror: When it came to vanity, my sister made Becky Sharp look like one of the Sisters of the Holy Humility of Mary—an order with which she was forever comparing me (unfavorably, I might add).

She was capable of examining herself for hours in the looking glass, tossing her hair, baring her teeth, toying with her pimples, and pulling down the outer corners of her upper eyelids to encourage them to droop aristocratically like Father's.

Even in church and already primped to the nines, Feely would consult a little mirror that she kept hidden inside *Hymns Ancient and Modern* so that she could keep an eye on her complexion while pretending to refresh her memory with the words to Hymn 573: *All Things Bright and Beautiful*.

She was also a religious snob. To Feely, the morning church service was a drama, and she its pious star. She was always off like a shot to be the first at the communion rail, so that in returning to our pew, she would be seen with her humble eyes downcast, her long white fingers cupped at her waist, by the maximum number of churchgoers.

These were the facts that had sifted through my mind as I planned my next move, and now the time had come.

With the little white Bible Mrs. Mullet had given me on my confirmation day in one hand and the tire kit in the other, I headed for Feely's bedroom.

This was not as difficult as it might seem. By following a maze of dusty, darkened hallways, and keeping to the upper floor, I was able to make my way from Buckshaw's east wing towards the west, passing on my way a number of abandoned bedrooms that had not been used since Queen Victoria had declined to visit in the latter years of her reign. She had remarked to her private secretary, Sir Henry Ponsonby, that she "could not possibly find enough breath in such a wee dwelling."

Now, behind their paneled doors, these rooms were like furniture morgues, inhabited only by sheet-covered bedsteads, dressers, and chairs which, because of the dryness of their bones, had been known sometimes to give off alarming cracking noises in the night.

All was quiet now, though, as I passed the last of these abandoned chambers, and arrived at the door that opened into the west wing. I put my ear to the green baize cloth, but all was silent on the other side. I opened the door a crack and peered through it into the hallway.

Again nothing. The place was like a tomb.

I smiled as the strains of Bach's *Jesu, Joy of Man's Desiring* came drifting up the west staircase: Feely was busy at her practice in the drawing room, and I knew that my work would not be disturbed.

I stepped into her bedroom and closed the door.

It was a room not totally unknown to me, since I often came here to filch chocolates and to have a good old rifle through her drawers. In design, it was much like my own: a great old barn of a place with high ceilings and tall windows; a place that seemed better suited to the parking of an aeroplane than the parking of one's carcass for a good night's sleep.

The greatest difference between this room and my own was that Feely's did not have damp paper hanging in bags from the walls and ceiling: bags that during heavy rainstorms would fill up with cold, dripping water that turned my mattress into a soggy swamp. On those occasions, I would be forced to abandon my bed and spend the night, wrapped in my dressing gown, in a mousy-smelling wing chair that stood in the one dry corner of the room.

Feely's bedroom, by contrast, was like something out of the cinema. The walls were covered with a delicate floral pattern (moss roses, I think) and the tall windows were bracketed with yards of lace.

A four-poster with embroidered curtains was dwarfed by the room, and stood almost unnoticed in a corner.

To the left of the windows, in pride of place, was a particularly fine Queen Anne dresser, whose curved legs were as slender and delicate as those of the ballet dancers in the paintings of Degas. Above it, on the wall, was fastened a monstrous dark-framed looking glass, too large by far for the dainty legs that stood beneath. The effect was rather Humpty Dumpty–ish: like an obscenely oversized head on a body with leprechaun legs.

I used Feely's hairbrush to prop open the Bible on the dresser top. From the tire repair kit, I extracted a tin of magnesium silicate hydroxide, better known as French chalk. The stuff was meant to keep a freshly patched inner tube from sticking to the inside of the rubber tire, but this was not the application I had in mind.

I dipped one of Feely's camel-hair makeup brushes into the French chalk and, with one last glance at the Bible for reference, wrote a short message across the mirror's surface in bold letters: *Deuteronomy 28:27*.

That done, I pulled a handkerchief from my pocket and gently dusted away the words that I had written. I blew the excess chalk from where it had fallen on the dresser top, and wiped up the few traces that had drifted to the floor.

It was done! The rest of my plan was guaranteed.

It would unfold itself through the inexorable laws of chemistry, without my having to lift a finger.

When Feely next parked herself in front of the mirror and leaned in for a closer look at her ugly hide, the moisture of her warm breath would make visible the words that I had written on the glass. Their message would spring boldly into view:

Deuteronomy 28:27

Feely would be terror-stricken. She would run to look up the passage in the Bible. Actually, she might not: Since it had to do with personal grooming, she might already have the verse off by heart. But if she did have to search it out, this is what she would find:

The LORD shall smite thee with the boils of Egypt, and with the emerods, and with the scurvy, and with the itch, whereof thou canst not be healed.

As if the boils weren't bad enough, "emerods" were hemorrhoids, the perfect added touch, I thought.

And if I knew my sister, she wouldn't be able to resist reading the rest of the verse:

The LORD shall smite thee with madness, and with blindness, and with astonishment of heart; and thou shalt grope at noonday, as the blind gropeth in darkness, and thou shalt not prosper in thy ways: and thou shalt be only oppressed and spoiled alway, and there shall be none to save thee.

Feely would toss up her marmalade!

Having seen the message materialize before her very eyes, she'd believe it to be a telegram from God, and—by the Old Harry!—would *she* be sorry!

I could see it now: She'd fling herself down and grovel on the carpet, begging forgiveness for the rotten way she'd treated her little sister.

Later, she would appear at the dinner table, haunted, haggard, and shocked into silence.

I chortled as I skipped down the staircase. I could barely wait.

At the bottom, in the foyer, stood Inspector Hewitt.

fifteen

THE INSPECTOR DID NOT LOOK HAPPY.

Dogger, who had only just let him in, closed the door silently, and vanished in the way he does.

"You should think about opening an auxiliary police station here at Buckshaw," I said affably, trying to cheer him up. "It would certainly save on petrol."

The Inspector was not amused.

"Let's have a chat," he said, and I had the impression that he was not entirely attempting to put me at my ease.

"Of course. I am at your disposal."

I was capable of being gracious when I felt like it.

"About your discovery at the fountain—" he began.

"Brookie Harewood, you mean? Yes, that was awful, wasn't it."

The Inspector seemed startled.

Damn! Ten seconds into the game and I had already made a serious misstep.

"You know him, then?"

"Oh, everyone knows Brookie," I said, recovering quickly. "He's one of the village characters. At least—he was."

"Someone *you* knew?"

"I've seen him about. Here and there, you know. In the village. That sort of thing."

I was sewing an invisible seam between truth and untruth, a skill of which I was especially proud. One of the tricks of the trade when doing this is to volunteer fresh information before your questioner has time to ask another. So I went on:

"I had returned to the Palings, you see, because I was worried about Gry. Gry is the name of the Gypsy woman's horse. I wanted to make sure he had food."

This was not entirely true: Gry could have survived for weeks by nibbling the grass in the glade, but noble motives can never be questioned.

"Very commendable," Inspector Hewitt said. "I had asked Constable Linnet to lay on some hay."

I had a quick vision of PC Linnet producing an egg in the straw, but I banished it from my mind to keep from grinning.

"Yes, I noticed that when I got there," I said. "And of course, I met Porcelain. She told me you had tracked her down in London."

As I spoke, the Inspector produced a notebook, flipped it open, and began to write. I'd better watch my step.

"I didn't think she'd be safe in the caravan. Not with whoever attacked her gram still wandering about. I insisted she come back with me to Buckshaw, and it was on our way here that we came across the body."

I didn't say "Brookie's body" because I didn't want to seem too chummy with him, which could only lead to more questions about our prior acquaintance.

"What time was that?"

"Oh, let me see—you were here when I got up, just around breakfast time—that was at about nine-thirty, I should say."

The Inspector riffled back several pages in his notebook and nodded. I was on the right track.

"After that, Sergeant Graves came straightaway to take my fingerprints—ten-thirty—perhaps eleven?

"At any rate," I went on, "Constable Linnet should be able to tell you what time I called to report it, which couldn't have been much more than ten or fifteen minutes after we discovered the body in the fountain."

I was stalling—treading water, delaying the time when he would inevitably ask about my so-called assault on Fenella. I decided to leap into the breach.

"Porcelain thinks I attacked her gram," I said bluntly.

Inspector Hewitt nodded. "Mrs. Faa is very disoriented. It often happens with injuries to the head. I thought I'd made that quite clear to the granddaughter, but perhaps I'd best have another word—"

"No!" I said. "Don't do that. It doesn't matter."

The Inspector looked at me sharply, then made another scribble in his notebook.

"Are you putting another *P* beside my name?"

It was a saucy question, and I was sorry as soon as I asked it. Once, during an earlier investigation, I had seen him print a capital *P* beside my name in his notebook. Maddeningly, he had refused to tell me what it meant.

"It's not polite to ask," he said with a slight smile. "One must never ask a policeman his secrets."

"Why not?"

"For the same reason I don't ask you yours."

How I adored this man! Here we were, the two of us, engaged in a mental game of chess in which both of us knew that one of us was cheating.

At the risk of repetition, how I adored this man!

AND THAT HAD BEEN THE END OF IT. He had asked me a few more questions: whether I had seen anyone else about, whether I had heard the sound of a motor vehicle, and so forth. And then he had gone.

At one point I had wanted to tell him more, just to prolong the pleasure of his company. He'd have been thrilled to hear about how I had caught Brookie prowling about our drawing room, for instance, to say nothing about my visits to Miss Mountjoy and to Brookie's digs. I might even have confided in him what I'd found at Vanetta Harewood's house in Malden Fenwick.

But I hadn't.

As I stood musing in the foyer, the slight squeak of a shoe on tile caught my attention, and I looked up to find Feely staring down at me from the first-floor landing. She'd been there all along!

"Little Miss Helpful," she sneered. "You think you're so clever."

I could tell by her attitude that she had not yet consulted her bedroom mirror.

"One tries to be of assistance," I said, casually dusting a few stray smudges of French chalk from my dress.

"You think he likes you, don't you? You think a lot of people do—but they don't. No one likes you. There may be a few who pretend to, but they don't—not really. It's such a pity you can't see that."

Amplified by the paneling of the foyer, her voice came echoing all the way down from among the cherub-painted panels of the ceiling. I felt as if I were the prisoner at the bar, and she my accuser.

As always when one of my sisters turned on me, I felt a strange welling in my chest, as if some primeval swamp creature were trying to crawl out of my insides. It was a feeling I could never understand, something that lay beyond reason. What had I ever done to make them detest me so?

"Why don't you go torture Bach?" I flung back at her, but my heart was not really in it.

IT ALWAYS SURPRISES ME after a family row to find that the world out-doors has remained the same. While the passions and feelings that accumulate like noxious gases inside a house seem to condense and cling to the walls and ceilings like old smoke, the out-of-doors is different. The landscape seems incapable of accumulating human radiation. Perhaps the wind blows anger away.

I thought about this as I trudged towards the Trafalgar Lawn. If Porcelain chose to go on believing that I was the monster who had bashed in her grandmother's skull with—with what?

When I had found Fenella lying on the floor of the caravan, the inside of the wagon had been, except for the blood, as neat as a pin: no bloody weapon flung aside by her attacker: no stick, no stone, no poker. Which seemed odd.

Unless the weapon had some value, why would the culprit choose to carry it away?

Or had it been ditched? I'd seen nothing to suggest that it had.

Surely the police would have gone over the Palings with a microscope in search of a weapon. But had they found one?

I paused for a moment to stare up at the Poseidon fountain. Old Neptune, as the Romans called him, all muscles and tummy, was gazing unconcernedly off into the distance, like someone who has broken wind at a banquet and is trying to pretend it wasn't him.

His trident was still held up like a scepter (he was, after all, the King of the Sea) and his fishnets lay in a tangle at his feet. There wasn't a trace of Brookie Harewood. It was hard to believe that, just hours ago, Brookie had dangled dead here—his body a gruesome addition to the sculpture.

But why? Why would his killer go to the trouble of hoisting a corpse into such a difficult position? Could it be a message—some bizarre form of the naval signal flag, for instance?

What little I knew about Poseidon had been gained from *Bullfinch's Mythology*, a copy of which was in the library at Buckshaw. It was one of Daffy's favorite books, but since there was nothing in it about chemistry or poisons, it didn't really interest me.

Poseidon was said to rule the waters, so it was easy enough to see why he was chosen to adorn a fountain. The only other waters within spitting distance of this particular Poseidon were the river Efon at the Palings and Buckshaw's ornamental lake.

Brookie had been hung from the trident much like the way a shrike, or larder bird, impales a songbird on a thorn for later use—although it seemed unlikely, I thought, that Brookie's killer planned to eat him later.

Was it a warning, then? And if so, to whom?

I needed to have a few hours alone with my notebook, but now was not the time. There was Porcelain to deal with.

I wasn't finished with Porcelain. As a token of goodwill, I would not be put off by her childish behavior—nor would I take offense. I would forgive her whether she liked it or not.

I can't claim that Gry was happy to see me arriving at the Palings, although he did look up for a moment from his grazing. A fresh bale of hay strewn nearby told me that Constable Linnet was on the job, but Gry seemed to prefer the green salad of weeds that grew along the river's edge.

"Hello!" I shouted to the caravan, but there was no answer. The delicate instrument that was the back of my neck told me, too, that the glade was deserted.

I didn't remember Porcelain locking the caravan when we left together, but it was locked now. Either she had returned and found the key, or somebody else had done so.

But someone had been here and—if I could believe my nose—quite recently.

Warmed by the sun, the wooden door was releasing an odor that did not belong here. As I would do in my laboratory with a chemical, I used my cupped fingers to scoop air towards my nostrils.

No doubt about it: A definite odor lingered near the door of the caravan—an odor that most certainly had not been on the outside of the caravan before: the smell of fish.

The smell of the sea.

sixteen

"YOU'RE IN MY LIGHT," DAFFY SAID.

I had intentionally planted myself between her book and the window.

It was not going to be easy to ask my sister for assistance. I took a deep breath.

"I need some help."

"Poor Flavia!"

"Please, Daff," I said, despising myself for begging. "It's about that man whose body I found at the fountain."

Daffy threw down her book in exasperation. "Why drag me into your sordid little games? You know perfectly well how much they upset me."

Upset her? Daff? Games?

"I thought you loved crime!" I said, pointing to her book. It was a collection of G. K. Chesterton's Father Brown mysteries.

"I do," she said, "but not in real life. The antics you get up to turn my stomach."

This was news to me. I'd file it away for later use.

"And Father's almost as bad," she added. "Do you know what he said at breakfast yesterday, before you came down? 'Flavia's found another body.' Almost as if he was proud of you."

Father said that? I could hardly believe it.

The revelations were coming thick and fast! I should have thought of talking to Daffy sooner.

"It's true," I said. "I did. But I'll spare you the details."

"Thank you," Daffy said quietly, and I thought she might actually have meant it.

"Poseidon," I said, taking advantage of the partial thaw. "What do you know about Poseidon?"

This was throwing down the gauntlet. Daffy knew everything about everything, and I knew she couldn't resist showing off her uncanny power of recall.

"Poseidon? He was a cad," she said. "A bully and a cad. He was also a womanizer."

"How can a god be a cad?"

Daffy ignored my question. "He was what we would call nowadays the patron saint of sailors, and with jolly good reason."

"Which means?"

"That he was no better than he ought to be. Now run along."

Ordinarily I might have taken umbrage at being dismissed so high-handedly (I love that word, "umbrage"—it's in *David Copperfield*, where David's aunt, Betsey Trotwood, takes umbrage at his being born), but I didn't—instead, I felt rather an odd sense of gratitude towards my sister.

"Thanks, Daff!" I said. "I knew I could count on you."

This was shoveling it on, but I was honestly pleased. And so, I think, was Daffy. As she picked up her book, I saw that the corners of her mouth were turned up by about the thickness of one of its pages.

I WAS HALF EXPECTING TO FIND Porcelain in my room, but of course she was gone. I had almost forgotten that she'd accused me of attempted murder.

I'd begin with her.

PORCELAIN (I wrote in my notebook)—Can't possibly be her grandmother's attacker since she was in London at the time. Or was she? I have only her word for it. But why did she feel compelled to wash out her clothing?

BROOKIE HAREWOOD—Was likely killed by the same person who attacked Fenella. Or was he? Did Brookie attack Fenella? He was on the scene at the time.

VANETTA HAREWOOD—Why would she kill her own son? She paid him to keep away from her.

URSULA ?—I don't know her surname. She mucks about with bleaches and willow branches, and Vanetta Harewood said she was fiercely protective. Motive?

COLIN PROUT—was bullied by Brookie, but what could Colin have had against Fenella?

MRS. BULL—threatened Fenella with an ax—claimed she'd been seen in the neighborhood when the Bull baby vanished years ago.

HILDA MUIR—whoever she may be. Fenella had mentioned her name twice: once when we saw the Bull child perched in a tree in the Gully, and again when I cut the elder branches in the Palings. "Now we are all dead!" Fenella had cried. Was Hilda Muir her attacker?

MISS MOUNTJOY—was Brookie's landlady. But why would she want to kill him? The theft of an antique plate seems hardly a sufficient reason.

I drew a line and under it wrote:

FAMILY

FATHER—very unlikely (although he once drove Fenella and Johnny Faa off the Buckshaw estate).
FEELY, DAFFY, DOGGER, and MRS. MULLET—no motive for either crime.

But wait! What about that mysterious person whose fortune Fenella had told at the church fête? What was it she had said about her?

"A regular thundercloud, she was." I could almost hear her voice. "Told her there was something buried in her past . . . told her it wanted digging out . . . wanted setting right."

Had Fenella seen something in the crystal ball that had sealed her fate? Although I remembered that Daffy scoffed at fortune-tellers ("Mountebanks," she called them), not everyone shared her opinion.

Hadn't Porcelain, for instance, claimed that her own mother, Lunita, had such great gifts of second sight that the War Office had funded her crystal-gazing?

If Lunita had actually possessed such great powers, it wasn't too great a stretch of the imagination to guess that she had inherited them from Fenella, her mother.

But wait!

If Fenella and Lunita both had the power of second sight, would it be unreasonable to assume that Porcelain, too, might be able to see beyond the present?

Was that the real reason she was afraid of me? She had admitted that she was.

Could it be that Porcelain saw things in my past that I could not see myself?

Or was it that she could see into my future?

Too many questions and not enough facts.

My shoulders were seized by a shudder, but I shook it off and went on with my notes.

THE PALINGS

There is a feeling about this place that cannot be easily explained. To my ancestor, Lucius de Luce, it must have seemed like the Great Flood when the river was diverted to form the ornamental lake. Before that time, it had been no more than a quiet, isolated grove where Nicodemus Flitch and the Hobblers came for baptisms and beanfests. Later, the Gypsies had adopted it as a stopping-place in their travels. Harriet had encouraged this but after her death, Father had forbidden it. Why?

Another solid line, under which I wrote:

FISH

(1) When I surprised Brookie in the drawing room at Buckshaw, besides alcohol, he (or his creel) reeked of fish.

(2) There was also a fishy smell in the caravan when I found Fenella beaten on the floor. By the time I discovered Porcelain

sleeping there the next morning this odor had vanished—but it had been there again today, this time on the outside of the caravan. (Q): Can odors come and go? Like actors in a play?

(3) Miss Mountjoy smelled of fish, too—cod-liver oil, judging by the vast quantities of the stuff that she keeps about Willow Villa.

(4) Brookie was killed (I believe) by a lobster pick shoved up his nostril and into his brain. A lobster pick from Buckshaw. (Note: Lobster is not a fish, but a crustacean—but still . . .) His body was left hanging on a statue of Poseidon: the god of the sea.

(5) When we found him hanging, Brookie's face was fish-belly white—not that that means anything other than that he had been dangling from the fountain for quite a long time. Perhaps all night. Surely whoever had done this thing had done it during the hours of darkness, when there was little chance of being seen.

There are probably people abroad on the earth at this very moment who would be tempted to joke "There's something fishy here."

But I am not one of them.

As any chemist worth her calcium chloride knows, it's not just fish that smell fishy. Offhand, I could think of several substances that gave off the smell of deceased mackerel, among them propylamine.

Propylamine (which had been discovered by the great French chemist Jean-Baptiste Dumas) is the third of the series of alcohol radicals—which might sound like boring stuff indeed, until you consider this: When you take one of the alcohols and heat it with ammonia, a remarkable transformation takes place. It's like a game of atomic musical chairs in which the hydrogen that helps form the ammonia has one or more of its chairs (atoms, actually) taken by the radicals of the alcohol. Depending upon when and where the music stops, a number of new products, called amines, may be formed.

With a bit of patience and a Bunsen burner, some truly foul odors can be generated in the laboratory. In 1889, for instance, the entire city of Freiburg, in Germany, had to be evacuated when chemists let a bit of thioacetone escape. It was said that people even miles away were sickened by the odor, and that horses fainted in the streets.

How I wish I had been there to see it!

While other substances, such as the lower aliphatic acids, can be easily manipulated to produce every smell from rancid butter to a sweaty horse, or from a rotten drain to a goat's rugger boots, it is the lower amines—those ragged children of ammonia—that have a most unique and interesting characteristic: As I have said, they smell like rotten fish.

In fact, propylamine and trimethylamine could, without exaggeration, be given the title "The Princes of Pong," and I knew this for a fact.

Because she has given us so many ways of producing these smelly marvels, I know that Mother Nature loves a good stink as much as I do. I thought fondly of the time I had extracted trimethylamine (for another harmless Girl Guide prank) by distilling it with soda from a full picnic basket of Stinking Goosefoot (*Chenopodium olidum*), an evil-smelling weed that grew in profusion on the Trafalgar Lawn.

Which brought me back to Brookie Harewood.

One thing I was quite certain of was this: that the riddle of Brookie's death would be solved not by cameras, notebooks, and measuring tapes at the Poseidon fountain, but rather in the chemical laboratory.

And I was just the one to do it.

I was still thinking about riddles as I slid down the banister and landed in the foyer. Nursery rhyme riddles had been as much a part of my younger years as they had anyone else's.

Thirty white horses upon a red hill
Now they tramp, now they champ
Now they stand still.

"Teeth!" I would shout, because Daffy had cheated and whispered the answer in my ear.

That, of course, was in the days before my sisters began to dislike me. Later came the darker verses:

One's joy, two's grief,
Three's marriage; four's a death.

The answer was "magpies." We had seen four of these birds land on the roof while having a picnic on the lawn, and my sisters had made me memorize the lines before they would allow me to dig into my dish of strawberries.

I didn't yet know what death was, but I knew that their verses gave me nightmares. I suppose it was these little rhymes, learned at an early age, that taught me to be good at puzzles. I've recently come to the conclusion that the nursery rhyme riddle is the most basic form of the detective story. It's a mystery stripped of all but the essential facts. Take this one, for instance:

> As I was going to St. Ives
> I met a man with seven wives.
> Each wife had seven sacks
> Each sack had seven cats
> Each cat had seven kits.
> Kits, cats, sacks, wives
> How many were going to St. Ives?

The usual answer, of course, is "one." But when you stop to think about it, there's much more to it than that. If, for instance, the teller of the rhyme happened to be overtaking the man with the traveling menagerie, the actual number—including sacks—would be almost three thousand!

It all depends upon how you look at things.

MRS. MULLET WAS HAVING her tea at the window. I helped myself to a digestive biscuit.

"The Hobblers," I said, diving in with both feet. "You said they'd have my blood for sausages. Why?"

"You keep clear o' them lot, miss, like I told you."

"I thought they were extinct?"

"They smells just the same as everybody else. That's why you don't reck'nize 'em till somebody points 'em out."

"But how can I keep clear of them if I don't know who they are?"

Mrs. M lowered her voice and looked over both shoulders. "That Mountjoy woman, for one. God knows what goes on in 'er kitchen."

"Tilda Mountjoy? At Willow Villa?"

I could hardly believe my good fortune!

"The very one. Why, it was no more than this morning I saw her in the Gully—headed for the Palings, she was, just as bold as brass. They still go there to do things with the water—poison it, for all I know."

"But wait," I said. "Miss Mountjoy can't be a Hobbler—she goes to St. Tancred's."

"To spy, most likely!" Mrs. Mullet snorted. "She told my friend Mrs. Waller it was on account of the organ. The 'Obblers got no organs, you know—don't 'old by 'em. 'I do love the sound of a good organ well played,' she told Mrs. Waller, who told it to me. Tilda Mountjoy's an 'Obbler born and bred, as was 'er parents before 'er. It's in the blood. Don't matter whose collection plate she puts 'er sixpences in, she's an 'Obbler from snoot to shoes, believe you me."

"You saw her in the Gully?" I asked, making mental notes like mad.

"With my own eyes. Since that Mrs. Ingleby come into her troubles I've been havin' to stretch my legs for eggs. All the way out to Rawlings, now, though I must say they're better yolks than Ingleby's. It's all in the grit, you know—or is it the shells? 'Course once I'm all the way out there, it makes no sense to go traipsin' all the way back round, does it? So it's into the Gully I go, eggs and all, and take a shortcut through the Palings. That's when I seen her, just by Bull's bonfires, she was—no more'n a stone's throw ahead of me."

"Did she speak to you?"

"Ho! Fat chance of that, my girl. As soon as I seen who it was I fell back and sat on a bank and took my shoe off. Pretended I'd got a stone in it."

Obviously, Mrs. M had been walking in the same direction as Miss Mountjoy, and was about to overtake her—just like the person who was walking to St. Ives.

"Good for you!" I said, clapping my hands together with excitement and shaking my head in wonder. "What a super idea."

"Don't say 'super,' dear. You know the Colonel doesn't like it."

I made the motion of pulling a zipper across my lips.

"Oon ewdge?"

"Sorry, dear. I don't know what you're saying."

I unfastened the zipper.

"Who else? The other Hobblers, I mean."

"Well, I really shouldn't say, but that Reggie Pettibone, for one. His wife, too. Reg'lar stuffed hat, she thinks she is, at the Women's Institute, all Looey the Nineteenth, an' that."

"Her husband owns the antiques shop?"

Mrs. Mullet nodded her head gloomily, and I knew she was reliving the loss of her Army and Navy table.

"Thank you, Mrs. M," I said. "I'm thinking of writing a paper on the history of Buckshaw. I shall mention you in the footnotes."

Mrs. Mullet primped her hair with a forefinger as I walked to the kitchen door.

"You stay away from them lot, mind."

seventeen

LIKE SEVERAL OF THE SHOPS IN BISHOP'S LACEY, PETTIBONE'S had a Georgian front with a small painted door squeezed in between a pair of many-paned bow windows.

I bicycled slowly past the place, then dismounted and strolled casually towards the shop, as if I had only just noticed it.

I put my nose to the glass, but the interior was too dim to see more than a stack of old plates on a dusty table.

Without warning, a hand came out of nowhere and hung something directly in front of my face—a hand-lettered cardboard sign.

CLOSED, it said, and the card was still swaying from its string as I made a dash for the door. I grabbed the knob, but at the same instant, the disembodied pair of hands seized it on the inside, trying desperately to keep it from turning—trying to drive home the bolt before I could gain entry.

But luck was on my side. My hearty shove proved stronger than the hands that were holding it closed, and I was propelled into the shop's interior a little faster than I should have liked.

"Oh, thank you," I said. "I thought you might be closed. It's about a gift, you see, and—"

"We *are* closed," said a cracked, tinny voice, and I spun round to find myself face to face with a peculiar little man.

He looked like an umbrella handle that had been carved into the shape of a parrot: beaked nose, white hair as tight and curly as a powdered wig, and red circles on each cheek as if he had just rouged them. His face was powder white and his lips too red for words.

He seemed to stand precariously on his tiny feet, swaying so alarmingly backwards and forwards that I had the feeling he was about to topple from his perch.

"We're closed," he repeated. "You must come back another time."

"Mr. Pettibone?" I asked, sticking out a hand. "I'm Flavia de Luce, from Buckshaw."

He didn't have much choice.

"Pleased to meet you, I'm sure," he said, taking two of my fingers in his miniature fist and giving them a faint squeeze. "But we're closed."

"It's my father, you see," I went on breathlessly. "Today's his birthday, and we wanted to—my sisters and I, that is—surprise him. He's expressed a great interest in something you have in your shop, and we'd hoped to—I'm sorry I'm so late, Mr. Pettibone, but I was folding bandages at the St. John's Ambulance . . . "

I allowed my lower lip to tremble very slightly.

"And what is this . . . er . . . object?"

"A table," I blurted. It was the first thing that came to mind, and a jolly good thing I'd thought of it. There must be dozens of tables in a place like this, and I'd be able to have a good old snoop round while searching for the right one.

"Could you . . . er . . . describe it?"

"Yes," I said. "Of course. It has four legs and—a top."

I could see that he was unconvinced.

"It's for stamps, you see. Father's a philatelist, and he needs something he can spread his work on . . . under a lamp. His eyes are not quite what they used to be, and my sisters and I—"

He was edging me towards the door.

"Oh—just a minute. I think that's it," I said, pointing to a rather sorry bit of furniture that was huddled in the gloom beneath an ormolu clock with plump-bellied pewter horses. By moving to touch it, I was six or eight feet deeper into the shop.

"Oh, no, this one's too dark. I thought it was mahogany. No—wait! It's this one over here."

I had plunged well towards the back of the shop and into the shadows. With Pettibone bearing down upon me like a wolf upon the fold, I realized that I was now cut off from the door and freedom.

"What are you playing at?" he said, making a sudden grab for my arm. I leapt out of his reach.

Suddenly the situation had turned dangerous. But why? Was there something in the shop Pettibone didn't want me to see? Did he suspect that I was on to his shady antiques dealings?

Whatever the cause of his aggressiveness, I needed to act quickly.

To my right, standing about a foot out from the wall, was a massive wardrobe. I slid behind it.

For a while, at least, I was safe. He was too big to squeeze behind the thing. I might not be able to come out, but I'd have a moment to plan my next move.

But then Pettibone was back with a broom. He shoved the bristles into my ribs—and pushed. I stood my ground.

Now he turned the broom around and began prodding at me furiously with the handle, like a man who has trapped a rat behind the kitchen cupboard.

"Ouch!" I cried out. "Stop! Stop it! You're hurting me!"

Actually, he wasn't, but I couldn't let him know that. I was able to slip far enough along the wall that I was beyond reach of his broom.

As he came round the wardrobe to have a try from the other side, I slithered back to the far end.

But I knew I was trapped. This game of cat and mouse could go on all day.

Now the wardrobe had begun to move, its china casters squealing. Pettibone had put his shoulder to a corner and was shifting the thing out from the wall.

"Oh!" I shrieked. "You're crushing me!"

The wall of wood stopped moving and there was a brief pause in his attack, during which I could hear him breathing heavily.

"Reginald!"

The voice—a woman's—cut through the shop like a falling icicle. I heard him mutter something.

"Reginald, come up here at once! Do you hear me?"

"Hello upstairs!" I shouted. "It's Flavia de Luce."

There was a silence, and then the voice said, "Come up, Flavia. Reginald, bring the girl here."

It was as if she'd said "fetch."

I slipped out from behind the wardrobe, rubbing my elbows, and shot him a reproachful look.

His eyes strayed to a narrow staircase at the side of the shop, and before he could change his mind, I moved towards it.

I could have made a break for the door, but I didn't. This could be my only chance at scouting out the place. "In for a penny, in for a pound," as Mrs. Mullet was fond of saying.

I put my foot on the first step and began my slow trudge upstairs to whatever fate awaited me.

The room at the top came as a complete surprise. Rather than the rabbit's warren of little cubicles I had imagined, the place was unexpectedly large. Obviously, all of the interior walls had been knocked out to form a spacious attic which was the same size as the shop beneath.

And what a contrast with the shop it was! There was no clutter up here: In fact, with one exception, the room was almost empty.

In the middle of the floor stood a great square bed hung with white linen, and in it, propped up by a wall of pillows, was a woman whose features might well have been chiseled from a block of ice. There was a faint bluish—or cyanotic—tinge to her face and hands which suggested, at first glance, that she might be the victim of either carbon monoxide or silver poisoning, but as I stared, I began to see that her complexion was colored not by poison, but by artifice.

Her skin was the color of skim milk. Her lips, like those of her husband (I presumed that the parrot-man was her husband) were painted a startling red, and, as if she were a leftover star from the silent cinema, her hair hung down around her face in a mass of silver ringlets.

Only when I had taken in the details of the room and its occupant did I allow my attention to shift to the bed itself: an ebony four-poster with its posts carved into the shape of black angels, each of them frozen into position like a sentry in his box at Buckingham Palace.

Several mattresses must have been piled one atop the other to give the thing its height, and a set of wooden steps had been constructed at the bedside, like a ladder beside a haystack.

Slowly, the icy apparition in the bed lifted a lorgnette to her eyes and regarded me coolly through its lenses.

"Flavia de Luce, you say? One of Colonel de Luce's daughters—from Buckshaw?"

I nodded.

"Your sister Ophelia has performed for us at the Women's Institute. A remarkably gifted player."

I should have known! This landlocked iceberg was a friend of Feely's!

Under any other circumstances, I'd have said something rude and stalked out of the room, but I thought better of it. The investigation of murder, I was beginning to learn, can demand great personal sacrifice.

Actually, the woman's words were true. Feely *was* a first-rate pianist, but there was no sense going on and on about it.

"Yes," I said, "she's quite talented."

Until then I had been unaware that Reginald was close behind me, standing on the stairs just one or two steps from the top.

"You may go, Reginald," the woman said, and I turned to watch him descend, in uncanny silence, to the shop below.

"Now then," she said. "Speak."

"I'm afraid I owe you and Mr. Pettibone an apology," I said. "I told him a lie."

"Which was?"

"That I'd come to buy a table for Father. What I really wanted was an opportunity to ask you about the Hobblers."

"The Hobblers?" she said with an awkward laugh. "Whatever makes you think I'd know anything about the Hobblers? They haven't existed since the days of powdered wigs."

In spite of her denial, I could see that my question had caught her off guard. Perhaps I could take advantage of her surprise.

"I know that they were founded in the seventeenth century by Nicodemus Flitch, and that the Palings, at Buckshaw, have played an important role in their history, what with baptisms, and so forth."

I paused to see how this would be received.

"And what has this to do with me?" she asked, putting down the lorgnette and then picking it up again.

"Oh, somebody mentioned that you belonged to that . . . faith. I was talking to Miss Mountjoy, and she—"

True enough—I *had* been talking to Miss Mountjoy. As long as I didn't actually say that she'd told me, I'd be guilty of no great sin. Other than one of omission, perhaps. Feely was always going on and on about sins of commission and omission until your eyes were left spinning like fishing lures.

"Tilda Mountjoy," she said, after a long pause. "I see . . . tell me more."

"Well, it's just that I've been making a few notes about Buckshaw's history, you know, and as I was going through some old papers in Father's library, I came across some quite early documents."

"Documents?" she demanded. "What kind of documents?"

She was rising to the bait! Her thoughts were written on her face as clearly as if they were tattooed on her cheeks.

Old papers relating to Nicodemus Flitch and the Hobblers? she was thinking. *Now here's my opportunity to pull the rug out from under dear, dull-as-ditchwater old Tilda, and her long-winded papers in the* Hobblers' Historical Society Journal. *Former librarian be blowed! I'll show her what* real *research can bring to light.*

And so forth.

"Oh, just odd bits and pieces," I said. "Letters to one of my ancestors—Lucius de Luce—about this and that—

"Just a lot of names and dates," I added. "Nothing terribly interesting, I'm afraid."

This was the cherry on the icing—but I would pretend to brush it off as worthless.

She was staring at me through her lenses like a birdwatcher who has unexpectedly come upon the rare spotted crake.

Now was the time to keep perfectly still. If my words hadn't primed the pump of curiosity, then nothing would.

I could almost feel the heat of her gaze.

"There's more," she said. "What is it? You're not telling me the who truth."

"Well," I blurted, "actually, I was thinking of asking if I might be allowed to convert to the Hobblers. We de Luces are not really Anglicans, you see—we've been Roman Catholics for ages, but—Feely was telling me that the Hobblers were non—non—"

"Nonconformists?"

"Yes, that's it—Nonconformists, and I thought that, since I'm a nonconformist myself . . . well, why not join?"

There was a grain of truth in this: I remembered that one of my heroes, Joseph Priestley, the discoverer of oxygen, had once been the minister of a dissenting sect in Leeds, and if it was good enough for the esteemed Joseph—

"There's been a great deal of debate," she said reflectively, "about whether we're Nonconformists or Dissenters, what with our Reconstitution in 17—"

"Then you *are* a Hobbler!"

She stared at me long and hard, as if thinking. "There are those," she said, "who work to preserve the foundations upon which their forefathers built. It is not always easy in this day and age . . . "

"It doesn't matter to me," I said. "I'd give anything to be a Hobbler."

And in a way it was true. I had visions of myself limping cheerily along a country lane, my arms outstretched for balance, teetering like a tightrope walker, as I veered crazily from hedge to hedge.

"I'm a Hobbler," I would shout out to everyone as I stumped past.

As I was hobbling to St. Ives . . .

"Most interesting," the woman was saying as I came back to reality. "And is your father aware of your aspirations?"

"*No!*" I said, aghast. "Please don't tell him! Father is very set in his ways and—"

"I understand," she said. "We shall let it be our little secret, then. No one but you and I shall know about any of this."

Hey presto!

"Oh, *thank you,*" I breathed. "I knew you'd understand."

As she rattled on about the Act of Toleration, the Five Mile Act, the Countess of Huntingdon, and the Calvinist Connection, I took the opportunity to look around the room.

There wasn't much to see: the bed, of course, which, now that I had time to think about it, reminded me of the Great Bed of Ware in the Victoria and Albert Museum. In a far corner near a window was a small table with an electric ring and a small kettle, a Brown Betty teapot, a biscuit tin, and a single cup and saucer. Reginald Pettibone was evidently not in the habit of having breakfast with his wife.

"Would you care for a biscuit?" she asked.

"No, thank you," I said. "I don't use sugar."

It was a lie—but an excellent one.

"What an unusual child you are," she said, and with a wave of the hand towards the tin, she added, "Well, then, perhaps you won't mind fetching one for me. I have no such scruples."

I went to the window and reached for the biscuit tin. As I turned,

I happened to glance outside—down into the fenced area behind the shop's back door.

A rusty green van stood with its double doors open, and I knew instantly that it was the one I'd seen parked outside Willow Villa.

As I watched, a powerful man in shirtsleeves stepped into view from somewhere below. It was the bulldog man—the man who had almost caught me in the coach house!

Unless I was sadly mistaken, this would be Edward Sampson, of Rye Road, East Finching—whose name I had found on the papers in the glove compartment.

As I stood rooted to the spot, he reached into the back of the van and dragged out a couple of heavy objects. He turned and, perhaps feeling my eyes upon him, looked straight up at the window where I was standing.

My immediate reaction was to shrink back—to step away from the glass—but I found that I could not. Some remote part of my mind had already spotted a detail that was only now leaking slowly into my consciousness, and I'm afraid I let out a gasp.

The objects gripped in the hands of the bulldog man were Harriet's firedogs—Sally Fox and Shoppo!

eighteen

"WHAT IS IT?" THE WOMAN ASKED. HER VOICE SEEMED TO BE coming from a very great distance.

"It's—it's—"

"Yes, dear . . . what is it?"

It was the "dear" that brought me snapping back. A "dear" or "dearie" to me is about as welcome as a bullet to the brain. I've had places reserved in the ha'penny seats of Hell for people who address me in this way.

But I bit my tongue.

"It's—just that you have such a smashing view from your window," I said. "The river . . . Malplaquet Farm . . . all the way to East Finching and the hills beyond. One would never suspect, walking in the high street, that such a—"

There was a floor-shaking crash from downstairs as some heavy object was dropped. A couple of muffled curses came drifting up through the floorboards.

"Reginald!" the woman shouted, and there was an awkward silence in the depths.

"Men!" she said, loudly enough to make herself heard downstairs. "Windmills on legs."

"I think I'd better go," I said. "They'll be expecting me at home."

"Very well, dear," she said. "Run along, then. And don't forget about those letters. You may bring them whenever you're able."

I did not tell her what I was thinking, but rather, gave a very small mock curtsy, then turned and made my way down the narrow stairs.

At the bottom, I glanced towards the back of the shop. Reginald Pettibone and the owner of the van stood staring at me from the shadows. Neither of them moved or spoke, but I knew, in the way we females are supposed to know, that they had been talking about me.

I turned my back on them and walked to the door, stopping only to write my initials casually in the dust that covered an ebony sideboard. I wasn't exactly afraid, but I knew how an animal trainer in a steel cage must feel when, for the first time, he turns his back on the fierce gaze of a pair of new tigers.

Although she didn't say so, Gladys seemed happy to see me. I had parked her against a tree across the high street from Pettibone's shop.

"There's dirty work at the crossroads," I told her. "I can feel it in my bones."

I needed to get home at once to inspect the drawing- room hearth.

THE TREES WERE MAKING late afternoon shadows as I cycled through the Mulford Gates and up the avenue of chestnuts. I'd soon be expected to put in an appearance at the dinner table, and I wasn't looking forward to it.

As I opened the kitchen door, the sound of a Schubert sonata came floating to my ears.

Success! I knew instantly that my psychic booby trap had been sprung.

Feely always played Schubert when she was upset, and the opening of the Piano Sonata in B Flat Major when she was especially distraught.

I could almost follow her thoughts as the piano's notes went flying past my ears like birds from a forest fire. At first there was the tightly controlled anger, with threats of rolling thunder (how I loved the thunder!), but when the full storm broke, Feely's fierce talent could still make me gasp with admiration.

I edged closer to the drawing room, the better to hear this remarkable outpouring of emotion. It was almost as good as reading her diary.

I had to be careful, though, that she didn't catch sight of me until dinner, when Father would be there to save my hide. If Feely so much as suspected that I was responsible for the spirit message on her mirror, there would be buckets of blood on the carpet and entrails dangling from the chandeliers.

The drawing room would have to wait.

I did not realize how tired I had suddenly become until I was dragging myself up the stairs. It had been a long day, and it was far from over.

Perhaps, I thought, I would have a nap.

As I approached my laboratory, I came to an abrupt halt. The door was standing open!

I peered round the corner, and there stood Porcelain, still wearing Fenella's black dress, toasting a slice of bread over a Bunsen burner. I could hardly believe my eyes!

"Cheer-oh," she said, looking up. "Would you like some toast?"

As if she hadn't just recently accused me of bashing in her grandmother's brains.

"How did you get in?"

"I used your key," she said, pointing. It was still inserted in the lock. "I watched you hide it in the hollow bedpost."

It was true. I had long before discovered Uncle Tar's secret hiding place for keys and other things he wanted to keep to himself. My bedroom had once been his, and over time all, or most, of its secrets had been revealed.

"You've got your bloody nerve," I said. The thought of someone invading my laboratory made my skin crawl, as if an army of red ants were swarming up my arms, fanning out across my shoulders, and up the back of my neck.

"I'm sorry, Flavia," she said. "I know it wasn't you that attacked Fenella. I can't have been thinking straight. I was confused. I was tired. I came back to apologize."

"Then you'd better get at it," I said.

I was not going to be mollified—wasn't that the term Daffy had used when she'd said the same thing to me: "mollified"?—with just a couple of token words. There are times when "I'm sorry" is simply not enough.

"I'm sorry," she said. "I really am. It's all so upsetting. It's just too much."

Suddenly she was in tears.

"First there was Fenella—now they won't let me see her, you know. They've got a constable in a chair watching the door to her room. Then there was that awful business of the man we found hanging from the fountain—"

"Brookie Harewood," I said. I'd almost forgotten about Brookie.

"And now this latest body they've dug up in—what do you call it?—the Palings."

"What?"

Another body? In the Palings?

"It's all too much," she said, wiping her nose on her forearm. "I'm going back to London."

Before I could say another word, she dug into her pocket and pulled out a five-pound note.

"Here," she said, prying open my fingers and pressing them closed upon the banknote. "That's to feed Gry until Fenella's discharged from hospital. And . . ."

She looked straight into my eyes, still gripping my hand. Her lips were trembling. "If she doesn't recover, he's yours. The caravan, too. I came here to tell you I'm sorry, and I've done it. And now I'm leaving."

"Wait! What did you say about another body?"

"Ask your inspector friend," she said, and turned towards the door.

I made a lunge for the key and slammed the door shut. We tussled for the doorknob, but I managed to grab the key, jam it into the inside lock, and give it a frantic twist.

"Hand it over. Let me out."

"No," I said. "Not until you tell me what you saw in the Palings."

"Come off it, Flavia. I'm not playing games."

"Nor am I," I told her, crossing my arms.

As I knew she would, she made a sudden snatch at the key. It was an old trick often used by Daffy and Feely, and I suppose I ought to have been grateful for having learned it from them. Being ready for the next move, I was able to hold the key out, at arm's length, away from her.

And then she gave up. Just like that. I could see it in her eyes.

She brushed her hair away from her face and walked back to one of the laboratory tables, where she splayed her fingers out upon its surface, as if to keep from toppling over.

"I went back to the caravan to pick up my things," she said, slowly and deliberately, "and the police were there again. They wouldn't let me anywhere near it. They were lifting something out of a hole in the ground."

"Lifting what?"

She was staring at me with something that might have been defiance. "Believe me, it wasn't gold."

"Tell me!"

"For God's sake, Flavia!"

I waved the key at her. "Tell me."

"It was a body. Wrapped in a carpet, or something—not very big. A child, I think. I only saw one of the feet . . . or what was left of it.

"A bundle of old green bones," she added.

She clapped her hand across her mouth and her shoulders heaved.

I waited patiently for more, but if there were any further interesting details, Porcelain was keeping them to herself.

We stared at each other for what seemed like a very long time.

"Fenella was right," she said at last. "There is a darkness here."

I held out the key and she lifted it from my open palm with two fingers, as if it—or I—were contaminated.

Without a word, she unlocked the door and let herself out.

What was I supposed to feel? I wondered.

To be perfectly honest, I think I had been looking forward to having Porcelain dog my every step as I went about investigating the attack upon Fenella and the murder of Brookie Harewood. I had even thought of ways of giving her the slip, if necessary, as I traipsed about the village, digging up information. And perhaps I had too much anticipated sitting her down and patiently explaining the trail of clues, and the ways in which they pointed to the culprit—or culprits.

But now, by walking out, she had deprived me of all of that.

I was alone again.

As it was in the beginning, is now and ever shall be, world without end. Amen.

No one to talk to but myself.

Except Dogger, of course.

DOGGER WAS SITTING IN THE last shaft of sunlight in the garden. He had brought an old wooden chair from the greenhouse and, perched upon the edge of its seat, was hammering nails into the tin stripping that sealed the wooden tea chest that lay before him in the grass.

I lowered myself into the wheelbarrow that was standing nearby.

"They've found another body," I said. "At the Palings."

Dogger nodded. "I believe that's so, Miss Flavia."

"It's the Bull baby, isn't it?"

Dogger nodded again and put down the hammer. "I should be surprised if it weren't."

"Did you hear about it from Mrs. Mullet?"

Although I knew it was not a done thing to inquire of one servant about another, there was no other way. I couldn't just ring up Inspector Hewitt and pump him for the details.

"No," he said, preparing to drive home another nail. "Miss Porcelain told me."

"Porcelain?" I said, gesturing up towards the east wing—towards my bedroom window. "You knew about Porcelain? That she was staying here?"

"Yes," Dogger said, and left it at that.

After a few seconds I relaxed, and there fell between us another one of those luxurious silences that is part of most conversations with Dogger: silences so long and profound and golden that it seems irreverent to break them.

Dogger rotated the tea chest and began to apply stripping to another edge.

"You have very fine hands," I said at last. "They look as if they belong to a concert pianist."

Dogger put down the hammer and examined both sides of each hand as if he had never seen them before.

"I can assure you that they are my own," he said.

This time, there could be no doubt about it. Dogger *had* made a joke. But rather than laughing condescendingly, I did the right thing and nodded wisely, as if I knew it all along. I was learning that among friends, a smile can be better than a belly laugh.

"Dogger," I said, "there's something I need to know. It's about nosebleeds."

I had the impression that he looked at me sharply—even though he hadn't.

"Are you having nosebleeds, Miss Flavia?"

"No," I said. "No—not at all. It's no one here at Buckshaw. Actually, it's Miss Mountjoy, at Willow Villa."

And I described to him what I had seen in that dank kitchen.

"Ah," Dogger said, and then fell silent. After a time, he spoke again—slowly—as if his words were being retrieved, one by one, from some deep well.

"Recurrent nosebleeds—epitaxis—may have many causes."

"Such as?" I urged.

"Genetic predisposition," he said. "Hypertension—or high blood pressure . . . pregnancy . . . dengue—or breakbone—fever . . . nasopharyngeal cancer . . . adrenal tumor . . . scurvy . . . certain diseases of the elderly, such as hardening of the arteries. It may also be symptomatic of arsenic poisoning."

Of course! I knew that! How could I have forgotten?

"However," Dogger went on, "from what you've told me, it is none of these. Miss Mountjoy's nosebleeds are most likely brought on by the excessive consumption of cod-liver oil."

"Cod-liver oil?" I must have said it aloud.

"I expect she takes it for her arthritis," Dogger said, and went back to his hammering.

"Gaaak!" I said, making a face. "I hate the smell of the stuff."

But Dogger was not to be drawn out.

"Isn't it odd," I plowed on, "how nature puts the same pong in the liver of a fish as it does in a weed like the stinking goosefoot, and in the willow that grows by the water?"

"Stinking goosefoot?" Dogger said, looking up in puzzlement. And then: "Ah, yes, of course. The methylamines. I'd forgotten about the methylamines. And then . . . "

"Yes?" I said, too quickly and too eagerly.

There were times when Dogger's memory, having been primed, worked beautifully for a short time, like the vicar's battered old Oxford which ran well only in the rain.

I crossed my fingers and my ankles and waited, biting my tongue.

Dogger removed his hat and stared into it as if the memory were hidden in its lining. He frowned, wiped his brow on his forearm, and went on hesitantly. "I believe there were several cases reported in *The Lancet* in the last century in which a patient was recorded as exuding a fishy smell."

"Perhaps he was a fisherman," I suggested. Dogger shook his head.

"In neither case was the patient a fisherman, and neither had been known to be in contact with fish. Even after bathing, the piscine odor returned, often following a meal."

"Of fish?"

Dogger ignored me. "There was, of course, the tale in the *Bhagavad Ghita* of the princess who exuded a fishy odor . . . "

"Yes?" I said, settling back as if to hear a fairy tale. Somewhere in the distance, a harvesting machine clattered away softly at its work, and the sun shone down. What a perfect day it was, I thought. "But wait!" I said. "What if his body were producing trimethylamine?"

This was such an exciting thought that I sprang out of the wheelbarrow.

"It would not be unheard of," Dogger said, thoughtfully. "Shakespeare might have been thinking of just such a complaint:

" *'What have we here? a man or a fish? dead or alive? A fish: he smells like a fish: a very ancient and fish-like smell.'* "

A chill ran up my spine. Dogger had slipped into the loud and confident voice of an actor who has delivered these lines many and many a time before.

"*The Tempest,*" he said quietly. "Act two, scene two, if I'm not mistaken. Trinculo, you'll recall, is speaking of Caliban."

"Where do you dig up these things?" I asked in admiration.

"On the wireless," Dogger said. "We listened to it some weeks ago."

It was true. At Buckshaw, Thursday evenings were devoted to compulsory wireless listening, and we had recently been made to sit through an adaption of *The Tempest* without fidgeting.

Other than the marvelous sound effects of the storm, I didn't remember much about the play, but obviously Dogger did.

"Is there a name for this fishy condition?" I asked.

"Not to the best of my knowledge," he said. "It is exceedingly rare. I believe . . . "

"Go on," I said, eagerly.

But when I looked up at Dogger, the light in his eyes had gone out. He sat staring at his hat, which he held clutched in his trembling hands as if he had never seen it before.

"I believe I'll go to my room now," he said, getting slowly to his feet.

"It's all right," I said. "I think I will, too. A nice nap before dinner will do both of us good."

But I'm not sure that Dogger heard me. He was already shambling off towards the kitchen door.

When he was gone, I turned my attention to the wooden tea chest he had been nailing shut. In one corner was pasted a paper label, upon which was written in ink:

THIS SIDE UP - Contents - Silver Cutlery - de Luce - Buckshaw

Cutlery? Had Dogger packed the Mumpeters in this crate? Mother and Father Mumpeter? Little Grindlestick and her silver sisters?

Is that why he'd been polishing them?

Why on earth would he do such a thing? The Mumpeters were my childhood playthings, and the very thought of anyone—

But hadn't Brookie Harewood been murdered with one of the pieces from this set? What if the police—?

I walked round to the far side of the crate: the side that Dogger had turned away from me as I approached.

As I read the words that were stenciled in awful black letters on the boards, something vile and sour rose up in my throat.

Sotheby's, New Bond Street, London, W.C., it said.

Father was sending away the family silver to be auctioned.

nineteen

DINNER WAS A GRIM AFFAIR.

The worst of it was that Father had come to the table without *The London Philatelist*. Instead of reading, he insisted upon solicitously passing me the peas and asking, "Did you have a nice day today, Flavia?"

It almost broke my heart.

Although Father had spoken several times of his financial troubles, they had never seemed threatening: no more than a distant shadow, really, like war—or death. You knew it was there but you didn't spend all day fretting about it.

But now, with the Mumpeters nailed up inside a crate, ready to be taken to the train for London and pawed over by strangers at the auction rooms, the reality of Father's predicament had hit home with the force of a typhoon.

And Father—the dear man—was trying to shield us from the reality by making bright table chatter.

I could feel the tears welling up in my eyes, but I dared not give in to them. It was fortunate that Daffy, who sat across from me, did not even once look up from her book.

To my left, at the far end of the table, Feely sat staring down into her lap, her face pale, her colorless lips pressed together into a tight, thin line. The dark circles under her eyes were like bruises, and her hair was lank and lifeless.

The only word to describe her was "blighted."

My chemical wizardry had worked!

The proof of it was the fact that Feely was wearing her spectacles, which told me, without a doubt, that she had spent the day staring in horror at the spirit message that had materialized upon her looking glass.

In spite of her occasional cruelty—or perhaps because of it—Feely was a pious sort, whose time was devoted to making bargains with this saint or that about the clarity of her complexion, or the way in which a random beam of sunlight would strike her golden hair as she knelt at the altar for communion.

Where I generally believed in chemistry and the happy dance of the atom, Feely believed in the supernatural, and it was that belief I had taken advantage of.

But what had I done? I hadn't counted on such utter devastation.

Part of my brain was telling me to leap up and run to her—to throw my arms around her neck and tell her that it was only French chalk—and not God—that had caused her misery. And then we would laugh together as we used to in the olden days.

But I couldn't: If I did, I should have to confess to my prank in front of Father, and I wanted to spare him any further grief.

Besides, Feely would more than likely stab me to death with whatever came to hand, snow white tablecloth or not.

Which made me think of Brookie Harewood. How odd! There hadn't been a word at the dinner table about murder. Or was it now *murders*, plural?

It was then, I think, that I noticed the cutlery. Instead of our usual silver utensils, I realized that each of our places had been set with the yellow-handled knives and forks that were kept in the kitchen for the use of the servants.

I could contain it no longer. I scraped my chair back from the table, mumbled something about being excused, and fled. By the time I reached the foyer, my tears were splashing about me like rain on the black-and-white checkerboard of the tiles.

I THREW MYSELF ONTO THE BED and buried my face in the pillow.

How could revenge hurt so keenly? It didn't make any sense. It simply didn't. Revenge was supposed to be sweet—and so was victory!

As I lay there, flattened by misery, I heard the unmistakeable sound of Father's leather-soled shoes outside in the hall.

I could hardly believe my ears. Father in the east wing? This was the first time since I had moved into it that he had set foot in this part of the house.

Father came slowly into the room, shuffling a little, and I heard him pause. A moment later I felt the bed sink a little as he sat down beside me.

I kept my face pressed tightly into the pillow.

After what seemed like a very long time, I felt his hand gently touching my head—but only for a moment.

He did not stroke my hair, nor did he speak, and I was glad he didn't. His silence spared both of us the embarrassment of not knowing what to say.

And then he was gone, as quietly as he had come.

And I slept.

IN THE MORNING, THE WORLD seemed a different place.

I whistled in my bath. I even remembered to scrub my elbows.

It had come to me in the night, as if in a dream, that I must apologize to Feely. It was as simple as that.

In the first place, it would disarm her. In the second place, it would impress Father, if Feely had told him what I had done. And finally, it would make me feel all warm and self-righteous about doing the decent thing.

Besides, if I played my cards right, I could also pump Feely for information about Vanetta Harewood. I would not, of course, tell her about the lost portrait of Harriet.

It was the perfect solution.

THERE'S NOTHING AS BEAUTIFUL AS the sound of a piano in the next room. A little distance gives the instrument a heart—at least to my sensitive hearing, it does.

As I stood outside the drawing-room door, Feely was practicing something by Rameau: *Les Sauvages,* I think it was called. It sometimes made me think of a moonlight glade—the Palings, perhaps—with a tribe of devils dancing in a circle like maniacs: So much more pleasing, I thought, than that sleepy old thing on the same topic by Beethoven.

I straightened my back and squared my shoulders. Feely was always telling me to square my shoulders, and I thought she'd be happy to see that I'd remembered.

The instant I opened the door, the music stopped and Feely looked up from the keyboard. She was learning to play without her spectacles, and she was not wearing them now.

I couldn't help noticing how beautiful she looked.

Her eyes, which I had expected to be like a pair of open coal holes, shone with a cold blue brilliance in the morning light. It was like being glared at by Father.

"Yes?" she said.

"I—I've come to say I'm sorry," I told her.

"Then do so."

"I just did, Feely!"

"No, you didn't. You made a statement of fact. You stated that you had come to say you're sorry. You may begin."

This was going to be more humiliating than I thought.

"I'm sorry," I said, "for writing on your mirror."

"Yes?"

I swallowed and went on. "It was a mean and thoughtless trick."

"It was indeed, you odious little worm."

She got up from the piano bench and came towards me—menacingly, I thought. I shrank back a little.

"Of course I knew at once that it was you. *Deuteronomy? The boils of Egypt? The emerods? The scurvy and the itch?* It had Flavia de Luce written all over it. You might just as well have signed the thing—like a painting."

"That's not true, Feely. You were devastated. I saw the circles under your eyes at dinner!"

Feely threw her head back and laughed.

"Makeup!" she crowed. "French chalk! Two can play at that game, you stupid moke. A bit of French chalk and a pinch of ashes from the grate. It took me all afternoon to get it just the right shade. You should have seen your face! Daffy said she almost had an accident trying not to laugh!"

My face began to burn.

"Didn't you, Daff?"

There was the sound of a wet snicker behind me, and I spun round to find Daffy coming through the doorway—blocking my route of escape.

"'It was a mean and thoughtless trick,'" she said, imitating me in a grating, falsetto, parrot voice.

She had been eavesdropping on my apology from outside in the hallway!

But now, rather than flying at her in fury, as I might have done even yesterday, I gathered up every last scrap of inner strength and attacked her with a new and untried tool: clear, cold calm.

"Who is Hilda Muir?" I asked, and Daffy stopped moving instantly, as if she had been frozen in a snapshot.

The appeal to a superior knowledge. And it worked!

By coming to one of my sisters in humility and keeping my temper with the other, I had gained in just a few minutes not one, but two new weapons.

"What?"

"Hilda Muir. She's something to do with the Palings."

"*Hilda Muir*," Fenella had said, when we'd first spotted Mrs. Bull in the Gully. "*Hilda Muir.*" She'd said it again when I brought the elder branches to the caravan. "*Now we are all dead!*"

"Who is Hilda Muir?" I asked again in my new and maddeningly calm voice.

"Hilda Muir? The Palings? You must mean the Hildemoer. She's not a person, you idiot. She's the spirit of the elder branches. She comes to punish people who cut her branches without first asking permission. You didn't cut any elder branches, did you?" (This with another wet snicker.)

Daffy must have seen the effect her words had on me. "I truly hope you didn't. They sometimes plant them on a grave to indicate whether the dead person is happy in the next world. If the elder grows, all's well. If not—"

The next world? I thought. Hadn't Porcelain watched the police pull a baby's body from the very spot—or very near it—that I had cut the elder for firewood?

"The Hildemoer's a pixy," Daffy went on. "Don't you remember what we told you about the pixies? For heaven's sake, Flavia—it was only a couple of days ago. The pixies are the Old Ones—those horrid creatures who stole Harriet's precious baby and left *you* in its place."

My mind was an inferno. I could feel the anger rushing back like the Red Sea after the passage of the Israelites.

"I hope you didn't cut elder from someone's grave," she went on. "Because if you did—"

"Thank you, Daffy," I said. "You've been most informative."

Without another word, I brushed past her and stalked out of the drawing room.

With the mocking laughter of my darling sisters still ringing in my ears, I fled down the echoing hall.

twenty

IN THE LABORATORY I LOCKED THE DOOR AND WAITED TO SEE what my hands were going to do.

It was always like this. If I just relaxed and tried not to think too hard, the great god Chemistry would guide me.

After a time, although I'm not sure why, I reached for three bottles and placed them on the bench.

Using a pipette, I measured half an ounce of a clear liquid from the first of these into a calibrated test tube. From the second bottle I measured three ounces of another fluid into a small flask. I watched in fascination as I combined the two clear fluids with several ounces of distilled water, and before my eyes a reddish color appeared.

Presto chango! Aqua regia . . . royal water!

The ancient alchemists gave it that name because it is capable of dissolving gold, which they considered to be the king of metals.

I have to admit that manufacturing the stuff myself never fails to excite me.

Actually, aqua regia is more orange than red: the precise color of pomegranates, if I remember correctly. Yes, pomegranates—that was it.

I had once seen these exotic fruits in a shop window in the high street. Mr. Hughes, the greengrocer, had imported the things on a trial basis, but they had remained in his shop window until they blackened and caved in upon themselves like rotted puffballs.

"Bishop's Lacey's been't ready for pomegranates yet," he had told Mrs. Mullet. "We don't deserves 'em."

I had always marveled at the way in which three clear liquids—nitric acid, hydrochloric acid, and water—when combined could produce, as if by magic, color—and not just any color, but the color of a flaming sunset.

The swirling shades of orange in the glass seemed to illustrate perfectly the thoughts that were swarming round and round, mixing in my mind.

It was all so confoundedly complicated: the attack upon Fenella, the gruesome death of Brookie Harewood, the sudden appearance and equally sudden disappearance of Porcelain, Harriet's firedogs turning up in not one but three different locations, the strange antiques shop of the abominable Pettibones, Miss Mountjoy and the Hobblers, Vanetta Harewood's long-lost portrait of Harriet, and underneath it all, like the rumble of a stuck organ pipe, the constant low drone of Father's looming bankruptcy.

It was enough to make an archangel spit.

In its container, the aqua regia was growing darker by the minute, as if it, too, were waiting impatiently for answers.

And suddenly I saw the way.

Lighting a Bunsen burner, I set it beneath the flask. I would warm the acid gently before proceeding with the next step.

From a cupboard I took down a small wooden box upon the end of which Uncle Tar had penciled the word "platinum"; and slid open the lid. Inside were perhaps a dozen flat squares of the silvery-gray mineral, none larger than an adult's fingernail. I selected a piece that weighed perhaps a quarter of an ounce.

When the aqua regia had reached the proper temperature, I picked up the bit of platinum with a pair of tweezers and held it above the mouth of the flask. Aside from the hiss of the gas, the laboratory was so quiet that I actually heard the tiny *plop* as I let the platinum drop into the fluid.

For a moment, nothing happened.

But now the liquid in the flask was a darkening red.

And then the platinum began to writhe.

This was the part I liked best!

As if in agony, the bit of metal crept towards the glass wall of the flask, trying to escape the acids that were consuming it.

And suddenly *poof*! The platinum was gone.

I could almost hear the aqua regia licking its lips. *"More, please!"*

It wasn't that the platinum had not put up a noble fight, because it had. The important thing, I reminded myself, was this: *Platinum cannot be dissolved by any one acid!*

No, platinum could *not* be dissolved by nitric acid alone, and it merely laughed a jolly "ha-ha!" at hydrochloric acid. Only when the two combined could platinum be broken down.

There was a lesson here—two lessons, in fact.

The first was this: I was the platinum. It was going to take more than a single opponent to overcome Flavia Sabina de Luce.

What was left in the flask was bichloride of platinum, which in itself would be useful to test—in some future experiment, perhaps—for the presence of either nicotine or potassium. More to the point, though, was the fact that although the platinum chip had vanished, something new had been formed: something with a whole new set of capabilities.

And then quite suddenly, I caught a glimpse of my face reflected in the glassware, watching wide-eyed as the somewhat cloudy liquid in the flask, shifting uneasily, took on, perhaps, a tinge of sickly yellow, as if in the drifting mists of a Gypsy's crystal ball.

I knew then what I had to do.

"AHA! FLAVIA!" the vicar said. "We missed you at church on Sunday."

"Sorry, Vicar," I told him, "I'm afraid I rather overdid myself on Saturday, what with the fête and so forth."

Since good works do not generally require trumpeting, I did not feel it necessary to mention the assistance I had offered to Fenella. And as it turned out, I was right to hold my tongue, because the vicar quickly brought up the subject himself.

"Yes," he said. "Your father tells me you were allowed rather a luxurious Sabbath lie-in. Really, Flavia, it was most kind of you to play the Good Samaritan, as it were. *Most* kind."

"It was nothing," I said, with becoming modesty. "I was happy to help."

The vicar got to his feet and stretched. He had been snipping away with a pair of kitchen scissors at the tufts of grass growing round the wooden legs of the St. Tancred's signboard.

"God's work takes many strange forms," he said, when he saw me grinning at his handiwork.

"I visited the poor soul in hospital," he went on, "directly after Morning Prayer."

"You spoke to her?" I asked, astonished.

"Oh, dear, no. Nothing like that. I'm sure she wasn't even aware of my presence. Nurse Duggan told me that she hadn't regained consciousness—the Gypsy woman, of course, not Nurse Duggan—and that she—the Gypsy woman, I mean—had spent a restless night, crying out every now and then about something that was hidden. The poor thing was delirious, of course."

Something hidden? What could Fenella have meant?

It was true that she had mentioned to me the woman whose fortune she had told just before mine: something about something that was buried in the past, but would that count as hidden? It was worth a try.

"It's too bad, isn't it?" I said, shaking my head. "Hers was the most popular pitch at the fête—until the tent caught fire, that is. She was telling me how startled someone was—the person who went in just before me, I believe—when she happened to guess correctly something about her past."

Had a little cloud drifted across the vicar's face?

"Her past? Oh, I should hardly think so. The person whose fortune was told immediately before yours was Mrs. Bull."

Mrs. Bull? Well, I'll be blowed! I'd have been willing to take an oath that Mrs. Bull's first encounter with Fenella in several years had taken place in my presence, on Saturday, in the Gully—after the fête.

"Are you sure?" I asked.

"Quite sure," the vicar said. "I was standing near the coconut pitch talking to Ted Sampson when Mrs. Bull asked me to keep an eye on her tots for a few minutes. 'I shan't be long, Vicar,' she said. 'But I must have my fortune read—make sure there are no more of these little blighters in my future.'

"She was joking, of course, but still, it seemed a very odd thing to say, under the circumstances." The vicar reddened. "Oh, dear, I fear I've been indiscreet. You must forget my words at once."

"Don't worry, Vicar," I told him. "I won't say a word."

I went through the motions of sewing my lips shut with a needle and a very long piece of thread. The vicar winced at my grimaces.

"Besides," I said, "it's not the same as if the Bulls were your parishioners."

"It *is* the same," he said. "Discretion is discretion—it knows no religious bounds."

"Is Mrs. Bull a Hobbler?" I asked suddenly.

His brow wrinkled. "A Hobbler? Whatever makes you think that? Dear me, that somewhat peculiar faith was, if I am not mistaken, suppressed in the late eighteenth century. There have been rumors, of course, but one mustn't—"

"Was it?" I interrupted. "Suppressed, I mean?"

Could it be that the Hobblers had gone underground so effectively that their very presence in Bishop's Lacey was disbelieved by the vicar of St. Tancred's?

"Whatever her allegiances," the vicar continued, "we mustn't pass judgment upon the beliefs of others, must we?"

"I suppose not," I said, just as the meaning of his earlier words struck home.

"Did you say you were talking to a Mr. Sampson? Mr. Sampson of East Finching?"

The vicar nodded. "Ted Sampson. He still comes back to lend a hand with the tents and booths. He's been doing it man and boy for twenty-five years. He says it makes him feel close to his parents—they're both of them buried here in the churchyard, you understand. Of course he's lived in East Finching since he married a—"

"Yes?" I said. If I'd had whiskers they'd have been trembling.

"Oh dear," the vicar said. "I fear I've said too much. You must excuse me."

He dropped to his knees and resumed his snipping at the grass, and I knew that our interview was at an end.

GLADYS'S TIRES PURRED ON THE tarmac as we sped north towards East Finching. It was easy going at first, but then as the road rose up, fold upon fold, into the encircling hills, I had to lean on her pedals like billy-ho.

By the time I reached Pauper's Well at the top of Denham Rise, I was panting like a dog. I dismounted and, leaning Gladys against the stone casing of the well, dropped to my knees for a drink.

Pauper's Well was not so much a well as a natural spring: a place where the water gurgled up from some underground source, and had done so since before the Romans had helped themselves to an icy, refreshing swig.

Spring water, I knew, was a remarkable chemical soup: calcium, magnesium, potassium, iron, and assorted salts and sulphates. I grabbed the battered old tin cup that hung from a chain, scooped it full of the burbling water, and drank until I thought I could feel my bones strengthening.

With the water still dribbling down my chin, I stood up and looked out over the countryside. Behind me, spread out like a handkerchief for a doll's picnic, was Bishop's Lacey. Through it, this side of the high street, the river Efon wound its lazy way round the village before ambling off to the southwest and Buckshaw.

Now, almost two weeks into the harvest, most of the countryside had traded its intense summer green for a paler, grayish shade, as if Mother Nature had nodded off a little, and let the colors leak away.

In the distance, like a black bug crawling up the hillside, a tractor dragged a harrow across a farmer's field, the buzz of its engine coming clearly to my ears.

From up here, I could see the Palings to the south, a green oasis at a bend in the river. And there was Buckshaw, its stones glowing warmly in the sunlight, as if they had been cut from precious citrine and polished by a master's hand.

Harriet's house, I thought, although for the life of me I don't know why. Something was welling up in my throat. It must have been something in the well water. I took Gladys from her resting place and shoved off towards East Finching.

From this point on, the journey was all downhill. After a couple of jolly good pumps to get up speed, I put my feet up on the handlebars, and Gladys and I with the wind in our teeth came swooping like a harrier down the dusty road and into East Finching's high street.

Unlike its neighbors, Malden Fenwick and Bishop's Lacey, East Finching was not a pretty bit of Ye Olde England. No half-timbered houses here—no riot of flowers in cottage gardens. Instead, the word that came to mind was "grubby."

At least half the shops in the high street had boarded-up windows, while those that were apparently still in business had rather a sad and defeated look.

In the window of a tobacconist's shop on the corner, a crooked sign advertised: *Today's Papers.*

A bell above the door gave out a harsh jangle as I stepped inside, and a gray-haired man with old-fashioned square spectacles looked up from his newspaper.

"Well?" he said, as if I had surprised him in his bath.

"Excuse me," I said. "I wonder if you can help me? I'm looking for Mr. Sampson—Edward Sampson. Could you tell me where he lives?"

"What you want with him, then? Selling biscuits, are you?"

His mouth broke into a ghastly grin, revealing three horrid teeth which appeared to be carved from rotted wood.

It was the same thing, more or less, that the abominable Ursula had said to me at Vanetta Harewood's door: a bad joke that was doing the rounds of the countryside, the way bad jokes do.

I held my tongue.

"Selling biscuits, are you?" he said again, like a music hall comic beating a joke to death.

"Actually, no," I said. "Mr. Sampson's parents are buried in St. Tancred's churchyard, in Bishop's Lacey, and we're setting up a Graves Maintenance Fund. It's the war, you see . . . We thought that perhaps he'd like to—"

The man stared at me skeptically over his spectacles. I was going to have to do better than this.

"Oh, yes—I almost forgot. I also bring thanks from the vicar and the ladies of the Women's Institute—and the Altar Guild—for Mr. Sampson's help with the fête on Saturday. It was a smashing success."

I think it was the WI and the Altar Guild that did it. The tobacconist wrinkled his nose in disgust, hitched his spectacles a little higher, and jabbed his thumb towards the street.

"Yellow fence," he said. "Salvage," and went back to his reading.

"Thank you," I said. "You're very kind."

And I almost meant it.

THE PLACE WAS HARD TO MISS. A tall wooden fence, in a shade of yellow that betrayed the use of war surplus aviation paint, sagged inwards and outwards along three sides of a large property.

It was evident that the fence had been thrown up in an attempt to hide from the street the ugliness of the salvage business, but with little effect. Behind its boards, piles of rusting metal scrap towered into the air like heaps of giant jackstraws.

On the fence tall red letters, painted by an obviously amateur hand, spelled out: SAMPSON—SALVAGE—SCRAP IRON BOUGHT—BEST PRICES—MOTOR PARTS.

An iron rod leant against the double gates, holding them shut. I put my eye to the crack and peered inside.

Maddeningly, there wasn't much to see—because of the angle, my view was blocked by a wrecked lorry that had been overturned and its wheels removed.

With a quick glance up and down the street, I shifted the rod, tugged the gates open a bit, took a deep breath, and squeezed through.

Immediately in front of me, a sign painted in blood-red letters on the hulk of a pantechnicon said BEWARE OF THE DOC—as if the animal in question had gone for the artist's throat before he could finish the letter G.

I stopped in my tracks and listened, but there was no sign of the beast. Perhaps the warning was meant simply to scare off strangers.

On one side of the yard was a good-sized Nissen hut which, judging by the tire tracks leading to its double doors, was in regular use. To my right, like a row of iron oasthouses, the towering junk piles I had seen from outside the gates led away towards the back of the lot. Projecting from the closest heap—as if it had just crashed and embedded itself—was what surely must be the back half of a Spitfire, the red, white, and blue RAF markings as fresh and bright as if they had been applied just yesterday.

The fence had concealed the size of the place—it must have covered a couple of acres. Beyond the mountains of scrap, spotted here and there, scores of wrecked motorcars subsided sadly into the grass, and even at the back of the property, where the scrap gave way gradually to an orchard, blotches of colored metal glinting among the trees signaled that there were bodies there, too.

As I moved warily along the gravel path between the heaps of broken machinery, hidden things gave off an occasional rusty *ping* as if they were trying to warm themselves enough in the sun to come back to life—but with little success.

"Hello?" I called, hoping desperately that there would be no answer—and there wasn't.

At the end of an L-shaped bend in the gravel was a brick structure: rather like a washhouse, I thought, or perhaps a laundry, with a round chimney rising up about thirty feet above its flat roof.

The windows were so coated with grime that even by rubbing with my fist, I could see nothing inside. In place of a knob, the door was furnished with what looked like a homemade latch: something cobbled together from bits of iron fencing.

I put my thumb on the tongue of the thing and pressed it down. The latch popped up, the door swung open, and I stepped into the dim interior.

The place was unexpectedly bare. On one side was a large fire chamber whose open door revealed a bottom covered with cold ashes and cinders. On its side was mounted what appeared to be a motor-driven blower.

These things hadn't changed in four or five hundred years, I thought. Aside from the electric fan, there was little difference between this device and the crucibles of the alchemists that filled the pages of several vellum manuscripts in Uncle Tar's library.

In essence, this furnace was not unlike the gas crucible that Uncle Tar had installed in the laboratory at Buckshaw, but on a much larger scale, of course.

On the brick hearth in front of the furnace, beside a long steel ladle, lay several broken molds: wooden chests that had been filled with sand into which objects had been pressed to make an impression—into which the molten iron had then been poured.

Dogs, by the look of them, I thought. *Spaniels indented in the sand to make a pair of doorstops.*

Or firedogs.

And I knew then, even though I had not yet had a chance to test them for authenticity, that it was here, in Edward Sampson's washhouse foundry, that copies of Sally Fox and Shoppo had been cast: the copies that were likely, at this very moment, standing in for the originals on the drawing-room hearth at Buckshaw.

But where were Harriet's originals? Were they the fire irons I had seen in Miss Mountjoy's coach house—the antiques warehouse in which Brookie Harewood kept his treasure? Or were they the ones I had seen in the hands of Sampson, the bulldog man, at the back door of Pettibone's antiques shop? I shuddered at the very thought of it.

Still, I had already accomplished much of what I had come to do. All that remained was to search the Nissen hut for papers. With any luck, a familiar name might well pop up.

At that moment I heard the sound of a motor outside.

I glanced quickly round the room. Save for diving into the cold furnace, there was nowhere to hide. The only alternative was to dash out into the open and make a run for it.

I chose the furnace.

Thoughts of Hansel and Gretel crossed my mind as I pulled the heavy door shut behind me and crouched, trying to make myself as small as possible.

Another dress ruined, I thought—and another sad-eyed lecture from Father.

It was then that I heard the footsteps on the stone floor.

I hardly dared take a breath—the sound of it would be amplified grotesquely by the brick beehive in which I was huddled.

The footsteps paused, as if the person outside were listening.

They moved on . . . then stopped again.

There was a metallic *CLANG* as something touched the door just inches from my face. And then, slowly . . . so slowly that I nearly screamed from suspense . . . the door swung open.

The first thing I saw was his boots: large, dusty, scarred from work.

Then the leg of his coveralls.

I raised my eyes and looked into his face. "Dieter!"

It was Dieter Schrantz, the laborer from Culverhouse Farm—Bishop's Lacey's sole remaining prisoner of war, who had elected to stay in England after the end of hostilities.

"Is it really you?"

I began dusting myself off as I scrambled out of the furnace. Even when I had come out of my crouch and stood up straight, Dieter still towered above me, his blue eyes and blond hair making him seem like nothing so much as a vastly overgrown schoolboy.

"What are you doing here?" I asked, breaking out in a silly grin.

"Am I permitted to ask the same?" Dieter said, taking in the whole room with a sweep of his hand. "Unless this place has become part of Buckshaw, I should say you're a long way from home."

I smiled politely at his little joke. Dieter had something of a crush on my sister Feely, but aside from that, he was a decent enough chap.

"I was playing Solitaire Hare and Hounds," I said, making up rules wildly and talking too fast. "East Finching counts double for a compound name, and Sampson's scores a triple S—Sampson's, Salvage, and Scrap— see? I'd get an extra point for having someone with a biblical name, but today's not a Sunday, so it doesn't count."

Dieter nodded gravely. "Very complex, the English rules," he said. "I have never completely grasped them myself."

He moved towards the door, but turned to see if I was following.

"Come on," he said, "I'm going your way. I'll give you a lift."

I wasn't particularly ready to leave, but I knew that my nosing around was at an end. Who, after all, can carry out full-scale snoopage with a six-foot-something ex–prisoner of war dogging one's every footstep?

I blinked a bit as we stepped out into the sun. On the far side of the path, Dieter's old gray Ferguson tractor stood tut-tutting to itself, like an elephant that has stumbled by accident upon the elephant's graveyard: a little shocked, perhaps, to find itself suddenly among the bones of its ancestors.

After closing the gate, I climbed onto the hitch between the two rear wheels, and dragged Gladys up behind me. Dieter let in the clutch, and we were off, the Fergie's tall tires sending up a spray of cinders that fell away behind us like dark fireworks.

We flew like the wind, basking in the September sunlight and drinking in the fresh autumn air, so it was only when we were halfway down the south slope of Denham Rise that the penny dropped.

My posterior was braced firmly against one of the Fergie's wings and my feet on the clanking hitch. As we sped along, the ground beneath was just a rushing blur of greenish black.

But why, I thought suddenly, *would a farmer be so far from home with no trailer rumbling along behind; no plow, no harrow swaying in the rear?* It simply made no sense.

I felt my hackles beginning to rise.

"Who sent you?" I shouted above the whistling wind and the roar of the Fergie's engine.

"What?"

I knew from my own experience that he was stalling for time.

"What?" he said again, as if I hadn't heard him, which made me suddenly and inexplicably furious.

"It was Father, wasn't it?"

But even as the words came out of my mouth, I knew that I was wrong. There was no more chance that Father would telephone Dieter than that the Man in the Moon should ring up the rat catcher.

"Inspector Hewitt!"

I was clutching at straws. The Inspector was equipped with his own official transportation, and would never send a civilian on one of his errands.

Dieter shoved up the throttle in its quadrant and the tractor slowed. He pulled off into a small lay-by where a wooden platform was piled with milk containers.

He turned to me, not smiling.

"It was Ophelia," he said.

"Feely?" I screeched. Had my sister sent Dieter to follow me? All day? How dare she! How doubly-damned dare she! This was an outrage.

That I should be thwarted—torn away—kidnapped, virtually, from an important investigation—by my own sister made me see red.

Bright red.

Without a word, I jumped down from the tractor's hitch, lifted Gladys onto the road, and set off walking down the hill, my head held high and my pigtails swaying.

When I got far enough away to remember it, I put one foot onto a pedal and mounted, shoving off shakily, but recovering enough to begin an offended but dignified coasting.

Moments later, I heard the tractor's engine rev up, but I did not look back.

Dieter pulled alongside, driving precisely to keep pace.

"She was worried about you," he said. "She wanted me to see that you were all right."

Feely worried about me? I could hardy believe it. I could count on one finger the times she had treated me decently in the past couple of years.

"To spy on me, you mean," I shot back.

It was a mean thing to say, but I said it. I quite liked Dieter, but the thought of him being under my sister's thumb made me livid.

"Come on, hop up," Dieter said, bringing the tractor to a full stop. "Your bicycle, too."

"No, thank you very much. We prefer to be alone."

I began pedaling to get ahead of the tractor. I suppose I could have pulled over and waited, then climbed aboard for a graciously accepted ride into the village.

But by the time I thought of it, I was already halfway up the high street.

I WAS DISAPPOINTED NOT TO FIND Dogger at work in the greenhouse. It was always such a pleasure to slip in, sit quietly down beside him, and fall into easy conversation, like two old gaffers on a bench beside the duck pond.

Second choice, when I wanted information, was Mrs. Mullet, but as I discovered when I stepped into the kitchen, she had already gone home for the day.

I'd have given anything to be able to pump Daffy about the Hobblers, but something kept me from asking any more of her. I still hadn't taken my revenge for her part in the cellar inquisition, even though I had already twice broken my injured silence to ask her about Poseidon and about Hilda Muir—or Hildemoer, to be more precise—and the pixies.

It seemed to me that you couldn't possibly win a war in which you were forever going over to the other side for advice. Also, fraternizing—or whatever you call it when sisters do it—with the enemy diluted one's resolve to kick them in the teeth.

My head was fairly fizzing with information, and there had been little time to sort it all out.

Some of the more interesting points had already begun to come together in my mind, clustering and curdling in much the same way that silver chloride (good old AgCl) forms a sort of chemical cheese when a soluble chloride is added to silver nitrate.

Soluble! That was the word. Would I ever be able to solve this complex tangle of puzzles?

One thing was immediately clear: I needed to know more—much, much more—about the Hobblers, and it was clear that no Hobbler of my immediate acquaintance was going to make my life easier by spilling the beans.

twenty-one

I AWAKENED TO THE ROAR OF WATER ON THE ROOF TILES AND in the drains—the sound of Buckshaw in the rain.

Even before I opened my eyes, I could hear that the whole house had come alive in a way that it never did in dry weather—a deep, wet breathing in and out—as if, after a mad dash down the centuries, the tired old place had just thrown itself across the finish line.

There would be little winds in the corridors, I knew, and sudden cold drafts would spring up in out-of-the-way corners. In spite of its size, Buckshaw had all the comfort of a submarine.

I wrapped myself in my blanket and stumped to the window. Outside, the stuff was coming straight down, as if it were lines drawn with pencil and a ruler. It was not the kind of rain that was going to pass away quickly—we were in for hours of it.

Father acknowledged my presence at the breakfast table with a curt nod. At least he didn't try to make chipper conversation, I thought, and for that I offered up a little prayer of thanksgiving.

Feely and Daffy, as usual, were busily pretending that I didn't exist.

Rainy days cast a darker than usual pall over our morning meal, and today was no exception.

Our September breakfast menu had been in force for almost two weeks now, and the base of my tongue shrank back a little as Mrs. Mullet brought to the table what I thought of as our daily ration of T.O.A.D.

*T*oast
*O*atmeal
*A*pple *J*uice
*D*ates

The dates, stewed and served with cold clotted cream, were another of Mrs. Mullet's culinary atrocities. They looked and tasted like something that had been stolen from a coffin in a midnight churchyard.

"Pass the dead man's," Daffy would say, without looking up from her book, and Father would fix her with a flickering glare until the latest philatelic journal dragged his attention back to its pages—a time span of, usually, no more than about two and three-quarter seconds.

But today Daffy said nothing, her arm reaching out robotically and shoveling a few spoonfuls of the vile mess into her bowl.

Feely wasn't down yet, so I made a relatively easy escape.

"May I be excused, please?" I asked, and Father grunted.

Seconds later I was in the hall closet, fishing out my bright yellow waterproof.

"When cycling in the rain," Dogger had told me, "being visible is more important than keeping dry."

"You mean that I can always dry out, but I can't be brought back to life when I'm impaled on the horns of a Daimler," I said, partly joking.

"Precisely," Dogger had said with a perfect tiny smile, and gone back to waxing Father's boots.

It was still coming down like lances as I made a dash for the greenhouse, where I had left Gladys. Gladys didn't much like the rain, since it made her skirts muddy, but she never complained.

I had plotted my course to Rook's End with great care, avoiding both the Gully and the house of the dreaded Mrs. Bull.

As I pedaled along the road towards Bishop's Lacey in my yellow mackintosh, I remembered what Dogger had said about visibility. In spite of the mist that hung like tatters of gray laundry over the soaked fields, I could probably be seen for miles. And yet, in another sense, because I was only eleven years old, I was wrapped in the best cloak of invisibility in the world.

I thought of the time Mrs. Mullet had taken me to see *The Invisible Man*. We had gone on the bus to Hinley to replace an Easter dress that I had ruined during a particularly interesting—but failed—experiment involving both sulfuric and hydrochloric acids.

After a sickening hour in Fashions by Eleanor, a shop in the high street whose windows were bandaged over with paper banners in dreadful shades of pink and aqua—"Latest Easter Frocks for Young Misses!" "New From London!" "Just in Time for Easter!"—Mrs. Mullet had taken pity on me and suggested a visit to a nearby A.B.C. tea shop.

There we had sat, for three quarters of an hour at a table in the window, watching people stroll by on the pavement outside. Mrs. M had become quite chatty and, forgetting perhaps that I wasn't her friend Mrs. Waller, had let slip several things that, although they were not important at the time, would probably come in handy when I was older.

After the tea and the pastries, with most of the afternoon still ahead of us ("You was a real trouper about the frock, dear—in spite of them two witches with their tapes and pins!"), Mrs. M had decided to treat me to the cinema she had spotted in the narrow street beside the tea shop.

Because Mrs. Mullet had seen it years before, she talked all the way through *The Invisible Man*, nudging me in the ribs as she explained it to me minute by minute.

"'E can see them, like, but they can't see 'im."

Although I was amused at the mad scientist's idea of injecting a powerful bleach to render himself invisible, what truly shocked me was the way he treated his laboratory equipment.

"It's just a fill-um, dear," Mrs. Mullet said, as I gripped her arm during the smashing of the glassware.

But all in all, I thought, looking back on it, the entertainment had not been a success. Invisibility was nothing new to me. It was an art I had been forced to learn from the day I took my first step.

Visible and invisible: the trick of being present and absent at the same time.

"Yaroo!" I shouted to no one in particular as I splashed past St. Tancred's and into the high street.

At the far end of the village, I turned south. Through the rain I could just make out in the distance the Jack o'Lantern, a skull-shaped formation of rock that overhung my destination, Rook's End.

I was now running parallel to and a half-mile due east of the Gully, and before many minutes had passed, I was gliding along the edge of one of the great lawns that stretched off in three directions.

I had been at Rook's End once before to visit Father's old schoolmaster, Dr. Kissing. On that occasion I had found him in the decaying solarium of the nursing home, and was not looking forward to setting foot in that particular mausoleum again today.

But much to my surprise, as I leapt off Gladys at the front door, there was the old gentleman himself sitting in a wheelchair beneath a large, gaily colored umbrella that had been set up on the lawn.

He waved as I plodded towards him through the wet grass.

"Ha! Flavia!" he said. "'It can be no ill day which brings a young visitor to my gate.' Horace, of course—or was it Catullus?"

I grinned as if I knew but had forgotten.

"Hello, Dr. Kissing," I said, handing over the packet of Players I had filched from Feely's lingerie drawer. Feely had bought the things to impress Dieter. But Dieter had joked her out of it. "No, thank you," he said when she offered him the packet. "They ruin the chest," and she had put the cigarettes away unopened. Feely was uncommonly proud of her chest.

"Ah," Dr. Kissing said, producing a box of matches as if from nowhere and striking one expertly as he was still opening the packet of cigarettes. "How very kind of you to think of my one great weakness."

He inhaled deeply, holding the smoke in his lungs for what seemed like an eternity. Then, letting it escape as he spoke, he gazed off into the distance, as if addressing someone else.

> *"Thus he ruins his Health, and his Substance destroys,*
> *By vainly pursuing his fanciful Joys,*
> *Till perhaps in the Frolick he meets with his Bane*
> *And runs on the weapon by which he is slain."*

And runs on the weapon by which he was slain?

My blood chilled as he spoke the last line. Was he referring to his own smoking of cigarettes—or to the bizarre death of Brookie Harewood?

A conversation with Dr. Kissing was, I knew, a game of chess. There would be no shortcuts.

"The Hobblers," I said, making the opening move.

"Ah, yes." He smiled. "The Hobblers. I knew you would ask me about the Hobblers. One should have been disappointed if you hadn't."

Could Mr. or Mrs. Pettibone have told him of my interest? Somehow, it seemed unlikely.

"Surely you don't suspect that I am one of them?"

"No," I said, struggling to keep up with him. "But I knew that your niece—"

Until that very moment I had nearly forgotten that Dr. Kissing was Miss Mountjoy's uncle.

"My niece? You thought that Tilda was keeping me briefed on your . . . ? Good lord, no! She tells me nothing—nor anyone else. Not even God himself knows what Tilda's left hand is doing nowadays."

He saw my puzzlement.

"One needs look no farther than one's own hearth," he said.

"Mrs. Mullet?"

Dr. Kissing coughed a wheezy cough—which reminded me uncomfortably of Fenella—and consoled himself by lighting another cigarette.

"It is common knowledge that you are situated, as it were, in close proximity to the estimable Mrs. Mullet. The rest is mere conjecture.

"One has not, of course," he went on, "communicated personally with the good woman," he said. "But I believe she *is* known far and wide for, ah—"

"Dishing the dirt," I volunteered.

He made a little bow from his waist. "Your descriptive powers leave me in the dust," he said.

I could easily grow to love this man.

"I know about Nicodemus Flitch," I told him, "and how he brought his faith to Bishop's Lacey. I know that there are still a few practicing Hobblers in the neighborhood, and that they still gather occasionally at the Palings."

"To conduct baptisms."

"Yes," I said. "For baptisms."

"A much more common practice in years gone by," he said. "There are nowadays few Hobblers left of childbearing age."

I tried to think of who they might be. Certainly not Tilda Mountjoy or Mrs. Pettibone.

"I believe poor Mrs. Bull was the last," he said, and I noticed he was watching me out of the corner of his eye.

"Mrs. Bull?"

Was Mrs. Bull a Hobbler?

"Mrs. Bull, who lives in the Gully?" I asked. "The one whose baby was taken by Gypsies?"

I couldn't help myself. Even though I didn't believe it, the fearful words slipped out before I could think.

Dr. Kissing nodded. "So it is said."

"But you don't believe it."

I was in fine form now, catching every shade of the old man's meaning.

"I must confess that I don't," he said. "And I expect that you would like me to tell you why."

I could only manage a stupid grin.

Although the rain was still beating down upon the umbrella with a monotonous drumming, there was a surprising stillness and a warmth beneath its protective cover. Across the lawn, the dreadful house that was Rook's End crouched like a giant stone toad. In one of its tall windows—in what had once perhaps been the ballroom—two old ladies, in outlandish and outdated costumes, were dancing a stately minuet. I had seen this pair on my last visit to Dr. Kissing, executing their timeless steps beneath the trees, and now they had obviously spotted me.

As I watched, the shorter of the two paused long enough to wave a gloved hand and the other, seeing her partner's greeting, came almost to the glass and made a deep and elaborate curtsy.

By the time I brought my attention back to Dr. Kissing, he was lighting another cigarette.

"Until last year," he said, watching the smoke vanish into the rain, "I was still able to make my way to the top of the Jack o'Lantern. For a young man in tip-top physical condition, it is no more than a pleasant stroll, but for a fossil in a wheelchair, it is torture.

"But then, to an old man, even torture can be a welcome relief to boredom, so I often made the ascent out of nothing more than spite.

"From the summit, one can survey the terrain as if from the basket of a hot-air balloon. To the northwest, in the distance, is Greyminster School, scene of my greatest triumphs and my greatest failure. To the west, one has a clear view of the Palings, and behind it, Buckshaw, your ancestral home.

"It was at the Palings, incidentally, that I once asked the lovely Letitia Humphrey for her hand in holy matrimony—and it was at the Palings that Letitia had the jolly good sense to say no."

"I'll bet she lived to regret it," I said gallantly.

"She lived—but without remorse. Letitia went on to marry a man who made a fortune adulterating wheat flour with bone dust. I am given to understand that they made each other very happy."

A cloud of tobacco smoke made his sigh suddenly visible in the damp air.

"Did *you* regret it?" I asked. It was not a polite question, but I wanted to know.

"Although I scale the Jack o'Lantern no more," he said, "it is not entirely because of my infirmities, but rather because of the increasingly great sadness that is visible from the summit—a sadness which is not nearly so noticeable from the lower altitudes."

"The Palings?"

"There was a time when I loved to gaze down upon that ancient crook in the river as if from the summit of my years. In fact, I was doing so on that day in April, two and a half years ago, when the Bull baby disappeared."

My mouth must have fallen open.

"From my vantage point, I saw the Gypsy leave her encampment—and later, saw Mrs. Bull pushing the baby's perambulator along the Gully."

"Hold on," I said. "Surely it was the other way round?"

"It was as I have described. The Gypsy woman hitched her horse and drove her caravan north along the Gully. Sometime later, the Bull woman appeared, wheeling her baby south towards the Palings."

"Perhaps the pram was empty," I ventured.

"An excellent point," Dr. Kissing said, "except for the fact that I saw her lift out the infant whilst she retrieved its lost bottle from the blankets."

"But then Fenella *couldn't* have kidnapped the baby."

"Very good, Flavia. As you may have perceived, I've long ago come to that same conclusion."

"But—"

"Why did I not inform the police?"

I nodded dumbly.

"I have asked myself that, again and again. And each time I have answered that it was, in part, because the police never asked me. But that will hardly do, will it? There is also the undeniable fact that when one reaches a certain age, one hesitates to take on a new cargo of trouble. It is as if, having experienced a certain amount of grief in a lifetime, one is given pass-slip to hand in to the Great Headmaster in the Sky. Do you understand?"

"I think I do," I said.

"That is why I have kept it to myself," he said. "But oddly enough, it is also the reason that I am now telling you."

The silence between us was broken only by the sound of the falling rain.

Then suddenly, from across the lawn, there came a shout: "Dr. Kissing! Whatever are you thinking?"

It was the White Phantom, the same nurse I had seen on my previous visit to Rook's End, now looking ludicrous in her white uniform and huge black galoshes as she came galumphing across the grass towards us through the falling rain.

"Whatever are you *thinking*?" she asked again as she stepped beneath the umbrella. I've observed that domineering people like the White Phantom often say everything twice, as though they're on a quota system.

"I am thinking, Nurse Hammond," Dr. Kissing said, "of the sad decline in English manners since the late war."

His words were met with a silent sniff as she seized the handles of his wheelchair and shoved off rapidly with it across the lawn.

As she paused to open the conservatory door, Dr. Kissing's words came floating back to my ears—

"Tally-ho, Flavia!"

It was a call to the hunt.

I waved like mad to show him that I had understood, but it was too late. He had already been wheeled indoors and out of sight.

twenty-two

I THINK THERE MUST BE A KIND OF COURAGE THAT COMES from not being able to make up your mind.

Whether it was this or whether it was Gladys's willfulness I can't be sure, but there we were, suddenly swerving off the main road and into the Gully.

I had been going here and there about the village, avoiding the unpleasant Mrs. Bull in much the same way as a housefly avoids the folded newspaper. But the Gully was a shortcut home to Buckshaw, and there was no time like the present.

Although Gladys's black paint was now spattered with mud, she seemed as frisky as if she had just been curried with a bristled brush and wiped down to perfection. Her nickel handlebars, at least, glittered in the sun.

"You're enjoying this, aren't you, old girl?" I said, and she gave a little squeak of delight.

Would Mrs. Bull be standing guard at her gate? Would I have to pretend again to be Margaret Vole, niece of that fictional—but beloved—old character actress, Gilda Dickinson?

I needn't have worried. Mrs. Bull was nowhere in sight, although the hovering smoke from the rubbish heaps made it difficult to see much of the property.

Her redheaded boy—the one who had been perched in the branches when I rode through the Gully with Fenella—was now sitting in the ditch at the edge of the road, digging his way to China with a piece of cutlery.

I brought Gladys to a slithering stop and put both feet on the ground.

"Hello," I said, rather stupidly. "What's *your* name?"

It was not the most brilliant opening, but I wasn't accustomed to talking to children, and hadn't the faintest idea how to begin. It didn't matter anyway, because the little wretch ignored me and went on with his excavating.

It was difficult to judge his age, which might have been anywhere between four and seven. His large head wobbled uneasily atop a spindly body, giving the impression that one was looking at rather a large baby or a small adult.

"Timofey," he said in a froggy croak, just as I was about to shove off.

"Timothy?"

There was another awkward pause, during which I shifted uneasily from foot to foot.

"Timofey."

"Is your mother at home, Timofey?" I asked.

"Dunno—yes—no," he said, giving me a wary sideways glance, and he returned to his digging, stabbing fiercely at the soil with his bit of tableware.

"Digging for treasure, are you?" I asked, going all chummy. I leaned Gladys against a bank and climbed down into the ditch. "Here, let me help."

I casually worked my hand into my off-side pocket and closed my fingers around a stick of horehound.

With a quick darting motion, I reached down into the hole he was digging, and pretended to extract the sweet.

"Oh, Timofey!" I cried, clapping my hands. "Look what you've found! Good boy! Timofey's found a sweet!" Although it jarred, I couldn't bring myself to call him by any name other than the one he called himself.

As I held out the horehound, he snatched it away from me with a lightning-fast movement and shoved it into his mouth.

"Preasure!" he said, gnawing nastily.

"Yes, treasure," I cooed. "Timofey's found buried treasure."

With the horehound stick jutting out of the corner of his mouth like a sickroom thermometer, Timofey put down his digging implement and attacked the hole with his bare hands.

My heart gave a leap as my mind registered what now lay exposed in the dirt: the silver . . . the prongs . . . the figure of the lobster punched from the handle . . . the de Luce monogram . . .

The child was digging with one of the de Luce lobster picks! But how could that be? Dogger had already shipped the silver to Sotheby's for auction and the only piece that had been overlooked, perhaps, was the one that had been used to put paid to Brookie Harewood. And that, unless I was sadly mistaken, had, until quite recently, been shoved up Brookie Harewood's nostril and into his brain. How could it possibly have made its way from there into the hands of an urchin grubbing in the Gully? Or could this be a copy?

"Here," I said. "Let me help you. I'm bigger. I can dig faster. Find more sweets."

I made digging motions with my hands, scooping like a badger.

But Timofey snatched up the lobster pick, and was holding it away from me.

"Mime!" he said around the horehound. "Mime! Timofey foumd it!"

"Good boy!" I said. "Let's have a look."

"No!"

"All right," I said. "I don't want to see it anyway."

If there's anyone on earth who knows the ways of a child's mind, I thought, *it's me—Flavia de Luce—*for I had not so long ago been one myself.

As I spoke, I reached into my pocket and extracted another stick of horehound—this one, my last. I gazed at it fondly, held it up to the sunlight to admire its golden glow, smacked my lips—

"Give over!" the child said. "I wants it!"

"Tell you what," I told him. "I'll trade you for that nasty digger. You don't want that old thing. It's dirty."

I pulled a horrid face and went through the motions of retching, sound effects and all.

He grinned, and inserted the prongs of the lobster pick into one of his nostrils.

"No, Timofey!" I said in the most commanding voice I could summon. "It's sharp—you'll hurt yourself. Give it here.

"At once!" I added sternly, putting on the voice of authority, as Father does when he wants to be instantly obeyed. I held out my hand and Timofey meekly laid the silver lobster pick across my lifeline—the very part of my hand that the Gypsy—Fenella—was it only three days ago?—had held in her own and told me that in it she saw darkness.

"Good boy," I said, my head swimming as my fingers closed upon the murder weapon. "Where did you get it?"

I handed him the horehound stick and he grabbed it greedily. I shoved my hand into my empty pocket, as if I were digging into a bottomless bag of sweets.

I locked my eyes with his, noticing, for the first time, the strange transparency of his irises. I would not look away, I thought—not until—

"Danny's mocket," he said suddenly, his words oozing out around the sticky horehound.

Danny's mocket? Danny's *pocket*, of course! I was proud of myself.

But who was Danny? It couldn't be the baby—the baby wasn't old enough to have pockets. Did Mrs. Bull have an older son?

My mind was buzzing with possibilities as I shoved the lobster fork into my pocket. It was a mistake.

"Mam!" the child shrieked, "Mam! Mam! Mam! Mam! Mam!" each cry louder and higher in pitch.

I scrambled out of the ditch and made for Gladys.

"Mam! Mam! Mam! Mam! Mam!"

The little rotter had been set off like a blasted alarm.

"You!" came a voice from out of the smoke, and suddenly Mrs. Bull was coming towards me, lumbering through the smoldering heaps like something out of a nightmare.

"You!" she shouted, her raw arms already extended, ready to seize me. Once she laid hands on me, I knew, I was done for. The woman was big enough to tear me apart like a bundle of rotten rags.

I grabbed at Gladys and pushed off, my feet slipping wildly from the pedals as I threw myself forward, trying to put on speed.

Oddly enough, I was thinking quite clearly. Should I try to divert her by shouting "Fire!" and pointing at her house? Since the place was surrounded by smoldering rubbish heaps, it seemed both a good and a bad idea.

But it was no time for tactics—Mrs. Bull was bearing down upon me with alarming speed.

"Mam! Mam! Mam! Mam! Mam!" Timofey went on maddeningly from the ditch.

The woman's huge hands snatched at me as our paths intersected.

I needed to get past her to be safe. If she managed to seize even so much as one of my sleeves, I was sunk.

"Yaroo!" The cry came out of me quite unexpectedly, but I recognized it at once. It was the battle cry of a savage—a fierce, fearless bellowing that rose up out of my ancestral lungs as if it had been lying in wait for centuries.

"Yaroo!" I let another fly just for pleasure. It felt good.

Mrs. Bull didn't stop—but she faltered—missed a step—and I shot past.

I looked back over my shoulder and saw the woman standing in the road, her fists shaking, her red face contorted with fury as she screamed: "Tom, get yourself out here . . . and bring the ax!"

I SAT ON THE RIVER'S EDGE letting the water cool my feet. There was an unearthly silence in the Palings, and I shivered a little at the thought of the things that had happened within the past few days. First there had been the attack on Fenella, followed almost immediately by the death of Brookie Harewood. Then, too, Porcelain had told me, just before she'd cleared off, that the police had found the body of a baby—probably the Bulls' baby—right here in the grove. I suppose I should have felt sorry for the mother. She may have been mad with grief, for all I knew. Perhaps I should have taken my life in my hands and expressed my condolences.

But life is never easy, is it? If only one could make time run backwards, as it does in those short subjects at the cinema where dynamited factory chimneys fall upwards and restore themselves, and shattered bits of glass fly together to form a vase . . .

In such a world I could, if I wished, bicycle backwards up the Gully, dismount from Gladys, and give the woman a hug. I could tell her I was sorry they'd found the body of her baby buried here in the Palings, and that if there was anything I could do to help, she had only to ask.

I sighed.

Across the river and through the trees, not far from where Fenella's caravan was parked, I could see a mound of fresh soil. That must be the spot where the body had been found.

Other than the fact that she'd seen the baby's foot—"Wrapped in a carpet, or something," she had said, "a bundle of old green bones"— Porcelain hadn't given me any more of the details. And it was too late now—Porcelain was gone.

I could hardly ask Inspector Hewitt about the discovery of the body, and until I had the opportunity to find out from Mrs. Mullet what the village was saying, I was on my own. I would wade across and have a look.

The river was not very deep here. The Hobblers, after all, had been coming to this spot for centuries to baptize their babies. The water was of just sufficient depth for a good old ducking, and I was no more than a hundred feet from the disturbed spot where the police had evidently made their gruesome find.

I hitched up the hem of my dress a couple of inches and started across.

Even a few feet out from the bank, the water grew noticeably colder on the bottom as I waded slowly towards the center, my arms widespread for balance, taking great care not to lose my footing in the ever-strengthening current.

Soon I was at the halfway point—and then I was past it. The water level had receded to just below my knees when I stepped on something hard, stumbled, missed my footing, and went flailing tail-over-teakettle into the water. Total immersion.

"Oh, rat spit!" I said. I was furious with myself. Why hadn't I taken Gladys and walked her across the little bridge?

"Double rat spit!"

I scrambled to my feet and looked down at myself. My dress was completely soaked.

Father would be furious.

"Damn it all—dash it all, Flavia," he would say, as he always did, and then would begin one of those silences between us that would last for several days until one of us forgot about my offense. "Being at loggerheads," Daffy called it, and now, as I stood knee-deep in the water, I tried to imagine that I had been suddenly transported to a cold, rushing river somewhere in the Canadian north woods, with the severed heads of the loggers bobbing past me in the current like bloated, grizzled apples.

But practicality brought me back to Bishop's Lacey. I knew that when I got home to Buckshaw, I would have to sneak into the house, make my way upstairs, and rinse out the dress in the sink of my laboratory.

In the water, the little cloud of mud stirred up by my feet was clearing quickly.

It was odd—although I could easily see the tops of my feet on the river's bed, there were no stones in sight. And yet I had certainly tripped on something hard. I had nearly broken a toe on the stupid thing. *As I had done before!*

I stood there for a moment, already feeling a chill in the September air. Something in the water shifted: a bubble . . . a ripple of water . . . of light. Slowly I bent at the waist and reached carefully into the river's depths.

A little deeper . . . a little farther to the left. Although I couldn't see it, my fingers closed around something hard. I took a firm grip and lifted it towards the surface.

As the object came up towards me through the water it became visible. It was eerie.

Hard . . . transparent . . . invisible in the water . . . becoming visible as it came into the air.

A sudden sinking feeling told me that my heart already knew what the thing was before my head did, and both had already begun to pound as I realized that the object I was holding in my streaming hands was Fenella's crystal ball—the ball with which some unknown person had bashed in her skull: the ball with which someone had tried to kill her.

The thing had been lying on the river bottom for days, its transparency making it invisible in the water even though it was in plain sight. No wonder the police had missed it!

Only if they had waded around in the shallows—and only then if they had stepped upon it by accident, as I had—would they have found the object of their search.

I would, of course, take it to Inspector Hewitt at once.

As I climbed the bank, I noticed that a silence had fallen upon the Palings, as if the birds were afraid to make even a peep.

The crystal ball was cold in my hands, refracting distorted images of earth, trees, and sky, its swirling colors like dye dropped into water.

If it hadn't been for the glass, I might have missed the flash of blue among the trees—a color that didn't belong there.

I stopped in my tracks as if preoccupied. *Don't look directly at it,* I thought.

I twisted the hem of my dress uselessly, as if trying to wring it dry, then made a little hammock of the material in which to sling the crystal ball.

Would my wet hands leave fingerprints? Who knew? It was the best I could do.

"Blast it all!" I said loudly, more for effect than anything, but signaling that I thought I was alone.

With my peripheral vision, I could see that there was a swatch of color among the bushes. By shifting my gaze slightly, I could see that it appeared to be a scarf—a flowered scarf.

Could it be one of the pixies Daffy and Feely had told me about—one of those malevolent water sprites that stole babies? Perhaps it was the very one that had taken Mrs. Bull's child! But no . . . pixies didn't exist. Or did they?

I let my eyes drift slowly to the right.

Quite abruptly, as if by magic, an image snapped into place. It was like one of those optical illusions in *The Girl's Own Annual* in which a silhouette of two faces in profile is suddenly seen to be an egg cup.

Gray hair . . . gray eyes, staring straight at me . . . a scarf at the throat . . . riding breeches—even the monocle hanging by a black cord round the neck.

It was Vanetta Harewood's companion, Ursula, standing motionless among the bushes, counting on the camouflage of stillness to keep me from spotting her—Ursula who gathered willow withies from the riverbank to twist into her dreadful baskets.

I let my eyes meet hers, then drift away, as if I hadn't seen her. I looked to her right—to her left—and finally above her, letting my mouth fall open slackly.

I scratched my head, and then, I'm afraid, my bottom.

"I'm coming, Gladys," I shouted. "It's only a squirrel."

And with that, I made off across the bridge, muttering away to myself like the mad daughter of an eccentric squire.

Damn! I thought. I hadn't had a chance to examine the police diggings.

Still, my day had been remarkably productive. In my pocket was the silver de Luce lobster pick that I was quite sure had been used to put an end to Brookie Harewood, and cradled in my skirt, the crystal ball that was almost certainly the object with which Fenella had been bashed. After all, if it wasn't, then why would it have been tossed into the river?

An idea began to take shape.

Of course I would hand over these weapons at once to Inspector Hewitt—I had planned to do so all along, for various reasons.

But first, I wondered, was it possible to retrieve fingerprints from an object that had been immersed for days in running water?

twenty-three

I HAD CLIMBED NO MORE THAN A DOZEN STAIRS WHEN FATHER'S
voice, from somewhere below me in the foyer, said, "Flavia—"

Thwarted!

I stopped, turned, and came down one step out of respect. He was
standing at the entrance to the west wing.

"My study, please."

He turned and was gone.

I trudged down the steps and trailed along behind him, making a
point of hanging well back.

"Close the door," he said, and sat down at his desk.

This was serious. Father usually delivered his little lectures while
standing at the window, gazing out into the grounds.

I perched on the edge of a chair, and tried to look attentive.

"I've had a call from Nurse Hammond on the—" He pointed in the
general direction of the telephone, but could not bring himself to say
the word. " . . . instrument. She tells me that you took Dr. Kissing out
into the rain."

The hag! I'd done no such thing.

"He wasn't in the rain," I protested. "He was sitting under an umbrella
on the lawn, and he was already outside when I got there."

"It makes no difference," Father said, holding up a hand like a policeman directing traffic.

"But—"

"He's an old man, Flavia. He's not to be bothered with nonsensical intrusions upon his privacy."

"But—"

"This gadding about the countryside must stop," he said. "You're making a confounded nuisance of yourself."

A nuisance! Well!

I could have spat on his carpet.

"I've given this a great deal of thought recently," he said, "and come to the conclusion that you have far too much time on your hands."

"But—"

"Part of that is my own fault, I'll admit. You've not been provided with sufficient supervision and, as a result, your interests have become rather—unhealthy."

"Unhealthy?"

"Consequently," Father plowed on, "I've decided that you need to be more among people—more in the company of your peers."

What was he talking about? On the one hand I was wandering about the village excessively, and now, on the other, I was in need of human companionship. It sounded like something you might say about a rogue sheepdog.

But before I could protest, Father took off his glasses, very deliberately folded their black, spidery arms across the lenses, and put them away in their hard-shelled case. It was a sign that the conversation was nearing its end.

"The vicar tells me that the choir is in need of several extra voices, and I've assured him that you'd be happy to pitch in. They've laid on an extra practice this evening at six-thirty sharp."

I was so astonished I couldn't think of a single word to say.

Later, I thought of one.

"DON'T DAWDLE," FEELY SAID, as we marched across the fields towards the church. She had been summoned to sit in, as she sometimes did, for Mr. Collicutt.

"Where's old Cockie, then," I had asked, and waited for the inevitable explosion. Feely, I think, was half in love with the handsome young man who had recently been appointed organist at St. Tancreds. She had even gone so far as to join the choir because of the superior view of his bobbing blond curls afforded by a seat in the chancel.

But Feely wasn't biting—in fact, she was strangely subdued.

"He's adjudicating the music festival in Hinley," she said, almost as if I'd asked a civil question.

"Do, re, mi, fa, so-what?" I sang loudly, and intentionally off-key.

"Save it for the sinners," Feely said pleasantly, and walked on in silence.

Half a dozen boys in Scout uniforms, all members of St. Tancred's choir, were shoving one another about in the churchyard, playing a rough game of football with someone's hat. One of them was Colin Prout.

Feely stuck her first and last fingers into her mouth and let out a surprisingly piercing and unladylike whistle. The game broke up at once.

"Inside," Feely ordered. "Hymns before horseplay."

Since its scoutmaster and several of the boys were also members of the choir, the Scout troop would not meet until after choir practice.

There were a couple of anonymous groans and whispers, but the boys obeyed her. Colin tried to scuttle past, his eyes fixed firmly on the ground.

"Hoy, Colin," I said, stepping in front of him to block his way. "I didn't know you were a Scout."

He put his head down, jammed his hands into the pockets of his shorts, and sidestepped me. I followed him into the church.

The older members of the choir had already taken their places, chatting away to one another as they awaited the arrival of the organist, the men on one side of the chancel, the women facing them, on the other.

Miss Cool, who was both Bishop's Lacey's postmistress and its confectioner, shot me a beaming smile, and the Misses Puddock, Lavinia and Aurelia, who owned the St. Nicholas Tea Room, gave me identical twiddles of their fingers.

"Good evening, choir," Feely said. It was a tradition that dated back into the mists of Christian history.

"Good evening, Miss de Luce," they responded, automatically.

Feely took her seat on the organ bench, and with no more than a "Hymn number three hundred and eighty-three," barked out over her shoulder, launched into the opening bars of "We Plow the Fields and Gather," leaving me scrambling to find the page in the hymn-book.

"We plow the fields and scatter," we sang,

"the good seed on the land,
but it is fed and watered
by God's almighty hand;
He sends the snow in winter,
the warmth to swell the grain,
the breezes and the sunshine,
and soft refreshing rain."

As I sang, I thought of Brookie's body dangling from Poseidon's trident in the downpour. There had been nothing soft or refreshing about
that particular storm—in fact, it had been one hell of a cloudburst.

I looked across the chancel at Colin. He was singing with intense
concentration, his eyes closed, his face upturned to the day's last light
which was now seeping in through the darkening stained-glass windows.
I'd deal with him later.

"He only is the Maker
of all things near and far;
He paints the wayside flower,
He lights the evening star;
the winds and waves obey Him—"

The organ screeched to a halt in the middle of a note, as if someone
had strangled it.

"De Luce," a voice was saying sourly, and I became aware that it was
Feely's.

She was addressing me!

"The voice cannot emerge through a closed mouth."

Heads turned towards me, and there were a couple of smiles and
titters.

"Now then, again—from 'the winds and waves obey Him—'"

She struck a leading note on the keyboard, and then the organ roared
back to life and we were off again.

How dare she single me out in that manner? The witch! *Just you*
wait, Ophelia Gertrude de Luce . . . just you bloody well wait!

To me, the choir practice seemed to go on forever, perhaps because there's no joy in simply mouthing the words—in fact, it's surprisingly hard work.

But at last it was over. Feely was gathering up her music and having a jolly old chin-wag with Cynthia Richardson, the vicar's wife, whose fan club did not count me among its members. I'd take the opportunity to slip away unnoticed and tackle Colin in the churchyard with a couple of interesting questions that had come to mind.

"Flavia—"

Drat!

Feely had broken off her conversation, and was bearing down upon me. It was too late to pretend I hadn't heard her.

She seized my elbow and gave it a furtive shake. "Don't go sneaking off," she said in an undertone, using her other hand to wave a cheery good-bye to Cynthia. "Father will be here in a few minutes, and he has asked in particular that you wait."

"Father here? Whatever for?"

"Oh, come off it, Flavia—you know as well as I do. It's cinema night, and Father was quite right—he said you'd try to dodge it."

She was correct on both counts. Although I had since put it out of my mind, Father *had* announced suddenly several weeks earlier that we didn't get out enough as a family—a situation that he intended to rectify by subscribing to the vicar's proposed cinema series in the parish hall.

And sure enough—here was Father now with Daffy, at the church door, shaking hands with the vicar. It was too late to escape.

"Ah, Flavia," the vicar said, "thank you for adding your voice to our little choir of angels, as it were. I was just telling your father how pleased I was to see Ophelia on the organ bench. She plays so well, don't you think? It's a treat to see her conducting the choir with such verve. 'And a little child shall lead them,' as the prophet Isaiah tells us . . . not, of course, that Ophelia's a little child, dear me, no!—far from it. But come away, the Bijou Cinema awaits!"

As we strolled through the churchyard towards the parish hall, I noticed Colin flitting from gravestone to gravestone, engaged apparently in some elaborate game of his own invention.

"I worry about that boy," I heard the vicar confiding to Father. "He has no parents, and now, with Brookie Harewood no longer around, as it were, to look out for him—but I'm chattering—ah, here we are . . . shall we go in?"

Inside, the parish hall was already uncomfortably warm. In preparation for the pictures, the blackout curtains had been drawn against the evening light, and the place was already filling with that humid fug that is generated by too many overheated bodies in a confined space.

I could distinguish quite clearly the many odors of Bishop's Lacey, among them the various scents and shaving lotions; of talcum powder (the vicar); of bergamot scent (the Misses Puddock), of rubbing alcohol (our neighbor Maximilian Brock); of boiled cabbage (Mrs. Delaney), of Guinness stout (Mr. Danby), and of Dutch pipe tobacco (George Carew, the village carpenter).

Since Miss Mountjoy, with her pervading odor of cod-liver oil, was nowhere in sight, I circulated slowly round the hall, sniffing unobtrusively for the slightest whiff of fish.

"Oh, hello, Mr. Spirling. It's nice to see you. (Sniff) How's Mrs. Spirling getting on with her crocheting? Gosh, it's such a lot of work, isn't it? I don't know where she finds the time."

In the center of the room, Mr. Mitchell, the proprietor of the photographer's shop in the high street, was grappling with writhing snakes of black cine film, trying to feed them into the maw of a projector.

I couldn't help but reflect that the last time I'd been in the parish hall, it had been on the occasion of Rupert Porson's final puppet performance—on this same stage—of Jack and the Beanstalk. Poor Rupert, I thought, and a delicious little shudder shook my shoulders.

But this was no time for pleasantries—I had to keep my nose to the grindstone, so to speak.

I rejoined Father, Daffy, and Feely just as the front row of houselights was being switched off.

I will not bother quoting the vicar's preliminary remarks about "the growing importance of film in the education of our young people," and so forth. He did not mention either Brookie's death or the attack upon Fenella, although this was perhaps neither the proper time or place to do so.

We were then plunged into a brief darkness, and a few moments later the first film flashed onto the screen—a black-and-white animated cartoon in which a chorus of horribly grinning cats in bowler hats bobbed up and down in unison, yowling "Ain't We Got Fun?" to the music of a tinny jazz band.

Mercifully, it did not last long.

In the brief pause, during which the lights came up and the film was changed, I noticed that Mrs. Bull had arrived with Timofey and her toddler. If she saw me among the audience, she did not let on.

The next film, *Saskatchewan: Breadbasket of the World*, was a documentary that showed great harvesting machines creeping across the flat face of the Canadian prairies, then rivers of grain being poured into railway hopper cars, and the open hatches of waiting cargo ships.

At the end of it I craned my neck for a glimpse of Colin Prout—yes, there he was at the very back of the hall, returning my gaze steadily. I gave him a little wave, but he made no response.

The third film, *The Maintenance of Aero Engines: Part III*, must have been something left over from the war—a film that was being shown simply because it happened to be in the same box as the others. In the light reflected from the screen, I caught Father and Feely exchanging puzzled glances before settling down to look as if they were finding it terrifically instructive.

The final feature on the program was a documentary called *The Versatile Lemon*, which, aside from the narrator's mentioning that lemons had once been used as an antidote to a multitude of poisons, was a crashing bore.

I watched it with my eyes shut.

THE NEW MOON WAS NO MORE THAN a sliver of silver in the sky as we made our way homeward across the fields. Father, Daffy, and Feely had got slightly ahead, and I trudged along behind them, immersed in my own thoughts.

"Don't dawdle, Flavia," Feely said, in a patient, half-amused voice that drove me crazy. She was putting it on for Father.

"Squid!" I said, warping the word into a sneeze.

twenty-four

MY SLEEP WAS TORN BY IMAGES OF SILVER. A SILVER HORSE IN a silver glade chewed silver grass with silver teeth. A silver Man in the Moon shone in the sky above a silver caravan. Silver coins formed a cross in a corpse's hand. A silver river glided.

When I awoke, my thoughts flew back at once to Fenella. Was she still alive? Had she regained consciousness? Porcelain claimed she had and the vicar said she hadn't.

Well, there was only one way to find out.

"SORRY, OLD GIRL," I said to Gladys in the gray dishwater light of the early morning, "but I have to leave you at home."

I could see that she was disappointed, even though she managed to put on a brave face.

"I need you to stay here as a decoy," I whispered. "When they see you leaning against the greenhouse, they'll think I'm still in bed."

Gladys brightened considerably at the thought of a conspiracy.

"If I look sharp, I can hare it cross-country and catch the first bus for Hinley this side of Oakshott Hill."

At the corner of the garden, I turned, and mouthed the words, "Don't do anything I wouldn't do," and Gladys signaled that she wouldn't.

I was off like a shot.

———

MIST HUNG IN THE FIELDS AS I flew across the plowed furrows, bounding gracefully from clod to clod. By catching the bus on a country road, I wouldn't be seen by anyone except those passengers who were already on board, none of whom would pose much risk of reporting me to Father, since they were all heading for destinations away from Bishop's Lacey.

Just as I climbed over the last fence, the Cottesmore bus hove into view, clattering and flapping its wings like a large, disheveled bird as it came jolting towards me along the lane.

It stopped with a rusty sigh, and a tendril of steam drifted up from its nickel radiator cap.

"Board!" said Ernie, the driver. "Step up. Step up. Mind your feet."

I handed him my fare and slipped into a seat three rows from the front. As I had suspected, there were few other riders at this time of day: a pair of elderly women who huddled together at the rear, too much in the grip of their own gossip to pay me the slightest bit of attention, and a farm worker in overalls with a hoe, who stared sadly out of the window at the darkly misty fields. Sunrise would not be for another quarter of an hour.

THE HOSPITAL AT HINLEY STOOD AT the end of a steep street that rose up precariously from behind the market square, its windows staring down glumly onto the black cobbles, which were still wet from the night's rain. Behind the high wrought-iron gate, a porter's lodge bore a sign written in no-nonsense letters: *All Visitors Please Report*.

Don't loiter, something told me, and I took its advice.

To the left, an archway of stained stone led to a narrow passage in which a couple of square gas lamps flickered with a sickly light.

Hearses Only, it said on a discreet plaque, and I knew I was on the right track.

In spite of my trying to walk in silence, my footsteps echoed from the wet cobbles and the seeping brick walls. At its far end, I could see that the passage opened into a small courtyard. I paused to listen.

Nothing but the sound of my own breathing. I peered cautiously round the corner—

"Beck!" said a loud voice, almost at my ear. I shrank back and flattened myself against the wall.

"Beck, get yourself out here. Quench's man will be along directly, and we want to have her ready to hand over. You know as well as I do what happens when we keep them waiting."

Ellis and Quench, I knew, was Hinley's largest and oldest undertaking firm, and was known far and wide for the shininess of its Rolls-Royce hearses and the gleam of its Daimler mourners' cars.

"When Ellis and Quench buries you, you're buried," Mrs. Mullet had once told me. I could easily believe that they would not like to be kept waiting.

"Old Matron gets her knickers in a knot," the voice went on, "if we're not all shipshape and Bristol fashion on the loading dock. And when old Matron's not happy, I'm not happy, and when I'm not happy, you're not happy. Beck? Get yourself out here, will you?"

There came the sound of boots shuffling on the timbers of the dock, and then a voice—a surprisingly young voice; perhaps a boy's voice—said: "Sorry, Mr. Martin. I forgot to tell you. They rang up about twenty minutes ago. Said they'd be round later. Had a call out to the Old Infirmary, they did."

"Oh, they did, did they? The buggers! Think nothing of leaving the likes of us twisting in the wind, whilst they go larking about the countryside in their bloody Bentleys. Well, I'm going down to the boiler room for a cup of tea, Quench or no Quench. Matron's up on Anson Ward with the latest crop of nursing sisters. Poor wee things—I hope they remembered their asbestos uniforms!"

I waited until I heard the heavy doors close, then quickly, before I could think better of it, scrambled up onto the loading dock.

"Blast!" I said under my breath, as a sliver of wood pierced my knee. I pulled the thing out and shoved it into my pocket so as not to leave any evidence behind. I dabbed at the oozing blood a bit with my handkerchief, but there was no time for compresses. It would have to do.

I took a breath, pulled open the heavy door, and stepped into a dimly lighted corridor.

The floors were marble, and the walls were painted—brown for the first four feet, then a ghastly green from there all the way up to the ceiling, which appeared to have been whitewashed in another century.

On my right were three small cubicles, one of which was occupied by a wheeled cart, upon which lay a sheeted figure. It took no great stretch of the imagination to guess what lay beneath. This was the real thing: the genuine article!

I was dying to undo the buckles on the straps and have a peek under the sheet, but there wasn't time.

Besides, there was part of me that didn't want to know if the body was Fenella's.

Not just yet. Not in that way.

From where I stood, I could see the full length of the corridor, which stretched away from me into the distance. It seemed endless.

I began to move slowly, putting one foot in front of another: right foot . . . left foot. On one side of the corridor was a double door marked "Laundry." From behind it came the muffled rumble of machinery and a woman laughing.

Left foot . . . right foot . . . toe to heel . . .

The next door was the kitchen: dishes clattering, voices chattering, and the powerful, clinging smell of greasy cabbage soup.

Soup for breakfast? I realized that I hadn't eaten since yesterday, and my stomach gave a heave.

For the next dozen paces, the walls were inexplicably moss green, and then, just as quickly, a queasy mustard yellow. Whoever had chosen the paint, I decided, wanted to ensure that anyone who wasn't sick when they entered the hospital jolly well would be before they left.

The next set of doors on the left, judging by the bracing whiff of formalin, belonged to the morgue. I gave a little shiver as I passed: not one of fear, but rather of delight.

Another room was marked "X-Ray," and beyond that point, open doors on both sides of the corridor, with room numbers on every one. In each room, someone was sleeping, or rolling over. Someone was snoring, someone moaned, and I thought I heard the sound of a woman crying.

These are the wards, I thought, *and there must be others on the first and second floors.*

But how could I find Fenella? Until then, I hadn't given it a moment's thought. How does one quickly find a needle in a haystack?

Certainly not by examining one straw at a time!

I had now arrived at a doorway that opened into a sort of large foyer, in the center of which a woman wrapped in a black woolen sweater was staring intently at a spread of playing cards on her desk. She did not hear me come up beside her.

"Excuse me," I said, "but you can put the five of diamonds on the black six."

The woman nearly fell out of her chair. She jumped to her feet and spun round to face me.

"Don't *ever*—" she said, her face going the color of beets. "Don't you *ever* dare—" Her fists clenched and unclenched spasmodically.

"I'm sorry if I startled you," I said. "I didn't mean to, really . . . "

"What are you doing here?" she demanded. "No visiting until one-thirty this afternoon, and it's only just gone—" She shot a glance at her watch, an impossibly tiny lump strapped to her wrist.

"I'm waiting for my cousin," I explained. "She's just slipped in to bring our grandmother some . . . "

I took a deep breath and wracked my brains for inspiration, but the only thing that came to mind—to my nostrils, actually—was the nauseating odor still leaking from the kitchen down the corridor.

"Soup!" I said. "We've brought our gram some soup."

"Soup?" The woman's voice—and her eyebrows—went up into an inverted V. "You've brought *soup*? *Here*? To a *hospital*?"

I nodded meekly.

"Who's your grandmother?" she demanded. "What's her name? Is she a patient here?"

"Fenella Faa," I said without hesitation.

"Faa? The Gypsy woman?" she asked, sucking in her breath.

I nodded dumbly.

"And your cousin, you say, has brought her *soup*?"

"Yes," I said, pointing haphazardly. "She went that way."

"What's your name?" the woman asked, snatching up a typewritten list from her desk.

"Flavia," I said. "Flavia Faa."

It was just implausible enough to be true. With a snort like a racehorse, the woman was off, down a wide corridor on the far side of the foyer.

I followed in her wake, but I don't think she noticed. Still, I kept well back, hoping she didn't turn round. I was in luck.

Without a backwards glance, she vanished into the second room but one on the left, and I heard the sound of curtains being swept open.

I didn't stop, but continued on past the open door. A single glance revealed Fenella in the farthest bed, her head swathed in bandages.

I ducked down out of sight behind a draped cart that was parked against the wall.

"All right, come out of there!" I heard the woman say, followed by the *click* of a door being opened—probably the room's W.C.

There was a silence—then a low, muttered conversation. Was she talking to Fenella—or to herself?

The only word that came clearly to my ears was "soup."

Another brief silence, and then the sound of the woman's shoes went echoing away down the corridor.

I counted to three, then flitted like a bat into Fenella's room, closing the door behind me. A whiff of ether told me that this must be the surgical ward.

Fenella was lying motionless on her back, her eyes closed. So frail, she looked—as if the bedsheets had absorbed the last ounce of her juices.

"Hello," I whispered. "It's me, Flavia."

There was no response. I reached out and took her hand.

Ever so slowly her eyes came open, fighting to focus.

"It's me, Flavia," I said again. "Remember?"

Her wrinkled lips pursed, and the tip of her tongue appeared. It looked like the head of a turtle emerging from its shell after a long winter at the bottom of the pond.

"The . . . liar," she whispered, and I grinned as stupidly as if I had just been awarded first prize at the spring flower show.

Licking her lips feebly, Fenella turned her head towards me, her black eyes now suddenly fierce and imploring in their sunken sockets.

"Sret," she said quite distinctly, giving my hand a squeeze.

"Sorry," I said, "I don't understand."

"Sret," she said again. "Puff."

A light went on at the back of my brain.

"Cigarette?" I asked. "Is that what you're saying?"

She nodded. "Sret. Puff."

"I'm sorry," I said, "I don't smoke."

Her eyes were fixed upon mine, imploring.

"Tell you what," I said. "I'll go find you one, but first, I need to ask you a couple of important questions."

I didn't give her time to think.

"The first is this: Do you really believe I did this to you? I'd die if you did."

Her brows knitted. "Did this?"

"Put you here—in the hospital. Please, Fenella, I need to know."

I hadn't meant to call her by her given name—it just slipped out. It was that kind of moment. Daffy had once told me that knowing and using someone's name gave you power over them.

There was no doubt that, at least for now, I had power over this poor injured creature, even if it was only the power to withhold a cigarette.

"Please, Fenella!" I pleaded.

If this was power, I wanted no part of it. It felt dreadful.

Without taking her eyes from mine, she moved her head slowly from side to side.

"No," she whispered at last, replying to my question.

No? It was not the answer I was expecting. If Fenella didn't think I had attacked her, then Porcelain had lied!

"Who was it, then?" I demanded in a voice so rough that it surprised even me. Had that savage snarl issued from my throat?

"Who was it? Tell me who did this to you!"

For some inexplicable reason, I wanted to seize her and shake the answer out of her. This was a kind of anger I had never known before.

Fenella was terrified. I could see it in her fuddled eyes.

"The *Red Bull*," she said, accenting each of the two words. "It was . . . the *Red Bull*."

The Red Bull? That made no sense at all.

"What's going on here?"

The voice came from the doorway. I spun round and found myself face-to-face with a nursing sister. It wasn't just the white uniform and stockings that made her seem so intimating: The blue cape with its red lining and piping had turned her into a human Union Jack.

"Flavia?"

The familiar voice took me by surprise.

It was Flossie Foster, the sister of Feely's friend Sheila!

"Flossie? Is it really you?"

I'd forgotten that Flossie had gone in for nursing. It was one of those trifles that had been mentioned at the dinner table by Feely, somewhere between the salad and the sausage rolls, and put out of mind before the plates were cleared away.

"Of course it's me, you goose. What on earth are *you* doing here?"

"I . . . ah . . . came to visit a friend," I said, making a sweeping gesture towards Fenella.

"But visiting hours aren't until this afternoon. If Matron catches you, she'll have your toes on toast."

"Listen, Flossie," I said. "I need a favor. I need a cigarette, and I need it quickly."

"Ha!" said Flossie, "I should have known! Feely's little sister is a tobacco fiend!"

"It's not like that at all," I said. "Please, Flossie—I'll promise you anything."

Flossie reached into her pocket and pulled out a packet of Du Mauriers and a monogrammed cloisonné lighter.

"Now light it," I told her.

Surprisingly, she did as she was told, although a little furtively.

"We only smoke in the nursing sisters' tea room," she said, handing me the cigarette. "And only when Matron's not around."

"It's not for me," I said, pointing to Fenella. "Give it to her."

Flossie stared at me. "You must be mad," she said.

"Go ahead, give it to her . . . or I'll tell Matron what you had in the hip flask at the vicar's garden party."

I was only teasing, but before I could shoot her a grin, Flossie had inserted the cigarette between Fenella's dry lips.

"You're a beast," she said. "An absolutely horrid little beast!"

I could tell she wanted to slap me, as I gave her a triumphant smirk.

But instead, we both of us broke off to look at Fenella. Her eyes were closed, and smoke was rising from her mouth in a series of puffs, like smoke signals from an Apache campfire. They might well have been spelling out the word "b-l-i-s-s."

It was at that very moment that Matron barged into the room.

In her elaborate cocked hat and starched white bib, she looked like Napoleon—only much larger.

She sized up the situation at a glance.

"Nurse Foster, I'll see you in my office."

"No, wait," I heard myself saying. "I can explain."

"Then do so."

"The nurse just stepped in to tell us that smoking is forbidden. It's nothing to do with her."

"Indeed!"

"I heard you coming," I said, "and stuck my cigarette into that poor woman's mouth. It was stupid of me. I'm sorry."

I snatched what was left of the cigarette from Fenella's lips and shoved it between my own. I took a deep drag and then exhaled, holding the thing between my second and third fingers in the Continental manner, as I had seen Charles Boyer do in the cinema, and all the while fighting down the urge to choke.

"Then how do you explain this?" Matron asked, picking up Flossie's lighter from Fenella's blanket, and holding it out accusingly towards me.

"It's mine," I said. "The *F* is for Flavia. Flavia de Luce. That's me."

I thought I detected a nearly imperceptible squint—or was it more of a wince?

"Of the Buckshaw de Luces?"

"Yes," I said. "It was a gift from Father. He believes that the occasional cigarette fortifies one's lungs against vapors from the drains."

The Matron didn't exactly gape, but she *did* stare at me as if I had suddenly sprouted a beak and tail feathers.

Then suddenly, and without warning, she pressed the lighter into my hands and wiped her fingers on her skirt.

There was the sound of professional shoe leather in the corridor, and Dr. Darby walked calmly into the room.

"Ah, Flavia," he said. "How nice to see you. This, Matron, is the young lady whose prompt action saved the life of Mrs. Faa."

I stuck out a hand so quickly that the old dragon was forced to take it.

"Pleased to meet you, Matron," I said. "I've heard so much about you."

twenty-five

"BUT HOW IS SHE?" I ASKED. "FENELLA, I MEAN—REALLY?"

"She'll do," said Dr. Darby.

We were motoring home to Bishop's Lacey, the doctor's Morris humming happily along between the hedgerows like a sewing machine on holiday.

"Fractured skull," he went on when I said nothing. "Depressed occipital condylar fracture, as we quacks call it. Has quite a ring to it, doesn't it? Thanks to you, we were able to get her into the operating room in time to elevate the broken bit without too much trouble. I think she'll likely make a full recovery, but we shall have to wait and see. Are you all right?"

He hadn't missed the fact that I was sucking in great deep breaths of the morning air, in an attempt to clear my system of cigarette smoke and the horrid odors of the hospital. The formalin of the morgue hadn't been too bad—quite enjoyable, in fact—but the reek of cabbage soup from the kitchen had been enough to gag a hyena.

"I'm fine, thank you," I said, with what I'm afraid was rather a wan smile.

"Your father will be very proud of you—" he went on.

"Oh, please don't tell him! Promise you won't!"

The doctor shot me a quizzical glance.

"It's just that he already has so much to worry about—"

As I have said, Father's financial distress was no secret in Bishop's Lacey, particularly to his friends, of whom Dr. Darby was one. (The vicar was the other.)

"I understand," the doctor said. "Then he shall not hear it from me.

"Still," he added with a chuckle, "the news is bound to get about, you know."

I could think of nothing but to change the subject.

"I'm rather puzzled about something," I said. "The police took Fenella's granddaughter, Porcelain, to see her in the hospital. She claims Fenella told her it was me who bashed her on the head."

"And did you?" the doctor asked slyly.

"Later," I said, ignoring his teasing, "the vicar told me that he, too, had paid a visit, but that Fenella had not yet regained consciousness. Which of them was telling the truth?"

"The vicar is a dear man," Dr. Darby said. "A very dear man. He brings me flowers from his garden now and then to brighten up my surgery. But if cornered, I would have to admit that sometimes, on the wards, we are forced to tell him fibs. Little lies in little white jackets. For the good of the patient, of course. I'm sure you understand."

If there was one thing in the world that I understood above all others, it was withholding selected snippets of the truth. It would not be an exaggeration to say that I was an Exalted Grand Master of the craft.

I nodded my head modestly. "He *is* very devoted to his work," I said.

"As it happens, I was present when both the granddaughter and the vicar came to the hospital. Although the vicar didn't get as far as her room, Mrs. Faa was fully conscious at the time of his visit."

"And Porcelain?"

"At the time of Porcelain's visit, she was not. The victims of skull fracture, you see, can slip in and out of consciousness as easily as you and I move from one room to another—an interesting phenomenon when you come right down to it."

But I was hardly listening. Porcelain had lied to me.

The witch!

There's nothing that a liar hates more than finding that another liar has lied to them.

"But why would she blame it on me?"

The words must have slipped out. I'd had no intention of thinking aloud.

"Ah," said Dr. Darby. "'There are more things in heaven and earth, Horatio, than are dreamt of in your philosophy.' Meaning that people can behave strangely in times of great stress. She's a complicated young woman, your friend Porcelain."

"She's no friend of mine!" I said rather abruptly.

"You took her in and fed her," Dr. Darby said with an amused look. "Or perhaps I misunderstood."

"I felt sorry for her."

"Ah. No more than sorry?"

"I wanted to like her."

"Aha! Why?"

The answer, of course, was that I was hoping to make a friend, but I could hardly admit that.

"We always want to love the recipients of our charity," the doctor said, negotiating a sharp bend in the road with a surprising demonstration of steering skill, "but it is not necessary. Indeed, it is sometimes not possible."

Suddenly I found myself wanting to confide in this gentle man—to tell him everything. But I could not.

The best thing for it when you feel tears coming on for no reason at all is to change the subject.

"Have you ever heard of the Red Bull?"

"The Red Bull?" he asked, swerving to avoid a terrier that had dashed out barking into the road. "Which Red Bull did you have in mind?"

"Is there more than one?"

"There are many. The Red Bull at St. Elfrieda's is the first that comes to mind."

A smile crept over his face, as if he was recalling a cozy evening of darts and a couple of pleasant pints of half-and-half.

"And?"

"Well, let me see . . . there was the Red Bull on a Green Field, from *Kim*, which was the god of nine hundred devils . . . the Red Bull of the Borgias, which was a flag, and was on a field of gold, not green . . . the notorious Red Bull playhouse that burned in the Great Fire of London in 1666 . . . there was the mythical Red Bull of England that met the Black Bull of Scotland in a fight to the death . . . and, of course, in the days when priests practiced medicine, they used to hand out the hair of a red bull as a cure for epilepsy. Have I missed any?"

Not one of these seemed likely to be the Red Bull that had attacked Fenella.

"Why do you ask?" he said, seeing my obvious puzzlement.

"Oh, no reason," I said. "It was just something I heard somewhere . . . the wireless, perhaps."

I could see that he didn't believe me, but he was gentleman enough not to press.

"Here's St. Tancred's," I said. "You can let me off at the churchyard."

"Ah," said Dr. Darby, applying the Morris's brakes. "Time for a spot of prayer?"

"Something like that," I said.

ACTUALLY, I NEEDED TO THINK.

Thinking and prayer are much the same thing anyway, when you stop to think about it—if that makes any sense. Prayer goes up and thought comes down—or so it seems. As far as I can tell, that's the only difference.

I thought about this as I walked across the fields to Buckshaw. Thinking about Brookie Harewood—and who killed him, and why—was really just another way of praying for his soul, wasn't it?

If this was true, I had just established a direct link between Christian charity and criminal investigation. I could hardly wait to tell the vicar!

A quarter mile ahead, and off to one side, was the narrow lane and the hedgerow where Porcelain had hidden in the bushes.

Almost without realizing it, I found my feet taking me in that direction.

If her claim about Fenella had been a lie, she couldn't really have been afraid of me, as she had pretended. There must, then, have been some other reason for her ducking into the hedgerow—one that I had not thought about at the time.

If that was the case, she had successfully tricked me.

I climbed over the stile and into the lane. It had been just about here that she'd slipped into the shrubbery. I stood for a moment in silence, listening.

"Porcelain?" I said, the hair at the back of my neck rising.

Whatever had made me think that she was still here?

"Porcelain?"

There was no answer.

I took a deep breath, realizing it could easily be my last. With Porcelain, you could always so quickly find yourself with a knife at your throat.

Another deep breath—this one for insurance purposes—and then I stepped into the hedgerow.

I could see at once that there was nobody hidden here. A slightly flattened area and a couple of trampled weeds indicated clearly where Porcelain had squatted the other day.

I crouched beneath the branches and wiggled myself into the same position that she must have assumed, putting myself in her shoes, looking out at the world as if from her eyes. As I did so, my hand touched something solid . . . something hard.

It was shoved inside a little tent of weeds. I wrapped my fingers round the object and pulled it into view.

It was black and circular, perhaps a little over three inches in diameter, and was made of some dark, exotic wood—ebony, perhaps. Carved into its circumference were the signs of the zodiac. I ran my forefinger slowly across the carved image of a pair of fish lying head to tail: Pisces.

The last time I had seen this wooden ring was at the fête. It had been on the table in Fenella's tent, supporting her crystal ball.

There was little doubt that Porcelain had pinched the ball's base from the caravan, and was making off with it when I had surprised her in the lane.

But why? Was it a souvenir? Did it have some sentimental attachment?

Porcelain was simply infuriating. Nothing that she did made any sense.

Finding the base reminded me that the ball itself, hidden safely away in plain sight among my laboratory glassware, was still awaiting careful study.

My intention had been to examine it for fingerprints, even though most traces had likely been washed away by immersion in the river. I remembered how Philip Odell, the wireless detective, had once pointed out to Inspector Hanley that the glandular secretions of the palms and fingers consisted primarily of water and water-soluble solids.

"So you see, Inspector," he had said, "Garvin's fatal mistake was in running his fingers through his hair. The barber had scented it with brilliantine containing bay oil, which, of course, is soluble in alcohol, but not in water. Even after a night at the bottom of the millstream, the fingerprints

*on the handle of the knife were still plain enough to put his villainous neck
in a noose."*

Philip Odell aside, I had my own ideas about underwater fingerprints.
There was, for instance, a quite readily available household substance
that would fix and harden any traces of residual grime that might be left
by a killer's hands. Given time, I would do the laboratory work, write it
up, and present it to Inspector Hewitt on a silver platter. He would, of
course, take my paper home at once and show it to his wife, Antigone.

But there had been no time. The compulsory cinema night and choir
practice at St. Tancred's, followed by my visit to Fenella in hospital, had
robbed me of the opportunity to carry out the necessary research.

I would hurry home and begin at once.

I had no more than one foot out of the thicket when I heard the
sound of an approaching motor. I ducked back into hiding, remembering
to turn my face away as the thing swept past. By the time I judged it safe
to come out again, the machine had vanished in the direction of
Buckshaw.

I DID NOT ACTUALLY SPOT the Inspector's blue Vauxhall until I had
already set foot between the griffins of the Mulford Gates. It was parked
off to one side beneath the chestnuts, and he was leaning patiently
against it, waiting.

Too late now to turn and bolt. I'd have to make the best of it.

"Oh, Inspector," I said, "I was just about to ring you up and tell you
what I've found!"

I was aware that I was gushing, but I didn't seem to be able to help
myself. I held the wooden base out to him at arm's length.

"This was in a thicket by the side of the lane. I think it's part of
Fenella's crystal ball."

He pulled a silk handkerchief from his breast pocket and took the
wooden O from my hands.

"You shouldn't have touched it," he said. "You ought to have left it
where it was."

"I realize that," I told him. "But it was too late. I touched it before I
saw it—without meaning to. It was hidden under some weeds. I'd just
stepped into the bushes for a moment . . ."

The look on his face told me that I was skating on thin ice: I had already used the "sudden call of nature" excuse, and it wouldn't bear repeating.

"You saw me, of course, didn't you? That's why you stopped and waited for me here."

The Inspector ignored this neat bit of deduction.

"Get in, please," he said, holding open the back door of the Vauxhall. "It's time for a talk."

Sergeant Graves turned round and shot me a quick, quizzical glance from the driver's seat, but he did not smile. Only then did I realize how much trouble I was in.

We drove to the front door of Buckshaw in silence.

IT WAS MY SECOND FULL CONFESSION in as many days.

We were sitting in the drawing room—all of us, that is, except Father, who was standing at the window, staring out, as if his life depended on it, across the ornamental lake.

He had insisted that we all of us be present, and had summoned Feely and Daffy, both of whom had annoyingly come at once, and were now seated primly side by side on a flowered divan like a couple of toads come to tea.

"It is regrettable," Inspector Hewitt was saying, "that our investigation has been so badly compromised. Crime scenes disturbed . . . evidence tampered with . . . crucial information withheld . . . I hardly know where to begin."

He was talking about me, of course.

"I have tried to impress upon Flavia the seriousness of these matters, but with little success. Therefore, I'm afraid I'm going to insist, Colonel de Luce, that until such time as our work is complete, you keep her confined to Buckshaw."

I couldn't believe my ears! Confined to Buckshaw? Why not have me transported to Australia and be done with it?

Well, so much for choir duty and future cinema nights. So much for Father's decree that we needed to get out more as a family.

Father mumbled something and shifted his gaze from the ornamental lake to the distant hills.

"That said," the Inspector went on, "we come to the real reason for our being here."

Real reason? My heart sank as if it already knew something that I did not.

The Inspector brought out his notebook. "A statement has been taken from a Miss Ursula Vipond, who says that she witnessed the removal from the river of what she described as . . . " He opened the notebook and flipped through a couple of pages. " . . . a glass sphere . . . "

My eyes widened.

" . . . by a child whose name she has reason to believe is Flavia de Luce."

Confound the woman! I knew at once that this busybody could be none other than that troll, Ursula, who haunted Vanetta Harewood's cottage in Malden Fenwick. I'd listed the odious creature in my notebook, but hadn't known her surname.

She'd been standing hidden among the bushes at the Palings, watching as I pulled Fenella's crystal ball from the river.

"Well?"

I could tell by his tone that the Inspector was becoming impatient.

"I was going to give it to you straightaway," I said.

"Where is it?" he asked.

"In my laboratory. I'll go get it and—"

"No! Stay as you are. Sergeant Graves will see to it."

Surprised, the sergeant broke off gazing at Feely and leapt to his feet.

"Just a moment, Sergeant," she said. "I'll show you the way."

The traitor! The minx! Even with her little sister under attack, Ophelia could think of nothing but courtship.

"Wait," I said. "The laboratory is locked. I'll have to go fetch the key."

Before anyone could think to stop me, I had swept past Feely and the sergeant, out the door, and was halfway down the hall.

The truth was that the key was in my pocket, but without turning me upside down and shaking me, they had no way of knowing that.

Up the stairs I dashed, taking them two at a time, as if all the demons of Hades were at my heels. Into the east wing I fled, and down the long corridor.

I fumbled at the lock of the laboratory, but something inside the mechanism seemed to be mucked up, as if—

I gave a fierce shove and the door flew open, propelling me almost into the arms of . . . Porcelain!

twenty-six

"WHAT ARE YOU DOING HERE?" I HISSED, MY HEART STILL pounding like a trip-hammer. "I thought you were in London."

"I might have been," Porcelain said, "but something made me come back to apologize."

"You did that once before," I said, "and you botched it. I can live without another of your so-called apologies."

"I know," she said, "and I'm sorry. I didn't tell you the truth about Fenella. She wasn't conscious when I went to the hospital. And she didn't tell me you'd attacked her. I made all of it up because I wanted to hurt you."

"But why?"

"I don't know. I wish I did, but I don't."

Suddenly she was in tears, sobbing as if her heart would break. Without thinking, I went to her, put my arms around her, and pulled her head against my shoulder.

"It's all right," I said, even though it wasn't.

But something inside me had undergone a sudden shift, as if my interior furniture had been rearranged unexpectedly, and I knew, with a strange new calmness, that we would sort things out later.

"Wait here until I come back," I said. "Father's expecting me downstairs, and I mustn't keep him waiting."

Which was true, as far as it went.

———

AS I WALKED BACK INTO THE drawing room, Sergeant Graves was still standing quite close to Feely, a look of disappointment on his face.

"I put it in this," I explained, handing Inspector Hewitt a square cardboard box, "so that there would be the least number of points in contact with the glass surface."

I did not explain that, because it was precisely the right size, I had pinched the box from Feely's bedroom, nor did I mention that I had flushed a pound of Yardley's lavender bath salts down the toilet for want of a better place to put it on short notice.

The Inspector lifted the top flap gingerly and glanced inside.

"You'll find a ring of faint smudges on the glass," I said. "Most likely whatever's left of the fingerprints—"

"Thank you, Flavia," he said in a flat voice, handing the box to Sergeant Graves.

" . . . and perhaps a few of mine," I added.

"Take this straightaway to Sergeant Woolmer, in Hinley," the Inspector said, ignoring my small joke. "Come back for me later."

"Yes, sir," Sergeant Graves said. "Hinley it is."

"Hold on a minute," I said. "There's more."

I carefully pulled one of Feely's embroidered handkerchiefs from my pocket.

"This," I said, "might well be a copy of the silver lobster pick that killed Brookie Harewood. Or perhaps it's the original. It's got the de Luce monogram on it. One of the Bull children was digging with it in the Gully. If there *are* any fingerprints on it besides his and mine, you'll quite likely find that they match the ones on the crystal ball."

I looked round the room to watch the reactions on everyone's faces as I handed the thing over to Inspector Hewitt.

As Mrs. Mullet once said, you could have heard a pin droop.

"Good lord!" Father said, stepping forward and reaching for the thing even as the Inspector was still unwrapping it.

I had almost blurted out that the rest of the family silver was on its way to Sotheby's, but something made me hold my tongue. What a bitter blow to Father it would have been had I let *that* slip out.

"Please, Colonel, don't touch it," the Inspector said. "I'm afraid this must now be treated as evidence."

Father stood staring at the silver lobster pick as if he were a snake that had come unexpectedly face-to-face with a mongoose.

Daffy sat bolt upright on the divan, glaring at me with what I took to be hatred in her eyes—as if she held me responsible for all of Father's misfortunes.

Feely's hand was at her mouth.

All of these details were frozen on the instant, as if a photographer's flash had gone off and preserved forever a thin and uncomfortable slice of time. The silence in the room was audible.

"Killed Brookie Harewood?" Inspector Hewitt said at last, turning to me. "This lobster pick? Please explain what you mean by that."

"It was in his nose," I said, "when I found his body hanging from the Poseidon fountain. Surely you saw it?"

Now it was the Inspector's turn to stare in disbelief at the object in his hand.

"You're quite sure?" he asked.

"Positive," I said, a little peeved that he should doubt me.

I could see that the Inspector was choosing his words carefully before he spoke.

"We found no lobster pick at the scene of the crime—and none has turned up subsequently."

No lobster pick at the scene of the crime? What a ludicrous statement! It was like denying the sun in the sky! The thing had been there, plain as day, stuck up Brookie's nostril like a dart in a corkboard.

If the pick had fallen out through force of gravity, for instance, the police would have found it in the fountain. The fact that they hadn't could mean only one thing: that someone had removed it. And that someone, most likely, was Brookie's killer.

Between the time Porcelain and I had walked away from the fountain, and the time that the police arrived—no more than, say, twenty minutes—the killer had crept back, scaled the fountain, and removed the weapon from Brookie's nose. But why?

The Inspector was still staring at me intently. I could see his cogs turning.

"Surely you don't think I killed Brookie Harewood?" I gasped.

"As a matter of fact, I don't," Inspector Hewitt said, "but something tells me that you know who did."

I didn't move a muscle, but inwardly I positively preened!

Fancy that! I thought. *Recognition at last!*

I could have hugged the man, but I didn't. He'd have been mortified, and so—but only later, of course—would I.

"I have my suspicions," I said, fighting to keep my voice from sliding into an upper register.

"Ah," the Inspector said, "then you must share them with us sometime. Well, thank you all. It has been most illuminating."

He summoned Sergeant Graves with his eyebrows, and went to the door.

"Oh, and Colonel," he said, turning back. "You *will* keep Flavia at home?"

Father did not reply, and for that, I decided on the spot, his name would be inscribed forever in my private book of saints and martyrs.

And then, with a rustle of officialdom, the police were gone.

"Do you think he likes me?" Feely asked, making a beeline for the looking glass on the chimneypiece.

"I should say so," Daffy replied. "He was all green eyes, like the monster cuttlefish in *Twenty Thousand Leagues Under the Sea.*"

With no more than a look of perplexity, Father left the room.

Within minutes, I knew, he would be submerged in his stamp collection, alone with whatever squids and cuttlefish inhabited the depths of his mind.

At that moment I remembered Porcelain.

IT DIDN'T COME EASILY TO ME to knock at the door of my own laboratory, but knock I did. No point in startling Porcelain and ending up with my throat slit from ear to ear.

But when I stepped inside, the laboratory was empty, and I felt my anger rising. Blast her! Hadn't I told her to stay where she was until I returned?

But when I opened my bedroom door, there she was, sitting cross-legged on my bed like a malnourished Buddha, reading my notebook.

It was too much.

"What do you think you're *doing*?" I shouted, running across the room and snatching the book from her hand.

"Reading about myself," she said.

I'll admit it: I saw red.

No, that's not quite true: I first saw white—a silent, brilliant white that erased everything—like the A-bombs that had been dropped on Hiroshima and Nagasaki. Only after this deadly burst of flower petals had begun to cool and fade, passing first from yellow through orange, did it at last simmer down to red.

I had been angry before, but this was like something ripped from the pages of the Book of Revelation. Could it be some secret fault in the de Luce makeup that was manifesting itself in me for the first time?

Until now, my fury had always been like those jolly Caribbean carnivals we had seen in the cinema travelogues—a noisy explosion of color and heat that wilted steadily as the day went on. But now it had suddenly become an icy coldness: a frigid wasteland in which I stood unapproachable. And it was in that instant, I think, that I began to understand my father.

This much was clear: I needed to get away—to be alone—until the tidal wave had passed.

"Excuse me," I said abruptly, surprising even myself, and walked out of the room.

I SAT FOR A WHILE ON THE STAIRS—neither up nor down.

It was true that Porcelain had violated my privacy, but my response had frightened me. In fact, I was still shaking a little.

I riffled idly through the pages of my notebook, not really focusing upon its written entries.

What had Porcelain been reading when I interrupted her? She had been reading about herself, or so she claimed.

I could hardly remember what I had written. I quickly found the spot.

PORCELAIN—Can't possibly be her grandmother's attacker since she was in London at the time. Or was she? I have only her word for it. But why did she feel compelled to wash out her clothing?

The answer to that remained a puzzle, but surely, if Porcelain had come back to do me in, she'd have done so by now.

As I closed the book, I remembered that at the time my last notes were made, I had not yet met the Pettibones. I had promised the Queen

Bee that I would bring her some papers from Buckshaw relating to Nicodemus Flitch and the Hobblers.

The fact that I had fabricated these juicy documents on the spur of the moment was really of no importance: with a library like Buckshaw's, there might very well be documents lurking that would satisfy the woman's obvious greed.

If the library was unoccupied, I could begin my search at once.

I was feeling better already.

I LISTENED WITH MY EAR GLUED to the door. If Daffy was inside reading, as she usually was, I could swallow a teaspoon of pride and ask her opinion, perhaps under cover of an insult, which almost always resulted in her taking the bait.

If that didn't work, there was always the Solemn Truce. Under these rules, I would, immediately upon entering the room, drop to one knee on the carpet and declare "Pax vobiscum," and if Daffy replied, "Et cum spiritu tuo," the cease-fire went into effect for a period of five minutes by the mantel clock, during which time neither of us was allowed to offer any incivility to the other.

If, on the other hand, she flung an inkwell, then the peace pipe was declined, and the whole thing was off.

But there was no sound from the other side of the panel. I opened the door and peeked round it.

The library was empty.

I stepped inside and closed the door behind me. For safety's sake, I turned the key in the lock and, although it probably hadn't been operated in the past hundred years, the bolt slid home in perfect silence.

Good old Dogger, I thought. He had a way of seeing that essentials were taken care of.

If anyone questioned me, I would claim that I was feeling somewhat peaked, and had hoped to have a nap without being disturbed.

I turned and had a good look round the library. It was simply ages since I'd been alone in this room.

The bookshelves towered towards the ceiling in strata, as if they had been formed geologically in stacks, by the upwards shifting of the earth.

Near the floor and closest to hand were the books that belonged to the present generation of de Luces. Above these, and just out of reach, were those that had been hoarded by the house's Victorian inhabitants, above which, piled to the ceiling, was the rubbish left behind by the Georgians: hundreds and hundreds of leather- and calf-bound volumes with thin worm-eaten pages and type so small it made your eyes go buggy.

I'd had a squint once before at some of these relics, but had found them devoted mainly to the lives and sermons of a bunch of dry old sticks who had lived and died while Mozart was still crawling around in diapers.

If ever there was a graveyard of religious biography, this was it.

I'd work methodically, I thought, one wall at a time, top of the north wall first, then top of the east wall, and so forth.

Books about dissenting clergymen were not exactly kept at one's fingertips at Buckshaw. Besides, I wasn't sure exactly what I was searching for, but I knew that I would likely find it nearer the ceiling.

I dragged the rolling library ladder into position and began my climb: up, up, up—my footing more precarious with every step.

Libraries of this design, I thought, *ought to be equipped with oxygen bottles above a certain height, in case of altitude sickness.*

Which made me think of Harriet, and a sudden sadness came over me. Harriet had scaled these very same bookcases once upon a time. In fact, it was stumbling upon one of her chemistry texts in this very room that had changed my life.

"Get on with it, Flave," said a strict-sounding voice inside me. "Harriet is dead, and you've got work to do."

Up I went, my head still cocked at an uncomfortable angle from reading titles on book spines at the lower levels. Fortunately, at this higher altitude, the older volumes had sensible, no-nonsense horizontal titles stamped deeply into their spines in gold-leaf letters, making them three-dimensional, and relatively easy to read in the perpetual twilight near the ceiling:

The Life of Simeon Hoxey; Notes on the Septuagint; Prayer and Penance; Pew's Thoughts Upon Godliness; Astronomical Principles of Religion Natural and Reveal'd; The Life and Opinions of Tristram Shandy, Gentleman; Polycarp of Smyrna; and so forth.

Just above these was *Hydraulicks and Hydrostaticks*, a relic, no doubt, of Lucius "Leaking" de Luce. I pulled the book from the shelf and opened it. Sure enough, there was Lucius's bookplate: the de Luce family crest, with his name written beneath it in a surprisingly childish hand. Had he owned the book when he was a boy?

The title page was almost completely covered with dense, inky calculations: sums, angles, algebraic equations, all of them more hurried than neat, crabbed, cramped, and rushing across the page. The entire book was somewhat rippled, as if it had once been wet.

A folded paper had been inserted between the pages which, when I opened it out flat, proved to be a hand-drawn map—but a map unlike any I had ever seen before.

Scattered upon the page were circles of various sizes, each joined to the others by lines, some of which radiated directly to their targets, while others followed more rectangular and roundabout paths. Some of the lines were thick; some thin. Some were single; others double; and a few were shaded in various schemes of cross-hatching.

At first I thought it was a railway map, so dense were the tracks—perhaps an ambitious expansion scheme for the nearby Buckshaw Halt, where trains had once stopped to put down guests and unload goods for the great house.

Only when I recognized the shape at the bottom of the map as the ornamental lake, and the unmistakeable outline of Buckshaw itself, did I realize that the document was, in fact, not a map at all, but a diagram: Lucius "Leaking" de Luce's plan for his subterranean hydraulic operations.

Interesting, I thought, *but only vaguely*. I shoved the paper into my pocket for future reference and resumed my search for books that might contain some mention of the Hobblers.

Sermons for Sailors; God's Plan for the Indies; Remains of Alexander Knox, Esq.

And suddenly there it was: *English Dissenters*.

I must say—it was an eye-opener!

I suppose I had been expecting a dry-as-dust account of hellfire parsons and dozing parishioners. But what I had stumbled upon was a treasure trove of jealousy, backbiting, vanity, abductions, harrowing midnight escapes, hangings, mutilations, betrayal, and sorcery.

Wherever there had been savage bloodshed in seventeenth- and eighteenth-century English history, there was sure to have been a Dissenter at the heart of it. I made a note to take some of these volumes up to my bedroom for a bit of horrific bedtime reading. They would certainly be more lively than *Wind in the Willows*, which had been languishing on my night-table since Aunt Felicity had sent it to me for Christmas, pretending to believe it was a history of corporal punishment.

With *English Dissenters* in hand, I climbed down the ladder, dropped into the upholstered wing-back chair that Daffy usually occupied, and began flipping through its pages in search of the Hobblers.

Because there was no index, I was forced to go slowly, watching for the word "Hobblers," trying not to become too distracted by the violence of the religious text.

Only towards the end of the book did I find what I was looking for. But then, suddenly, there it was, at the bottom of a page, in a footnote marked by a squashed-spider asterisk, set in quaint old-fashioned type.

"The mischief of Infant-baptism," it said, *"is an innovation on the primitive practice of the church: one of the corruptions of the second or third century. It is, moreover, often made the occasion of sin, or is turned into a farce as, for example, in that custom of the sect known as the Hobblers, whose dipping of a child held by the heel into running water, must be understood as no more than a bizarre, not to say barbaric, survival of the Greek myth of Achilles."*

It took several moments for the words to sink in.

Mrs. Mullet had been right!

twenty-seven

UP THE EAST STAIRCASE I FLEW, *ENGLISH DISSENTERS* CLUTCHED in my hand.

I couldn't contain myself.

"Listen to this," I said, bursting into my bedroom. Porcelain was sitting exactly as I had left her, staring at me as if I were a madwoman.

I read aloud to her the footnote on infant baptism, the words fairly tumbling from my mouth.

"So what?" she said, unimpressed.

"Mrs. Bull," I blurted out. "She lied! Her baby drowned! It had nothing to do with Fenella!"

"I don't know what you're talking about," Porcelain said.

Of course she didn't! I hadn't told her about the encounter with the enraged Mrs. Bull in the Gully. I could still hear those frightening, hateful words in my mind:

"*Gypsy! Gypsy! Clear off!*" she had screamed at Fenella. "*'Twas you as stole my baby. Tom, get out here! That Gypsy's at the gate!*"

Thinking to spare Porcelain's feelings, I skated quickly over the story of the Bull baby's disappearance, and of the furious outburst its mother had directed at Fenella in the Gully.

Mrs. Mullet's friend had told her the Hobblers dipped their babies by the heel, like Achilles in the River Styx. She didn't quite put it that way, but that's what she meant.

"So you see," I finished triumphantly, "Fenella had nothing to do with it."

"Of course she didn't," Porcelain scoffed. "She's a harmless old woman, not a kidnapper. Don't tell me you believe those old wives' tales about Gypsies stealing babies?"

"Of course I don't," I said, but I was not being truthful. In my heart of hearts I had, until that very minute, believed what every child in England had been made to believe.

Porcelain was becoming huffy again, and I didn't want to risk another outburst, either from her, or worse, from me.

"She's that redhead, then?" she said suddenly, bringing the topic back to Mrs. Bull. "The one that lives in the lane?"

"That's her!" I said. "How did you know?"

"I saw someone like that . . . hanging about," Porcelain said evasively.

"Where?" I demanded.

"About," she said, locking eyes with me, just daring me to stare her down.

The truth hit me like a slap in the face.

"Your dream!" I said. "It was her! In your dream you saw her standing over you in the caravan, didn't you?"

It made perfect sense. If Fenella really *could* see into the past and the future, and her daughter, Lunita, could impress the Air Ministry with her powers, there was no reason Porcelain couldn't summon up such an unpleasant woman in her sleep.

"It was like no dream I've ever had before," Porcelain said. "Oh, but God . . . I wish I'd never had it!"

"What do you mean?"

"It didn't seem like a dream. I'd fallen asleep on Fenella's bed—didn't even bother taking off my clothes. It must have been a noise that roused me—somewhere close—inside the caravan."

"You dreamed you'd fallen asleep?"

Porcelain nodded. "That was what was so horrible about it. I didn't move a muscle. Just kept taking deep quiet breaths, as if I was asleep, which I was, of course. Oh, damn! It's so hard to explain."

"Go on," I said. "I know what you mean. You were in my bed, dreaming you were in Fenella's bed."

She gave me a look of gratitude. "There wasn't a sound. I listened for a long time, until I thought they were gone, and then I opened my eyes—no more than a sliver, and . . . "

"And?"

"There was a face! A big face—right there—just inches away! Almost touching mine!"

"Good lord!"

"So close I couldn't really focus," Porcelain went on. "I managed to make a little moan, as if I was dreaming—let my mouth fall open a bit . . . "

I have to admit I was filled with admiration. I hoped that, even in a dream, I should have the presence of mind to do the same thing myself.

"The lamp was burning low," she went on. "It shone through the hair. I could only see the hair."

"Which was red," I said.

"Which was red. Long and curly. Wild, it was. And then I opened my eyes—"

"Yes, yes! Go on!"

"And it should have been your face I was looking at, shouldn't it? But it wasn't! It was that face of the man with the red hair. That's why I flew at you and nearly choked you to death!"

"Hold on!" I said. "The *man* with the red hair?"

"He was beastly . . . all covered with soot. He looked like someone who slept in a haystack."

I shook my head. In a weird way it made sense, I suppose, that in a dream, Porcelain should transform Mrs. Bull, whom she had perhaps glimpsed in the Gully, into a redheaded wild man. Daffy had not long before been reading a book by Professor Jung, and had announced to us suddenly that dreams were symbols that lurked in the subconscious mind.

Ordinarily, I should have written off the contents of a dream as rubbish, but my recent life seemed so flooded with inexplicable instances to the contrary.

In the first place, there had been Fenella's vision—in her crystal ball—of Harriet wanting me to help her come home from the cold, and even though Fenella had claimed that Feely and Daffy put her up to it, the whole thing had left me shaken; wondering, in fact, if her confession was not itself a lie.

Then, too, there had been Brookie's tale about the restless Gray Lady of Buckshaw. I still hadn't decided if he'd been having me on about the so-called legend, but there'd been simply no time to look into it on my own.

I must admit, though, that these nibblings of the supernatural at the base of my brain were more than a little unnerving.

"Why didn't you tell me this before?"

"Oh, I don't know, everything's so confusing. Part of me didn't trust you enough. And I knew that you no more trusted me."

"I wasn't sure about your clothes," I told her. "I wondered why you had to wash them in the river."

"Yes, you put that in your notebook, didn't you? You thought I might have been soaked with Fenella's blood."

"Well, I . . . "

"Come on, Flavia, admit it. You thought I'd bashed in Fenella's skull . . . to . . . to . . . inherit the caravan, or something."

"Well, it was a possibility," I said with a grin, hoping it would be infectious.

"The fact of the matter is," she said, giving her hair a toss, then winding and unwinding a long strand of it round a forefinger, "that women away from home sometimes feel the urge to rinse out a few things."

"Oh," I said.

"If you'd taken the trouble to ask me, I'd have told you."

Even if it wasn't meant as such, I took this as an invitation to ask blunt questions.

"All right," I said. "Then let me ask you this: When the man in the caravan was leaning over you in your dream, did you notice anything besides his hair?"

I thought I knew the answer, but I didn't want to put words in her mouth.

Porcelain knitted her brows and pursed her lips. "I don't think so—I . . . wait! There *was* something else. It was so ghastly I must have forgotten it when you woke me so suddenly."

I leaned forward eagerly.

"Yes?" I said. Already my pulse was beginning to race.

"Fish!" she said. "There was the most awful reek of dead fish. Ugh!"

I could have hugged her. I could have put my arm around her waist and—if it hadn't been for that curious stiffness in the de Luce blood that keeps me on an invisible tether—danced her round the room.

"Fish," I said. "Just as I thought."

Already, my mind was a flask at the boil, the largest bubbles being: Brookie Harewood and his reeking creel, Ursula Vipond and her decaying willow withies, and Miss Mountjoy with her lifetime supply of cod-liver oil.

The problem was this: Not a single one of them had red hair.

So far, the only redheads in my investigation were the Bulls: Mrs. Bull and the two little Bulls. The little ones were out of the question—they were far too young to have attacked Fenella or murdered Brookie.

Which left the obnoxious Mrs. B who, in spite of her other failings, did not, to the best of my knowledge, smell of fish. If she did, Mrs. Mullet couldn't have resisted mentioning it.

Fish or no fish, though, Mrs. Bull had an obvious grievance against Fenella, whom she believed to have kidnapped her baby.

But whoever left the fishy smell hanging about the caravan was not necessarily the same person who fractured Fenella's skull with the crystal ball.

And whoever had done *that* had not necessarily murdered Brookie.

"I'm glad I don't think as hard as you do," Porcelain said. "Your eyes go all far away and you look like someone else—someone older. It's quite frightening, actually."

"Yes," I said, even though this was news to me.

"I've tried to," she said, "but it just doesn't seem to work. I can't think who would want to harm Fenella. And that man—the one we found hanging from the fountain—whoever would want to kill *him*?"

That was the question. Porcelain had put her finger on it.

The whole thing came down to what Inspector Hewitt would call "motive." Brookie was an embarrassment to his mother and had stolen from Miss Mountjoy. As far as I knew, he had no connection with the Pettibones, other than the fact that he provided them with stolen goods. It would be odd indeed if those two old curios had murdered him. Without her husband's help, Mrs. Pettibone could never have manhandled Brookie's body into the position in which Porcelain and I had found it. Even *with* her husband's help—old Pettibone was so frail—they'd have needed a motorized crane.

Or the assistance of their friend Edward Sampson, who owned acres of rusting machinery in East Finching.

"I can think of only one person," I said.

"And who might that be?"

"I'm afraid I can't tell you."

"So much for trust," she said in a flat voice.

"So much for trust."

It hurt me to cut her off in that way, but I had my reasons, one of which was that she might be forced to spill the beans to Inspector Hewitt. I couldn't have anyone interfering when I was so close to a solution.

Another was that Brookie's killer and Fenella's attacker were still at large, and I couldn't possibly put Porcelain at risk.

She was safe enough here at Buckshaw, but how long could I keep her presence a secret?

That's what I was thinking about when there came a light tap on the door.

"Yes?" I called out.

A moment later, Father walked into the room.

"Flavia—" he began, then stopped in his tracks.

Porcelain leapt from the bed and backed towards the corner of the room.

Father stared at her for a moment, and then at me, then back at Porcelain again. "Excuse me," he said, "I didn't realize—"

"Father," I said, "I should like to introduce Porcelain Lee."

"How do you do?" Father said after an almost imperceptible pause, then sticking out his hand at once, rather than waiting for her to do so first. He was obviously flustered.

Porcelain came forward a couple of halting steps and gave him a single shake: up-down.

"Lovely weather we've been having," Father went on, "when it isn't raining, of course."

I saw my opportunity and I took it.

"It was Porcelain's grandmother, Mrs. Faa, who was attacked in the Gully," I said.

What seemed like an eternity of shadows fled across Father's face.

"I was saddened to hear of that," he said at last. "But I'm given to believe she's going to make a splendid recovery."

Neither of them knowing what to say next, they stood there staring fixedly at each other, and then Father said, "You'll join us for supper, of course?"

You could have knocked me down with a moth-eaten feather!

Dear old Father! How I admired him. Generations of breeding and his natural gallantry had turned what might have been a sticky situation into a perfect triumph, and my bedroom, rather than the anticipated field of battle, had suddenly become a reception chamber.

Porcelain lowered her eyelids to signal assent.

"Good!" Father exclaimed. "That's settled, then."

He turned to me. "Mrs. Mullet returned not ten minutes ago to retrieve her purse. Left it in the pantry. If she's still here, I'll ask her if she wouldn't mind—I believe she might still be in the kitchen."

And with that, he was gone.

"Crikey!" Porcelain said.

"Quick," I told her. "There's not a minute to lose! You'll probably want to have a wash-up and change into something more . . . fresh."

She'd been wearing Fenella's dowdy black outfit for days, and looked, to be perfectly frank, like a Covent Garden flower seller.

"My things won't fit you," I said, "but Daffy's or Feely's will."

I beckoned her to follow, then led her through the creaking upstairs corridors.

"That's Daffy's room," I said, pointing, when we reached the west wing of the house. "And that's Feely's. Help yourself—I'm sure they won't mind. See you at supper. Come down when the gong is struck."

I don't know what makes me do these things, but secretly, I could hardly wait to see how my sisters reacted when Porcelain came down for supper in one of their favorite frocks. I hadn't really had the chance to pay them back properly for the humiliation in the cellars. My jiggered looking glass had backfired horribly, but now, suddenly, out of the blue, dear old Fate had given me a second chance.

Not only that but Mrs. M had turned up unexpectedly in the kitchen, which presented a perfect opportunity to ask her the question that might well stamp this case "Closed."

I flew down the stairs and skipped into the kitchen.

Hallelujah! Mrs. Mullet was alone.

"Sorry to hear you forgot your purse," I said. "If I'd known sooner, I could have brought it to you. It would have been no trouble at all."

This was called "storing up credits," and it operated on the same principle as indulgences in the Roman Catholic Church, or what the shops in London called "the Lay-away Plan."

"Thank you, dear," Mrs. M said, "but it's just as well I come back. The Colonel's asked me to set a few things on the table, and I don't mind, really, seein' as it's Alf's lodge night, and I wouldn't have much to do anyway but knit and train the budgerigar. We're teachin' it to say 'Eee, it was agony, Ivy!' You should 'ear it, dear. Alf says it's ever so 'umorous."

As she spoke, she bustled about the kitchen, preparing to serve supper.

I took a deep breath and made the leap.

"Was Brookie Harewood a Hobbler?" I asked

"Brookie? I'm sure I couldn't tell you, dear. All I knows is, last time I seen 'im slinkin' round the church, I told the vicar 'e'd best lock up the communion plate. That's what I said: 'You'd best lock up the communion plate before it goes pop like a weasel.'"

"What about Edward Sampson? Do you know anything about him?"

"Ted Sampson? I should say I do! Reggie's half brother, 'e is, a reg'lar bad bun, that one. Owns that salvage yard in East Finchin', and Alf says there's more'n old tin goes through them gates. I shouldn't be tellin' you this, dear. Tender ears, and all that."

I was filling in the blanks nicely. Pettibone and Company, under cover of a quiet shop, an out-of-the-way salvage yard, and an eccentric religion, were operating an antiques theft and forgery ring. Although I had suspected this for some time, I had not seen, until now, how all of it fitted together.

Essentially, Brookie stole, Edward copied, and Reginald sold treasures removed from stately homes. The ingenious twist was this: After the original objects were copied, they were returned to their owners, so that they would seldom, if ever, be missed.

Or were the originals replaced with the copies? I had not yet had time to find that out, but when I did, I would begin by making a chemical analysis of Sally Fox and Shoppo's metallic content. I had originally intended to begin with the de Luce lobster pick I had found in the hands of Timothy—or was it really "Timofey"—Bull. But the demands on my time had made that impossible.

With his gob full of sweets, Timofey had been very difficult to understand.

I smiled as I recalled the child mucking in the lane.

"Danny's pocket," he had replied when I'd asked him where he got his pretty digger. In retrospect, he was almost cute.

"And Mrs. Bull, of course. Is she a Hobbler, too?"

"I couldn't say," Mrs. Mullet said. "I've been told Tilda Mountjoy was one of 'em, but I never heard it said that Margaret Bull was, even though them two is as thick as thieves! Them 'Obblers goes traipsin' round to one another's 'ouses of a Sunday to sing their 'ymns, and shout, and roll about on the floor as if they was tryin' to smother a fire in their unmentionables, and God knows what all else."

I tried to picture Miss Mountjoy rolling around on the floor in the grips of religious ecstasy, but my imagination, vivid as it is, was not up to it.

"They're a rum lot," Mrs. M went on, "but there's not a one of 'em would let Margaret Bull through their front gate. Not in a month o' Sundays! Not anymore."

"Why not?"

"Somethin' 'appened when that baby of 'ers got took. She was never the same after—not that she was much of a marvel before—"

"What about her husband?"

"Tom Bull? 'E took it real hard. Nearly killed 'im, they say. 'E went off not long after, and my friend Mrs. Waller said 'is wife told 'er, in confidence, mind, that 'e wouldn't be comin' back."

"Maybe he went off to find work. Dogger says a lot of men have done that since the end of the war."

"'E had work enough. Worked for Pettibone's brother-in-law."

"Ted Sampson?"

"The very one we was talkin' about. A foundryman, Tom Bull was, and a good one, so they say, even though 'e'd 'ad 'is troubles with the police. But when that baby girl o' 'is got took, somethin' 'appened, inside, like, and 'e went off 'is 'ead. Not long after, it were, 'e was up and gone."

How I longed to blurt out to her that the body of Tom Bull's baby daughter had been found in the Palings, but I dared not breathe a word. The news had not yet reached the village, and I didn't want to be accused of leaking information that the police would sooner keep to themselves—at least for the time being.

"You'd better run along and clean up for dinner, dear," Mrs. Mullet said suddenly, breaking in upon my train of thought. "The Colonel says you're 'avin company to supper, so 'e won't want to see dirty 'ands at the table."

I held my tongue. In ordinary circumstances, I should have lashed out against such an impertinent remark, but today I had a new weapon.

"Quite right, Mrs. M," I heard myself saying, as I trotted instantly and obediently to the door.

Here I paused, turned dramatically, and then in my best innocent-as-a-lamb voice, said, "Oh, by the way, Mrs. Mullet, Vanetta Harewood showed me her portrait of Harriet."

The clatter of dishes stopped, and for a few moments there was a stony silence in the kitchen.

"I knew this day would come," Mrs. Mullet said suddenly in an odd voice; the voice of a stranger. "I've been 'alf expectin' it."

She collapsed suddenly into a chair at the table, buried her face in her apron, and dissolved into a miserable sobbing.

I stood by helplessly, not quite knowing what to do.

At last, I pulled out the chair opposite, sat down at the table, and watched her weep.

I had a special fascination with tears. Chemical analyses of my own and those of others had taught me that tears were a rich and a wonderful broth, whose chief ingredients were water, potassium, proteins, manganese, various yeasty enzymes, fats, oils, and waxes, with a good dollop of sodium chloride thrown in, perhaps for taste. In sufficient quantities, they made for a powerful cleanser.

Not so very different, I thought, *from Mrs. Mullet's chicken soup*, which she flung at even the slightest sniffle.

By now, Mrs. M had begun to subside, and she said, without removing the apron from her face: "A gift, it was. She wanted it for the Colonel."

I reached out across the table and placed my hand on her shoulder. I didn't say a word.

Slowly, the apron came down, revealing her anguished face. She took a shuddering breath.

"She wanted to surprise 'im with it. Oh, the trouble she went to! She was ever so 'appy. Bundlin' up you lot of angels and motorin' over to Malden Fenwick for your sittin's—'avin' that 'Arewood woman come 'ere to Buckshaw whenever the Colonel was away. Bitter cold, it was. Bitter."

She mopped at her eyes and I suddenly felt ill.

Why had I ever mentioned the painting? Had I done it for no reason other than to shock Mrs. Mullet? To see her response? I hoped not.

"'Ow I've wanted to tell the Colonel about it," Mrs. Mullet went on quietly, "but I couldn't. It's not my place. To think of it lyin' there in 'er studio all these years, an' 'im not knowin' it—it breaks my 'eart. It surely does—it breaks my 'eart."

"It breaks mine, too, Mrs. M," I said, and it was the truth.

As she pulled herself to her feet, her face still wet and red, something stirred in my memory.

Red.

Red hair . . . Timofey Bull . . . his mouth stuffed with sweets and the silver lobster pick in his hand.

"Danny's pocket," he'd said, when I asked him where he got it. "Danny's pocket."

And I had misheard him.

Daddy's pocket!

Red and silver. This was what my dreams and my good sense had been trying to tell me!

I felt suddenly as if a snail were slowly crawling up my spine.

Could it be that Tom Bull was still in Bishop's Lacey? Could he still be living secretly amid the smoke that blanketed his house in the Gully?

If so, it might well be *he* who'd been outside smoking as I crept with Gry past his house in the dark. Perhaps it was *he* who had watched from the wood as Inspector Hewitt and his men removed Brookie's body from the Poseidon fountain—he who had removed the pick from Brookie's nose when Porcelain and I—

Good lord!

And Timofey had found the lobster pick in his father's pocket, which could only mean—

At that very instant, the gong in the foyer was rung, announcing supper.

"Better get along, dear," Mrs. Mullet said, poking at her hair with a forefinger and giving her face a last swipe with her apron. "You know what your father's like about promptness. We mustn't keep 'im waitin'."

"Yes, Mrs. Mullet," I said.

twenty-eight

THE HOUSEHOLD HAD BEEN SUMMONED, AND WE ALL OF US stood waiting in the foyer.

I understood at once that Father had decided to make an occasion of Porcelain's presence in the house, perhaps, I thought, because he felt remorse for the way in which he had treated her grandparents. He still did not know, of course, about the tragic death of Johnny Faa.

I stood at the bottom of the stairs, a little apart from the others, taking in, as if for the first time, the sad splendor of the de Luce ancestral home.

There had been a time when Buckshaw rang with laughter, or so I'd been told, but quite frankly, I could not even imagine it. The house seemed to hold itself in stiff disapproval, reflecting only the sound of whispers—setting dim but rigid limits on the lives of all of us who lived within its walls. Other than Father's gorgon sister, Aunt Felicity, who made annual expeditions in order to berate him, there had been no guests at Buckshaw for as long as I could remember.

Daffy and Feely stood with annoyingly perfect posture on either side of Father, both of them scrubbed to disgusting perfection, like the well-bred but rather dim daughters of the local squire in a drawing-room drama. Just wait till they saw Porcelain!

To one side, Dogger hovered, nearly invisible against the dark paneling, save for his white face and his white hair—like a disembodied head afloat in the gloom.

Glancing at his military wristwatch, Father made a slight involuntary frown, but covered it nicely by pulling out his handkerchief and giving his nose an unconvincing blow.

He was nervous!

We stood there in silence, each of us staring off in a different direction.

Precisely fifteen minutes after the gong had sounded, a door closed somewhere above, and we focused our attention upon the top of the staircase.

As Porcelain appeared, we gasped collectively, and Mrs. Mullet, who had just come from the kitchen, gave out a cry like a small nocturnal animal. I thought for a moment she was going to bolt.

Porcelain had not chosen from Daffy's or Feely's wardrobe. She was dressed in one of my mother's most memorable outfits: the knee-length, flame-colored dress of orange silk chiffon that Harriet had worn to the Royal Aero Society Ball the year before her final journey. A photograph had been taken by the *Times* that evening as Harriet arrived at the Savoy—a photograph that created a stir that to this day has never been quite forgotten.

But it wasn't just the dress: Porcelain had pulled her hair back in the same way that Harriet had done when she was riding to the hounds. She must have copied the style from the black-and-white photo on Harriet's desk.

Because I had rifled my mother's jewel box myself from time to time, I recognized at once the antique amber necklace that lay against Porcelain's surprisingly well-developed bosom, and the stones that glittered on her fingers.

Harriet's—all of them Harriet's!

Porcelain paused on the top step and looked down at us with what I took at the time to be shyness, but later decided might well have been contempt.

I must say that Father behaved magnificently, although at first, I was sure he was going to faint. As Porcelain began her long, slow descent, his jaw muscles began tightening and loosening reflexively. As with most military men, it was the only permissible show of emotion, and as such, it was at once both nerve-wracking and deeply endearing.

Down and down she came towards us, floating on the air like some immortal sprite—a pixy, perhaps, I thought wildly. Perhaps Queen Mab herself!

As she neared the bottom, Porcelain broke into the most heartbreaking smile that I have ever seen on a human face: a smile that encompassed us all and yet, at the same time, managed to single out each one of us for particular dazzlement.

No queen—not even Cleopatra herself—had ever made such an entrance, and I found myself gaping in openmouthed admiration at the sheer audacity of it.

As she swept lightly past me at the bottom of the stairs, she leaned in close upon my neck, her lips almost brushing my ear.

"How do I look?" she whispered.

All she needed was a rose in her teeth, but I hardly dared say so.

Father took a single step forward and offered her his arm.

"Shall we go in to dinner?" he asked.

"MACAROONS!" PORCELAIN SAID. "How I love them!"

Mrs. Mullet beamed. "I shall give you the recipe, dear," she said. "It's the tinned milk as gives 'em the extra fillet."

I nearly gagged, but a few deft passes of my table napkin provided a neat distraction.

Daffy and Feely, to give them credit, had—apart from their initial goggling—seemed not to have turned a hair at Porcelain's borrowed costume, although they couldn't take their eyes off her.

At the table, they asked interesting questions—mostly about her life in London during the war. In general, and against all odds, my sisters were charming beyond belief.

And Father . . . dear Father. Although Porcelain's sudden appearance in Harriet's wardrobe must have shocked him deeply, he managed somehow to keep a miraculously tight grip on himself. In fact, for a few hours, it was as if Harriet had been returned to him from the dead.

He smiled, he listened attentively, and at one point he even told rather an amusing story about an old lady's first encounter with a beekeeper.

It was as if, for a few hours, Porcelain had cast a spell upon us all.

There was only one awkward moment, and it came towards the end of the evening.

Feely had just finished playing a lovely piano arrangement of Antonín Dvorak's *Gypsy Songs, Opus 55: Songs My Great-Grandfather Taught Me*, one of her great favorites.

"Well," she asked, getting up from the piano and turning to Porcelain, "what do you think? I've always wanted to hear the opinion of a *real* Gypsy."

You could have cut the silence with a knife.

"Ophelia . . . " Father said.

I held my breath, afraid that Porcelain would be offended, but I needn't have worried.

"Quite beautiful in places," she said, giving Feely that dazzling smile. "Of course I'm no more than half-Gypsy, so I only enjoyed every other section."

"I THOUGHT SHE WAS GOING TO leap over the piano stool and scratch my eyes out!"

We were back upstairs in my bedroom after what had been, for both of us, something of an ordeal.

"Feely wouldn't do that," I said. "At least, not with Father in the room."

There had been no mention of Brookie Harewood, and apart from a polite enquiry by Father ("I hope your grandmother is getting on well?"), nothing whatever said about Fenella.

It was just as well, as I didn't fancy having to answer inconvenient, and perhaps even embarrassing, questions about my recent activities.

"They seem nice, though, your sisters, really," Porcelain remarked.

"Ha!" I said. "Shows what little you know! I hate them!"

"Hate them? I should have thought you'd love them."

"Of course I love them," I said, throwing myself full length onto the bed. "That's why I'm so good at hating them."

"I think you're having me on. What have they ever done to you?"

"They torture me," I said. "But please don't ask me for details."

When I knew that I had gained her undivided attention, I rolled over onto my stomach so that I couldn't see her.

Talking to someone dressed in my mother's clothing was eerie enough, without recounting to her the tortures my sisters had inflicted upon me.

"Torture you?" she said. "In what way? Tell me about it."

For a long while there was only the sound of my brass alarm clock ticking on the bedside table, chopping the long minutes into manageable segments.

Then, in a rush, it all came spilling out. I found myself telling her about my ordeal in the cellars: how they had lugged me down the stairs, dumped me on the stone floor, and frightened me with horrid voices; how they had told me I was a changeling, left behind by the pixies when the real Flavia de Luce was abducted.

Until I heard myself telling it to Porcelain, I had no idea how badly shaken the ordeal had left me.

"Do you believe me?" I asked, desperate, somehow, for a "yes."

"I'd like to," she said, "but it's hard to imagine such ladylike young women operating their own private dungeon."

Ladylike young women? I'm afraid I almost uttered a word that would have shocked a sailor.

"Come on," I said, leaping to my feet and tugging at her arm. "I'll show you what ladylike young women get up to when no one is looking."

"COR!" PORCELAIN SAID. "It's a bloody crypt!"

In spite of an occasional electric bulb strung here and there on frayed wiring, the cellars were a sea of darkness. I had brought from the pantry the pewter candlestick that was kept for those not infrequent occasions when the current failed at Buckshaw, and I held it above my head, moving the flickering light from side to side.

"See? There's the sack they threw over my head."

"And look," I said, holding the candle down close to the flagstones. "Here are their footprints in the dust."

"Seems like rather a lot of them for a couple of ladylike young women," Porcelain said skeptically. "Rather large, too," she added.

She was right. I could see that at once.

Distinct footprints led off into the darkness, too big to be Daffy's or mine or Feely's, which mingled near the bottom of the stairs. Nor were they Father's: He had not come all the way down the steps, and even if he had, his leather-soled shoes left distinct impressions with which I was quite familiar.

Dogger's footprints, too, were unmistakeable: long and narrow, and placed one in front of the other with the precision of a red Indian.

No, these were not Father's footprints, nor were they Dogger's. If my suspicions were correct, they had been made by someone wearing rubber boots.

"Let's see where they go," I said.

Porcelain's presence bucked up my bravery no end, and I was ready to follow the prints to wherever they might take us.

"Do you think that's wise?" she asked, the whites of her eyes flashing in the light of the candle. "No one knows we're down here. If we fell into a pit or something, we might die before anyone found us."

"There are no pits down here," I said. "Just a lot of old cellars."

"Are you sure?"

"Of course I'm sure. I've been down here hundreds of times."

Which was a lie: Prior to my inquisition, I had been in the cellars just once, with Dogger, when I was five, hunting for a pair of eighteenth-century alabaster urns that had been put away at the beginning of the war to protect them from possible air raids.

Candle held high, I set off along one of the black passageways. Porcelain could either follow, or stay where she was in the dark shadows between the widely spaced electric bulbs.

Needless to say, she followed.

I had already formed the theory that the footprints had been made by Brookie Harewood—the *late* Brookie Harewood—but there was no point in mentioning this to Porcelain, who would probably get the wind up at the very idea of following in a dead man's footsteps.

But what on earth could Brookie have been doing in the Buckshaw cellars?

"Poachers know all the shortcuts," Father had once said, and again, he was probably right.

As we passed under a low brick archway, I let my mind fly back to the night I had caught Brookie in his midnight prowl of the drawing room. It was hard to believe that had been only five days ago.

I still had a perfect mental image of our strange interview, which had ended with Brookie warning me against housebreakers who might have their eyes on Father's silver. "Lot of that going on nowadays, since the war," he had said.

And then I had opened one of the French doors and made it quite clear that I wanted him to leave.

No—wait!—I had first *unlocked* the door!

The door had been *locked* when I entered the drawing room. And there was no earthly reason to believe that Brookie had locked it behind him if he had broken into the house from the terrace. He'd have wanted it ready for a quick escape, had he been in danger of being caught.

It was reasonable, therefore, to assume that Brookie had gained entry to the house by some other route: through the cellars, for instance.

And the footprints now before us, disappearing into the darkness—quite clear impressions of a fisherman's gum boots, now that I stopped to think about it—suggested that my assumption was correct.

"Come on," I said, sensing that Porcelain was hanging back. "Stay close behind me."

I thought I heard a little whimper, but I may have been wrong.

We had passed the end of the string of electric lights, and were now in an arched passageway lined on both sides with piles of decaying furniture. Here the footprints—more than one set of them, but all made by the same pair of boots—revealed that they had ventured more than once into, and out of, Buckshaw. The most recent prints were razor sharp, while the older impressions were softened slightly by the incessant sifting of dust.

"What's that?" Porcelain cried, seizing my shoulder with a painful grip.

Ahead of us, a shrouded object half blocked the passage.

"I don't know," I said.

"I thought you'd been down here hundreds of times," she whispered.

"I have," I told her, "but not in this particular passage."

Before she could question me, I reached out, took hold of the corner of the sheet, and yanked it away.

A cloud of dust went billowing up, blinding us both—making us choke as if we had been caught in a sudden sandstorm.

"Oooh!" Porcelain wailed.

"It's only dust," I said, even though I was stifling.

And then the candle guttered—and went out.

I gave a silent curse and felt in my pocket.

"Hold this," I said, finding her hands in the darkness and wrapping her fingers round the candlestick. "I'll have it going in a jiff."

I dug deeper into my pocket. Drat!

"Bad luck," I said. "I think I left the matches in the pantry."

I felt the candlestick being shoved back into my hands. After a brief moment, there was a scraping sound, and a match flared up brightly.

"Good job I thought to pick them up, then," Porcelain said, applying the match to the candle. As the flame grew taller and more steady, I could see the object over which the sheet had been draped.

"Look!" I said. "It's a sedan chair."

The thing looked like an early closed-in motorcar whose wheels had been stolen. The wood paneling was painted light green with hand-drawn flowers clustered in the corners. The gold medallion on the door was the de Luce crest.

Inside the chair, fleur-de-lis wallpaper had peeled away and hung down in tongues upon the green velvet padding of the seat.

There was an odd musty smell about the chair, and it wasn't just mice.

To think that some of my own ancestors had sat in this very box and been borne by other humans through the streets of some eighteenth-century city!

I wanted nothing more than to climb inside and become part of my family's history. Just to sit, and nothing more.

"This is owned by a woman," Porcelain said in a slow, strange voice that sounded, more than anything, like an incantation. "Silk dress . . . powdered wig . . . white face, and a black spot—like a star—on her cheek. She wants—"

"Stop it!" I shouted, spinning round to face her. "I don't want to play your stupid games."

Porcelain stood perfectly still, staring, black eyes shining madly out of her white face. She was entirely covered with dust, Harriet's flame-colored dress now faded to an ashen orange in the light of the flickering candle.

"Look at you," she said in a voice that sounded to me accusing. "Just look at you!"

I couldn't help thinking that I was in the presence of my mother's ghost.

At that moment, a metallic *clang* came from the passageway ahead, and both of us jumped.

It sounded like iron on iron: chains being dragged through the bars of a cage.

"Come on," Porcelain said, "let's get out of here."

"No, wait," I said. "I want to find out what's down here."

She snatched the candlestick from my hand and began to move quickly back towards the stairs.

"Either come back with me, or stay here alone in the dark."

I had no choice but to follow.

twenty-nine

THE FLAME COLOR BEGAN TO BRIGHTEN AS SOON AS I SHOVED the material into the beaker.

"See?" I said. "It's working."

"What is that stuff?" Porcelain asked.

"Dry-cleaning fluid," I said, giving Harriet's dress a poke with a glass rod, and stirring gently. "Carbon tetrachloride, actually."

I couldn't say its name without recalling, with pleasure, that the stuff had first been synthesized in 1839 by a Frenchman named Henri-Victor Regnault, a one-time upholsterer who had produced carbon tetrachloride through the reaction between chlorine and chloroform. One of the early uses of his invention had been to fumigate barrels of food in which various unpleasant insects had taken up residence; more recently, it had been used to charge fire extinguishers.

"Father uses it to scrutinize watermarks on postage stamps," I said.

I did not mention that I had recently liberated the bottle from one of his storage cupboards for an experiment involving houseflies.

"Look at the dress. See how clean it is already? A few more minutes and it will be as good as new."

Porcelain, who had wrapped herself in one of my old dressing gowns, looked on in awe.

I had changed into a cleanish dress and left the dusty one soaking in one of the laboratory's sinks. Later, I would hang it from one of the gas chandeliers to dry.

"You de Luces are a strange lot," Porcelain said.

"Ha! Less than an hour ago you thought that at least two of us were ladylike young women."

"That was before you showed me the cellars."

I noted that our little tour of the Chamber of Horrors had changed her mind.

"Speaking of cellars," I told her, "I'm not easily frightened, but I didn't much care for that stuff about the lady who owned the sedan chair."

"It wasn't stuff. I was telling you what I saw."

"Saw? You're asking me to believe that you saw a woman in a powdered wig and a silk dress?"

For someone with a scientific mind, like me, this was hard to swallow. I had still not decided what to make of Brookie Harewood's Gray Lady of Buckshaw, or Fenella's cold woman who wanted to come home from the mountain. To say nothing of the pixies. Did everyone take me for a gullible fool, or were there really other worlds just beyond our range of vision?

"In a way, yes," Porcelain said. "I saw her with my mind."

This I could understand—at least a little. I could see things with my own mind: the way, for instance, that trimethylamine could be produced by allowing *Bacillus prodigiosus* to grow on a sample of Mrs. Mullet's mashed potatoes in the heat of a summer afternoon. The resulting blood-red specks—which were known in the Middle Ages as "Wunderblut," or "strange blood," and which for a whole week in 1819 had appeared on various foods at Padua—would release not only the smell of ammonia, but also the unmistakeable odor of trimethylamine.

When you come right down to it, I suppose, there is no great difference between ghosts and the invisible worlds of chemistry.

I was glad I had remembered dear old trimethylamine: my chemical friend with the fishy smell. I had discussed it with Dogger several days ago and formed certain opinions which I had been prevented from acting upon.

It was time now to pick up the threads and follow them, wherever they might lead.

"I'm tired," I told Porcelain, yawning vastly.

Five minutes later we were tucked up in bed, one of us drifting rapidly towards oblivion.

I WAITED UNTIL SHE WAS ASLEEP, then slipped quietly out of bed.

It was just past midnight when I eased shut my bedroom door and crept silently down the curving staircase.

I remembered that Dogger kept a high-powered torch in the butler's pantry for what he called "midnight emergencies," and it took only a moment to find it.

No frail candle this time, I thought: I had at my fingertips sufficient power to light up the Palace Pier at Brighton. I hoped it would be enough.

The cellars seemed colder than I had remembered. I should have worn a sweater, but it was too late now.

I was quickly at the point where the electric bulbs ended: beyond them, a cavernous blackness that led—who knew where?

I switched on the torch and pointed it along the passageway. Far ahead, I could see the outline of the sedan chair. I no longer relished the thought of climbing into the thing and recalling days gone by; in fact, I would be relieved to get past it.

"There is no lady," I said aloud, and to my relief, there wasn't.

Ahead, the passage took a slight shift to the right. Since I had essentially set off to the right from the bottom of the kitchen stairs, I was heading east—now a little southeast, towards the Visto and the Poseidon fountain.

The gum-boot footprints were easy to follow now, no longer overprinted with Porcelain's and mine. There were several sets, I noted, three coming and two going. If, as I suspected, they were Brookie's, he had made his first trip to steal one of the firedogs, his second to return it and make off with the second. On his last visit he had left by way of the French doors.

A sudden cold draft swept past me. Good job I'd brought the torch—the candle would certainly have blown out.

With the draft came a dark and a dank odor: an odor I could not at once identify, but one which suggested the reservoirs of neglected water closets: green corrosion with more than a whiff of zinc.

Well, I thought, *I'm not afraid of zinc, and green corrosion is something that has always interested me.*

I pushed on.

When I had been down here earlier with Porcelain, I had heard a definite metallic *clank*, but now the passage—which had begun to narrow—was as silent as the tomb.

In front of me was an archway with an open door, beyond which, or so it seemed, was a room.

I took two careful steps down into the chamber and found myself surrounded on all sides with metal pipes: zinc pipes, lead pipes, iron pipes, bronze pipes, copper pipes; pipes running up, down, and across, all interconnected with right elbows and great metal bolts with here and there a huge valve like the steering wheel of a motorcar.

I was at the very heart of Lucius de Luce's subterranean waterworks!

And then I heard it—a metallic clanking that echoed round and round the chamber.

I'll admit it—I froze.

Another *clank*.

"Hello," I called, my voice shaking. "Is anyone there?"

From somewhere came another sound: an animal sound for certain, though whether it was human, I could not tell.

What if a fox had made its way into the tunnel? Or a badger?

If that was the case, it would likely run away from a human with a torch—but what if it didn't?

"Hello?" I called again. "Is anyone there?"

Again a muffled sound, weaker. Was it farther away, or was I imagining things? One thing was certain: It could only be coming from somewhere behind a giant pipe that rose up out of the stonework, leveled off, bent ninety degrees, and headed off towards the far side of the chamber.

I scrambled up onto the thing, straddled it for a moment—then dropped down on the other side.

The passageway into which the pipe led was lower, narrower, and damp. Moisture beaded on the walls, and the floor, between bricks, was wet earth.

Just ahead, the tunnel was blocked by an iron gate: an iron gate that was chained shut and locked on the other side with a large, old-fashioned padlock.

I gave the thing a rattle, but it was absolutely solid. Without a key, there wasn't a hope of getting past.

"Damn!" I said. "Damn and double damn!"

"Flavia?" someone croaked.

I must admit that I came very close to disgracing myself.

I shone the beam through the bars and picked out a shape huddled on the ground.

For as long as I live I shall never forget his white face staring up at me, blinded by the torch's beam. He had managed, somehow, to lose his spectacles, and his pale eyes, blind and blinking, were those of a baby mole pulled from its hole and dragged out suddenly into the daylight.

"Colin?" I said. "Colin Prout?"

"Turn it off!" he pleaded in a ragged voice, twisting away from the light.

I swung the torch away, so that the passage beyond the bars was once more in near-darkness.

"Help me," Colin said, his voice pitiful.

"I can't. The gate is locked."

I gave the massive thing a shake with one hand, hoping it would spring open—perhaps by some as-yet-undiscovered magic—but that did not happen.

"Try it from your side," I told him. "There might be a latch . . . "

I knew, even as I said it, that there wasn't, but anything was worth a try.

"Can't," Colin said, and even in the darkness I could tell that he was on the verge of tears. "I'm tied up."

"Tied up?" It seemed impossible, even though I had once or twice been in the same position myself.

"I've got the key, though. It's in me pocket."

Praise be! I thought. *Finally, a bit of luck.*

"Wiggle yourself over to the gate," I said. "I'll try to reach the key."

There was a painful silence, and then he said, "I'm . . . I'm tied to somethin'."

And he began to whimper.

It was enough to make a saint spit!

But wait: The padlock was on Colin's side of the gate, wasn't it? I had noticed this but not given it my proper attention.

"Did you lock yourself in?" I asked.

"No," Colin snuffled.

"Then how did you get in there?"

"We come through the door in the fountain."

A door in the fountain? We?

I chose to ask the most important question first.

"Who's 'we,' Colin? Who did this to you?"

I could hear him breathing heavily in the darkness, but he did not answer.

I realized at once the futility of it all. I was not about to spend the rest of my life trying to pry answers out of a captive from whom I was separated by a wall of iron bars.

"All right, then," I said. "It doesn't matter. Tell me about the door in the fountain. I'll come round and let you out."

It made me furious, actually, to think that I should have to ask a stranger about a secret door at Buckshaw—and secret it must be, for I had never heard of such a thing myself. Such mysteries were surely meant to be handed down by word of mouth from one family member to another, not practically pried from a near-stranger who skulked about the countryside in the company of a poacher.

"Simon's toe," Colin said.

"What? You're not making any sense."

The sound of sobbing told me there was no more to be got from him.

"Stay here," I said, although it made no sense. "I'll be back before you know it."

"No, wait!" he cried. "Give me the torch. Don't leave me alone!"

"I have to, Colin. I need the torch to light my way."

"No, please! I'm 'fraid of the dark!"

"Tell you what," I said. "Close your eyes and count to five hundred and fifty. It won't be dark with your eyes closed. When you finish, I'll be back. Here—I'll help you start. One . . . two . . . three . . . "

"Can't," Colin interrupted, "I 'aven't learnt my hundreds."

"All right, then, let's sing. Come on, we'll sing together:

"God save our gracious King,
Long live our noble King,
Long may he . . .

"Come on, Colin, you're not singing."

"Don't know the words."

"All right, then, sing something you know. Singing will make me come back sooner."

There was a long pause, and then he began in a cracked and quavering voice:

"London Bridge is . . . fallin' down
Fallin' . . . down, fallin' down
London Bridge is fallin' down . . . "

I turned round and began to pick my way carefully back along the passage, the sound of Colin's voice soon becoming no more than a faint echo. Leaving him there, alone in the darkness, was one of the most difficult things I've ever had to do, although I can't say why. Life is full of surprises like that.

The return journey seemed endless. Time had surely slowed as I made my way back beneath the low arched ceilings to the cellars.

Up the steps I went and into the kitchen. Although the house was in perfect silence, I paused anyway to listen at the door.

Nothing.

Technically, I knew, I was not being disobedient. I had been forbidden to leave home, and I had no intention of doing so. The Poseidon fountain was well within the bounds of Buckshaw, which allowed me to have my cake and jolly well eat it, too.

I slipped quietly out the back door, leaving it unlocked, and into the kitchen garden. Overhead, the stars twinkled like a million mad eyes, while the moon, already halfway to its first quarter, hung like a broken silver fingernail in the night sky.

Ordinarily, even though it wasn't far to the Poseidon fountain, I'd have taken Gladys with me, if only for company. But now, when a single one of her excited squeaks or rattles might awaken the household, I simply couldn't risk it.

I set out at a brisk walk through the wet grass, across the east lawn towards the Visto. Somewhere, an owl hooted, and something tiny scurried through the dead leaves.

Then suddenly, almost without warning, Poseidon was looming above me, odd angles of his metal anatomy catching the starlight, as if some ancient part of the galaxy had fallen to earth.

I climbed up the steps to the base. What was it Colin had said?

"*Simon's toe.*" Yes, that was it—but what had he meant?

Of course! *Poseidon's* toe!

He must have heard the name from Brookie and got it muddled.

I scrambled up onto the fountain's lower bowl. Now Poseidon's giant foot was almost in my face, its big toe curled back as if someone were tickling his tummy.

I reached out and touched the thing—shoved it down as hard as I could. The toe moved—as if on a hidden hinge—and from somewhere below came a distinct metallic *snick.*

"Simon's toe," I said aloud, smiling and shaking my head, proud of myself for having solved the puzzle.

I climbed down to the ground and—yes!—there it was! One of the large sculptured panels of water nymphs that formed the fountain's decorative base had sprung out slightly from the others.

How devilishly clever of old "Leaking de Luce" to have hidden the lock's release in one of the statue's feet, where it wouldn't be easily discovered.

The hatch swung open with a groan and I stepped carefully into the fountain's base. As I had suspected it might, a single lead pipe emerged from one of several grottos below and bent up sharply to feed water to the fountain. A large arm-valve was obviously meant to control the flow, and although a heavy covering of cobwebs told me that it had not been used for ages, I was surrounded by the sound of dripping water which echoed unnervingly in the dankness of the confined chamber.

A dozen precarious steps led down into a wide, rectangular pit at the bottom of the fountain.

They were splattered with blood!

On the edge of the bottom step was a large stain, while diminishing dribbles marked the ones higher up.

The blood had been here for some time, as was evident from its brown, well-oxidized appearance.

This must be the spot where Brookie met his death.

Avoiding the splotches, I picked my way gingerly to the bottom.

The pit was surprisingly spacious.

To one side, overhead, an iron grating revealed slits of the night sky: the stars still shining brightly, giving off so much light, in fact, that even the towering outline of Poseidon himself was visible far above. Gaping upwards at this novel viewpoint, I somehow managed to misstep. I twisted my ankle.

"Damn!" I said, pointing the torch at the ground to see what had caused my injury.

It was a rope, and it lay coiled in the circle of light like a self-contented viper sunning itself after a particularly satisfying lunch.

I can't say that I was surprised, since I had already deduced that there would likely be a rope. I had simply forgotten about it until I tripped on the stupid thing.

What *was* surprising, though, was that the police had not discovered such a crucial bit of evidence: a surprising misstep, not only for me, but also for them.

Better not touch it, I thought. *Best leave it in place for Inspector Hewitt's men*. Besides, I already knew as much as I needed to know about this particular remnant of the crime.

With a couple of halting steps, I limped towards an open tunnel.

But wait! Which of these openings would lead me back to Colin?

The one on the left, I thought, although I could hardly be sure. Lucius de Luce's plan had shown a bewildering maze of subterranean waterworks, and only now that I thought about it did I remember shoving the folded map into my pocket.

I grinned, realizing that help was right here at my very fingertips. But when I reached for it, my pocket was empty.

Of course! I had changed my dusty dress for a clean one, and I let slip a mental curse as I realized that Lucius's priceless hand-drawn map was, at this very moment, soaking its way to blankness in a laboratory sink!

There was nothing for it now but to follow my instincts and choose a tunnel: the one on my left.

Here at its eastern extremity, the corridor was not only lower and more narrow, but had fallen into scandalous disrepair. The brick walls and pieces of the roof had crumbled in places, covering parts of the floor with broken rubble.

Careful, I thought. *The whole thing might cave in and—*

Something slapped my face—something dangling from the roof like a dead white arm. I let out a little yelp and stopped in my tracks.

A root! I had been frightened by a stupid root that had been put down, perhaps by one of the long gone borders which had, in earlier times, shaded the walkways of the Visto.

Even though I ducked under the thing, its slimy finger still managed to caress my face, as if it were dying for want of human company.

I limped along, the light of the torch sweeping wildly in front of me.

Here, on both sides of the tunnel, a dusty assortment of ladders, ropes, pails, watering cans, and galvanized funnels had been left, as if the groundskeepers who had used them had wandered off to war and forgotten to return.

A sudden flash of red brought me to a stop. Someone had written on the wall. I let the light play slowly over the painted letters: *H.d.L.*

Harriet de Luce! My mother had been here before me—found her way through this same tunnel—stood on these same bricks—painted her initials on the wall.

Something like a shiver overtook me. I was surrounded with Harriet's presence. How, when I had never known her, could I miss her so deeply?

Then, faintly, from far along the tunnel, there came to my ears the sound of a voice—singing.

"London Bridge is fallin' down . . . my fair lady."

"Colin!" I shouted, and suddenly my eyes were brimming. "Colin! It's me, Flavia."

I lurched forward, tripping over fallen stones, feeling the ooze in my shoes from the tunnel's seepage. My hands were raw from clutching at the rough wall for support.

And then, there he was . . .

"My fair lady," he was singing.

"It's all right, Colin. You can stop now. Where's the key?"

He winced at the light, then stared at me with a strange, offended look.

"Untie me first," he said gruffly.

"No—key first," I said. "That way you won't run off with it."

Colin groaned as he rolled slightly onto his left side. I reached into his pocket—Ugh!—and pulled out an iron key.

As he twisted, I could see that Colin's wrists were bound firmly behind him and lashed to an iron pipe that rose up vertically before vanishing into the roof.

The poor creature could have been tied up here for days!

"You must be in agony," I said, and he looked up at me again with such blank puzzlement that I wondered if he knew the meaning of the word.

I struggled with the knots. Colin's efforts to free himself and the moisture from the seeping walls had shrunken them horribly.

"Do you have a knife?"

Colin shook his head and looked away.

"What? No knife? Come on, Colin—Boy Scouts are born with knives."

"Took it off me. 'Might hurt yourself.' That's what they said."

"Never mind, then. Lean forward. I'll try the key."

Putting the torch on the ground so that its light reflected from the wall, I attacked the knots with the business end of the key.

Colin groaned, letting out little yelps every time I applied pressure to his bonds. In spite of the clamminess of the tunnel, sweat was dripping from my forehead onto the already saturated rope.

"Hang on," I told him. "I've almost got it."

The last end pulled through—and he was free.

"Stand up," I said. "You need to move around."

He rolled over, unable to get to his feet.

"Grab hold," I said, offering my hand, but he shook his head.

"You have to get your circulation going," I told him. "Rub your arms and legs as hard as you can. Here, I'll help you."

"It's no good," he said. "Can't do it."

"Of course you can," I said, rubbing more briskly. "You need to get some circulation into your toes and fingers."

His lower lip was trembling and I felt a sudden surge of pity.

"Tell you what. Let's have a rest."

Even in the half-light his gratitude was hard to miss.

"Now then," I said. "Tell me about the blood on the fountain steps."

Perhaps it wasn't fair, but I needed to know.

At the word "blood," Colin shrank back in horror.

"I never done it," he croaked.

"Never did what, Colin?"

"Never done Brookie. Never shoved that sticker in his nose."

"He roughed you up, didn't he? Left you no choice."

"No," Colin said, managing somehow to pull himself to his feet. "It weren't like that. It weren't like that at all."

"Tell me what happened," I said, surprised by my own coolness in what could prove to be a tricky situation.

"We was chums, Brookie an' me. He told me stories when we wasn't scrappin'."

"Stories? What kind of stories?"

"You know, King Arthur, like. 'Ad some right lovely talks, we did. Used to tell me about old Nicodemus Flitch, an' 'ow 'e could strike a sinner dead whenever 'e took the notion."

"Was Brookie a Hobbler?" I asked.

"'Course not!" Colin scoffed. "But 'e wished 'e was. 'E fancied their ways, 'e used to say."

So there it was: I should have asked Colin in the first place.

"You were telling me about the sticker," I said, trying to steer Colin gently back to the moment of Brookie's death.

"He showed it to me," Colin said. "Ever so pretty . . . silver . . . like pirate treasure. Dug it up behind your 'ouse, Brookie did. Goin' to make dozens of 'em, 'e said. 'Enough for a garden party at Buckin'ham Palace.'"

I dared not interrupt.

"'Give it 'ere,' I told 'im. 'Let's 'ave a gander. Just for a minute. I'll give it back.' But 'e wouldn't. 'Might stab yourself,' 'e said. Laughed at me."

"''Ere, you promised!' I told 'im. 'You said we'd go halfers if I carried the dog-thing.'

"I grabbed it . . . didn't mean nothin' by it—just wanted to have a gander, is all. 'E grabbed it back and gave it such a tug! I let go too quick, and—"

His face was sheer horror.

"I never done it," he said. "I never done it."

"I understand," I said. "It was an accident. I'll do whatever I can to help, but tell me this, Colin—who tied you up?"

He let out such a wail that it nearly froze my blood, even though I already knew the answer.

"It was Tom Bull, wasn't it?"

Colin's eyes grew as round as saucers, and he stared over my shoulder. "'E's comin back! 'E said 'e'd be back."

"Nonsense," I said. "You've been here for ages."

"Goin' to do me, Tom Bull is, 'cause I seen what 'e done at the caravan."

"You saw what he did at the caravan?"

"'Eard it, anyhow. 'Eard all the screamin'. Then 'e come out an' tossed somethin' in the river. 'E's goin' to kill me."

Colin's eyes were wide as saucers.

"He won't kill you," I told him. "If he were, he'd have done it before now."

And then I heard the sound behind me in the tunnel.

Colin's eyes grew even larger, almost starting from their sockets.

"'E's 'ere!"

I whipped round with the torch to see a hulking form scuttling towards us like a giant land crab: so large that it nearly filled the passage-way from roof to floor, and from wall to wall; a figure bent over nearly double to negotiate the cramped tunnel.

It could only be Tom Bull.

"The key!" I shouted, realizing even as I did so that it was in my hand.

I sprang for the lock and gave the thing a twist.

Damn all things mechanical! The lock seemed rusted solid.

No more than a dozen paces away, the huge man was charging along the tunnel towards us, his rasping breath now horribly audible, his wild red hair like that of some raging madman.

Suddenly I was shoved aside. Colin snatched the key from my hand.

"No, Colin!"

He rammed it into the lock, gave it a fierce twist, and the hasp sprang open. A moment later he had yanked open the gate and pushed me—dragged me—almost carried me—through.

He slammed shut the gate, snapped the lock closed, and pushed me well away from the bars.

"Watch this un," he said. "'im's got long arms."

For a moment, Colin and I stood there, breathing heavily, looking in horror at the blood-engorged face of Tom Bull as it glared at us from behind the iron bars.

His great fists grasped the heavy gate, shaking it as if to rip it out by the roots.

The Red Bull!

Fenella had been right!

I jerked back in horror against the wet wall, and as I did so, my twisted ankle gave way and I dropped the torch.

We were plunged instantly into inky blackness.

I dropped to my knees, feeling the wet floor with outstretched fingers.

"Keep clear of the bars," Colin whispered. "Else 'e'll grab you!"

Not knowing which way was which, I scrabbled in the darkness, fearful that at any instant my wrist would be seized.

After what seemed like an eternity, the back of my hand brushed against the torch. I closed my fingers around it . . . picked it up . . . pushed the switch with my thumb . . . nothing.

I gave it a shake—banged it with the heel of my hand . . . still nothing.

The torch was broken.

I could have wept.

Close to me, in the darkness, I heard a rustling. I dared not move.

I counted ten heartbeats.

Then there came a scraping—and a match flared up.

"'Ad 'em in my pocket," Colin said proudly. "All along."

"Go slowly," I told him. "That way. Don't let the match go out."

As we backed away from the gate into the tunnel, and Tom Bull's face faded into darkness, his mouth moved and he uttered the only words I ever heard him speak.

"Where's my baby?" he cried.

His words echoed like knives from the stone walls.

In the horrid silence that followed, we edged farther back along the tunnel. When the first match burned out, Colin took out another.

"How many of those do you have?" I asked.

"One more," he said, and he lit it.

We had gained some ground, but it was still a long way to the cellars.

Colin held his last match high, moving slowly again, leading the way.

"Good lad," I told him. "You've saved us."

A sudden gust of cold air blew out the match, and we were plunged once again into blackness.

"Keep moving," I urged him. "Follow the wall."

Colin froze.

"Can't," he said. "I'm 'fraid of the dark."

"It's all right," I told him. "I'm with you. I won't let anything happen."

I pushed against him, but he would not be budged.

"No," he said. "Can't."

I could have gone on without him, but I was incapable of leaving him here alone.

And slowly, I realized that somehow, even in the darkness, I could dimly see Colin's white face. A moment later, I became aware of a growing light that had suddenly filled the passageway.

I spun round, and there, to my amazement, was Dogger, holding a large lantern above his head. Porcelain peered round him, fearfully at first, and then, when she saw I was quite safe, running to me, almost crushing me in her embrace.

"I'm afraid I ratted on you," she said.

thirty

"AND DOGGER, YOU SEE, HAD ALREADY LATCHED THE DOOR at the fountain. It only opens from the outside, so there was no way Tom Bull could get out."

"Well done, Dogger," Father said. Dogger smiled and gazed out the drawing-room window.

Daffy shifted uneasily on the chesterfield. She had been torn away from her book by Father, who insisted that both she and Feely be present at the interview. *It was almost as if he was proud of me.*

Feely stood at the chimneypiece, pretending to be bored, stealing quick, greedy glances at herself in the looking glass while otherwise simpering at Sergeant Graves.

"This whole business about the Hobblers is intriguing," Inspector Hewitt said. "Your notes have been most helpful."

I fizzed a little inside.

"I gather they've been carrying out their baptisms in the Gully since sometime in the seventeenth century?"

I nodded. "Mrs. Bull wanted her baby baptized in the old style, and her husband, I think, probably forbade it."

"That he did," said Sergeant Graves. "He's told us as much."

The Inspector glared at him.

"She went to the Gully with Miss Mountjoy—Dr. Kissing saw them together. There might have been other Hobblers present, I really don't know.

"But something went horribly wrong. They were dipping the baby by the heel, as Hobbler tradition requires, when something happened. The baby slipped and drowned. They buried it in the Palings—swore to keep the truth to themselves. At least, I think that's what happened."

Sergeant Graves nodded, and the Inspector shot him *such* a look!

"Mrs. Bull thought at once of blaming it on Fenella. After all, she had just passed the caravan in the lane. She went home and told her husband, Tom, that their baby had been taken by Gypsies. And he believed her—has gone on believing her—until now."

I took a deep breath and went on. "Fenella told Mrs. Bull's fortune at the fête last week—told her the same nonsense she tells everyone: that something was buried in her past—something that wanted digging out."

Only at that instant, as I spoke, did the full force—the full aptness—of Fenella's words come crashing into my consciousness: *"Told her there was something buried in her past; told her it wanted digging out—wanted setting right."* I had actually copied these words into my notebook without understanding their meaning.

She couldn't *possibly* have learned of the Bull baby's supposed abduction until later—she had been gone from the Gully before the bungled baptism began.

Mrs. Bull, to reinforce her lie, must have been forced to follow through by filing a false report with the police. Tom, because of his shady associations, must have managed to keep well in the background. Hadn't Mrs. Mullet let slip that he'd had his troubles with the law?

How I wished I could ask the Inspector to confirm my conjecture—especially the part about Tom Bull—but I knew he wouldn't—couldn't—tell me. Perhaps some other time . . .

At any rate, Fenella had almost certainly been tracked down and questioned by the authorities during their investigation of the missing child—tracked down, questioned, and cleared. That much seemed obvious.

So that when Mrs. Bull had wandered unexpectedly into her tent just last week at the fête, it must have seemed as if Fate had sent her there for justice.

"There's something buried in your past. Something that wants digging out . . . wants setting right," Fenella had told her, but it was not the baby she meant—it was Mrs. Bull's accusation of kidnapping!

"Revenge is my specialty," Fenella had said.

Revenge indeed!

But not without cost.

Surely the woman had recognized Fenella's caravan at the fête? Whatever could have possessed her to enter the tent?

I could think of only one reason: guilt.

Perhaps, in her own mind, Mrs. Bull's lie to her husband and the police was beginning to come unraveled—perhaps in some odd way she believed that a fresh confrontation would deflect any growing suspicion, on Tom's part, of her own guilt.

What was it Dr. Darby had told me? *"People can behave very strangely in times of great stress."*

"Well?" the Inspector said, interrupting my thoughts. He was waiting for me to go on.

"Well, Mrs. Bull, of course, assumed that Fenella had looked into the crystal ball and seen the drowning. She must have gone home straight-away and told her husband that the Gypsy who had taken their baby was again camped at the Palings. Tom went to the caravan that very night and tried to kill her.

"He still believes his wife's lie, most likely," I added. "Even though the baby's body has since been found, I'll bet he's still blaming it on the Gypsies."

I glanced over at Sergeant Graves for confirmation, but his face was a study in stone.

"How can you be so sure he was at the caravan?" Inspector Hewitt asked, turning to a new page of his notebook.

"Because Colin Prout saw him there. And as if that weren't enough, there was that whole business about the smell of fish," I said. "I think you'll find that Tom Bull has a disease that causes his body to exude a fishy odor. Dogger says that a number of such cases have been recorded."

Inspector Hewitt's eyebrows went up slightly, but he said nothing.

"That's why, as it's grown worse, he's kept to his house for the past year or more. Mrs. Bull put about the story that he'd gone away, but he'd all the while been right here in Bishop's Lacey, working after dark. He's a foundryman, you know, and probably quite handy at melting down scrap iron and molding it into antiques."

"Yes," Inspector Hewitt said, surprising me. "It's no secret that he was once employed at Sampson's works, in East Finching."

"And still is," I suggested. "At least after dark."

Inspector Hewitt closed his notebook and got to his feet.

"I'm very pleased to tell you, Colonel, that your firedogs will soon be restored. We found them in the coach house where Harewood kept his antiques."

I was right! The Sally Fox and Shoppo at Brookie's *had* been Harriet's! Having replaced them with reproductions, Brookie was just waiting for a chance to sell the originals in London.

"There are others involved in what proved to be a very sophisticated ring of thieves and forgers. I trust that, in due time, you'll read about it in the newspapers."

"But what about Miss Mountjoy?" I blurted it out. I felt quite sorry for poor Tilda Mountjoy.

"She may well face charges as an accessory," the Inspector said. "It's up to the Chief Constable. I don't envy him his task."

"Poor Colin," I said. "He hasn't had an easy life, has he?"

"There may be mitigating circumstances," Inspector Hewitt said. "Beyond that, I can say nothing."

"I knew for certain he was mixed up in it when I found the rope."

I regretted it as soon as the words were out of my mouth.

"Rope? What rope?"

"The rope that fell through the grating at the Poseidon fountain."

"Woolmer? Graves? What do we know about this?"

"Nothing, sir," they said in unison.

"Then perhaps you will favor us by taking yourselves to the fountain immediately and rectifying the oversight."

"Yes, sir," they said, and marched, red-faced, from the drawing room.

The Inspector again focused his fierce attention on me. "The rope," he said. "Tell me about the rope."

"There had to be one," I explained. "Brookie was far too heavy to be hoisted onto the fountain by anyone but the strongest man. Or a Boy Scout with a rope."

"Thank you," Inspector Hewitt said. "That will do. I'm quite sure we can fill in the blanks."

"Besides," I added, "the rubbed spot on the trident showed quite clearly where the rope had polished away the tarnish."

"Thank you. I believe we've already noted that."

Well, then, I thought, *you've no one to blame but yourselves if you didn't think of looking for the rope that caused it. Colin is a Boy Scout, for heaven's sake.* There were times when officialdom was beyond even me.

"One last point," the Inspector said, rubbing his nose. "Perhaps you'd be good enough to clear up one small question that has rather eluded me."

"I'll do my best, Inspector," I said.

"Why on earth did Colin hang Brookie from the fountain? Why not leave him where he was?"

"They had struggled for the lobster pick inside the base of the fountain. When Colin let go of the thing suddenly, Brookie's own force caused him to stab himself in the nostril. It was an accident, of course."

Although this was the way Colin had told it to me, I must confess to gilding the lily more than a little for the Inspector's benefit. I no more believed Colin's version of the story than I believed that dray horses can fly. Brookie's death, in my estimation, was Colin's revenge for years of abuse. It was murder, pure and simple.

But who was I to judge? I had no intention of adding so much as another ounce to the burden of Colin's troubles.

"Brookie fell backwards down the stone steps into the chamber. That's probably what actually killed him."

Oh Lord, forgive me this one charitable little fib!

"Colin fetched a length of rope from the tunnel and hauled him up onto Poseidon's trident. He had to tie Brookie's wrists together so that the arms wouldn't slip out of the coat later. He didn't want to risk the body falling."

Inspector Hewitt gave me a look I can only describe as skeptical.

"Brookie," I went on, "had told Colin about the Hobblers' belief that Heaven was right there above our heads. You see, he wanted to give Brookie a head start."

"Good lord!" Father said.

Inspector Hewitt scratched his nose. "Hmmm," he said. "Seems rather far-fetched."

"Not so far-fetched at all, Inspector," I said. "That's precisely the way Colin explained it to me. I'm sure that when Dr. Darby and the vicar allow you to question him further . . . "

The Inspector nodded in a sad way, as if he'd rather suspected it all along.

"Thank you, Flavia," he said, getting to his feet and closing his notebook. "And thank *you*, Colonel de Luce. You've been more than generous in helping us get to the bottom of this matter." He walked to the drawing-room door.

"Oh, and Flavia," he said rather shyly, turning back. "I almost forgot. I came here today somewhat as a message bearer. My wife, Antigone, would be delighted if you'd come for tea next Wednesday . . . if you're free, of course."

Antigone? Tea? And then it sank in.

Oh, frabjous day! Callooh! Callay! That glorious goddess, Antigone, was summoning me, Flavia Sabina de Luce, to her vine-covered cottage!

"Thank you, Inspector," I said primly. "I shall consult my calendar and see if I can set aside some time."

UP THE STAIRS I FLEW. I couldn't wait to tell Porcelain!

I should have guessed that she'd be gone.

She had torn a blank page from my notebook and fastened it to one of my pillows with a safety pin.

Thanks for everything. Look me up in London sometime.
Your friend,
Porcelain

Just that, and nothing more.

At first I was seized with sadness. In spite of our ups and downs, I had never met anyone quite like Porcelain Lee. I had already begun to miss her.

I FIND IT DIFFICULT TO WRITE about the portrait of Harriet.

Leaving the painting at Vanetta Harewood's studio with its face against the wall was out of the question. She had, after all, offered it to me, and since Harriet had paid in full for the work, it belonged rightly to her estate at Buckshaw.

I would hang it secretly, I decided, in the drawing room. I would unveil it for my family with as much ceremony as I could muster. I could hardly wait.

In the end, it hadn't been terribly difficult to arrange the transfer. I'd asked Mrs. Mullet to have a word with Clarence Mundy, who operated

Bishop's Lacey's only taxicab, and Clarence had agreed to "lay on transportation," as he put it.

On a dark and rainy afternoon in late September, we had rolled up at the gate of the cottage studio in Malden Fenwick, and Clarence had walked me to the door with an oversized black umbrella.

"Come in," Vanetta Harewood said, "I've been expecting you."

"Sorry we're a bit late," I said. "The rain, and so forth . . . "

"It's no trouble at all," she replied. "To be truthful, I've been finding the days rather longer than usual."

Clarence and I waited in the hall until the glowering Ursula appeared with a large object, wrapped in brown paper.

"Keep it dry," Vanetta said. "It's my best work."

AND SO WE BROUGHT HARRIET'S portrait to Buckshaw.

"Hold the umbrella for me," Clarence said, preparing to wrestle the package from the backseat of the taxicab. "I'm going to need both hands."

Shielding the parcel from the slanting rain, we dashed to the door, as awkward as three-legged racers.

I had handed Clarence the fare and was halfway across the foyer when suddenly Father emerged from his study.

"What have you dragged home now?" he asked, and I couldn't find it in my heart to lie.

"It's a painting," I said. "It belongs to you."

Father leaned it against the wall and returned to his study, from which he emerged with a pair of shears to cut the several turns of butcher's string.

He let the paper fall away.

THAT WAS TWO WEEKS AGO.

The portrait of Harriet and her three children is no longer in the foyer, nor is it in the drawing room. Until today, I'd searched the house in vain.

But this morning, when I unlocked the door of my laboratory, I found the painting hanging above the mantelpiece.

I've mentioned this to no one.

Father knows it's there and I know it's there, and for now, that's all that counts.

In order to provide sufficiently dramatic lighting for this story, I must admit to having tinkered slightly here and there with the phases of the moon, though the reader may rest assured that, having finished, I've put everything back exactly as it was.

acknowledgments

The writing of a book is, among many other things, an extended journey with friends: a kind of pilgrimage. Along the way we have met, sometimes parted, shared meals, and swapped stories, ideas, jokes, and opinions. In doing so, these friends have become inextricably woven into the book's fabric.

My heartfelt gratitude to Dr. John Harland and Janet Harland, to whom this book is dedicated, for many years of friendship and countless excellent suggestions.

To Nora and Don Ivey, who not only opened their home to me, but also saw to it personally that one of my lifelong dreams was made to come true.

To my editors: Bill Massey at Orion Books in London, Kate Miciak at Random House in New York, and Kristin Cochrane at Doubleday Canada in Toronto. And particular thanks to Loren Noveck and Connie Munro, at Random House, New York, my production editor and copy editor respectively, who toil away quietly behind the scenes doing much of the work for which I get the credit.

To Denise Bukowski, my agent, and Susan Morris at the Bukowski Agency, who fearlessly juggle all the mountains of detail with astonishing efficiency.

To Brad Martin, CEO of Random House Canada, for his abiding faith.

To Susan Corcoran and Kelle Ruden of Random House, New York, and Sharon Klein of Random House, Toronto, for their phenomenal support.

To Natalie Braine, Jade Chandler, Juliet Ewers, Jessica Purdue, and Helen Richardson of Orion Books, London, who have relieved me of so much of the worry.

To Jennifer Herman and Michael Ball for making the miles fly by and delivering me safely.

To Ken Boichuk and his Grimsby Author Series, with gratitude for a most memorable evening.

To my old friend Robert Nielsen of Potlatch Publications, who published some of my earliest fiction, and who honestly seemed as happy to see me again as I was to see him.

To Ted Barris, author and longtime friend, whose focused energy is always such an inspiration.

To Marion Misters of Sleuth of Baker Street in Toronto, and Wendy Sharko of The Avid Reader in Cobourg, who welcomed me back to my birthplace and hometown respectively.

To Rita and Hank Schaeffer, who coddled me in Montreal.

To Andreas Kessaris of the Paragraphe Bookstore, Montreal.

To the Random House "Ladies of Westminster": Cheryl Kelly, Lori Zook, Sherri Drechsler, Pam Kaufman, Judy Pohlhaus, Camille Marchi, Sherry Virtz, Stacey Carlinia, Emily Bates, Amiee Wingfield, and Lauren Gromlowicz, with whom I shared a ton of books and two tons of laughs.

To Kim Monahan, Randall Klein, and David Weller of Random House, in New York City.

To Tony Borg, Mary Rose Grima, Dr. Joe Rapa, Doris Vella, and Dr. Raymond Xerri, who will probably never realize what a great difference they made. Their many kindnesses and courtesies during the writing of this book will never be forgotten.

To Mary Jo Anderson, Stan Ascher, Andrea Baillie, Tim Belford, Rebecca Brayton, Arlene Bynon, Stephen Clare, Richard Davies, Anne Lagace Dowson, Mike Duncan, Vanessa Gates, Kathleen Hay, Andrew Krystal, Sheryl MacKay, Hubert O'Hearn, Mark Perzel, David Peterson, Ric Peterson, Craig Rintoul, M. J. "Mike" Stone, Scott Walker, Lisa Winston, and Carolyn Yates, who made it seem easy by asking all the right questions.

To Skip Prichard and George Tattersfield at the Ingram Book Company, in La Vergne, Tennessee; and to Claire Tattersfield, who did me the great honor of skipping school to have her book signed, and to Robin Glennon for arranging a most memorable day.

To fellow authors Annabel Lyon, Michael McKinley, Chuck Palahniuk, and Danielle Trussoni, for sharing part of the journey.

To Paul Ingram of Prairie Lights Books in Iowa City, Iowa, and to Wes Caliger. In spite of having entertained President Obama the day before I arrived, Paul's welcome was the kind that every author dreams about.

To my "Evil Twin" Barbara Peters at The Poisoned Pen, in Scottsdale, Arizona, who leaves the most astonishing plot ideas on my voice mail.

To the memory of my dear friend David Thompson of Murder by the Book in Houston, Texas, whose shockingly early death in September 2010 has deprived the world of mystery fiction of one of its cornerstones. Known for his encyclopedic knowledge of mystery fiction, David was universally loved by authors and readers alike.

And to David's wife, McKenna Jordan of Murder by the Book, and McKenna's mom, Brenda Jordan, for gentle kindnesses too numerous to count.

To Dan Mayer and Bob Weitrack of Barnes and Noble, New York; to Ellen Clark, Richard Horseman, Dane Jackson, and Eric Tsai of Borders, Ann Arbor, Michigan.

To Barb Hudson, Jennie Turner-Collins, and Micheal Fraser of Joseph-Beth Booksellers, in Cincinnati, Ohio, and to Kathy Tirschek, who got me safely to wherever I needed to go.

With love to the Brysons: Jean, Bill, Barbara, John, Peter, and David, who have always been there.

To the Ball Street Gang: Bob and Pat Barker, Lillian Barker Hoselton, Jane McCaig, Jim Thomas, and honorary member Linda Hutsell-Manning: together again after half a century. Thomas Wolfe was wrong: You *can* go home again.

To Evelyn and Leigh Palmer and to Robert Bruce Thompson, who helped with the chemistry. Any errors remaining are my own.

I must also acknowledge particular indebtedness to the books that inspired the invention of that peculiar sect, the Hobblers: *History and Antiquities of Dissenting Churches and Meeting Houses, in London,*

Westminster, and Southwark; Including the Lives of Their Ministers, from the Rise of Nonconformism to the Present Time, Walter Gibson, London, 1814, and *The History of Baptism,* Robert Robinson, Boston, 1817.

And finally, as always, with love to my wife, Shirley, who makes my life easy by cheerfully doing whatever I leave undone, besides doubling as my personal computer technician. No one is more brilliantly adept at rejuvenating worn-out keyboards and, while she's at it, removing the crumbs.